THE LAYOUT

J. DAVID ROBBINS

iUniverse, Inc.
Bloomington

The Layout

iUniverse books may be ordered through booksellers or by contacting:

iUniverse
1663 Liberty Drive
Bloomington, IN 47403
www.iuniverse.com
1-800-Authors (1-800-288-4677)

ISBN: 978-1-4620-0757-8 (sc)
ISBN: 978-1-4620-0758-5 (ebook)
ISBN: 978-1-4620-0759-2 (dj)

Library of Congress Control Number: 2011905533

Printed in the United States of America

iUniverse rev. date: 8/15/2011

To Nancy,
my wife, my greatest critic and my best friend.

ACKNOWLEDGEMENTS

A work with so many words is seldom a solo accomplishment. With that in mind, I thank my wife Nancy and my children Adam, Ian and Courtnay for all of their art and their support. Thanks to my amazing brother Mike Robbins who is always there when I have a question and who I have been pestering with technical quandaries for the last sixty-five years. My appreciation goes out to my wonderful friends Lisa Martin and Jack Schroeder for volunteering to edit my many errors and to Jeff Haas who offered invaluable early encouragement and advice. Also, a tip of the hat to three authors who helped guide me through the process of publishing: Paul Patengale, Peter Steckel, and my long time intellectual sparring partner Jay Douglas.

ACKNOWLEDGMENTS

Track One
PILOT

*S*O THIS HERE'S WHAT I'M HEARIN'; Y'want the whole plate a free-holies, refried, from the top. Right? Even the stuff about me? Don't mind lettin' ya in on a little secret, bro. I get tired a tellin' it. Ya know, at first, it was like, dude, I'm gonna be on TV an' shit. But damn, homie, after the cops, and the insurance guy, and the hottie from the five o'clock news an' shit...well, it get's old.

That thing on'r what? Yeah? Okay. Here goes.

So, like I tol' all the others, I'm Derri Caseman. You probably gonna wanna write Derrick, but only my mom calls me that. Work for a plater over there in Cheech-an'-Chong-ville? El Barrio, TJ North. I stand out, this head I got. Somebody told me only like two percent a the whole world's got red hair. What do ya think it is in old San Juan de Boyle Heights? Ya might wanna write that in your notes 'cause ya can't see it on the tape. Local color, right. Like, human in'erest. Yeah, well, I'm down with that. Even speak a little Mex so I can get lunch at the truck. I been there five years. I'm twenty-three. Pretty much learned the plating trade. Brass, chrome, all that shit. Ya wanna Goldfinger your bitch, I'm the guy. Idea was t'open my own shop, ya know, when I got good at it, but, fuckin' EP an' A! Know what I mean? Like the planet's gonna be around longer if it's up to some fuckin' polar bear!

So, the day a the thing, see, I come down San Fernando from Glendale. Deal is, I stay way up there in Tujunga, but I say Glendale 'cause most dudes know where that is. Tujunga, they kind a heard a maybe, but couldn't find it in the Thomas like it was in Pennsyl-fuckin'-vania or some shit. You can bleep out any a this ya want. 'S'okay with me ya pick an' choose. Anyways, I keep my ass off the freeway as much as I can 'cause a the traffic, catch San Fernando over there in Burbank, then it's pretty Parnelli-smooth over to Fig, through Lincoln Heights, an' it's all low rider heaven after that, right on up to the shop.

So, this particular mornin', I'm doin' my regular thing. Got a little Zeppelin in the dash 'cause I'm like into old school shit an' all I'm gonna hear all day at work is thumpa thumpa fuck dis bitch an' mariachis, right? Five years a this gig an' I got fuckin' mariachis comin' out a my ass. Nothin' wrong'th that shit, but it's all fuckin' day! So I'm tootin' along t' Jimmy Paige, just cruisin', see, 'cause I could give a shit what time I get there, like anyone else's ever on time in Mañanaville, an' like out a nowheres this car makes a left goin' the other way an' that's all I see at first. But as I pass where she turned...I didn't know it was a she 'til the cops tol' me...I hear this bang, an' I know that sound. Dented a few a my own when I first got my license. Like most dudes. I mean, what are ya, sixteen? Like you're gonna drive careful? Fuckin' brain dead at sixteen! So, I check out the rear view, not like I'm one a them ambulance chasers or nothin' or one a them voyagers that peeps int' people's shit, but, dude, ya hear the crunch an' ya can't help takin' a little peek. We all been there, know what I mean?

This is right over there in front a the plumbing supply and the titty bar. They got pictures a the girls up on the outside. You know the one? I see this car kind a bounce up onto the tracks an' fuckin' stop. Jus' kina roll up an' stop an' I can see the driver's head up against the winda an' it looks like she ain't movin'. I mean, like what the fuck do I know? She's a ways off by now 'cause I didn't stop right on the button. What is movin's the fuckin' gate thing. I think she must a blew the turn there an' hit the pipe or whatever that holds up the gate. An' hit it pretty hard too 'cause this bitch's out for the night, seemed

J. David Robbins

t'me. Pitcher this shit now, I mean, on the fuckin' t-racks! Gates come down on both sides a her, so even if she's just kickin' it, I'm all, this is a place I don't wanna be. I pull over. I guess I said that. There's no parking on the signs, but shit, they can give me a break on this one. I mean, I am bein' the good sumerian, ain't I? So, I get my ass out a the car an' my heart's pumpin' like a mother fucker, know what I mean? 'Cause, dude, I don' know if the bitch's dead or knocked out or what. An' then I seen it. This big ass headlight fixin' to do some serious damage to this bitch's wheels, punk-ass horn goin' all apeshit. I get a little closer. Not too close. I don't want ya readin' 'bout me in no paper. Don' wanna be one a them sadistics. Fuck no! I'm all, lady, lady, get your ass out a the fuckin' car. She don't move. He-l-l-l-o-o-o! Choo choo comin' your way! I'm like gettin' a sore throat tryin' t'get her attention, an' the Metro ain't gettin' any smaller. An' before ya know it, it's like a fuckin' Stallone flick out there. All fuckin' blam, crash. Shit flyin' everywhere. I'm all, Jesus, God, the fuck! An' this train keeps comin' like it hit a Matchbox truck. This lady's car kin'a like folds itself around the front a the train. I never seen nothin' like that. I never heard no noise like it. I mean, louder than the fuckin' AM-and-C in Dolby. Sparks everywhere, pieces a the car rippin' open like, I don' know, like a huge-ass balloon. An' then, this fuckin' kaboom, like it's all she wrote, see, an' there's like this kind a fire ball and shit, an' I'm all, shit, fuckin' Iraq! Fuckin' Operation Iraqi Freedom. 'S'what I'm talkin' about. An' the bitch in the car? Toast. You jus' know it. The heat gets me out int' the street. This chick's a crispy critter by now or I wasn't there. Deep fried. KF-and-C. Slam bam, thank ya, ma'am! I don't see the train stop 'cause I'm all hurlin' up my breakfast 'bout then. Tell ya this, dude, I never seen shit like this. On TV, sure, but ya don't like smell the fuckin' TV. Know what I mean?

(Recorded transcript)

4

Track Two
MIXED CONSIST

STOCKTON

I

Taylor Bedskirt steps out of the shuttle into a summer that sucks the moisture from his very bones. He imagines crackling, shriveling, decomposing into the shrapnel of his former self, melting like frozen yogurt into the asphalt. Prominent Rorschach pools of sweat define his underarms, beads of valley heat shimmer like mercury on his forehead, his eyelids, in the shadow of his nose. He trundles — Taylor is no runner — toward the glass doors, enters the lobby and is momentarily on the divide between the dark and light sides of the moon, at once freezing and boiling. He removes the damp straw hat from his vulnerable pate, takes a breath of half-body relief, and proceeds to the folding table next to the sign that reads, in simple, portable white letters, "Welcome Members STEAM & TRACTION HISTORICAL SOCIETY OF AMERICA, SIERRA REGIONAL CHAPTER."

Dale Moncton, former physician from Chico, is there with the roster, sitting next to Patty Moncton, president and first lady in stately welcome behind their table. Dale is wearing his trademark red vest with the various enameled pins of his favorite trunk lines: the Rio Grande, sister Western Pacific, Santa Fe; fallen flags and cherished memories, and obscure surviving short lines like the nearby Stockton Terminal & Eastern. He is also wearing an M. H. Grossman conductor's hat, to which Patty has expertly affixed a large brass badge with the word PRESIDENT hugging the curve of the dome top, the raised initials in an archaic font of railroad roman, S&THSA seriffed and elegant in shiny nickel across the bottom, and in the center, traveling left, a high stepping four-four-oh locomotive morphing into, going right, a streetcar with clerestory and trolley.

It is Dale's turn to coordinate the show — his first time in six years — and he is already shrugging off what appears to be at least a three percent drop in the expected registered attendance. Stan Franco, last year's chair from the moldy northwest, had warned Dale six months before, *Next time, with any luck, they'll be blaming all this on you.* Stan is not exactly Nostradamus, but he gets it right this time.

"Welcome there Taylor, m'boy." Dale is all white on gold smiles and cheery loudness, and Taylor grins back, not sure of *m'boy*: he predates Dale by about six years. He feels a bit too large to be anybody's *boy*.

"Dale. Patty," he acknowledges.

"Buyin' or sellin'?" Dale inquires.

"You know me," says Taylor.

Dale thinks, *If there's anyone I don't know, it's Taylor Bedskirt.* Taylor is a quiet quandary, and if there are depths to Taylor, Dale certainly hasn't plumbed them. *A retired mechanical engineer, but that's about all. Master of all things railroad; fumbler of all else.*

"Can't let anything go. Just here to browse."

"This *is* the place for that, you betcha," Patty affirms like an ageing cheerleader. She is virtually salivating on her optimism. She winks up at Taylor, awash in his infernal excretions; a secret conspiracy, meaning something else entirely, which in time, he knows, she will get on to.

Taylor never knows how to react to these nice people. He doesn't exactly dislike them. But they unnerve him, make him feel conspicuous: as if he is too large, too strange, too alien, as if there is something unpleasant stuck in his teeth or a nugget of wax riding the ore car out of his ear. They mean well, all the members mean well — most all of them, anyway. They are good people of the kind fifties sitcoms were made — salt of the earth, hard working tax-paying citizens, stable retirees riding out their last slow freights to the terminal — and any slight, any asperity, is incidental. Taylor avoids wholesome banter, would rather these folks just leave their wares on display for him alone to choose and covet, to massage in the silence of an empty hall.

Unconsciously, he crinkles his dehydrating brow, brushes invisible particles from his shoulders, and worries perhaps that his fly is open, the evil inanimate zipper teeth hatching a plan, conspiring some malicious pain, maybe not wide open, not enough to let the train leave the station — as his father would tell him those many years ago — just enough for one anguished peek that everyone would know about but would never, ever mention publicly, telling it only in eyebrow gossip, a nearly invisible inferential dip of chin as Taylor happens by.

He excuses himself to examine a display of easels offering shellac-coated twelve-by-fourteens, a preview of tomorrow's show; a digital rainbow tease of stark contrasts; the Coast Daylight in action, all streaking orange and yellow and great mushrooms of black smoke. He surreptitiously checks his zipper, finds it appropriately engaged and proceeds, relieved, to the registration line.

Harlan Brewster is there, two Jack Daniels-fogged steps in front of him, staggering up to the counter, leaning forward onto unsteady elbows, setting his eyes on a trajectory of interception with the plastic black name card riding snuggly upon Lynette's perfect breast — the best proportioned Brewster has ogled since leaving the airport and its parade of stewies — and proceeds to leer and foam with critical approval, his crimson face lathered like a fumarole.

"Mr. Brewster, welcome to Chivalry Timbers Suites. How long will you be staying with us?" Lynette's is a girlish voice, but professional and to the point.

A foot off the Formica, Brewster tries to swagger, encounters a protest of somnambulate synapses, and is nailed to the industrial grade carpet beneath his Montrails from Shopzilla.com. "I will stay with you, Ginette, as many nights as you'll have me."

The membership finds the sober Brewster somewhere south of bearable: soused, he is the headliner on the boorish belt of the American rail circuit. Taylor is wishing that he hadn't been seduced by the photos. He could have been first in line, comfortably registered, and proceeding solo up to his room.

"I'll put you down for two," Lynette forces through her float-queen smile. She is like a float herself: glittery and bejeweled, white on blond, with razor-thin black eyebrows sketched in lieu of prototypes. She looks about twelve, never mind the precocious curves and faint hint of nipples, too young for plastic restructuring.

"Got a friend?" Brewster asks. "Put us down for three." He wheels around slowly — very slowly, a very partial wheel, hour-hand sluggish — winks at Taylor, wheels incrementally back again, creaking like a mechanical soldier in an old clock.

Lynette has heard them all and gives no sign of cracking. She's been to the training, done the simulations. Off to the side, the evening manager, a blue blazer cut too long and tan trousers cut just too short, breathing a savory hint of curry, watches Brewster carefully, as if Harlan were a Pakistani terrorist about to embark on some unspeakable misbehavior. He comes with his own baggage, Mr. Chandra; has attended his own managerial training. His hands are clasped behind his back, a learned stance, tried and true, officious, vigilant; perhaps these hands cautiously embrace a candlestick, a lead pipe, something with which to protect his clerk, something to leave out of the summary to the head offices in Cedar Rapids. There will be no shenanigans in his lobby, no prurient impropriety with his employee.

Taylor considers leaving the line, sacrificing his place, heading over to the brochure rack to check out the outlet malls, water parks and other possible attractions of the Great Central Valley. He glances apologetically at the Cramers — next in line, Mr. & Mrs., white-silver-gray — who have been coming here forever; he for the Adlake lanterns; she for the dining car china.

"Okay, then," says Lynette, "One. I've got you down for one. And smoking?"

"A little too much on the plane," concludes Mrs. Cramer to Mr. Cramer, indignantly loud enough for Taylor, who hunches his shoulders again for lack of words, feeling he should perhaps intervene, which he knows he won't; that perhaps by association, by membership, by a curious mistake of inbreeding, he is somehow responsible.

Brewster is in his Levi jacket, the one with the Union Pacific shield blazing patriotically on the back, and khaki shorts between which and his unseasonable thick woolen hiking socks quiver alabaster-pale legs with flea bite tracks like *Sphonaptera* stepping stones. Brewster will blame, *The dog. My wife's fucking dog.* His eyes are the red of the Canadian Pacific herald and he sports what Mr. Cramer has famously referred to as his *Rudolf nose* — bulbous and demarcated like a track map for American freight lines — set atop baleen whiskers triangulated into a locomotive's pilot: what the layman calls a *cowcatcher.* "The flight wasn't long enough for *too much*," he protests, and then, to Lynette, "So tell me, sweet pie, what goes on in this fine burgh after dark?"

"Street lights," she says. She is ready for trainloads of Brewsters. "The buffet shuts down in about an hour. The bar is open until two and they've got a limited menu of soups and sandwiches. I recommend the buffet. Also, there's an ice machine and vending machine on each floor. There's a portfolio in your room that gives you the skinny on room service. Which is limited, and doesn't go on all night, so if that's where you're leaning, you'd better check it out first thing."

"You on it?"

"Nope. I just do the desk."

"'Bout the buffet?"

"Nope, *just* the desk!"

"Look, cupcakes, there's gotta be more than stroganoff under heat lamps in a town this size." He is leering. His hands form the shapes of breasts — hers, she doesn't doubt.

At the sight of invisible boobs pliant in Brewster's grip, Lynette places her own elbows on the counter. They are elbow parallel, eye to eye. Mr. Chandra's fingers twitch anxiously behind his back. His bittersweet chocolate face, flat like *naan*, ET's forward on extended neck, his tiny ears swivel for possible nefarious transmissions. There is a dangerous tension in the air, an undercurrent, a going over the line breach of sub-level clientele deportment. Lynette levels her emerald gaze on Brewster's befogged pupils. He tries to edge downward, following the directional plunge of retreating cleavage, but she lasers him to attention, and whispers — thankfully soft enough for Taylor to pretend not to hear, and too directional for Chandra — "Let's take a little inventory, you old school, dickhead pervert. You're registering at a fucking train show in Stockton. Maybe you set your sights a smidge high." She never loses the smile, all sugar and spice to Brewster, all cardamom and *garam masala* to Chandra; the same smile she used when she lost Miss Fresno to that Hmong bitch who probably wasn't even legal; probably just got it to right some simmering affirmative action wrong that had nothing to do with either of them. There are hidden rapiers in her retro mini beehive.

Brewster's curved hands flatten in defense. He attempts to back up, and takes a half step forward. He attempts to push himself upright, but Brewster can't even draw a straight line, let alone be one. His mail-sack lids hang weighty over eyes that seem to have excused themselves for the night. Even Brewster, diminished as he is, must now understand that this is a family hotel, and that the gentlemen's club must be elsewhere. There will be no lap dance forthcoming from Lynette's pallid white behind.

He staggers across the lobby as if he is avoiding sniper fire. Mr. Chandra approaches him, asks, "Are we having a problem?" in sub-continent singsong. Brewster hears, "R-V having a problem?" and says, "Then announce it over the PA, Sahib, I don't own a camper!"

II

THIS PARTICULAR CHIVALRY TIMBERS SUITES IS one of a small chain of roadside hotels, the kind that find themselves planted among tall corn and alfalfa fields and enough flat, fertile land for populations in search of seasonal employment. For reasons known to no one now alive, its conceptualizer — a Hotel Management grad from Iowa State — envisioned a series of medieval-themed hostelries to punctuate the American prairie, fortified outposts of cheap cloistered comfort for the weary. Like its sisters, the Stockton branch sports crenellated rooflines, half-timbered walls — no doubt, the chivalric timbers suggested by the sign — a moat with two or three over-fed ducks avoiding the *pâté* crowd, even a *faux* drawbridge.

The stucco walls are cleverly imagineered to resemble weathered gray stone, and the watchtower is high enough, and bright enough to keep people awake in San Diego. It is topped by a massive, neon knight. The knight is armored and mounted, one glaring blue eye on the lookout for dragons, his gaze Egyptian-perpendicular to his profile. It is an agrarian lighthouse, a beacon for the bleary-eyed millions on US Ninety-nine. Its beam repeats itself on bug splattered windshields, chronicles the endless grind of eighteen wheelers, the transient whoosh of SUVs, a logistical landmark in diesel humidity over the otherwise nullified acreage. Travelers watch for it. It is Chimney Rock, a red map pinprick in the navel of California, a landmark of familiar welcome in a gaseous fuzz and blinking in the torrid night air. It announces civilization to new home owners in the miles of tracts that sit upon the fields like upturned take-out boxes of Chinese grazing up orchards and sinuous channels of Huck Finn delta, a bright phallic insult reflected on the lazy San Joaquin.

Next door, there is a compatible Olde English Miniature Golfe and Arthurian Mini Speed Racer Track, where young Lancelots can vie for Guenivere's kerchief. The message, unmistakably, is, *Have a nice day* and *be sure to have it here.*

Inside the Inn, plague-era architects from wheat states have obliged the company's vision with crests and shields and heavy, wrought iron chandeliers prickled with spear points. Ye Oldes are everywhere: Ye Olde Lobby, Ye Olde Vending Machines, Ye Olde Elevator to Ye Olde Guest Suites, Ye Olde This, Ye Olde That. The Ye Olde signs are newly distressed with whipping chains and the letters wood-burned by Ye Olde Smithy. There are unhealthy portions of Ye Olde Beef in Ye Olde Buffet, which, never the less, Lynette recommends over the sandwiches in Ye Olde Pub. Her own dinner generally involves a Double-double combo from Ye Olde In-and-Out across the freeway. Ladies seek out Ye Wenches. Brewster surrenders an airport snack to the throne in Ye Squires. A must stop for tourists is Ye Olde Gift Shoppe, which offers post cards of nearby national parks, buffalo and salmon jerky, locally made cheeses from which toothpick-speared cubes are set out to tempt, wines from local vintners, roasted cashews and almonds, and a line of Official Chivalry Timbers Suites tees and sweats, shorts and bathing suits, all with little galloping Lancelot logos, made in USA: which in this case means Samoa.

Chivalry Timbers is a favorite of families on the way to Universal Studios, to Yosemite, to the Gold Rush Country in the Sierra foothills. It is a place to unplug and air out the kids. It is a bit under the weather, but clean — *you know what to expect* — and economical. And, *What the hell, we're only gonna sleep here.*

For similar reasons, and also for its ample Ye Olde Conference Room, it is a favorite of third tier convention planners and sees its share of financial planning tutorials, guns and ammo shows, farm product displays, and, *twice* each year, despite clinging to the Olde Annual label of a past scheduler, the toy and model train and railroad antiques gathering.

This is the Jerusalem of Taylor's pilgrimage; his transcendence to a higher plane, to a more sustainable and comprehensible way of life, to a time of vanished gallantry, his Camelot of hurtling tonnage, of red hot fire boxes and dining cars with waiters in starched white at sixty miles per.

※

Taylor reclines in his boxers on the double bed closest to the window. It is not relaxation. Rather, it is depletion and replenishment, in that order. He has this day been packed into a sardine can at Bob Hope Airport, in legless proximity to strangers with keyboards for laps, and has waited agonizingly second to Harlan in the lobby. He enjoys the non-human rattle of the air conditioner, the blue knight's eye blinking through the curtains. The room is poorly lit and he feels as gray as he looks. He breathes in, he breathes out.

Surely, the venerable Cramers feel no contrition for Brewster's performance: they have the clarity of good Puritan stock to guide them and live in an autumnal assurance of righteousness. But Taylor is shaken by Brewster's public inebriation. Not that he pities Brewster. There is not enough love lost between the two for that. Yet, there is this nagging fraternal responsibility: they carry the same membership cards in their pockets — The Railway & Locomotive Historical Society, Friends of the California Railroad Museum — and they both wear tiny cross sections of rail on their lapels. It is sibling-like, a brotherhood; they have drunk from a chalice of the same order, and members and non-members alike will register such peerage.

But a drunken railfan!

Taylor can hardly bear the shame. He wants to slip back into his trousers, head down to the lobby, and beg Lynette's forgiveness; try to convince her that *we are not really like that. Really.* About now, Mr. Cramer is paging through his binder with lists and photos of trainman's lanterns he already owns, and is dreaming of an etched B&O tall globe he is told will be available in the morning — a brass presentation lamp for some long-deceased engineer — and is casually dismissing Brewster as, *Not all that bad a guy for an asshole.* Mrs. Cramer, without answering, scowls at his language. Admonishment enough. But Taylor needs closure, a young woman's kind smile as she lifts the pale of responsibility from him. The thought calms him and he breathes normally. He will go down and express his sympathy over her ordeal. Show what nice guys train nuts can be, just like any other nuts — the gun people, the realtors, the tractor vendors. He sits up on the bed, wipes the beads of sweat from just below his vanishing hairline, even sticks an encouraging finger into one of his belt loops and tugs the trousers an inch or so upward.

But he doesn't put them on. He is really ready just to be here, right here, in the room and alone. Doesn't want to call more attention to himself, or let someone else do the calling for him. He doesn't want to see Brewster stagger off the elevator — his shirt stained, his Union Pacific patch tie-dyed in vomit — or ponder the breeding mystery of how a man can throw up on his own back. Did he remove the jacket and lay it on the tile floor as he proceeded to expertly miss the bowl; did he fail to find the stall and lay down in his own despicable effluence? Perhaps Chandra intervened, lugging comatose Harlan from under his humid arm pits, parading him through the lobby of gawkers and into the Squire's, perhaps to help him to the sink for a rinse, or to drown him in the toilet — what ever the popular delinquent control in Peshawar these days — and, perhaps, has kindly wiped Brewster's face with the guest's own clothing.

By now, Lynette has probably shined the whole thing on. She's been through this before. Certainly she knows the ropes. Maybe they have a manual or something, tells them how to handle this sort of thing. They probably get together in the locker room and unload after work, have cathartic sessions of support; round tables, if you will. That must be what they do. You couldn't deal with Brewsters all day for the kind of money she makes. Not that Taylor has any idea how much an associate at Chivalry Timbers makes, but there must be some sort of compensation: combat pay like they talk about for teachers, an employee of the month cake, her color eight by ten on the wall. Lynette is fine, like a rock, Taylor decides. Why, just the way she leaned into Brewster, that look that could kill, the slight widening of her nostrils that said it's a good thing for you that this counter separates my knee from your balls. Whatever the appropriate action, it can wait for tomorrow. In the event of probable non-action, it can wait considerably longer.

Taylor calls down for the Turkey Club and Diet Coke described in the guest book under *Ye Lite Repasts*. The Club in the picture looks like Emeril Lagasse assembled it; the one that will wind up in Taylor's mouth will be wafer-thin, with a mysterious flap of turkey sucking up a cheese-like substance with the efficiency of a sanitary pad, and a brittle stick of bacon aged and cured somewhere on the back of a lorry in a far distant land. It will be delivered by a young man with shaved head and zits that sparkle and gleam like Christmas lights wired to his face. He will be dressed in attire that bespeaks what someone in Cedar Rapids thinks English squires wore when the Sac and the Fox were hunting buffalo on the site of corporate headquarters.

Soon, ensconced with his sandwich, pickle wedge and microwaved fries on the bed he will not sleep in, Taylor forgets all about Lynette and Brewster and settles in for a night of flat screens. He grabs the remote, secure with its plastic-coated, steel-wound cable that enters a secure hole in the night stand, no doubt disappearing into a secret conduit that wends its way to a junction of anchors hidden in amber waves of mid-continent ethanol, and there chaperoned by a vigilant security officer waiting for the telltale tug of petty theft half a continent away.

But Taylor is here to click, not to take, and the evening's video menu appears with the skillful depression of his chunky thumb. There are the perennials — CNN and Fox. Cars are exploding on HBO. And there is porn. *Secret* porn. Over a Yani sound track, the guide informs him that any adult movie ordered will be charged to his credit card under a coded name and no one, absolutely no one, will know if he masturbated to "Desert Hot Sluts III; The Director's Cut," or "Harry Potter." Not that Taylor has someone to hide his viewing habits from. Even when he had, eons ago, he would not have chosen such fare. He shuts off the TV, releases an iBook from his bag, along with several of his own DVDs, plucks a bit of calcified bacon from his teeth, and queues up the well reviewed "Pere Marquette 1225 Freight Special", ninety-eight, heart-throbbing minutes of cinder and fume photo run-bys. Not exactly masturbatory fare, but a hardy rush nonetheless. For a night away from his own domain, there is not much more that Taylor can imagine needing.

There is, in actuality, more hotel room here than Taylor Bedskirt requires. It is ages since he has requested two beds, but hotel designers, not unlike Brewster, assume that such rooms are made for at least two people who apparently will not be cuddling. Lost in a world of drive wheels and running gear, he barely notices the framed prints of distressed damsels and knights errant screwed to the walls — the prints, not the damsels — and the bolted mace made into a lamp, the swords X'ed like an RR Crossing sign in threatening, razor-sharp styrene above the bed. Taylor, large that he is — six three, a torso like a Dietz lantern globe, bowing out at a low waist, ham sized hands, boxcar-sized shoes, sealed in insulation that begs to be rendered and burned in lamps — is a miniaturist, a scale modeler, three point five millimeters to the foot, a painter of baggage men held in the grip of tweezers, a sticker of decals, a gluer of balsa wood.

Two of the many sore points in his marriage were this scale of things and his immunity to life-sized décor. For Taylor, but not for Helen, there was solace in the tiny and awe in the controlled. It was a marriage nearly torn asunder by current and grease, coal, and size, and a healthy serving of acrimonious screaming and respondent silence, and would have dissolved completely had not a fortuitous commuter train interceded on their behalf.

Later, sandwich, wedge, stick and Coke all prey to voracious stomach acids, Taylor replaces the disc in its jewel box, dons his shopworn pajamas, and, yawning, he heads for the facilities. He washes the sticky nougat off of his fingers — he has hit the courtesy bar for a Three Musketeers — and works diligently on his teeth: brush, floss, rinse. His dentist has been threatening receding gum surgery and he wants no part of it. He pops his statin, his inhibitors, the recommended children's aspirin, his Prilosec, all from a little plastic box with the first letter of each day of the week molded three dimensionally onto the separate covers. He has yet to open the Viagra prescription, though he has had it for over a year. One pill makes him larger, one pill allows him to swallow, one pill keeps his arteries flowing like traffic over the Tehachapi Loop.

He lowers his ample buttocks onto the toilet, adjusts for the inevitable overlap, and cracks the new copy of <u>Trains Magazine</u> that he has remembered to bring in with him. He prefers <u>Classic Trains</u> or <u>Railroad & Railfan</u>; too much contemporary rail news in <u>Trains</u>. He is something of an antiquarian, our Taylor; he likes varnish and narrow gauge, high balls and trolleys. He hums to the rhythms of steam whistles and taps to the chug of drivers, of electric sparks crackling on the catenary. Helen liked modern, clean things. She disdained the clutter that seemed to perspire from Taylor's very flesh.

He savors the last run of the Cumbres & Toltec steam rotary plow, sets the magazine on the rim of the plastic molded tub over the neatly folded bath mat, completes the ritual at hand, tugs up his bottoms, and proceeds to the sink for another wash. Hands sanitized, he runs them through a memory of hair. Taylor's hair is the only thing about him that is light. His already overlarge skull seems to be annexing new forehead all the time, a continual hostile takeover. But the mostly still-blond wisps are weightless like a baby's; silky, with spacious pink real estate between each follicle suburb. He has taken to wearing hats in the sunlight on the advice of his brother-in-law. Even with so little fertility, there is a hint of persistent dandruff motes, highlighted by the reddish rays of the heat lamp.

He wipes the mist from the mirror with a Kleenex. More agonizing memories announce themselves, Helen at her venomous best: *Moron, you're schmearing up the mirror which I just Windexed. Go ahead, live in a pigsty! Should I bother?* Or, *Hey, Mr. Snow Globe, light powder and a promise of some decent skiing in the john today.* One Christmas, she gave him a case of Head and Shoulders. He had wanted an antique Jersey Central Assistant Station Master's hat that had collected six or seven bids on eBay.

He knows he is disheveled, rough along the edges, but he is clean, and is told, by the very few females of his acquaintance, that he is not unhandsome, does not lack for attractive features: a strong square jaw, striking eye pools the color of the B&O's Royal Blue, large, but gentle features that advertise a certain kindness, a certain red state wholesomeness that a nice divorcee or widow would find, if not sexy, secure. He is a Volvo of a man: square-ish and brawny and as safe as an air bag on impact. He hears this from Betsy, his older sister, over the table, over the phone, with husband Leo in the background pleading, *Leave the guy alone. He's a big boy. He doesn't need some tragic reject to eat up his money at this stage of the game.* Betsy says, *Shut the fuck up, will ya! He shouldn't be alone this time a life. What if something happens?* and proceeds to inventory Taylor's attributes with a clarity that is not always obvious to the naked eye, Leo's or otherwise.

Taylor lies atop the made bed, the one away from the detritus of Club sandwich, et al. He is tired but anxious for morning. Without Helen, even all these years later, this is Christmas, right here at the Chivalry Timbers Suites, ninety-eight moisture-laden degrees outside, frigid Freon clattering in through the vents, the world rushing by on Ninety-nine, the bugs splattering, the windmill churning at the miniature golf, the price of gas at the Shell across the road flipping in a blur faster than you can serve up burgers at the adjoining drive-thru, and Ye

Olde Conference Center packed with railroad antiques, like goodies under Leland Stanford's tree. He can almost hear reindeer prancing on the roof.

III

H E WAKENS TO THE RASP OF the air conditioner: sounds like screws have loosened in a full night's labor. The room is frigid — penguins could mate here, Laplanders could herd reindeer. Climatologically motivated, Taylor acts with the verve of a smaller man, is soon showered, shaved, wiped, rolled and powdered, and probably combed, although you wouldn't know it the way his weightless coif misbehaves as he exits the elevator and hustles through the lobby, tellingly, without a glance at Ye Olde Check In. He is dressed incognito in nondescript Target specials, with only the vastness of the material to betray his whereabouts. His jeans are the color of track ballast, his long sleeve shirt off-off-white, except for the gray ponds already seeking level under his arms. He lumbers on hoppers of tan sneakers. Yet, ultimately, he is outed by the rail-slice lapel pin.

The vendors have advanced to the Conference Room to wrestle with the tables and uncrate railroadiana. That is what it is called, this assemblage of old, discarded things, parts and parts of parts of lost industry.

Taylor grabs a tray and joins the buyers in the buffet line. There is a sprinkling of non-members too; families anxious to occupy small spaces at high speeds, now in respite from the ever more difficult task of seeing how long they can stand each other in a Toyota Sequoia's rarified air, and nomadic tribes of salesmen, suited up by Men's Warehouse, thinking commissions as they down bagels and caffeine.

Taylor helps himself to the equally itinerate eggs running like fugitives in the stainless vat. He nods to Bill Stiles who, like Taylor, is a collector of timetables, digs deep into the steak fries, takes a pat on the back from Hank what's-his-face who seems to show up at all of the shows west of Chicago. Tonging into a rasher of bacon, a slice of ham with a tiny navel bone, and three burnt sausage pellets, he greets that character Peter-something, once again in engineer's overalls and Seaboard cap as if he is doing living history, piles up a weighty stack of pancakes hatted with butter square and invasive syrup, and sees, across the room, granite-mugged Carl "Nightstick" Derouche, the former Burlington company dick. Then, rewarding his ticker with melon and seedless grapes, he winks convincingly at a couple who he can't identify for the life of him, gathers up orange juice railed from Florida, coffee, sugar packets, several napkins, some bent and chewed cutlery, and heads towards a lonely corner table for two with a chair that faces out through tinted glass to the swimming pool. He has forty-five minutes to enjoy the flapping kids, empty the plate, head back to the warming lamps, suck down seconds, hit the ATM in the lobby, and set off to diminish his funds filling the rare gaps in his collection.

Stars collide. It is not to be so easy: in Taylor's experience, it seldom is. The Geldorfs are two at a table for four. Jack kicks out one of the empty chairs: Darlene will not be denied.

"Jesus!" summonses Jack, estimating the post sea level elevation of Taylor's breakfast. "Expecting Sir Edmund Hillary? You could hide Katmandu right there between the steak fries and dead pig strips."

Taylor fails to understand the analogies, offers a surrender grin, sinks reluctantly into the assigned seat, gets busy with the business at hand.

"Must be sharing," says Darlene. "Who is she?" She pretends to look about the room for Taylor's mysterious flame.

"Maybe he's pregnant," Jack says. "You pregnant, Taylor?"

Mouth full, Taylor shakes his head, mumbles through egg and syrup-drowned potato, points to his chest in some sort of denial that, although obtuse, is understood by the Geldorfs. "You on for tomorrow?" from Jack. "Moncton has put together something with the Modesto people. He thinks he can wheedle a cab ride on old Six Hundred."

Taylor shakes his head again. "Projects," he manages. "Didn't drive up this time."

"You flew? Traitor to the cause." Both Geldorfs have plates that reveal the devastation wrought by vegans: gnarled pits, naked seeds and stems, spent bags of green herbal tea. They are faddists, haven't always been fauna free; probably won't continue to be so.

"You?" asks Taylor, and immediately feels foolish.

"You're kidding, right!" scolds Darlene. They are both in black leather cycle garb, hers with squaw fringe, their helmets perched like love birds on the empty chair. They have come up, as usual, on matching Harley Dyna's, and are as tan as hobos. Jack wears his hair in long cyclonic whorls. Darlene's is cut chemo-short, though the dangerous plunge of zipper connotes choice rather than surgery. She has a hard punkish sensuality and is not exactly pretty; he is prematurely craggy — he prefers sculpted — and not exactly handsome. But at thirty-five and forty-one respectively, they are the gossip darlings of youth in the Inland Empire Chapter of gray beards. They enjoy a trailer in Hemet, and Taylor knows them from meets at the San Gabriel Valley trolley museum, where Jack is known to don a full Pacific Electric uniform and pilot a Big Red Car around the loop. It is rumored that Jack once delivered nitrous oxide tanks to dentists, had a small house and a wife, and that Darlene was a hygienist with an alternate plan. It is rumored, also, that Jack was merchandising out the tanks to the un-certified, and did a short, license-voiding stint in a white-collar facility. When he got out, it was Darlene, not the wife, that was there to receive him.

Patty Moncton and Mrs. Cramer enjoy hours of speculation. Perhaps from forming license plates, Jack is said to be good with his hands. *I'd like to confirm that with Darlene*, Brewster has famously announced. Jack builds intricate model streetcars that receive current from brass trolleys and overhead wires. Darlene makes stained glass windows whose themes alternate between interurban electrics and couples coupling. Together, they tune their own bikes, graft cactuses, and ply each other with home-etched tattoos. Patty Moncton has noted that there is often an aroma of some illegal substance in their wake, and Mrs. Cramer has it on good account that their love life is sometimes a wider community experience.

Like Neighborhood Watch? Patty offers. *What was that line in that movie,* I like to watch? The train husbands accuse the wives of catty delusion; the train wives are cautiously aware of an envious undercurrent among the husbands.

"This taken?" Stan Franco is standing with tray and speaking to the Geldorf helmets. "They're with us," says Jack, clearing the chair, dropping the headgear loudly to the floor. "Stan the Man, set your aging ass down."

To Taylor's mild chagrin, Stan obliges. "One aging ass down," he says. "The big question is, Houston, can I get it back up?" He proceeds slowly to dismantle a waffle. "Been out? 'S'gonna be a scorcher."

"What d'ya think, we sleep in leather?" from Darlene.

"It's been said," Stan chuckles.

"Fuck off, Stanley," snorts Jack, aware of the group chatter. Nearby, a family of four shudders through thankful devotions for the Chivalry Timbers and God's bounties.

"Somebody's got his kick stand up his ass this morning," Stan observes. "And it *is* a bit Mojave out there."

It is all friendly. They have been attacking each other for as long as they can remember. Dr. Franco lives in ghostly Eureka where, he says, *the coast sort of evaporates into sea. There is no line of demarcation between what is liquid and what is solid.* Retired from the mill offices in Scotia, and working for the last four years on the construction of a diminutive live steam loco, he still manages to teach an occasional evening class on Forest Husbandry at Humboldt State. Owning no Stockton-appropriate clothing, he is dressed like a lumberjack all in flannels and sleeves; looks like he just lost the logrolling event. He belatedly notices Taylor, and asks, "And how're you? Long time, no see. Joinin' the boys in Modesto tomorrow?"

Taylor finds a narrow empty passage in his otherwise occupied yowl. "Plane tonight."

"Plane? Jesus, short hop like yours! Salt and pepper there, Darlene?"

"So we've been saying," says Jack.

"Stuff to do, you know," Taylor defends. "The house. Always something."

Stan agrees. "Don't I know it. I have spent most of my retirement on deferred maintenance."

"And boiler fitting," Jack corrects.

"Yeah, well, that's the down time. But Taylor's right. Particularly an old Victorian like mine. I tell Linda, let's unload this joint. For chrissakes, how much space do two old farts need? I'd do the fixing myself if I were the tender age of my Hells Angel pal here. If it's not plumbing, it's electrical. We got some dry rot in the basement and the pest control folks can't seem to evict the rats running a tap dance academy in the attic. Anyone you call you get nickeled and dimed, anyone that knows what they're doing. I got a carpenter thinks he's Frank-fucking-Gehry, scuse the French, hon. Not a level or a square to be seen on this guy's tool belt. Sure, you can cruise the Home Depot for a Mexican or two, and don't get me wrong, these people'll work their asses off, I got nothing against 'em, but it's all grunt work, hauling, digging, you're lucky if you can get one understands a plumb line enough to set a fence post. But finish carpentry? Install an outlet? Don't even go there."

Taylor is suddenly grateful that Stan has joined them. He feels redeemed. They can all believe he needs to get home early to un-stuff a toilet with a bent coat hanger and save a bundle from some pirate with regulation electric snake. He finds himself once more consulting his watch, shoveling larger and larger quantities of fuel into his mouth.

"Sure stokin' the swill," Jack remarks.

"Speaking of which," says Stan, "you two missed the Harlan Brewster show last night," an announcement that gets Darlene's attention and draws a sharp scowl. "We are on the brink of the decline and fall of western civ, my friends. I don't know why they don't just kick his rude ass out. Brewster the Rooster, cockadoodling through another badly acted scene. The lower classes shall inherit the earth, and Harlan shall be the executor of the estate. My day, wouldn't let a dope like that get a leg in the door. Shows to go ya, when ya got nothing but colonials in all the managerial positions. Not that I've got anything against our subcontinent brethren. Very industrious people. But, Christ, there was a time when a good, old fashioned American hotel management class would…"

"Here to have a good time, Stan."

"Sure, who's stoppin' ya? But Christ, Jack!"

"And Jack Christ, at that, speaking of reasonable carpenters." Jack stands, takes one last sip of his grapefruit juice, and makes the appropriate face. "You know, you academes are spoiled by the five star amenities you got up there in Arcata or U-reek-a or wherever, but us low life railfans, we're just bumpkins agog down here in Gotham. And, well, I can't say it hasn't been a slice a life, because it's been *at least* a slice, and I'd really like to sit here and visit'th y'all through the weekend, discussing garbage disposals and lawn jockeys, and as certain as drivers in LA will continue to try and beat the Blue Line at the grade crossing, I hope I've remembered to TiVo The Brewster Chronicles: How Not to Get Laid, and we've certainly enjoyed, the wife and I, listening to you and Little Taylor here, old vets as you are, bewail the trials of contemporary domesticity, but, alas, me thinks, it's just about show time."

"What's the rush? Prices go down consistent with the seller's desperation," lectures Stan. "No one wants to lug all that crap home."

"We're simplifying our lives," says Darlene. "Downsizing. Shrinking our footprint. We don't buy anything anyway, so's might as well *see* it all. There is a museum quality to this thing." She stands beside Jack, who adds, practiced, as if they've run this routine before, "We are railroad's answer to realty, choo choo looky-loos, and Stan, looks as if you've got kind of a museum quality yourself."

"I'll give you what to look at, son." Doctor Stan, one week short of seventy-two, leans back in his chair, and says, "Why'n't you and Taylor here run off and enjoy yourself with the toy trains while I take Darlene up to my room to see a few etchings, find out what she's missed all these years wasted on the likes of you?"

"Promises, promises," she dismisses.

"Gettin' a little carried away with this Brewster thing, Doctor Damp," says Jack. "Tell ya what, barring rigor mortis, you get a hard-on sometime this decade, you be sure to give us a ring."

"Jeez-us, cheapskate," Darlene complains. "*I* haven't even gotten a *ring*! Except the ones I make myself."

Taylor wants to get up too, leave while the three of them are still entangled in what he assumes is humor. Stan's arrival had thankfully reduced him to irrelevancy, allowed him to avoid the bulk of the banter. "See you inside," he says, hoping not to. He stands, too abruptly, catching his belt buckle on a lip of table, rattling plates of breakfast detritus. Taylor can be his own unsteady fault line. No space in the actual world seems large enough for him.

"Whoa, *toro!* Mind the china shop," says Jack, stepping back into his chair, shoving it, hoping to avoid the expected shrapnel. "'Night of the Living Foamers!' Contain yourself, nothing sells before the doors open."

"Leave 'im alone, Jack," says Darlene. "Tell him, Taylor, to leave you alone. Jack's not exactly Gene Kelly himself."

"I am grace on earth, my dear," Jack insists.

"Sorry. I'm so sorry, I…I…"

"'S'nothing," from Darlene, always the one to comfort. "It's why we wear leather. Cleans up real easy." She is checking about her v-neck, wiping a napkin across her zipper collection, just in case, just a precaution. She doesn't overdo it, doesn't want to further embarrass Taylor. "Anyway, Jack, tell Taylor about the time your forgot there were *three* steps down from the trailer."

"No, no, no, no. We don't go there. I was captive of a depth-distorting, alien substance."

Taylor quickly apologizes again, receives denials from the trio of stand-ups, and hurries away; like a sloth hurries away, a great swaying of extra insulation and disconnected steps, two out of three frames missing from the picture. Returning his tray, he pauses momentarily, breathes in, breathes out, relishing his escape, however clumsy, at once saddened by the lost opportunity for seconds and heartened by thoughts of sugar-plum switch stands, nickel and brass, spit and polish, high iron and high gloss, and the need to speak of nothing but what is essential: The Great American Train. Unconsciously, he checks his fly with a swift pass of fingers, and, self-consciously, brushes a minor drift from his shoulder. The action recalls a classic Helenism — flung his way as he modeled protective tunnels for a mountain pass — *Forget the trains, snowflake, maybe you can craft tiny snow sheds to wear on your shirt like epaulettes.*

Foamer, huh! he thinks, as Jack, catching up at the tray return, winks a brotherly wink, and calls out, "All a-fuckin'-board, Casey Jones!"

And all a-fuckin'-board it is.

IV

THE HALL IS A STARK RECTANGLE with removable walls to accommodate any number of numismatists, time share peddlers, *pow wow* delegates, sales associates earning points on the cosmetics pyramid, Tupperware party planners there to snap, suck and seal. It is lit yellow from cans in the acoustic ceiling. There are no windows, no real doors, just panels that vanish to accommodate the events, and one cinderblock load-bearing wall between the conventioneers and the sizzling parking lot. Today, from concrete anchors on the one firm barrier, the red/white/blue banner of the National, with its steamer and trolley car in Chang and Eng perpetual fusion, hangs a bit too small, revealing eight horses' legs a-running, four armor clad boots a-hanging, the butt ends of dual lances a-charging, and plumes a-flying on the aggregate wall. How these jousting puzzle parts relate behind the banner is left to Ye Olde Imagination.

Mr. Napuri, the day manager — his black hair slicked like a roundhouse floor — is making last minute gesticulations, adjustments, apologies and ministrations, and spreading just a whisper of jasmine incense over the platform signs, spittoons, and tie spikes arrayed neatly on the tables. There is a general hum of expectation. A bustling of enterprise. Last minute table linens, Pullman blankets, and whole sinks ripped from the compartments of sleepers are edged apart to accommodate one last Pyrene fire extinguisher from the Santa Fe, one final double-sided REA red diamond. There is a compressor in the room and someone is already tuning the Leukenheimers, heavy polished brass steam whistles, the orchestra of restless movement, the night callers, the banshee screamers of freedom and adventure straddling a dusky horizon. There is the buzz of a small city depot, the sweet-sour electrical whiff of model trains, and the cheerful salutations of semi-annual cronies.

Taylor takes mental inventory of the regulars from all the chapters on the Pacific Slope: the Sierra, the Redwood, the Inland Empire, the South Bay, the Border, and the possible new kids on the block, the non-joiners, the curious. There are locals and circuit sellers, the ones who do Buena Park, Gaithersburg, Austintown, The Great American Train Show, with religious consistency. They are mostly men, white men, *very* white men, and a smattering of resigned wives; *the camp followers,* Brewster says. Most are reasonably spry, but there are the inevitable canes and aluminum walkers; one member glides about in an electric cart, his booty neatly stashed in a basket behind him; another, lugged about by a stalwart wife of half a century, runs tubes up his nose, drags a dolly with what appears to be diving gear — Lloyd Bridges come up out of the drink. The High School Reunion Principle of Subtraction is strictly adhered to and each meet sees fewer participants from the old guard. Theirs is a hobby plagued by attrition.

But still, the survivors show up. They are, or were — mostly were — teachers, mechanics, bankers, owners of mom and pop shops, attorneys, CEOs, sellers of all the things Americans buy. Some have enjoyed the blessing of a munificent god and have actually worked on the railroad all the livelong day. They are middle-aged and old and a few scrappy youngsters in their formative fifties. They are people who remember when the things in this room were not avocational, were the things of commerce, bore the stamp of some of the world's greatest industrial conglomerates — Pullman, Baldwin, St. Louis Car. There are historians here, inveterate collectors of stuff no one will ever need again, Renaissance men of all things rail, myopic specialists looking for padlocks, *only* for padlocks, or *only* for Chicago & Eastern Illinois padlocks, or some of the very few items extant that say the words *Hocking Valley R.R.* on them, and *only* those words. Sig Heffernan is all about the New York, Ontario & Western. Bob Westfield lives only for narrow gauge. Bennett Ingolffson is obsessed by logging engines, customized for curves and grades and creeping headway among the conifer stumps, the Shays, the Heislers, the Climaxes — *My fave,* Brewster had told Darlene Geldorf at a previous show, to which she congratulated him for finally reaching puberty, offered him best wishes from her repertoire of familiar Universal Sign Language gestures, and proceeded to grant him a *buena vista* of the wonderful half moons of her leather shiny-black ass as it diminished on the way to the closest sunset.

Don't bother these guys with Pennsy. Don't try to entice these minimalists with the *Broadway Limited* or the *Phoebe Snow*. Gus Nathan knows from memory every Pacific Electric spur line, street stop, milepost and switch stand that no longer exists. Some are here for the garden railways, the LGB gargantuans, looking for a sweet deal on a slightly used Uintah articulated to chug around the geraniums. There is a legion of HOers. There are husky O gauge buffs, delicate N gaugers with less space than time on their hands. And though there is a stark absence of former porters and dining car waiters, there are, instead, a sizable number of older boys who have actually pulled a throttle or thrown a switch in their day. They are, many of them, wrinkled and palsied, with the calluses of hard manual labor, and tales of boomers and run-aways, and sleet so blinding you couldn't see the steam domes from the cab. And they are all as straight as the trans-Australian; although, based on percentages in the general population, of which we can only assume they are representative, one out of ten of them has a secret to conceal that might make him unpopular in a work gang.

These are men's men in the traditional industrial sense. They don't *decorate* their rooms: they just hang stuff — heavy, metal stuff. They get men's diseases like prostate cancer and angina and can't for the life of them — these solid, to-the-core-sensible guy's guys who have been hitched to the same women for forty or fifty years — understand how anyone from a decent family can contract HIV. They are mostly Christians of varying degrees; few wear Jesus on their sleeves but most prefer Merry Christmas to Happy Holidays. One or two Jews have come out of the closet: Ruben Goldenberg, an itinerant time table peddler based in Broward County and a refugee from Toronto winters, has taken to wearing a patch of blue silk on his head that has caused some minimal, yet tolerant, comment, and there is a clean cut Mormon from St. George, sweating in his storied mystic underwear, who makes his appearance with locomotive builder's plates on an occasional basis.

Sometimes there's a new face. Today, a fellow in a suit with a *Marv Hibbler* name tag who is rep-ing a small radio scanner outfit to the seriously stricken, those fans who need to know the location of every long freight winding through rattlesnake infested canyons. Ridge Canfield was the first of this bunch to sign on to such technology, had been known in those days of yore to race *The Sleek Geek* — his fifty-five De Soto Firesweep — cab to cab with Electro-Motive diesels, an equally devoted buddy hanging out the shotgun window and recording the action on Super 8. None are people who cause much attention at airports. More are Republicans than Democrats. A few plead Independent. Nightsitck leans toward Ron Paul, Jack is solidly in the Kucinich camp. Taylor hasn't voted since...well, ever. Not even for Moncton as Chapter Chair. He likes to imagine he would have supported Charlie Crocker's bid for governor, but imagine he must. Few of these stalwarts get pulled over by urban police for minor vehicle violations. They do not raise eyebrows at Walmart. Taylor has seen them all, but knows few names. Names, faces, are not what interests him.

The Monctons are set up in mock permanence, with black, felt-skinned backdrops for their Mimbreno creamers and Seaboard Air Line cruet sets. There are one or two sellers — Taylor knows them as clients of the High Ball train shop — making final amendments, truing a battered Cleveland Union Station sign, tweaking a short globe into a bent Dressel lantern frame disinclined to accept it. Brewster is there with his uniform buttons and badges, looking shrunken, ill and ill at ease, as colorless as the amber lights will allow.

Now the buyers are wandering in, a little uneasy with the burden of things fried debasing into arterial sludge. They nod to Taylor, poised like a rent-a-cop at the door. Eyelids flick his way. A few hands tap his back, no doubt releasing an avalanche that no longer worries Taylor, not here, not now. There are scattered *"Heys"* and *"Hi yas"* and *"Howdy-dos,"* even a *"S'up"* or two, and a *"My man"* for good measure.

Taylor is as gracious as Taylor gets. He even smiles. There is a cheery pinkness to his ample face, his slits of eyes unusually spacious and illuminated, his meaty lips parted, moist, and ready for the passage of words. Taylor verges dangerously on congenial. The talk in this room will be of solid things, relevant things; conversations he can enter without prodding, arguments to which he can lend credence, expertise.

The issues will involve Amtrak closures, a fund drive at the Nevada Northern, the latest Walther's catalogue of miniatures. The topics will be born of Alco, EMD, the Jewitt Car Co., the parlance rooted in places like Lima, Ohio, Cheyenne, Wyoming, Promontory, Utah, and Barstow. Some of the babble will be of current interest: is the Administration squeezing the purse strings of public transit? Will there ever be anything approaching a bullet train blurring the landscape between LA and San Francisco? Are short lines on the upturn?

But most of what Taylor will hear and what Taylor will say is residue, nostalgic, of lost possibilities, of unfair perks for truckers, of corporate conspiracies to do in the trolley and to damn the steam boiler. This is where Taylor Bedskirt goes for a rush. This is his adrenalin-charged bungee jump, his rappel into the black void of Moaning Cave, his Mammoth Mountain slopes. This is where Taylor goes to catch a wave, his Bonneville, his I-Max, his Riverside Five Hundred. His whitewater. He breathes in. He breathes out. He steps in and comes home.

Taylor's senses are on acute alert, amplified; he can actually taste and smell what is on those mismatched folding tables. He proceeds to thresh his way down the rows, here and there squeezing a crop sample for ripeness. He has a practiced pattern to his harvest, always beginning on the furrow farthest to the right from the entrance, winding his way dutifully through the antiques, and only then proceeding through the next divider into the electric train room. He is not a dodger, does not switchback across aisles, but slowly trots up one side, down the other; a connoisseur, taking a taste here, a sniff of cork there, rolling it all about on his educated tongue, breathing in the dynamic bouquet of oils and lubricants.

Nightstick Darouche has beaten him to the first table. The vendor, a youngish, fit fellow in his mid-fifties, is someone Taylor doesn't know if he knows. The faces blend; the features shape change, all of a kind to Taylor whose thoughts are on the tables, settled there with a soft hiss like morning steam. Darouche is telling the vendor that when he was knocking heads on the high iron, "We didn't have these kinds a graffiti problems all over the rolling stock. *We* sent a message. Vandals didn't have rights in my day. Property was property."

Darouche has a smokestack physique and a rugged angry scowl that announces itself in the set of his jaw, the broad reach of shoulders, the planted trunks that hold him up. He is wearing a tight black Norfolk Southern t-shirt, and over that, a tan corduroy sport coat, unseasonable, with a missing button on the right sleeve and an elbow patch lifting like a scab from the opposite elbow. He is a short man, topped by thinning needles of crew cut defined by the corners of his block of head, itself set tightly on his larger cube of torso. His neck is currently on sabbatical. The years of chasing vagrants across the tops of boxcars have left him burnished; he has come up through the ranks and earned his swarthiness, resembles a creosoted crosstie in proportion and hue. The vendor listens intently to his tales of yard enforcement, nods a quick greeting to Taylor who is studying a display case. Taylor has no idea how old Darouche is, but is certain it is older than he looks.

Nightstick doesn't so much as acknowledge Taylor as stake him out. His conversation veers one way, his suspicious beads of eyes the other, dissecting Taylor as if he is suspected of smuggling spray paint into the building. "Taylor?" says Darouche, interrupting himself. "It's Taylor, right?" He knows full well it is Taylor: he likes to act out — dismissive and superior — as if Taylor isn't worth remembering by people with authority.

"Yes, that's right," Taylor mumbles. He doesn't want to be drawn in.

"I knew it!" he says, as if, *ah ha! It is* not *all right to be Taylor.* In his hand, Derouche is holding a gleaming, seven point Market Street Railway detective's shield in mint, over which he and the vendor have been having some polite dispute as to authenticity. "We got counterfeits up the ying yang," Darouche explains. "The Chinese could replicate your thumb print so well the Feds couldn't tell the difference. I worry when I come across an item in this kind a condition. A little wear tells me something. This here, I don't know."

The vendor doesn't argue. It is too early in the day to lay on the pressure. Darouche is his first looker, and he will hold the haggling for the late afternoon crowd.

"What do you think...Taylor, is it?" He is interrogating, trying to get Taylor to slip, give a different name. Darouche knows more than Taylor about railroad police badges, of which he has a well-known and comprehensive collection, beginning with the badge he wore on the job, and through which he has managed to maintain a thread of continuity through these difficult, fallow years of retirement. If you feign interest, he will remove a fading snapshot from his wallet, show you how they are arranged on a wall behind glass, how the strobe glares back at you from the sheen. He longs to hurl a vagrant through an open boxcar door. It's been years since he's practiced his pitch, has felt useful.

Taylor is wise enough to defer with a shrug and move on. Darouche watches him go, stays on him until the Geldorf's cross his path, and he is satisfied to intercept these possible new scofflaws. The room is swarming with perps. "When I was their age," he mutters to the vendor, "you were expected to do a little work before you saw that much of a girl. Makes ya wonder who's buying and who's selling." If he were outside on the tracks, he would spit: has a good mind to do so anyway.

"How's the hunt?" Jack asks Taylor in passing.

"Oh, you know," Taylor responds, which means sufficiently nothing to either of them, but which frees him to move on to the next display.

And so it goes. He buys little. *The prices, the prices!* He feels like he is in line at the pump. One would think the economy would devalue such non-essentials. In any case, he needs to be on a jet and there won't be space for anything sizeable, himself included. But that's okay. He, like Jack, like Darlene, can be Chauncey *the* Gardner too. He likes to look, and if he comes home with nothing other than what he carries in a bag, he will still have come home with something.

The next vendor, a Reno tax accountant by day, and an active member of the Nevada State Railroad Museum, lectures Taylor on the evils of eBay. "You guys'er killing us," he complains. "We feel a certain abandonment." Taylor has heard the whine before. It has become a mantra. The accountant, he remembers, is a reasonable guy, who is constantly thinning out his collection and using the funds to fatten it up again. Taylor can't for the life of him remember if he has ever heard the man's name, though they have faced each other over the portable table six or seven times in the last few years. Taylor has given him personal checks, written to *Cash* — most of the vendors accept them, usually accompanied by a cautionary remark like, *Haven't been ripped off yet,* or, *At least you got your address there. Truth is, Here, everyone knows everyone.*

Taylor says, "There's a limit to what one can afford."

"There's a limit to a profit margin as well. I got overhead here."

"I understand, but still..."

"And you come in here and you get to handle the goods. Far as I know, the virtual tech isn't there to let you do that yet. How many times have you opened a package and found the contents to be not as represented? That doesn't happen here. This is the real deal. That alone's worth the five bucks that got you in here."

"You're right there."

"So, my friend, make me an offer on the St. Joe badge."

Taylor hefts it in his hand, runs his ample thumb over the Herren Bros. hallmark imprinted on the back. It is solid, cold. "I can do fifty."

"Fifty! I paid fifty! I look like eBay to you!" It is friendly, it is banter, but there is a soul to it, a portent.

By the third aisle, Taylor is still empty handed. *Nothing gained, nothing lost*, he thinks, not even the time spent with the used book venders, the perennial pushers of <u>Railroads of Nevada & Eastern California, Vols. I</u>, <u>II</u> and <u>III</u>, with or without dust jackets, the over thumbed, discredited editions of Beebe & Glegg with their splotchy black and whites on cheap matt paper, or the specialty titles covering traction and short lines: the Visalia Electric, the Yosemite Valley, the Apalochicola Northern. He has most of them, dressed in clear library liners, some new, the used ones inducted into his collection after a stint in his garage freezer stuffed in zip locks like extra meat; the cold kills the earwigs who would rather eat pages than read them. He has most of the used magazines too, also in their prophylactic security — Taylor practices safe railfaning — boxed and indexed, yet, happily, he thumbs through them once again, discusses prices, shakes his head, and heads off down the line wagging his plentiful caboose.

"Hey, Bedskirt, over here." It is Brewster. The voice grates, an effort to call above a whisper. Taylor has already seen him, averted his gaze, but as easy as Taylor is to ignore, he is that difficult to miss, even in bland, Target camouflage. He forces an almost pleasant upturn of mouth and reluctantly approaches Brewster's neat little rows of uniform buttons. They are set on a soft, synthetic cotton linings in thin black cases piled one upon the other.

"I don't do buttons," Taylor lies. It is okay to lie to Brewster. It is okay to lie to his sister Betsy, to the guys at the High Ball, to imagine a lie to the once-pretty waitress at the diner he usually lunches at. It is pretty much okay just to lie in order to enjoy anonymity. A good white lie from a good white man like Taylor can be the key to happiness.

"Sorry to hear that," says Brewster without his usual enthusiasm. "How're you with zippers? That Darlene, now, I saw you at breakfast trying to get a peak of prime over the subdivision on your plate. I think the view lots are worth the premium. Talk about zippers. The broad's got more teeth on her chest than you'd find in a shark's mouth!" Despite the Brewsterisms, Brewster is looking under it all this morning; feels like a keg rolled over him.

Taylor pretends to study the cases, the little gold and silver coat and lapel buttons, the rope anchors for conductor's caps. "How're you feeling this morning?" he ventures, at once sorry he has done so, not wishing to hear a tale of woe that will move him not.

"I feel nothing. Absolutely nothing." A torn Alka-Seltzer wrapper peeks from his shirt pocket and the Levi jacket is not to be seen, no doubt dripping away on the extendable clothesline up in his room. He swallows down some insistent bile. "And I'm a guy who likes to feel."

"Wow," says Taylor, "Boston Elevated! Don't see those everyday." Maybe every other day, and they both know it.

"Forget the do dads, Tailsman. I'll *treat* you to the B.E. if you want it. Let me ask you something. As you came through the lobby this morning, did you take note whether that little number from last night was at the desk?" Taylor looks puzzled, doesn't like the route this one is on. It is a mixed train he doesn't want to board. "One with the jugs," pleads Brewster. Taylor doesn't remember the Juggs; perhaps that was a couple he waved at in the buffet.

Taylor's density competes admirably with his girth. Not that he is stupid. He holds an engineering degree from Cal State Fullerton — not exactly MIT, but no small feat. But Taylor doesn't listen to, doesn't hear, doesn't covet anything that can't toot or whistle. His is a practiced, hard-earned naiveté, an energetic screening of most of the things that pass for human activity. He has TV, but no cable, no antenna, and uses it exclusively for his DVDs. The hundreds of bookmarks on his computer are exclusively rail sites and rail chat rooms. And eBay; the drain down which much of his income flushes. Though not immune to their charms, in particular a certain aforementioned waitress who will subsequently introduce herself, he tends to avoid women, even the safe ones he is related to, and actively detours around any encore of matrimonial warfare.

Nor is he much attuned to hanging with the guys, hasn't learned their jargon, doesn't get their jokes. Doesn't want to. His rare forays into male bonding have been miserable failures; when long time counter man Benny Canola threw himself a stag retirement bash upon exiting the High Ball — a bacchanal that assumed the proportions of a Blue Ray marathon of great Super Bowl highlights — though not caring very much if he came or didn't, the guys in the shop insisted, cajoled, embarrassed, and all but bludgeoned Taylor into attending. It was the right thing to do. *Just pick up a six-pack and drag your sorry ass on over,* Benny, the man of the day, ordered. Taylor showed up with refreshments from Costco, pulled out the contents and set it down on a coffee table reflecting Benny's TV. *This is what?* Benny asked. *Sixpack,* Taylor defended. *You said a sixpack.* Benny shook his head. The others covered their mouths. *Of beer, dipshit! Not a sixer of Berringer White Zin! Key*-riste — which, briefly, Taylor figured to be a Flagler-bridged islet off the southern coast of Florida. *Man, you need to get out and do some serious catching up.* It was the last time they invited him, sorry as they felt; it was the last time he would be coaxed.

And now, Brewster is saying, "Help me out here, bud. See, I think she kind a liked me. I felt this buzz. However, being a bit uncoupled, I think I missed my signals. Boy, I'd like to show that little piece a freight around the hump yard! You saw the signs, right? Right?"

"Gee, I don't know, Brewster. I was kind of browsing the brochures, getting a feel of where I'm at. I'm not all that adept at reading women. Been single for a while."

"All the more reason! Fuckin' *Stockton,* Bedibye! What to feel was…" The Geldorfs are passing; Darlene is giving Brewster a look that could derail tank cars with toxic loads, evacuate whole neighborhoods. Brewster can nearly smell the seepage and his stomach, in dissonant concert, wires up another acidic load.

"Got to roll," Taylor says. "Take care, now."

"Yeah, you roll. Want the B.E.? Go on, 't's yours."

"I really don't do buttons. Maybe I'll be back around later."

"Be sure you are. I could use a little help with this problem, Taylor."

It is not clear to either of them of what help Taylor can be, and Taylor is already rummaging through old employee rule books from the Illinois Central and the Florida East Coast, spread like a lady's fan on another table. A row away he sees Nightstick, ominously exploring the heft of a four foot wrench that would be at home dismantling passenger engines, and casting furtive glances both at Brewster and Taylor. Surely, Nightstick has seen them huddled together, planning, plotting, considering all kinds of terrible eventualities à la Stephen King. When their eyes lock, Taylor's and Nightstick's, the latter does not avert his gaze.

Soon, like many others in the growing crowd of shoppers, Taylor actually makes a purchase. The object of his desire is a tattered cardboard sign in black and gold that reads, PULLMAN TICKETS. It is worth a fraction of what he manages to pay for it. Taylor does not need to advertise the sale of tickets to defunct parlor cars, but it will fit snuggly into his sense of cluttered aesthetics and home décor. Taylor, of course, has never been plagued with HGTV; seldom uses terms like *mid century, eclectic* or *whimsy.*

He scans the brochures of the Broward Jew, is in love with an ornate <u>Route of the Minute Men</u> lithoed folder from the Lexington & Boston Street Railway, circa 1905, for which Ruben would like to realize one hundred ten dollars, minus the customary ten percent, as stated on the little round tag stuck to the back of the clear map envelope. Taylor heaves from one stout oak of a leg to another, pulls a pair of battered reading glasses from his shirt pocket, adjusts the duct tape over one hinge with pressure from his fingers, hesitates. "I don't know, I don't know," to which equivocation Ruben adds the extra perk, "If you buy more than one item, we can play with the numbers a bit." Taylor, having seen the same booklet rescued from cyberspace for forty-six fifty after three bids, promises to think about it, and continues to browse up the final antique row.

The humanity is now as thick as cornbread stuffing and elbows have assumed the importance of appliance *de rigueur.* Checks are being written and cash surrendered. There is a significant absence of receipts or Mastercards, and Halsey Carmeno, late of the IRS field office in Sacramento, feels the full weight of guilt more than that of the great, solid brass Burnham, Parry, Williams & Co. builder's plate that clings to his underarm like solid deodorant, and stares at the worn carpet as he passes the table of the Reno tax accountant.

There is now the odor of perspiration and hot dogs and old metal in the filtered air. Taylor finds himself in front of a familiar case with a few common hat badges: the tallish Long Island Assistant Conductor, the Canadian National Porter, the never-miss-a-show New York Railways in its simple aluminum backing. He dons the glasses again; they are thick with compromised black frames that make him look like a raccoon, and the lenses are smudged and scratched like they had landed on Omaha Beach.

"How much for the St. Paul Union Depot?" Taylor inquires. The object of attraction is a simple nickel plaque, curved to embrace a hat, from Attendant 39.

The woman behind the case is grandmotherly and agrarian, wears jeans and a blouse she probably fashioned herself from an old saddle blanket. It is certain she would rather be pickling produce in jars than vending cap badges in Stockton. She removes the badge from the case, checking on the back for a price. "He's got it marked sixty-five."

"What can he do?"

"Papa," she calls over to a slight gentlemen who his matching a license to a check to a face, and holding up a weathered palm for an extra ounce of time. "Gentleman wants to know what you can do on the SPUD badge."

"What I got on it?"

"Sixty-five."

"That's what I can do." He finishes up with his customer and offers Taylor an end of discussion smile.

Taylor rubs his hands together, breathes in, breathes out, licks his lips and sweeps a sweaty paw over his left shoulder. "You've been lugging the same badge to the last three shows."

"Not much to lug."

"I can go fifty-five."

"I paid more than that."

"Okay," Taylor surrenders, retrieving a battered wallet that has been bravely enduring geologic pressures between his substantial posterior and the multitudes of folding chairs, tufted booths, concrete benches and shuttle seats it has caressed. Taylor *needs* this badge; one never knows when one will be called upon to attend to something in a Twin Cities train station. Just look what goes on at the airport.

The last table in the row is the Moncton's. A tangy smog of deli mustard, onions and relish is rising from the charred dogs and Polish on a nearby grill and settling like dew over Patty's Harriman Blue butter pats, her Milwaukee Road parfait glasses.

"Well, I see you've made a few kindly adoptions," she says to Taylor. Dale is busy unloading a rare Rutland silver crumber for Mr. Cramer, under the surveillance of the missus who is ready to amputate one each of arm and leg to pay for it.

"Not so much. The sign," Taylor shows shyly. "A badge. These prices, Patty!"

"Nothings cheap in love and war, so I hear."

"I suppose. Things moving?"

29

"A little slow. The Internet, you know. And speaking of love and war, how've you been keeping yourself busy these last few months?"

"Oh, you know. This and that?"

"Any of *that* involve the company of an eligible female?"

"Been there, done that," Taylor excuses.

"I could take sisterly offence. We're all getting up there, if you don't mind my saying. Time will come you might appreciate a little warmth at your side on a cold night. Someone to discuss <u>Law & Order</u> with, stir the Ready Whip into your hot chocolate."

"I'm just a bit diabetic. Just on the edge."

"I've seen you with the Cokes, you old fibber."

"Diet! Anyway, I do well on my own. I keep busy. Thanks for asking."

"My cousin Grace lives in your neck of the woods, Taylor. She lost her husband several years ago. Stroke, you know. I have mentioned you to her. She's only a bit younger than you, I believe, but she has taken care of herself. Has managed to maintain her girlish figure. I've heard tell she resembles Jane Fonda, visually anyway. Not the politics. Heavens, no! Dale says she's still a looker. I wouldn't know, but Dale says."

Dale overhears and winks. "I wasn't so tied up, I'd take a shot myself."

"Go peddle your silver, dear," Patty scolds.

Mrs. Cramer sets down a precious Union Pacific carafe, stiffens, arches her back, arches her brows, arches her tight little Vermont lips, chapped and dry and nostalgic for some real maple syrup, and says in a voice like finger nails on asphalt, "Men! I swear, Patricia, 'f'we didn't need 'em to open an occasional jar, we all might just as well be lesbians." Her husband is clutching a lantern in each palsied hand, a slight jumbled tremor mixing the liver spots like cubes in a shot glass, his eyes pale with worry.

"I'll take a rain check, Patty. I'm kind of involved now." Taylor is making it up. He is thinking of the waitress in the diner next to the High Ball. If he *were* involved, if he was *interested* in involvement, she'd be a candidate whose campaign he could support. "Don't know if it's going anywhere, but, you never know."

"Taylor, I would be overjoyed if you were less of a liar. You get lonesome, you know where to find us. We will keep Grace's number at the ready, snug under my Pinocchio fridge magnet. Though how long Grace will keep is anybody's guess. I'd consider the early bird tactic, I was you."

Taylor is already excusing himself, stepping surreptitious steps in reverse. He forks over the last of his cash for a foot long with the works and a Coke Zero, and will have to hit the ATM before long. He is down to two checks. In two or three ponderous strides he has inhaled the dog and bun and is sucking the last of the battery acid remover, and promotes the can to the top tier of the recycle bin — done under the protest of a defensive yellow jacket here to see what all the fuss is about.

As is his pattern, he hits the electric trains last. It is the climactic moment of the show for Taylor, a world of comforting contrasts for the big man, where all is small and predictable and cooperative, where a man like Taylor can be an empire builder, a Jay Gould, a Vanderbilt, a Grenville M. Dodge, laying down the lines of commerce unopposed, full of grit and gumption, sans the stock holder's wail, the busybody trust busters, the rate wars, the beleaguered farmers; where a creative mind can mark the spot of towns and junctions, bring sustenance to some and ruin to others; remake the map, make a new map, a new topography; be a nation builder, a land baron, a captain of industry, a Rockefeller, a Morgan, inscrutable, fierce, judgmental; structure the weather, water the forests and drain the deserts, be the decider; bringer of luxury and want, writer of tables and charts, compiler of statistics; a venue maker, a playwright, an inventor, the one who holds the patent; cloud seeder, road builder, canyon bridger, draftsman of the very horizon. He can be the imposer of awe.

Taylor is known in this room, if not better known: a minor celebrity. It is said that he is a fixer, that can he slip a tweezers into the cab of a locomotive with a frozen motor and get it humming like a bird, that he can unlock the paralyzing crud of years of neglect, coax the magnetized fibers from the gears, tenderly oil a piston so that the rods slide like eels. Taylor doesn't just fix: he gets into, he becomes of a size like a genie after wish number three, fits himself into the tiny hot box, flows through the imaginary tubes of boilers. Taylor jostles and caresses his way into a locomotive's brass heart, a mighty King Kong peering in the window, gently cradling the reluctant engine, working his tiny magic with massive digits. In this room, Taylor Bedskirt has been called *the train whisperer.*

He need go no further to feel a spasm of spending taking hold and decides on a quick, impersonal visit to the money machine. This must be a non-judgmental venture, so he wends his way across the antiques room avoiding anyone that might chance a conjugal discussion. Stan is just coming in the entrance prepared for the last minute fire sale, having finally devoured breakfast and the <u>Fresno Bee</u>. He nods as Taylor rushes by, anxious to get his hands briefly on some twenties.

Glancing over at the desk, Taylor notices a new girl fending off Brewster. She is Asian, and is at once wearing all of the cosmetics she owns in the world. Looking like the star of a Chinese opera, she can be expected to belt a few crooked shrieks at any moment. Both anxious managers are huddled near the brochure rack, perhaps with twin truncheons behind their backs, keen eyes on Brewster, who, on break from the furious, break-neck labor of moving uniform buttons, is gesticulating with an unlit cigarette in one hand and a paper coffee cup, ostensibly warmed by coffee, in the other. He is practicing new material from his realm of obnoxia, cajoling the girl for extra towels, extra soaps, anything to keep him planted at the desk.

Nightstick has made his stealthy way in and is lecturing the Indians on the virtues of the pre-emptive strike, how, in his day, the authorities knew how to divest a bum of a free ride in an empty, and nobody asked questions or demanded an incident report. The Indians give him polite, but less than rapt, attention.

Taylor shuffles the ten Andrew Jacksons that slide smoothly from the slot like TP in the men's room. He scampers his rather primitive scamper back through the displays, minding his circuitous route of evasion, and is able to *borrow* a sack from the hot dog man. Soon he has shed some easy come bills and proudly clings to a used Pacific Fast Mail, fully loaded Mikado engine, in its original box, that has a burned out motor to account for a more than reasonable price. It is all unpainted and caparisoned in a skin of polished brass, a limited edition jewel mined, cut, and burnished overseas for a very select American audience.

With the addition of a few loose trucks and couplers from a man he knows only as The Parts Guy, Taylor is now anxious to get home to display his new treasures. And it is nearing flight time. He heads out a back door, makes one last trip up to the room, the bathroom; gathers up his things in his carryon, and delivers his card key to the Asian girl behind the grease paint mask.

Outside, there is to endure one last sight of Brewster, the cigarette now lit, curdling in a hot wind that seems to turn the very sidewalk soggy like wet cardboard. Harlan is now leaning up against two neatly parked Harleys, centered perfectly between, and exactly parallel to, the angled white lines. The Geldorfs creep up on rubber soles, snuggling their heads up into helmets, neatly and compactly wrapped like surfers in wet suits.

Jack says, "Brewster, you schmuck, if you are sniffing those seats…" to which Brewster announces, "I am all nostrils to you, sweethearts."

Disapproving, Nightstick steps out across the drawbridge, into the shadow of Rapunzel's tower, to see if he can be of service. There are miniature racers grumbling, kids melting into the greens on the golf course, and pterodactyl-sized moths committing mass ten lane suicide. In-and-Out fries waft canola perfume on the crest of a current as hot as breath while Taylor waddles to the courtesy shuttle.

In stockinged feet, Taylor and his miniature two-eight-two causes some consternation with the TSA. They smile and are officious, but only after a call to a supervisor, and a conference with the nose of a very large German shepherd, is Taylor, re-shoed, allowed to proceed down the tarmac. The aisle on the plane is as tight as a two-foot gauge coach in Maine, and getting Taylor into the window seat is like filling sausage derma.

It turns out that Ruben Goldenberg, in a festive skullcap the size of a monk's bare pate, has the seat next to Taylor. He is garrulous, explains that before returning to the swamps and the flying cockroaches, he plans to visit his in-laws in Studio City and consume a picture perfect corned beef and side of slaw at Art's Deli. With a snarl, he offers the required epithet for eBay, an organization he considers only slightly elevated from Hezbollah, then prods Taylor to discuss his purchases. "I'll show you mine, you show me yours. By the way, I unloaded that brochure," Ruben brags. "Full price. But I'm a nice guy, and I massaged him with a ten percent discount, not including tax. Could have been yours."

"Yes, well, there's always another." Taylor suspects Ruben will pay no tax.

"You're from the High Ball, aren't you? You're…you're?" Ruben conjures with his hands, points to Taylor's eyes with extended index finger, trying to find the big man in a box of mental file cards.

"Taylor," Taylor rescues.

"Yes, Taylor. I have heard of you, Taylor." He is animated now, almost wondrous. "The talk is you got a setup to make Vanderbilt envious. That's what I hear. They say, you got enough track to span continents, that your locos take on the trappings of fleets. Is this so, what I hear?"

"It's an adequate layout."

"Don't be bashful. I'm told it traverses rooms; that it takes hours for a fast limited to circumnavigate the system. That the house is nothing but trains."

"It's not a large house."

"My Hannah has banished anything train to the garage. Half the garage, actually. Twenty-eight hundred square feet of *tchatkis* and not one tiny spike, not a waybill, not a ticket, not a transfer, crosses the threshold in that house. Not that I got what to complain, but tell me, man to man, how do you get away with it?"

Taylor is mooshed in place like a preserved peach. He thinks a moment. He breathes in, he breathes out. Seat belts are fastened and the flight attendant is doing karaoke with the masks and floatation devices. Taylor gives an affirmative shake of his head, brushes off his shoulders, glances down — past the <u>Model Railroader</u> unfolded in his lap — to check the zipper he has forgotten he can't see, feels a instant surge in his gut, unidentifiable, not dread, not excitement, but connection, a coming together, a liberating flash of clarity — a weightlessness as if the plane is already aloft, as if a brief spasm of turbulence has been encountered and left behind in the jet stream — turns to face poor Ruben, still wandering in his desert diaspora, deprived of that promised place to milk his goats and leaven his bread and run his trains, smiles broadly at the wonderment of the human condition, and answers simply, concisely, with a sudden realization of his own stunning good fortune, "I'm a widower!"

FIRST HELEN

It's the only way to hurt him, breaking one of his infantile trains. Christ, he looks pitiful, as if somebody close suddenly died. He's in pajamas — mismatched — and wearing those idiotic glasses with the silver tape. His hands shake slightly. He does that stupid breathing thing of his. What is he, twelve? Christ, what a retard! She leaves Taylor muddled in disbelief, locks herself in the bedroom, hot with rage, thinks of calling Betsy, but that's tricky. She is his sister, after all, the matchmaker, blood first, then the friend. Not that Betsy is adverse to ripping him a new one now and then...more than just now and then...but she is the sibling. It's like ethnic humor. There are taboos, rules. For all her bluster, Betsy is not exactly a disinterested party. So she lifts the phone and makes a different call, slips on her new red pumps, grabs her purse and heads out to the garage. Taylor is still standing over his broken toy like a moron. He says, It was a work of art. Do you know how much this cost? *She says,* Cry me a river, lardass. The mood I'm in, how much that piece a crap costs is not something you want to share with me! *She wants to lock him into his little train room, set it afire, wall it up, unleash hordes of rats to gnaw his wires and consume his ridiculous papier-mâché mountains. She slams the back door as she leaves, hits the remote to raise the automatic garage door, squeals the big Buick's radials off the oily concrete and out into the street.*

THEBES

I

His Honor, Socrates Caldawalder Phipps-Rouge — P-R to nearly everyone — buffs the fender mirror with his monogrammed hanky, adjusts for angle, steps back inside the mud-brown, thirty-one Willys-Knight, like Walter Prezhki, its owner, the last of its breed and grudgingly out of its element.

"A night so crisp you can almost taste the moonbeams," P-R exclaims. He eases onto the right side of the seat, snuggles up in his long, wool nightrider's coat, puffs the generous collar high up on chapped cheeks. "Y'all an aficionado of weather?...Walter?"

"Whether what?" Prezhki answers flatly.

"Weather! The many moods of fickle nature. Pressing us to the extremes of our endurance, challenging our intelligence to make-do. Weather. Climate. Meteorological perversity." He uses his sleeve to wipe away the condensation on his window, offering a fading view of the mirror.

"Not something I devote too much time too, other than figuring out what to wear before I leave the house. Not really up to me, is it?"

"You've got to have control to enjoy? Is that what you're telling me?"

"I tend toward not banging my head into walls, that's all."

"Where's the fun in that? Need to take a good plunging risk now and then. Especially when the plunging has to do with necklines. A good life is an edgy life. Got to stick your neck out."

"Neck, you say? I'm fine as I am, thank you."

From an inside pocket, P-R withdraws a silver flask, also monogrammed, works his fingers around it to keep them from fusing, unscrews the pearl-inlaid lid, and puts brandy to lips. The warmth eases into his system like liquid love, caresses his chest, soothes his gut, insulates his loins. He lets out a long hiss of comfort and wordlessly hands the flask toward Prezhki.

"No, no. On the clock," Prezhki protests softly. His breath is tangible; sequins of silky frost glitter along the cut end of his formidable mustachios. His words are muted between the crafted handlebars. He, too, defends against the night with fur; promotes his cowboy persona in animal skins an inch thick and as heavy as armor.

"By-the-book man, you are. Noble servant of the public," P-R. compliments, unsurprised, withdrawing the flask. "Confirms the wisdom of expending so much of my time and effort getting y'all re-elected."

Through blue lips, Prezhki offers a sardonic chuckle. His craggy, pocked face lies in the shadow of a hunters cap with great Basset-ear flaps falling low enough to edge onto the lambskin. His shield is pinned directly in its center. "I like to fantasize, P-R, that maybe a couple of folks actually voted for me on the basis of merit."

"That would be my vote. And the missus assures me that she trusts my political wisdom. But when it comes to stirring up the shanty folks, Darktown, the bottoms by the rail yards, the hobos not even registered, considerable palms must be greased, as you well understand, seasoned as you are. That's just the tip of the iceberg, as they say. Three fourths or more, I hear, lies submerged, and under the watchful eye of sharks employed by the opposition. It's democracy, Walter. How the big fish swallows his public." He again offers up the flask, pokes it nearly into Prezhki's face.

"You know me better."

"Can't wear y'all down? Long after sundown, you know. Takes the chill out. Granted, you are a careful man. And I am certain that circumspection rewards its practitioners. But you do lack that certain *joie de vivre* that a little detour invites. A man needs to pick up the beats every now and then. Get some gristle in his teeth. Feel the wind in his hair."

"Caution works for me," Prezhki says dismissively, lightly nudging away P-R's extended arm. He hasn't the slightest idea what P-R is gabbing on about. P-R enjoys being obtuse, enjoys pitching a fog of verbosity to regale and confuse.

"Caution or tedium? No inclination at all to wander? Let your pecker do the leading?"

"I am a man set in my ways, and I have convinced myself to be satisfied with them. Fine wife, healthy son. Steady income, for which I am heartily grateful. I would not be comfortable on the high wire."

"I would not be balanced without it," assures P-R proffering the flask once again, this time only a gesture, only briefly. He wipes the window again. Nothing yet in the mirror: the narrow streets of Thebes are deserted. They often are.

Thebes has never achieved that place on the hill that P-R's father envisioned as he laid his patchwork grid of Utopian company town down the gorge and up the escarpments — a map stenciled from the bone structures of beached whales, and now, with loss of the mines, smelling of decaying flesh. Even the name has lost its Hellenic magic: the locals now emphasizing both syllables equally, so that it sounds like *Thē-bus*, much in the style of *Kay-ro*, Illinois, or *Lima*, like the bean, Ohio. The waning heat of the Willys-Knight still pops-clicks, cooled by the great stone viaduct of the Uncas Falls, Tishomingo & Gulf mainline looming before them in classical majesty, a series of repetitive arches conforming to the concave swell that bottoms at Pinewood Gorge Road. Chiseled into the rock is a neat diamond of concrete, with screaming comet and V-channeled letters that read, THE TISHOMINGO BRINGS IT ALL TO YOU and A.D. 1914.

P-R concentrates expectantly on the rear-view. From a cold distance, there comes a heart-wrenching moan that he prematurely imagines is the cuckold's torment expressed through a heavy hand. "I'm told," he tells, and he is told much, as he tells it, "that each engineer, if you get to know the notes, if you can master the english laid on, that each and every engineer has a sort of signature that can be read in the whistle as a grade crossing approaches, the notes molded of the pressure applied the cord and the innermost character of the one who yanks it. Each one: his own style, his own elements of self-identification. It is an aesthetic — an industrial aesthetic. I don't know that this is an exclusively New World thing, but it does bespeak a certain native individuality, a testosterone-flushed momentum, this need to announce, even if fleeting, this claiming, this boasting, like pissing on a tree. Urine, you see, being our most basic of surveying tools."

Prezhki shivers. The shiver undulates, follows the fault line up his spine for a mighty shaking of shoulders. He is lost to P-R's musing. "All the same to me, boss. Wakes you out of sleep just the same. Stops you at the crossing just the same. Tells you what you'll miss, and what you won't, according to the clock, just the same."

"Well, for instance, Walter. Take that there moan of a minute ago. That's the six-thirty. We know that from the clock. But at the throttle, that's Moses Brown. See, it's a long call, longer than most, a reluctant call. Not quite sure of itself. A little edgy dip, a whoop gone sour. Not quite sure of anything right now. It is suspicious and vague, and doesn't know why. Moses Brown does not compose a happy tune."

"I don't know any Moses Brown."

"And this too, Walter. *I* am on that train."

"Could of fooled me. Let's hope's it's a contagious deceit."

"I am on that train, *at this very moment*. I touch cloth to lips, having just consumed an admirable t-bone brought to me still sizzling by a very deferential colored boy, identified only as *No. 3* by the little pin on his coat. It is a good t-bone; not Delmonico's, but I tend to be sated. It is slightly dry, though. I like a little fight left in my meat."

"Can only imagine."

"So, heavy with this near-elegant repast, I leave *No. 3* a handsome gratuity, and embark on a stroll toward the observation lounge for an aperitif, something with licorice, perhaps, a hint of cinnamon, and a soothing armchair conversation with one of the finer fulminating products from our neophyte client state in the Gulf. An hour or so by the schedule, barring some unforeseen mishap, I will be in the marble halls of The Capitol, mingling with certain influential assemblymen, doing my very best lobbying for the deserving citizens of Tishomingo, laboring, I suspect, in their interest, into the wee hours of this frigid, star-crusted night, and, by morning, shall be back in the warm embrace of matrimony, Mrs. P-R's confident snores gentle in my ear."

P-R consults the reflection again and begins to feel a minor agitation with the passing of time. He is not a man who tolerates tardiness in others. He encourages it in himself to allow time for adoration to build. And build it does.

Behind them now, at the final trolley stop on the Five Line, just before the pavement ends, a streetcar eases slowly to a stop — one big box of light in the darkness — and like illuminated cornflakes cascading from the bowl, sparks rain down on the car. A man gets off, well bundled, heads across the avenue to The Roadhouse where laughter breaks like glass from the open door. A woman steps down, loaded with packages, lugs them in the opposite direction up the street. The motorman makes a show of stretching, winds down the rear trolley, proceeds slowly along the car, inspecting undercarriage, winds up the forward trolley, flips over the THEBES END OF LINE board to expose 9TH & MAPLE TISHOMINGO, in such process converting back to front and front to back, welcomes a bottle in a bag from the conductor, re-boards, clangs the bell, and begins to pilot the little Birney car back up the line towards where the sign board predicts it is going. Another electric complaint on the wire. A celebration of crystals, a distant dollhouse Fourth of July explodes and vanishes. A figure throwing out trash is briefly lit by The Roadhouse.

"What's this!" P-R complains. "Where is she?" He is not really angry: he is seldom publicly that distracted. He is a paragon of control, not so difficult in a life virtually without adversity. This explains his boyish face, his plentiful scalp still greased and black, hiding now under his Knox Vagabond with the brim pulled low over his brow. It is his charm, this self-mastery. Alone with the Chief on a dark, failed edge of municipal detritus, or before a throng in straw boaters on Election Day, P-R sports his roundish bright cheer on clean shaven face, the college varsity star's face, now sixty-two years along in carefree good cheer and only a little worse for wear, the big TR teeth in contagious smile, those sterling pools of eyes like Uncle Sam's, multi-directional, *I want you*, and you, and you; people return to P-R like swallows to Capistrano. They want to be wanted. They want to be had.

"She was supposed to be on that car?"

"How else? Jesus! That was the Five." He winds down his window, invites in meat-locker vapor, shoves his head out and stares up the gravel slope.

"Maybe..."

"What's that?" He brings his head back in, adjusts his hat, rolls the window back up.

"Maybe she got off the car farther back. Maybe, for caution's sake, she's walking the rest of the way."

"The way *y'all* would do it maybe. Not her. Not in this chill." P-R offers the flask again and again Prezhki waves it away."

"*Consistently* cautious, I see."

"Me to a T."

On the viaduct, an elongated triangle of yellow light, the abrasion of steel on steel, a loud chaos of Streamline Moderne locomotive right off of Raymond Loewy's sketch pad; great spinning discs stepping high on vaudeville legs, a whiff of bituminous, a flash of brightly lit squares queued up on the Pullmans; the humanity in the windows busy with the tasks of being carried off into darkness;

roaring now, screaming now; and, finally, the marker lights casting green and red over the rear platform.

Yet P-R is distracted by a brief silent flash on the rear view, turns his head to track a geriatric Ford pick-up piled high with bed springs, brass headboards and discarded plumbing, that perambulates to exhaustion half a block back but well out of the street light beam at the trolley stop.

A woman steps out. She is wearing a hat, a thick coat. She is a shadow sack, featureless. She leans her head back into the cab, perhaps to say something of appreciation, a *drive carefully, now*, and, perhaps, a caution, *this didn't happen*. She comes intently down the grade at the edge of the road, sidles up to the Willys-Knight but pays it no attention other than to extend her gloved hand, trace a jagged line in the frost of the rear door window, accept a key on a wooden token from P-R who has reopened his window, and proceed to the base of the gulley, just below the line of stone arches. She follows the rutted drive up to the collection of cabins nestled along the UFT & G roadbed, under the hissing neon placard that reads, in syncopated indigestion, B IDG VIEW MOT R CO RT, *VACANCY*, and finds her way to the very last porch light. A fenderless Chevy outside Number Two is the only vehicle in the lot, and that cabin is as dark as the others. The woman points the gifted key at Number Seven, struggles with it in her cumbersome gloves, pushes open the door, switches on a light, looks in, goes in, closes the door and draws the curtains. The room light goes off, then the porch light. There is only a soft glow from what must be the bathroom.

Prezhki ponders the surprise Ford truck. "Was me, this'd be a good time to reconsider my options."

"Was you, we'd both be home enjoying domestic bliss."

"Front of a crackling log."

"I appreciate your taking this time. I owe you one."

"On the clock. To serve and protect and all that. I'll be back around about midnight."

"Give me a half-hour window either direction. That okay?"

"I'll wait in The Roadhouse. I believe we might see a frost tonight and I don't want you to go to the trouble of prying my stiff, blue fingers from the wheel. Car'll be in the lot. Just honk twice. I'll hear you."

The porch light at Number Seven blinks once, blinks twice. "What a gal!" P-R approves. "Y'all have yourself an eventless evening, Walter."

"And what do I wish you, P-R?"

"As in olden days, my complicit friend, wish me joy."

II

THE VIGILANT, LEAD BOGIE ENTERS UPON the viaduct. Moses Brown glances over at the fireman coughing coal dust from his lungs like a miner and shaking out his red bandana, and can see, out the fireman's window, a split second sputter of the wounded Bridge View Motor Court sign, and two yellow head lights opening like cat's eyes in the darkness. In the distance, the Number

Five trolley worries itself up out of Pinewood Gorge to crest on the porous border of Tishomingo. It is hot and acrid in the cab as he shifts his buttocks on the wooden seat, adjusts his left leg to keep it from frying by the open firebox.

Sardo Cardenelli, dark as a Negro, coaxes the stoker with another generous load of fuel, accompanied by the grunts of his labor. Sardo is a grunter. A complainer. A man who notices inadequacies, failings, injustices.

Brown, on the other hand, is the stoic hero an engineer is supposed to be: silent, grim-faced, bedecked in Oshkosh overalls and striped cap and a tuxedo of grime, his substantial Ellsworth & Thayer Great Western gloves maintaining a determined lock on the regulator, releasing more and more steam to take advantage of the flat plane above the gorge and make up time lost on the grade between Tishomingo Junction and the bridge approach.

Moses Brown, with only grade school education, a seemingly coarse man when in polite society, unlettered, uncultured, a sort of iconic dignitary among the working classes, is the master of one of the most complex pieces of technology in the collectanae of invention. He composes and conducts its throbbing symphony. He is the underpaid hero of boys. The pragmatist. Commander Thunder. Captain Bolt Lightning. He is the patron saint of things that move: cargoes, people, the fluid spirit of the land. The stuff of dime novels and <u>Railroad Man's Magazine</u>. He is a fiction all of his own. A captain. A man in charge. A commander who, by definition, has a following, would not be there at all but for such congregation.

All of this makes Moses Brown a very serious sort of fellow, taciturn even, not easily given over to distraction. He is a decision maker, a hegemonic leader of men and gauges and valves to direct without the distractions of language and undue thought. He is a reactor, a first responder, the finest the Tishomingo Line has to offer. He is a racing idiom of speed, straight as a rail, the mercury of positional instability, with forty-one thousand superheated pounds of iron at his disposal, sucker punching his skeletal structure at seventy stunning miles per hour in unchallenged responsibility, nearly four thousand pounds of tractional effort on six seventy-nine inch flanged drivers, allowing the big Alco Hudson to string along nine heavy cars and a small town's population as easy as a load of cotton on staked flats.

Moses nods at Sardo. He seldom speaks — reserves speech for prophylactic moments. He takes seriously the SAFETY FIRST and THIS SHOP HAS HAD NO ACCIDENTS SINCE _____ signs plastered like bandages over the scars of gruff commerce all through the Tishomingo roundhouse. But Sardo doesn't notice. "Leave up," Moses growls over the rumble. All around him things of iron and brass grumble and hiss, belch and fart, horrendous gastric complaints, the incineration of carbon, the expelling of waste, a brutal digestion with the sole purpose of heating water, as if they ride some mythic tea pot, of pressurizing vapor. Moisture sizzles briefly on stove-hot surfaces, clock sounds, crying sounds, sounds of pain and screams of passion, a wailing of mysterious night things in unspeakable agony. Moses hangs on the throttle, sliding, rubbing, yanking, teasing, priming, cajoling, and the massive lover swoons and pumps, the leaf springs hanging like genitalia from axles; the running gear locked to wheels under its skirts. Chug, clack, in and out, the lubricated rods probe the pistons, and genies rise spent from the stack.

"Christ, what'd you rather be doin'?" Sardo wonders aloud. The hogger doesn't answer, as is his want. Sardo knows the answer. The only thing he himself would rather be doing is sitting in Moses' seat massaging the iron. A few scattered lights lose themselves to propulsion in the crevice that is Thebes. There is no longer a station here. Sardo finds his thermos with one hand as he adjusts the bandana with the other. It is all joe. Moses abides no spirits in his cab, even, to Sardo's chagrin, sniffs and tastes from the thermos before Sardo is allowed to carry it up the ladder.

It is a mostly proportioned, well regulated shop there in the engine, with strictly delineated tasks for the crew, serving the needs of the sleek streamliner, rounded on its headlight end like an overturned silo, with only a minor toxic of envy and remonstrance, neither a match for Engineer Brown's mastery of domain.

Brown has a shaved bullet head, shaved square chin, both mottled with manly stubble, and from which soot is easily rinsed and resistant air is smoothed on its way. The big engine is linear cream and green, the UFT&G corporate colors, requires two knowledgeable men to govern her. Moses and Sardo have more eyes than a gang of flies crashing a picnic. Five Oh One, *The Socrates Phipps*, as labeled on the cab sides, is all gauges about the firebox door: water level, boiler pressure, brake vacuum, even the gleaming Seth Thomas clock. There are levers in abundance for acceleration, for slowing, the J-bar for shunting in reverse, the blower for releasing steam to the stack. Even the hot footplate provides a sanding gear, drain cocks, injectors, dampers, enough to keep them both from dozing.

Sardo's coffee is kept warm by its proximity to the firebox. Moses, with near-Mormon abhorrence, hangs a thermos of water outside his window for the air to cool. There is much for them to study and absorb — most of it in the fluid readings of fretting needles — for they tempt a mechanism that is capable of explosion, and, short of that, hosts a gallows sense of humor that has claimed two fingers from Sardo, cracked a rib for Moses, and planted grim purple asterisks on their arms and foreheads. This is not a job for the easily intimidated.

III

CHOC BONJOUR DROPS IT DOWN INTO first, coaches the old truck up off the gravel and over the edge of the pavement, the load chattering amongst itself about his questionable driving and road maintenance in Caldawalder County. He ventures second gear through a bar of light escaping from The Roadhouse, and proceeds up the gorge road past shuttered storefronts. He is careful to avoid dipping a tire into the groove of the trolley tracks as he makes a right and down shifts again, urging the asthmatic Ford to wheeze its way up Glassworks Street, riding the ascending ridge along the gorge escarpment with the precise steps of a seasoned pack mule. He attains the summit, which flattens into a shallow tableland, with the old Gifford Bottling Plant wasting away in its center. Just beyond, Choc once again forsakes pavement, follows his own ruts up behind the plant to the loading dock, over the grade crossing to the other side of the spur that has gone nowhere on either end for the last twenty-three years.

Originally, the spur served Gifford's as the Caldawalder County Belt Rail Road, a twice weekly mixed train shunting loads out and empties back with occasional stops at Whetstone's Mill & Furniture Factory, crossing a cut of the Tishomingo main line, swooping down to Sunset Point Park Boating and Camping near the dam that created Phipps Lake out of the Lower Gorge, and following the summer shuttle route down to the UFT&G station. There, it gifted western Tishomingo with the added prestige of Junction. In the Great Flood — *great* as all remembered floods are — of 1910, the line beyond the Point was washed out. Combined with declining revenue, after Whetstone's moved to more secure Uncas Falls, the line — unable to maintain itself on the motor car summer tourist traffic to the Lake, or the loads of soda pop from Gifford's — applied for abandonment, forcing Gifford to tail Whetstone north.

What is left of the Belt Line facility has become Choc's home, un-purchased and equally unchallenged. Sitting on the spur is the old Maintenance of Way Department crew car — MW-003 — that Choc sleeps in, surrounded as it is in his sculpture garden with bedsteads, chiffoniers, abandoned commodes, and ungainly tire towers threatening to implode. There are the obligatory rusting hulks of stripped autos, switch stands sans switches, tin Chew Mail Pouch signs, a Signal Oil pump with the glass broken out and the hose long since converted to siphon use in a cattle cistern.

Careful not to graze the wood sides of 003 — a virtual splinter farm awaiting harvest — Choc drags his worn body up the washbasin step, into his all-purpose room of kitchen/bedroom/parlor. He performs his natural obligations in an outhouse out back, a precision-measured distance accounting for aromatic concerns, and set in a protective depression to avoid the undue influence of a wind not of his own making.

Earlier, at the coal tipple in Junction, he had helped himself to some scattered lumps rejected by the Five-Oh-One in its interminable ritual of warming up. MW-003 is colder than Mordant Cave, the county's number one tourist draw: LIVE THE MYSTERY, say the billboards. Choc's first task is to burn some oil for light and some anthracite for heat. The balance of his estate consists of more unwanted appliances, some of which Choc will actually be able to convert into a small profit, and an old gasoline railcar; a bus on tracks really, an aerodynamically unsound, knife-nosed McKeen product, gutted on the inside. A salvage company has rescued the trucks, leaving the car up on concrete blocks, to be inherited by Choc for storage. As if the whole lot wasn't storage.

Choc is an old man; very old for a black man who has had to dodge hypertension, TB, poverty, and the un-plumbed ways of white folks. It takes him as long to warm up as it does the Hudson to produce a head of steam. There is constant pain in bones he didn't know he had. Three or four times an hour, he urinates into a Ball jar — it is too cold to bare his tired penis in the draft of the outhouse. He flexes arthritic fingers for the return of sensation, then cups his hands to relieve the agony it brings. If he had teeth, they would chatter. Choc guesses to be in his late seventies; born, perhaps, just around the time of Emancipation. In an oval frame on the front inside wall, pulled from a dumpsite near Uncas Falls, he has hung a portrait of Mr. Lincoln: it is so faded that the homely form is barely distinguishable from the Brady backdrop.

Still wrapped for the outdoors, he revives himself in the cane-back by the stove. He consumes Booth's Sardines from a keyed tin and what is left of a can of Betty Lou's Shoestring Potatoes. He washes it down with Nash's Coffee, black and strong, poured from an old blue pot pocked with white pustules. He is tired and dirty: more tired than dirty. His old elephant skin hangs from his neck and cheeks as if the epoxy has dried up and broken loose, as if there is less bone scaffolding than surface flesh with which to drape it. His eyes are milky; the left one of limited virility, and if he had a mirror, if he could see himself, he would look less like the Choc he remembers than an old Tom Turkey worrying the holiday season. His nose runs, draining the frost from his mind, and he wipes with the back of his gnarled claw at the ten or so bristles that once passed as mustache. The coffee has cleared some space for a bourbon chaser and Choc shares some of his own warmth with the old Peerless caboose stove. And then he begins to ponder the strange and perilous journey he has made that day with the reckless white woman.

He takes this reverie back a month or so ago. It was another day that he was picking around the tipple. A side tanker was composing a train of hoppers and reefers between him and the station and not until too late did he see the yard bull approaching from behind the signal tower.

The bull is a squat man with a lineman's shoulders. He wore a derby and his shield was affixed prominently on his coat jacket. Choc knew of this one, a man with a reputation for avocational head cracking, whispered to have bludgeoned to death an offending tramp one night after work hours, not even on company property. Though dark complexioned, with cropped black hair and a thick smear of blue-black on his upper lip, he is naturally known, affectionately, and not so, as Mr. Red. Rhedezhvetski, his payroll moniker, is all but unpronounceable to piney wood folk. He was walking fast and determined, kicking up ominous signals of dust, and yelling, *Hey, boy, hol' on up there.*

Choc froze. He has reached a futile time of life when death takes on an acceptable level of inevitability, but hopes to meet his maker without the preface of a good pummeling. *Ah ain't lookin' t' hop no freight,* he excused weakly. *Jus' f'in' t' tote dis here coal on back t' where's Ah finds it.* The lameness of his own remarks numbed him; held his warn, salvaged loafers affixed to the hard ground. Red, he knew, would just as soon beat him senseless as have a discussion.

Red was suddenly standing before the interloper, looking up into his clouded eyes, the fierce scowling lips slashed into his own pumpkin head as if by blade. Choc could not sustain his glare and turned away to await punishment.

But Red, club in hand, sniffed the smoky air, and said, not unkindly, *Y'all's that junkman, ain'cha?*

Ah ain' took nuffin' but a few chunks.

Whacha called, boy?

Dey calls me, Choc, suh.

Chalk? Like Chalkboard?

No, suh. Choc like Choc-oh-late.

Well, don't that figger? You a handy man, I hear.

Da's right.

I got me half a fence done up'n my yard. He motioned behind him to company housing, using his truncheon as pointer. *Kind a waited too long an' the ground froze up an' I sort a lost in'erest. How much y'all set me back t' sink three fence posts? Can do the rest m'self.*

Fo' by fo's? Choc was still trembling, not quite trusting the turn of events. He had wet himself and hoped the coal smoke masked the smell of it.

That's right. Mind ya now, that yard's 'bout as hard as a young buck's dick in a rain a virgins.

Twen'y cent, Choc said with little reflection.

Tell ya what. I give ya thirty-five, ya'll out a my hair in one day's time.

So rather than playing a peg to Red's mallet, Choc dug Red some holes. Red was pleased, gave him another two bits to complete the short line of pickets, and then began to recommend him up and down Railroad Avenue as a *colored boy* who could be trusted to lift and install a sink pump, though you wouldn't know it to look at him, or replace a hinge on a storm cellar door. Choc worked for the telegrapher, the ticket agent, the men in the tower, a car knocker and a jam buster.

And this was how, just this very day, he wound up hunched over like a cotton picker plucking weeds from a hogger's wife's kitchen garden. He thinks back on how he wiped his brow with the old straw hat, straightened his overalls, and proceeded to tap timidly on the screen door outside her mudroom. It was a while before she opened the solid door and looked through the screen.

Okay den, Miz Brown, he said, offering no other explanation for standing on her porch.

You done? Her voice was tentative, as if she hesitated to speak to him at all, or as if she had other things on her mind. She spoke softly so as not to wake her husband who was sleeping through the early afternoon in their upstairs bedroom in preparation for a night shift. Behind the screen, he could barely make out her features, as if she had no definition, no form whatsoever.

Y'might wanna come on out'n see Ah's done whatcha'll ast.

I can see from the window. She cracked the screen door, offered him a gratuity from her tiny alabaster hand, as white as a new tombstone, shut and hooked the screen again. *Mr. Red tells me y'all stay somewhere over to the Gorge. Is that so?* She was speaking as if they shared some sort of conspiracy.

He didn't like her tone, was always wary of white folk's questions. *Ah'm jus' a po' color' man makin' a libin',* he thought, *what mo' dey needs a know?*

I have another chore for you. I see you have a truck. I want you to bring your truck and meet me at seven tonight, seven exactly, up at the Flying A on Broadway. I will be around the back but I will be able to see the street. I will come out when I see you. Be sure the passenger door is unlocked and do not shut off the engine. Can y'all do that?

D' hell, he thought, *gotta dog could do dat!* He began to sweat again, out there in the cold before this screened-in lady. There was a strange buzzing in his ears. He didn't answer. Didn't know how to get out of this without raising her ire, wished he had forfeited his pay, simply walked off without knocking on her screen door.

Please, ma'am. Ah ain' lookin' for no trouble. Y'gots sumpin' else needs fixin'...

It will be worth two dollars, she says.

Now he was truly confused as to course. *Two dollars t' tote a woman! White peoples got no sense, da lot a'em!*

She felt a need to explain, even to him. *I'm visiting my sister over to Thebes.*

*Da Fibe Car...*he began to offer.

I know about the Five Car, she snapped. *A bargain at a nickel round trip. I shall give y'all two-fifty, and that's final, and for two-fifty you don't need to know anything that I have not already told you.*

Ah weren't lookin' fo' no mo' money, ma'am. Da two's more'n fair. Bu'cha'll knows how folks does 'rive t'conclusions.

She gave him a cold Medusa stare. *Let me come to some conclusions for y'all.* Her voice struggled between locked teeth now, though he couldn't see clearly through the screen, came through the cross-haired holes on the dust and grit of the old wire. *Imagine this. My husband, who is about to wake, comes down into my kitchen and sees three buttons rent from my blouse. There are tears streaming down my face. I can tell him that I was scrubbing the linoleum and as I stood, I accidentally caught my blouse on the handle of the coffee grinder. Or, I can tell him that the old boo in the garden come up to the door for his pay and got himself worked up the way they do, shoved his foot between the door and the jam and made an inappropriate advance upon my person. I will show him the buttons on the floor of the mudroom.*

Fo' y'wanna do dat? Ah ain' done ya'll no harm.

'Cause I can. How about that ride?

Yes, ma'am.

You'll be there? Seven? You have a way to know it's seven?

He shook his head *yes*, afraid to offend further. No good comes from offending people like this. He would park far enough away from the street lamp at the back of the station so that no one would see her come out to him.

Yes, ma'am.

The door is to be unlocked.

Yes, ma'am.

Seven. Y'all tell time?

Yes, ma'am, he answered, and thought, *T'ink she credit me a' leas' bein' able a'count church bells!*

And later, a full load from his day of junking cautioning from behind that there must be something amiss; a lone Black man, even a harmless old uncle such as himself, should have sense enough not find himself in the company of a young white woman, driving with her into a dark night. If he were a younger man, if there was time left for him, he would have found a way out of this situation, not excluding the possibility of moving to another county. But as of this day, he had outlived all of the people he had ever cared about, and all that had cared for him. And *two dolla' fifty in times like dese!*

He came by the Flying A, a few minutes early by his pocket Bulova. Only the minute hand functioned under the cracked glass, but Choc could read the sky well enough to call the hour, and he could count to seven. *Bitch! he mumbled. Ah seen circus horses could count t' seben.* The short hand hung flaccid on the tarnished face and Choc related to the watch as he did to the truck, as temporal visitors awaiting the final torch.

As he drove by the first time, he noticed the night man servicing a couple of cars under an arc of light by the pumps and an empty service bay without illumination. Upon circling the block, only one car was left and he paid it little attention as he crept into the dark back lot behind the station, the engine on and struggling to stay so. She dragged a cutout of the shadow she came out of, shaped vaguely like her, an inscrutable tracing of a women, and when she got into his cab he could still barely make her out, so protected with yards of fabric was she, so insulated from the cold, indistinct, as if still behind a screen door.

She spoke curtly, without looking at him. "Take me down past The Roadhouse and park out of the light just beyond the car stop, down onto the gravel. I will get out, y'all'll be compensated, and neither of us will ever mention this again."

Expecting *compensated* meant *paid*, he pulled the choke on the old Ford, gave the wheel an affectionate caress, and knew suddenly what it was he was not supposed to know and what he didn't want to know. Because on the grade beyond the car stop, just before the railroad viaduct, after Pinewood Gorge Road reverts to gravel, there is nowhere to go but the Bridge View Motor Court.

Choc generously dilutes the last of the coffee with the brandy. He is not a man with the luxury of choice in the matter of drinking. This bottle was payment for a washer in a leaky faucet. Sometimes he is gifted a beer or two, and once even a quarter bottle of champagne, his first experience of the bubbly, poured into an unwashed empty can so that it tasted very much like carbonated baked beans. *White folks drink some funny shit*, he thought.

He cracks a thin film of ice in the washbasin, lets his fork and cup soak in the grease of his breakfast dish. He looks forward to summer when he can cook over the old steel drum in the yard, can sit in the shadow of a rusty O'Keefe & Merritt on his old Dodge rear seat resting on palettes lifted from the glassworks, foisting unpaid vacations on the resident mice, swatting flies and wasps, sharing tales with a transient or two. Things tend not to hurt as much in summer. He thinks that maybe he can use today's earnings down at Poole's Drugs & Notions, just at the corner where he turns off out of Thebes. Maybe there is a potion he can take that will make his fingers work the way they used to, give release to the joints; not for always, just for these winters, how ever many he has left. "Lawd aw'mighty," he says aloud, "a ol' man can has some gloomy t'oughts, he can!"

The dog is scratching on the door outside. It is sometime before Choc finds the motivation to let it in.

IV

CHIEF PREZHKI YANKS THE WHEEL A hard left, attempts the U on gravel crackling like popping corn, stops on the dime of soft shoulder, backs into the narrow lane and proceeds up toward the pavement. As he realizes the civilized west side of Pinewood Gorge Road, he stops and lets the cold engine idle and catch its breath in the thin air. He can see the one working taillight on the pickup slowly attain the grade, then veer unexpectedly off to the right to vanish behind the drug store. Soon a pair of headlights blink in the pines coming back west, but on a grade, up, up, picking their way ridge-ward and over the top with one last wave of cyclopean tail light. He tugs with his gloves on his frozen lower lip. "Hell's going on?" he wonders aloud.

He moves up to the empty lot next to The Roadhouse. It is busy tonight. The curb in front is parked up with everything from Chevies to Daimlers, and the lot too is nearly full with frosted windshields. Prezhki doesn't like being here. Thebes is at best a retrograde town. There is a light or two peeking off the hillside, and an occasional streetlight installed in more hopeful times, but The Roadhouse is the only sign of ambulatory organic life. *This is not something I want to be involved in.* He is not a man to sneak about, not a man to abet the sordid. And Thebes is not even really in his jurisdiction. Because the village cannot afford its own services, the county reimburses Tishomingo to provide the minimum, to keep the body on life support; the County, in turn, is compensated by the state. Periodically, the Thebes town council petitions the Tishomingo town council to annex, and periodically it is sent packing. As long as service costs are kept down, the city is taking in more than it offers in water and power and an occasional fire truck. This is the way it will remain. Thebes has no tax base to use as enticement.

Prezhki would have sent Donald McCallum, as was usual when P-R calls, for the favor. But Donald's young bride was giving birth. *I don't know,* Prezhki hedged into the phone. He is not a man who enjoys pleading. *Donald's off tonight. Henrietta's laid-up at Angel of Grace about to deliver and I don't blame him for wanting to be close. If this baby's ugly as Donald, someone's got to be there to shove it back,* to which P-R responded, *Anything Officer McCallum needed to do in this situation was successfully completed some time back. She's better off without him. Even so,* Prezhki said, which opened up the void to P-R's, *And what's on y'all's calendar this evening, Walter, that's so goddamned important?* Preshki owes P-R. The Mayor, with the usurer's enthusiasm, sees to it that everybody is a debtor.

So here he is, getting out of the Willys-Knight, this frozen Thursday in February, stepping up to the commotion of The Roadhouse. There is a crowd inside. There is noise. A piano is being played but barely heard. Any available space not occupied by a person is filled with smoke, not the least of which comes from the poorly vented kitchen.

The Roadhouse abhors a vacuum. There are men and women and an occasional family gnawing racks of ribs not much smaller than the steers they rode in on, shelling salty bowls of prawns and crawfish coated with corn meal, drenched in the local ale, and fried in sizzling pots of lard like Dante's sinners. There is laughter and the clatter of plates cut from the bottom of the the lard vats, huge tin barrels of pig rendering, its porcine perfume coating every breathing nostril in the room. Via Rock-ola, Al Jolson begins to compete with the upright and neither can be heard worth recognizing.

A couple of janes glance Prezhki's way; he consciously shifts the manacle on his ring finger and they look elsewhere.

Once a juice joint, The Roadhouse is a notorious dive. It is dirty and abused and there is blood on the sawdust floor that is either animal or human or both. But there is no other food served in Thebes, and none better in either Tishomingo or Uncas Falls. The concierge at your swank city hotel will direct you there across the tracks for a night of slumming and cheap, hearty cuisine, and to see how the natives cavort. The fried chicken, it is said, is coated in herb-toasted breadcrumbs from loaves baked on the premises by Anatoli himself, and the drumsticks are gift-wrapped in crisp bacon that he has cured. Customers have been known to swoon. More than few have not slept through the night after such a meal.

Prezhki reaches the counter. Anatoli, the big Greek owner of The Roadhouse, is sweating pounds of his own suet into the brew, his shirt and face and balloon-stack cook's hat drenched in enough Athenian tallow to make candles.

"Chief. What I can do you outta?" The Chief admires Anatoli; relates to his immigrant gumption in being able to succeed during such hard times in a business that could not have been an easy fit for a first generation American. Prezhki's own family immigrated from the poverty of Silesia to the poverty of Manhattan, then emigrated to the middle class of Cincinnati.

"How's it going, Toli?" They are shouting.

Anatoli shrugs, seems to say, *look around.* "It's going. How? Beats me! You closing me for home-made hooch or you are to eat? Got fresh sinkers, you want?"

"I'm going to use your pay phone." Prezhki takes off the cap with the mud flaps and sets it on Anatoli's counter. "I'm putting you in charge of this here. Try not to drip anything on it." He unbuttons his coat as all the chill seems to be inside of him now, as if he's been marinated in it, and the room air is warm on his sandpaper face. He puts his nickel in the slot, takes the receiver of the hook, rings up June, the Gorge Bell night operator for Thebes, and says into the little black horn, "Evening, June. This is Chief Prezhki. Give me my office." There is a series of ticks, the sound, perhaps, of voices being compressed and sent their loquacious way in a molecular chain reaction.

Mike Voorhiis is on dispatch, hears, "This here's Walter. I'm over at Toli's."

"What Toli's? The Greek's?"

"No, Toli the Eskimo! Of course, the Greek! I catch you napping? Anyway, you want me to pick you up something?"

"Nope, but thanks for the consideration. I sent a car on over to the Chinaman's. Brought back egg foo young and some a that chopped soo-wee. And a tub a that there noodle juice they clean the tables with. What zactly is *soo-wee* anyhow? Pig talk t'me. "

"No idea. Was me, I'd call home to make sure my terrier was still chained in the yard." Prezhki does not trust foods that hide their origins in alien characters, as if ashamed. "Your funeral and none of my own. Anything on the board?"

"Been deader than a possum in traffic. Couple a quiffs in lockup. And a bellbottom up from the coast up-chucking all over 'is bunk. Better t'keep him here than dredge the lake tomorrow: there be another war, they may need 'im. Also, we gotta few domestic squabbles we're able t' talk down. Sister Agnes Marie on over to Holy Trinity rung up t' say they had themselves a peeper outside trying t' get a look-see through the dorm window at the bubs on them wayward girls they got up there. Ain't exactly how she said it, a course. Anyways, I sent a car, but no sign a no gate-crasher."

"Hold on there a minute," the Chief shouts over the din. "June! Get the hell off my line, woman! Christ, you'd think we were the <u>Evening Traveler</u>!" He hears *click;* there are always clicks. "Okay, Mike, what else?"

"Your missus called 'bout an hour ago. Said the plumbing froze up an' she didn't know what' all t'do. I sent up a car, an' they got it thawed. When y'all comin' on back?"

"Late. Very late. Seeing you don't want anything. Hold the fort and I'll cover your rounds." The Chief is weary. Times like this, he feels like a scoutmaster, hankers for a real crime, a slasher, a bank knocked over, a compulsive firebug, a vacuum cleaner salesman flung from a train, a sacrificial virgin tied to a log at the sawmill. "You just hang in there on dispatch, Mike. If things slow down, you can get the boys to clean their guns and polish their shields. Do a door to door to see if any old ladies are planning to cross a street in the coming days. Be prepared." Mike does not register such cynicism. Prezhki sees him as *summa cum laude* from the University of Subalternation. On Prezhki's roll-top, there is a sign that reads:

THIS DEPARTMENT HIRES SYCOPHANTS.
ALL OTHERS NEED NOT APPLY.

Mike asks, "Whatcha'all got in Thebes, anyways?"

"You don't want to know. And June, neither do you," he says, and hangs up.

He goes back to the counter and inspects his hat. "Give me one of those hamburgers with cheese and extra onions, Toli. Wrap it to carry. Pickles too. A couple of those little sliced pickles." And before he can say, *Some Heinz too, but don't drown it, I want a ketchup burger, I'll ask you to hold the sawdust,* Anatoli already has a third pound of ground chuck bleating and hissing its last and erupting molten fat like a tiny Krakatoan event on The Roadhouse Ring of Fire. "And a cup of that motor oil passes for java in this joint. And, Toli, what can you tell me goes on up at the Glassworks?"

"Kids shoot the cans, mostly. Knock each other up. I don't go to there."

"Any squatters?"

"Just junkman. Old colored fella. What's junkman's name?" he calls behind him.

"Junkman!" says a boy scrubbing pots.

Anatoli's son, Little Toli, comes into the kitchen with an armload of hickory for the hearth stove. There is an open oven with a spit roast twirling and splattering like Joan of Ark's last day in France. "Choc," he offers. "Junkman's name is Choc."

"Choc Bonjour," the pot scrubber gives up.

Prezhki gets a group effort for one colored's name. "This Choc," he says, "he known to get in trouble now and then?"

"Choc? What he do?" asks Big Anatoli with genuine surprise.

"You tell me."

"Fix things Choc. Radiators, weather vanes, you name it. Gentle as *ka-bob* lamb. Choc okay."

The teenage dishwasher nods in agreement. He has just come in from a visit to the trashcans and is trying to stall near the ovens.

When the hardworking burger arrives it has already sweated through its sack. Prezhki lifts it off the counter and it embarrasses itself with the slick little puddle it leaves behind. There is no discussion of payment, none of the civilian/cop banter of *What I owe you? And G'wan, you nuts? Just take it.*

With every intention of eating in the car, the Chief steps out onto the sidewalk. A gray rat, the size of Oliver Hardy, is frozen to the pavement in the middle of the street, waiting for a tire tread tattoo. The mercury has now dropped faster than Amelia Earhart in her recent misfortune. Resigned, he turns and goes back in and finds an empty stool near the piano man. The guy has done himself up with bowler and sleeve garters and is playing "The Maple Leaf Rag" about seven times faster than Joplin intended. Prezhki knows this by the movement of the fingers across the yellow teeth of the old upright. He can only hear every fifth note. The juke is featuring banjos on the other side of the room. It sounds like a Charles Ives jam session.

Prezhki lays the Cop Burger Special down on the counter to bleed out. He considers calling the station, have them send a car and rush it up to Emergency. He lifts the top bun, grabs a knife from a convenient bean tin, and scrapes most of the ketchup onto the flattened bag. Anatoli sees this, chalks it up to spite. And then, without eating, Prezhki sets it down again, and considers with wonder how very foolishly flippant P-R really is. *One would think,* he thinks, *that a fella with so much to lose would be mindful of the risk, leave a little in the bank rather than flash it all about town. Was me, which it wouldn't be…Hell, none a my own!*

V

P-R YANKS OFF HIS GLOVES — the first with his teeth, the other with the free hand, as if to demand satisfaction on the field of honor — cups his hands to his mouth and summonses warmth from some interior fire. He alternates stomping feet. The only light in the room reveals a thin crack under the bathroom door. But he knows she is here with him, can smell her, like springtime in a meadow. There are other scents in the room, none nearly as enticing: stale mold, a throw rug doused in urine, ancient dust frying on the ticking radiator like breading on the Sunday hen, eons of cigarettes, alcohol. *This is where stinks are made*, P-R considers.

He feels around for a dresser, finds it, sets his hat down with delicacy. He is finicky about his attire, believes this to be a requirement of his status. His eyes are starting to adjust. He can see her forming on the bed; still a mound, not a woman yet. He pulls his flask from his coat, unscrews the cap, sets it on the lamp table. She has left a large sewing bag embroidered with roses on the floor: inside, perhaps, a change of clothing. The wire trashcan is nakedly stuffed with something crumpled — maybe tissue paper — from which she has unwrapped a bottle and two stemmed glasses.

"Y'all miss me?" She has the high rural voice of a Blue Ridge singer, with just a tincture of rasp from cigarettes. It is a seductive voice, just the suggestion of brash, in other circumstances within the bounds of respectability.

"Is the Pope?" he says in his magnolia scented drawl. He removes his tie, monogrammed, silk, about as wide as a standard gauge caboose, folds it with formality and sets it down with the gloves and hat, then gets to work on pearl buttons.

She had hoped for something more labored, something to build upon, and is shaken that he has invoked the Supreme Pontiff while preparing her damnation. She is Black Irish, American by virtue of a potato-loving fungus, a churchgoer. "Cuddle now. Come and warm me up," she says. It is at once promise and tease. She is starting to rematerialize, all angles and curves under the sheets, a sinuous map of the Hallawatchee River awash in the white adrenaline of Uncas Falls.

He fumbles with the buttons, less careful than before, and he is become hard with his impatience. He can see her now as she lifts the sheets, alluring, yet so expected. P-R is a man who knows his way around a woman. He knows beforehand every twitch, every drop of moisture, every cry. He knows this woman's form better than some, perhaps, less than others. He is no novitiate.

"Hurry, I don't change my mind," she says.

He is finally nude, still cold but warmer, and strides across the frozen floorboards and slips in beside her. Though sixty-two, he retains his collegiate urgency and the firmness to back it up, only recently beginning to take on a few pounds. She wraps the cover around them and they cling together like cave formations. Soon they are lost to that less seemly activity of men and women that goes by names both wondrous and crude, the primal junction of mammals caught in the web of attraction: they paw and thrust and take things in their hands not generally held in polite company; tongues flick like snake tongues; they claw and scratch and leave marks that may have to be lied away; they bite, they even chew, they are each other's protein, take objects into their mouths without knowing where they've been; they invade each other's secret passages, enter the types of places that others have been prosecuted for entering; and they make sounds fit for a hog slaughter, they grunt and hiss, they snort; their breath is labored and uneven; they admonish, they encourage, they threaten, and she parades a vocabulary she was not previously aware she possessed; they scream, oh, do they scream; they are soothing and hurtful, gentle and brutal, caring and abandoned, blessed and damned. Limbs flair, torsos gyrate, pelvises clash like tectonic plates, the earth shakes, hearts stop, celestial trumpets blare, there are tympanic rumblings and The Beast's laughter and a mighty sonic disturbance drowns the juke across the road and up the grade at The Roadhouse as a long line of reefers trundles over head. She shrieks, he growls, a Philco in a battered, Bakelite box soft shoes across the nightstand. Framed ads from magazines — Dr. Pepper, Chesterfield — rat-a-tat-tat on the walls, and the earth yowls like the end of days.

She is younger than him by nearly twenty years but has earned the padded hips that he clutches, the round bottom, milk shake thick, that he lays her on, the breasts assuming a certain mature elasticity. P-R likes a little blood in his meat, likes handholds and crevices to ease his climb, likes rediscovering the hidden reaches and subtle whorls, a pasture of soft hair, a dark mottled disc of areola as pedestal to thumb-firm nipples, the twitter of a nerve, the involuntary undulation of spine, the pleasurable arch of sole, the generation of heat in the meeting of thighs. Months back, when they had started in on each other, she had been hesitant, terrified even, as immutable as the Confederate general mounted in the town square. But P-R was the pedant of tongue and hand and genital, and as a gift he gave her flex, gave her rhythm, gave her the feral athleticism she practices now. The plaster behind them will never be the same.

Later, when all is memory, they will credit at least a portion of the chaos to the big Lima Berkshire pounding iron with a drag freight on the viaduct. But — and they have done this sort of thing before — tonight they will each leave satisfied that, as such human congress goes, this has been an event of some magnitude.

She has turned to gelatin: jiggles like a mold, feels abused, debased, broken and entered. "Again," she says.

"A moment. I *beg* you."

When they are sated and lying abreast on their backs, it occurs to him to say, "Tell me about the truck."

For her, it comes out of nowhere. She turns to look at him with still pretty face, only beginning to surrender to a faint crackling, like old china washed too many times. Her nose is a bit sharp for some tastes, a bit sculptured and masculine, her lips a fraction too narrow, and her tired, gray-blue pools of eyes would shade better with awnings of much longer lashes. She does not stop traffic anymore, and fewer heads turn, but there is about her the sexuality of the not quite beautiful, the ones who just have to try harder. "Tell me about the cop car," she counters.

"What cop car?"

"Don't do that. I know the car. I can see him drive up several times a day from the office window."

"As a gentleman, I am compelled to await my turn."

"You are a married man, buck naked with a married woman not your own in a room that rents by the hour. Y'all may be the Mayor of Tishomingo, but you are no gentleman."

"You wound me, my love." She is a challenge, this one.

"A small price to pay for my ruination," she scolds.

"Nevertheless, I lay here humbled, scarred."

"Poor baby. But I do see signs of imminent recovery." She brushes her hand through his dense pelvic hair. "You want to smoke?"

"Not just yet."

She strikes a match, is briefly yellow porcelain, takes a Camel from the nightstand, and a drag from the Camel. She lays on her back again and forms several manly and concentric rings. "No one to worry about, lover. Just an old colored junkman that's got what to lose from idle talk."

"Why didn't y'all avail yourself of the public transport as planned? Do your civic duty?"

"Too bright on the trolley. What if someone I know got on? And I just *did* my civic duty, Your Honor, you should be so good as to recall."

"You're visiting your poor sister in Thebes who is ailing. Who'd doubt you?"

"This is easier for y'all. You're political. You can take a lie in stride. I've never done anything like this before. The fewer people I have to fib to, the better off we both are."

"You're feeling guilty?"

"No. Well, maybe." She retreats tentatively, assurance lost in her tone. "I'm not cut from stone, P-R."

"As I hope some day to be. In the civic square, I imagine. This is about him."

"This is about *us*." She is emphatic, peeved. "Keeping it from being about him is something I alone am burdened with."

"You're certain the colored boy won't talk."

"If I weren't, I wouldn't have gone with him."

"Who is he? I think I know the truck."

They can hear sounds from outside: tires, transmissions, a rattle of trashcans colliding. And the Rock-ola.

"There is no need for you to know the truck or the driver. This is my part of our arrangement."

"No, y'all's part was the trolley. How will you get back? Not the way you came, I hope."

"No, not the way I came."

"Then how?"

"Why would you need to know that?" She doesn't want to add a new element to the equation, does not fall back on her sister, a spinster, who has no one but her, and will cover any lie she needs covered. The story will be that she has spent the day with her sibling, they cooked dinner together and discussed their mundane domestic lives, and since her husband was at work, she decided to stay the night and ride the streetcar home in the morning. The latter part of the story will be true.

They are silent a while. He thinks about the word *arrangement*. He hadn't expected her to be so pragmatic.

"Now you," she coaxes. She is working a finger around his naval, then down along his thigh to where he is sticky with her memory. Her other hand holds the cigarette and out of the side of her mouth she blows away a fossil of ash.

"I'm always brought in a squad car. Can't very well drive my own car. I am, after all, at this very moment on a train to the capital."

"That was not the usual cop car." She wears a gotcha smirk and little else but a simple wedding band; plated, not pure.

"If y'all know that, you've answered your own question."

"So now *you've* involved another party."

"And this is my part of the...*arrangement*. The part *I* am responsible for. It is about calling in a debt. Not the first, not the last. It has nothing to do with you. With *us*."

"He knows what you're doing. This place."

"He doesn't know who with, and, like your colored, it is to his advantage not to."

He gets up, a big naked man in dim light, retrieves a cigar from his coat, lights it, sucks mightily, and tucks himself back in, and slips the cigar ring on her finger over the wedding band. "I think I know my people." His smoke mingles with hers, with the mold, the urine, the sex drying but pungent. It is not a pleasant brew; the room takes on the olfactory persona of a well-used armpit.

"D'y'all trust me?" she asks.

It is not the question he expected. He had thought, perhaps, a play on the paper ring, to which he was prepared to disillusion her as to symbolism or promise. Yet he doesn't hesitate in saying, "No, I don't. I'm political, remember?" P-R is nothing if not adaptable.

"I can take care of things. I'm not incapable."

"We are not alluding to a fourth spouse here, are we?" His head faces true to the ceiling as his eyes wander to hers.

"Of course not. I wouldn't do that. I want you to feel you can trust my judgment."

"I don't trust judgments." It comes harsher than he means it to. "Not yours, not mine. Judgments are amorphous, subjective to a fault. I look for signs. Concrete things. Things I know that tell me that what I think is happening *is*, in fact, happening."

"What kind of things?"

"Well, for instance...And y'all should know this. Each engineer on a locomotive..."

"Let's not."

"No, hear me out. Each engineer has his own distinctive pull on the whistle. His own aural John Hancock. Anyone in the business of making sounds, for whatever purpose, has it. The trolley motorman his bell. The fish man his call. If I hear a piece by Brahms that I've never heard before, I know it's Brahms because his mark is on it. When I hear *The Limited* on the viaduct, I know whose hand is on the throttle."

"That is a cold perspective," she observes. It is a critique. She is no longer playing.

He reaches over and takes her rosary from between her recumbent breasts and into his moist fingers. It is copper with a diminutive brass Jesus that is so authentic you can feel His pain. "Is this you?" he asks. "Is this your warmth?" He is spreading the scent of her from his fingers onto the Savior.

"It is, yes."

"Hard to figure, at this moment."

"Again, consequences that I agree to face without you."

"There's always confession, the letting in of even another party to share the shame."

"I didn't make the system, though I suppose I will be judged by it. And what about y'all, P-R? Do you believe in anything at all? Do y'all fear anything?"

"Well, I must say I do have a great deal of faith in myself. All based on precedent. Beyond that, I didn't design the system either, but I know how to work with what I've been given. If there is a plan in that, so be it. As to fear...I have yet to have had the pleasure."

"Such confidence is vanity," she tells him.

"Cardinal sin. I've been accused of worse."

"Worse than cardinal sin? I am marked by you. I fear you've monogrammed me on some part of my soul that I can't see."

"Keep it well hidden, and no one will be the wiser."

"Okay to say if you don't believe in anything but yourself. You've only yourself to inform, to answer to. Me? I guess I'm kind of a chump for God. What can I hide from Him? I can't just shrug off all of this...whatever this is. I can't just say *I didn't make the system.*"

"Y'all brought up the system. Not I."

"If there *is* a system, rules."

"To be broken."

"Yes, of course. We are evidence of that. But do you ever feel that its all a set up, like we're dangling at the ends of strings, being manipulated, both the following and the breaking of the rules?"

"A naked philosopher, no less. Goya would have painted you supine, clutching a bust of Aristotle, perhaps."

"No, really, things we do, I do, I sometimes feel like I can't help myself, like I'm being moved along mindlessly, without my permission, and I know these things are wrong, but do them anyway."

"If they're wrong, these things we do, then knowing how to get away with them is the ticket."

"But, what if even that, the lie, the subterfuge, is part of the plan?"

"Preordained? Not very Catholic of you. Is this where you're going? A conditioning? What do they call them? Those things in the movies? The cover of Popular Science...Robots? Us, mechanized."

"Yeah, maybe. Someone up there winds us up in the morning and sends us on our way."

"With an old colored man in a pickup?"

"Yes. Or in an unmarked cop car."

"Why? What for? Seems so senseless, doesn't it?"

"I don't know. Maybe it passes the time."

"In eternity? We're told there is no time."

"Maybe, like this, us here, its just something...something to do."

"Then you were right in the first place. You didn't make the system. Nor did I. We are guilt free."

"No, y'all are. Y'all were designed guilt free. Then there's the rest of us."

Come Sunday, anonymous and closeted in the confessional at St. Augustine's of Hippo, she will whisper, *Forgive me Father, for I have sinned.*

Father Gilead, who's heard it all, will stroke his brow and jiggle his beads, massage away thoughts of the choir boy with the auburn locks he will have just led up from the boiler room, and will think: *Christ, who hasn't?*

PASADENA-HIGHLAND PARK

I

T AYLOR BEDSKIRT IS A MAN WHO cherishes space, walls, fences: a man to whom the buffer is integral to the whole. As concerned with the safety of his things as he is with the seclusion of his person, he has assembled all the latest accoutrements of domestic fortification. Automatic floods and security cameras ring the periphery of the compound. Wrought iron bars enclose the two outer porches and roll down metal shutters conceal the windows. It is as if he's operating a meth lab. The doorbells have been removed and the doors themselves re-skinned with knock-proof steel sheeting. Taylor envies the Chivalry Timbers its moat, wonders if there is an ordinance in Pasadena prohibiting cauldrons of steaming hot oil for pitching over entryways. Once there was a roof siren, the kind used in the Fifties to convince Americans that an early warning would save them from nuclear annihilation; the siren was stolen.

Some of his neighbors worry that an Al-Qaeda cell is operating a *madras* here; others are certain they have seen a house like Taylor's used as a set for a porn flick that mysteriously popped up mid-surf on their PCs; in the oral telling and on Facebook, the story has devolved from triple X to snuff film. Fred Elkhorn, a neighbor three addresses up, peers over his Sears power mower and tells Mrs. Devore, pruning her hedge, that he is convinced that the big man on the corner harbors a Vietnamese sex slave chained by the ankle next to the furnace in the basement — probably a missing coed on her way home from school — her geometry book thrown unceremoniously into the crawl space below the house as feed for a family of mice. But as vigilant as the neighbors are with their Neighborhood Watch decals, their Bosch binoculars and their creative suspicions, no one has ever seen anyone but Taylor go in or out of the modest corner house. Nor are there telltale noises at night. Certain domestic rumblings emanate from the house next to his. Elsewhere is heard the occasional whirl of a Makita tool, not so different from any number of houses on a block where garages are converted to wood shops and Asian teens customize their own Acuras. But Taylor's house is quiet.

The postman brings the usual: bills, throw-aways, sheets of coupons for Q-tips and toilet paper and one-hour film processing; and packages, perhaps more than the usual amount of packages. He shoves them through the bars that prevent anything or anyone wider than six linear inches from getting anywhere near the mailbox. Mrs. Gettzleman, across the street, the most senior of the block's veterans, has theorized that Taylor is the custodian of a CIA safe house, and awaits anxiously a glimpse of Matt Damon skulking around with silencer erect. Curtains open — she sits in her living room window with her Zankou chicken take-out, a hot pepper, and Armenian garlic sauce neatly arranged on a doily she made forty years before, and stakes out the perplexing corner.

Secure as the island of Diego Garcia, coinage could safely be banked at Taylor's house; stacks of big bills from Al Capone's vault stashed in Geraldo-safe containers: bricks of gold, ingots of silver, Academy Award nominations, the Hope Diamond, the decayed corpse of Jimmy Hoffa. He could be breeding ferrets, gerbils, black mambas, endangered and venomous toads, the world's last passenger pigeon — any variety and number of illegally imported creatures — monitor lizards let out at night to consume pit bulls, schools of piranhas, Big Foot or Nessie. Maybe he has grafted together some primal pair or assembled a monster out of parts retrieved from the trash bins of County Hospital. He could be building a bomb, breeding Ebola, poisoning cranberries, injecting LSD into packages of *chicharrones* for restocking on super market shelves, conducting covens for naked Wiccans. Maybe Elvis lives in the ad-on behind the kitchen.

And though he seems like an okay guy — waves hello, doesn't make any noise or complain when next door's sprinklers overshoot onto his El Dorado, never hurts anybody, never utters an unkind word, is quiet, keeps to himself — his are qualities of omission, not revelation, the stuff of dark matter that spawns imagination and suspicion; the kind of things people say about the guy who suddenly flips and blows holes in holiday shoppers at the K-Mart or the deacon who has secretly been stashing bodies in his garage freezer. Who knows? Who really knows?

While Taylor was off in the Central Valley, his distraught sister Betsy cajoled husband Leo into an espionage mission. They parked up the next block for forty-five minutes looking in vain for signs of life, hopefully Taylor's. For no reason Betsy could find germane to their covert operation, tangential Leo noted, with disoriented chronology, that, *Had Texas revolutionaries found shelter in Taylor Bedskirt's house instead of a decrepit adobe mission in San Antonio de Béxar, way back in that fateful February and March of 1836,* if they had instead ensconced their *motley volunteers in Taylor's breach-proof redoubt,* on a quiet lane of two and three-bedroom Spanish styles behind trim lawns with sprinklers and palms in Pasadena, California, *Travis might have lived to command again, Crockett could have had an additional adventure to lie about, and Bowie, perhaps, would have invented an even bigger knife. And Santa Ana, that wily coyote; he and his band of strident illegals would have been rounded up by the INS to cries of la migra, la migra, echoing over chlorinated pools and satellite dishes, and carted back across the river.* For Taylor's house, according to Leo, is nearly as *impenetrable as a Lone Star martyr's truth.*

Betsy, having found the momentary wisdom to ignore him, was sucked into the double circular truths of her now opaque girlhood, two fuzzy-edged peepholes through her Bushnell's. For perspective, she scanned the forgotten lawn, the cracked-asphalt street, the pepper tree on the opposite side populated by wild parrots in loud Talmudic debate, and scanned in on Mrs. Gettzleman peering back at her through opera glasses. Betsy dropped the lenses and attempted to look elsewhere and innocent. Mrs. Gettzleman gave her a neighborly wave with a Kleenex clutched in her ancient talon.

Taylor, back from broiling Stockton to simmering Pasadena, plops from the shuttle van like Cheese Whiz from a tube. All eyes — the obvious from behind the tinted glass of the van and the covert pairs of local spies — are upon him as he proceeds over a lawn the color of a market bag, lighting up the spots as if there is going to be a film premiere, and disappears behind the first wrought iron barricade of his maximum security facility. His key sticks momentarily in the deadbolt: he must remember to squirt in a little WD-40. Then he tackles the combination lock, pulls up on the handle to combat any expansion wrought by the heat, and enters the air conditioned purity — always, exactly, sixty-eight degrees — that preserves his world like life in a Petri dish. He resets the combination electrically, throws the bolt, and disarms the alarm at the panel by the door. His shoes come off and are placed in an entry closet with the few other pairs he owns. Then he flips on a light and, as if Scotty had beamed him up, Taylor Bedskirt leaves the planet of men, gets sucked through his own personal star gate of the mind, Gullivers his way to Lilliputia, and rematerializes in a place that is all his very own.

The layout.

The Layout. The layout suggests the immensity of Kansas, the scale of Delaware, the diversity of California, the braggadocio of Texas, the antiquated lethargy of rural Louisiana, the touristy quaintness of coastal Maine. It is a cliché of Edward Hopper's America on a Bierstadt field, vertically elongated and purposefully majestic, where no one really looks at one another, a grimy realization of Bernice Abbot clarity and Walker Evans palpability. It soars from blue floors, its seascape base, rising to beach and coastal palisade; it flattens in city grids and furrowed plains; undulates into hills; thrusts upward to forested uplands and craggy peaks; blends into painted skies of muscular Thomas Hart Benton clouds. There is a lone Charlie Russell desert with good-postured saguaros and organ pipes and ocotillos like huge cephalopods stuck into the hand-sculpted earth. There are sugar pines and fir trees and redwoods, even a Christmas tree plantation.

And there are the works of man, our One Man: intricate networks of roads and trails — some well traveled thoroughfares with vans and commerce; others, eucalyptus-framed lanes with a single horse and produce wagon — and every imaginable variety of human manifestation from city hall to five and ten, from charcoal kiln to canning factory, from manor house to out house; gas stations, bus depots, small town jails, tenements, saloons, white churches and red school houses; places to live, places to work, parks for play and cold bench slumbers, gray cemeteries with tilted stones. All are woven with rivers and streams, dry gullies lined with chaparral, and peopled with hand-painted metal figurines shorter than a thumb joint. These are policemen in uniform, bums with bindle sticks, suited men with business on their minds, even a naked women perpetually sun bathing in her garden, night and day, with three boys in short pants peering through the knot holes in her fence. And she is not ashamed.

Of course, there are railroads. There are trunk lines spanning the plywood continent with high speed specials; long, laborious freights creeping behind hinged Mallets; industrial lines with switchers delivering raw materials and dispensing finished products; logging lines denuding the forests on the backs of log cars behind geared engines seeking the mill; the little Plymouth and Davenport gas locomotives hauling ore from the mines; electric traction cars carrying the people to work.

It is a grand point-to-point layout meandering between climate zones and time zones and escalating elevations; actually goes from place to place and with geometric indifference disdains the common oval. It is standard gauge — HO, three point five millimeters to the foot — where space allows, narrow gauge — HOn3 — where curve radii govern its premium of solid footing. Higher up, in the illusion of miles, the tracks get narrower, the trains get smaller, N gauge and tiny Z gauge, so that the eye takes in vast expanses of territory with variegated ecosystems and changing bases of industry.

And with the rails come their incumbent structures: the roundhouses with their big lazy-Susans; the depots and terminals, towers, shops, coaling stations, car barns; the train sheds with massive steam vents; the water towers; the dependent constructions of fences and walls, phone poles with concave lines, trolley poles with taught wire down the centers of streets, retaining walls, culverts, trestles, piers for ocean plying ships.

Taylor has planned the menu, authored the recipe, stirred and seasoned the brew: two cups coal dust, one half teaspoon conifer needle, a pinch of rust, a tablespoon of grime, tincture of asphalt, essence of soil, balsa wood to taste, paint and pastels and other ingredients of decay and weather, a quick swirl of stain, a roux of slag left near a mine, all sprinkled with the crisp, unmistakable coating of electric current browned to a golden hue.

Overhead: a light for sun, a light for moon, and attendant lights for stars, riding their own rails on a continual twenty-four hour cycle, spreading long shadows and high noon glare over Taylor's planet, casting darkness over the twinkling of firefly lights in houses and shops, following the trains at scale speeds from living room to dining room, up the hall, into and around two of the three bedrooms, and back into the add-on — what Taylor's parents once referred to as *the lanai* — where extensive yards allow storage for rolling stock, and facilities for construction and repair.

As master of his universe, Taylor inventories the domain, sets down his bag, unhitches a hand vac and frees a boxcar from the consuming greed of a dust mote, and sucks the life from a cobweb covetously consuming an icehouse. He is without peer here. He has set the sun and moon in motion and given twinkle to stars. He is all the utilities in one giant trust. He makes rivers flow and seasons change as if they were in some more variable meteorological latitude than Pasadena. He brings the circus. He is Mussolini making the trains run on time, James J. Hill lacing the snail path of rails over great divides, Carnegie ripping the very guts from the earth and leaving libraries in exchange. Nothing happens here without the blessing of Taylor Bedskirt: not the razing of buildings; the plowing of fields; the raping of forests; nor the movement of the minute beings that inhabit this aesthetically weathered wonderland.

During the coming autumn, Taylor will remove scores of deciduous green trees to be placed away in Tupperware containers, keeping them as fresh as vacuum sealed deviled eggs, and will replace them with near clones morphed to reds and yellows and screaming oranges. When winter arrives, these too will retire as hillsides reforest with leafless successors. When it snows, it is Taylor's gift; when it dries, it is Taylor cleansing away the hardest months. Occasionally, he is arsonist, burns to the scorched plaster earth a squatter's cabin, and is the fire company poised in mid-douse at the crime scene, and brings the dozer to tear it all down and clear the lot, and is the contractor who replaces it with something more substantial: a general store, an outlet for men's furnishings, a greasy diner with stainless siding.

Vac at the ready, Taylor proceeds to his scheduled track inspection a suck at a time. All about him on the textured walls are signs and posters and bits and pieces of vanished commerce advertising, WAGNER PALACE CARS, RAILWAY EXPRESS MONEY ORDERS, 1854 EASTERN & NORTHERN EXPRESS R.R. ROUTE BUFFALO TO BOSTON DIRECT AND RELIABLE. Passengers are warned to AVOID STANDING ON PLATFORMS, that a FLAG OVER CROSSING is just ahead in the dining room, that the Maine Central tolerates NO TRESPASSING in the second bedroom. Destination plaques from streetcars promise YALE BOWL, the 8 CAR TO AVE 28 CAR HOUSE. Displayed are drum heads from the backs of observation cars, THE HIAWATHA, THE MOUNTAINEER, THE SUPER CHIEF, and logos from the Camas Prairie, the Georgia, the winged shield of the Bangor and Aroostook, the earnest beaver of the Canadian Pacific, the Dashing Commuter of the Long Island headed for the bar car. From every available inch of lath and plaster ceiling hang lanterns with their clear, amber, red, green or blue globes dripping down like wine bottle baskets at a neighborhood *ristorante*.

It goes like this from front room to dining room, as Taylor carefully squeezes through the open trestle of main line that curves off to the hall to deliver loads to other towns in other rooms. He passes a white aspen forest where a hunter is forever shooting an elk, just at the door to the kitchen, stops, sucks, moves on to his refrigerator, hunts for a Diet Coke among his shelf-wide stash of soda cans, pops the tab and watches the can sweat into icy beads, chugs a good long chug, lets out a deep, primal, gastric bellow — the kind you produce when you're all alone — farts in a pleasurable staccato series, grabs a sack of Dandy's Shrimp Flavored Chips, and proceeds back to the living room.

Here he mounts the platform allowed by the vaulted ceiling; three feet off the oak flooring, Taylor padding up the plywood steps in stockinged feet, as buoyant as Taylor ever is, assumes his swivel director's chair in front of a multiphased digital control panel that would make nearby JPL blush. He breathes in. He breathes out. He polishes his dispatcher's visor on his pant leg, slips it snuggly over the arid expanse of his head. He flicks a switch. Geometric lines of conjoined LCD's pop across the panel, one string for each train that begins to shrug off paralysis, chugging in scale sound and syncopated rhythms to assume increasing speeds. Signals flash, crossing gates descend, smoke ensues from every oily stack, and the oversized voices of trainmen no more than twenty millimeters tall call out things like, *B-o-a-a-a-r-r-r-d, Tie 'em on, Throw 'em in the hole,* and, of course, *Tickets please!* Headlights skip down the ties. Trolleys sizzle on the lines. There is hustle everywhere: speed and thunder, the crashing of knuckle couplers in the yards, the boomerang call of whistles, the clang-clang-clang of all the bells in dissonant fanfare. The spirit of Taylor hovers over all. And Taylor, with low cal cola and salty sea chips, looks down from the firmament and sees everything that he has made, and behold, it is very good. And there is evening and there is morning.

II

"C UNT!" HE HEARS, A DISEMBODIED VOICE from the nameless neighbor, the one with the concert t-shirts and the extended-cab pickup seven feet off the ground. "Fucking cunt!" a redundancy Taylor fails to appreciate.

Inescapably, there is a conjunction of Taylor's two worlds: a subset cocktail party where the actual of Pasadena is forced to mingle with the sub-actual of the layout. It is a crossroads netherworld, a purgatory, a discordant commingling of oppositional forces that drags him from his reverie, causes him to switch off the omnipotent, animating switch. The trains stop with electric suddenness; the din disperses; the twinkling lights blink once and are gone. And the earth stands still.

Taylor tilts his head westward, cocks an ear. At first, the sounds from outside are but premonition. Taylor has come to expect them and is strangely drawn, so disturbingly magnetic are they, so alluringly subversive, so utterly sublimated to the cacophony of the layout, that he is not sure if he is hearing them at all or just recalling a subtext from previous evenings or a scenario from a trackside shanty somewhere in the detritus of his living room. He sets down his soda, checks his fly automatically, squints to filter his senses that he may hear all the more, and chews the last of the shrimp chip caught mid-world in his mouth. He is annoyed by his own loud mastication. The best auditory vantage point is the bathroom, tiled in yellow and black Checker Cab *nouveau* and providing the perfect acoustics for tapping into the chaos of the family next door. He cracks the window.

An ear stuck to the glass, he repeats it quietly. "Cunt!" It is unfamiliar in his mouth, sticks like cotton to his teeth. *Who talks like this?*

"FUCKING STUPID CUNT!" It is a growl, a groan, wet with saliva, rancid with anger, vaulting over the four foot concrete block wall that demarcates their respective properties, jabs like a lance under the frame of Taylor's bathroom window, demanding his attention, renting the fabric of his fantasy evening.

There are breaking sounds — Glass? China? *Bones?* Someone whimpers — the woman? Occasionally Taylor has seen her in pink wool robe, even in summer, tiny geisha-steps out to the local throw-away, crushing snails on her driveway, her head hung unnaturally close to the asphalt — a scolded cur, *bad dog, BITCH!* — long dark hair streaming ragged and unwashed down one side of her face, the other covered in conscientious disguise by her left hand; grabbing the paper, quickly retreating beneath the red tile roof, and, lastly, picking up a diapered child who waits by the door.

Taylor breathes in, breathes out. Clears his throat, clears the cotton musk of *cunt* from his esophagus. He hears the neighbors' phone ring once, twice; a parade of insistent rings underlying the screaming. He shuts the window, slowly, and thinks, *One day I will call the police. He shouldn't think I won't.*

As it was not yesterday, *one day* is not today.

But the phone keeps on ringing. Louder now, as he leaves the bathroom. It is not the neighbors'. "Darn!" he says, "where is the stupid thing?" Somewhere in the bedroom, under the bed? In the entry closet? Stuffed in a coat pocket? Locked away in the carton his latest Lehigh Valley boxcar came in? Sidling up to a Marie Callender frozen fettuccine in the freezer? He can't remember when he last used it, or where. It stops. He stops. He knows it is only a reprieve — Taylor entertains no more than four categories of call: the traditional hang up, the solicitation, the apologetic wrong number usually asking for Paco or the Housing Authority, his sister Betsy, who insisted he install the phone in the first place. As prophesied, it rings again, seems louder this time, more urgent, a phone on crack, ring, *ring*, **RING**, double ring-ring, rings on tops of each other, rings that won't give up, Chinese-water-torture rings beating on his forehead.

He finds the phone uncharacteristically snug in its cradle next to his bed, charged and ready, actually hollering now, levitating into his reluctant pink palm, arm wrestling up to his ear. "Hello?" It is more question than greeting.

"My God, you're okay!" It is Betsy. Nobody can ring as loud as Betsy. He hears shuffling, a hand cupping the mouthpiece, and she mumbles to Leo somewhere nearby behind the Business Section, *"He picked up."*

"Course he picked up," says Leo in the distance, *"the phone was ringing. That's what people do when the phone rings."*

"Hello," Taylor says again. It is lame, he knows, a stall. He awaits the harangue.

"Do you know how worried we've been?" It sounds more like anger than worry. The words are slow, deliberate, labored. He is surrounded by anger.

"You've been, you've been," Leo corrects. *"I could give a shit!"*

"Worried?" Taylor wonders aloud. He worries that she worries, a sort of sibling exchange of perpetual discomfort.

"Worried! Worried! You know. Like when people who care about you don't know where you've disappeared to for days at a time? When you just suddenly, what? Fall off the edge of the earth?" She is forcing her best thespian sobs. The words have lost their formal deliberation, come hectic and ragged over the wire.

"I was in Stockton." This should explain everything.

"I said, *edge of the earth!*"

"Since Friday."

"One of your...*train* things, I suppose." Betsy is made for phones; can sneer audibly.

"Yes. Stockton's twice a year. You know that."

"He was in Stockton, he says."

"My condolences," Leo offers.

"I've been calling and calling."

"I wasn't here."

"How would I know that? You could've told us you were going to be out of town." Said like, *why wouldn't even you know this?*

"I didn't think...I didn't know...Why?"

"So we'd know where you were!"

He is honestly baffled. It takes him some seconds to say, "And then?"

"And then! And then we wouldn't worry."

"I didn't worry, Taylor," Leo calls. *"Spend a weekend in Spitsbergen, for all I care!"*

Leo can make Taylor — if not laugh, smile — and is one of the few real people who can. Leo's humor tends toward the obsessive, the haphazard. It profits from more corn than Archer-Daniels-Midland.

"Worry about what, Betsy?" It drips innocence.

"What if something happens to you?"

"Nothing *ever* happens to me."

"Shit happens to everybody, Tay! You're special? Touched by God? And when something does happen? At least get yourself a cell. They're essential these days. Everyone has one. First graders. People without drivers' licenses. Deaf mutes! Illegals. Everyone. I saw a Sprint ad in <u>The Times</u>. They're giving them away."

"I don't want a cell phone. I've told you. I have no need..."

"I'll pay for it. *Won't we, Leo?*"

"He's sixty-two years old, for chrissakes, let him buy his own phone. Or not!"

"I don't need you to pay for it. Anyway, you said they're giving them away."

"With the service. You pay for the activation, the service. Where've you been?"

"Stockton, I said."

"Not what I meant, shithead." It arrives as affectionately as *shithead* can.

"Okay."

"Then I can count on you to buy your own?"

"No, no you can't. I don't need one."

"What if there's an accident and we don't know where you are? What if you come down with something?"

"If you know where I am, there can still be an accident. I can still get sick."

A phone, after all, is not a vaccine.

"How would we get to you? How would we get you help?"

"Well, I don't know, Betsy. I suppose, if everyone else has a cell phone, somebody would call nine-one-one or something. I mean, if I'm laying under a bus..."

"Don't even fucking go there, Taylor! I don't want to hear it."

"Then I'll tell them not to call."

There is a short silence, inseminated as it were. "I don't mind telling you, Taylor," she says with adjustment, more measured now, sounding like she really does mind, "that being your sister is no walk in the park."

"Okay."

"You never grow up."

"Leave 'im alone, Betsy!"

"Leo. I'm having a conversation here with my brother!"

"And I'm reading the paper, minding my own business, and the entire mortgage industry is going belly up, so let this shit alone already. He doesn't want a cell phone, so what?"

"With my *brother, Leo."*

"I can take care of myself, Betsy."

"Don't make me laugh." She laughs — see how he manipulates? "You could never take care of yourself. You were the last kid on the block to learn to tie your shoes."

"How could you know this? Were you even born yet?"

"I know it. I just know it."

"But how?"

"Mom told me things."

"About me? Mom told you things about me?"

"She was worried about you."

"'Cause you didn't have a cell phone."

"Then she should've told *me.* What was she worried about?"

"The way you...*are!* The way you live! You've always been so...so fucking weird, Taylor, with your...*trains!* She worried, that's all. She couldn't talk to Dad. He encouraged you, if anything. You were always obsessed. She couldn't get you out of the house to make friends, play football, shoplift Matchbox cars, anything normal. She worried that you had no color. That you ate at odd hours. You were just never a regular kid. Detached. Like you were always daydreaming. No one ever called for you. No friends. Certainly, no *girl* friends. You just never did the kind of things everyone else did. I bet you still can't ride a bike! When you went to college, Daddy filled out all the applications. He even mailed them. You never did anything for yourself that didn't involve trains. You didn't even watch TV! Sweet Jesus, Taylor, who the fuck doesn't watch TV? Only the blind! So she talked to me? So what! Sometimes she cried. Did you know that?" Betsy offers a sniffle or two of her own. "And did you know what this was all like for me? I mean, being Taylor Bedskirt's kid sister? I used to pretend we weren't related. Pretended I didn't even know you. When I would get a teacher you already had and they'd call roll that first time and say, *Don't you have a brother?* I'd say, *No, I'm an only child.*

Must be a different Bedskirt. Like anyone believed there was a different Bedskirt! The *teachers* weren't even *that* dumb! I was so ashamed of you. Kids said you were a retard. A pervert. And I would pretend that I didn't know you. Sometimes I'd agree with them, just to take the focus off of me. You can't blame me. You really can't. I was a kid, see. It wasn't my fault you were such a fuck-up. To this day, I don't know how you take care of yourself. Do you even have food in the house? I bet you eat out every night." She pauses, all ears for denial.

Taylor has been thumbing through a soft-cover edition of <u>1001 Track Plans for the HO Modeler</u> that he keeps by the bed; he is familiar with this particular rant. "Well, as a matter of fact, I just ate dinner. Right before you called. Was just getting ready to do the dishes."

"You have dishes? What did you eat? Something that said, *Tear here and reseal?* Meat in a bag?"

"I had leftovers. Thursday, I made a roast. With carrots and potatoes. And gravy."

"You're *such* a liar, Taylor. It's pathological, you know. You really need to have that head of yours examined. You know, I pray for you."

"Okay. Thank you."

"I pray they won't find you..."

"They?"

"...in a pool of your own blood some day..."

"Eight foot at the deep end," Leo calls, *"for the diving board."*

"You know, I'm fine, Betsy. I really am. I've always been fine. I was a happy kid. A real happy kid! I was."

"Like you know how to be happy!"

"What's to know?"

"There you have it. What's to know, huh! Being happy is more than just not being miserable. Let me ask you something, Taylor."

"Okay."

"And don't lie to me."

"Okay."

"When's the last time you got laid?"

"Okay, alright!" moans Leo. *"Enough! Basta!* TM-*fucking*-I, already! I am out of here, Betsy. You have driven me from my favorite reclining chair, from the comfort of my den. I am taking my diminishing* <u>Times</u> *to the Kohler, where, hopefully, it will be just me and the stock market shitting our way down to Santa Monica Bay. There I will live out my diaspora. And Taylor, you hear me, guy? Don't answer that question. Because the next question is going to be who is she? and how many times? and,* I hope you didn't use one of those cheap Chinese condoms that have about a seventy-eight percent failure rate and will make of you the oldest guy at the *Lamaze class since William O. Douglas!"* Taylor hears papers crumbling while Leo's voice trails from the room.

Taylor is slumped on his bed. He lays the book over his chest. He is thinking about whether or not to restore the innards of the two-eight-two he picked up in Stockton, or simply give it a cosmetic touch up to sit on a siding. "Okay then,

Betsy. It's been really nice talking to you. Want to get to those dishes. Don't want to be up half the night with my hands in the sink."

"You're not getting off the hook so easy, big brother."

"Okay."

"We're not done here."

"Okay."

"Have you got a calendar? I don't know what you'd put on it. Have you got one?"

"Yes. Sure. You mean like an appointment calendar?"

"That's what I mean."

"Sure."

"Go get it."

"'S'right here."

"Right where?"

"Here in the kitchen. Hanging on the wall. Next to the phone. Right *here*."

"I want you to save a date. I was calling in the first place to get you to save a date. And then you didn't answer…For days, you didn't answer and I thought…"

"Okay. What date?"

"Save September Twelfth. It's Steven's birthday."

"Okay. I have it right here. Saved. BD-Steven."

"Asshole, his birthday's the Tenth. We're *doing* it on the Twelfth because it's a Saturday."

"I meant…"

"Don't forget to buy him something. Last year you forgot."

"No. I had something ordered and it never came. From…what's that web site? The one that sells everything in the world? Congo, that one."

"Amazon."

"A video game or something. Didn't I give it to him later?"

"Taylor, do you even know which one Steven is?"

"What kind of a question is that?" He tries to sound offended. How does she intuit such things?

"Do you?"

"I'm not answering that. It's demeaning. The Twelfth. I'll be there."

"Of September."

"Okay."

"Comes shortly after Nine Eleven."

"Okay."

"Nine Eleven's not a convenience store."

"I know that."

"Dress nice. Slacks. No jeans. No shorts. I'm having someone from the library."

"What kind of a someone?"

"A new girl. A widow. A very nice, unpretentious gal. This has nothing to do with you, so don't get a switch stand up your ass. You are not the fucking naval of the universe, you know. Sometimes people just get invited places for totally non-Taylor reasons. Just don't come like a slob. Don't wear any of those little railroad pins or anything. I don't want to have to explain away my dork brother to someone who doesn't know you."

"Betsy. I don't want to meet anybody."

"This is not a fix up, Taylor. Are you even listening? I don't even know if she's looking. Probably has a boy friend, a pretty thing like her."

"Well, I'm not looking."

"That's understood. The air is cleared. I didn't invite her with you in mind. But, you know…it wouldn't hurt to be close to somebody again. How long's it been? Ten, twelve years? Let me think. I was pregnant with Steven, getting over the shock of it at my age, and then the accident."

He is quiet. When he speaks again, his voice is hollow, weary. "There was no accident, Betsy."

"Well, you stick to that, Taylor. The police thought so. And the insurance. No previous attempts. No note. But you know best."

"There was no accident. I told them. They didn't take me seriously."

"No shit! Anyway, what I was getting at is that it's been long enough. Stop pining away."

"I never pined. I've told you this. This was not a great marriage."

"I don't want to hear it! The woman's dead! And she was my friend."

"Okay. But she wasn't mine."

"Don't wanna hear it, don't wanna hear it, don't wanna hear it!"

"I'm not saying anything bad about her. We just…probably should not have been married. We didn't like the same things."

"Taylor, Taylor, Taylor. How you wear a person down. Do you think you are ever going to find a woman who gets wet when a trolley rolls by?"

"Why do you talk like this? Like my lunatic neighbor? We didn't learn this kind of language at home. Who taught you such language?"

"I had peers. Look, all I'm saying is, it's time that you get yourself out a little. Have some fun. There would be no shame in sharing a pot of coffee with…"

"Well, if it'll make you feel better, I already have someone." There it is, out there. Now what? He smells trestles burning.

"You're involved with somebody!"

He thinks briefly. What exactly does *involved* entail? He dodges with, "It could happen!"

"A woman?"

"Of course, a woman. What did you think?"

"A saint! I thought a fuckin' saint! Who is she?"

"Leo told me not…"

"Leo's a dickhead! Who is she?"

"It's…it's somebody. It's just…I don't know. I don't know if it will go anywhere." Now he's being frank. The bridge recedes to a smolder.

"Why won't you tell me who it is? Are you making this up? Because, this lying, this is not normal. I'm your sister. Just about your only living family. I have a right to know."

"I thought I'd wait, you know, until I have a better picture of how things are working out."

"Who is she?"

"Well, she's a woman I met."

"No shit!"

"At the coffee shop next to the High Ball. She's in the restaurant business. She's very nice."

"So what's she doing in that dive next to the High Ball?"

"I don't know. See what the competition is up to."

"Competition! What is she? A cockroach? She gotta name?"

"Yes."

"Well?"

"Cory Ann. Her name is Cory Ann."

"Sounds like a name from an old murder ballad. Brambles and roses and riverbanks. Joan Baez. I didn't know they gave people double names anymore. Except, maybe, in Tennessee, West Virginia. One of those places where cousins and sheep all sit at the same table."

"She was probably named a number of years ago."

"And you've gone out? You and this St. Cory Ann?"

"Once or twice."

"Once or twice?"

"Twice. I meant twice. The first time was kind of the initial thing, you know."

"'S'called a date, Taylor. Bring her."

"Bring her where?"

"To Steven's birthday."

"Oh, I don't know, I mean, isn't that, what...kind of abrupt. I mean, two dates, and off to meet the family?"

"Taylor. You're not twenty-three. You're not bringing her to meet your parents. Look, Tay, just bring her. I won't entertain a no."

"Okay."

"Okay? You will?"

"If you want. What about your friend?"

"What friend?"

"From the library? The unpretentious one?"

"Oh, her. I made her up. Just to scare the shit out of you. So you'll know how it feels. So next time you go off to one of your sleepovers with your little train pals maybe you'll call and give us a heads up or something. Maybe you'll get yourself a cell phone. Maybe having a lady friend will remind you how it is to relate to people that are taller than salt shakers."

"Is that a pathology? Making up unpretentious women from the library?"

"Never having known you to be particularly clever enough to be a wise ass, I will assume that was a serious question. Just bring her, Taylor. The table will be set."

"Okay, then."

"Bullshit! You won't."

"I will."

"Taylor?" There is a new, cautious edge to her voice. "What *lunatic neighbor*? Is somebody bothering you?"

"No, not at all. Not me."

"Then what is it?"

"This guy next door. Where the Maplebys lived when we were kids. I think he beats his wife. I hear all this language. Filthy, angry language. And things breaking."

"Are you spying on them?"

"It's just pretty loud."

"Probably the TV."

"Sometimes, I see the wife the next morning. She covers her face."

"Most women cover their faces in the morning. Maybe she's Muslim."

"And there's a little kid."

"Look, Tay, don't get involved. You never know with people. It's like on TV, on the cop shows. They go out on a domestic violence call and the wife who's all beat up tries to kill the cops when they cuff the husband. They probably have great make-up sex."

"I don't know. What if he kills her or something?"

"Puts a damper on the make-up sex! You just stay out of it. And Taylor? If it's not too late, you and that Cory Ann person might want to get tested for HIV. You never know these days. Do you have a doctor? Do you get regular check ups? Pressure, sugar, cholesterol, finger up your ass?"

He's beginning to sweat. His ear hurts. "Everything's taken care of."

"What'd they find that had to be taken care of?" Betsy is a woman of some nuance.

"Nothing! Nothing at all. I'm fine."

"You still see that screwy, old quack, Radly?"

"He's younger than me. And he's not a quack."

"He couldn't be more of a quack if he fell out of the mouth of a duck! My friend, Ani Menhedrian? The one who runs the volunteer program at the Library? She took her mother-in-law to your young Dr. Kildare to have him look at a small discoloration on her arm. We're talking an eighty-seven year old woman who's never been sick in her whole life, lives alone, still drives. So Dr. Jekyll, he takes one look at her and has her admitted to Glendale Adventist for tests and observation. Three weeks later the woman's dead. Not one sick day in her life until she meets your Kevorkian-in-training."

"She was eighty-seven! People die! Lot's of people do."

"He's too old, Taylor. God knows what has changed in medical science since he bled his first patient. You need a young man. Someone who is current, who doesn't keep a jar of leeches on his desk. And Taylor, I don't mind saying so, but your best bet is to find some Jew doctor. I don't know what it is with those people, but they sure do manage a fine Pap smear. Might cost a few bucks more, but you get what you pay for."

"I don't need a pap smear."

"You're seeing a witch doctor, dumb ass. How would you know what you need?"

"I like Radly. I've been seeing him for years. I'm comfortable with him."

"You want comfort, go to a mattress salesman. You want to stay alive, see a Goldberg or a Cohen. I know what I'm talking about." She works part time at the Main Branch Library; spends hours with all the knowledge of human kind.

"He tells me all the right things. About watching my diet, exercise…he says I should walk at least twenty, thirty minutes, three days a week."

"So, you live on a street as flat as Twiggy. Do you walk three days a week?"

"No."

"See."

"It's not Radly's fault I'm lazy."

"He's your doctor, isn't he? If he can't get you do take care of yourself, who the hell can? Radly can kiss my ass!"

Taylor has a visual: Radly, resembling a rather large mallard, bent over, his stethoscope flipped over his shoulder, planting a smooch on Betsy's bare bottom. It is Boschian; gives Taylor a chill, sets him to breathing in and out.

After the call, he is left with this new quandary about the semi-imaginary woman he is to bring to the party for Steven. He thinks of this woman as the waitress in the dive next to the High Ball, the one with the coincidental Cory Ann name tag, the one he speaks to only to order an egg salad sand or a tuna melt. He is also left with a rapid thumping and a muffled curse from next door. One problem calls for no immediate response; the other, he worries, will be the price of his white lie. And unless Armageddon fortuitously strikes prior to the time Betsy commiserates with her dear friend Betty Crocker, he will have to have a woman to bring on a third date. Betsy, Patty Moncton, Darlene Geldorf. What is it with women that they can leave no man unturned, no bouquet uncaught, no bachelor's life uncomplicated? *You should have married a conductor,* Helen had once told him. *Someone who'd really punch your ticket!*

III

To the uninitiated, mention of the High Ball can conjure visions of dark bars with oak stools and vinyl booths and plastic bowls of peanuts set out at strategic intervals to encourage thirst. True, the High Ball is a back room, an exclusive gentlemen's club, the specialized inner sanctum of males out to drop more than a few bucks on shared pleasures, to covet, to lust, to speak the good old boy jargon of such places that pop up, infrequently, in all American cities. But it is a far cry from the implied scenario, located as it is behind the Smoke 'n' Whistle, itself, not the barbeque joint *its* name suggests. The High Ball, named for a certain type of obsolete railroad signal, from whence also derives the name of the drink that is not served here, is a fairyland of lost boyhood; a breathtaking commissary of model trains, a hands-on, miniaturized experience of nostalgia to die for. Peter Pan could cavort here forever.

The Smoke 'n' Whistle is actually the more accessible of the two. As the younger sibling, it is now enjoying its twelfth year as a purveyor of specialized toys. Toby Baylor, inheritor of the original business, has expanded from scale replicas to play things for the young and the ever young. The newer section occupies the front two thirds of an old brick-faced building on north Fair Oaks, only blocks above the Two-ten — *freeway close,* says the ad in the Yellow Pages.

It is bright in The Smoke, painted like a Dunn Edwards ad, decorated to capture the imagination of pre-schoolers visiting with nannies or young moms — infants papoosed to their bellies — down from the bluffs above the Rose Bowl. From the gentrifying craftsmans in Bungalow Heaven, kids come here to shove Thomas the Tank up inverted U's of wooden bridges, locomotives all aglow with cheerful smiles, happy to belch around in their grooves and bring commerce to daring figure eights, cocooning for the night behind plastic doors in the greaseless engine house.

Weekends, you will find these same premises shared with enthusiastic dads trying to scam the latest Lionel passenger sets — with their loop of tri-rail and transformers — onto twelve-year olds; their gray matter compressed between Hitachi-padded headphones, their eyes red, lost to the spell of thumbs beating Gameboys to death. Dad's with yards dream longingly of something larger — big outdoor leviathans from LGB or Bachmann — and scheme as to how to get the wife to share a plot of garden for a turntable, to allow rail traffic to industrialize the begonias, to accept a trestle spanning the *koi* pond.

But the serious stuff goes on at the High Ball, a fifty-nine year old institution secreted behind a mahogany door, itself lifted from an abandoned Southern Pacific station, with TRAINMEN ONLY etched to its frosted pane, just under the antique American Flyer light fixture at the back of the Smoke 'n' Whistle.

This is Taylor's part-time door, entered two days a week, where he dons his station agent's vest, weighted like Dale Moncton's in a pox of *cloisonné* pins in deep burgundies and forest greens, all the many colors of the logo rainbow. There is a rare niche for Taylor here amongst the brass imports and laser cut kits. He has earned a modicum of distant respect from his colleagues in matching vests. Unlike the others, Taylor operates within an extremely small window of interests, has, according to one of Betsy's well-worn jibes, *a one-track mind.* Taylor doesn't know which celeb was most recently arrested for driving under the influence, which one is currently being entered into the ledger at the Betty Ford Clinic, doesn't follow who's screwing or adopting who in the potential Oscar set, hasn't seen a movie in ten years that wasn't coal fired; has never heard the words *Brittany Spears;* doesn't know the zip code for Beverly Hills.

Also, Taylor is apolitical; doesn't differentiate Giuliani from *masticoglia*, Hilary Clinton from DeWitt; barely knows global warming from bagel warming; has no idea that the value of his house tripled in the last ten years and dumped forty percent in the last three months; is not sure which of the –stans our troops are currently dying in — Afgani-, Kurdi-, Kazhiki-; thinks the greatest drawback to building a wall along the border is that it will be covered in graffiti before the mortar dries, like everything else in the Southern Californian neo-desert.

But he knows his trains. He knows Baldwin from Lima, EMD from GE, Pullman from St. Louis Car. He knows light from heavy rail, trolleys from pantographs. He knows how a locomotive tire is changed, the approximate cost of re-tubing a boiler, and probably how many spikes it takes to fill the Albert Hall. He can tell a customer which company makes the best knuckle coupler to keep his trains from breaking apart like Yugoslavia, the year that the city of San Francisco took over the Market Street Railway, the radius of the Pennsy's great Horseshoe Curve, the category of hurricane that wiped out the Florida East Coast to Key West, the psi attained by the world's only four-eight-eight-*eight*-four that just couldn't do the trick for the Erie. Taylor is a walking Britannica of the flanged wheel set. Customers seek him out for solutions to their most technical of problems; authors of treatises on obscure short lines vie for his insights into branch closures and stations abandoned. He is the George Bancroft of steam, the Henry Steele Commager of electric traction. He knows how many ties Death Valley Scotty salvaged for fire wood at his desert castle; which interior designer chose the book titles for the library at Jay Gould's Lindenhurst estate; which model makers cast steel and which use only brass, what is the best glue to use when modeling a wooden combine car from original Union Pacific plans.

He is a savant of motive power, a breathing catalogue of tiny side rods, marker lights, superchargers, hand rails and smoke stacks, the source of record on antique china from the *Super Chief,* the bios of commercial artists hired by the Northern Pacific and the Santa Fe to capture the visual splendors of indigenous peoples along their routes. Taylor is verification, bottom line and final word. And though those who work with him find him odd to the point of vexation, hugely detached and remarkably naïve, they recognize that he also possesses a stroke of significantly myopic genius.

Barry Styles opens the High Ball this morning. "Hey, Tail," Barry calls, his voice cracking like gum, using a nickname not particularly a favorite of Taylor's. "Get up to Stockton?"

Barry is young for the High Ball, young for a hobby weighted heavily on nostalgia. He is only eight years out of high school and a perpetual student at Pasadena Community College — each year he majors in whatever he hasn't flunked out of the year before. Barry is a nice kid, all agree, but his great pustules of never receding late term acne, as well as his constant barrage of questions on whatever seems particularly irrelevant at any given moment, tends to put people off. Toby likens him to a Matt Groening creation, gangly thin and bent over, squeaking away through his Monday morning interrogation of Taylor, who has come in just behind him.

"Always do," Taylor smiles, checking for new inventory behind the glass cases. The handcrafted locomotives and streetcars are lined up and ready for commerce with their price tags, face down, in the hundreds and low thousands of dollars, waiting for admirers to foam like salted snails.

Barry slurps from a Monon mug. All the men at the High Ball have their special mugs, each with a favorite railroad emblem, hanging on a Pullman coat rack in the warehouse; the place referred to simply as *the back* — as in, *I'll see if we got one in the back.* Being a fellow member of the dandruff brotherhood, Taylor, in continued evidence of his singularity, feels compelled to smile *good morning* and prepare for the young man's onslaught.

"I couldn't go. Had a Bio exam to cheat through. Good turnout?"

"Moncton seemed happy, I guess. Or maybe not."

"Who showed? Like all the regs?"

"Pretty much. We get anything new from Rivarossi?"

"Nope. Just the Athearn shipment, as far as I've seen. Check the back. Maybe there's something unopened. Baylor's been screwin' with the G gauge set up in the front window. At least since I got in."

"You just came in."

"Yeah, well, explains why I don't know nothing. Anyway, Baylor seemed to be all into whatever he was doing, so I figured he's been there a while doing it. 'Til someone pops the cherry on the back room, the secret remains. So who'd ya bump into up there?"

"Oh, I don't know. The Monctons."

"Yeah, you said."

"Bill what's-his-name? You know. The Cramers. Stan, doctor from Eureka?"

"Don't know him. Want a Winchell's?"

"Sure. What've you got?"

"Usual mixed. I got glazed left. A bear claw. One a those pink one's no one ever asks for." He sets the stained cardboard box — also pink — on the counter with a small stack of square napkins. Taylor opts for a cruller with dripped chocolate riding the ridges.

"Ruben Goldenberg."

"The Jew guy?"

"Yes."

"Was he wearing the beanie?"

"Yes."

"What's with that, anyway? I mean, how much rain can you keep off with that thing? What about those hippie Geldorf's? She's some hottie, huh, Taylor!"

"I guess. She's very nice."

"Nice! You bet your ass she's *nice!* Wouldn't mind a little a such *nice a my own!* Shit, that Geldorf's a lucky bastard! And Brewster?"

"Brewster?"

"I don't mean, like, Brewster's a lucky bastard. I mean, like, was Brewster there?"

"Oh, yes. Brewster was there."

"He cracks me up. Guy's, like, this mega-asshole!"

"I guess."

"So tell me, Tailgate, my man, how is it you can afford to bum your way across the country every time a whistle blows? I mean, you get out to Winterail, and Durango when they run the Goose, and Mid-Continent! I'm lucky I can swing for a trip to Traveltown. You're just working the two days right? And most of what you earn's'gotta get eaten up with all the freight you haul outta here. Baylor says you're a better customer than the customers. That he cleans you out every payday. That would suck royal for me! What gives?"

Taylor smiles through a mouth full of cruller. "Good pension."

"Yeah, from?" They pause, a tandem realization of the inappropriateness of the question.

Taylor answers anyway. "I was an engineer for many years."

"No shit! I'm impressed."

"Not a hogger. I worked for a toy manufacturer. I designed the sound boxes. You know, how you pull a string in a bear or a duck or something, and it says a few words. Random. Different each time. *Hello. I'm Teddy. What's your name?* We developed these…what were essentially little phonograph records."

"Bears and ducks, huh! Pretty old school. Pulling strings is something I've tried instead of studying. There's no future in it. Everything's all about chips now. Like Elmo. You know Elmo, right? My niece has this Elmo that's got a better vocabulary than me. So this must a been before CDs, huh? Chips? And then what? You had this pension, so you just retired? Don't you have to be older to retire? I mean, like sixty-five or seventy? My Dad retired and he just about went nuts. There was nothing for him to do so he moped around all day pissing off my mother. He pissed her off before he retired too, I guess, but, it's like he didn't have as much time to do it. Then, last year, he died. Just like that. Retired for eighteen months. Brick shithouse of a guy. And he dies. Do you worry about that? I don't mean checking out, I mean, not having nothing to do."

"The layout keeps me pretty busy."

"I shouldn't have another one of these," Barry says, poking the bear claw. "My girlfriend says it's bad for my skin. If she finds something to replace these with that's good for my skin, then we'll think about it." He sucks his lips in over his teeth; gives a resentful sniff. "Not exactly smooth as an iPhone screen herself! So the layout does the trick for you, huh? I never had more than about four by four to work with. That's why I'm stuck with an N gauge pike."

"Keeps me very busy."

"Yeah, Baylor says you're some kind a perfectionist or something. Set your own spikes. No prefab track for you. And, I guess, like, callin' all the shots for your own little piece a the planet. Must be something else. And you just get by on the pension? Some a this stuff's like left-ball-expensive! And you have a house and all? Baylor said you live near by."

"In Pasadena. House is paid for. It's an inheritance. And I came into some other money."

"Oh, yeah?"

"Yeah. I'm okay. I'm set." Taylor has picked up a feather duster and is working himself around the cases. He has requested that Baylor purchase a hand vac for the shop, which Baylor agrees would be wise, but it never seems to happen. Baylor is low on expenditures and big on profits, is responsible for the Smoke 'n' Whistle's past success, which, nonetheless, Taylor finds a bit sacrilegious — as if the store is a public trust, the fulfillment of a societal priority.

"Well, good for you, Taillight!"

"Isn't it?"

"Just came into money?"

"That's right. *And* the pension."

"How'd'ya just come into money's what I wanna know. Like you come into a room, come into the store. How do you just, like, come into money?"

"You don't make it happen, if that's what you mean."

"I'd like to see the layout sometime. You ever do an open house?" Taylor is evasive, says, "Sometime, maybe." The kid wants to know, "Like when?" Taylor counters with, "It's a work in progress."

"Aren't they all? Well, whenever. You'll give me a heads up, right?"

"Okay."

"This is so not gonna happen, is it?"

"No, I don't think it will."

"You got pix?"

"I don't do pictures."

"You don't do pictures? You *so* don't let anybody see the setup? What's it for?"

"Me! It's for me!"

"One more a these isn't going to do my face any further damage, y'think? Like, what's one more meteor crashing into the moon? You know, you're a smidge off the deep end, Taylor. Funny kind a guy."

"Okay."

"This isn't like one a those epiphanies to you, is it?"

"My sister has commented...occasionally. But you know. It's okay with me. I'm really into the layout. And, I think, that donut will do a guy more harm than I will." He says this reaching for the bear claw.

"That's my Tailpipe! 'S'all good, dude. You got it figured."

IV

LEO VALVERDE IS HOME TODAY. HE is coming down with something replete with scratchy throat, sniffles and forehead pressure. *The summer cold is the worst,* he thinks, so he boots up the BTU's and stays wrapped in his robe, wondering who passed it on to him, as if such knowledge would bestow comfort.

It should be a quiet day. Both boys are at camp, enjoying the stings of flying things and other bounties of nature, and Betsy is scheduled to volunteer at the library this afternoon. Leo has called in to the shop, now confident it is left in able hands, so he decides to review invoices, worry about the property he is trying to unload before the real estate market goes completely belly up, and, perhaps — most importantly — update his Netflix queue. He is hunched in viral misery in his upstairs office, crammed with signed bats and balls, an autographed Kobe jersey framed like a Rembrandt, his golf clubs. He suffers over his PC with a box of tissues and some of that nasal spray advertised on TV by talking boogers. Any product that can give voice to mucous is okay with him.

Betsy, looking drawn, looking quartered even, in T-shirt and gray sweats, is lumped in the stuffed chair under a noble profile of Seabiscuit. Her knees are curled to her chest; she mumbles into them. "I'm not here. To you, I might as well not be here."

Reluctantly, he swivels in his chair and faces the lounge where she slumps with a crestfallen grimace right out of Lee Strasburg's studio. "We're talking about...?" he opens, nodding toward the door, a long-term couple's code for the phone downstairs in the den. Leo says Betsy can creep into a room and look over your shoulder with all the subtlety of a red Hummer H3, vertical exhaust pipe rising from the hood, tailgating your Prius with the driver's elbow Crazy-glued to the horn; you look back in the rearview and see some lunatic's nostrils about to swallow your hybrid. *Like a worm from* <u>*Dune*</u>. This is Betsy, being subtle.

Leo marvels that she still looks so good in a T-shirt; for a gal her age, worn down by the abrasion of two active boys, she has somehow kept it together. He recognizes that she is a big boned woman; largeness is a hereditary thing with the Bedskirts. She has to be careful about what she eats, so he makes sure his comments rarely reference body fat. He has her out daily, jogging around the Rose Bowl, has converted the guest room into a depository for torture devises sold on late night commercials by Swedish models with masculine biceps, and in all ways attempts to manage Betsy's preservation as his very own prom queen.

Leo, too, is fit. He doesn't have the natural inclination to annex unwanted territory; is one of those despicable people who can eat anything at any time of day or night and keep it concealed. He doesn't need to be bribed and cajoled or insulted to take to the tennis courts or to enter a marathon. Sinus problems invade his space with some regularity, but when it comes to serious illness, he opts not to participate. All of which makes him even more miserable when stricken by the little viral necessities that dog him just like everybody else. Bob Dylan, he remembers, noted that even the President was occasionally as exposed as Adam in the Garden. This thought comforts him, assures him that he is not the specific target of divine malevolence.

"I'm dot going to argue wid you," he declares. It is a disingenuous remark, spoken through his nose, a language that he muses is a dialect of *phlegmish*.

Despite such aberrant moments as this one, Leo's stay here on the mother planet has been mostly a good one. He has successfully redefined his father's onetime chop shop in Boyle Heights to a first rate body shop in Pasadena, catering to the Masaratis and Jaguars sold nearby, then to a small chain of garages in three counties. He has wisely, until the present moment, invested in real estate; buying up repos in bankruptcy auctions, throwing in a few cosmetic bucks, and cleaning up on the resale. The large, white Casa de Valverde is high enough above the Arroyo to boast *view lot* status, and, as its *patron*, Leo enjoys the amenities of country clubs and yearly cruises to Costa Rica's rain forests and the Bahamas.

Steven and David are two wonderful, healthy boys; California bronze-skinned like their old man. He is delighted that they have made it a full week without a camp counselor calling for a conference. Last year, he was asked to take them home on day three because they had buried a kid with glasses under a weighty collection of Harry Potter tomes. *Boys will be boys.* So what if Steven is somewhat of a bully — athlete that he is, he has the Darwinian predisposition to be so.

And David? Why, *the little tyke's fork may be one tine short* when it comes to human interaction, and he may be a sometime follower in his brother's kiddy sadism, but it's only because the kid's brilliant in his way, *can eke the juice from a pre-squeezed orange,* notices odd ball stuff that gets by the average second grader, such as: *Zebras must be black with white stripes 'cause their pee pees are black,* which, though perhaps not definitive in zoological circles, is a fairly perceptive observation for a child. For all anyone knows, David is secretly pressing Steven's buttons, monopolizing his remote, writing the dialogue his older brother uses to spread his particular brand of juvenile Nazism like Skippy's on white bread. And, of course, David's unwritten contract with his brother arises from his terribly prescient observation that the best defense against perpetual pummeling is to be himself a signatory to the local axis of evil.

Leo counts these things as blessings. As he does his marriage, which, he rationalizes, *is as good as such arrangements generally get.* Betsy is a good mom, if overbearing; a good wife, if, also, overbearing. Occasionally, Leo still gets laid, sometimes with a modicum of enthusiasm, in his own hillside tri-level with three-car garage, Direct-TV, pool with spa, and many less fortunate Mexicans to clean up his debris and pitch manure onto his lawn. He's okay with the Mexicans; considers himself a *near other-white*, having been born in Taos. Everyone with a Spanish surname in Taos is descended directly from Cabeza de Baca who, in his turn, must have fucked his away toward Cibola like an inquisitional porn star. Just ask them, the Taoists.

She uncurls her legs, stretches, a wind up for her pitch. "What do you know? An only child. Probably the only Latino without at least ten siblings in LA County. Nothing but yourself to worry about. Don't think I don't envy you."

He tells her to "pant, pant, breade," that he himself is feeling poorly, that they are drifting into well-covered ground, that he is losing money and wishes to avoid bloodshed; hers. "I got stock in de toilet. Dot American Standard, *in* de *actual* toilet!" He fears he will need the sheriff to collect the rent on the three Riverside rentals. That another is vacant as long as Anasazi cliff dwellings. That he can't even get a bite from termites on the spec in San Berdoo.

"Are we okay?" She momentarily surfaces from her bell jar gloom. Leo's talking about money, after all. He says they are as long as people keep on driving into each other; the body shops are the upside. She adds dimension to her slump, manages to become almost a seat cushion: invertebrate, a mere gel of her former self. "So we're in trouble? I need to know, because I'm already having a breakdown!"

"Yes, you are." It is a continuum, her breakdown, so he treats it with less concern than she would like. Right now, he's feeling a creeping dampness of spirit himself, a general fatigue, his usually animated hands now occupied with the constant labor of wiping his nose, covering his mouth. "Take one of dose pills ob yours."

"I took a fucking pill! I took two fucking pills!" She has taken three and will probably have to opt out of the children's story telling hour at the library. Drooling on Dr. Seuss is frowned upon in the big comfy room with the fireplace.

"While dey were bucking, or did you at least let dem binish?"

She says, "See, Leo, this is a big part of the problem. The stupid jokes. This is why I can't talk to you," which germinates the obvious, "You're *always* talking to me! *Dat* is de problem!"

"So, whaddya saying? I shouldn't talk to you? I just have the breakdown all by myself? What about *share and share alike?* Community property state, asshole." She is working on a good, plump tear — a chrysalis of emotional transformation.

"I'll habe a breakdown too? Dat would be good, ib we bob lost it togeder. It's just, it's jus dat sometimes you can talk stuff to deab."

"*I* can?"

"You're a probessional killer. Come brom out of town wib a biolin case. One night bisits. Payment in a locker at LAX. And you reach a point…some determining point…where you habe to conclude dat all de talking is getting you doding more dan two bucking pills!" He speaks softly, bored with the current rehearsal. He knows his lines too well. It's a long running, off-Broadway production, the Valverde marriage and the mysterious Taylor Triangle.

Betsy says she can't keep everything bottled up like Leo, that Taylor will lead her to an early grave. Leo concurs, says, "You're letting him."

"Who else is going to give a shit!"

"Question is, sister-ob-de-year, is dere a shit dat deeds to be giben?" It is said without enthusiasm, through a chilled shimmer.

"You know, this…this attitude of *yours* is a big part of the fucking problem." He agrees that she has made this point. "You encourage him," she accuses.

"*I* encourage him?"

"You damn well do. Every time I try to do something for him, you make a joke out of it. He even said on the phone, *Leo said, I don't have to answer.*"

"He said dat?" Suppressed pride; spoken to a multi-ply Kleenex practiced in absorbing innuendo.

"Yep. And no matter what the gravity of the conversation, you make one of your idiotic little jokes and he giggles like you scruffed his hair." Idiotically faithful, he says, "He doesn't really have hair." Confirmation in tow, she parries, "See? This is what I'm talking about. I know what he looks like. Why even make such a stupid comment?"

He shrugs, slouches, seems to melt into the chair like hot cheddar. She is not amused. "You're mad at me or him?" he asks.

"You." She sits up, skeletal again, like a sudden bone marrow transplant has taken hold. She is wounded, dangerous, eyes him like a lioness to his doomed okapi. "You're the one that's supposed to be the fucking adult! How can I get mad at *him*? He's like a fucking pet. If he shits in the house, I'll whack 'em with the newspaper, but I can't get mad at him. I feel sorry for him."

"Come on! You're *always* mad at him."

"Just mad. Not *at* him."

"A distinction I somehow bail to grasp. Ain't his mama, kiddo."

"We say that about people who grow up. I'm his fucking *surrogate* mother. It is my burden to bear. And I could use a little help with the weight. Instead, you encourage this...weird behavior of his. You're just like my father."

"Dead? I'm not dead."

"The fuck you talking about! I rest my case."

"Good idea." While the juries out he intends to have a good cry over their fiscal losses. He runs yet another Kleenex over his reddening nose. The spec houses were *sure things* before they weren't.

"Don't you turn your back on me." He is pre-warned; doesn't dare turn. "Everything in life is not made right by some line from an old movie...or some cockeyed play on words."

"Comic relieb," he says without conviction. "Works bor Whoopi and Robin."

She frisbees a Dodgers coaster at him, gets him square in the jugular. He wisely resists the opportunity to cry, *Wow, Odd Job, on the mark!* Her tears are welling to the surface. He is convinced she must just have come up from slicing onions in preparation for this particular performance. They are tears big enough for Leo to reflect in.

"You know," she says, suddenly thoughtful, poised, "when we were kids, my father thought a good bonding moment with his boy was a Sunday afternoon in some grungy rail yard, each of them burning through enough film to put us in the poor house. They'd go on vacations, just the two of them. They didn't go rock climbing in Joshua Tree. They didn't go camping at the Grand Canyon. They didn't go to the Baseball Hall of Fame. They went off for days with a stack of railroad magazines to see the last run of some broken down streetcar somewhere, the closing of the short line to Fuckall, Nebraska. My dad at least had a social grace or two tucked up his sleeve, but my wacko brother is clueless, and I think that's Dad's fault for encouraging this asinine obsession. So don't screw with *me* now. I'm not in the mood." He knows he is obligated to ask about where her dad took her. "Fucking nowhere! Not that I wanted to be dragged off to Owens Valley to collect spikes from the last narrow gauge, what ever that is."

"A streak of sibling ribalry, shooting across de dight sky."

"I am not...*jealous*...of that stunted, overgrown...moron! Don't even fucking go there. So help me, I will throw something you'll really feel. So watch it, Poncho. You know, at times like this it is hard to remember why I married you."

He suggests his charm, his wisdom, his precocious insights. She suggests that he's a prick.

"Could *dat* habe been de attraction? Dat certain, uncontrollable drall into which you spiraled?"

She is breathing slower now, settling into the banter. Leo can be disarming. "I don't remember you being such a mega-asshole when you were trying to get into my pants."

He begs to differ, that he has always been an asshole of some considerable magnitude, that when you're young, assholes possess a magnetism that will only wane with time and familiarity. "You'be just come to outgrow assholes. Happens. De downside of long-term relationshibs."

She shakes her head, wipes her eyes with the back of her hand. Smears the black sludge dripping down her cheeks. Calmly now, she asks, "So what about Taylor?"

"What about Taylor?' he repeats. "Taylor's Taylor. Once a Taylor, always a Taylor. You're absolutely right. Dere is no hope bor Taylor. On his own planet. Leabe him dere and gibe yourself, myself, a break, Bets. He's dot exactly in his bormatibe, malleable years. Only de inebitable decrepitude is going to make any dibberence, and, eben den, he's still going to be our stunted, hair-brained Taylor wib de *Broadway Limited* shobed up his behind."

She pretends to mull over what he has said while she measures the time she thinks mulling should take. Then she says, "I can't be such a quitter. He's my brother."

"A Sisyphean challenge."

"Don't go speaking New Mexican on me, Pedro." When she is angry with Leo she calls him by every Iberian name she can think of, rattles them off like a Spanish baby naming book. "He says he's bringing someone to Steven's birthday."

"And?"

"Well, he's lying."

"Why would he lie?"

"He's a liar. And, to shut me up." He thinks both are good reasons. "I mean, Leo, look at him. Look how he carries himself, how he lets himself go. How many times have I pointed out the dandruff? Does anything change? Does he listen? His head looks like a fucking cup cake with vanilla sprinkles! And where does the man shop? How can they allow such combinations to leave the store? Plaid with stripes, dots with more dots! Have they no shame! You haven't seen the shirt with chickens or parrots or whatever fowl-fucking-bird. So I ask you, who'd go out with him? What kind of reject could he possibly bring to Steven's birthday?'"

"Maybe he exhumed a Harbey Girl. What did he say?"

"She's a business woman. Owns a chain of high-class bistros. Ha! My ass, she owns restaurants. If she slops kraut on dogs at the Home Depot parking lot, I'll be shocked."

"I didn't credit him for de imagination."

"So who's he going to bring? Some skank running a booty sale on Western and Sunset?"

"Beliebe me, Betsy, Taylor wouldn't dow a hooker brom a Brownie Scout."

"He can read what it says on the box of cookies! So, Jaime, enlighten me. What's the deal? Is he going to cancel at the last minute? Break Steven's heart?"

This brings a smile to Leo's congested face; one that cracks the glaze hardening on his upper lip. "Our Stebie has a heart? Look, I'm sure de kid couldn't gibe a shit about de uncle-in-de-closet."

"Do you think he's gay?" He should have seen this one on the horizon, denies it's what he meant. "But he could be?" she persists.

"Ten percent of us could be."

"I don't believe that West Hollywood bullshit!"

"I dink he's indibberent."

"What? He doesn't get erections?"

"Dot someding you want to ponder about your broder, Bets."

"I pray he doesn't do something stupid to ruin Steven's birthday."

"You pray with that mouth? Does Jesus dow you talk like dat?"

"Look, Leo, Jesus isn't a fucking baby, after all. I think He understands the importance of emphatic expression."

"If God didn't want us to curse...." Only the buzzing in Leo's head continues unabated.

"You're so smug." Her nostrils flare and her eyes and cheeks flame like red ink on wet newsprint. "You know nothing of God. You don't believe in God," she accuses.

"In whom? I don't beliebe in bairy god mobers eiber. But I'be heard de rumors. Ib God's boss ob de whole shebang, how could dibberent cultures come up wib dibberent gods?"

"Some cultures are just...stupid!"

"Uh uh! Too easy!" He tells her that God is like the telephone whose time had come. Wishes he held the patent. That folks see their gods in ways they've been described. Like UFO nuts with their saucers; just as they appear in movies. "When we habe a dighttime encounter in de middle of Debada, it's an image imprinted ober popcorn and JooJoo Bees." And ghosts. Why are they always clothed? Because, that's the way Mrs. Muir saw them. Or do clothes die too? Do sport shirts have spirits of their own? He throws ups his arms in frustration. "Jesu..."

"Don't!" she snaps, *crack!* Like a croc in a swamp.

He surrenders, can't argue the self-evident to the irrational. "My head hurts."

"Take a couple a pills." She has tuned him out. Betsy subscribes to a form of incremental evangelism that will settle for appeasement in a pinch. A weakened opponent is opportunity to savor. After a while, she says, "It was a mistake letting him buy me out of the house with his half of the inheritance."

"Who? God?"

"Good, Leo. Make God a joke. That's rational. And real grownup too. It was a mistake to leave him alone like that. You're the smart real estate mogul. You should never have…"

"B.C.E.! Let it alone, already. How bar back do you want to blame?" He tells her to blame her father for fertilizing her mother's seed, her Irish ancestors for fleeing the potato. He reminds her that she didn't want the house; that they were in the market for something entirely different. "And dere was Helen den, too. Dobody lebt Taylor alone except some Metrolink engineer whose dame we don't eben dow. Don't gibe me dis house donsense again. I'be got house donsense enoub ob my own right dow." His nose is now running like a Rolex.

"Do we even know what he's done to the place?"

"What's de dibberence? I don't care ib he's opened a titty bar in dere!"

"I'd prefer a titty bar. Badda-*fucking*-bing, Leo, pimping would be more normal for a sixty-two year old bachelor…"

"Widower."

"Whatever. Widower playing with toys all day. This was the house I grew up in."

"And naked pole dancers is more your idea ob wholesome dostalgia?"

"I'd just like to know what goes on in there. When Helen was alive, at least there was a sofa in the living room. Helen didn't replace the dining room table with a fucking thingee to turn trains around."

"Well, my guess, bor what it's worth, is dere's a whole shit load of dese tiny little people hanging around who deber, eber mobe, let alone wiggle deir g-strung asses."

"Deber eber mobe?" She giggles, then recalls the mood. "It's not normal."

"Good. Make fun. Dat's mature too. Anyway, I'm dot a tiny little person. I'be do brame of reberence. Anyway, we all habe our toys." He motions around to the bats, the signed mitts and balls.

"Do you think, maybe, he never…I mean, in his own peculiar way, never got over what happened to Helen?"

He rubs the next Kleenex vigorously under his nose; like trying to staunch lava. He says he doubts that Taylor has given Helen much thought since Goodwill hauled her clothes away. "Betsy, Betsy, Betsy. What we habe here is Taylor, who says he's going to bring a woman to Steben's birbday. You *want* him to bring a woman. But you don't beliebe he really dows a woman, so you are angry, why? Because, ib he doesn't dow a woman, as you suspect, he is eider going to habe to make up some excuse dot to come, like, like, maybe, a scheduled derailment ob tank cars loaded wib toxic chemicals dat he just can't miss, or, he is going to habe to somehow binagle some broad who could be what, a bag lady? A junkie? To join him, perhaps in exchange bor lucre, perhaps bor some sinister bavor, perhaps bor a ride on her caboose? Or dot!"

"So, then what do we do?'

"Whoeber de hell walks in wib him, let her eat cake."

She realigns her switches. "Do you think David takes after him?"

"Oh, boy!"

"Do you? Do you think maybe it's like a genetic thing in my family?"

"Mercy, woman, don't hand me straight lines! Look. Admittedly, our younger son is a bit bruitcake-ish, I'm de birst to admit, well, maybe dot de birst, but one ob de birst in line, and I don't mean *bruit* bruit, you dow, widout de cake, so don't go obb on anoder one ob your paranoid tangents. But I haben't seen de kid shobeling coal lately, dor habe I had to tell gangs of coolies waiting on be lawn dat we're dot doing any grading today, so take your sledge hammers and go on home to Hang Chow, or Hang Toub, or where eber de hell dey hang, and wash a bew shirts."

"But he's strange, our David. You know he is. The things he knows."

"He's a genius! Geniuses *are* different!"

"He knows weird shit."

"Since when is dowing bings a bad idea?"

"But the *kind* of things he knows! You know what he told me at breakfast today?"

"Ice water is an oxymoron?"

"No. I haven't heard that one. I said, *Good morning, sweetie,* handing him his cereal, and he says, *Did you know that at one time some cereals had so much iron in them that they were actually magnetic?*"

"Is he right?"

"Yes! I googled it. That's not the point. Why would a seven year old know that? Why would he care?"

"Bis is de bing, Bets. I mention bis dow to put an end to all your conbusion. One dight, I surreptitiously turkey basted your womb wib your broder's sperm. You didn't dotice because you were watching 'Briends.' You dow, de one where de two retards are playing Boozball. You're pretty easy to put one ober on when caught in de grip ob great drama. I admit, in retrospect, I should dot habe done it. Ib I could only say dree Hail Marys and turn back time. Short ob bat, bis should at least explain our David."

"You are *such* an asshole!" He offers no argument. "But you're such a *major-fucking-asshole!*"

"I'be honed a skill or two."

"You know, one time, when he was in the fifth grade..."

"David?"

"No, Cisco, Taylor! In the *fifth* grade...Mom told me this sometime near the end, 'cause you see, Leo, this is the kind of thing a mother worries about, even on her death bed, that her child won't ever fit in, won't ever live a normal life. So she told me that Taylor, in the fifth grade, takes this history test that has a section where you're supposed to identify the terms. And my dork brother, for Ferdinand Magellan, writes, *The name of a railroad car Franklin Roosevelt used.*"

"And he was right too?"

"Yeah, he was. Roosevelt, and I think Truman, had this fancy railroad car named *Ferdinand Magellan* that they would hook to the back of trains and on the platform in the back — you've probably seen the news photos; they had this row of mikes so they could ride around and give speeches. Natch, the teacher marks it wrong, but Taylor digs out some book somewhere and proves he's right."

"So de teacher concedes de point and dobody's any worse bor wear."

"No, that's not it. You fucking know it's not it. Because the fucking *it* here, Tiburcio, is that fifth grade boys know baseball scores and super heroes. Some of them even know the name of a real explorer or a pirate or someone out of history. But no fucking, fifth grader other than my weird ass brother, knew that *The Ferdinand*-fucking-*Magellan* was a railroad car! It is this relating to things from way out in left field. Coming up with the least appropriate response to almost anything. I am seriously worried about my lunatic brother *and* our strange little boy."

"I'm seriously worried about de turkey baster. Do us all a babor, pop on ober to Bed, Bab and Breakbast, or whateber, and pick up a dew one bebore Banksgibing, will ya, hon? You're saying bat de correct answer is de least appropriate?"

She tells him she could ring his fucking neck. She wipes her eyes, lifts herself sluggishly from the chair. "Watch your back, *cabrón!*"

"Eberyone else you want to sabe. Me you want to strangle. Go figure."

"Waste a prayer on a fucking papist idolater? Not on your life. You are beyond redemption. See if they laugh at your dumb-ass jokes in hell!"

"I'll tell dem to Taylor. Sometimes he laubs."

She stomps from the room with whatever drama she has left in the tank. He turns back to the computer. The news isn't good. Real estate is falling like a monochromatic Kansas farmhouse on a Technicolor witch. He becomes nostalgic for his money, for his sense of wellbeing, even for his late spat with Betsy. The tickle in his throat has reached his ear, his nose is plugged like a spiked canon, his organs unite in devilish conspiracy to ruin his day. It is time to put a stop to this. Reluctantly, he lugs himself up, goes out to the balcony overlooking the entry hall.

Betsy is making an effort to find car keys buried in her bag. She doesn't look up. "Don't come down here. I don't want to catch anything."

"Too late. Look, I'm sorry you're upset about Taylor."

"You're sorry I'm upset? You can't apologize for me. Do you have my fucking keys?"

"Why would I habe your keys? What do you want me to do, Bets?"

She stops the rummaging, picks up the bag, sees the keys on the table under it next to the framed photo of the four of them, Betsy and Leo, Taylor and Helen. "See him once in a while. Take him to dinner, a ball game. Talk to him."

"About?"

"I don't know! Carburators. Football. What do old farts talk about?"

"In Taylor's world?"

"Do this for me, Leo. It's not such a big deal. And take me seriously, for once."

He represses an urge to say something akin to *flipping off the flippancy.* He watches her amble off to the dining room, beneath his study and out of his vision, hears the movement of a chair, imagines her slump into it, a sort of parallel surrender to his own.

In somewhat diminished voice, she says, "I don't know where I think I'm going in these clothes."

"You want me to call de Library, tell dem you OD'ed, dat I'be got you hooked up to de pool vac and am about to pump your stomach?"

"Yes, Leo, that would be very helpful."

"Bets?"

"Still here. Kind a."

"I am trying to be helpful, you dow. Wib Taylor. Shitty day, and I'm in some kind a mood, but I am trying."

"So you say."

"I am."

"Show me." She has succeeded in extracting guilt from her flippant husband. On some level she finds satisfaction; on another, in some secret recess of her maternal being, she knows there is a certain justification for Leo's impatience, that Leo, as per the whole Taylor aggravation, is not so much bothered by her tenaciousness as he is by it's duration. This is an argument that calls for term limits.

He closes his eyes tightly, wiggles his nose to try to loosen up a non-functioning nasal passage. He doesn't commit, but they both know he has been given an assignment that does not involve creative options. "We're gonna be okay, you dow," he says. "De money bing, I mean. We'be got a cushion. If dis is de rainy day we'be been sabing bor, get out de old slickeroos and let it pour, let it pour, let it pour."

She collapses into a big stuffed chair. "You always do this," she says. "Whenever I have something on my mind you try to divert me with the abysmal state of our finances, or you've got a cold, or you're worried about Tio Miguel's shingles in Santa Fe." She has summoned her last line of defense; fighting diversion with diversion.

"Who could blame me? Anyway, dibersion is a cherished tactic ob combatants since Cane killed Abel. Or maybe since a little later. What do I dow? De point is: we *will* be okay because we're dibersified. We may be a little less okay dan we're accustomed to, but relatibe to eberyone else, I can guarantee we won't be libing in a camper shell on PCH. But Betsy, understand, dat outside of dese sterile halls, dis drywall bacuum of ours, dere is a *recession*. And do you know what a *recession* is? It is a word used to replace *depression* because, abter Herbie Hoober, *depression* became just a little too…well, depressing! And you dow what *depression* replaced? *Panic!* Bummer, huh? Dat's why we see de placebo of *adjustment* on de horizon. And I *do* habe a cold. Anyway, I will take my Swiss Army Porsche Design Original ober to Engineer Bill's and make him my blood brober, and we, *us*, you and me, will be okay. Okay?"

"We'll see."

"We will. You dow, it deber occurred to me before how many times we use the letter b in conversation."

"B?"

"No, b. T,u,*b!*"

"Sh-*ut up!*"
"You too?"
"We'll see."
"Last word."
"Enough!"

V

"H I YA, HON!" IT IS loud, brash, a salutary fanfare. She is the *hon* and *doll* kind of waitress you get in places that serve chicken fried steak in Love Canal gravy. "'S'it gonna be?"

Taylor scans the chalkboard at the end of the counter. "How's that pot pie special?"

She leans forward, pathetically ignorant of the view she affords him; cramped breasts crushing the tiny cross that struggles to keep them apart. She speaks softly in deference to Enrique, the short order chef, who is sadistically dumping frozen potato twigs in a metal basket and dipping the basket into an *autodafé* of molten cholesterol. To unrepentant tubers, Enrique is Torquemada. "You goin' for a stomach pump later today, pot pie's the ticket." The twang is a hint of north Texas, a whiff of southern Okie, an arrow point of Choctaw. Taylor thinks trailer.

"Thanks for saying. What about the *pollo de oro?*"

"The *toe*-maine tenders? Ya ever wonder what part a the chicken's the nugget, doll?"

"Okay then. How about the chili fries?"

"Lumps a frozen spud swimmin' in doggie diarrhea doo-doo."

"Why are you telling me this?"

"What? A gal can't have a conscience?"

"I'm running out of options. What would you have?"

"I bring my lunch from home. Your best bet's the burger. It ain't one a them black Agnes things, who ever the hell she is, and it does have enough filler t'stuff a sofa. Enrique's last *pro*-fession was auto upholstery. Filler's dry as the LA River in August. But once he gets it all oiled up on the grill there, it'll shimmy down like a newt."

"And the patty melt?"

She is still leaning down. He is still trying not to look, but he is not very good at trying. Taylor can sympathize, but is nearly devoid of empathy. Perhaps it is because he is a *cold fish*, as Betsy says. Or perhaps it is because he has had so little life experience of his own that he has no comparable unit of measure. He sees Earth from a distance; lurks in his own peripheral space. Even with this limited capacity for compassion, he can get himself to feel something akin to sorry for Cory Ann the waitress. She's a tiny thing, but chesty, with great curls of red hair, wall to wall freckles, a little hour glass figure with the sand running out, and more make-up than Helena Rubenstein. None of which arouses anything more in Taylor than the filling of certain pelvic veins with meltdown quantities of hemoglobin. What he feels bad about is her apparent poverty, struggling as she does on minimum wage and the cheap tipsters from the train shop next door. So poor, in fact, that she can't afford to wear clothing her size, as if she is still growing at forty or so, stuffing all that woman economically into blouses that are so small that buttons hang on for dear life, seeking a purchase on the very minimum of frayed thread and revealing little blimp-shaped windows on grainy flesh, as jam packed as the third class coach out of Calcutta. Today is no exception, and, either by accident or a restraint of physics, she has left open her three top buttons.

"*Paddy* melt? If ya like liquid Irishman. Just kiddin'. Actually, Enrique does a wicked melt. He's best with grease. Kind of a ethnic thing."

"Then I'll take the melt."

"Cow'r turkey?"

"Excuse me?"

"The real McCoy or ya watchin' the pounds?"

"Do I need to?" he asks, alarmed.

"You're just right, babe, have the beef. Jack'r cheddar?"

"What do you like?"

"I like a good foot massage, but it ain't on the menu an' I ain't orderin'."

"Jack then."

"Jack it is. Onion, pickle, mayo, mustard, ketchup, lettuce, tomato?"

"On a melt?"

"Why not? He can grill the onions, 'f'ya want."

"Okay."

"Comes with fries 'r fruit."

"Fries. I like them kind of well done. Crispy. Actually, kind of burnt. And a diet Coke."

"Pepsi do it?"

He nods.

"You want it on the special?"

"What's the difference?"

"Well, 'f'you're gettin' the drink, the special'll save you a buck." She arches her head toward the kitchen and belts, "PMJ, the works for my sweetie, and Enrique, kill the fries would ya, *cabrón*?"

Taylor gets up from the stool and takes a booth along the wall. Three very dead flies on the napkin dispenser pay silent tribute to Enrique's culinary skills. Taylor likes the cafe; there are photos of old dining cars all around the room, some with additional flies squished under the glass, and a few posed shots of African-American waiters grinning like crocodiles, just tickled pink, as it were, to be servin' the white folk. He is the only customer, having purposely come in late to avoid the regulars.

Somehow, he has to get to know Cory Ann, has to make a move in the waning days before Steven's birthday. But picking up a woman is not a subject Taylor has ever had much of a handle on. He has brought the latest Walther's model railroad catalogue with him, thumbs through pages of cattle cars and hoppers, feigning interest and searching desperately for some secreted hint on the art of attraction. There is, of course, much in life to imitate literature, but Taylor's access to the written word is confined by chain link and YARD LIMIT signs. He fears it will be difficult to attract her with sweet nothings about *five-pole, skew wound can motors* even with *dual flywheels*. And *rear-mounted air horns?* Probably not a subject to be broached in mixed company.

Cory Ann brings his plate, sets out bent flatware, spills a brown drop as she sets down the plastic cup. The melt is open-faced and traditional, oozing red, yellow, white, a raft of pickle, salad veggies on the side to be handled at buyer's discretion. The fries look like Richmond after the Yankees arrived. She sits on the bench opposite Taylor, pushes off each tennis shoe with the opposite toes, and rests her heels on the torn Naugahyde next to his thigh. He is unnerved, fears he won't be able to swallow. She is barefoot, practices a long, relaxed sigh, and says, "This girl's dogs'er hunted out."

He has no idea what she is talking about.

"Rub my feet, will ya, dearie? Save my life."

"While I'm eating?"

"What'm I thinkin'? You take your time. If nobody else comes in, y'can do me later."

"This is...well...unusual," he says.

"Hey! I ain't askin' ya t'climb up in my drawers, am I? Been on my feet all day, you're in here two-three times a week, seem like an okay sort a guy, so-o-o..."

He waits, removes his wounded glasses, then says, "So?"

"So maybe we should get t'know each other."

"Two times. Just two times a week," he says, but thinks, *This is not so hard after all. Happy birthday, Steven!*

"Look, just kiddin'. No sense a humor, huh!"

"Yes, that's right. Very little."

"So, chuckles, what's that you're readin'?" She has left her naked feet next to his warming thigh.

He hesitates, nearly whispers, "Model railroad catalogue."

"I *thought* ya were from next door. You guys have a look 'bou'cha. Kind a like glazed over, like you got ambers in your eyes."

"Embers. I think you mean embers."

"What ever. Say, so tell me. Whaddya guys do over there all day?"

"Sell this kind of stuff." He points to the Walther's with both hands linked to Jack-drenched toast.

"An' for fun?"

"It is fun!"

She squints, sends little lines of wonder outward from her blue eye shadow. "No, like after work? Weekends?" There is clip to her twang, an urgency to her lilt.

"Same as everybody else."

"Everybody else don't go home an' play'th little trains. In your case, sugar plum, a busman's holiday." She responds quickly, thinks on her feet, or, currently, her ass. And what an inspirational ass it is — even Taylor can find adjectives for it.

"I'm not into busses. Some of the guys…Anyway, it's not like that. These are not toys. Come by sometime and I'll show you. They're scale models, little works of art made by serious…artisans. Like fine jewelry."

"Think I'll stick'th baubles, 'cause baubles is a gal's best friend." With fire-engine-red Fu Man Chu nails, she flicks an earring the size of a chandelier from an Iranian import shop. There is the unmistakable tinkling of quality rhinestone. "Whadda your wives think? Grown men playing with little…what'd y'say? Scale models?"

"I don't have a wife."

"Well, ain't that a shock!"

"I *was* married," he replies defensively. "Some time ago. Her name was Helen."

"So what happened t'this Helen? She have it up the wahoozits with the trains?"

"She died…actually."

Cory Ann readjusts her feet down the seat, a few inches away from his thigh. He is instantly sorry he has mentioned Helen. Nothing good ever comes from mentioning Helen.

"Sorry," she says looking like she means it. "Didn't mean t' be…all la-di-da 'bout it. I gotta mouth size of a horse's, sometimes."

"It's okay. Do you want to know how it happened?"

She is doubtful. "Ya wanna tell me?"

"She was hit by a train."

"A *real* train!" She has a visual of something Lionel running over the late Helen's toes, breaking the skin, causing it to fester and develop into gangrene, from which she expires weeks later, despite a series of amputations.

"Yes."

They are silent for a while. Then they both begin to laugh nervously. "You're shittin' me, right?"

"No. We had a fight. We always had fights. I don't know why. Everything just always seemed to end up in a fight. Actually, she did most of the fighting. I know it takes two, but Helen could fight all by herself. She kind of fought *at* me. Helen was a very unhappy woman. This one morning, we had a terrible fight. She hit me with a very expensive passenger car. I still have this little scar over my eye. The car shattered." He shows her the scar, doesn't know why he's talking so much but continues on. "She gets in the car, for some reason drives all the way over to San Fernando Road in Glendale, over near the Home Depot, and she's just driving and along comes the Metrolink, and she hangs a left right on to the tracks and stops."

"Jesus!"

"Yes. The Police thought the car stalled out. I don't think so. She was depressed. We fought. She had no business being over on San Fernando Road. Really no business being on the tracks."

"That sucks! Must a been like devastated." Again, he finds the little fault lines in her makeup, a worried delta edging out from the corners of her eyes and mouth, hints of graver foundational instability. Not even the Corps of Engineers would scoff at such evidence. She is perhaps older than he originally thought; maybe forty-five, fifty even.

"No, actually, no I wasn't. At first, I was confused. *What now?* I thought. I went into the third bedroom where she allowed me to keep my layout. A pretty modest set up then. I stared at a grade crossing for a while. You, know, the place where the road crosses the track. After a while I found myself putting cars on the track, then imagining a train coming. Before I know it, I'm running trains into the cars to see what happens at impact. Of course, I understand, it's not exactly what Helen experienced, but, I kind of needed to see it to understand. I'm not a bad person, or anything, I don't want you to think I am. But it was later that night, after the police had come to the house and told me I would have to come in and identify the body…or whatever was left of the body…Helen's body…It was later that night that I started getting the inspiration for the train layout. What rooms I could use. What furniture I could get out of the way."

Her lower lip is hanging into her unbuttoned blouse. *"Now* you're shittin' me!"

"Okay." He does not want to disappoint.

There is a moment of thoughtful silence.

"The wife's in three parts on the tracks an' you're makin' garage sale signs'th a Sharpie?"

"No. I guess…I guess I just made it up."

"So y'do have a sense a humor. Like *mondo bizarro*, but ya can sure spin one."

"Okay."

"You're creepin' me out there for a minute, cutie pie."

"Okay. I'm sorry," he says, taking his first bite of the patty melt he's been holding. His fingers are awash in cheese sweat. "Cory Ann? It is Cory Ann, right?"

"What it says right here on the boob." She points, despite the obviousness of both boob and name plate.

"I don't usually talk this much."

"That's probably a good thing."

"Probably."

"Taylor, huh? Fan-*cy!*"

"It was a surname. My grandma on my father's side was descended from Zachary Taylor."

"Oh, yeah, I remember him from them old cowboy movies. Remember that old Saturday night movie show called the 'Fabulous Fifty-two'? Guess I'm datin' myself, but somebody has t'. When my mom and her bozo *d'jure* would get pretty much schnockered, which was most a the time, I got t' stay up late mostly 'cause they forgot about me, an' I watched these old black an' whites, and there was a lot of cowboy movies back then."

"I don't think Zachary Taylor was in any of them. He's been dead for maybe a hundred fifty years."

"What ever. They were *old* movies. Zachary-somebody or somebody-Taylor. I was just a kid."

"Do you want to go out with me? Like on a date?"

She directs a talon toward his lips. "Got a little...no right there, a little mustard thing goin' on."

He attacks the little mustard thing with his napkin. "Do you?"

"Ya ever get anywheres with this approach? Shit! Kind a direct, doncha think?" She has narrowed her eyes, pulled away her legs and rested her feet on the clogs. She reaches for one of his fries; it is as crispy as Formica. "I mean," she crunches, "do the girls go for the dead wife thing an' all?"

"I've never told anybody else. Just my sister, Betsy, but I don't think she takes me too seriously. You'd like Betsy. She swears a lot too."

"Oh, honey! As the man says, y'ain't heard nothin' yet."

He doesn't hear, is distracted by the gravity of his own next move. "So, what do you think? You want to go out on a date? With me?" It is out of the bag now, tabloid naked, soaked in light.

Enrique is leaning on the counter, his shaved head beading with sweat, a soiled rag over his shoulder. He has bargain-basement tattoos that look like they'd been etched with the tooth of a comb. "Yo, Taylor, how the choos-choos hangin'? Coralita, *mi novia*, y'gonna sit there on your sweet futon all afternoon? *En* that case, my little *chicharona*, I'm gonna take *cinco* out back for a toke or two so you give me a holler we happen to attrac' some clientele. An' you, dawg, watch out for this one. She soak you in *Tapatillo* an' eat you alive!"

"Go out in the lot and shoot up or somethin', asshole," she calls to his back. "Don't mind him, honey buns. A reject from our Bad Moves Division. You wanna go out, okay. I gotta few empty slots on the old dance card. I kind a like you, I think. I like the innocence. You are so...*not* Enrique...so *not* what I'm used t'."

No dinners are served in the Dining Car. It is purely an omelet and sandwich joint. Taylor and Cory Ann make arrangements for the next evening and Taylor steps outside bolstered by his newfound charisma with the opposite sex. It is summer, and the smog is heavy enough to bend car antennas. He glances north toward the sickly brown curtain that makes it seem he is looking through a dirty window screen. He wonders what they have done with the mountains, how they store them during the warmer months. By New Year's Day, in concert with local ordinances, the sky will be as transparent as O.J. Simpson, and six thousand foot peaks will support prickly ridges of transmission towers against a sky so blue it hurts the eyes; all this so that folks bundled in the Snow Belt can watch Miss South El Monte cruise the elbow of Orange Grove and Colorado with teeth as big as dominoes and barely three square inches of bikini.

Nightstick Darouche, in shades and USMC cap, is the surprise guest holding up the front wall of the Smoke 'n' Whistle, scowling at traffic with its passacaglia of horns *à la* Frescobaldi. "If I was GM or Ford," he mumbles, "I'd charge extra for the fucking horns, make them an option, and dun the driver each time they're used."

"What's up, Carl?" Taylor asks, only imperceptibly slowing.

"Just checking on an order."

"Come on back and I'll see to it for you."

"I'll pass. Baylor wrote it up. I'll talk to Baylor." His fists are clenching, opening, clenching.

"Okay." Taylor reaches the door.

"Long lunch, huh?" Slits replace his eyes.

"Monday slow. I'll make it up."

"Baylor's too easy on you guys."

"Well, we all pitch in when we need to."

"Got something going in the greasy spoon?"

Taylor stops, half in, half out. "Yes," he says with confidence. "I think I do. Were you looking in the window?"

"Some things are so obvious you don't need to creep up on 'em."

"I made a date," says Taylor.

"A date?"

"Uh huh."

"Kind a new ground for you, isn't it?"

"No. I'm not unknown to the ladies."

"I'll phone Ripley's. You be careful, Taylor. I've known some waitresses in my time."

"What's wrong with waitresses?"

"You just be careful, son."

"Okay." He breathes in and out; a cadence attuned to Nightstick's fists.

"Okay then, to you," says Nightstick. "And Taylor?"

"Yes?"

"You're gonna wanna zip your fly before you traipse through the kiddie section."

Taylor falls for it, walks sideways along the storefront, checks the zipper as he passes through the vestibule.

VI

I T IS NEARLY DARK, BUT STILL steaming hot, as Taylor slowly edges up Cory Ann's street. He notes the landmarks she has indicated: the Cali-Mex Market, the elementary school bungalows, the corner *tienda* with the big banner reading, TODOS TIPOS DE CARNE ASADA CARNITAS LENGUA. The receding sky behind them is chemical red.

The streets are steep and ragged and the trees are old, having seen the neighborhood grow out of the hills, decay, and semi-gentrify right up to the current recession. Taylor's Caddie with its great raccoon's tail of black exhaust seems right at home with the cars parked on lawns: Nissans lowered to the ground like caskets and sporting disguises of huge spoilers and wheel-well covers, gold-flecked Impalas with names of sweethearts on the rear windows and pinstriped like old zoot suits, battered Buicks with one or two primed fenders and welded chains for license plate frames, *macho* black Suburbans with silver nudes on the mud flaps and suffering under the weight of enough amps and woofers to entertain capacity crowds at Burning Man. Some are missing hubcaps; others roll on chrome wheels whose value exceeds the Blue Book on the vehicle. Still others perch on concrete blocks, hoods ajar like whale jaws with caged shop lights hanging over the engine blocks.

Hers is a street of sidewalks cracked by roots and pitched like skate board ramps. Every available hard-scape surface not defended by iron bars is decorated with spray paint scrolls, as if begging for increased attention to spelling in the LA Unified Schools. These are the Avenues, Highland Park, in the crotch between Eagle Rock and the old Southern Pacific facility — the Taylor Yards; no relation. East LA's overflow.

Some of the neighboring streets sport remodels. Young couples of various ethnic and gender-preference backgrounds find themselves blessed to be able to sign onto sub-prime loans for two bedroom wooden fixer-uppers that have been stuccoed on the outside, the ceilings cottage cheesed on the inside, with gasping floor heaters in the front room only. All for fifteen thousand above the asking price of half a mil. The houses sag and tilt on 1915 foundations, wind their way up narrow lanes to shame San Franciscans. Pit bulls behind chain link outnumber people, all of them perpetually frantic and ready to make the morning paper with a half-eaten mailman trophy or the blood-stained uniform of the meter reader.

Cory Ann rents a small one bedroom in a court right out of Raymond Chandler. Few of the units have air conditioners and most of the tenants are out on the stoops sucking beer cans to competing *tejano* beats. The men are shirtless to display their illustrated torsos. The women, even the pregnant ones, sport exposed midriffs glistening brown in the ozone glare and weighted to the ground with pounds of piercings, as if they had just emerged from the jungles of Borneo.

Taylor seems extraordinarily out of place, is sure the locals are commenting in Spanish on his Hilo Hattie shirt with *nene* birds tucked away under broad palm fronds, his High Ball baseball cap, and yellow double-knits designed by octogenarians for the *bocci* court at Leisure Village, He carries a wax cone of flowers from Trader Joe's. He hears a teasing, *¡Qué bonito! ¿Para mí?* followed by laughter, and, *Fuck bitch! Leave the homie alone!* The homie is grateful for the admonishment. He breathes in, he breathes out, and is too self-conscious to check his zipper while in the gauntlet between the grandstands. There is a stink of tobacco and weed and a sting of chili peppers. A company of cockroaches is drilling on the parade ground sidewalk.

He reads, "Kowntertaup" on the mailbox. The numbers have been stolen from the doorjambs, leaving nail holes and a half of a seven on hers. He thinks it a good omen, even half of a seven; one mustn't expect too much. She has the screen door ajar, is leaning in the doorway like a barefoot pinup, wearing hip-low jeans with amputated knees, legs dipped snuggly into to them like they are the chocolate shell at the Tastee Freeze. Her legs are short woman long, her waist cowgirl high. Her blue halter has its work cut out for it, a project of suspension to challenge the Roeblings. A small purple butterfly enjoys a particularly favorable perch on her left breast.

One of the revelers calls, "*Chica! Ba-a-ad accident, no? I see you're air bags inflated.*"

Taylor is suddenly thrilled speechless, an emotion for which he finds no precedent, and blurts a high pitched, "Hi," fears it will be the extent of his vocabulary. His back burns from the *jalapeño*-dusted stares coming at him from the suddenly quiet stoop party.

But he is immersed in her scent, lush and tangy, Avon calling, a bit too loudly. There is also the definite competition from pungent spaghetti sauce. Taylor likes spaghetti sauce, often fingers it cold directly from the jar. And all at once, he likes Cory Ann very much. Betsy should be a fly on the wall. Betsy would have a cow: a big cow, white with black spots, and great pink bagpipes dripping milk between her rear legs. Betsy's massive episiotomy would forever remind her to no longer underestimate big brother.

"So, sweet pie," Cory Ann says, a whispery high voice, reedy with a bouquet of Gallo red, "my home girl Griselda seems t'like the flowers, so'f they're for me y'best hand 'em over before she mugs your ass."

He hands her the flowers as she holds the door open. They are her only real flowers; she is heavy into floral plastics, scent provided by aromatic nightlights stuck in several outlets. The apartment is small, a front room with a TV, a sofa and a coffee table that holds up a black ceramic panther shining like coal, and three threadbare issues of <u>Apartment Life</u> tastefully arranged in the shape of a fan. The TV is on, softly — a handsome young man is making faces as he attempts to drink a dark brew alive with brine shrimp. Above the TV, cord hanging askew, a large print of Paris, the city, textured like oils and with street lights that actually light up. Beat that, Utrillo. The bedroom and bath apparently reside behind the doorway with the plastic beads raining down and reflecting light patterns over the walls.

Cory Ann gives Taylor a quick peck on the cheek, an action that causes her to step up high on her kernels of toes and crane her neck, and burns a steaming crater into Taylor's shaven face. Then she runs off to the kitchen to trim the stems and plunge what remains into a Betty Boop beer mug filled with tap water. "These'er real pretty," she says, placing the mug down on the center of her table, so that the purple flowers clash with the gingham oilcloth cover and the thrift store Melmac plates it is set with. A big pot is gurgling on the O'Keefe & Merritt two burner. "Hope I don't kill 'em. Ain't so good at keepin' shit alive."

"Aren't we going out?" he asks from the kitchen door. "I was going to take you somewhere nice. Fuddruckers has steaks now."

"What a prince!" she remarks. "But y'know, hon, like *my* busman's holiday? No big thrill for me t'go somewhere an' see a wetback flip burgers. You okay'th homemade spaghetti? I mean, I didn't make the sauce exactly, but I did kick it up a bit, like that Emerald guy says on the food show."

"I love spaghetti."

"See? We're compatible. Passed the first big test. Besides, my feet are hurting all the way up t'my ears and I'm all about kicking back right now. Close the door, will ya, sugar lips. I'm gonna flip on the air." She makes a few adjustments on the Sears window model; it clatters and howls into action and blows the napkins off of the table. He gets a chance to appraise the reptile squiggling down her lower spine and flicking its forked tongue at the crack of her ass. *Cracked or not*, he decides, *it's a pretty nice ass.* "So whaddya drinkin'?"

"Nothing. I just came in."

"Mr. Liter-*al*, jeez! What can I ge'cha?"

"I don't know. I'm not much of a drinker."

"Well, let's see if we can fix that." She rescues a Tecate from the fridge, pops the cap and hands it over. It is Arctic-cold on this cactus-hot night. "I got appetizers too, so lug your brew back t'the *say*-lon and take a load off. Loose the loafers 'f'ya want."

She follows him into the front room and the battered sofa, snuggles up next to his great haunch of thigh, her wine in a water glass in her delicate hand, his beer in his. They are like a baby-back rib sidling up to a side of beef. She prepares a small cocktail napkin for him, adorns it with a square of Velveeta stabbed through the heart with a little plastic sword, a tortilla chip suffocating in a recyclable tub of guacamole, and a dripping cocktail dog, the size of a child's thumb, skewered like a trophy sent with a ransom note.

She removes his hat, says, "Stick around for a while," spins it across the room. "I was thinkin'," she says, "'bout what you said 'bout your wife. At first, I'm thinkin', shit, what's the story! I mean, I was weirded out an' all. Then I thought you were pullin' my leg. Don't I wish! Then, I'm thinkin', he means it. It's true. But you're so innocent about it. So...I dunno...*Honest.* Honest is kind a refreshin'. And I can understand the sense a relief. Even with somethin' so horrible. Like Jesus wants ya t'go on. Like Jesus wants ya t'make plans an' go right on. The way ya just come on out with it. Like it was the most natural feelin' in the world."

He chews the little dog and she dutifully dabs his lips with another napkin. "I like this sauce," he says. "My mother used to serve these up for her bridge parties."

"Let's not go t'mothers just yet. A bit early in the whatever-this-is. I know, speakin' a sauce, that I already mentioned mine, but I'm ready to put that behind me 'til I'm pinned an' we're goin' steady."

He is blank faced. Devours the Velveeta. Her hand is fumbling along the lobe of his ear. He tries to remember if he Q-tipped and hopes his dandruff behaves.

Cramped at her little table, they suck pasta like the Lady and the Tramp. The spaghetti is just south of *al dente*, more like *calamari*, like rubber bands, but nonetheless smooth and lubricated. Their four lips smack happily. Her halter, not so happily, suffers the tensions of stress, threatens to burst like the Johnstown Dam. Taylor is embarrassed by an insistent erection.

"Now, ya owe me," she says. "Rub my feet." And no sooner is it said than she plops her left foot onto his leg.

Hesitantly, he takes it in hand, starts to rub, pinch, flex toes. He is inventing, has no idea how this works, and, being himself excruciatingly ticklish, doesn't understand the point. Helen would never have asked him to touch her feet; would never have touched his. Yet he likes the feel of Cory Ann shoeless, the callused pads, the gentle protrusion of ankle, the wiggle of her painted toes. So immersed does he become in this rare giving of pleasure, that only slowly does he realize that her right foot is now snuggly seeking the warmth of his crotch, that her big toe is exploring, probing away with practiced confidence. Her lips part, just barely; her eyes narrow and sparkle. Taylor is all heat and blush and wonder. And he realizes that it has been a very, *very* long time.

Afterward, clinging to each other in her double bed under the fleshy light of a lava lamp, the bulge of his belly slotted nicely into the curve of her spine, a hand cupped to breast, sweet wheezes of snoring ruffling Cory Ann's pillow, Helen once again enters his new found Oz like the Wicked Witch of the West. Helen, who, even in the beginning was dry and distant, still and bloodless, had never prepared him for Cory Ann. Cory Ann the primitive, the creator, the texture of avocado, the moistness of citrus, pitons secure, climbing the mountain of man flesh; she is Shiva the Cosmic Dancer, her many arms swaying like seaweed in the depths, her many fingers probing topographic contours, depressions and rock-hard spires explored previously only in clinical lab tests. She has more tongues than a good Jewish deli.

It is an experience so remote to Taylor, so fundamentally new, that, with silent apologies to Cory Ann, he cannot help comparing it to his fumbling, and just a little grotesque, obligations with Helen. He has no context for this kind of joy, can only think in familiar analogies, that, while Helen was un-fired and sandbox dry, IRT tight, and as resistant as Donner Pass in winter, Cory Ann is the supercharged fairy queen perfection of the fuck; is, though not exactly Penn Station roomy, spacious and accommodating, and lubed for the long haul. If he could, Taylor would get up a head of steam and blow smoke, heating the night air with sated cinders and ash and, whatever, glowing *ambers* to write home about.

At five in the morning, showered — powdered, oiled, anointed, Avoned to the marker lights and fresh as new rotary-plowed snow — she aims her hair dryer, slips into another too small blouse with her name stitched to the boob, gives him a lip brush across the brow, and tells him to stay as long as he likes but to lock the door when he leaves, *babe*.

At seven, Taylor is sitting naked in front of the tube. It hasn't been turned off since he arrived the night before; may, in fact, never have been turned off since she moved in. "Good Morning America." He has never seen it. He helps himself to a breakfast of dry frosted flakes with a tiger on the box, a bottle of Bacos that he throws into his mouth like nuts, topped with a dessert of Reddy Whip shot directly onto his tongue. He takes orange juice straight from the carton. Distractedly, he scratches his spent cock and breathes evenly. Excluding the time on the top of Mt. Washington when he peered over a stack of flapjacks erupting in butter and floes of maple syrup, all the while mesmerized by the crooked little cog engines puffing up the impossible grade, this is the best breakfast he has ever had.

SECOND HELEN

She's surprised a cop hasn't pulled her over: all the stop signs she's rolled through, the yellow lights she's run, setting off a flutter of angry horns as she roared up the car pool ramp onto the Two Ten. How could Betsy ever have thought that this could be a good idea? How could she, for that matter? You're more vulnerable with your own shelf life nearing expiration. The last shopper standing finds slim pickings. And Taylor, when he hasn't got that baffled boy look on his face, isn't all that bad looking. She thought he was just shy. And his innocence seemed kind of cute. Who knew how much more than innocence it was? Absolute cluelessness wasn't what she signed on for. A bungler, lost in his own little world, an autistic's sense of intimacy. Time to pack the Samsonite. Wipe her hands of the whole dismal failure. Rather be alone. Fuck it! I'm already alone. Kind of.

TISHOMINGO

I

"THERE WAS NOTHING. ALL WAS UNFORMED. A void. A vacuum if you will. The unnatural was the natural. An unnatural condition lacking the tangible. A darkness beyond black. The darkness of nothing. The deep without depth, the earth unformed, without substance. There was no time. Try to imagine. Not only no clocks, no calendars, no passage of sun across the ether. There was no ether! And no time. And there had been no time for *all* time. Only the hovering spirit of the Lord. The keenest eye of the first and greatest of artists. The Father before offspring. The Creator before Creation. An unfathomable consciousness. Old before age. Ageless. Wise beyond wisdom. Praise the Lord."

"Praise the Lord." It is repeated throughout the congregation, follows the brimming basket down a row of pews, up the next, switchbacks through the families starched and white.

"How to explain the unexplainable?" he asks. "My mind rolls over on itself. Free fall. I feel I am having one of those dreams, you know the ones, we all have them, where you are falling and falling and never touch bottom? Unsettling dreams that wake us from sleep in a cold sweat, make us latch onto something solid, a stone, a slab of wood, the Good Book. Keep it by your bedside. Keep it for such dreams. Keep *it* to keep *you*."

Heads shake. They know those dreams. It has been nearly a decade of things rolling over on themselves.

"But this is before sweat. Before solid." He scans their eager faces. "From *nuh*-thing. Not *even* nothing! *Before* nothing. Think about it. Let your mind roll over on itself and never ever reach bottom because there is as yet no bottom. No rolling. No mind. No thought. *Nothing* for you to grab onto." His voice is deep, unearthly, as the particular acoustics of the room gather it up, process it, wind it through rafters, filter it back down from the transoms.

He slips out of his old frock coat, hangs it gently on a corner of pulpit, and offers up his famous paternal smile. He does all this purposely, movements of conviction, of punctuation.

They smile back, conjoined, the smile of the flock, a conspiracy of the righteous, a cabal. He could take his staff and lead them to water, lead them to graze, lead them to chasms and over the edge.

He rolls up first one sleeve, then the next, immune to the cold in the winter room, the insulating gray stone of its walls, the vaulted ceiling gathering up to itself all available warmth. But he is warm; jacketless, wrists bare. He dwells in the warmth of the Lord.

They shake heads. They know what is coming. They anticipate. They are cold — wrapped in Sunday austere, woolens, flannel — but are warming. He warms them, as he leans an elbow onto the rostrum, closes the Book with an audible thump, plays the crowd with gun-metal blue eyes, beatific, transmitting the love, the heat. "Which reminds me of a story," he says slowly, cocking his head, intonations of the approaching aside. Twinkles alight in his eyes like Christmas bulbs.

"Here it comes."

"Oh, yes."

"Wouldn't ya know?"

They are with him, hanging on his every breath. Some lean forward in their seats, Bible's comfy like babes on their laps.

"Will you bear with me, my friends?"

"Yes." Of course they will. He speaks rhetorically.

"Hear my story?"

"Yes!"

"Praise Jesus."

"Praise Him."

"It was just this last year, as I recall," he starts, moving down the three steps into the midst of the congregants, shaking a hand or two as he preaches, ruffling the hair of a youngster in passing. He becomes one of them, un-elevated, integral leader-follower, pitching, playing off their responsive commentary. His voice now comes not from some levitating source; it pours sweetly from his own lips. He speaks slowly, in a higher register, words almost painfully enunciated, as if nothing he says should be missed, as if great value compounds every verb, enriches each noun, assays every article. "You'all remember, I am sure, for how could you forget? The visit of the Great D. W. Plunderblast's Wild Animal Circus to the fairgrounds in Uncas Falls? I would bet the collection basket...may I be forgiven the sinful lapse of the wager...that many of you attended a performance or two during that most magical of weeks. I may use the word *magical?* In a totally secular sense? No harm, no harm. Bear with me."

They nod affirmation. They bear with him. They remember bears; bears and tigers and cotton candy and troops of clowns all ejected from the world's most ornate and colorful train, a great coupled stream of golden carved floral and belching calliopes, smelling of elephants, hay and dung.

"My good wife," gesturing towards the becoming blush of the pious woman, "and I, like you, good friends, gather our little brood...there they are, next to the missus, Praise Jesus, does it not give you'all a glow, an inner comfort?...Pile into our humble Ford, clutching our tickets for the eight o'clock performance in the big top. We are as steady in intent as the tightrope walker herself. We are as one, breathless with excitement and expectation. Who amongst us, here today, wasn't?

The fifteen familiar miles, remember? They seem an alien eternity, yet, somehow, we are there with time to spare, and time to spare is a dangerous thing for humans, as we all know, a breeding ground for temptation, the spore of deviltry, the welcome mat at the door of Satan's intervention. Get ye away, Say-*tan!*"

"Get ye away!" Some of them actually wave their hands, push forward with splayed fingers, thrust Satan from the room. He doesn't go willingly.

The speaker reaches down to kiss the soft cheek of the swaddled Milford baby, brushes his arm so unconsciously over the pliant breast of nubile Mrs. Milford, in the process, reduces her to paralysis, to shivering liquid puddles. "As it happens, we have an hour to spare and are drawn, perhaps perversely so… Who amongst us has not so sinned?…To what is, I think, given the unfortunate nomenclature of *freak show*. Say it, try it out, *freak show.*"

"Freak show," tentative, halting. He has stepped into the briefest of rainbows, a planetary elongation of triangle, sunlight piercing a cloud, entering the church through stained glass, casting him in clown colors, then vanishing with the coming storm.

"I think it is important to say it. To feel it on your tongue. There but for fortune, dear friends. Say it again. Say it loud. Not *side show. Freak show.* A piteous assemblage of God's anointed that He in is wisdom has chosen to bear the millstone of hideous affliction, those poor unfortunates encumbered with gnarled limbs, tethered in perpetuity like Chang and Eng, skulls pointed like mountain peaks: The Human Skeleton, The Bearded Princess, The Pretzel Man tied in the knot that is himself, The Wolf Boy; grotesqueries that baffle all of our complacent rationality, that chill us to the marrow, repulse us with their crippled abominations, *yet*…hear me now, draw…us…*on* like Moses into the sea. I saw you there, Mayor, Sarai, leading your own little troop of grandchildren."

The Mayor and his wife nod confirmation, beam around at the crowd in the comfort of this special recognition. Some of the women stare down at their shoes; one glares towards P-R, an un-Christian glare of accusation conceived at once by the sperm and egg of several cohabiting deadly sins.

"We all alike suffer the sometime trespass of curiosity. That is part of our humanity. And just beyond the tent of The Fish Woman, a poor thing suffering a terrible flesh of scales from head to toe, breathing through gills slashed into the sides of her neck…"

Some recoil now, kerchiefs to lips, more eyes cast down. The Fish Woman is the most reprehensible of all.

"…we arrive at the brightly adorned tent of Aslam the Magnificent. And magnificent he is in his heathen manner; make no mistake, in his bejeweled turban and ballooning pantaloons, as if a genie just emerged from his vessel, dark like a Bantu warrior, a Goliath with great golden earrings and scimitar smile, the golden orb eyes you might expect of a pirate on his salt air prowl."

Children shiver with the fearful image; they have seen the N.C. Wyeth illustrations in <u>Treasure Island</u>. Grown-ups comfort them with reassuring hugs.

"Ah, Chief Prezhki, there in the last pew, hiding, as it were? Hoping to be called away by the timely behavior of some miscreant? How many, many Sundays has it been?"

Heads turn to acknowledge the Chief. Prezhki feels compelled to nod.

"We surrender our hard-earned buffalo nickels." He pivots, slowly treads back toward the pulpit. "And as we advance toward Aslam's Saharan abode we are joined by two stylishly attired gents, professorial sorts, in sartorial exactness, rolling their eyes, shaking their heads, but nonetheless riding the crowd inside and sitting, as it so mysteriously happens, in the same row as my family and myself. So, by such coincidence, I am afforded, by the nearness of their conversation, an insight into their shared thoughts. And, to the relief of some of you, dear friends in Jesus, who have so patiently agreed to accompany me on this exercise of memory, I approach the crux of my tale."

"We're with you, brother."

"Amen."

"I deduce from their words, most of which I will spare you in Christian charity, that the two gentlemen are of the educated class, perhaps, even, professors from our great secular institution in the capital. They are highfalutin sorts, scoffers, out for a night with the general muck of men, yours truly, unabashedly indicted. And one of these benighted professors...I shall herein call them Professor One and Professor Two...Professor Two leans over to Professor One and says, 'Watch this guy, watch him *con these rubes.*'"

There is a rumble of disapproval.

"No, no, no," with palm flat, pivoting around in the aisle. "The Lord loves a sinner. Take no offense. A rube, maybe. But better a rube in Christ Jesus than the misguided dupe of our poor Charlie Darwin. Am I right? Of course, I'm right. And, so...back to our exotic Mohammedan...In the course of Aslam's smooth delivery he produces, with a great flourish that sets his turban aflight," his voice building, ascending like stairs, "a white dove, then another, then another, ten, fifteen, twenty in all, like clowns from their tiny car, all from this one turban," accelerating, a heavy hand to the throttle, "and then...as three or four of the newly emancipated creatures return to perch on his great extended arm, set like a great tree bough, he places them back into the turban, turns it over, bundles it like waste paper, crushes it in his powerful hands," he pantomimes, crushes invisible feathers and bone, "and unravels it until it is but a length of wrinkled cloth. And the doves inside? *Gone! Vanished! Nowhere!* From nothing to nothing! The crowd gasps. *I* gasp. How has he done it? Professors One and Two chuckle. *Cheap trick! Something from nothing! The American Way.* These are *rational* men, our good professors."

A few are nodding now. They see the parable; know where he is going.

"So here are these two brilliant minds of the University of Great Knowledge. Men of Learning. Readers of the Thinkers: the Galileos, the Platos, the Newtons, et al. Able to spot a cheap trick from a mile away. A falcon's vision, these wise men. Able to laugh away the making of doves from nothing; the returning of doves to nothing. Think about it. Think about it."

They think about it; how can they not.

"How can two such prodigies scoff at the creation of something from nothing there in the tent of this inscrutable barbarian, yet tomorrow find themselves lecturing pliant students on a creation absent a Creator? Impossible to procure a lowly dove from the empty turban, yet possible to elicit all that *is* from a void? *I ask you!*" He is back to the podium, a barely perceptible transit. *"In the beginning God created the heaven and the earth.'* Without the hovering spirit of God there is no mechanism of Genesis, there is no light, there is no firmament. There are no creatures of the sea, none walking upon the land, none alighting into the air on wings. My two learned professors, who I thank for their *scientific* insights, are correct on one score. Nothing comes from nothing. Praise Jesus."

"Praise Jes/Praise/Jesus/Prai/sus." All at once, apart by milliseconds.

"Let me confess a sin," he says quietly. They crane forward, shake heads in the negative. "No, no, no, please, brothers and sisters, allow me to purify my transgression. A transgression of omission, but a transgression nonetheless. I make no excuses. I faltered. For it was my duty to call them out, these doubters, and I said nothing." He raises his heels, flattens his toes, bows his knees to sink mechanically to the floor, smoothly, as if being lowered at some measured pace, as if held at the shoulders by invisible wires. He faces the rafters, the nearing storm, splays his hands, his arms. "There and then, oh, Lord, I should have called them out. Prostrate, humble, I should have beseeched them to hear the Word and know the Truth and turn their stiffened spines toward damnation. Satan, get thee behind me." A modulation of voice, of body, he rises like the dead Christ, as if someone has rolled the stone from his cave, an effortless ascent from a man P-R's contemporary, a grandfather, un-afflicted by age, knees retreat with rubber smoothness, an elbow sets casually down upon the podium. "We learn from our mistakes. We grow. We become worthy once again."

Their mouths are agape; some smile. They are on the edge of their seats when he releases them from his thrall.

"Matthew tells us, *'Beware of false prophets, which come to you in sheep's clothing, but inwardly they are ravening wolves.'* Guard against the –ologies of *canus lupus:* anthropo-, archaeo-, geo-, bio-. Seal yourselves from the unbelievers, however learned. Drum out the cacophony of howling science, thrust down the naysayer, the doubter, the contrarian. It is going to rain today, not because of the arrogance of some hydrographer with enough degrees to shame a thermometer, but because it is God's intent for it to do so. Three words I leave you with on this forbidding Sabbath. Short, elegant words, to inform your week until next we meet. You'all know them. Say them with me."

And they all say together, *"Read your Bible.* Read your Bible. *Read your Bible."*

He pauses, reads them through his eyes, his ears; measures the tension palpable in the room, and then, and only then, says, "Certain Orientals have their chants that they repeat ad infinitum. They call these *mantra*. Strange heathen word. This is our mantra, good friends of First Baptist. This is our mantra in Christ."

"Read your Bible. READ YOUR BIBLE. *READ YOUR BIBLE.*"

His arms are extended; he is gathering them up. His skin has a sheen, a glow some say, dry wax and candle lit. He says, *"And ye shall know truth from falsehood. Amen."*

"AMEN!"

He pauses. Catches his breath. Finds support from the pulpit. The congregation swoons with his resurrection. "I'm wondering," he continues in a business-like tone, "if I can impose upon our lovely contralto, Mrs. Praetoria Humboldt, to join me before you and lead us in *What a Friend We Have in Jesus*. Praetoria?"

Mr. Humboldt beams, gives his wife a gentle shove. Mrs. Humboldt protests all too briefly, gathers up great clouds of satiny shroud and stones from the mouths of oysters, straightens her long form in an effort to free herself from the knees jutting into the row in which she sat, fairly glides up to the pastor's side, all full to the brim with the Spirit, redolent with Christian charity, shows her regal sculpted chin to advantage. He takes her hand. P-R awaits another scornful glare his way; it doesn't come. When she begins to sing, it is as if she is transformed, evolved even. Her eyes turn to crystal and you can see through them to her very soul. Her voice, too, has that velvet sheen and is pitched with strings of pearls. The congregation stands, holds hands like a line of paper dolls.

On the roof, the clatter of rain begins. Below the ceiling, the Sabbath is celebrated in song.

II

THE GOOD PASTOR ARPACHSHAD SHEM STANDS in total humidity, shaking the hurried hands of his parishioners. The clouds have tired of threatening; they unleash their torrents, what are called *sheets* of rain, an all encompassing sob to soak these friends in Jesus as they race to their automobiles, the muck of the church yard gathering layer upon stratified layer to the soles of their shoes to be scraped off with rags and tire irons and the rims of running boards. They thank Jesus for having reminded them to bring their wraps and umbrellas, blooming suddenly like a spring-fed garden and bursting huge protective petals over the hallowed ground. The dead who are required to lay in the mud are probably not nearly as grateful; they are all but forgotten in the mad flight, these stalwarts of Tishomingo — the founders, the surveyors, the tillers, the builders, the very pioneers under their slabs.

Sister Shem, as plain as a pauper's headstone, urges dapper and benighted Pastor Shem not to dally in the rain. "Y'all'll catch your death," she chides.

"In all likelihood, me it or it me, eventually. Get the children quickly up to the house and be sure that the girl has that fire roaring. I will be home shortly. You can begin the lesson with Jeremiah, Seventeen. Sin should dilute well in so much water." The rain forms a veil from the brim of his hat; he is the only one coming out of the church without added protection. Moisture percolates up his trousers and darkens his socks nearly to the garters.

"A silly stunt," she scolds.

"In a good cause. I am confident that in His wisdom, the Good Lord will spare me any debilitating consequences."

"That, or He will think you a fool not worth the effort." She grabs the children by the shoulders and with them slogs toward the parsonage, making room for the line of worshipers.

"Wonderful sermon, Pastor."

"I do love y'all's asides."

"Another lollapalooza, Brother Shem. Don't know how you do it."

Still flushed, Mrs. Milford passes with her tented infant, barely offering a glance.

"Thank you for allowing the song, Pastor, though it took me somewhat aback."

"Thank the Lord, Mrs. Humboldt. It was He that gave you voice."

"But I do so appreciate your comforting words." Mr. Humboldt has already passed, cannot hear his wife's conversation.

"I am but the messenger. Praise Jesus, Mrs. Humboldt, that He may offer forgiveness, and you may find solace."

"Next Sunday, Pastor."

"You'all be here now."

"With bells on."

"Chief Prezhki! How kind of you to grace our portal. You know, on high an accounting is being made."

"Do they vote on high? All the little cherubs lining up to mark their ballots? I like to make the rounds, Pastor. Law enforcement comes easiest to the department that knows its public."

"I'm certain that the two commissioners who worship in these humble surroundings will appreciate such sensitivity."

"And I'll trust in your certainty, Pastor." He will not say *Brother*. "I wish you a fine, and hopefully drier, Sabbath."

"And I wish you'all one scofflaw-free."

Prezhki answers with a wry smile. "That may already be too late." He leans forward so that only Shem can hear. "When Satan comes a'shoppin', I hope at least one of us still has a soul to bargain with."

Shem's glare freezes raindrops; there is a brief clatter of hail. Stiffly, he says, "And Mrs. Prezhki? I haven't seen her in a blue moon. Does she too mourn lost opportunities?"

"She is a reading woman and a skeptic. Peas in a pod, her and me." Prezhki moves on.

"What was that about?" asks P-R, coming up with Sarai loose on his arm.

"The Chief can be a challenging man, don't you think?"

"We get on. One reaches an understanding with such folks. It's the politic thing to do."

"Speaking of which, indulge me with a short visit in my study. If Mrs. P-R wouldn't mind taking the car. I'll have the custodian run you back later."

"Can you handle the ark, dear?"

"As well as you. It's not that far." She feigns a brush of P-R's cheek; you could drive their Lincoln through the gap. "Brother Shem," she acknowledges, and is off slump-shouldered into the storm, sinking into the muck, dwindling as she goes. Her life with P-R has been a continuous dwindling of sorts.

"You know," says P-R, forgetting her affront, "I had considered eighteen holes at Meadow Green."

"The Lord, it seems, has other plans. Why don't you'all get out of this deluge, make yourself comfortable in my study. I will be on up as soon as the congregation disperses. First file cabinet to the right of the door, second drawer from the bottom, you might find something to combat the chill."

"Had better not be a Bible. I'm chilled enough to burn it in the stove."

Brother Shem enters his study sans glow, fish wet and puddling the floorboards, lacquering them with a deep-grained sheen. His hat brim droops like earflaps. He looks suddenly humbled, fragile as wet parchment. The room is plain, last white washed eons ago, with thick dark scuffed molding, chipped plaster dusting the floor, a smell of things growing in colonies, an infectious sprawl like British Africa. His desk is covered with paper in unkempt stacks: pencils, pens, an inkwell advertising the Tishomingo Lines, and a calendar, the gift of Bishop Pedrasti at the Uncas Falls St. Nicholas of Myra Cathedral, with the stations of the cross celebrated monthly — sans Simon and Veronica.

Arpachshad is liberal by Baptist standards, is a great promoter of inter-faith fraternization, keeps up a regular line of commentary with Christian clergymen of numerous denominations, opinions neatly delineated in curving script to bring envy to the writers of indentures. In his formative years, it was his father's dictum that *penmanship is next to godliness,* for the first Pastor Shem was a man of precision, a rigid exemplar of tradition, an enthusiastic agent of damnation for all those who weren't. The father's church was built on a firm foundation of brimstone, unlike the nebulous concrete underpinnings of his son's organization. Arpachshad is his father mellowed and cured, an evolution of Old to New Testament.

P-R is already coatless, low in his chair, boots slumped on the Pastor's desk. He has helped himself to Shem's brandy, now fills a second glass and pushes it across the cluttered blotter. "Well, don't y'all look like Jonah," he says, "puked up from the gut slathered in whale sputum?"

"And you, Socrates, you don't occasionally roll up your pant legs and slog around in the mud?" He is the only person to call P-R *Socrates*; they have known each other that long. Shem slips into an anteroom, drops out of his wet clothing.

"I don't court pneumonia," P-R says.

The pastor comes back into the room wrapped in a Pendelton, adjusts a spittoon on the floor to intercept a slow stream of leakage from the roof, sits down and contemplates the brandy. "I am standing out on the porch greeting the faithful under their umbrellas, and I am uncovered and drenched. So what do you think the message is?" He begins to shiver, reaches out a trembling hand to clasp the glass.

"That you don't know to come in out of the rain!"

"The message is the invincibility of faith. How many of those folks walked off shaking their heads, wondering about my absolute disdain for the forces of nature, believing I am shielded from the damp?"

"They can believe what they like. Fact is, you're not any more inoculated than they are, and if you drop dead from this little stunt, don't come haunting me." He refills his own glass.

Shem wipes his face and hair with the edge of the wool blanket. He purchased it on a trip west to visit the Whitman mission and other memorials to Christian martyrs. He adjusts another cuspidor just behind his chair. There are leaks throughout the room ending in cooking pots and chamber pots, a wide mouthed vase and a washtub. They add an extra layer of rhythm to the rain. "In ancient times, pharaohs and priests claimed divine lineage in order to separate themselves from the common man. As for us, that would lack a certain element of humility. So we compensate by celebrating our singularity in other ways. It is our tip of the hat, so to speak, to the age."

"Y'all want to read the L. Frank Baum version of the Old Testament, go right ahead. I like a more pragmatic approach. One that doesn't put me on a gurney."

"Do you in fact? I wonder, how many sham promises have you made in your career. The number of crises you have spawned to thwart them. We are all wizards of a sort. All of us, sacred or profane. All politicians are preachers; all preachers, politicians."

"You know, Shad, sometimes, when I see you levitate across the floor back there, stroking the crowd with one of your tales, I think, shit, this guy really believes what he's saying! I'm flabbergasted by my reaction: I know better. Y'all're that good."

"I believe in the beneficence of what I'm saying. All is well that ends well."

"Yeah, and all the theatrics? Just more dirt swept under the rug?"

"So tell me, why do you come here then?"

"What's this? Turning the other cheek, or turning the question back on me? I'll tell you this: I don't drag my ass out on a Sunday morning to save my immortal soul!"

"I didn't expect you did? Why climb sand hills? Then why?"

P-R is warming his hands by vigorously rubbing them together. It looks like enthusiasm. "I'm on the job. I'm making the rounds. As always, I have the wellbeing of the constituency on my mind, you know. If I drink the Baptist brandy this week, I'll imbibe the Catholic wine the next. Some loon out in the boondocks wants me to pray with his snake, I ask him how he's registered and hiss along to Jesus. Maybe the water moccasin stands upright, maybe even votes. Hebrews consolidate their voting bloc, they can clip off my foreskin in the town square. If I've got to act like I'm enjoying some greasy ham hock in Darktown, cuddle a wop baby, or sport a Chink to lunch…well, let's just say, I know what I've got to do. You can line up a rainbow of bare asses, Pastor, and I'll give each one of them a smooch. And I too will be comfortable in the beneficence of my performance."

"Kind of like standing in the rain and pretending you're not bothered by the moisture."

"Kind of like. One man's bullshit, another man's religion. All the same to me. You too, I think. Anyway, y'all didn't pray for rain so I'd spend the afternoon watching you catch cold over a discussion of our relative purposes in public life. This have something to do with the Chief?"

"Prezhki? Why do you ask?"

"Come on. You're holding out. I saw that look in your eyes. Your only slip up of the morning, your only moment of un-Oz-like behavior. If you could have gotten yourself a Prezhki doll to stick pins in, you would have converted to heathenism in a minute flat, a bone in your nose, sacrificed one of your grandkids with a stone knife."

Shem shivers and shrugs all at once. "You're projecting. Rather fancifully. Prezhki can be something of a nuisance. You see, for a man in the public eye, he tends to be incautious, tactless. I find it unbecoming, perhaps unwise. Yet, he is who he is, and if the Lord has a use for him, so have I. In that context, I have hit him up for a little donation. The kind of thing a responsible public servant expects once in a while."

"And he didn't like you waving a couple of Bible-thumping police commissioners in his face, I bet."

"You know him. He thinks there is value in the last word."

"Isn't there?"

"Only if it's The Word. For no matter what else is spoken, it will be final."

"Yeah, well, there's last words and Last Words. Look, Prezhki's all right. It's all give and take. If he needs to let you know how he feels about it, well, that's just his interpretation of integrity. And, bottom line, he gets to keep his job and you get whatever it is you squeezed out of him. So, I suppose I'm here to get sucker-punched too, that it?"

"At least you'all won't have to be circumcised for the Baptist vote."

"No, and you're not going to hold me under water until I cry out *Uncle John*, either. So, look, I'm on the edge of my seat, what are we talking about? A change in zoning for the new Sunday School? I supply the stakes for the next tent meeting? I take Prezhki up the hill and crucify him between a couple of vagrants he's got locked up at the jail?"

"Short of making you a total immersion Mayor, Socrates, or marching out the Praetorian guards, perhaps you could simply assist with the roof. You may have noticed there is a problem of a porous nature just begging for attention."

"Plug it with prayer. You're talking out of pocket? You know the city can't..."

"Of course out of pocket."

"*My* pocket. Poor Prezhki. He's not even a Baptist, is he?"

'So? He's the chief of Baptists. You're not a Baptist either."

"Today, I am. Next Sunday, who knows? Burn a little incense for Shiva? How much are we talking about?"

"Your share or the total?"

"What do I care about the total? The gross is y'all's business. Throw me a net."

"Now who sounds like Jonah? It's a slate roof. I'll need to get estimates."

"You sure will. You make sure you get your Commissioners to cough up too. Let me see if I've got a contractor that owes me some steeple climbing. Then you get me ballpark, and I'll twist a few gilded arms at city hall. But I need to know what we're talking about first. You know, they don't usually do slate anymore. Not a local item either. You're going to have to pinch the railroad a little to see about freight rates. The materials will be dear enough. Give old Ferrous a ring. Maybe he'll do something for you, y'all being a church and all."

"I knew I could count on you."

"I bet you did. Is it written? So, is that it? You done counting?"

"That's *one* of the its?"

"There is more?"

"Of a more personal nature."

"Begging money isn't personal?"

Shem stands, removes the blanket — a man of God in damp, full-body BVD's. He moves back to the anteroom where his outer garments are roasting on a ticking radiator, avoiding streams of water as he goes. He flips the clothing over, wants them evenly browned on both sides. Standing in front of the radiator, he rotates forty-five degrees, then again, then again, to warm himself. "How long have we been friends?" he calls through the door.

"Are we friends?" P-R calls back.

"I like to think so."

"Of convenience, maybe."

"In any case, a long time I think."

"Friends don't blackmail each other for new slate roofs on their chapels."

"We make no profit. We simply asked for assistance. You'all generously complied."

"Now it's *we*. You can spread the sin around the congregation like butter on toast. You know, you've whet my appetite with this *personal nature* thing. Let's lay it out on the table already." They can't see each other now; they talk to the room, their voices just that much raised.

"Once, when I was a boy, my father beat me raw with the slat from a broken chair back. It wasn't his weapon of choice: he had an old bridle that he had saved for such instructive opportunities. But in a rage he reached for the nearest object that he reasoned wouldn't actually kill me. You see, he had discovered that I had spent an afternoon with you'all in front of the Polack's drug store."

"Wazhelefski's. I spent a whole summer learning to say it."

"A licentious afternoon. We were there to peruse the girls just out from school. Do you remember?"

"So many girls under the bridge. But, the Polack's was a bliss of prime sightings. With the soda fountain and the two straws in one mug."

"To my father it was a prime portal into the inferno. I was informed on by a vigilant parishioner."

"So your old man, never the most measured and tolerant of gents, beat holy shit out of you because you spent the afternoon with me. He probably would have laid into me with the rest of the chair if my father didn't own the land the church was built on. My father had a connection with a higher power as well."

"There was a girl you ruined in high school."

"Not at the Polack's, I didn't. Anyway, *ruin* is such a relative term. A woman isn't a matchstick, after all. Strike it once and it's all used up. Where are we headed with this?"

"I'm just filling in some pertinent background."

"To what? Y'all want ancient history, read Gibbon. Where *is* this going?"

"I could go on and on with such examples."

"You would shortly be talking to an empty room."

"There is a considerable catalogue of your proclivities."

P-R pushes himself up, scrapes the chair loudly. "Send me the ballpark."

The pastor appears in the doorway. He has his trousers on now, the suspenders loosely draped like straphangers on a streetcar. "Please, Socrates, sit down. We are going to have this conversation."

"Tell it to Jesus."

"Don't you think I have?"

P-R sits back down and suppresses the anger he thinks unbecoming a good shepherd. The sheep have feelings. "So what is this?" He waves a curious index finger. "You digging up some dirt? A little local archaeology? What have you got?"

"Nothing at all like that. I wouldn't presume to…At present, just rumors." He stands in the doorway still, his backside soaking up the heat from the radiator. "Little rumblings. I thought, as a prophylactic, I'd lay it all out on the table. A friendly gesture even if on an unseemly topic."

"About? I'm all ears." He cups them for emphasis.

"A certain member of my congregation, a woman, it appears, complains of being compromised."

"A woman! Thank heaven! You know, before we go any farther down the line on this, let's remember that my appeal to the electorate does not derive from sainthood. I never pretend it does. I don't flagellate myself with bell chains or fast atop pillars. There are men in this town who'd give their manhood to be me. Not of course, the best choice of sacrifice. What point would there be in being me without it? So, there are rumors? Fine. They stay rumors. Dew on morning lawns. A puddle on a hot afternoon. There are always rumors. The basic building blocks of conversation. And if I know anything at all, I know discretion."

"Do you? But the woman spoke to me."

"Did she? Did she? Which one? She's lying. A married one? A recent virgin? A spinster trying to discover what all the fuss is about? A member of the auxiliary? A chorister? The whole fucking chorus, perhaps? They're *all* lying. Not an honest bone in their bodies, not even the rib we gave them."

"You'all have the gall to ask, *which one?*"

"You have the gall to mention rumors? You just bilked me out of some slate roofing. Don't press your luck."

"I am asking you not to use my congregation as a crop ripe for harvesting. This is not the Polack's."

"Talk about ripe, you hypocrite, Mrs. What's-er-whoozes nearly dropped her baby this morning as you went to pet its head on the way past a teat, you surreptitious little prick. You know me. I don't care who y'all are. I don't care if God's your brother-in-law, or what thunderbolts you think you wield. I'm not part of your lackey flock. What exactly are you threatening me with? The papers? The radio? What?" His anger is not loud; shrillness does not become him.

Shem bravely re-enters the room, his room, and sits in his chair. "I think you're overreacting."

"Overreacting, my ass! You haven't begun to see me overreacting. Did you think I would fall down on my knees so you could immolate me with a chair slat? I thought you were smarter. I own the fucking ground we're on!"

"So now you're blackmailing me!"

"If necessary. No second thoughts. Y'all crawl up my ass, I'll crawl up yours!"

"It's not me, you see, Socrates. The woman. The women. They are emotional about these things. The hurt and guilt gets the better of their discretion. She, they, are likely to slip. To blurt out something to the wrong...Look. Hear me. I'm the last one to challenge you. We are symbiotic, you and I. We each profit by our association."

"This does not get brought up again. You want to stick your nose in other people's souls, so be it, just stay out of my trousers. And here's a little free tutoring on local real estate for y'all. There are three categories of property here in Tishomingo: Column One, you've got your properties that I own outright, Column Two, your plots owned by people I own outright, and Three, little swampy holes of pestilence that just aren't worth shit. Why do y'all think this church is at the very end of the trolley line, not a neighbor in blocks, overlooking the rail yards and a hog corral? My father was not an over generous sort. But he was a nicer fellow than me. It does not profit you to go down this road, believe you me."

"Very well, Socrates. Very well. But I can only control my own mouth. And my advice to you is to disengage, to avoid aggravating any possible situation that comes pregnant with political risk."

"Good choice of terms. You know, Shad, I'm glad your old man beat you. Not that you learned anything by it, but I do get some satisfaction in knowing it hurt. I listened to you today, righteous, aglow, actually fucking aglow, like an angel in one of those big illuminated Bibles, cheeks ruddy, eyes hot with wattage, Professors One and Two, The Grand Swami What's-his-puss, and that voice, that lilt, smooth like an infant's bottom, and I've got to wonder, I do; does Shad Shem believe in any of it? Or is it all illusion? A side show trick? A way to make a buck? Be important? Center stage, Shem the Magnificent, slays the doubters, screws the rubes. Y'all are something else! I give you that!"

There follows an extended period of silence, a time of recouping, of evaluation, a time to catch one's breath and assess the level of the new playing field. In all their years of pushing and pulling they have never approached the bitterness, the personal nature, of the present exchange. They can hear each other breathing, hear the rain in the pots mocking the slate on the roof. P-R lowers his head, a trained peel of hair caving down over his brow, over the furrows of some new strategy, and he begins to laugh, quietly, then just barely audibly, a vibration in his shoulders, a shaking of his head from side to side, and he says, looking down at his glass of gifted brandy, "I've always known you to be a fairly assertive political schemer, Pastor Shem, but I have never known you, before this morning, to have the audacity to kick a man in his privates. Just what do you gain by fucking me?"

There is more silence. "Is that what I'm doing? In the vernacular?" Shem begins to laugh as well. "I have a responsibility to my flock."

"You do," P-R says looking up, filling both their glasses again, "but it is a little too skewed toward the ewe's at the expense of the rams."

"They come to me with their deepest problems, their fears. I am their counselor before God. They tell me things they cannot share with spouses, parents, friends. I am neutral ground, a charged neutral ground, as it were, helping to bring them back to Christ. I offer sanctuary. Eternal grace. Cleansing."

"Listen to yourself! How much of this...? Look, I know you. How much of this do you really believe? How much of this do you really expect me to believe y'all believe? All this shepherding crap! We spent pubescent summers watching the tits grow, you and I, and that old tyrant father of yours beat your ass raw not because of the afternoon with me but because he was afraid you were going to follow your divining rod straight to hell. There are things I know about you too."

"This is not a contest."

"It certainly is! Every conversation, every fleeting exchange of words, is a contest."

"I don't claim sainthood either. We abide no canonization here. How many times have you heard me preach the shared commonness of us all?"

"Oh, countless times. But all from an elevation of about three inches above the floor gravity subjects the rest of us to. It's not so much the words from your mouth. That you do well. It's the direction of your nose I find offensive."

"*Sin coucheth at the door but thou mayest rule over it.* I don't deny it's there, I simply deny it purchase."

"I don't deny it either. I open the door to see what it's selling. And what about Mrs. Young Mother? Even Sarai flinched. I felt just the slightest shiver from her... of distaste...about as passionate as she gets these days."

"I patted the child on the head. I don't need to justify my actions to you. I have only one judge. Nor am I aware of any other...egregious contact...of... intent."

"No, but she is. The mother. On her deathbed she will think back and wonder what that brush of the Pastor's arm meant that rainy morning years before. Was it invitation; was it provocation? Was the Devil tempting her? Was it a comfort that still tortures her so? Was it inadvertent, a chance contact of the innocent kind that occurs so frequently between men and woman? Is there such innocence? She will blame herself and forever long for some closure, all at once, all the same, and she will find simple human curiosity every bit as forceful as the pull of God."

"Do you'all believe in anything, Socrates? Are you concerned for your soul?"

"This has come up a lot lately. I'm not sure I know exactly what a soul is, where it is: in my mind, my heart, up my ass. Is it vestigial like an appendix? Is it connected to the nervous system? Does it require the continuous pumping of blood?"

"Ask yourself these questions. Ask yourself some less mundane questions. The soul is our connection to a higher power, the source of our continuance. We, as a collection of organs and fluids are its custodians in the brief interlude in which all of our various mechanisms are in operation. The soul is the eternal us. All else is temporal, fleeting, the blink of God's eye."

"How can you know this?"

"It is a matter of faith. How can you not?"

"So that's it? The end of all argument. *A matter of faith.* Four little words. Five syllables. No questions asked."

"That's right."

"Y'all believe that?"

"I do."

"Y'all're a literal reader of your Bible?"

"I am."

"You have no questions, no doubts?"

"It is not for me to question. I do not dissect Truth as if it's a pinned frog in a lab."

"A virgin gave birth?"

"That's what It says."

"And Cain knew his wife? Where did *she* come from? There were what? Four people on the whole planet and suddenly Mrs. Cain comes bursting into town to check out the eligible bachelors?"

"I am not privy to all of God's mysteries."

"But don't you wonder? All of a sudden the fellow's in Nod getting laid by some mystery woman from nowhere. This doesn't beg a question? Let's begat our way down to Noah. So he takes two of each beast of the field, right? How does he get...say, kangaroos? Gila monsters? Llamas from Peru? This is a fellow living somewhere in the Holy Land, near the Holy Land, and if I'm not mistaken, he just didn't call an agent at the railroad to give him a break on the freight and run them all over to the ark? And how big was this ark? Do you know how many animal species there are? Why didn't they eat each other? Why didn't they fucking eat Noah?"

"If the Lord God can create all the beasts of the field, it seems no great stretch of the imagination for him to lead them unto the ark."

"A tale of immense elasticity, if you ask me."

"I don't ask you. I don't ask. That's what faith is. And I'm sorry you have none."

"Don't worry about me."

"So what questions do you ask?"

"About what?"

"About," he throws his woolen arms outward into the room, "all of this? All creation?"

"How would I know what to ask? Maybe your boy Charlie Darwin has a few insights. Sounds reasonable. The record's everywhere, written in the earth. It doesn't come hawked by some itinerant vendor in a Ford or stuck into the nightstand drawer of a hotel room. Or, maybe y'all'er right. Maybe there is some big chief up there who puts it all together, some omnipotent force slipping into His work gloves and boots, making mountains, daylight, time itself, setting the moon to ride across the sky, volcanoes to erupt, people to move around the landscape doing what they do in acceptance or in doubt, the faithful, the scoffers, turning coal into energy, making airplanes take flight, buildings combust, make the trains run, make gravity to hold it all down under the fucking firmament. A big guy all alone with nothing else to do. How the fuck should I know? How would you? You know, everybody's a little Spinoza these days, a little Nietzsche. Trying to figure it all out. See, you guys, you guys of the cloth, you're a little more like me. You've got it figured. You've got a manual, instructions, commandments. And guys like me, we've got it figured too. It is, whatever the fuck it is. I have faith in that. What more do I need? So what? I've got a city to run. People to direct. Some precious acres to manage. I have little time to ponder the meaning of life."

Shem taps his nails on the desk, then makes a final appraisal of his drink. He is warm now, even in this room damp with vapor. "And I know. I know because faith intercedes. What more do *I* need?"

"Y'all need a roof. Pray that problem away."

"I have. And here you are."

The rain has not let up. From under his umbrella, P-R notes a figure sitting in the gazebo where the Number Two trolley does its circle on the route back Downtown. The figure motions to him. Prezhki's car is still in the lot.

Sitting on the bench, the Chief says, "That was the hungriest collection box I've seen in a month of Sundays."

"It's a greasy system," says P-R matter-of-factly. "I grease yours, you grease mine."

"Hit you up for the roof too? Remind you of the faithful Baptist voters?"

"Oh, Pastor Shem's alright. Man does what he's got to do. Look. I won't be carried home by a church custodian. Y'all going to offer me a ride, save me the nickel, or does the Mayor of Tishomingo have to ride the trolley with the rubes?"

III

EACH SABBATH MORNING, THE FOUR-MEMBER THEBIAN contingent of the Ladies Auxiliary at St. John Chrysostom rides the electric car over the hill into Tishomingo — there are no longer any churches in Thebes — and, after Mass, traditionally gather at the Five and Ten on Phipps-Rouge Street. They are elderly women, one married, two widowed, and a spinster pure as Mother Mary. They rattle and tap their decaying forms onto the hardwood floors, past the pneumatic message tubes, down to the end of the long lunch counter — all mahogany and striated marble and gleaming under the intense polishing of the waitresses — dragging with them their collective infirmities like a mobile hospital ward: their gnarled arthritic fingers, their gout-ridden and varicose-veined legs, their bowel complaints and poor vision, their irascibility from sleeplessness and constant pain.

They choose the far end of the counter, opposite and away from the golden National register, over where the counter forms an L, so that, two opposed to two, they can sit at a conversant angle to each other in happy combat and an exchange of intelligence, and plop their two commodious, one pleasantly girlish, and one skeletal, bottoms down upon the stools. They are three dried prunes and one astonishingly ageless plum preserve, in from the rain, anxiously awaiting the usual smear of egg salad on thin, toasted white bread, washed down with limeade and a chaser of cobbler or cherry pie fresh from under sparkling glass domes. Because it is Sunday, and most other businesses up and down the block are shuttered, trade in the Five and Ten is sporadic, and usually one or both of the waitresses, themselves comparative spring chickens, joins in the sharing of news and speculation.

And their conversation — if one cups an ear, tilts a head in their direction, and is cautious that the sipping of coffee coincides with the pauses in their speech — may be heard to proceed something like this:

So, dear, what's the poop on the line? And I don't mean the pigeons!

Now that you ask, there was something. Just Thursday night, my shift. Chief Prezhki is ringing up the station.

Don't say? That's news! Next you're gonna tell us the mailman rung up the post office!

I will tell you what I will tell you, providing you can hold your tongue. Why don't you eat something, keep your mouth occupied.

You two! Go on, June.

I was saying... The Chief asks me to ring up the station. And guess where he's calling from?

Now how in all creation are we to guess that?

He is calling from The R.H. I can here the goings on in the background.

So the man was hungry! Nothin' to write home about.

But in Thebes?

Now wait. Hear me out before you go wagging your lips all over my story. So, you see, as requested, I plug him into Tishomingo P.D. That nice Officer Voorhis picks up. Mike doesn't know why the Chief's over at The R.H. He asks, what for?

He's eating! Has no one any sense?

I don't like Officer Voorhis. He scolded me once about crossing the street outside of the crosswalk. And I wasn't even. The nerve of young people today!

Don't blame him. The way you walk, hon, you're a danger to the autos. Ought a hook you up to the trolley tracks t' keep ya outta trouble.

I'm sure he was just concerned about your safety, dear. Just doing his job.

Are you girls listening?

When there's something to listen to!

Well, if you don't listen first, how will you know if there's something worth listening to?

Voorhis tells the Chief...You see the Chief offers to bring Voorhis something to eat...

Wha'd'I tell ya?

And Voorhis says Thank you, no, *he sent some patrolmen over to the Chinaman's...*

So now what, we got the whole force out with the runs? There's a headline for ya. That Chinaman's out to kill us all, I tell ya. You ever hear a anyone askin' what's in all that phooey and what not? Those people eat rats. I have it on good authority. Horse's mouth. I've spoken to one of the cooks. As much as you can talk to those people before they break off into all that gibberish a theirs. You won't hear more gobbley-goop over at the Pentecostal's. And dogs. They eat them too. You get yourself some a that chow suey young, or whatever, and you'll never know what kind a chow-chow you're stickin' in your pie hole.

Three dogs have gone missing over in Thebes just this week. You don't suppose...?

One of 'em was my Ofelia, and anyway, the bitch come back last night.

Heavens, dear! The language!

That's what she is! A bitch! Look it up'n'your Webster's.

I do not believe that that nice Mr. Webster would...

Would and did. That's the word. Bitch...Bitch, bitch, bitch. Nothin' special about it. Comes after bit and in front a bite.

Okay, now ladies. Remember, we are churchwomen in a public place. Appearances, please. June, go on, dear. I'm sure there is more to tell about than what policemen eat for dinner.

I was going to say that Officer Voorhis said something about that nice Officer McCallum, the one with the baby face, looks no more than fifteen...That Officer McCallum's wife was giving birth, which of course, we all know by now.

Don'go tell us again then.

A boy, I think. Or...a girl. Anyway, the Chief then accuses me of listening in. Of all the nerve...

You were *listening in!*

Since I am your main source of news, I would expect you not to take his side. He actually told me to get the H *off his line. Maybe his call, but it's my line.*

It's the phone company's line, seems to me.

He actually shouted at me! Called me June.

That is your name, dearie.

And what did you say?

I said nothing. I'm not supposed to be listening.

But everyone knows you do! I can hear you breathing when I call up to my sons in Uncas Falls.

I do not breath into the mouth cup.

Oh, yes you do.

Like Webster's bitch in heat.

Ladies!

Yes, ladies. A little decorum, ple-e-e-ase!

Anyway, yesterday, I am talking to my nephew Mort who has himself an after school job at the R.H....Oh, I forgot.

Sign a imminent decrepitude.

They discussed the evening's crimes. That came before this other.

Before what other?

Her nephew, Mort. Get the wax out, will ya!

They had some hobos sleeping off a drunk in the cells, apparently. They call it the tank. I don't know why. I can't imagine something with bars looking like a tank.

That's 'cause a you havin' no imagination. Tank, bars, drunks. I see the connection.

With my job, things what I hear, I don't need imagination. Imagination's all right, I suppose, if you don't have sufficient reality. For instance, I hear the deskman tell the Chief that they had a peeping tom up at the Girls' Home.

Weren't for the sisters, I'd burn that den a evil down.

My word, they're just children!

Not no more!

Peepin' tom don't surprise me. It's a wonder they don't paint the windas black.

When I was a girl...

In days a yore.

I'll give ya yore in a minute! All over yore behind, ya don't hold yore tongue!

Ladies. Ladies.

I was just sayin', that when I was a girl we kept our knees buttoned up tight as a Wells Fargo vault. Houdini couldn't a gotten in.

Or out!

Well, that was long before they invented the vagina.

I don't know what's gotten into you today, but I recommend a good scrub with borax of your vocal regions!

Check your Webster's. It's in there too. Somewhere front a vagrant and...

I don't believe Mr. Webster...

Well, ya gotta call it something! Every bitch has one!

Well, I don't believe we need to call such things anything at all. And I'm sure I know who'll be dominating the confessional come next Sunday. And it's only this *Sunday today!*

At my age, I'd be delighted if I were capable of something that'd warrant absolution! And if I did, would I remember it in the confessional?

I hope I make it to next Sunday!

There are sins and there are sins.

What does that mean? I never know what people mean when they say there are this and that and both this *and* that *are the same thing.*

It's true that when we were coming up there was no such thing as a special home if you got in trouble. Our fathers would have made sure we didn't live long enough to check in.

Seems a bit drastic.

I suppose it was, but it kept our knickers up.

There's nothin' like fear to motivate a child. Trouble today is, parents mostly has shucked their responsibility. You see how these young women go about with all their business hangin' out. It's a wonder they just don't put 'em all in a home when they turn twelve and let 'em out again when they grow up. About thirty.

Spare the rod at your peril, I say.

Amen to that.

Anyway, you all going to listen or you going to bicker all day? Now, about my grandnephew Morty, he's a good, industrious boy. He's always worked, that one. From the time he was little. Not like his no good father. Big as a minute he was and he...

Chief Prezhki. Stay focused, June, you're all over the map.

Mort's got a part in it. You see, I mentioned to Mort that I had heard...not on the line mind you, that doesn't leave the counter here. That I heard that the Chief stopped into The R.H. on Thursday night and I asked, as a concerned citizen, was there a problem? And Mort says, no, not that he knows of, but that a curious thing did happen before the Chief came in to use the phone and order up some carry out.

He called for carry out from The R.H.?

No, no. Follow the story. You sticking that egg salad in you ears or what?

I still got sense to know what goes in what hole.

He orders up The R.H. carry out and uses the phone to ring up the station, like I told you. Now Mort, he totes the trashcan outside. The Greek's boy just sits there on his bee-hind while Morty does all the toting.

Gotta start somewheres. Before you work your way on up to sittin' on your own.

That was the night we all nearly froze to death and the poor thing's outside dragging hundreds of pounds of bone and gristle and whatnot. That Greek does take advantage.

Foreigners! When I was a girl, we didn't have so many foreigners.

A little hard work don't hurt nobody.

I'd like to see you do it!

I'm seventy-eight years old! And I don't pretend to be no face-stretcher like the rest a ya. You want to see me draggin' hundred pound cans a hog bones out into the sub-zero night? Lordalmighty, if you ain't the dumb Dora, I don't know who is!

Mort says he sees the Chief's car parked 'cross the street, some ways past the last trolley stop, but on the Greek's side of the road, over where it turns to dirt. He sets up on the loading dock a while to see what he could see.

The night we nearly froze to death?

He was warmed by his curiosity. The young can be foolish that way.

Young fools' ll be old fools, by and by.

You ought t' know, dear.

If I was forty years younger….

You'd still be old!

Mort says that a truck comes by. Old Choc's truck. Stops at the curb just past the trolley stop, and a woman gets out, heads down the dirt road towards the bridge.

Outta the truck or the Five Car?

What woman?

He didn't say? The truck.

Did you ask?

Well, what do you think? It's the dark of night and cold as Arctic ice and this woman he sees is wrapped up like an Eskimo.

She ridin' a sled and whippin' dogs?

She better keep clear a that Chinaman, she don't want him to boil up her team!

I don't believe that old colored man'd get himself into anything untoward. He has always been a proper one, that Choc. An example for the rest of them.

Nevertheless, that's what Mort says he sees. And Chief Prezhki, while he's waiting on his burger…he likes his French fries extra crisp, don't you know…Asks the Greek if he knows who drives the truck and if he knows where to find him. Mort learns this later from the dishwashing boy. The woman, meanwhile…

This is a colored woman, right?

White or colored, a hussy all the same.

There are hussies and there are hussies.

What does that mean?

…goes on by the Chief's car, Mort says. And then she goes over to the motor court like she lives there, just high steps it on up to the last room, opens the door like she's got a key, and slips inside. Lights on, then lights out.

He sees all this in the pitch dark?

Well, he's got no call to make it up!

Kids tell stories.

Not Morty. He's a very serious young man. Wants to be a pharmacist.

The things that go on in that place! They ought a burn it down!

What things go on?

Things, dear. Things.

But what things?

Carryin's on! If you don't know by now, you don't need to know.

There's more. A man gets out of the car.

I knew it.

What man?

The boy doesn't know. He's looked away 'cause a rat was digging in his trash.

Don't tell the Chinaman that either!

When he turns back, there's this man. He doesn't know what side the man got out on. And the windows are fogged so he can't see if anyone's still inside the car. But a man has gotten out. A big man. Now I'm not saying anything, but Mort says, from the back…

And in the dark.

…you could mistake this man for Mayor P-R.

You don't say?

I am not accusing anybody.

That old weasel!

Always been the cake-eater.

And this big man? He does what?

The woman in the room, she flips the lights. Like a signal. And this big man...

P-R?

I didn't say that. Just his size, his walk, reminded Mort, that's all. This man goes on up to the same room...

Your nephew told you this?

They really ought a burn that dump down! I was forty years younger...

...and slips in easy as she did.

Not all he slipped in, you ask me.

Are you telling us that your nephew is telling you that the Chief drove a man that looks like the Mayor to one a them there lee-asians with some vamp that herself got driven by Choc the junkman up to the motor court?

Wouldn't surprise me if it was the Mayor. More's been said on that subject.

Didn't I just say?

I don't need to tell you, my curiosity got the better of me too.

What'd I say 'bout old fools?

So I make it a point to run into Mrs. Martinez at the motor court...

The greaser's wife?

I believe they are Spanish. She has red hair and freckles and is whiter than a maggot. Anyway, since she works in the office...She and her husband trade off...

So they never have to see one another.

Foreigners!

Why would a man wanna see a wife looks like a maggot?

...so, kind of round about, I approach her on the subject of the strange woman...

The Eskimo.

...and the big man, and she says, rather quiet like, her hand cupped over her mouth, that the room is reserved by phone. And payment comes in cash by mail.

Let me guess: no return address?

She mentioned that, yes.

This's happened before?

I understand it's a fairly regular thing.

Is it now!

Ain't the tourist trade keepin' that cesspool open.

This may be just a coincidence, girls, but I am acquainted with a lady I met at the library. A Mrs. Red-something-or-other. An Eastern Orthodox lady with some kind of accent,...

Another foreigner! What are we, Ellis Island now?

...but a nice woman nonetheless. And just the other day, we are discussing books we've read, and she, out of the blue, tells me this funny story she's heard from her husband who works at the rail yard as a watchman. I promised her I wouldn't repeat a word because she didn't want to get anybody into trouble, but since this is a closed club we

have here, I know what I tell you will be handled with absolute discretion. On Thursday evening, according to this woman's husband, who has an official position with the railroad, so I figure he'd know of what he speaks, our very proper colored junkman picks up a neighbor lady of his up at the Signal Station and drives off with her.

A neighbor lady of the junkman?

No. Of the watchman, of course. Are you listening?

I am listening. But when I taught school...

Shortly after the Deluge.

...a pronoun, *dear, was used to modify the preceding subject in the phrase or sentence, so that you're* his *would connote the colored junkman.*

An abduction?

No, no such a thing. She gets into his truck of her own accord.

No!

This is what she says.

This cheap ticket, she lives in railroad housing?

She does. Both she's do, Mrs. Red and our mystery gal.

You're telling us this is a white woman?

White as a maggot!

I tell you what I was told. I come to no conclusions.

What is this world coming to?

I've a good mind to confront that old fool myself.

Oh, I wouldn't do that. I wouldn't want to get my nose caught in other people's business. Still, one does wonder.

And if the conversation is so heard, and the four venerable ladies of St. John Chrisostom — however tight lipped on their ride back over the hill on the Number Five — had piqued their imaginations, and how could they not have, then each on her own would plumb secret sources, lean a little on known informers, so that next Sunday, over the marble counter, they would each have a new tidbit to serve up with egg salad, limeade and pie.

One's coffee can now be indulged without fear of missing a word.

Doreen the waitress wipes up the counter where the old women have spent over an hour. Livonia the waitress serves a man a cup of joe near the register, then sidles up to Doreen and says, "Did you hear what June said? Chief Prezhki told her, kind a quiet with his hand cupped over his mouth...seems she run into him at The Roadhouse, that some old colored man brought a white woman from 'Mingo to have some kind a you-know-what with Mayor P-R at that old Motor Court near the railroad bridge."

"On the level?"

"Only repeating what I heard."

"From the horse's mouth?"

"That's what I heard. Clear as day."

"You don't say!"

"We're outta ketchup."

"You don't say!"

IV

L IKE SWAMP GAS, A LOW, MILKY haze hugs the ground, pierced here and
there by the oddments of Choc Bonjour's eclectic finds. There is no swamp
here to feed the soup. Chief Prezhki steps carefully, intent on not tangling
a trouser cuff on the handle of a rusting coffee grinder or to trip on a random
piece of plumbing abandoned in the dirt below the fog. It is Monday morning
and the skies have cleared some, leaving expanses of cobalt on goose down and
low sun-stretching shadows in thin, elastic forms. It is cold and dank in the
Gifford Glassworks yard, a smell of decay. Prezhki has a taste on his tongue: old
mushrooms, lichen on a stump, a dull gray flavor of abandoned things. He wears
a long, leather overcoat, open in front to reveal more formal attire: woolen sports
coat, also ajar, vest arced by a watch chain, and signature winter cap concealing
his brow. The hem of the sports coat is bunched up over his holster.

Choc wakes with a start. He hears someone clanking about, picking things
up, dropping them down again. He rubs the crust from his eyes and the fog
from his window, sees puffs of breath expelled from under the hat, another near
formless figure hunched in study of some object with its details erased by mist.
He pulls up a tattered blanket, wraps it around him as he rises, all stiffness and
pain, a call from the lower back that streaks down his leg, a dull cramp in the
arch of his left foot, a stitch in a shoulder that needs working out. He hears his
own joints cracking in ambulatory distress, feels bands of sinew and ligament
audibly mourning the loss of suppleness. He creaks and crackles and moans
his way upright, shuffles to the door, over the hump of near-deaf dog dreaming
of youth, and steps out onto the stoop he has fabricated of packing crates and
shipping pallets.

"Mornin'" he offers, his eyes lowered. Choc knows better than to stare into
the pink face of a white man, particularly one with the vestigial pearl handle
describing the peril he brings.

Prezhki ignores him, focuses on a line of old hand pumps piercing the fog
like tombstones.

"He'p y'all, boss?" The words come out in a funny-paper balloon of vapor.

A geriatric bulldog mix ambles out from behind him, angrily wheezes canine
imprecations in Prezhki's direction.

"Call off your bitch," the Chief snaps.

"Dat jus' Yuleti'. Don' pay'er no min'. She gotta say 'er piece an' den be done
wid it, gonna slunk on ober t'un'er d'car t'sleep 'way da day."

"You leash that bitch or I'll shoot her." It is said matter-of-factly, as if it is
news to no one.

"Okay. Okay. She don' mean no harm," says Choc, "She jus'a ol'man's ol'dog."
He comes off of the porch with a length of twine he has hanging off a date nail
near his door, loops it around Yuletide's neck and hooks her up to a rusting gas
pump. "She gib 'erse'f t'me one Chridmas, 's'why Ah calls'er dat." Yuletide is white

with black continents, has a bent tail, and a series of infected bare spots festering along her rump. In summer, she's known up and down the flea circuit as a biter's best friend.

With the dog secure, Prezhki continues to rummage. He has spotted a table-load of old radios suffering from peeling veneer's disease: Zeniths, Kolsters, Apollo-Dynes, and boxes of old tubes. Then he turns to a Mail Pouch sign tilted up against a door-less phone booth, phone-less as well, upon which hang license plates twisted and dented and shot at to make brown splatter spots.

Prezhki fires a metal plate like a discus; it saucers upward, peaks and descends into the anonymity of the ground mist. It must land on something soft: there is no sound of collision. "You ever sell any of this crap?"

"Now'n'den. Can't complain."

Prezhki lifts up a copper and brass Western Inspection Company fire extinguisher, inspects it, gives a twist to the hose which cracks and withers at his touch, little particles of rubber fleeing the heat. "Because most of this shit looks like it's been here for a while."

"Well, suh, d'stuff been boughten's gone, Ah 'spect."

Prezhki puts down the extinguisher, none too gently, turns to Choc and takes a step forward. Automatically his hands find their place at his thighs, his elbows back, fluffing out both coats, showing the gun in better light. "You sassing me, uncle?" he asks. His words too are visible.

"No suh," Choc answers. "Ah jus' means dat what ain't here no mo' jus' ain't here no mo'."

"A logic to that. You're Choc, right?"

"Choc Bonjour. He'p y'all fin' sumpin' 'ticular?"

"A world of throw-away crap, isn't it? You have a Zenith back there looks something like one reported stolen from a nice old cobbler in town. Said it kept him company on lonely days spent re-soling folks' shoes."

"Ain'uttin' here 'cept what Ah finds put out 'r what folks brings me. Sometime' Ah trades an' ol' faucet'r sumpin' for a radio, a ice box, one a dem little Union cook stoves wid da Eisenglass dat peoples use t'heat a small room come a day like dis here a one."

"Uh huh. Bet you've got receipts on all this here too. What's up there?" He points to the McKeen rail car up on its construction blocks.

"Dat's where Ah keeps d'better class a merchandise. C'n go on up der'n have a look see, ya'all wants."

"Words out of my mouth. I'll have myself a *look see*, I will. I am a discriminating shopper. I'll be sure to check out the Tiffany shades, the Hope Diamond, the Queen of Sheba's pearl studded brassiere." The fog begins to lift; he can see the ground clearly now, takes long strides up the slight grade. He lifts himself up into the motorcar. *"Crème d'la-*fucking-*crème*! My word, old man!"

Wrapped in his blanket like ground chuck in cabbage, Choc reluctantly trudges behind. "Ah could put up some coffee."

"Culinary skills too! I'll be damned, uncle, you are a gentleman of refinement. Thank you, no. Keep a thermos in the car."

There is little light in the rail bus. The interior fixtures have been stripped, replaced by makeshift tables piled high with boxes of unrelated things: tools and pepper shakers, a pistol without a cylinder grouped with fading portrait studio photos, heavy, black pots and pans and glass door knobs turned purple. There are no prices on anything; Choc believes in impromptu evaluations and his own prescience as to a customer's affordability.

Prezhki thumbs some dust from old book jackets. "Upton Sinclair," he reads. "Frank Norris. Wouldn't have taken you for an aficionado of social criticism, but hell, you're a muckraker yourself, I guess. How much for the O'Henry here?"

"Gen'rally da'd be a nickel. Whyn't ya'll jus' take it an' have yo'self a good read."

"Now why would you do that?"

"He'p out a servant a da peoples."

"You know who I am?"

"No, suh. Ah c'n guess what ya does."

Prezhki replaces the book. "This box of china here? Gold leaf and all the fixings. Looks a lot like the plate they serve up at the Empire Grill."

"No suh. Diff'ren' flowers. Empire Grill's got red roses. Ah don'know what t'call dose li'le yella ones."

Prezhki sets down a dish. "You know, uncle, I have been to the Empire Grill but once, about six, seven years ago. Anniversary dinner with the old lady. Cost me an arm and a leg. Of course, it's kind of a classy joint and they leave you with your favored arm so you can lift your fork and reach your billfold. You must move a tolerable load of this here...*merchandise*...to dine so frequently at the Empire, you being able to recognize the finer nuances of the china."

"Spen' 'nough time washin' 'em t'give 'em names. Come Saturday evenin', dey sometime hires on extra kitchen he'p. Ah don't stan' up straight like dat for so long no mo', but dere wud a time..."

Prezhki turns his head and spits out the door into the ground-clung fog. "You know, Mr. Bonjour, sometimes it's better to curtail the commentary. Sometimes a wise man leaves a whole hell of a lot unspoken. That being said, you're beginning to piss me off just a little. So why don't we just play a little cop and guilty-looking-old-colored-man in which the cop asks all the questions and the old colored man shuffles and nods and doesn't speak out of turn. What do you say?"

Choc stares downward. His feet are frozen and he feels as if he's left his toes down at the work car.

"That's your truck down on the drive?"

Choc nods.

"You wouldn't be using it to cart white women around in the dark for nefarious purposes, would you?"

Choc shakes his head.

"But you do know to what I refer? You do know this sort of thing is a very bad idea, don't you?"

"Ah..."

"No, no. Don't speak. You don't want to ruffle me, old man. I don't want a reason. I don't want a story. I don't want to know if she paid you...in some way. Cold night, doll needs a ride, who knows? See, unlike Mr. Sinclair and Mr. Norris, I am not a muckraker. All I want to know is that it won't happen again. That never again in your wildest imaginings do you allow a white female bottom to lit upon your car seat. You just sell your shit here and do your fixing and let the taxi company do what it does. And one more thing, uncle, if you have told anybody about the particular ride of which I speak, which would have been foolish indeed, you will now deny having said it if it comes up again, pretend you are just a doddering old fool who put his memory out with the garbage, and that's the end of it. And if, somewhat more sensibly, you have not discussed this sordid adventure, you will keep it as secret as if it were buried treasure and you were the world's champion miser. Don't speak. *Shhh.*"

Prezhki steps out of the McKeen, descends back down to the car, his breath trailing him like an old hog in the engine yard. Choc keeps his eyes to the ground, transfixed on the spot where his lifeless feet must be. Halfway, Prezhki stops, turns, and calls up, "You know? I did some checking with the county down in Uncas Falls. They have no record of a Choc Bonjour ever acquiring a piece of property out by the old glassworks. In fact, seems the original owners never actually relinquished title. With such an unstable dilemma involving his real estate, a smart man would tread lightly in places unfamiliar to him, or not tread at all. You have yourself a safe and profitable day now, hear."

Choc, lifting his eyes, sees the man's back float along the crust of the fog, decides that he could identify the pistol before he could the cop. Pistols don't all look alike.

Prezhki takes the Willies down the hill, pulls up on the wrong side of the street at the corner market, goes inside for a Nehi orange. He is suddenly sweating in his too many coats, even on a chilled day like this. He sits back in the car, gulps down the soda in three manly chugs, flings the empty to the floor, and enjoys the confluence of cold from inside of him and from the air outside. He is angry with himself; disappointed really: driven to harass a harmless old colored man like that. Sometimes he thinks P-R's favor just isn't worth all the humiliation of the little chores and cover-ups he is forced to engineer, the constant application of bandages and the free-form truths. He will need to talk to P-R. A favor is one thing, but there needs to be a discussion of parameters, a little give and take, a civil meeting of civic minds.

Choc installs himself back on the cot, his feet in a bucket of hot water from the stove, still wrapped in the blanket and enjoying all the various painful encumbrances of being old and not all that far from passing out of the annoyances of body and coppers and the daily drudgery of being. He feels he is being pulled in different directions. There is that nasty white woman and her threats, and the police with his. He has seen this kind of trouble but has never before had it visited upon himself. He senses change in the frigid morning, alterations, a different spin to the earth to be not too eagerly anticipated.

The old, spotted kettle works itself to a frenzy and the aroma of strong coffee blankets that of things mutating around him. *Time,* thinks Choc, *t'pay a visit up to da Power 'n' Light Chapel a da Holy Gobspel an' plumb da well a Rev'ren' Salvation's wi'dom.*

Yuletide slumps back in, snuggles up under the cot, and eyes the old man's soaking feet with a look of deranged hunger.

V

U NCAS FALLS IS A SPIDER'S BODY on the map, a junction city where several railroads dominate an energetically grimy parcel of real estate. The chromosphere — a reeking miasma of one part air and two parts spent fuel — is brown-black, a soft focus of thick smudge and patterns of acidic floating particles. The back score is the constant din of locomotives and factories and big trucks acting important; the wail of forges; the gargantuan thump of stamp mills; the hiss of solid things reduced to white-hot industrial gravy.

The Tishomingo has but a minimal presence here, its northern terminus being Union Station — just enough space to load and unload passengers in the relative comfort of a canopied platform, and several lengths of freight sidings from the transfer yard nearby. It is a place to exchange cattle and everything useful or superfluous from cabbages to coal: milled lumber, automobile suspensions, coils of electrical wire, chromed toasters, farm machinery ranging from hoes to harvesters, bakelite combs and brushes, boxes of the new pastime Monopoly from the Parker Bros., cartons of obsolete and flammable vulcanite trolley tokens on their way to burial, an order of ten thousand straight pins, cookware, Bibles, and reams of newsprint. There are more than a few hobo rats and silverfish, and often some human transients beaten to retardation by the bulls with their truncheons.

The two long haulers — the Uncas Falls, Tishomingo & Gulf, and the Gulf and Northern — meet in relative conciliation here at the Tishomingo's extremity. They will run roughly parallel to each other for the three hundred or so iron miles to the sea, but because of widely divergent spheres of interest, see themselves as something less than rivals.

The Gulf Line is shorter, newer, and maintains a modern double-track operation from point to point. Though an ideal passenger route, advertising as "The Short Line," it competes with equally up to date macadam whose flexibility and appeal to independence has deprived it of most of its human traffic. Instead, its adaptable management has analyzed the handwriting even as it materializes on the wall, no matter how fast the vantage point barrels by, and has decided to reduce passenger revenue to a few slow local mixed trains; a bulletin to those along the way that it's time to purchase an automobile. "The Short Line," therefore, has come to rely upon its vibrant freight traffic, mostly generated by the ports at its southern end, and by the coal mined along the route at the dingy company town of Bituminy.

On the other hand, the more circuitous Tishomingo snakes from one failed community to another and, calling itself "The Scenic Route to the Gulf," —

a euphemism for the decaying quaintness it serves — suffers from geriatric ownership, poorly funded maintenance, and a mostly single track main line that causes agonizingly long delays to a schedule that looks good only on paper. It has hired a famous eastern artist to create distinctive color brochures, boasting the delights of the pine forests, the great Thebes Viaduct, water falls, ante-bellum villages and cotton plantations that the wise tourist can simply drive to with the help of a free road map from the local filling station. Hampered as they are, they run the *fast* train with all its streamlined *moderne* sleekness and glistening chrome fixtures. It has not gone unnoticed in railroad journals that the Tishomingo's main attribute is redundancy. There are rumblings that days, as well as rolling stock, are numbered.

On this day of Prezhki's menacing visit to Bonjour, Moses Brown and Sardo Cardineli have left their showcase train set to the maintenance crew to primp and provision for its next run out. To get home from UF, they have wangled a ride in the caboose of a slow cattle train painfully trudging behind an ageing mogul. The caboose stove is warm and inviting and the coffee better than can be expected, although neither Moses nor Sardo are particular about what warms them; while Sardo simply lacks discrimination, Moses knows that he can endure any hardship.

Outside pass stark, leafless trees, drained of color, tree gray on sky gray, the whole world in rectangles of smoky glass rocking like a ship at sea; an occasional gray crow, looking for lunch, flaps in sinister flight, a gray hawk glides by with the late Mr. Mouse dangling from its beak. In a clearing, a few gray cattle stand huddled and stupid, dreaming of grass blades and other bovine delights and comforted by the fulsome odor of their own unwashed bulk and continuous methane release.

The equally unwashed men in the crummy, smelling of grease and kerosene and a considerable crepitation of their own, and with facial wrinkles etched in coal dust, sit huddled in wraps of woolen with the Line's logo fading on the strands. The men talk of the work day, of baseball scores, of things that ail them, of wives and children, girlfriends and, mostly, the good ladies of Maiden Lane just beyond the yards in Tishomingo. It is all spiced with insults about their comrade's mothers, diminutive canards about genitals, prowess at work or at love, punitive remarks and counter-remarks about intelligence. Moses Brown does not participate: he sits with eyes closed, pretending to sleep, silent and stoic and above, or at least outside of, the fray. No one prods him to join in. They respect his station, his aloofness. In return, he barely considers them at all.

TISHOMINGO-YARD LIMIT: an inverted triangle sign, freights being assembled by the dinkies, filthy geysers of spent carbon emanating from the stacks of the little tankers, the mainline engines sidling up to the long wooden dock, the hoppers and reefers and flats swaying in a seductive chorus line on the slack track width of four feet eight and one half inches — the span, it is erroneously told, of Roman chariot axles.

Here sprawls a town-sized acreage just off the main line of sidings and structures: the boiler shop, the coaling station, the machine shop where locomotives are repaired, converted and, some, even constructed. Rolling stock is maintained here, blacksmiths argue iron into unnatural contortions, a seventy-foot turntable spins perpetually before the doors of the thirty-stall roundhouse. Company offices are in Downtown, Uncas Falls, where the execs can enjoy a civilized lunch; but this, this yard complex, this is the heart beat, the systemic pump of living fluids, where the real work is done; where cars commune into trains; where fuel is loaded and water dispensed; where a huge steel tire is changed on a whale-sized machine that has been hoisted off its track by an overhead crane. Big Baldwins begrudge space with grunting Alcos, five brand new Lima superpower two-eight-fours impertinently commence their apprenticeship. It is a sea of motion swum by pods of goliaths spouting in less than convivial displays of forged masculinity.

This is the nerve center of The Tishomingo. This is the core and soul of Tishomingo.

A goodly chunk of the city's labor force has made its way down to these yards and shops. The railroad issues the largest payroll in the county, even more so than the larger Uncas Falls "Short Line," whose several divisions are headquartered in other burgs along their mainlines or in Eastern commercial hubs. Much of what goes in and out of Tishomingo, animate or not, has traditionally gone through here, then to be relayed over to the trolleys and the draymen and now the truckers. The macadam here in these rugged hills is still quite inadequate, so if you operate a factory, or shop, or sell something that isn't of local manufacture, chances are your bills of lading will include some mention of the Tishomingo Yards, or a siding spun off from it will wind up at your loading dock attended by a by-weekly box car or two. There is, conceivably, no Tishomingo without The Tishomingo. Despite the physical contrast, the self-adulation, Tishomingo is but a railroad away from Thebes.

Sardo is typically effusive; thanks the train crew as he disembarks. Moses considers himself covered by the fireman's niceties and drifts off on his own separate path, allowing the trainmen only a somber nod.

Mr. Red, rolled like a *piroshki* in a hefty woolen jacket, his nickel-plated shield pinned to the lapel, a fur cap with ear flaps — much like, perhaps in imitation of, Chief Prezhki's — sucked down snug upon his anvil of skull, is stamping his boots and expelling frosty puffs of breath at the base of the wooden stairs that lead up the ridge to the employee tenant housing; a stark row of brick and board clones in need of paint and a good scrubbing. Moses suspects that Red has been waiting on him; not to confirm, Red stuffs a copy of the current employee timetable into his coat pocket and tries to look surprised at their encounter.

"Hey, Cap'in," calls Red. He has a reedy, suspicious tone. The lids of his eyes slant downward on the outside, perpetually looking askance, his view of the world one of constant query.

Maybe Moses nods; it is hard to know for sure. His is not a face of overt expression.

"Good run?" Red asks, seemingly dubious that it could be.

"Kind a all the same," Moses offers with economy.

"More'n that, I'd think. Beats freezin' your hin'quarters watchin' fer bums. Y'alls hoggers're looked upon'th some favor, I guess ya know."

"Puts the occasional t-bone on the table."

Red has positioned himself in front of the stairs. Moses is not pleased.

"Got a minute?"

"Kind a tired."

"Won't take but a minute."

Moses sniffs; spits tobacco carefully between the bull's boots, waits for Red to air his business.

Red eases back, a slight give in his knees, a slump of hulking shoulders. "See, I was wonderin', Cap'in, seein' as part'a my purview's company property on the ridge same as below, if maybe your house guest might not be familiar with, you know, certain proprieties we generally recognize here abouts."

"I'm real tired, Mr. Red. That, and I got no house guest and no fuckin' idea what you're goin' on about."

"No disrespect intended, Cap'in. Just keepin' an eye out on the neighborhood; the ladies in particular with the low-lifes and whatnot we got ridin' these here freights."

"I got no houseguest, Mr. Red, not that it's any a y'all's concern."

"Well, that's the curious thing."

Moses pushes past him — would walk through him had not Red the good sense to step aside.

"I seen a woman come outta your place Thursday night. She was pretty bundled for the cold. Headed on up toward town. Was it Mrs. Brown, I'd a offered a tote her up t'the market or whatever, it bein' night time an' cold like it's been. I come up from the other end a the block an' I give a wave, see, but she just crossed over t'the other side a the street, so I figure it ain't the missus, must be some guest, particularly since no sensible woman'd be out at…"

Moses stops on the steps. "Would not be wise t'offer some sort a judgment at this point." He speaks softly, slow and direct. His lips barely part.

"No, suh. Definitely ain't my place. I know my place, Mr. Brown."

"Do you, Mr. Red?"

"Suh, I do. And I wouldn't'a said nothin' t'all 'cept I seen this woman later on at the fillin' station up on Seventh."

"You followed her?"

"No, suh. Absolutely not. Seein' that she weren't Mrs. Brown, I concluded I got no business gettin' my nose outta shape over some woman with such poor sense as…"

"Y'all's point, Mr. Red? I'm gettin' no less tired."

"I'd already clocked out. Just needed a fill up. So I'm at the pump, see, and this same woman comes outta the ladies'…I know that from what she wore… and this old colored boy who does the odd job 'round here…a junk an fix-it man, well, he drives on up to the station an' this woman hops in the cab with him an' off they go like it was nat'ral."

"Like I said, I got no house guest. I wouldn't concern myself, I was you." It is said calmly, but Red senses he has unnerved the engineer, pierced just a little bit of tissue.

"I wouldn't a mentioned it 'cept..."

"I clocked out too, Mr. Red. Could be we'll talk another time. But I doubt it."

Red watches Brown's purposeful footfalls on the steps. He is satisfied with himself, Red is. *That'll keep the smug bastard on edge,* he thinks. *Give 'im reason t'come down t'earth.*

She is at the kitchen sink, her arms sunk in suds like dock pilings in a polluted lake. She tenses up as she hears him swing open the screen door, the hairs on her arms tingling as if an alien presence were about to enter. She tries to swallow but has no saliva and her gut contracts in complaint of him.

She expects the usual. Like the iceman he is, he will shower under the spigot he has installed in the mudroom and ruminate on getting around to replacing the rusty pipe before him that rattles like a loose shutter in the wind. He will come into the kitchen wordless, wrapped in a towel, will lead her by the hand up the stairs to the bed of capitulation and undress her. He will expect her to suffer the chore of removing her things: things she bought, things she sewed, things she darned, things she leveled with a flat iron. He will expect her to drop them crumpled to the floor, as he will drop her crumbled to their bed for half a minute of perfunctory penetration; wordless, noiseless, above all, joyless; a contractual fuck over-rehearsed, by the numbers, line by line; her face to the ceiling, his to the pillow, slick and neat like a train schedule. She plays opossum, he claims his right over her, as it condones on the cross stitch framed over the headboard — to have and to hold and to enter and to plant seed that will die in her fallow womb. After, he will roll over with his back to her, sleep for an hour and awake famished. But not for her. She is resigned; it will all be over soon and her evening can go on; perhaps a shawl to knit by the hearth; Jolson on the RCA; the president with encouraging words from his own fireside. And Moses, sated, will read the paper and slip back to bed, out for the night this time. She will clean up the kitchen; get it ready to start all over in the morning. When she finally sleeps, there will be space enough between them to pave for traffic.

But this day unfolds differently. This day unravels.

He enters the kitchen fully dressed, tracks in the filth of his locomotive.

"Mercy, my floor, Moses!"

"You'll scrub it later," he says evenly. It is the monotone of threat. He plops the lunch box down on the table, drops his heavy work gloves to the floor. They crumple like an old wife.

"Ain't there no supper, Flora?" It is accusatory. Certainly he smells the meal; the close kitchen air is thick with it.

She stands back to the sink, kneading a dishtowel. "I thought...You usually..."

"Yes?"

"After a run, you usually have…a somewhat different appetite."

"Is there supper or ain't there?"

"Yes. Isn't there always? I'll warm it for you."

She lights the oven already full, busies herself with cleaning spatulas and tongs, pouring a pot of grease into a mason jar — two mason jars, three — and avoids facing him for an interminable interlude while the stove stokes itself and Moses, she knows but does not see, sits before his virgin place setting and waits, swathed in quiet tension. When it is time, perhaps too soon because she can no longer endure the silence and the uncertainty, she serves up re-heated fried chicken and mashed potatoes swimming in a brown reservoir, and biscuits billowed like pillows, then sets down a pitcher and a mug and seats herself across from him.

He stares at the plate. It is his favorite supper, crackling crisp with plenty of pepper and a side of rhubarb alone in a satellite bowl. He stares for a long time, his hands down at his side. "I'm done. Take it away."

"You haven't touched it."

"Take it away."

"It's your favorite."

"Have y'all gone deaf?

"What's wrong? Something's wrong?"

"What's wrong is that it is still in front a me and my wife's forgotten how t' listen. My wife thinks it's argument a man needs after work."

She stands suddenly, angry and afraid, grabs the plate, the bowl, discards his favorite meal out the screen door for the neighbor's dogs to discover. They could choke on the bones; she hopes they do. She hopes the neighbor barges in to complain, occupying Moses with travail directed elsewhere. When she returns, he has already left the room.

Much later, turned away from her in the bed, he asks, "What do y'think'd happen if I caught ya'll'n a lie?"

"Have you?"

"You tell me. Have I?"

"What has gotten into to you?"

"Could ask you the same?"

They have had this conversation. Since the child passed, so many years ago, they have had it in cycles. Never a joyous man, he is now morose, calculating, looking for devils in all the details. She has asked him if he imagines things of her when he is in the engine cab, and he has said that he doesn't imagine her at all when working, that he has responsibilities to his employer and that the paying public has a reasonable expectation of getting to their stations alive. Thoughts of a woman's foolishness seem puny in comparison.

"I'm not doing this again," she says.

"Rather t'hear what ya *are* doin' than what y'ain't." He is without dimension in the dark room. She smells his metallic breath more distinctly than she sees his features.

"Why don't you tell me then? What is it y'all think is going on?"

He looks away from her; something on the wall, perhaps; speaks with his head diverted. "Last Thursday?"

"Is that a question?"

"Only if there's an answer t'tell."

"I went to my sister's over in Thebes, like I told you."

"She'll vouch, a course."

"Of course."

"An' ya left outta here when?"

"What are you asking me?"

"It's so hard to understand? What time ya'll went on up t' your sister's over in Thebes?"

"I went in the early afternoon. Like I told you. I took the trolley. I wore the earrings with the little bells made of pearl. The black hat you bought me. Right before I left, I stopped to piss. I wiped, as usual with my right hand, but when I washed I did the left as well. I don't know why. Just in case, I suppose. You'd think the right was enough. What else do you need to know? How many people rode the car? What they wore? Who smelled of garlic, who of rose water? Was the motorman polite?"

"I can call your sister."

"Do it. Call her."

He pauses. "I did. While ya did your dishes or whatever it is ya do in the kitchen 'til all hours."

"I plan meals to throw out. What do you think I do?"

"She said she don't know what time ya got there. She'd gone t' he'p a neighbor lady who's ill. So she said. You was there when she got back."

She is cautious; doesn't know if this is a trap. She says nothing. He can't twist *nothing*.

"I won't abide no lie," he says.

"I won't tell one."

"I spoke t' Mr. Red."

"That must've made your day."

"He said a woman left from here on Thursday evening."

"Is that it? Is that what this is about?"

"He thought we had a house guest."

"Mrs. Grady asked to borrow the Singer. I saw no harm in letting her stay while I was away."

"Mr. Red said he saw her up at the fillin' station. That she got into a nigger junkman's truck."

"Mr. Red, it seems, is all over town."

"That's what he said."

"I'm sure it is. What he saw is probably a different matter. Mr. Red has been known to indulge a bottle now and then."

"I could call up this Mrs. Grady."

"You could. Y'all could get down the Directory and call the whole damned town. I would think you'd embarrassed yourself enough already, but go on, give it a go. Let everybody from here to Uncas Falls in on your petty little suspicions based on inebriated gossip from an old yard bull. My Lord, Moses, you can be a fool when the need arises!"

"That's the point, Flora. I won't be no fool. I won't, in particular, be no woman's fool. Take it t'heart."

"I've no heart left, I fear. You have culled it from my chest. I am cold and empty like you."

"Go t'sleep, Flora. Y'all're tired. After all the cookin' an' moppin'. Maybe we won't have t' talk'a this no more. I am sick t' death a this…this thing we do. But y'are on notice. I will not be your fool. Take it t' whatever vacant cavity and step lightly. Step very lightly. The floorboards creak. The windows'er invitations t'look see. And who knows what'all tales ride the wires pole t' pole?"

"Mother of God, Moses, do you hear yourself?"

"Sleep now, wife. Clean slate 'n'a mornin'."

"I think not!"

"Ain't your place t'think, is it? Ain't your place 't'all."

"I still *feel*. I will have the memory of feeling."

"Which ya'll kindly keep t'your-own-self. This here's done. Go t'sleep."

She watches him in the dark, a gray cross-hatched figure in shadow. He is always dark, something about him; perhaps a mood, the depth of his lightless eyes, the perpetual shadow of stubborn beard clinging to him like coal filth that cannot be cleansed. People are afraid of Moses, she thinks. He thinks it is respect, their distance, a sort of curtsy.

The morning will be a reprise of past pretenses. Motions will be gone through. Meals cooked. Work performed. And at night he will come home, suffer the icy mud room shower, emerge in towel and lead her upstairs, where he will crumple her down on the marriage bed like dirty linen and sleep as obliviously as death itself. And she will think, lying a world away on the other side of the bed, *Damn you, Moses Brown, and the iron horse you rode in on.*

VI

CHOC IS AN UNSTEADY HAND ON a ladder these days. With the uncertain benefit of prayer and the strong grip of Brother Holynation Salvation bracing the rungs from below, the old man manages to scrape paint chips from a rain gutter, eighteen feet above the point at which a wiser septuagenarian would be standing.

"Ah don' fall so good dese days," Choc remarks, the scraper screeching shrilly down his spine.

"Closer t' God, surely a force stronger than gravity," Salvation assures.

"Don' know 'bou' dat. Righteous'er not, ain' neber seen a mans fall up."

"I got y'all here, my brother. Pray an' scrape. We shall have this here chapel prepped 'n' painted faster than a serpent can tell a lie."

Choc mumbles, *"All's Ah needs now's serpents 'n' grabity an' dese here ol' bones dry as kin'lin'."*

"That you say, Brother Choc?"

"Jus' a little prayer for da mans on da high wire, Brother Holynation. Leas' it ain't rainin'."

"No, suh, I prayed that ol' rain away."

"Sumpin' burnin' o'er t'da junction." Choc can see beyond the tenant houses, beyond the rail yards. The crystal day comes blurred through the gauze of his vision. A cauliflower of new smoke announces itself on the horizon.

"Prob'ly jus' some old engine'th a little heartburn. 'Melt away, O Philistia, all a thee; For there cometh a smoke outta d'nort'.' Isaiah, fou'teen thirty-one."

"Sumpin' bigger up t'da sawmill, could be." A confirmation of sirens is heard in the distance. "Believe it mo' 't'da sout'."

"Prob'ly some poor vagabon' 'at set up 'is camp fire up un'er a pulp mound. See here, Brother Choc, we can leave off this concern t'God an' the TFD. Why'n't y'all come on down here an' avail yo'self a some a Elisheba's home squeeze' lemonade? A 'lixor 'f I ever tastes one."

"Do it douse fires?" Choc does not need a second invitation. He slowly gets purchase on rung after rung, a rickety old skeleton of a man no longer in his element. Brother Holynation takes him up to the front of the old generating house. A pitcher with tin cups is set up on the steps, a curved frosted reflection of POWER & LIGHT skirting the lip, the partial word MUNICI___ white washed out, and replaced with CHA___to misspell with PAL, an economy at once of orthography and paint.

Choc and Salvation sit together on the cold stone steps, tap their cups together, *ting*, enjoy the Sister Wife's acid brew. "Hit d'spot!" Salvation says. He is very dark and healthy round and has a shine to him like new loafers. There is bulk to his shoulders, a girth not of over abundance but of simple wellbeing, of a man at peace with himself and his higher power. He is a wise and kind man, sees trouble where it lies, quotes the Old Testament but lives the New. The beaten-down, the trod-upon, see him as a beacon of possibility in a bleak temporal world.

Choc smacks his lips, happy to be seated. He is Salvation's antitheses, purple brown and crackled like lava; a pink patch of partial white man on his neck; gray-white, razor wire, petrified wool on his scalp; yellow eyes diverging to different marks on the landscape. "Ah gots a worry needs airin', ya'll don' min'." A palsy annoys his hands; the lemonade fails to level.

"'With the merc'ful, Thou dost show Thyself merc'ful.' Second Samuel, twen'y-two twen'y."

"'M'Ah mercy full, Brother?"

"Upright an' pure. What'all's ya trouble?"

Choc twirls his cup. Lemon rind rounds the vortex like opalescent specs of floating skin. "Happens dere dis here white woman. Not wha'cha think. Ah don' seek no truck'th her bu' she t'reatened me an' Ah gots so muddle', Ah di'n' know wha't'do."

"'The mouth of a strange woman 's'a deep pit.' Proverbs, twen'y two fo'teen."

"If'n ya'll don' min', could we might do dis here 'thought no quotationisms? 'Cause Ah's truly at a loss here."

Salvation chuckles from deep in his throat. "The Word does get th'better a me at times, that's for sure. But, mercy, Brother, a *white* woman?" *White:* an incredulous spray to bead both of their cups.

"Ah's doin' some work'n'er kitchen garten an' she up'n' ax me t'carry'er on o'er t'T'ebes dat bera ebenin'. Ah protes' as much's Ah can 't'out rousin' no ire, see, but y'knows how dey is. She done made up'er min'....an' mine too. Ah picks'er up at da Signal up dere on Sebent' an' carry'er down where she wanna go."

"That bein'?"

"Near dat ol' motor court down by d'railroa'. She ge's out, tells me t'keep my mouf shut, da fac' bein' she don' need a tell me nuttin. Den she t'ro' some change my way, an' me, Ah go on off home an' Ah don' look back 'cause Ah don' wanna know no more'n I already does."

"Time come, Brother Choc, th'harlot be th'one t'splain herself. You in th'clear with th'Lord, no question."

"Well, now, if dat be dat, awright by me. Bu' dis mornin', Ah gots a *po*-lice pokin' roun' my yard, pickin' up stuff, sayin' dis an' dat maybe don' belong t'me, sayin' maybe Ah don' hol' no title t'the yard, an'Ah be a wise ol' uncle Ah can keeps my mouf shut, like Ah don' alrea'y know dat. How dumb dey t'ink we is?"

"Now, dere's a specalation da smart brother'd give some thought. Tell me, he was *re*-ferin' t' this woman?"

"He don' mention *no* woman by name. Ah don' taxi no udder one, neider. He talkin' 'bout a Mr. Sinclair, a Mr. Norris, an' Ah don' know none a dem folks from a fence pos'. Y'knows how dey talks."

"Babel Tower ziggurat all there own selves." Choc's old ears hear, *rabble tower cigarette.*

"Don' neber say wha' dey means an' den dey sez ya sassin' if ya ax a question. Ah'm a ol' man, Pastor, ain' no secret t' dat, an' Ah ain' gots myse'f dis far not havin' no such triple-ations, an' now, all a dis come up outta nowheres. Lawd knows, Ah's jus' tryin' t'get by 'till one mornin' Ah wakes up'n'a better place 'thout no rope burns up'n dis here ol' chicken neck. So, Ah guess Ah jus' askin' Jesus give a man some slack dis one mo' time an' Ah dies happy'n my own bed. Sell me a few mo' trinkets, suck me out a good marrow bone now'n'den, an' lay me down t'sleep when d'good Lawd 'ques' my company."

Salvation claps his hands together. His feet do a little bounce. "Praise, Jesus, Brother Choc. Praise Him for grantin' y'all these here trials for t'overcome. This be th'test, my good brother. 'Create me a clean heart, O God; An' renew a steadfast spirit within me.' Psalms, fifty-one twelve."

Choc glances over at him with censoring amber eyes.

"Sorry," says Salvation. "We was dispensin' with scripture for th'momen', wasn't we? It's jus'...y'know, this sort a thing fan the flame 'th'in this here preacher's heart o' hearts. The 'ternal burnin' bush a truth foun' in th'souls a men. Can ignore it, but ya can't quench it. Can't douse it. An'therein lies all th'answers t'all th'questions. Y'don' ax th'cooper t'mend your drain, y'don' ax th'plumber t'band ya'll a barrel. 'Wisdom crieth 'loud in th'streets.'" *Proverbs,* he thinks, *one twen'y.*

"Ah's sure dat de trut', but ain't nuttin'n dese streets 'roun'ere gibin' dis Christian a chance'n ol' Gen'l Lee's army how t'void dat *po*-lice an' dat bad white woman. Scripture be okay wid me, bu' dis ol' junker sure cou' use a pin' a practicalitous common sense *ad*-vice roun' 'bout now."

Salvation delays his next words, feels admonished but admires the old man for his spunk. "Patience, Brother Choc. Patience an' faith. For The Lord taketh pleasure in them that fear Him, In those that wait for His mercy.'" *(Psalms one hun'er' forty seben eleben).*

"Uh huh. Dat true. Bu' right now, da fear Ah fear is a dat *po*-lice an' dat woman an' me, Ah ain' waitin' on no mercy from niet'er a dems."

Salvation clasps the old man about the shoulders, refills his cup in one motion. "I tell the children, when in a quandary, I'm 'bliged t'fall back on de t'ree D's."

"Dey is?"

"Dis, dat an' d'other." He enjoys a short chuckle. "Keep ya'll's eye open, ya mouth shut, an' don' hear nothin' ya ain' oughtin't'hear. Obey all th'traffic laws, keep y'all's' tire 'flated, an' otherwise don' call no unneeded attention on ya'selfs. All this other travail'll get et up by flies, like ofal always do, providin' y'don' go swat none a them aways. Make ya'rself small, Brother, camouflaged, like the mantis so's he can pray in peace. We are oil on th' water; light no matches." Salvation's bright eyes have returned to the roofline, a hint that all the pertinent remarks have been depleted. But he is worried about this occasional parishioner, knows there are no real comforts on this earth that can insulate the old man from his fears.

A hint of smoke idles by.

Much later, after an hour or two of paint chips and rust flakes and ash in the sky, Choc chugs up Forty-seventh with a neat basket of fried chicken and collard greens tucked under a crisp gingham from Elisheba's cupboard. The streets are broken here, bricks excavated to repair a wall and then forgotten, the sidewalks tortured by roots into tents of concrete. There is a row of neat cabins for the Pullman porters, the tiny yards planted in hedges and flowering plants not yet blooming.

This breaks down quickly by the hat maker's plant where the spur track splits off from the center of the street and curves abruptly to the platform out back, then meanders up to brick kilns, and back into the avenue. Here is a part of town that rattles like California when a short freight creeps by and the barber suspends his razor until the tremors pass, where grips tighten on cane-back rockers in the place old men gather with their dominos and checkers. There is a storefront chapel every block, soot stained: an equal contingent of bars with tired hookers hunkered down on a stairwell. Choc drives with caution; obeys speed limits, keeps his muddied vision on the road. An alley fight attracts a crowd; a wino tumbles off his bus bench and lays motionless; two cop cars skid up to a shack down a side street and officers bounce out with guns drawn. Choc sticks to the straight and narrow of his myopic vision. There is something grim in the air over Tishomingo, something dark and unsettling.

He tries to savor the good fragrance of the basket but can barely urge up the saliva of promise. And he thinks back on Reverend Salvation with his Psalms *dis* and his Proverbs *dat* and his Samuel *d'udder,* and in private blasphemy he thinks, *Wuf d'Lawd jus' a chile at play?* He chokes back the acid burn of citrus that Salvation has poured for him, and says out loud, "Da hell dat youn' fool preacherman tryin't'say?

VII

JUNE NEARLY SKIPS DOWN THE WORN carpet of the corridor. There is a weight of dry rot and rats rarified into the second floor air of the Thebean — locally shortened to *The 'Bee-ann* — Arms. She pounds excitedly on the number three door, evoking a shuffle from inside, a phlegmatic grumble, "Hold your horses. Can't be two places at once!"

The brass plate behind the peephole flips open revealing Loubella's milky cataract. "What's it? Sunday already?"

"Extri, extri," June cries out gleefully, "All the news that's fit to print."

"And all the ships at sea, I s'pose." Grudgingly, Loubella opens the door. Her sparse frame is barely occupying an old threadbare robe.

"That a teapot I hear whistling?" June inquires.

"Nope, just some sailor wants t'get in you're pants, June. You takin' sugar these days?"

"The doctor says I'm not to. So just one lump'll have to do it." June rushes in, unravels from her coat and scarf, places her hat and its fruit orchard carefully down on the table, and falls into the old sofa that huffs its way up around her behind. She feels she is falling into a well of goose down.

Loubella frowns at the hat. "I can go out an' find an Okie t'harvest that there for y'all."

"Just the tea, two lumps, dear."

Loubella slogs off to the kitchen past enough dark, overlarge mahogany furniture to denude Brazil. There are dim pictures of people long dead all around her. "I'll give ya three," she calls, turning off the pot, "one for the doctor." Her struggle to achieve the stove is a far cry from June's lithe energy. She is a slug to her friend's honeybee.

"Mercy, dear, crack a window, would you! The hall was bad enough, but it smells like the Greyhound depot in here."

"The supple fragrance of my own incontinence. Stay a while an' you won't notice it. I don't. With any luck, you'll be pissin' your own drawers soon enough."

She shuffles out with two cups, a string and a label draped out of each, and a small bowl in which to deposit the bags. "Bring anything to go with this?"

"Just things I hear."

"Can't eat things you hear."

"Oh, I don't know. Depends how meaty the things."

"Well, go ahead before I pass on to my reward. I haven't got all that much time. And trim the fat. Gives me gas. Not the very best introduction to St. Peter, I don't imagine."

June leans forward, pumps the tea bag up and down, and says mysteriously, "There are things going on, Loubella, that won't wait 'til Sunday lunch."

"Whatcha whisperin' for? Ain't nobody here but us, and I can't hardly hear you even in your normal voice."

"Yesterday morning, I am at my kitchen window, and who should drive by?"

"The Pope and six cardinals. How should I know?"

"Walter Prezhki."

"Don't say! Seems to be takin' an unusual interest in our forgotten burg."

"Yes, he does. And guess where he stops?"

"On the back of a whale! Jesus and Mary, June, just tell the darn story. I guarantee, y'all have my attention!"

"He takes the road up to Choc Bonjour's."

"He does, does he! My, my!" Interest defines the arch of her brows. "Seems a whole lotta white folks takin' account a the old boy a late. *You saw* this yourself? Not your nephew, now?"

"Plain as day."

"Easy for you to say. Day or night, all a blur to me. Got more cataracts than Niagara."

"He's up there quite a while, Chief Prezhki is. Thirty-seven minutes to be exact. I timed it."

"Betcha did."

"And then he comes on down and I am still at the window."

"Betcha are."

"He stops at the corner and gets himself a soda, and then goes back up over the hill to Tishomingo."

"Where he belongs, y'ask me. 'Course no one asks me nothin' no more. Ya know, June, I always did admire that street-facin' kitchen winda a yours."

"Consumed with envy, are you?" June is aglow with revelation.

"Listen to you. When you come down off a that high horse a yours, be sure to shovel up after the both a ya. And ya think this somehow relates to Thursday night?"

"Just thought I'd run that by you before I present to the girls on Sunday. I have no idea, myself." June shrugs a suit-yourself sort of shrug.

"What are we talkin' about at this new juncture? Mayor or...Chief a police?"

"Well, I don't really know, do I? That's what makes it interesting. Maybe... *both!*"

"They took turns! The Mayor first while the Chief gnawed his burger in The R.H.! Then the Chief goes up to the motor court and finishes up for the both of 'em!" Loubella sucks air; a long wretched hiss like it's the last time. She clutches her old Dalmatian hands up to her chin in a motion that resembles prayer. There is a wobble in the spindly fingers; arthritic bubbles in the joints. "We have ourselves some agile hussy? That what you're sayin'?"

"Oh, I'm not saying anything except what I know. You can put the pieces together as well as I."

"Sodom and Gomorrah, Junie bug! What's this world comin' to?"

"It's certainly not for me to know."

"Cost me a tea bag and three lumps a sugar. What else ya got?"

"I went over to Tishomingo yesterday. Treated my self to a new hat."

"*That's* what that is? I thought you got run over by a produce truck. This kind a weather, you'd better set it down by a smudge pot at night. Discourage Mr. Frost."

June scowls, tries to appear hurt. "The sales girl said it made me look young."

"The only thing's gonna make you look young is that there reincarnation. You're gonna wear yourself out keepin' the weevils out'a that patch a fertilizer."

"You're unkind."

"Well, at least I still know the difference 'tween a hat and truck farm. No young pup'v'a sales girl's gonna pull the wool over these old eyes."

June runs her fingers nervously over the rock hard fruit. "I think it has a flare," she defends.

"Flare, huh! Rockets red glare, SOS! You're lookin' a bit peaked, you are, dearie, under the weight a all them perishables. Want a refill? I can spike it up a bit."

"Heavens, no. I'm just trying...well, to compose myself. You're always so upsetting." She clutches a convenient hanky from out of her sleeve, pretends to dab dry eyes.

"Oh, Jesus, Joseph and Mary! So you bought a ...*hat.*"

"Yes I did, and guess who I ran into at the store. That little ladies shop near Phipps-Rouge Square with all those adorable things in the window?"

"Helen Keller! And she's still wonderin' who all *she* bumped into. Ha!"

"That's a *terrible* thing to say, Loubella. You can be a cruel woman!"

"See, that there's the wisdom a Catholicism, Junie-roonie, you're never more than a week away from absolution."

"Still..."

"So who *did* ya run into? That communist Eleanor Jewsevelt?"

"You're just doing this because it upsets me."

"And you keep gettin' upset! Don't you never learn?"

"I ran into," June interjects with conviction, "Ethel Goosander."

"Whoop-di-di! Never heard a'er."

"Oh, you remember. I used to work switchboard with her over at the Tishomingo Exchange. She's still over there, and, boy, does she ever get an ear full."

"Now you're gettin' interestin'. I'm on pins and needles…'course only in the three spots I can still feel anything. And I don't remember no Goosender."

"-Ander. Goos*ander*. A little discretion is in order. I need to protect my sources, after all."

"Who'm I gonna tell that you haven't already squawked to? Other than the girls, everyone else I know is dead. Least I think that's why they don't come 'round no more."

"I can think of other reasons," says June standing and proceeding toward an alley-facing casement. The room is a diorama of near-dead things. There is a stereopticon on a stand along side of a stack of yellowed Parisian views, wild Indians, National Parks; Victorian greeting cards of a romantic nature with embossed sweethearts and unraveling fringe borders; a tattered quilt; souvenirs from the Louisiana Purchase Exposition of nineteen aught four; a tea-stained damask table linen. It is a room where copper greens, brass browns, ceramic chips, and felt fades and turns to colored dust.

"What'er you up to, June?"

"I am going to provide us both with a little air. It's like an Edgar Allen Poe story in here." She shoves aside velvet curtains thick as whale hide. Clumps of dust powder her shoes. She offers a petite cough to her sleeve, all flowered patterns and airy like a doily. She hears Loubella wish her good luck and she flips the window latch, hunches her shoulders into the frame and pushes up.

"Painted shut," the older woman snickers.

"Are they all?"

"How would I know? No need to try 'em."

"Honestly, Loubella, I don't know how you live here!" She wanders about the room, studying pictures in dark frames, austere in their sepia formality.

"If ya call this livin'."

June stops in front of a picture of Loubella's late husband, spit and polish in nautical attire, and with her handkerchief rubs a smudge from the glass. "Your Nathan was a fine looking man," she muses.

"That's 'cause they only took his image fully clothed. In the all together, after the Great War and that influenza thing, and more'n'a few unwise choices made in tropical climes while in the merchant marines, that man's body looked like nothing more than Fort Sumpter after the siege, half a flag pole leanin' in the direction a the victors."

June sits back down into the sofa cushions. "You are an evil old crone, you know, Loubella?"

"And you're a saint to put up with me. I will pray for your beatification. Can we circle on back to the center ring?"

"Ethel is my best urban source. I am a little isolated out here in the sticks. And I think she has what they call a photographic memory. Anyway, she always has the goods for my money."

"My lips are sealed like an old wound. Shovel the dirt, Mrs. Pulitzer."

Once again, June leans in close, as if the walls have flies and the flies have ears. "Having no connection with our...*scarlet* lady, Ethel is privy to a call from a Mr. Ferrous up in Uncas Falls, who, further investigation reveals, to be none other than the regional supervisor of the Tishomingo Lines. The callee, if I may, is our very own Socrates Phipps-Rouge. Ethel, amongst her other talents, has a great appreciation for *certain nuances in human conversation* — her words, mind you, so that she can tell the relative emotions of the speaker, the speaker's mood, the speaker's place of origin, even the approximate status of one speaker in relation to another."

"This better be goin' somewhere."

"Ethel is absolutely, positively, one hundred percent certain that in this conversation between the railroad man and the Mayor, the Mayor is definitely a rung or two below the other."

"Are there words to this dressin' down?"

"Indeed, there are! This Mr. Ferrous, apparently in no uncertain terms and with as little small talk as possible, told P-R to get his you-know-what up to UF as soon as he can."

"He said that? 'His You-know-what?'"

"No, I believe he used a more forceful term which I would prefer not to repeat. Use your abundant imagination. The point is; he was talking *down* to P-R! Can you just imagine?"

"Well, I never!"

"No. And neither have I."

"So did P-R tell him to go you-know-what himself?"

"I'm not sure I know what *you-know-what* refers to, but he certainly did not. Instead, he says, meek as a mouse on the cat's birthday, *can it wait a day or two?* This was yesterday, understand. Mr. Ferrous literally barks, according to Ethel, *Wednesday at the you-know-what latest. One p.m., my office. It will be to your benefit to be there. I dare say,* he says, says Ethel, *I do not want to think of the consequences if you're not.*"

"I've never known P-R, sire or pup, to take a back seat to nobody. Sounds like hooey t'me!"

"Then wait until you hear this. Not a minute passes until P-R rings up Chief Prezhki and tells him to get *his* you-know-what over to the Sweet Briar Lounge for dinner. He's barking like a dog as well, P-R is, without a hello or how-di-do. *Six on the button,* he demands, *usual place,* and, without so much as by your leave, hangs up. Ethel says that the Chief then says a word that she wouldn't have expected of a fine man like him, and rings off."

"I'm speechless!"

"There *are* miracles. What d'ya think it all means?"

"Well, I wouldn't know. But I would think anybody who could talk to P-R like that and get away with it must know something about His Honor that we don't. Did P-R sound...I don't know...ruffled? Angry?"

"I only know what Ethel told me. And you are the first I've told. And you know what else, and this is all over Tishomingo? The boys at the police department and the fire department got quite a workout, I'm told, yesterday, and for all I know it's still going on today. Regular crime wave. Like there's something in the air, though you wouldn't know about air in here. Big fire over at the Cypress Creek sawmill; a shooting and some sort of melee in Darktown; a series of armed robberies Downtown, and I don't know what else. Not what were used to at this altitude, not at all."

"Full moon. That's what brings 'em outta the woodwork. Either that, or the Good Lord's taken leave a..."

"Don't you go and blaspheme now."

"I was gonna say, *a us.*"

IX

C HIEF PREZHKI RUNS HIS GLOVED FINGERS across a scar on the side of the Willis-Knight and spits onto the frosted cobbles. "*Shit,*" he says aloud, "*fuck me up right on the street in front of the station. Goddam Chief of fucking Police!*" *You'd think that would mean something.* He straightens up, tries to stretch the tension from his back, while the full moon and the neon of the Sweet Briar zigzags across his eyes,

L VE MAINE L BSTER
DANCING NIG TLY,

the first time he has seen a letter down, even a GE Mazda bulb out, or a fork out of place at the Lounge. It is the kind of high class eatery where they would pry the gum from underneath the tables — would have a specialized sterling utensil to do so — if the clientele were even inclined to chew gum.

It has been, Prezhki thinks, a bulb-out kind of day; a day off kilter; the tilt of the earth a fraction of a degree from true. He tallies three frozen winos — logs from the mill sailing in a queue down the Lower Gorge Branch of the Uncas toward the falls; a Negro man in a alley with a bottle of Stegmaier Porter jutting from his neck like a hose bib, not two blocks from a short hostage incident in which Mike Voorhiis takes a twenty-two slug across his shoulder, just before wrenching the gun away and closing a piano lid on the suspect. It is just a graze, but the first officer shot under Prezhki's watch. There are four fires, one at the sawmill, probably set, and three Downtown that do little damage but are preludes to an equal number of nearby robberies. And a naked inmate, again, from the County Sanatorium, falls from a second story window into a hydrangea, staggers out onto Tishomingo View Blvd., and winds up hospitalized with frostbite of the nether regions.

It is a grungy Uncas Falls kind of day in generally pastoral Tishomingo, as if someone has eaten of the wrong apple and riled God, and the legless, wily serpent has slithered off to conjure new mischief. It is a day of grand urban chaos in a town where police work generally consists of providing a tank for the tanked and returning lost children to wherever lost children are returned. And Prezhki, on a more humble scale, is as galled as God for the violation of his forbidden fruit.

And now this. This blatant hit and run abuse of his door panel, the impact of which was deadened by the light snow that thought to dampen the afternoon, coming as it did with a sudden chill that left a chunk of ice to derail a trolley where the line takes the trestle above the interurban to UF, a place where all of this misfortune would be more at home. On a better day, perhaps any other day, Prezhki would venture to inquire when the L BSTER was dancing, something he'd always wanted to see, but today he is tired and stiff, and not a little confused as to why his Department, and indeed his town, are being forsaken. And, he is beside himself with disdain for P-R who has ordered him to fiddle while 'Mingo burns.

He attempts to control his flow of breath, to contain his unseemly anger. He is a public figure in the common ground of the street, this very private man behind the very public shield, huffing and cursing before a well known chop house and watering hole, called out on this raw evening to pimp for the Mayor. He has, perhaps, shown a side of himself best kept concealed.

He barely notices that people passing by — a couple snug in the skins of dead animals, a man with a live dog — nod at him, perhaps offer a brief word of salutation that he doesn't hear. He leaves them unacknowledged and just a little bit bitter.

Tishomingo is a small city of complex connections, not unlike the circuitry of T Bell. It nourishes a barely subterranean intelligence network that links city hall to church to press to kitchen table to shop counter to bed. Garbage that stinks in Darktown reeks all the way to Thebes. The recruiting of a union man at the freight yards is cautiously noted in a VP's office in Downtown Uncas. P-R likes to remind cronies, of which category of brotherhood Prezhki is surely a card-carrying member, that, *If y'all piss in the Upper Gorge, they'all be drinking it in the Lower before the final shake of your dick.* The Chief is five steps beyond annoyed with P-R, and no less disgusted with himself.

It is dark and relatively quiet inside the Sweet Briar. He can hear ice clinking in the lounge. A few couples huddle in two-dimensional cutouts. Candles flicker between them, the unstable light preserving their anonymity. A woman's laughter pierces the smoky room, abates; a stack of dishes is set down somewhere. Sweet Briar is an old establishment of quiet respectability where the waiters are no more human than the table linen, faceless black men that otherwise would be porters. With ante-bellum detachment, you could wipe your mouths on them if so inclined.

The proprietor is one of the uptown Humboldts, a city commissioner and possessor of a pretty wife whose golden chords grace the hymnal under Pastor Shem's leaky roof. Humboldt prescribes a strict code of conduct in his establishment, himself checking the crystal for lipstick stains and the tines for particles of mint jelly and atoms of gristle. He flattens the whole under glass and inspects it through an ordered culinary microscope.

Out-of-towners linger here. They are business people, vacationers, manicured escapees from the grit of UF, long-married spouses chewing silently in talked-out resignation, borrowers and lenders of other people's money, a couple of non-natives so animated and delighted with each other that it will be known before morning at the Ladies Community Improvement and Garden Club that a blatant tryst was played out shamefully before all eyes over a shared porterhouse and a bottle of French wine. The *l bster*, apparently, is still in the dressing room applying whatever powder complements its exoskeleton under the hot lights: already red, it dispenses with the rouge.

A *maitre d'* with worm-thin moustache bows formally to Prezhki. The Chief holds up the palm of his hand to wave him off, beelines to the back room where P-R holds court, waits for the stationed waiter to peer in and announce him. It is six sharp and very little, if anything, is well.

P-R slouches in a padded chair big enough for the late Bill Taft. He is executing an enthusiastic assault on a hemorrhaging slab of prime rib, slicing boundaries into Texas-sized flesh as if he is his own League of Nations. A cigar smokes itself on the edge of a salad plate, democratically sharing the space with shreds of iceberg lettuce and chunks of imported bleu cheese. A pyramid of empty clamshells fills a bowl.

"Walter," P-R mumbles from a full mouth. He motions with his fork for Prezhki to take the only other chair, which sits across the large banquet table, lonely and categorically inferior. P-R eats European style; doesn't change silver from hand to hand, considers such highfalutin conceits a waste of time for a busy man.

Prezhki, more angry than humble at the moment, grabs the back of the smaller chair and brings it up alongside P-R's, falls back into it, and says, "I've got Chicken Little all in a huff back at the station. *I know it's falling*, I tell her, *but P-R's got a hard-on I've got to see to.*"

P-R barely arches an eyebrow, cuts a Hungary of prime from an Austria of fat. "You can still get the end piece," he says. "Blacker than a junkman. They call it the Mrs. O'Leary's Cow Cut."

"You know what kind of day it's been, P-R?"

"I have some idea. Eat. Then we'll talk."

"I don't have time to eat. Someone unlocked the asylum and all hell's breaking loose." He quickly catalogues the days trials.

"To say nothing of Chicken Little. I recommend the duck. The chicken was a bit dry last time the sky fell."

"Fuck you, P-R. I've got a job to do and I should be back at the station."

This gets the Mayor's attention. He puts down his fork and attends to his napkin. "*Fuck* me! Jeez, Walter, we *are* in a tiff. To what do we owe this uncharacteristic display of pique?"

Prezhki holds back; perhaps he has veered just a bit over the understood line. "Aw, g'wan, P-R! It's like Cicero during Prohibition out there. I don't have to tell you."

"No, you don't. I have all the sources I need. If I need you to tell me about naked loony tunes with their manhood in limbo, I'll add it to your job description. *Fuck me,* indeed! Enough to upset the gut of a sensitive man. Y'all sure you won't have anything? It's on me. Least I can do."

"Damn well is!" Prezhki leans forward, as if they're not alone in the room, places his hat on the table, splaying the flaps, absently gives the bowl of shells a little shake. "Phones haven't stopped ringing all day. I've got to get back."

"Let the chicken stew. Y'all want to avoid raw foul. And, you're entitled to a dinner break." He prepares the resumption of his meal, holds his knife and fork upright in his big fists. "Need you to do something for me."

"Am I talking to the clam shells?"

"If so, you have a skewed sense of your constituency."

"Cripes! Listen to yourself, P-R."

"Rarely do I listen to anyone else!"

Exasperated, Prezhky complains of "serious violations of law today."

"So I hear. Isn't that what the police are supposed be able to handle? Look, Walter, you're management, okay? No one, least of all me...and, don't worry about the commissioners, I'll take care of them...expects you do be out on every domestic, every missing poodle, every wino that falls asleep on the highway. See, a good manager surrounds himself with good people who can get the job done, thus freeing himself up for the superior burdens of wine and prime rib. Absent such competent underlings, he surrounds himself with a bunch of fools who can, at the very least, keep their mouths shut about how slipshod everything is."

"The hell you need, P-R? I don't have the luxury for this."

"I've got to see a man about a railroad tomorrow. In Uncas Falls. Thought I'd use my one stone economically, score a second bird in the process."

"A second bird? Or the same bird a second time? Or more?"

"That's not your affair, Walter. I want you to talk to someone at the railroad, Dispatching, or Employee Assignments, or whatever nomenclature they favor. Go down there yourself. Don't do this on the phone. I don't want every old biddy from here to Thebes knowing my business. I want you to see to it that a certain engineer is on a long shift tomorrow. Send him to the Gulf for a little salt air. Do him good. There may be a little tip on some real estate in it for y'all. Something up for grabs in the way of commercial property that just might cushion a man's old age."

"I don't want to do it. I'm *not* doing it."

"A matter of tense. You *will* be." P-R neatly places his utensils at either side of his plate. "Is this divorce, sweet heart? Irreconcilable differences?"

"I spend much of my time, much of my department's time, on poon runs for you. I even went up to check on the junkman, make sure he's on the up and up. Make sure you don't have to concern yourself with him. And most of the time, well...most of the time I *have* the goddamned time. But, see P-R, we have a situation right now. I don't know what tomorrow'll bring. And I have a responsibility to the job. I'm not your personal errand boy."

"You're not? I don't know the job descriptions in my own burg? You know, I could have the commission interviewing for chief by tomorrow. I could cut your pension down to the fat on this plate. We have a certain arrangement of operation, you and I, based on need, loyalty, gratitude, and certain facets of the facts of life that, while sometimes an embarrassment to discuss in mixed and cultured company, is...well, let's just say we all know where babies come from as well as we know the side best buttered on our morning toast, and the most propitiously kissed ass. So y'all went to see the junkman, on my account, did you? Well, I don't *know* of any junkman, Walter. You see, last Thursday, I was on the Flyer on my way down to The Capitol. I have the ticket stubs, a waiter who will say he remembers serving me, a legislator in my thrall who will recall meeting with me until the wee hours, in the interest of our shared love of public service, and a switchboard operator who overheard something about you driving down to Thebes Thursday night, parked right down there near the motor court by the viaduct, that there was some kind of exchange between you and some mystery woman who came down courtesy of an old colored man, perhaps the one you refer to, that you were seen shortly after at The Roadhouse, and after that, well, who knows? Because you certainly didn't go back to the office. Oh, and in case you figure you can outflank me on this, the wife of a certain engineer who you will get scheduled tomorrow and the next day, she spent the day at her sister's in Thebes. The sister will attest."

Prezhki feels ambushed, leans back in the chair and eyes P-R coldly. "So I'm the chump? This was all a setup from the beginning? Me driving you?"

"Y'all make it sound much more sinister than it is. I didn't exactly impregnate your officer's wife nine months ago so that he'd get the night off to join her for the birth. Wish I'd thought of it, though. Wish I had! But, you see, a smart man insures his investments. Don't y'all coppers call for back up once in a while?"

"So that's how it's going to be. I bust my keester for you, and that's how it's going to be."

"That's how it *is*! Tense again? What are you? Five? You've been around the block a few times. And you do nothing *for* me. You do it because your old lady likes an occasional bauble. Because your son throws a hell of a pigskin down there at the U but didn't have the academics to get in. Remember who wrote the reference, who had the pull. You do it because you don't have to walk the colored district in the dark with a nightstick on your belt. You do it because you have as much a sense of the order of things as I do, despite this charade of propriety. You know, Walter, I picked you for this job pretty much because you had a military background. Y'all knew rank. You knew how to take an order. Understood the natural hierarchy of things. But, see, we didn't have this conversation. What we did is, we shared a few clams, a sip of whatever this frog piss is supposed to be, and because I am a generous benefactor, as you well know, the commercial property I mentioned is still on the table along with the end cut of prime. And, Walter, as much as I love and respect y'all and will forever hold a certain admiration for your gumption and your decency, compromised as they are, I will expect you to see to it that, barring Armageddon between now and then, Casey Jones will be back at the throttle where he does his best work come the time. And the earth will keep on spinning in all its delicious debauchery, our compassionate president will put thousands to work mending the sky, there'll be a chicken little in every pot, the magic of modern medicine will defrost the naked guy's anaconda, and the TPD will continue its pussy run service for the Mayor. And you and I will be fast friends again, spinning yarns about Brother Shem, sucking at the breasts of our managerial good fortune, living the life, as it were, and serving the people. Because that's what makes it all go around. You sure I can't interest y'all in something to nibble?"

Prezhki is silent for some time while P-R resumes his meal. Then he says, "I get it from you. From the commissioners. From Shem, the pious son of a bitch! I won't be the patsy here. There will eventually be a line I will not cross. I don't know how long this nonsense can go on. I don't know."

"Well, I do. And I will let y'all know when it is over."

Prezhki retreats to headquarters, his tail snugly between his legs, his car door slashed, his blood boiling. A siren wails in the distance; he doesn't want to know.

In the morning P-R calls in Mrs. Brown, the part time typist, bids her take the interurban up to Uncas Falls within the hour, to proceed to the General Beauregard where a room will be reserved in the name of Della Cantrell, and to let her sister know what, if asked, she will be expected to say. *"Wear a veil or something on the car, something dark and concealed, sort of widow like, and take no rides from old colored men distracted from their junking."*

X

The Tishomingo Clarion-News
Sententia

Any long time reader of this journal will appreciate the fact that your editors, have often looked kindly upon the mutually beneficial relationship that this fair city shares with our premier industry, the Uncas Falls, Tishomingo & Gulf Railroad. We look upon such symbiosis as our maxim and have always received the same consideration from the company. Furthermore, we view it as our good fortune to have been served these many years through fair rates, efficiency, employment benefits for our citizens, outlets for our industry, quality passenger traffic, and an active participation by the company in the civic vitality of this community. It is, therefore, with some regret, that we find ourselves in the unfortunate position of opposing the street running extension plan being promoted by the esteemed T. Rail Ferrous, UFT&G Northern Division Superintendent. Mr. Ferrous is a reasonable man, an astute executive, and possesses the utmost reputation for ethics, decency, and intelligence. We trust, therefore, that he will attentively consider these musings, and respect, as sister city neighbors, our insights into, what we hope is, but a temporary lapse of good will.

First, a bit of background. The concept of street running was accepted practice fifty years ago. It allowed the railroad to route trains down city streets and benefited industries along the way. Several local firms constructed manufacturing facilities along the routes chosen, employing tens, if not hundreds, of our worthy laborers. But those were different times. Tishomingo was in its infancy, draymen with horse operations were sufficient to the task of hauling our then judicious volume of freight, the population along the route was sparse, and the city infrastructure was of such minimal proportions so as not to demand a considerable tax base. It seemed, at the time, perfectly reasonable to allow the railroad to run down the middle of a city street, for which the railroad need pay no taxes on a right of way it operated, but did not own.

Today, we find ourselves in a different era. The population has increased tenfold since our partnership with the line began, the impact of the freight trains on greatly increased auto traffic has reached critical proportions, the growing population has put more and more citizens, including a large number of children, in harm's way, and the coal exhaust from the locomotives has become a health hazard. To say nothing of our burgeoning freight traffic which causes the railroad to be an almost constant occurrence in our streets. Still, though leased in perpetuity, the line provides the municipality not one penny in annual revenue.

The railroad will no doubt argue that the indirect benefits accrued by the city through such operations are considerable. We agree, and are willing to hold the line as it is. However, it is brought to this paper's attention that our City Council has been asked to consider an amendment to our agreement. Superintendent Ferrous, we are told, has asked that august body to extend this unsightly and inconvenient traffic seven tenths of a mile further through a wholesome residential tract inviting to our better class of Negro; businessmen and working folks, many of the latter employed as porters and dining car staff for the railroad itself. The purpose of this new extension would be to connect with the now world famous Lone Arrow Brewery, whose output has snowballed in the last two years.

For the reasons mentioned above, it is this paper's position that such an extension would be detrimental to the quality of life along its route, For very little extra cost to the enterprise, Lone Arrow's fine new fleet of trucks could easily transport the product to the freight station, there to be loaded onto the cars. It is not our intention to detract from the railroad's profits, but in this case, we believe that the detrimental effect of extended street running would far outweigh the economic benefits to either the railroad or the brewery. In fact, considering the easy flexibility and cushioned ride of pneumatic transport on our modern macadam, we look forward to the day when the existing street running spur is recognized for the anachronism it is, and abandoned entirely. Barring this, it is not difficult to foresee a not too distant future when the railroad requests additional extensions, bringing even our finer white neighborhoods into close contact with noisome and polluting machinery.

We urge Mr. Ferrous and his representatives to join us in this friendly discourse, one, we feel, is to be had amongst the fond members of a happy family, and that our Mayor and Council will take a firm stand for the well being of their constituencies.

PASADENA

I

TAYLOR LURCHES, SUCKS AIR, PRESSES HIS back to the porch grill like batter to a waffle iron, stays to sizzle in the summer night heat. His bag of Church's fried chicken, having safely survived the vinyl ride on the commodious bench seat, spirals to the walkway; chicken crust cracking audibly; crackling, popping like corn, crushed Styrofoam, rat-a-tat-tat.

He is up on the steps, so that the neighbor, nearly as tall, seems much shorter, and Taylor looks down upon the shaved head, luminescent in the porch floods, the broken bend of nose, and a shapely ear pierced thrice with one big cross and two small in a lobed Golgotha-fashion statement. The neighbor wears the same neat fur frame around his lips that one in three LA County males wear, a Lakers hoodie, hood down, the sleeves chopped off with the disdain of an angry *mohel*, and great acres of thigh-length shorts that could accommodate both men at once. His tattoos, Maori-like, breed down his body, a virtual inscribed barbershop mirror of image upon infinite image. It is *him*, that urban terror, the wife beater, the child abuser, the guy just two slaps and a *BITCH, CUNT!* away from nine one one.

"Whoa, dude," the neighbor says quietly, concerned. He has a habit of jutting a lower lip when things seem out of whack. "Didn't mean to yank your chain." He bends down and picks up the bag of wounded legs and thighs, hands the broken bird back over to Taylor.

Taylor catches his breath; returns it to the eco-system with a long hiss — one pungent with industrial exhaust — generously lets it go. "Oh, that. I'm...I'm just all fingers."

"Sir?"

"I mean thumbs. Not fingers. Thumbs."

"Got it. Thumbs *are* fingers, I guess. Blake," he says.

"Excuse me?"

"Next door. Blake." He offers a hand. Taylor taps it as if he has been offered raw liver, still warm from its filtration assignment inside a late bison.

"Taylor."

"Yeah, I know," Blake says, handing over a package in a priority envelope. A timetable, a hat badge, a TOILET 5 CENTS sign from the Cotton Belt? "I brought your mail, sir. We get your shit all the time." His voice is a bit high pitched, a tone softer than the blunt chop of his words. "Usually I just throw it through the

149

bars here, kind a like they feed tigers at the zoo, but, well, I heard you drive up, so…I mean, I don't know how they hire at the old USPS these days, but it ain't what it was when my old man was a carrier. What ever happened to the fuckin' civil service exam? There should be some kind a reading test or something, huh? Here's a thought, a reading test in *English!* Match the numbers. Two to two, one to one, that-a-boy. I mean, do you believe this shit? I get your mail two, three times a week. I don't know who gets mine but it shows up eventually after visiting a few other families. Last week, I got a letter *for* some dude in Rhode Island. I don't even know where the fuck Rhode Island is to tell the truth. I never been on the Gulf Coast. There is not one thing on this envelope, not one number, not one word, that resembles my address. I'm all about responsibility, right? Good citizen. I think, *What would I want to happen if one a my letters goes to Rhode Island?* I'm down with *do unto others,* 's'what I'm saying. So I run it over to the station and ask to speak to the super, who, a course, is just another jerk, see?…Did I say *jerk?* Some mouth I got. I meant, *clerk.* 'Cause when they see you coming through the door they like just pass the nametag around to whoever's turn it is. It's, like, *Hey, LaTrisha, you up to face down some dickhead who thinks he ought a be getting his own mail?* Like, *Duh!* So, like it's really worth all the effort tryin'a do good to some poor fucker in Rhode Island whose wondering what happened to his Publisher's Clearing check, just so some skank in uniform can tell me that sometimes the letters get stuck together. I'm all, *So, unstuck 'em, bitch,* only that takes a little effort. A little common fucking sense. The six hundred people in line since before the last postal rate hike are pissed because someone's helping *me* when they been waiting like it's the friggin' DMV, or some shit. I want to tell them, *This ain't exactly help, people!* Half a these a-holes are waiting in line because they don't know they can buy a fucking stamp from the machine! Christ, civilians are stupid! No offense, but you know what I mean, dude. Anyway, so I guess I'm getting up on the volume dial a little, like who wouldn't with such lame-ass service? You reach a point, right? Mother fuckin' bottom line. You remember that flick, what's it's name, with that actor, you know, where this news guy on TV says…not *Anchorman,* old school, much older, saw it on Turner Classics, the guy in the flick, says he's so mad he ain't gonna take no more. Anyway, this manager-d'jury, 's'up in my fuckin' face close enough t'smell her breakfast grits, says to me, in this real serious cop voice, *I'm gonna have to ask you to step away from the counter, sir.* Here I am, still a little rusty on my Bethesda-rigged leg, and some raggedy-ass with a GED, who'd be washing cars in South Central if it weren't for that confirmative action shit, is telling me to *stand down, sir.* It's the uniform see. You take and put these little, powerless pukes in a uniform and this is what happens. Power. *Pow*-er. Power to the People. Every last fucking one a them. Power to the Little People!"

He slams fist to palm on *pow.* His lips are moist and he sniffs repeatedly mid-sentence.

"They fuckin' OD on it, the power. You see, in certain cultures, certain 'hoods, dressing one a the natives up in a uniform is like giving fire water to an Indian, you know what I mean? We're not talking epaulets and stars and brass buttons. Whatta they got? Little red tie cut like the one the Colonel wears when he's *smilin' down on ya* from the chicken sign, the blue shirt...or is it a white shirt? Is it a fucking blue shirt with white stripes or a fucking white shirt with blue stripes is what I wanna know, 'cause when they put these little pin stripes so close together you can't tell which is the background and which is the stripes. Who designs this shit anyway? You following me, dude?" He says it with conviction: the dude had better.

"Sure. Happens all the time." Taylor seems a dude who has read the dude job description. He doesn't really know why he is standing on his breached porch, clutching his convalescing fowl, feeling the heat and the juice wheezing from it in aromatic distress, not at all sure what he has just affirmed. Moreover, he fears his dinner is cooling, so that it will taste like an arm in a cast when he finally chomps down.

"What happens all the time?" It snaps out edgy, like the bite of a Coke Classic, but with a rum-pinch more attitude.

"The mail," Taylor justifies. "Stripes? I don't know."

"Yeah, well, probably not the million bucks you been waiting for, but, anyway..." He points to the package. "We've been here going on a year so, well, I thought it's time I just come by and say *Hey*." He gives a little unconscious salute.

"Hey it is," says Taylor, his hand possessively tight on the retrieved chicken bag, hoping that this discussion of things postal is about to come to a close without a round of shot gun pellets and a frantic visit from the swat team. The porch has taken on a deep fried aroma, like Georgia at breakfast-time.

But Blake the Terrible has no intention of leaving. His squinty red eyes — the right lid slightly uplifted as if he is taking Taylor in through a rifle sight — appraises Taylor's little San Quentin: all black wrought iron and missile silos and early warning technology. "So it's like 'Twenty-Four' in there, CT-fucking-U!"

Taylor doesn't know the reference, but puts it in context. "Oh, this old stuff. There was a time when the neighborhood kind of, you know...So I sprung for this setup. I'll dismantle it one of these days."

"Whattaya got in there? Sweatshop full a illegals smuggled out a Nam in containers? Sir?"

"No. Just..." he hesitates — what's come over him? — "trains." It is almost a relief to say. He rarely tells anybody. There is a certain clandestine element to his passion. There is to most people's.

"Trains? You get them out in trains? From Nam?"

"No, no. I *have* trains."

"What, like Thomas-the-fucking-Tank trains?"

Taylor feels a bit let down, betrayed even. "Wouldn't interest you," he says, a step back, a kind of retreat.

"You know what interests me? You some kind a clearvoyant?" Blake says. "Anyway, what I really came over for, well, in addition to the mail, you know, is, I wanted to apologize, sir."

"I don't understand."

"The noise. You know."

"It's the sound from the trains. I'm sorry."

"*My* noise. Our noise. Me and them." He nods back toward his house.

"These old houses are pretty solid. I don't hear much of anything."

"Nice a you to say. Anyway," he cups his mouth, offers a familiar wink, "Melissa's kind of a…you know, screamer."

"The baby?"

"Melissa's my wife!" The edge has taken on a new sharpness, ends in an admonitory precipice.

"O-o-o-oh! Like I said, lath and plaster, textured stucco. And with the air on…"

"She says I watch TV too loud. I mean, I don't think so. What's the purpose a surround if you can't hear it, right? But I guess that's a guy sort of thing. Fidelity. Anyway, I'm sorry if the TV gets on you nerves."

"No, it's fine."

"Melissa, she's alright, see, but she can get a bit…hysterical. Women! You gotta be a fuckin' chickologist to figure them out. The hot ones, like Melissa, are the worst. A little heifer with maybe two or three chins, she learns to tread water. I mean, who else would have her? But the hotties, they think they got your nuts on ice behind the bonbons, and who else'd have *you*? You know. She has this post pardon thing. Trouble dealing. She's kind a a whiner, Melissa. I mean, what's she got to do all day that's so fucking taxing? I'll tell you about taxing, dude. I'm in construction."

"I've seen the truck." It has double tire sets in the back and built-in metal cabinets along the side and a bumper sticker that says, FUCK YOU. Nothing else, just a sort of *hey there, you,* generic, all purpose, FUCK YOU.

"Licensed contractor, sir. Your ever need another bathroom, kitchen remodel, update some a this TJ iron crap you got all over…I got these guys, half of 'em don't speak a word beyond *lunche*…You'd think they'd have their own fuckin' *palabra* for something they do every day. I mean, if you're spending your days in prayer outside a the Home Depot, you'd think you'd wise up, learn the local lingo, and move up the career ladder to KFC or Wendy's or something else with a little class. Not this day-to-day shit for whatever the traffic'll bear. I gotta tell ya, bro, I ain't talkin' the hottest peppers in the *enchilada* by a long shot. So with busting my balls every day trying to get some illegal to understand the dif between a fir two-by-four and a sheet a drywall, and doing my books, payroll, using today's down on tomorrow's material, I mean, dude, this is one fucking margin kind a business, and I got some soccer mom whose off to the airport to pick up the rellies from Nebraska and needs the spare room completed like fucking yesterday so the Beverly-fucking-Hillbillies have a place to bed down…Well, shit, Taylor, dude, I come home for a little righteous R and R, you know what I mean? And *she's* burning down like the WTC, and will *I* get some take-out and change the little shit machine? I don't get woman sometimes. Sometimes they're like a whole different animal from us, sir."

"True enough," Taylor agrees, really agrees, trying to be congenial and hoping this will all come to an end soon, before this guy implodes, before they both become news at eleven: *This is Stan Chambers. I'm at the site of Taylor Bedskirt's house where an Iraqi War veteran imploded this evening only hours ago. Back to Eyewitness News.*

He thinks of Helen, the big EMD diesel humping her Buick, the screech of the world's largest chalk on the world's largest blackboard, the too easy crunch of metal, the pop of airbags, the woman's sudden trip through the safety glass; there is a stink of blood and seared flesh, Valero hundred octane, and of course, Church's fried chicken, and he hears Helen and her big sedan thump down the track like sage brush stuck on a bumper.

"Fuckin' A, it's true! They're different from us."

Taylor has switched channels to lighter fare: Cory Ann. "Yes, they are, they really are. Isn't that the attraction?"

"I don't mean the obvious. T and A. The plus side." He does an obscene finger slide with his hands. "With, I mean, the way their heads work. And how they deal and how they don't deal. That's why, on Super Tuesday, my buck was on the brother. My buck, not my vote. I'm not one a those Hollywood liberals, see. Pink's not my favorite color. But if a woman can't manage a kid smaller than your average Coho while she watches Oprah, how the hell's she gonna deal with Osama bin Laden and the rest a those crazy camel fuckers? I know what they're like, the A-*rabs*, sir. Been there, done that. Senator from New York, okay. Who gives a fuck! But it takes some balls to bomb shit outta people. So, I'm sorry if you sometimes hear Melissa come unglued and shit. A chick thing, 's all."

"Haven't heard a thing."

"Thing is, sir, ERA and burn your bra and all that, but I lost a knee for her right to sit on her ass and sing 'Rockabye' t'the rug rat, and I think, considerin' what I put out, I deserve a little fuckin' understanding. You wanna see my knee? Only thing I own not made by gooks. See, we were on R&R in the Green Zone. Safest spot in town, right? Me an' a couple jokers'er playin' Chinese checkers. The one that you play with marbles on a big Yid star. Y'ain't a Jew, are ya, Taylor?"

"Me? No. Not Chinese either."

"You making a joke, sir?" Blake eyes seem to transform with the topic, the mood. His eyes become deep-blue wells in blood stained white, wide and gravitational, blinkless. Taylor wonders if he has lids.

"Me? I don't think so. No."

"Chink checkers'er kinda like this war, see. Ya get t'jump over things you're not supposed to take out. Pretty soon they're on your flank or firin' up your ass. And like marbles, they all look alike. At least, the marbles are different colors. Anyway, we're kickin' back with the game, bullshitting about pussy which the back-ass-ward Hajjis ain't discovered yet, safe as money in the bank, when we hear this mega-ass whistle, like, *Wheeeeeeeeee,* and one a the guys says, *This sucks,* 'cause we got a pretty good idea what's next, and then the roof falls in and the *this sucks* guy just up and disappears, just fuckin' gone from the planet, and next thing I know I'm walking on a crutch with a bottle drippin' down my arm in Krautsylvania, where, I can tell ya, pussy has long been considered necessary t' the normal state of affairs. Civilized mother fuckers, the polka barrelers."

Blake's feet are shuffling huge lumpy Adidas that look like Detroit concept cars. "Tell ya the truth, Taylor, I know I can get a little loud too, on an off day. I got a lot on my mind. Saw some shit in the desert I don't even want to talk about. And when they decide to send you state side because a dude ain't as good in pieces…It's hard to adjust. Some a us function. Make a living. Others camp out on the streets. What I'm trying to tell you, dude, is…occasionally I can let the brewskie get the better a me. Not intentionally see, I'm all about sobriety, sir. But sometimes, you know, you knock down one or two in the evening to loosen up, and shit, like before you know it, Mr. Bud or Mr. Coors has snuck up on you, ambushed your ass, and you're fucking gone. And then with the kid and Melissa are all, *boo hoo, boo hoo,* in the fourth quarter of a whine contest…Sometimes a switch flips. Sometimes some bad shit comes down. Sometimes a guy gets loud. Sir. Whattaya gonna you do, huh?"

"It's really very quiet here."

"Yeah, yeah, that's white a you. But I, like…I'm on the step where I got to say I'm sorry to someone, and here you are. So…"

Taylor looks down at the step, the concept shoes, says, "Thank you." He sees that Blake is constructed on a slight tilt; his feet are not exactly parallel.

"I guess." Blake wipes his nose with the back of his hand.

"My dinner's getting cold."

Sniff. Sniff, sniff. "Shouldn't eat that shit anyway. Look, didn't mean to hog your evening, sir. Just go on in and nuke it or something and have yourself a good one."

"I'll do that," says Taylor, turning and aiming his keys.

Blake hasn't left. "Trains, huh?"

"That's right."

"Can I see?"

"See what?"

"The choo choos."

"Oh, no, place is a mess."

"Everywhere I go's a mess. That's why they call me. I've seen people livin' in shit you wouldn't believe."

"It's just that…that I've got a ways to go before it's all presentable."

"Some other time then?"

"Of course. Yes. Some other time when things are up and running."

"I'll hold you to that, sir."

"My sister's never even been here."

"You let me know."

"My girlfriend."

Neglect blankets the layout like smog. Engines hibernate in their roundhouses, a minor freight derailment in the Coast Yards has gone unnoticed, and most of the rolling stock sits still as tombstones in long furrows of silence. Elsewhere, trolleys are stranded mid-route, logs in flumes defy gravity, funiculars are forgotten on precipitous grades. Commerce is unwound like a Regulator Clock. Nothing moves, nothing sounds. No gears ratchet, no iron wheels whine on curves. There are no chugging compressors, no buzzing blades at the mills, no stamping of ore.

Taylor is here and Taylor is elsewhere, all at the same time. Taylor is suffering a passion deficit, as if passion is finite; has withdrawn from the layout and invested in Cory Ann. Lazily, he totes his bag of chicken, drags a thumb over a section of rail, considers how out of scale the dust has grown, gray as silt on a Dust Bowl ghost town. His compact world seems dry, brittle, vulnerable: there is a plague upon the land. A city hall sits tented by a web, a fraternity of gigantic silver fish have crawled growling and salivating from Tokyo harbor and have devoured the fabric awnings from streets of shops in a country burg. A theater marquee has capitulated onto an open Stutz, crushing the driver; there is no rescue, the ambulance unmanned, the fire brigade stiff as props, glued a-slide the pole and to the engine house floor. The sun has stopped. The moon is hidden. The visual memories of stars no longer there are no longer there. A Ford Tri-motor is frozen mid-flight. Not a church bell chimes.

The maker's thoughts are elsewhere. The bag of Church's careens into a steeple — *Enquirer* headline: GIANT CHICKEN PARTS, ALL DARK MEAT, TOPPLE CHURCH TOWER, UNDERWRITERS CALL IT ACT OF GOD. *In need of some perking up,* Taylor concedes, off to the microwave to radiate his dinner.

The drawbridge has been left up, cars still hugging the grade awaiting the passage of a ship that never comes down the South Fork of the Mourning Cloak River, and the air is mysteriously devoid of smoke. Even the naked lady who perpetually sunbathes — day and night, through all the seasons, in times without time, tanning through the primordial void, come home with Him like take-out in a bag, a thin terry cloth between her perfect plastic skin and the Adirondack lounger, on the bluff below a cottage much more modest than she, overlooking the white turbulence of the Shenanagalia near the bait shop and filling station known as Um Bridge; the brief speck of woman Taylor has endowed with black pubic hair from the tiniest of camel brushes in his jeweler-steady hands — has tipped from her chaise, and lays ass-up on face and bent knees. Taylor barely notices. The boys stuck to the knotholes — an HO scale knothole is 0.5833332 millimeters across, give or take — remain pruriently unfazed. One might be thinking, *I spy with my tiny eye.* Taylor has a knot hole of his own of late, a looking glass of wonder upon his own naked lady, vaginal hole through knot hole, his own barber shop infinity in the house of mirrors, an obsession to sublimate his obsession.

He sets the irradiated pieces of dismantled hen on a plate, sets the plate down on the work table in the back room, gazes over what he calls Taylor's Yard with its track upon track of freight and passenger cars, customized kits and scratch built, meticulously aged and weathered, some made to sag as if from years of wear, all of it languishing in the dim light of a gooseneck where he intends to eat. Locomotives, upturned, await cleaning, their dangling pilot trucks provocatively splayed.

But Taylor has left the air guns full, the soft lens paper packets unopened; precious brushes have dried, the lids of tiny paint bottles left upturned, leaching colors with names like Dust, Rust, Grime. Parts are scattered without design; hand rails, headlamps, under frame bracings, brake wheels. Several people and a dog are piled in a charnel house heap. The table abounds with powdered pastels and sealers, X-acto knives with triangular blades, lengths of rail, palettes of ties and matching spikes; neglected tools surround it all, compressors, clamps, tweezers, small precision drill presses and micro sanders, an array of needle nose pliers ajar like hungry alligators, and a lathe so unequivocal as to be able to hone post newels one sixteenth of an inch in diameter.

Normally, Taylor is more exacting: dust motes and cob webs are instantly vanquished, insects sprayed or crushed, engines oiled, cleaned and righted, the sun and moon aglow and in motion, the senses entertained with the sights and sounds of the macro-life. And food is never, ever allowed on the worktable. His is a pristine environment, as if he is nurturing sensitive cultures, sterilized down to particulate matter.

The devil here is truly in the details. Water ripples and foams, neon signs flicker, the grit and cinders nearly tangible to the nostrils. Dirt roads develop ruts, buildings burn and stand for months as charred reminders of Taylor's imaginative talents, trunks of great pines actually get transferred from logging line to mill and are stacked as boards on staked flats and trundled off to lumberyards in places like Conniption and Glasswort City. Even the shameless hussy in the Adirondack proudly displays fuchsia nipples meticulously Taylor-installed by dipping the tip of a needle into the paint. When off of her knees and righted on her towel, she will gladly offer them up for your appraisal.

But this evening, he faces the distractions of the neighbor, who he may need to inform on some day. Who, on another level, is not as sinister as imagined. Just a guy with things on his mind: an unstable wife, the stress of a child who — who knows? — may be colicky; money worries; and memories of things unspeakable. Perhaps, not a bad guy at all, victim himself of lapses, struggling with personal demons to stay on the wagon. A guy tolerant enough to want to see the trains. *Well, we'll see about that, after some sprucing up.*

And then there is Cory Ann, stamped on his forehead like the mark of a ticket dater. In the exactitude of his engineer's mind, he charts her topography as if it is a *papier-mâché* rendering of herself, of places he has touched, the elevations he has meticulously measured, breaking her down into precise quadrangles of grades and depressions, each exquisite detail swirled in successive contour lines, until he has mapped all of her angles, imagined a virtual archive of intersection, symmetry, porosity, a statistical analysis of terrain both firm and elastic, cool-dry and warm-moist, of glazed nail, velvet down, abrupt crevasses that morph to the touch, living slot canyons that threaten flash floods, that quake from light abrasion and open palm, the wisp of tongue, a tracing finger. Rather than needle points of nipple, Taylor surveys great pop-ups the shape of pencil erasers and as big as pinkies and stiffly resistant to the brush of papillae.

Taylor has never let his mind run so rampant. Could it be that Cory Ann has parts Helen lacked? He remembers no firmness about Helen, no cushion-soft gift of flesh. She had no fragrance, no sounds, no indescribable fine red line between ecstatic convulsion and the edge of pain, no sense of adventurous probing, no memory of experience, no litany of tricks. Helen had an angular, desert topography, sparse and forewarning, a plague of dry sediment, cracked and parched. He was told that the collision had been bloody, which surprised him: he hadn't considered her so sanguine.

❈

He wanders about the house of the layout, checking locks, turning off lights, economically tightening faucets. Peering out his bedroom window, he sees coach lamps and Mexican wrought iron fixtures lighting porches, blue light winking out of the windows at Mrs. Gettzleman's, the Devore's, and a massive aqua shadow from next door. The bass is thumping from Blake's surround. Taylor hears it clearly, *thump a dump, thump a dump*, as if all the tweeters have been recalled, all the mid-range lost in the insulation of the walls. There is no screaming tonight, no imprecations, no *cunts*, no *bitches*, not a thwack or ka-pow; just the homogenized domestic quiet of a young family of three enjoying the wholesome Blue Ray definition of Rambo and the bump, bump, bump of the bad guys going down and bleeding out.

He can't sleep. He has tried the usually soothing video of SP cab forward's battling snow on Sierra slopes, attempted to detail a half finished general store for Snowqualawana Crossroads, assembled a sundae of low sugar vanilla smothered in low sugar chocolate syrup and lite Reddi-whip for which he finds no appetite.

He falls upon the bed but can't even out the sheets, can't keep the covers tucked, get the proper angle of pillow under his distracted head. He practices his breathing. He tosses and turns, gets up to urinate, once, twice, three times. He listens without reward for Blake to open up on hysteric Melissa, snap a rib or two, rip an ear ring from a lobe, drag her around the house by the hair, and then he'd call nine one one, for sure this time, good guy or not, damaged war hero or not. So what if he wants to see the trains? What's that got to do with rage? With demons?

His mind wanders to Helen. She is there leering over his shoulder, listening for the commotion, note pad in hand, penciling down tips from the trained Marine, looking to add a little flourish to the flying waffle iron she had once directed at Taylor, to the hair dryer cord she had whipped across his thighs, to the locomotive she had threatened to hurl — but knew better, understood the limits of her husband's passivity — instead settled on a Pullman sleeper and then sped off to the Metrolink where, it turns out, locomotives were hurtling, and Helen found herself spread thin.

The phone is in his hand; how it got there he can only imagine. He taps it with all ten fingers, puts it down, picks it up, puts it down. The wireless understands his need, climbs off its cradle, begins to hum; nothing catchy, a monotone, a single note stretched beyond available breath. It crawls ever so slowly up his belly, careful not to disrupt sensitive hairs, switchbacks across his broad chest, nestles cozily up to his ear, and dials itself.

"Wha…?"

"Cory Ann? You there?"

"Jesus, sexy, the fuck time's it?" Her voice is husky, dampened in insulating phlegm and weariness.

For a moment, he is unsure. Considers hanging up. "It's me. Taylor."

"Know it's you, Feathers." The nickname has evolved from Tail, to Tail Feathers, to this. "Almost three in the morning! Y'okay?"

"I'm fine. I was missing you."

"I was sleeping. You outta try it."

"Cory Ann."

"Mmmmmm."

"You want to marry me?"

"————————————"

"Cory *Ann*? Do you? Want to marry me?"

"How come? Y'ain't pregnant, are ya?"

"It's Taylor," he says again.

"We talk 'bout this another time?"

"Can we talk about it now?"

"Jeez. Hotcakes, where's the fire, huh?"

"Can we?"

"Gotta take a breath, okay? Gotta take a piss. Can we talk 'bout it after?"

"I'll miss you."

"Christ Taylor! You drunk? I'm just gonna pee an' I'll be right back!"

He hears her walk, grunt, pee, flush. It is an eternity. Rivers erode to canyons.

"Are you mad at me?" he asks.

"Yeah. Actually."

"But will you marry me anyway?"

There is a long pause. "Taylor?"

"Uh huh."

"You're…like *serious?*"

"I think so."

"Ya *think* so?"

"Yep."

"Yep, ya think so?"

"Will you?"

"No."

"Why not?"

"It's three'n'a fucking morning! I gotta poison dickheads at seven. Go to sleep, Taylor."

"I can't. I'm horny."

"Not a reason t'spill for a ring. Take two aspirins, beat off, an' call me in the morning."

"I miss you, Snowy." The nickname is from Phoebe Snow; not the singer, the train — the same place Phoebe Snow the singer got it.

"Yeah, me too. Come in for breakfast an' I'll see if we can't get the greaser t'fuck up your arteries."

"Don't marry anyone else."

"Between now an' the morning rush! Won't even pick up the phone."

Click! Definitely, CLICK!

At seven thirty the next morning, Xochitl and Cuatémoc, the wife and husband miniature Mayan mow and blow squad — laid end to end they total but nine linear feet, with names so un-Mayan only Mel Gibson could get them this wrong — are patrolling the corner lot with space packs on their backs, rearranging leaves without exactly removing them from the property, and sending up great clouds of dust and pollen and fuel stench like Meso-American volcanoes. The lawn is mostly crabgrass and dandelions. Bleary eyed, Taylor staggers out onto the porch, their check in one hand, a Grand Trunk Western mug in the other.

The drapes part across the street and an ancient eye takes his measure.

He is in time to be discovered by Blake, surgically attached to his I-pod. Melissa is snuggled up under his substantial protective Semper Fi shoulder, safe from Tripolitan corsairs and Mexican cadets out to die for Chapultepec. They are out with the baby for some quality time, a stroll in the warming sun, the homey smell of blower emissions and car exhausts that are so binding for a young family and make wholesome pabulum for the young one.

"Hey, Taylor, chill for a sec." Blake gives Melissa a reassuring nuzzle on her frazzled blond strands, and she takes the stroller home over rumpled sidewalks tortured by the roots of the pepper tree.

Blake comes up on the porch, his Redskins thermos to his lips. "See the trains?"

"Heavens, no! There is some sprucing up to do. Quite a bit, actually. More than I thought." Taylor is sorry he has mentioned the trains to Blake.

Blake sits down on the steps. He invites Taylor to do the same, as if the property had just changed hands. Up and down the street, sprinklers are sucking Owens Valley dry. The men sit like gargoyles guarding the walk.

"Private kind a guy, huh?"

"I guess."

Blake holds up his drink. "Gatorade," he explains.

"Coffee," Taylor says in return.

"So, dude, bachelor huh?"

"Widower."

"Oh, that's too bad."

"No. Actually not."

"I get ya. You wanna talk about it?"

"I don't think so."

"I think we're gonna be fine, Melissa and me. Marriage Encounter. I'm looking into it. Melissa has agreed to see someone about some anti-depressants. Not like the ones that zombie you out or nothing like that, just something to take the ripples out, you know."

"I'm looking into getting married again."

"No shit! One of them Harvey Girls like in that old movie?"

"I think a Harvey Girl would be quite old."

"Just pullin' your watch chain, dude. You get used to that kind a shit in Allahwallastan. Only way to keep sane, the back and forth, you know. Even the bitches get into it. We had this one hard-ass lesbo sergeant could make your nuts shrivel before she even opened her mouth. 'Cause you knew whatever it was she was about to say was gonna lay some grunt lower than a raghead lookin' up at a smart bomb. You must a been in Nam, huh? What was that shit like? The jungle rumble? The fragging?"

"I don't know. I didn't have to go."

"How come? You weren't one a them hippie dippie fuckin' Jane Fondettes, were ya? Run off to Canada with all the other queens?"

"No, nothing like that. I was in school."

"What? Takin' over the admin' building? Growin' maryjane in planter boxes on your dorm window?"

"I lived at home. Right here, actually. I've always lived here. My brother-in-law says I'm apolitical."

"A political what? That's the question, right?"

"A political nothing. I'm not interested in politics. I don't get it."

"Well, nobody gets it. So fucking what? You're country needs you, you show up. That's the way it was in my house. The old man was Navy. His old man's old man learned to water board Filipinos after kicking Spanish ass. Nothin' knew under the hot tropical sun. School didn't have nothin' to do with it." He stands up, waves his thermos down at Taylor, removes the tiny headphones from his ears. "I sure hope you're not one a those faggot liberals, dude, who think all Saddam had in the old arsenal was a copy a the <u>Commi-sutra</u> and an inflatable, virgin fuck doll to practice his great love for all things American. I sure hope you're not. Later."

Taylor stays affixed to the porch. He toasts the spy across the street with his coffee. Xochi and Cuatémoc are grinning hopefully. They have dragged the trash and the recycling out to the curb and are wasting time in the hope that the *huero grande, pinche cabrón* will remember his obligations.

II

"SO, DID YOU THINK IT OVER?" he asks. "Get proposals eight times a day, sweetie. Hard t'even get'em t'stick to the faces, let alone, give'em consideration. Want any a these here, punkin? I can't eat it all, petite li'l thing I am."

They have agreed to meet for a picnic supper in the Arroyo Seco, snaking rural gash straddling the near-western edge of urban Pasadena and serving as demarcation, in lieu of the ever-so-popular wall, to keep out the undocumented riffraff from Eagle Rock and Highland Park and other less seemly working class districts of LA. It is a bit of the San Gabriels brought down to earth; from snow, to chaparral, to the train yards that supplied the train that bent Helen's car like a horseshoe and quartered Helen like USDA prime at the abattoir.

Famous people have lived here and near: the Anheuser Busches, Upton Sinclair, the chewing gum Wrigley's, the rake and ethnographer Charlie Loomis, Jackson Brown, and a Gamble from Proctor and___. The slopes are crowned by old money castles and Greene brother's craftsmans — local river rock, dark shingles, and beams overhanging sleeping porches in which to enjoy the mild, therapeutic nights. The Santa Fe main line to Chicago once went through here — now in a smaller scale impersonation performed by light rail. The trestles remain. Route Sixty-six roughly paralleled the tracks, but no more. Gone too is the Ostrich Farm, the Pacific Electric red cars, the suburban artist's utopia. Present is the Jet Propulsion Labs, a concrete channel that passes as a river in this domesticated part of the country, the Rose Bowl with its acres of parking flats, three freeways — one being the very first — a museum of old houses towed from places where they were no longer welcome, stucco apartments and ramshackle bungalows. Also, of course, an expanding gallery of graffiti is curated by the local talent: tagger posses, budding Riveras and Kahlos, bangers, *cholos*, and wannabes: any twelve year old who can get someone else to access the spray can cage at the local True Value Hardware.

"I never met anybody like you." He says this with a straight face; for him, it is not derivative.

"Don't think ya ever met anybody else at all. This shit ever work for ya? Corny movie lines? Jee-*zuz!* Ya can't be as out of it as ya act. Looky here, Feather, this marriage thing ya got 'n'your head, it's real sweet. God knows this ol' gal's flattered. But such a thing comes with a price. More'n'eatin' an'spoonin' which is about the extent a our relationship t' now. Don't know shit about each other."

She has brought a roll of paper towels guaranteed to withstand tsunamis, and something lemon-scented in a spray bottle. She scrubs the bird shit from the concrete table, sets out paper plates and plastic ware, the cheap white kind designed so that the tines always break off at the least threat of resistance. Un-bagged is a Styrofoam box with chicken fried steak for him and a mélange of Vons mayo salads in half pound cartons for her: egg, potato, pasta, chicken with celery and onion. There are assorted olives. Two brews canned in Colorado are popped and sweating their asses off like good blue collar drinks.

He ponders her last remark, rubs a palm over the thin veil of sweat on his brow. "What's to know?"

"Well, 'f'ya weren't born since the weekend, I'd figure a bunch. I never been t'your place, never met none a your people. We ain't even t' the stage we can fart in each other's company 'thout denyin' who done it."

"You want to fart? Fart." He is relieved to think he has discovered a solution to the current dilemma.

"Well, that's about the most tolerant thing a fella ever said t'me. Look, ya don't know me, Taylor. Maybe I ain't exactly the delicate flower ya think I am."

"I don't think you're a flower. I think you're sexy. I think...I think we have a great time together. I think you have gotten into my head and I can't get you out. I think you make great spaghetti. And you make me feel good. When I'm with you, anyway."

"There's the hitch, huh?"

"If we were married..."

"Speakin' a hitches!"

"...we could be together all the time and I'd be happy all the time."

Behind them, in the casting pond, a *sharpei* mix is playing in the water, as if it is not wrinkled enough. A couple is making out on a blanket under an oak. A Frisbee sails from nowhere, is lost with a thwack in dry brush.

"Nope," she says. "See, now there's the rub. Ya wouldn't, 'cause sometimes I'm a pit bull bitch. Sometimes I don't wanna be'th nobody, not even my own self. Sometimes I need my space. Sometimes I need a shit load a other people's space, an' they'd better fuckin' give it up to me when I do." She stares at the food, has maybe bought too much. "See, sweetbuns, in the matter a birds an' bees, you're about eight years old. I don't mean that you ain't *el toro*'n this gal's china shop, but Christ, you're like a kid all giddy from a first kiss. That's not a turn off. It's real cute, ya ask me. But, babycakes, you are a danger t'yourself an' are likely t'get yourself burned."

Several yellow jackets have set their sites on the chicken salad and are busy tying little bibs under whatever passes for chins on wasps. Taylor dares not swat at them, but keeps a wary eye. "I think I know what I want," he says.

"Think I know what ya want too. An' you're gettin' it. But I think we better put the skids on this *'till death do us part* stuff."

He sits quiet, dejected. How can he be so certain and she so cautious? She can see the disappointment dim his eyes. She smiles, gives him of touch of lips, leaves the thinnest hint of mayonnaise on his cheek. "Lemme tell ya 'bout me, hon, 'cause, thing is, I been around some blocks in neighborhoods ya might not wanna get out a the car."

"It won't make a difference." He shows no hesitation.

"Then we hadn't a ought a worry 'bout layin' it out on the table." She puts down the plastic wear, touches the back of her hand for a girlish swipe to the mouth, and adjusts herself into lecture posture *al fresco*, hands modestly folded in her immodest lap, legs tucked Indian-style under her denimed ass. "I come from some pretty screwed up folks," she says. "My old lady didn't exactly get the Good Housekeeping Seal of Approval. She wasn't the cover girl for <u>Parents Magazine</u>. I guess she may have been a looker at one time. The framework was there, ya could kin'a see the might-a-beens, but she was mostly all wear an' rust by the time I come around. An' she sure as shit didn't *act* pretty! Mostly, she was three'r four sheets t' the wind, an' I'm talkin' Katrina force gusts here. She wasn't around much. I don't remember the fresh smell a Betty Crocker when I come home from school. She hung around at this bar called Tootsies with a crew at least as no good as her.

I remember lovin' Lucy on the Crosley an' racin' roaches 'round the front room well into the night all by myself. Couldn't have been more than five."

It is welling up in her, begs to come out. Her lids puff and mottle, a thin crystal trail wends down her cheek, eroding mascara sediment. "Some times she'd come home'th a man I didn't know. If they lasted more'n fifteen minutes they were considered family. *SeeAnn, meet your Uncle Bill. A little hug for Uncle Marty.* Sometimes I'd look out the pitcher window and see some guy's ass in a car pumpin' like an oil rig an' hear my mother chortlin', like one a those chim-pan-*zees* they had in that Clint Eastwood movie, before the prick'd dump her out on t' the curb t' puke her guts out. Maybe that's how I got t' be. Back seat baby Cory Ann."

He has become transfixed on a tiny curl of pasta clinging to her mouth like Gutzon Borglum on Lincoln's lip. He wants to take it off, lick it off, press it between his lips. Has at least the good sense not to.

"Anyhow, she wasn't the kind t'sew Halloween costumes'r bake cup cakes'r turn up at Open House, is what I'm gettin' at. Don't know how she supported us, but she always had a few bucks stashed away when she needed it, so I guess there was like some sort a lucrative activity she engaged her sorry old ass in. I know. Sounds like one a them reality shows. An' it gets worse. Or better, if ya think a the ratings. Along comes Harold. *Sti*-ruttin' and tellin' tales an' all full a his nasty ol' self. Dug right up outta a shoppin' cart 'n'a weed lot, old Harold. Not bad lookin', 'f you like dull razors an' a shortage a teeth. If ever there was a guy looked like a vet from a perpetual bar fight, it was Harold. Now mind you, when Harold shows up'th his hand down Mom's bloomers, I'm, oh, no more than ten'er eleven. Got boobs the size a unpopped corn. Couple a kernels a their future selves. Don't think I'd been on the rag yet. I might a been a bit slow. Don' know see, 'cause Dorthea…bitch's name was Dorthea…never talked t' me 'bout nothin', thought I should learn by observation an' proceeded to provide text book examples a all the things I wasn't half ready t'learn 'bout jus'yet. Don't know whose pussy I was expected t'study when the flood come on. Anyways, Harold. I don' know what Harold did exactly. What sort a career path he followed. Sometimes, he had this bundle that he flashed 'till he didn't have it no more. Sometimes he was as flat as a parking lot. Sometimes a man'd come an' they'd go 'n'e backyard an' huddle t'gether a while an' pretty soon Harold would go on a little trip t'Lord knows where an' come home flush as a Kohler. Whatever it was, it wasn't somethin' he done regular, 'cause for long periods he just hung around the house front a the *tee*-vee makin' a general nuisance a himself, expectin' t' be waited on like he's some kind a VIP'ith too much on his mind t'take a piss by himself. *You wanna shake this here for me, sweetheart?* He thinks I'm Cinderella with a posse a birdies an' chipmunks an' whatever t' crease his trousers an' shine his shoes. Man had some raggedy ass shoes and clothes. When he was flush, he becomes this real sport. Takes us out t'eat two three times a week. All class, Harold is. Favorite restaurants all have wheels under 'em but I got t' admit I had some kick-ass tacos from this truck over by th' Texaco. All of a sudden, he even comes home'th a car. A Nash Ambassador with four colors a fenders an' upholstery looks like it rode'th Georgie Custard. No radio. No heater. We thought we were in th' lap a luxury. He starts takin' us t'movies. Mostly drive-ins, them grabbin' each other's goodies 'n'e back seat there, me crushed under a tub a butter corn 'n'e front feedin' my zits. There we was, a family, me, Dorthea, an' th' Lizard a Oz an' all his smoke'n'mirrors. A class act, Harold. A prince among assholes."

She pauses for breath. Her chest heaves. Taylor wonders if he should take her hand.

"But, Harold, you gotta hand it t'Harold. That man looked int' his crystal balls an' saw the future. Takes a look at Mom'n one ball, 'n'her no-worse-for-wear twilight, an' he takes a good long look at me in the other, an' Harold up an' says t' Harold, *Harold, see if ya can't see a ways down the road a bit an' ya just might sign yourself up for a twofer.* So Harold moves his shit the fuck in while Mom goes on bein' what ever it is Mom's always been, an' I set about harvesting a set a melons that gives Harold such a constant hard on that it comes a night the poor thing, try as he might, seekin' divine guidance as he does, just can't keep from brushin' up against 'em…Small house, see, kinda hard t' keep 'em out a everybody's way… The brushin' graduates t' feelin', an' pretty soon Harold's got himself a little two gal harem all his own. I rat t' the old cow, an' she says, *don' you fuck up this here good thing for me; ya could do worse than bonin' Harold Jardine.* She was probably right, an' I probably did. Gotta admit, I learned a lot they didn' teach at the junior high. Least not'n class. Real how-to. <u>Pedro-*feel*-ya for dummies.</u> An', t'tell the truth, I didn' know any a this wasn't the way it was supposed t'be. Y'know what y'know. I guess I thought all the kids had fifteen, sixteen uncles an' a step daddy who walked about the house wearin' nothing but a cigarette. Which reminds me. Best thing t'happen t'me at the old shotgun shack is Harold gettin' sick to death on his smokes. Man was a walkin' advertisement for one humped Camels. I never seen 'im that he wasn't suckin' on a bottle'r powderin' his nose'r had a lit one hangin' out a his sorry-ass pie hole, 'bout half a it gone t'ash. He ate with that cigarette, sat on the can'th it, screwed'th it, an' pretty much fell asleep'th it. Burned holes'n'a couch. Set fire t' the curtains. But like the Sturgeon General says, it gets ya in the end. Old Harold comes home from the VA one day, his face about as long as a road outta town, gets all teary eyed, calls us both over for a snuggle, an' gives us the low down on emphysema. I even felt bad for him for a minute there. But you know, even terminal disease has its good side. See, a man'th a tube up'is nose draggin'is scuba gear around on wheels is just no match for a young long legged gal 'n'a defensive state a mind. Hustle like he did, when they sang the Star Spangled Banana, old wheezy Harold was nowheres near the gold. And even schnarfin' up air through a tube, he's got the Joe Camel hangin' out a his sleazy grin."

She wipes a napkin over her eyes. "Smog," she blames. Taylor is still thinking about her hands.

"So, long story short, I'm on the street at fifteen. No tricks, just out'in'a night with a bunch a other kids an' its like we're learning the beauty a chemistry. Dead gone on our asses, most a the time. Boys come and go. In that order. It was a good thing too, bein' outta that shit hole, 'cause Harold finally succeeded in burnin' it down an' the both a them with it for good measure. *Oh, well,* I said. *Fuckin' orphan. So I thumbed my sweet little teenie bopper's ass out here t'where I thought I had an' aunt or somethin'*. Got busted 'n'a Safeway for liftin' some Twinkies, stuck'n'a shelter an' chucked off t'high school. Never found the aunt. Time I'm seventeen I got a fake ID, I'm married to a guy twice my age whose got a titty bar on La Brea where he kindly offers me a position 'n'a cage. I make enough'n'e old g-string t' dump him, get divorced, for what he gives me a good what for with a rubber dildo from the prop closet, before signing the papers, an' I wind up dancin' in a dump by a freeway, one a these places that advertises LIVE NUDE GIRLS, *live* bein' kin'a a stretch, you want an inside scoop. The money was okay, Taylor. Ya do what ya gotta do. I ain't makin' no excuses. Got turned down at Harvard, Yale, so, shit! I had my own place. Sometimes I had a boyfriend, some brave little Columbus, who'd pitch in before fallin' off the end a the earth. "Till I went on a bender. I'm told this. I don't remember."

By now, she has surrendered the chicken salad to the yellow jackets. The swarmers are so stuffed they find themselves kicked back in the plastic container, bloated and gassy, reminiscing on old times, other picnics, and picking their little *Vespidae* teeth and belching mayo out into the purple twilight, unable to attain flight. Taylor inches fingers forward; pulls them back.

"Wound up in some kin' a church shelter…shelter again, like a runaway dog, got damn near t'bein' put t'sleep…an' realized I'd become my mama an' my very own Harold was waitin' just around the next bender. So I cleaned up. Not that once ya stop doin' yourself in there ain't a line formin' t' take over the job. I go up an' down like everybody else, I suppose. But I like me a whole shit load better than I used to. Can keep myself 'n genuine costume bangles an' bath salts without wigglin' down a pole. Don't do hard drugs, watch my liquor allowance, don't smoke no more. Well, mostly I don't smoke. At the moment, you're the sum total a my vices. Discovered I had a talent for carrying several hot plates at once. A marketable skill'n these here parts, mister. Much admired an' sought after. I still get pinched occasionally, an' I still have t'out crude some horny piss ant joker whose old lady has him sleepin' on the couch, but you know what, sweetpie? I gotta talent for that too. Th-th-that's all folks. What ya see's what y'see, what ya get is what ya already got. There ain't no more to it."

"Sturgeon is a fish."

"Huh?"

"Fish."

"Fish? What the hell! Look, Tayli, don't feel sorry for me. I don't. I figure, ya sit at the table, ya get dealt some cards, right?"

"I guess." He has heard few enough of the words to have lost their context. Sounds are in flux, her slightly coarse twang, a hum of insects in the foliage hugging the stream bed, a truck on the freeway overpass. He sees her lips move. They hypnotize. He wants to touch fingers, lips. He says, "I'm okay with all that."

"Me too. Not exactly proud, but, at this point, okay with it all. Anyways, the point a me sharin' my shit is, I ain't the kind a girl ya drag home t'mother."

"She's dead."

"Christ on a cracker, Taylor, are you listening? What part a what I just told ya is it ya think worth marryin'?" She projects a big green olive across his chest, learns that olives perform poorly in high-speed collisions. WARNING TO CRASH TEST DUMMIES: STAY OUT OF OLIVES.

"So? Will you?" he asks.

"Is the Pope Hindu? Let's just like each other for a while an' see how that goes."

"I can do that, I think."

"Okay, then." She pretends to brush away a loose eyelash. "Don't let that poor steer t'have died'n vain. Eat, an' then we can go behind a bush an' I'll suck ya blind." This causes him some interpretive concern, which she registers as crestfallen. She says, "Don't worry, Tails, generally, that's a good thing."

"I'm sorry about your mother," he tells her.

"Don't be. I'm told they got her so morphed up, she feels no pain."

"I thought you said she was dead. In a fire."

"Did I? Sometimes it comes out that way. Makes more of a point."

The *shar pei* mix has come out of the pond and is shaking off water, too sensuous an attraction for a male Bassett with his left ear borne snuggly in his mouth, attempting to entertain her with some pathetic spinning like a canine dervish. The hound has been brought to the park by a young man testing the dog's chick magnetism: in the dog's world view, he has brought the young man in the hope that he has acquired a viable bitch magnet. At the moment, neither is particularly enamored of the other. The indifferent Amerasian lays down to sun herself, ponders the blur of the short French dog, as if to ask, *Does this really work for you, stubs?*

III

AS SUMMER WANES, IT BECOMES A custom of the lovers to spend a slow afternoon hour snug in their favorite booth at the Dining Car, listening to oldies on the digital juke. They pretend they're going somewhere, as Taylor did when, as a child, he could hear the *El Capitan* blow by in the night, a distant echo of adventure in far off places as exotic as Raton Pass and Albuquerque. Enrique spends the time scraping the grill and scowling.

"So what do I...do *we* get Steven?" Taylor is careful to speak in pairs, these late August days. They have become an item — indeed, *the* item in that very small corner of Earth that contains both the High Ball and the Dining Car; that which is not exactly fertile ground for any romance other than romance of the rails. He has let down his guard somewhat, and she continues to be as open as a twenty-four hour truck stop. Though she still hasn't seen where he lives, he has allowed her certain license with his person. She has shaved his head, thus banishing the dandruff to unpleasant memories of Helen, and has coerced him into getting new shades and an earring, and to growing a goatee so that, with all his bulk, he looks like a guy who lives on a camp in Idaho where he hordes suspiciously large quantities of fertilizer and keeps a data base on all of the synagogues west of the Mississippi. He sees only her; barely notices the changes in himself.

"Well, tatter tot, 'f'it's anything like it was when I was a kid, a little willing pussy would probably tide 'im over at least 'till Christmas."

"Gosh, babe, I don't think he's more than fourteen!"

"Perfect then. No one with too much experience. Don't wanna scare'im off."

They have come to serve each other as blinders to the outside world, do not notice as Toby, Barry Styles, and Nightstick Darouche slip in, take a booth at the side, and start thumbing through the menus stuck behind the napkins as if they can't already recite the un-annotated offerings, chapter and verse. In addition to the train pix, there are signed eight by tens on the walls, head shots of Hollywood celebrities; a guy from a carpet commercial, an older woman who has found relief from hemorrhoids, a good looking young man who has done a voice over for the talking cartoon booger so admired by Leo.

"You're no help," Taylor tells her. "I'll just find something next door."

"What? Like somethin' *you* would a wanted when you're his age? Not a primo idea, y'ask me. An', ya heard it first here."

"Hey, Cora d'whora," Nightstick grumbles. "Might negotiate a better tip if you find yourself able to dislodge your foot from Taylorailer's junction just long enough to tote over three ice teas, one of 'em heavy on the sugar, and scribble down our orders."

She leans out from the booth, nods indifferently. "Ah, Nightstick the douche. Didn't smell ya come in. Here's an idea, though," she says, "why'nt ya waddle your fat ass on over here, bend over an' touch your toes, an' I'll just lodge my pretty manicured foot somewheres else."

Barry howls, just up until the point that Darouche gives him the kind of lidless smile a Black Mamba bestows just before sinking its fangs into the fleshy part of your throat. Taylor is reminded of his neighbor.

Cory Ann slips into the fluffy gorilla slippers she has been wearing during the slow hours, pads on over to the only other occupied table. "Toby-Wan Kenobi. How's that sweet family a yours?"

"Everybody's well. I thank you for asking. And how're you keeping, hon?"

"You know me, dandy and randy."

"All talk."

"Could ask the Tailman over there. He might have a yarn or two."

"His would be a jaundiced view."

"Whatever. But the tales he could tell! Can I get ya?" Toby scans the specials over the counter, squinting. He has a habit of keeping his glasses in his shirt pocket where they are of debatable value.

"What's that chef's salad like?"

"Aren't going all PC on us, are ya?"

"Could afford to drop a notch."

"Well, tell ya this. It's the only thing in this dive the Health Department guya'll eat."

"Sold. Italian on the side. Low cal, if you got."

"Want the avocado for a buck more?"

"You only live once."

"'Bout you, dimples?" she asks Barry, leaning forward with her elbows on the table so that his face turns crimson and his zits begin to ooze like mud pots in Yellowstone.

"What's the toasted cheese like?"

"Like two pieces a burnt white bread held t'gether by one slice a scorched processed cheese. Can have a tomato on it if ya want."

"That'd be fine."

"Ya get two sides."

"Chili fries and coleslaw."

"Nice try. Chili fries ain't a side. What we call an *on*-tray. That's French, like the fries. Can have the regular fries though. Chili's extra."

"And the slaw. Regular fries and the slaw."

"An' the slaw." She arches her head towards Nightstick and asks Toby, "Can I put down a bowl for your pit bull?" Billy eyes follow the S-curve down her spine and around the crescent of her ass.

Darouche's finger juts forward faster than Billy's smile can form. "Problem started," Darouche says, "when they gave 'em the vote. Had eyes on *my* monkey shoes, I know where I'd be looking."

"Only way *you're* gonna see any. Anything ya want me t'read t'ya on the menu? We got a peanut butter'n' jelly on the kiddie page."

"Get me a Denver omelet, rye toast, home fries, cup a coffee. See if ya can't keep from grinding up a Coke bottle in the eggs and find somebody who knows how to warm the pot."

"Please," calls Taylor. There is an unfamiliar firmness in his tone. It surprises Taylor no less than the others. He reddens, sucks air, feels an inner heat.

"'Scuse me?" Darouche turns toward him, offers a razor thin smile of both satisfaction and menace.

"You treat her with respect, please." It comes out dry and phlegm blocked, and Taylor knows it does not carry the gravity he intended. Perhaps he should have dropped the *please.*

"Or what?"

Toby chants, "Na, na, na, na, na! Guys please."

Taylor leans forward, huffs toward Nightstick. "Or I'll see you outside." He has heard this somewhere and believes it to be some sort of threat.

Nightstick says, "Keep your lance in you chain mail, Galahad."

Taylor stands, like a great northern bear, on his hind legs and bigger than anybody else in the room.

Darouche observes, "Ain't this a Kodiak moment?"

There is a pinch of silence that conjures up adjectives like *pregnant* and *fulsome.*

"We're just playin', hon," Cory Ann says.

Toby blurts out, "Damn the torpedoes. Make it blue cheese and pour it on thick enough so that I don't see any green. Hell with Al Gore! And extra bacon bits."

Taylor is still fixed in the same place, his gaze on Darouche.

"I stand corrected," Darouche sneers. "I never knew *castratos* could grow 'em back."

"Okay, outside. You and me." Taylor is fuming, crimson creeping across his forehead, his cheeks.

Darouche stands up, throws his napkin on the seat. It's been a while since he has had such a tantalizing invitation.

"I'm gonna make this call," Enrique warns, waving his cell phone from behind the counter.

Darouche smiles, says, "See, here's the second problem. Never should a let 'em stay beyond the harvest."

"*¡Chinga cabrón!*" Enrique, still entrenched behind the counter, sweating in the heat lamps, produces a well-worn chef's knife. "We was here before you and your fucking leaking Mayflower. Ever heard a Columbus, dickhead? De Anza? Coronado? Leo Carrillo? Go home and rent yourself some Cheech and Chong and learn the local history you missed in Fourth Grade, asshole."

"That the knife your great grandpa took off a Bowie's dead body?"

"We can *all* go outside," says Enrique.

"Whoa, whoa," says Toby, laying a firm but unwelcome hand on Darouche's arm. "Let up, let up, let up. Everybody. We're here for a little lunch, a little break from the tumult of commerce. Let's see if we can't all just sit down, take a deep breath, and act like grownups."

"That's fucked, Tobe. This needle dick's a mega racist pig."

"That may well be, my friend, but short of chopping him up into *carnitas*, let's just let it ride for a while."

"Fucked up, Toby."

"Enrique. I've got a phone too," says Toby. "I could call the owner and tell him you're threatening a customer with the cutlery."

"That's cheap, man. You wouldn't do that."

"You may leave me no choice."

"I'm tired a this fucking racist shit around here. We been here since fucking Montezuma and Montezuma's people been here since the Quetzal bird sold 'em a piece a real estate for twenty-four *pesos*. And I got to put up with Darouche and trailer trash Mama over here…"

It is at this moment that Taylor defrosts, looses whatever dampened control he has employed up to now, pivots from Darouche to Enrique, gives either a grunt of exertion or a growl of anger — a point that will be debated later by those present as events are retold — and proceeds to lunge, rhino-like, in Enrique's direction for purposes only Enrique can imagine and Taylor has yet to divine. It has been some time since Taylor has practiced his lunge; never all that athletic, his was not a particularly impressive lunge to begin with. In this instance, he hurtles his bulk forward, a runaway train of wildly swinging arms — two sputtering propellers of rage — catches a size thirteen sneaker on a table leg, elevates high enough for a fleeing roach to escape beneath him with all three of its *blattidae* dimensions, and crashes like the *Hindenburg* on the flat floor New Jersey of the Dining Car. It is an impressive impact, if a mediocre leap, lacking only plumes of flame and a hysterical reporter crying, *the humanity, the humanity!*

Enrique, seeing his life of flipping burgers flash before him, an instant panorama of soundless cracked eggs, dipped white meat chicken compost, and slathered tuna salad on your choice of bread — white, rye or whole wheat — performs a lurch of his own, in reverse, loses the knife over his head, and lands on his TJ goat-hide wallet with it's tool-burned *vaqueros sombrero*-shaded in their saddles. Taylor lands on his face, the counter still between them, and Darouche is left feeling like he's been benched by the coach.

The knife, however, makes no attempt to look back, see if everybody's okay, takes on a mission of its own, proscribing an arc whose down slope finds it within an inch of the nose of Enrique's young nephew, Angel, who is spending summer back at the sink, arms deep in suds, oblivious in the grip of his noise-reducing Bose headphones, hemorrhaging brain cells with each sampled concussion, but still conscious enough to register that he has nearly just died. The knife, now ignored, and never one to empathize anyway, follows a trajectory toward an industrial-sized keg of mayo from Smart & Final, while Angel loses purchase on a stack of dishes that fall with a splash and a glurg and a great whirlpool of foam and bubbles into the sink, over the lip, onto the painted concrete floor with faux texture and tectonic cracks.

"The fuck, *Tío*, this's some messed up shit, homie!" They are the only words Angel has spoken all summer, and to this blessed recovery from muteness, Enrique's sister Parafanelia will be moved to light candles to St. Anthony.

Taylor rolls over, his breathing irregular, hot tears of humiliation settling in his goatee. Cory Ann kneels over him, caressing his face, wiping blood from his scrapes on to her apron, tenderly offering her lips to his bruises, while Barry, thanks to a short skirt cooperatively hiked up in all the action, gets a new vantage point from which to observe her upper thighs, and which earns Barry a firm punch to the shoulder from Toby's free hand.

"Enough," Toby commands. "No more knives. Darouche. Taylor. Corners. The bell has spoken...Please. What about you? You planning to go somewhere? Anybody outside you need to see about anything?"

"No sir," says Barry. "I'm just waitin' for my order."

"Wild west in here!" Toby complains and Taylor lugs himself up to his feet with Cory Ann's assistance. "Darouche," says Toby, his eyes darting from one to the other, "do me the favor of your company down here in the booth. I've got something to show you later. Find of a lifetime at an estate sale the other day. Haven't told anybody until now. Grand Avenue Railway Special Officer's badge. Only one I've ever seen. Sit down and eat your lunch and we may be able to negotiate its placement in a good home." Toby is speaking quickly, an earnest stopgap race to head off the insurrection.

"I'm intrigued," says Darouche calmly, settling back into his seat, a quick warning finger toward Enrique who has resurfaced from behind the counter to return the knife to its magnetized rack. "And, ma'am, if I could *please* get one a those cute little pitcher's a cream with that coffee, I'd be forever at your service."

Another impromptu interlude of silence follows. Cory Ann is palsied numb in her gorillas, as if some mobster had filled them with concrete. Taylor senses a deflation in the room, nods calmly to Darouche, and slumps sadly back into his booth. The clock on the wall resumes the telling of time. Cars once again pass in the street.

Cory Ann moves back to the chef's window, with trembling fingers clips the three orders to the stainless wheel and flips it around to Enrique.

"Can't be havin' this shit in here, girl," Enrique says. "The owners do a pop in and we're fucked. I got responsibilities. Can't afford t'be on no street."

"Not the time," she says. "Shut up an' fry something."

"You play too much, girl, all's I'm saying."

"'Bout me, Uncle Ricky?" from the sink. "Almost deviated my sputum, dude!"

Just after closing time, Taylor, sore, both literally and figuratively, hefts out a large Bachmann box complete with twenty lengths of indoor-outdoor G-scale track and a mixed train from the Eastern Tennessee and Western North Carolina. There is plenty of room in his brother-in-law's yard for a garden railroad.

As is his habit at the end of the day, he spends several minutes in a covetous swoon before the locomotive case: one full wall, under glass, with locomotives and Jewett cars for all. Steam dinkies from the mines, dummies in box cabs off the early els, low slung mudhens, tall striding Hudsons sheathed in *racy* skirts, compounds, well hung Beyer-Garret's from the thin lines of South Africa. They are gleaming brass or meticulously painted, some even weathered in a pantomime of age and long service. Taylor makes a mental note of his next acquisition, but finds it easier than usual to pry himself away and lug the Bachmann out the back door.

Toby is in the parking lot being embarrassed over his cigarette. "Trying to quit," he mumbles. He slouches up against his Camry, drops the butt, heel-crushes it into the asphalt.

"Okay."

"Can't fall off the wagon at home. The surveillance is too heavy. Talk about your *home*land security."

"I hear it's difficult. Quitting." Taylor's voice is flat, distant.

"You know how when you get a new car and suddenly everyone has the same car? When I was smoking, I mean, openly, I thought I was the last addict in California. Now, everywhere I go there is some reminder. A butt on the street, a smoke shop, a whiff of nicotine left in an elevator. Anyway, some crazy stuff in there, huh? Taylor?" He nods toward Dining Car's rear behind a line of dumpsters.

"I guess." Taylor is loading Steven's present into the Caddie's trunk, a space vast enough to stow the prototype.

"Getting pretty sweet on the waitress, it seems."

Taylor hoists his bulk out of the trunk, adjusts his belt, tucks in an errant shirttail. "Is this a problem?"

"Hair trigger on you today! No, sir, it is not a problem. Nor is it any of my business."

"Okay then."

"Mad as hatters, the bunch of you! Look, you gotta take Darouche with a grain of salt. Things he says. The guy's a jerk. Want's to feel important. Some people don't do so well with retirement. And Cory Ann's a big girl. She can hold her own you know. Always has."

Taylor slams the trunk shut. There is a whooshing sound, as if Taylor has vacuum packed the Great Basin in his infinite cargo space. "Maybe she shouldn't have to anymore."

"Well, okay, but we're talking about Darouche. You know, Taylor, Darouche does have some experience with blunt objects."

"You're saying?"

Toby absently crushes the cigarette a second time. "I'm saying, it might be wise to just let some things go."

"*The grain of salt?*"

"Well, yes, *the grain of salt.*"

"Look, Toby. I didn't start this thing."

"Christ, Taylor! What are we? Ten? Na na na *na* na! I know he can grate on a fellow, but nothing good will come of you calling him out."

"He needs to be respectful of my girlfriend."

"I have no argument with that." Toby himself is a respectful sort; takes the concerns of others seriously. He has a smooth baby face that tends to blush with little encouragement. Consistently neat and starched in short sleeved white dress shirts and black trousers, he would look appropriate riding a bike with Latter Day Saints, a mysterious backpack clinging like a papoose. "But, Taylor, just what were you planning to do if he had come outside with you, for chrissakes?"

"I don't know. Tell him how I felt."

"To what purpose?"

"He needs to know."

"You don't want to corner a man like that. This is why God in his wisdom gave us cheeks to turn."

"I'm not afraid of him."

"Should be. That old bastard will take out your knees before you can get your dukes up. Some of the older guys that come around, some of them retired from BNSF and UP, they've seen yard bulls work over a tramp or two. They tend to give Darouche a wide right-of-way. You should too, maybe."

"It's not about me, Toby."

"It's not about much of anything. That's my point." This is Toby being judgmental, and just a tad immoderate.

Taylor pats his trunk, checks his fly, thinks for a moment. "See, Toby, you've always been decent with me. But a lot of these guys...they treat me like I'm a little weird or something. And that's okay, see, because maybe I am. It doesn't bother me. They say things like I'm not in the room, and that's okay too because it's always been like that. No big deal. But being weird, being different, is not the same as being stupid. I understand what they say. Water off a duck's beak, or whatever. But as far as Cory Ann goes...New world order. They're going to have to be respectful or just shut up."

"I'll talk to Darouche."

"No. Don't do that. Comes up again, I will have to make myself understood."

"You've got a handle on this then?"

"I'll be okay. I will."

Somehow they are standing closer than they were. Toby stares down at his own feet, realizes that it is Taylor who must have moved, must have made some unconscious advance in his direction. The sound of the slammed trunk lid still seems to echo from the walls of the old brick buildings, the train shop, the cafe, the bike repair next door. The seven-space lot is shared. Sign's indicate where you're allowed to park. All others will be towed at their own expense. Darouche's Suburban is shoehorned into a compact only space, the Cadillac in another. What's left of Cory Ann's Corolla is fading paint in the alley behind and next to the dumpster. Taylor and Toby stand as if waiting for a whistle; two guys on break, contemplating a little one on one.

IV

TAYLOR REMAINS UNEASY WELL INTO THE evening. At home, he paces, trying to get involved in the maintenance of the layout, a task that has never before been so daunting. He manages a cursory dusting, ponders the afternoon pyrotechnics, forgets his place on the track, moves on to righting the derailed freight, pauses again and loses his thought of train. "What the heck," he says, and tromps out his front door, not even locking it, maneuvering around the juniper hedge along the neighbors' driveway, up onto Blake's and Melissa's porch. He rings the bell.

The house looks like it was built that afternoon. Blake always has an extra man or two around, scraping paint, installing double-pane windows, replacing a broken tile on the roof. Day in, day out, the driveway hosts cement mixers, generators, compressors, stacks of PVC, coiled wire, tubs of latex paint, miles of rebar. He entertains the workers with Mexican pop on a boom box, the whine of radial arm saws, cordless drills, the whack of air driven nails. Leo drives by Taylor's house occasionally on Betsy's urging, *Just make sure he hasn't torn the place down and replaced it with a roundhouse.* He has studied the action at Blake's, and told Betsy, *Taylor's house still looks like Big Bird's cage, but the place next door has become Dubai: foreigners are always building something.*

Blake opens the peep window, says, "Sir?" He is backlit from the blue constancy of LCDs.

"You want to come see the trains?"

A lock snaps, and Blake is standing full body in khaki pants and signature wife beater with his dog tag trapezed low on his chest. The T is stenciled with, **What I don't hurt won't know me,** and an American flag. "What trains?" He looks pale, older than he did on Taylor's porch. Something unseen tugs at the corners of his mouth.

"My place. The trains."

"Oh, the trains. Change a heart?"

"Do you want to see them?"

Blake flexes muscles so that his arms look like boa constrictors in the act of swallowing. He loses his slouch, and directs his red-white-blue eyes into Taylor's. "You're not some kind a faggot, are you Tailboy? 'Cause, if you are, you need to know there's no fucking *don't ask don't tell* on this block. You make a move for my bazooka and I'll light you up and call in air support."

It is not the first time today that Taylor feels dumbfounded, out of his element.

Blake smiles. "Just shittin' ya, bro. Let me tell Melissa." He arches his neck back from the door. "HEY, BABE, GOIN' OUT."

"DINNER'S ALMOST READY," she calls back.

"ALMOST IS ALMOST. I'M *ALMOST* BACK BY NOW."

She comes into the dining room, wiping her hands on a Hello Kitty apron. "I've been at this all afternoon."

"Life's a bitch." And to Taylor, "Not the only one around here, either, sir."

"It'll get cold, Blake."

"That's why we have a microwave, sugar cheeks," he says, coming out onto the porch and slamming the door to punctuate the end of the conversation. "Again, just shittin'ya, bud," he tells Taylor again. "That bitch thing: we're good, me an' 'Lissa. Co-pathetic. I been stickin' t'the book. My sponsor says I'm head a the class. Gonna make me CE-fuckin'-O a the A-fuckin'-A. By the way, I like the Jesse Ventura look, but what happened to your face? Looks like beach blanket summer on the sunny sands of Basra, sir."

"Ran into a switch stand."

"Yeah, and you should see the switch stand, huh?"

They are crossing the DMZ between Blake's perfect driveway and Taylor's lawn of the dead.

"I don't want to talk about it."

"Taylor, sir, dudes like me fight for the right of dudes like you t'shut the fuck up."

Down the street, Mr. and Mrs. Devore are pouring out a path of reddish stones in their drought resistant garden, cacti and succulents and native plants inspired by Caltrans freeway foliage. They stop to share a thermos. A young man in jogging attire pants by on the asphalt pushing a three wheel stroller with helmeted toddler — the kid's head thrust back, looking a lot like Yuri Gagarin at blast off. Mrs. Gettzleman — retreating from her twenty-one inch Magnavox where Anderson Cooper has been keeping her honest — takes up her post at the picture window and wonders what those two miscreants, Taylor and Blake, are up to.

Taylor pushes open his pawnshop security grill for Blake.

"Whoa-a-a-a, sir!" says Blake. "Your porch here's nearly AWOL. See that crack between the house and the concrete? Could hide snipers in there. Look, Taylor, what say I give you the Neighbors' Special on jacking that puppy back up? You're gettin' some big ass moisture in there. Serious breeding ground for all sorts a shit that'll eat your house: subterranean termites, dry rot, athletes' foot, suicide bombers, you name it."

"Athletes' foot?"

"So whattaya say? We got the go ahead t' shim this ski slope for ya?"

"It's always been like that."

"Yeah, well, then whatever's in there's had all the time it needs t'start takin' over the place like those alien seed pods in the movie...you know the one."

"An alien what?"

"Fuck's wrong with you? Sir? You a native speaker or what? Not one a them EDSLS, are ya?"

"Edsels? The car?"

"English as your Damned Second Language. You don't seem to know all the words. Don't get the jokes."

"That's true. "

"Yeah, well, I lost my sense a humor in the desert. What's your excuse?"

"I've always been this way. Like the porch." Taylor opens the door, slips out of his shoes, climbs up onto the control platform, sets things in motion.

"Hey-soos y Maria *Guacamole!*" Blake says, crossing the threshold with caution as if he expects land mines. "Now you're shittin' *me!* You unchained, un-whipped, free American sonofabitch! This is what we fight for, dude. Guys'r dyin' for this kind a liberty. *E* pubic fucking *unum,* sir. Christ in Saran Wrap, what'd this little setup put you back?"

"Put me back where?"

"Ooo-sama bin Yur Mama, Taylor! Easier gettin' an answer outta some *Fat-ima* burkabunny Ali Akbar Falousha at a checkpoint, Charlie. What language am I talkin', anyway?"

Taylor has no idea. Motions towards Blake's shoes; Blake pays no attention. "So, Blake, what do you think?"

"A this? Fuckin' sweet, dude! Not so much the trains and all this shit that goes with 'em, 'though it's pretty mind blowing if you're into that kind a thing. It's the point that you *get to do it!* You know how many guys'd give a nut to be able to push the whole fuckin' domestic thing...the dining room sets, the bedroom *on-som-bulls,* the matching dishes, Mikasa *es su casa...*just roll it all out on trash day. 'Cause, all a dude really needs, dude, which, apparently, you already got nailed, even though you don't seem t'speak the local tongue, is a fuckin' lounger with a cup holder, a fold-up tray with legs, a fridge, a big ass TV so's you can see the nose hairs on Kobe like they was Monster Cable, a futon for the occasional piece a snatch, and whatever the fuck it is that tickles your fancy: sports memberabilia, state a the art collection a porn, arcade games, beer cans a the world, even little fuckin' trains. Sir. Taylor, dude, you're somethin' of a nut case, but you're my hero."

"So, Blake, tell me. If you had a girlfriend. If you were single…"

"What's single gotta do'th it?" He winks in a clandestine fashion, the eyelid barely ajar in the first place.

"Well, if you were? And you were me?"

"Not gonna fuckin' happen, all due respect, sir."

"But if you were? And you brought your girlfriend here to your house, well, my house, but yours?"

"That's why the futon, dude."

"But what would she think? Your girlfriend?"

"They *think?* World's full a wonders! Le'me see. She'd probably be thinking how she could get all this crap outta here so's she could paint everything mauve or whatever-the-fuck puce, and put little floral patterns all over anything she could get her fellow cacklers to sit on while she tries to rip them off for some plastic storage containers famous for their suck."

"But would she think this is…*obsessive?* Would she walk out? My sister, who hasn't been here, but has an imagination, says that there is a pathology to all this."

"Whatever. Anyway, you fuckin' your sister?"

"Of course not!"

"Then who gives a shit what she thinks? Look, dude, women like cutesy, crafty shit like this. I mean, what is this if not the place the dollhouse lives in? Take Melissa. You don't know how many times a month I gotta tote her over to Michael's or Stat's so she can paint another fuckin' pine shelf for nic-nacs…I never seen so many fuckin' nic-nics!…Or holiday shit like Styrofoam turkeys and shells to glue all over Kleenex boxes, or stencil kits t'decorate the toilet seat cover. 'Course the stencils better than the shag carpet she used to put on the cover that wouldn't let the seat stay up while a guy took a leak. That was one mega-suck of an idea. Like they don't know what we do with our dicks when we ain't makin' them happy! It's all about them. Anyways, they *love* makin' shit. Scrap books, and crap ya really gotta have, like napkin holders, and hearts made outta dry flowers. Any chick, sir, that comes in here and sees Tinytown all decked out an' lit up is just gonna think she's glimpsed your feminine side. Why that cute little church over there's enough to get her wet enough to require snow chains before she sets her ass down on the potty." Blake has his palms firmly on Taylor's shoulders.

"You're sure?" Taylor steps back into in private space.

"Taylor. We are talkin' people that loose their cookies over a package a colored pipe cleaners. That they can twist around their little fingers as easy as they can their husbands. Ain't all that complicated. Sir. Now, have you given any thought t' doin' the right thing for that porch out there? I can give you a deal sweeter than a Hostess cupcake dipped in extra chocolate sauce and fried at the County Fair."

"I'm borderline diabetic. I shouldn't have the chocolate sauce."

"Fuckin' border line's a whole nuther *problema*. Look, bro, for you, fifty off the reg. Not your everyday, whoever-the-fuck-walks-through-the-door offer. Best I can do. I wouldn't give my own mother a break like that, but for you, sir, with all a this here, this license to be free, white and born in the US-of-A, and *single!* Fuck Springstein, *you* are the goddamned Boss. You are the Man! Tail*MAN*. King a men! King a fuckin' kings!" Blake falls to his knees, both made in America, kow tows, says, "Holy shit, you drive a hard bargain. How 'bout I throw in some fancy Spanish tiles on the risers? Give the place some a that curb repeal *as seen on TV?*"

V

B ETSY HAS TAKEN OFFENSE. YOU CAN hear the edge in her voice: fingernails on asphalt. She doesn't think the library is old school. Responsively, Steven sulks on his special day. Steven is at the age where sulking and seminal emissions war for his attention.

When piqued, Betsy pontificates — a term she herself would not use — and each such oration is preceded by a preamble to ease its way to ratification. "Everything that was ever written is there. Old, new, everything! The books fairly shout out ideas as you pass them. You can feel the vibes as you go; so eager are they to be shared. Ideas, facts, *us. We're* there. Each and every one of us can find ourselves on some page somewhere. We don't know it until we find it, but there we are. Everything that's ever happened, if it's been told or seen, handed down from one person to another, somebody wrote it down." She is speaking to both the children and the childlike that she has gathered to her table.

Leo is midway through his final chew of creamed veggies tucked snugly under a blanket of breadcrumbs. He doesn't touch the lamb; is snobbishly, if disingenuously, loyal to Mother Earth and all — or at least most — of her creatures. Or, maybe, just some of them. He clears his throat, follows the purge with, "Just choking on a bit of pedantry there, Bets. Feel like I'm on a field trip to the Library of Congress." Leo contends that the preambles peaked in seventeen eighty-seven: anything since is of the dead horse variety.

"I'm speaking to the *boys*, Leo!"

And perhaps *our guest*, Leo thinks. "Still, hon, the kids know what's in the library."

"Knowing isn't appreciating."

"Bor*ing!*" says Steven. "I can Google all that crap if I need to."

"Don't say *crap*, Steven," Leo admonishes through the filter of his napkin. He winks at Cory Ann. "The mouths on kids these days! My old man'd had me out at the woodpile by now. Say shit, son. It's so much more *now*."

Betsy is brimming with frustration, refuses to chalk it up to a generational theme. "Look, mister," she tells her son. "There is a dialogue in the stacks that's palpable, alive, a living, breathing celebration of words. See, just today, I was up there and I was torn from side to side; the stories brush up against me, they tantalize, emit scents, scream at me, *Pick me up*, trip me up, grab an arm. What're you wowed by? Space men, street chases, climb the Himalayas, killer sharks, penis size..."

"The k-*i*-ds!" Steven reminds.

"Yes, *the kids*, young man. Like ya don't know what's what. I clean your sheets, buckaroo. Anyway, a place with written words is the most exciting place I can imagine. It's never *old school*. No matter how old it is it's always new. Always saves a secret for next time. This I know, mister smartass. And the people that come in there? Readers, scholars, a prof from Oxy or Caltech, Thai massage therapists... you name it."

"I can get behind that," Steven says. "The Thai thing. Anyways, I thought Erlinda cleans the sheets."

Betsy ignores him. She hates when he's right. "And we get characters like you wouldn't believe. More characters than on USA."

David, speaking of which, adds, "Benjamin Franklin's Library Company had to order their first books from England."

"Very interesting, darling. Now see if you can*not* be heard for a while. Strain if you have to. I was saying, we get the odd client on a regular basis."

Leo says, "How odd for odd to be regular. There are conundrums in the library as well. They reach out for you too. Stink up the joint."

"We get a lot of homeless. There are several parks nearby that they sleep in, so they come to the library to use the toilets, wash up, hang out. Some read. Some voraciously. Others just stare at the chandeliers, talking to themselves."

"The chandeliers talk to themselves?" asks Leo. He gives Steven an elbow nudge and they both share a moment of preschool levity. David finds them juvenile, rolls his eyes.

"We don't hassle them unless they get loud," Betsy continues, in no mood to respond to the hecklers at the stage side table. "In that case, we get one of the security guys to politely remind them about the Golden Rule."

"The first library in Los Angeles County..."

"*David!* Let's invoke the Golden Rule right here, now, at this table for a while. Got it, Einstein-lite? Today, for example, we had a guy you wouldn't believe. I was up in the stacks with the cart, sometime after lunch, and I'm restocking shelves in the Biblical Studies Section, my fave, and I get this sense...you know how it is...like you're not alone."

"You're never alone, dear, particularly in religious studies. You've been setting this up, haven't you?" He starts playing with the forks and dinner rolls; does the little Chaplin dance from "The Gold Rush." The kids are delighted. He is delighted to have delighted them.

"And you've been channeling your inner rodent. Stuff it, Leo! Of course, it's a public facility so I know I'm not alone, but there was this *sense* of proximity. Weird. I get this little shiver. I have a Bible in my hand, and this voice said, *Did you read that? Many times*, I said, and then I tell him...it's this guy, see, nice voice, well spoken...*Just a minute and I'll get out of your way. Did you like it?* he asks. We're talking the Bible, right? So, already, I've got this guy pegged for some kind of shopping cart wacko, but when I turned to look at him, he's just this ordinary guy."

"An *irregular* ordinary guy," Leo amends.

"As it turns out, yeah. He's in a suit, very nicely groomed, forty, forty-five, wedding ring. I think, *okey dokey, wrong call. The guy's from the seminary nearby. Maybe he's testing me.* So, I said, *It's not to like or dislike. It is what It is. It is Truth.* And he said, *No, I don't see it that way. Are you a biblical scholar?* I asked him. He tells me, *On the contrary,* that he's an author. So, I see he's expecting the logical response to that, so I asked if he'd written anything I might know. He said, get this, *I wrote that one. The one in your hand.* I pointed out to him that I had a Bible in my hand and he said he knew that. As the author, he would. So I think he means he defaced the book, doodles, or his laundry list or something, it's all I can think of, and I, like a boob..."

The boys snicker. So does Leo. Boobs can be very funny. They compete well with dancing rolls.

"...thank him for confessing and that he can see the cashier to pay for any damage he did. So he looked at me like *I'm* nuts, and tells me he didn't just write *in* It, he wrote *the whole thing!* I didn't want to get in too deep with this guy, you can imagine, but I didn't want to be rude. Some of the crazy ones don't do well with rude. I didn't wanna set the guy off. So I said, with a smile, he must be much older than he looks, to which he says, *Oh, yes, much. It's a Mel Brooks kind of thing.* This probably means something to you, Leo..."

"It does, pass the nectarines."

"...but I have no f-..."

"Mo-*om!*"

"...no f-ing idea what he's referring to. Then he says, and I don't know if he's f-... fooling around or what, *It was never meant to be taken as truth.*"

Leo says, *And then he went into such a story...*

"I told him, *It's the word of God.* Why I'm arguing with a well-dressed stranger who's lost his crackers, is beyond me. I think, *whoops, he's going to start shouting. He's going to belt me.* Wrong again. Very calmly, he said, *Many people buy into the urban myth.*"

David says, quickly, so as not to be stopped, "Pope Urban the Second's pen pal was the Archbishop of Canterbury."

"Why do you know that?" his father asks.

"Shut *up*, David, or no Wikipedia for forty days and forty nights," Betsy warns.

"Rehab for you, kiddo," Leo adds.

"So this guy, this guy who wrote the Bible, says that the Book was his publicist's idea. A guy named Aaron, wouldn't ya know. *Put me in the book, show me in a good light, no warts, and I'll peddle this pot boiler for you,* is what the guy told him. *Something big, something epical, cast a thousands, lots of begetting, heads rolling everywhere, natural disasters, triumph of the meek over the mighty, frogs, gnats, murrain, first born.*"

"Gross!" says Steven. Not exactly learned biblical commentary, but to the point.

"*Don't forget the miracles. The reader'll sooner have a miracle than sense.* He tells him, so he tells me, that he's got a small art house in Canaan that goes in for such things. He calls it *faith pulp. First run, minimum, twenty thou. He says thou like he's in the biz. And just wait for the foreign language editions, Aramaic, Egyptian, the audience can do nothing but expand. By the time we go papyrus...etc.*, etc. And then this schmuck..."

"The author of the Bible?" Taylor asks.

"Yes, the author. I mean, pay attention, the guy who *says* he is. Focus, for mercy's sake, Taylor! He says something to the effect of, *We wanted dicey. We wanted a blockbuster. Who the hell knew people would take it literally? Like the Virgin on a tortilla, give me a break!* I have begun to back away now, looking for the stairs, looking for security, not that he'd done anything threatening, but there is this glazed look in his eyes that is not to be trusted. On the other hand, I'm getting pissed. I know he's a nut job, but let him blaspheme to someone else. I won't have it in my library. With my God. Then he goes into this long spiel about how none of what has resulted from his book's barnburner success was intended. But after a while, he says something like, *what the...hell, if the rubes wanna buy in, so be it.* But later, he tells me, and I'm feeling personally offended by this time...," glancing at Cory Ann, "me being observant, kind of born again lite and all that...."

"Not true," Leo protests. "Not true at all. Barely a mother would survive if people were born again, lite or full caloric. As I recall from my training in Lamaze, of which I am an alum, the cervix gives us ten centimeters and out we pop. Any more would be like the *Spinaltap* amp that goes to eleven. Even a vaginal opening of eleven centimeters is not going to allow the passage of a fully grown adult, prone and spasmodic in the ecstasy of his or her own second coming. Of course, they could slice you open like a coconut, but you're still not going to house a fully formed grown up, previously born in a much diminished state, babbling with about as much coherence as Lassie, in the allowable square centimeterage. Would be a violation of the laws of both physics and biology, and of the parameters of the parent/child relationship. The only thing getting stretched that far is the imagination."

Cory Ann heehaws little down home prickles of amusement. She understands little of what Leo has said but thinks he was cute saying it. This does not earn her the much-needed points with Betsy.

Betsy says, "We'll talk about this later, Leo. Anyway, he says, this nut job, the *other* nut job, not *this* nut job here, he says, he has had, of late, this change of heart. Not because his honest fiction has evolved into a crass, commercial scam that couldn't fit through the Eye of the Needle, etc., etc., and even so has spent three thousand years on the New York Times Best Sellers List, but because the notoriety is just too much of a burden. *I have created this major belief system. I can't deal with the responsibility. I feel like Frankenstein. I'm not your garden-variety L.*

Ron Hubbard, you see! Gotta go, I told him, and I mean like right this second before Igor shows up like Mr. Potato Head with his bucket 'o' parts, fresh outta Forest Lawn. *Responsibilities of my own.* And he says would I like him to sign the book? We have come full circle. I'm at the stairs now, and I tell him, *that's a no-no: first commandment, we don't write in the library books.*"

"You're making this up," says Leo.

"You'll never know," she says.

"And from this we are to conclude?" Leo asks.

"Sometimes our creations get the better of us." She is smiling at Taylor.

"And then what happened?" Taylor asks. Cory Ann gives him a solid kick under the table.

"Some Guttenberg Bibles," adds David matter-of-factly, "were printed on vellum, others on paper."

"Jeez, dork," says Steven. "Can't you just shut up for my birthday? Friggin' freak!"

"The Lord's name," Betsy scolds.

"Nickname, Mom. *Jeez* is just a nickname. Short for…"

"I know what it short for Mr. Rude. And you are going to rot in Hell for all eternity."

"All I meant," says Cory Ann, referring to days of yore before Betsy's current pique, "is that I don't get the whole liberry thing. Not much of a reader, I guess." Taylor has taken note of a substantial — if not one hundred percent — improvement in her grammar, as if she knows her audience and is no longer speaking to the street.

"We hold these truths to be self evident," Betsy mumbles.

"CAKE," shouts Leo. It bleats like a referee's whistle. "Time for cake."

They break for the kitchen, juggling plates smeared with lamb grease and garlic mashed potatoes, unadorned broccoli boring itself to death. All but Steven. It is Steven's birthday and he is entitled to sit on his young ass and be hovered over. David and Cory Ann return with cake plates. Cory Ann does this well, a certain balanced panache to her carrying technique. Leo and Betsy bang around in the kitchen cupboards looking for candles each thinks the other has bought. Taylor undoes the top button on his trousers and lumbers off to one of about a million toilets.

"Nickels are seventy five percent copper," David remarks for no apparent reason.

"And your head, shit-for-brains," adds Steven, "is one hundred percent poop."

"How come?" Cory Ann inquires, coming back into the room.

"Don't know," says David. "But they are."

"Why d'ya remember stuff like that?"

"Don't know. It's fun to know stuff."

"So, Cory," Steven says, his arms crossed, his head to a side, his eyes thin slits, "I got something to show you in my room. Wanna see?"

"Bring it here."

"It's already here. But I gotta *show* it to you in my room."

Cory Ann has adjusted the salad plates, feels like lobbing one over to Soupy Sales in the honor seat. She sits back down in her chair, stares knowingly into Steven's now reddish, brown face, "And after ya show me this little ol' thing a yours?"

"Then you show me something a yours."

"I'm gonna tell," David says.

"Won't live long enough, fish-bait," Steven cautions, not taking his eyes off of Cory Ann.

She smiles warmly, forces through her teeth, "I ain't the present, ya dirty little cretin."

David says, "Two bits is twenty-five cents. If five minutes is two bits, but you only want two and a half minutes, how do you pay twelve and a half cents?"

"What'm'I missin' here, boyos?"

David says, "Mom said you're a five minute, two bit whore. That Uncle Taylor paid you to come here and pretend to be his girl friend. We were listening."

"Little pitchers have big ears."

At that moment, the lights go out, and Leo and Betsy return with the cake ablaze like Mrs. O'Leary's barn. Taylor reappears, and the family starts singing four different versions of 'Happy Birthday' in as many keys. Penderecki would be delighted. "And you look like one too," Steven croons. The *two bit whore* chooses not to tax her vocal chords. She is gripping the tablecloth so tightly that the dessert plates on the opposite side have inched toward her on little invisible feet. Despite the incendiaries, the temperature in the room has dropped forty degrees.

"Make a wish," says Betsy through a tic brought on by the chill.

Steven smiles at Cory Ann and sprays the cake from flatulent lips. Betsy hands him the Henckel for the first cut, almost equal, percentage wise, to the amount of copper in a nickel. Cory Ann covets the Henckel.

"Tape worm," Leo explains.

"Gross," says Steven, with a face to prove it.

Cory Ann's molars are becoming sore from coupled pressure.

"I can't eat cake," Taylor says.

"On you nephew's birthday, you can eat cake," his sister says. "Won't kill you?"

"Don't worry, Taylor," says Leo, "Your sister'll pray you out of the diabetic coma. Hell, Bets, if he's not supposed to eat cake, he's not supposed to eat cake. Fuckin' French Revolution 'er what!"

"Da-*ad!*"

"What *is* he supposed to eat, Leo? Cory Ann?"

"Eats anything *I* put on his plate," says Cory Ann, an eye on the knife.

"So, Cory Ann," Leo says. "Taylor tells us you're in food services."

The evening, in Taylor's reckoning, is going well. Being a man for whom even the undercurrent is over his head, he sees Cory Ann already merged into the family as completely as the Santa Fe into the Burlington Northern. Betsy, he feels, with Leo's constant monitoring, is making the supreme effort, and Cory

Ann is showering her with compliments on her decorating skills. Both woman have, remarkably, lowered the lid on casual profanity. Even Betsy's remark, *How's the house, Taylor? The Dali Lama's been home more recently than me,* he accepted as good natured banter. *Kumbaya.*

Their reception in the formal entry hall was one of awe; even Steven couldn't take his eyes off of Uncle Taylor's new friend; so glamorous was she, so smartly dressed in new halter top, a stone-washed denim skirt that could double as a belt, and knee high boots with heels the length of the golden spike, an ensemble she had purchased especially to make the right impression. How could he blame them for ogling? He couldn't keep his eyes, his hands even, off of her himself. Under the table, like un-taxed salary, they had groped their way through Betsy's delicious meal, causing themselves to smirk at all the wrong moments, for Steven to elbow David which the younger boy took for some sort of subtle rebuke, for Betsy — only minimally soothed by how much in love her brother seemed — arching her eyes and nodding her head to Leo; her benevolent smile spreading faster than malaria in the Canal Zone, and subtly, unbeknownst to Taylor, just a hair less lethal.

The guest, for her part, requested the house tour as if visiting The Breakers in Newport. Leo was more than obliging. He took her under cavernous vaulted ceilings soothed by soffit lighting, a great flagstone fireplace and a bin of Prestologs to keep Pasadena cozy through the snow season. Contrasty, high gloss family groupings in gilded Gainsborough frames advertised the work of a local photographer; colors hand-enhanced; the deep royal blue backgrounds suggestive of celestial immortality.

He led her across bamboo floors to appease the Sierra Club: Leo is a passionate armchair contributor. The kitchen is a Jenn-Air showroom of stainless steel and hand-formed tiles baked in Mexico by — non-New — Mexicans, and secured by cherry wood custom cabinetry. There are two sinks, one for vegetables and one for all the other things that sinks are intended to do; dual dishwashers with an entertainment capacity for UN peace keeping forces; a counter-depth frig with three — count 'em, *three* doors — running filtered water, ice cubes, chopped ice, sculpted ice, glacial ice, designer ice, ice bergs, *and* an extra stand alone freezer for small herds of slaughtered bovines, well stocked on hog futures, tankards of low fat lactate, and an Iowa's worth of perishables that have escaped the covetous eyes of bio-fuel manufacturers.

Leo shows her the kids' rooms with built in desks and bookshelves and a switchboard worth of dedicated jacks. Steven's room has foldouts of the month tacked to the walls — what he calls *photographic mammaries* — a flashlight on his nightstand so that he can enjoy them after lights-out and keep his sheets in a constant state of encrustation, and a young constrictor curled in a twenty-gallon fish tank eyeing the world's most uninsurable mouse. David's has iconic black and white posters of Einstein, formulas reeling from his head, Hawkings and Newton, and a Habit-Trail to exercise his hamster; to keep it trim and desirable to the opposite sex. The hamster's name is Polly Math.

Betsy has a room of her own, for painting, which she does often but poorly; for floral arrangements, which she does seldom but well; for sewing, which she doesn't do at all: *Who the hell has the time?* Leo enjoys a study/office/man's cave bedecked in somber woods, chair rails and a desk you could play football on.

The library houses Betsy's fiction: Amy Tan, Isabelle Allende, literally anybody who writes about somewhere else, many in personalized first editions from the signings she attends; and Leo's history, focused mostly on Latin America or Chicano studies, bios of Bolivar, San Martín, Cesar Chavez, Juarez, Zapata, DeSoto, Pizarro; tracts on conquest and revolution, peasant upheavals, the secularization of missions; and fiction by Villaseñor, Vargas Llosa, long unreadable tomes of Octavio Paz. There is a photo on the wall of his great grandfather and Poncho Villa bandoleered to the nines after a fine day of happy manslaughter and recreational wenching.

The Valverde's each have a bathroom. Cory Ann is not surprised: she has her own as well. And there are others, one for the illegal help — don't ask don't tell, Erlinda, paid under the table she polishes right down to the glue under the veneer — one for the guests, and one for the hell of it that's a good fit for pool mooches placed as it is near the back patio and entered through an exterior door. The bathrooms have low-flow toilets that are quieter than Max Sennet movies, Jacuzzi tubs with more jets than Boeing, hand-painted, and signed, vessel-style sinks, showers rigged like carwashes with multiple shower heads up and down the walls that pulsate and throb, spit, squirt, explode in tactile delight in crevices the ordinary shower head is too polite to see, and bidets with geysers forceful enough to knock down mobs of angry protesters.

Leo likes to say, *Some folks around here may have more money, but the Valverdes have the most immaculate assholes on the block.* Cory Ann is appropriately gaga over it all; will whisper to Taylor later, *My Lord, honeysuckle, a gal could take a good dump with a lot less!*

Presents are traditionally opened in the great room, awash in comforting variations of tan the paint company calls *desert autumn*, the color of the children who betray much of their father's heritage under their thick mops of straight coal black hair in high gloss enamel. There are views of the lap pool and spa. Leo keeps the air on high so they can gather around the fireplace even in a September that the Santa Anas blow in from Palm Springs. As penance, he will write an extra guilt check for one hundred dollars to the League of Conservation Voters. The League will send him a gracious thank you, printed on re-cycled paper, to be presented to his accountant in February, when he will have an even grander conflagration designed to break Montana-sized bergs off the Antipodes. Leo is a constitutional Democrat, obeyer of most convenient laws, believer in *cheques* and balances, an aesthete of nuanced ambiance, a socially conscious guy trying desperately to bring a sense of coziness to a space the size of the Pentagon. It seems luxurious, but it's hard work, being Leo.

Betsy clears the coffee table of Ansel Adams, a large volume on seashells, and an antique Bible the size of a Plymouth. A flower arrangement, singed by Leo's pyromania, is set on the floor near the French doors. David hands Steven a lump wrapped haphazardly in the Sunday comics and says, from somewhere in a space of his own making, "The coast of Maine is three thousand miles long."

"How can that be?" Leo asks.

"I don't know, but it is."

Steven says, "Nerd-nostril," rips away the newsprint to reveal well-worked clay, amorphously shaped. "Looks like dog poop!"

"It's not," David protests. "I made it."

"You made dog poop?"

"It's a meteor."

Betsy says, "It's beautiful. Isn't it Steven?"

"If you like dog poop."

"From Dad and I," she says, handing him a cube neatly wrapped in appropriate Happy Birthday paper that glimmers from the hearth.

Leo says, "It's a globe from the Flat Earth Society."

"The CD's from my list?" says Steven. "Did you get them all?"

"Yes. And I have a new Bible for you too," says Betsy. "Yours is getting a bit worn."

Leo says, "The kid's about as spiritual as Christopher Hitchins. The smog kills pine trees, eats the cones in stereo speakers, and does a job on the skins of Bibles. Is this one signed?"

"Why don't *you* read it and find out, damned pagan!"

"I'm more into the Azimov kind of sci-fi."

"That big one is from Cory Ann and me," Taylor says.

"Actually, just from Uncle Taylor," says Cory Ann. "Sorry, I've *absolutely* nothin' for ya, kid."

Curious glances carrom about the room. Taylor insists, "No, no. It's from both of us. We decided together."

Steven anxiously tears through the ribbon and neatly folded tissue that Cory Ann has arranged. He is struck dumb by the Bachmann display.

"Runs inside and outside," instructs Taylor. "Rain won't hurt it."

Steven manages to lift his chin long enough to eke out a tiny, "Wow."

"Just from Uncle Taylor," Cory Ann reminds.

"Say thank you to Uncle Taylor," Betsy says.

"Thank you, Uncle Taylor."

David says, "Steven hates it. Can I have it?"

"Nonsense. Steven loves it. He's just…surprised," says Betsy. "Anyway, this kind of thing isn't for you." There is no possible way she is going to expose her immune-compromised babe to Taylor's viral spores.

"My meteor could crash that train in a trillion pieces," suggests the birthday boy.

"It's not for crashing," Taylor says with alarm. "Rain, okay. But remember boys, this is an adult toy, and requires a little care. We don't want to pummel it with space debris, do we?"

"Or ET dog poop," says Steven.

"I like it," David insists, sensing opportunity.

"It's not for you to like." Betsy is adamant. "Besides, Uncle Taylor says it runs outside, a place you never go, pale face."

"Inside too."

Betsy comes over to Taylor, gives him a kiss on the cheek, and whispers, "You're such a clueless asshole. And you spent too fuckin' much!"

"Taylor's idea entirely," says Cory Ann through clenched teeth.

"Not a big deal," Taylor says. "Toby gives me fifteen percent off."

"Wish you worked at Nordstrom's," says Betsy.

Following the gift giving, the dinner party divides by age and gender and retires to various retreats: the boys to their rooms, the women to the kitchen, and Leo leading Taylor to his study.

"Drink? Cigar? Amphetamines?" Leo offers.

"Thanks, no," Taylor says, sinking into a couch the shape of Fatty Arbuckle.

"Still the teetotaler, huh." Leo claims the swivel chair behind the desk. He is about as far from Taylor as he can be without crossing municipal boundaries and they speak in moderately raised voices, the way people do on the subway or when there are day laborers nearby rototilling dichondra.

"So? What do you think?"

"Oh, well, she's something else, Taylor. Quite the looker. What, in current parlance, is referred to as *hot*." Absently, Leo has picked up his glasses from the desktop. He relies on the comfort of the prop, dangling the frames between thumb and forefinger and using them as emphasis and pointer, a sort of extended body language.

"Hot. Yes, hot. I think this is it, Leo." Taylor has a new pair of reading glasses that Cory Ann forced on him during a soda run to CVS. They are perky and sleek, and peek proudly from his shirt pocket.

"So, gonna bite the old bullet, are ya? Look, Taylor, if it's all the same to you, why don't we just keep this one under our belts for a while. Let Betsy have some time to digest all of this."

"She's been on my case to find a woman since Helen."

"That's true. But, you know, your sister loves you very much and…and she's very protective of those she loves. Drives me crazy with vitamins and sweaters. If the kids aren't back from school by three thirty, she's got me organizing a posse to bring them back. Above all, she is a mother."

"Not mine."

"Tell her that! Look," he says, picking up his catcher's mitt, his thinking mitt, slapping a hard ball down into the leather, "She's gonna come around fine. You'll see. Why, in no time at all she'll be bragging she introduced you two."

Taylor looks uncomfortable: over-stuffed guy on over-stuffed sofa that resembles over-stuffed guy. Taylor looks fairly uncomfortable almost everywhere. His back somehow does not conform to the billows. He sits with his arms out and down, his hands curved on the convex cushions, hints of lamb in his neat goatee. "I think they're getting along fine."

"Probably in there exchanging recipes, stitching squares on a patchwork quilt for the victims in Darfur, discussing stretch marks and boob jobs. Soccer car pools. She have kids?"

"Gosh! I don't know."

"*Gosh?* What do you mean, you don't know? Children! Little parasites that eat you out of house and home, think you're a moron and then expect you to mortgage your nuts so they can go to college to smoke dope and diddle co-eds."

"She never said."

"You never asked?"

"It makes no difference."

"Not always the reason to find things out. Sometimes, Taylor, when we're close to someone, it's a good idea to know who they are."

"I know who she is."

"Does she know who you are?"

"Of course."

"She knows about the trains? She's been to the house?"

"I haven't been too…haven't had much time with the trains lately. This having a lady friend…kind of time consuming. I've let some things go. Deferred maintenance…" — on loan from Dr. Stan of Eureka — "…I need to attend to."

"She's been to the house?"

"We spend most of our time at her place."

"What's *more*? Has she…?"

"Soon. When I clean things up a bit."

"Uh huh. I see. Can't wait to hear how that goes."

"I'm a little tentative about it."

"Are you? A tad unsure?"

"Betsy's fault. She always makes me feel like I'm weird or something."

"Unique. She feels you're unique. Not everyone understands unique. Think how the Governor must've felt when Maria brought him home to meet all those Kennedys, what Sally Hemmings must a thought when she saw mammoth bones and all that crap from Lewis and Clark at Jefferson's house when he brought her home to meet the family. I'm rambling. You have no fucking idea what I'm talking about. Taylor, have fun, get laid, don't worry about your sister, buy low sell high, and keep Cory Ann away from the trains until you're sure she can't live without you. And, if Steven doesn't set up the G gauge, I'll play with it myself. Oh, by the way, Betsy thinks you spent too much money. I'm supposed to tell you."

In the kitchen, the gloves have come off, are laying crumpled on the terrazzo floor, those from Nordstrom's mingling with a mangy pair from the Salvation Army thrift store. If you're the sort that relishes female mud wrestling or a good catfight, this is a promising place to be. Me-*fucking*-ow! They are perched on the edge of barstools, blazing across the commodious island and through the steam of their coffee. A hot beverage is perhaps not the wisest selection for the current encounter; one would hope for iced tea on such a warm day, a gin fizz to take the edge off.

"Let's be frank," Betsy starts, a proponent of ground rules. She barely opens her mouth to reveal her own clenched teeth. Her foundation is receding into worry wrinkles around her eyes, the suck of tectonics, the shifting of plates, the further retreat from the unity of her facial Pangea. Leo would not approve.

"Girl t'girl," Cory Ann responds. She can sneer with the best of them.

"No bullshit."

"In the open."

"Cards on the table."

"What you see is what you get."

"Is what it is."

With each exchange they edge a bit closer, narrow eyes, the white coming to knuckles mediating fists to granite. Cory Ann adds the extra dimension of shifting shoulders, controlled heaves of her breasts and the squirm of the tattooed gecko, like the one that sells insurance, sandwiched between them. One of them may need his services shortly.

Betsy arches her back, leans to the rear, drums her fingers on the invisible ivory of the counter top. "Tell me, Cory Ann…It *is* Cory Ann?"

"Was when I got here, will be when I leave."

"What exactly do you do in the food services industry?"

"I'm the CEO at Betty Crocker."

"Are you now? And what exactly does that entail, dear?"

"Tail? Y'mentioned tail. I service the men employees. Occasionally the women. They tell me what they want, and I give it to'em. There's an exchange a currency, an' all's wet that ends wet. That's what waitresses do, y'know."

"You're a waitress?"

"Taylor likes t'get ahead a himself. You expected what? A five-minute, two bit whore?"

Betsy is flushed, hand-fans herself. "I never said that."

"I don't believe little diarrhea-mouth's got the guile t' lie."

Betsy is impressed with *guile*. Someone had said it on "The View" on a day Cory Ann was home with the flu. "It's gibberish, Betsy says. "Most of what he says makes no sense at all."

"Honest people have that problem."

"Look, I didn't mean to presume."

"'Bout what ya didn't say?"

"Look, understand, Taylor's like a child. He tells stories. Has imaginary friends. What was I to think?"

"Looky here, tinsel tits, I could give a flyin' fuck what *you* think. But I'd thank you t' keep me out a your potty mouth 'round those kids."

"This is my house, gutter bitch! I'll say what I damn well want about what ever the fuck I want in front a who ever the fuck happens to be here."

"If you weren't Taylor's sister, I'd haul your bitch-ass outside an' drown you in your own fuckin' chlorine."

"I'd like to see that."

"No. Actually, you wouldn't, Betsy Boop."

They eye their cooling coffee; posture from cooling passions. They are both a bit burnt out and sit still for several minutes. It is quieter than death but for the rustle of fabric on their tensed forms.

"Let's get beyond this shit," Betsy suggests at long last.

"Well beyond my ass already."

"Take a minute to calm the fuck down."

"Still water over here."

"You wanna refill on that?"

"Haven't thrown this one yet."

"You're not exactly what I expected."

"He tried t'get Angelina Jolie, but she was out adoptin' somethin'."

"I guess we got off on the wrong foot."

"Ya think?"

Betsy bites her lower lip, forces back an uninvited tear. "My brother makes me crazy. Leo says I get irrational when I talk about him."

"So why dump on me?"

"Because I don't know you. I don't know what you want. Taylor isn't like other adults. There's a whole universe of experience he's somehow skipped."

"What makes ya think I want somethin'?"

"Don't you? Doesn't everybody?"

"Can't think a what *you'd* possibly want. You're freezer's bigger than my whole apartment. I've had me some life that I don't think I want to go into right now, not with you, and that ya probably ain't very interested in anyhow. Sometimes I think I'm a magnet for assholes. I been married four times and got nothin' t'show for it. The last one sold cars. Chevies. GMC. Nothin' too classy. That lasted about three weeks. Then he sold Maytags and Kenmores. Last time I seen 'im he was handicappin' ponies at Santa Anita with some little Asian skank dippin' into his wallet pocket. An' he was the best of 'em. Taylor's a whole different ball game. Taylor don't know from takin' a'vantage. Is he a little strange? Fuck it, little sister, they're *all* strange! For me, he's a aerosol a fresh mint in the mornin' mouth a life. You think I'm some cheap hussy's gonna take him for all he's got, ka-ching, ka-ching? Fact is, I don't know what-all he's got. He's just this big, happy puppy in love with his trains an' he seems t'think I'm the cat's pajamas, an' that's all right with me. Fact is, in my experience...an' if I got anything, I got experience... nothin' much lasts longer than a episode a 'Family Guy' anyway, so enjoy the chuckles, an' when it's done, it's done. All's I want from Taylor's a little time, a little snuggle, a little affectionate pinch on the buns when it suits 'im, *and* when it don't? Ever'body goes their own way, no hard feelin's, no shit t' divvy up, these your CD's or mine? Your spatula? Your 'lectric tooth brush? No accountin', jus' out the door, have a good life an' maybe I'll bump into ya at the laundrymat some time." She too cues a welling tear.

"I owe you an apology. I guess. I didn't mean to …"

"Y'owe me nothin'. What's said is said and it ain't goin' nowheres. An' I got no expectations waitin' for paybacks. Just a whole shit-load a disappointment in that direction."

"He's so vulnerable. He's had a sad life."

"Cry me a river. He don't seem t'see it that way. He was happy as a clam in coal dust when we hooked up. Just an overweight guy startin' t'use his senior citizen discounts an' waitin' for his body t'crap out like every other guy'ats gotta pee more than three times a night. I been wavin' in this parade for some time, sister. Don't worry your designer-ass over Taylor. Taylor's just fine."

Betsy sits back, crosses her arms, steels her chin. "Have you been to his house?"

"He's sensitive 'bout that."

"Then we'll talk again when you have."

At the door, hugs and kisses are mimed as David announces that buffalos are actually bison. "Actually, you are," Steven tells him." Leo gives Steven an appropriate whack over the back of the head.

Cory Ann sports David a great bosomy hug which puts him close enough to the lizard to sign on the dotted line, and which will earn him one of Steven's masterful Indian burns later in the evening. She says, "Thanks, little cutie, you've taught me stuff I needed to know." David says, "There's more." "I'm sure there is," she agrees, turning to Steven as he moves in for an aborted attempt to meet the gecko, and says, "Happy birthday, Don Jew-wan." She busses his soft cheek and whispers in his ear, "Hope ya catch yourself some a that leopard-see like they got in Hawaii an' your measly little pencil drops off before ya get a chance t' stick it in the sharpener." Steven whispers back, "I love when you talk dirty."

In the car, Taylor — taking no notice of the incisor engraved on her lower lip, her glazed eyes planted on nothing through the open side window, or the Salem filter locked in her tight, still fingers supporting an impossibly long column of crooked ash worthy of Ripley's and held in place purely by lingering mortification — rolls down his window, smiles into his own reflection on the windshield, enjoys a little lamb burp, a tiny garlic mashed fart, breathes out in complacent relief, and says, "I think that went well. You?"

VI

B ETSY SURVEYS THE PILLAGE LEFT IN the wake of the unwashed hordes, then, without waiting for the official's whistle, calls, "Headache." Such a flag in the air generally announces the penalty of soiled dishes. Leo moans, curses under his breath, but Betsy is already tripping up the stairs to consume a bottle of Tylenol and retreat to the regulation safety zone of her bed.

Leo, surrendering to the *fait accompli*, is left to tidy the kitchen, hamper the tablecloth, bury the dead, and be drawn back to the fridge by the gamey odor of lamb. He opens the door, sees the platter covered in wrinkled foil, the irregular physique of leftover chops, Golden Fleece in CorningWare luring him with minty sirens' song. He looks backward, economically closes the stainless steel door, peruses the dining room, the stairs; is sure that he has inherited a minute or two of opportunity. He walks back across the terrazzo tiles of the kitchen, navigates around the shoals of the Maui-sized island in the center, and sees himself as a ghostly reflection in the hanging Babylonian garden of copper cookware.

He reopens the warehouse doors of the appliance and a too-pliant corner of foil from the tray emancipates one smallish — but not *the* smallest — chop from its swamp of frosting-thick, off-white fat, wonders briefly if Betsy has taken inventory of the leftovers, and gnaws the chalky musk of meat from the bone, gristle and all. His head falls back in a delirious rush, something he feels must be akin to a heroin high, and then purges with a hangover of responsibility and a promise to no one in particular that this sort of clandestine behavior will not be repeated as long as the earth needs him. He uses the bone to smooth out the visible suet sinkhole of the missing chop and discards it, re-covers the rack, and proceeds to check the locks on all the doors and windows as if he is security at the Bonaventure, pokes the fire into embers, turns down the air, and finds his way into pajamas decorated with golf clubs.

Betsy is buried to the neck in their dual control electric blanket, her side set to Cairo August, his to Bismark January. There are bags under her eyes you could load groceries into and she seems to have discolored to a mud gray under the fluorescents, like a figure coming out of cave walls in an old Flash Gordon serial.

"Hell on a hanger," he says, "you look like you've been hit by a bag a nickels!"

"Give it a break, will you?"

He knows what's coming, hears it in the rack and pinion ratchet of her nighttime plaint. When he is tired and she is despairing, her voice comes to him as something born of an errant nub of chalk on a blackboard, liberated calcium carbonate dust gathering in her throat. It carries chill arctic winds to solidify in his spine, leaving his still nubile bride to parch like ancient lakebeds, the rose of her cheeks receding to bleak, ashen pools. He has told her that her badgering makes his penis shrivel; she responded that if it shriveled any more, it would be harder to locate than a twelve-year old virgin in East LA. He reminded her that he is not a Mexican, not technically, and that hers is an un-Christian stereotype, to which she asked what was his frame of reference.

She says, "So, what's your take on Daisy Mae?"

He sits on his side of the bed, his back to her. It is futile to attempt imperviousness: he is Swiss cheese porous in Betsy's fulsome wake. "Well, if it gives you comfort," he says, "I checked all around and it seems that Dogpatch Dolly left the silver but walked off with the truffle peeler, three pairs of your favorite Victoria Secret panties, a bio of Dom Pedro II of Brazil, and Steven's virginity. Best of all, David's just rattled off the ingredients for a homemade explosive, some of which we have on hand in the larder. Other than that, we're buttoned up like a nun in a vault."

"Spare me. I'm worried."

He positions himself on his back above the covers. "Not now!"

"You tell me what he's doing with a woman like that."

"All the usual stuff is my guess. Isn't this what you wanted him to be doing?"

"No. Well, yes. But not with *her*. Look, I'm not saying she's as bad as I thought she'd be. Gotta admit, the girl's got more spunk than taste. But I'll tell ya this, Leo, as Jesus is my witness, as many screws as have come loose in Taylor's head, he *is* a college grad…an advanced degree, no less…from a good family, and at best she's the product of some shitty double-wide in a place like Victorville or Blythe with tarantulas and mangy dogs and feral cats everywhere, naked kids pissing in ravines, while their father's do target practice on highway signs."

"You've given this some thought?"

"He stands no chance with a woman like that."

"Betsy, I haven't seen your brother so jazzed since the last Railroad Fair in Sacramento. I'd say a hop in the old sack with a bundle like Cory Ann is a lot safer than snuggling up to some big Baldwin four-eight-nine or whatever the hell, with a hot firebox and twenty minutes left to get to Cheyenne."

"That's the fuckin' point!"

"The *fuckin'* point it is. We are in agreement."

She has a cold dishrag folded over her face, her eyes. "His experience is Teddy Bears that talk and his…*fucking* trains. What has he ever done to prepare him for Miss Overage Wild and Wet of 2008?"

"Helen comes to mind."

"Well, that turned out swell."

"You worried about Cory Ann or Taylor? This one doesn't seem likely to set herself up on the tracks at rush hour."

"So when she's had enough? When she discovers that he's about as exciting as fish farts? What happens then, Leo? What does he do?"

"Probably build a new siding to hold a few extra tank cars. Taylor, you recall, is not a guy of extended emotional episodes. I don't know what goes on in that head of his, but I do know he's the most self-contained son of a bitch I've ever known."

"Is that a reference to my mother, because if it is…?"

"Jesus, Betsy! Take a load off, would ya?"

"Don't compound the insult with blasphemy."

He turns to look at her. "Unless you have somehow ignited a sudden fire in your loins and require my further attention, I'm done for the day."

An hour later, in the dark, she is nudging his kidney with a sharp elbow. "Leo?" she says. It is a question, as if she expects he could be someone else.

Leo mumbles into his pillow. "Timeshit any…?" He has his half of blanket tuned to Gulag, December.

"Are we old, Leo?"

He struggles to heft himself onto his back. "'Pends who you ask."

"I had an old person's dream."

"Tell me in the morning."

"I'll forget by morning."

"Definitely an old person's...Nothing gained, nothing..." He surrenders to a yawn.

"Don't close me out. You always do that."

"Who's closing you out? I'm like 'The Night of the Living Dead' over here!"

"I dreamed it was the middle of the night."

"Is."

"And I couldn't sleep."

"This is not a dream."

"So I got up and went outside. I was all dressed. I don't know why. You know how dreams are."

"Maybe if I slept."

"So, I got in the car and drove around. Old Town, South Lake, and you know what?" He imagines shrugging. She says, "Everything was open. Supermarkets. Restaurants. Hardware stores. You could buy a pair of Birks or a Zippo lighter in the fuckin' middle of the night in this dream."

"Bet business was booming."

"It was. There were people everywhere. *Old* people. It seems, secretly, only the old people know this, in the dream, that long after the stores close for everybody else, they open again for all the old farts that can't sleep at night. Then they close up at about five so nobody else will know about it. Are you listening?"

"Choice do I have?"

"What does it mean?"

"If there's a buck to be made, somebody'll find a way to make it."

"But why did *I* dream it?"

"Because it's *your* dream. *I* couldn't dream it!"

"Is it because I'm thinking about age? About mortality?"

"I have no fucking idea."

"Because, if it is, then maybe I am old."

"Maybe you are."

"Fuck you."

"Please. Look, it's obvious that you think about death because you've come to believe that death is *something*. I don't think about it because I'm convinced that there's nothing to think about."

"God forbid, if something happens to me, what will happen to David?"

"Depends on what happens to you. I suppose if you get a hangnail, he'll probably survive the trauma."

"If I'm not here?"

"Then he'll be raised in a single family parent."

"You're falling asleep. But what *will* happen to David? You haven't a clue about his...disability."

"He has no disability."

"That's not comforting."

"That he has no disability? I'd think you'd be delighted."

"That you don't *know* he has a disability. The other day, he told me how old some scientist thinks the world is."

"I hope you didn't contradict him with visions of the Bishop of Usher."

"I didn't want a theology versus bad science spat with my baby."

"Bad science? What is that?"

"You're changing the subject."

"The subject is the weirdness of our youngest son. Thank God for primogeniture. At least the little whacko will not inherit our estates: the hunting grounds, the fens, the moors stalked by wolves with bellies full of peasants. David's fine. What isn't fine is that snake trainer you go to for spiritual immersion."

"There are no snakes. I've told you this."

"Betsy, the guy believes that Lot's wife was turned to salt, amongst other very questionable events. He's a moron!"

"The Lord moves in…."

"I know. How convenient. And I know where this is going. I know it *ad nauseum*."

"Okay, Nostradamus, where is it going?"

He rolls over to look at her, nearly burns himself on the tropical side of the Seeley's equator. "It's going to Taylor. It always does. You're going to ask what happens to Taylor if something should happen to you, something involving old age and expiration like a due date on a library book. First of all, he's older than you. Us guys, our warranties are far more limited than yours."

"You never know. All kinds of shit happens to people our age."

"One, maybe it's dangerous to shop in the middle of the night. All the *locos* are out and about. Two, when it's time for your internment, I will personally pick up Taylor and make sure he's wearing an appropriate tie without a silkscreen of some caboose on it, make sure his teeth are brushed, shirt tucked in, and get him to the service on time. Then, I will take him home, remarry, and give David a happy childhood. End of story. End of conversation. Go the fuck to sleep already."

"See. You're closing me out." She sits up, crinkles her nose. "And Manuelito, you fucking phony, I gotta tell you that you smell like something Mary had whose fleece was white as snow."

"I cleaned up. The kitchen reeks."

"The stink of the sacrificial lamb clings to you like sin. A mark of shame God has branded you with so that I will sense the transgression He has witnessed." She has only a partial tongue in her cheek.

Leo is angry, feels about his end table in search of a pair of glasses to jab at her. "So what? Even if, he's gonna kick my sorry ass out of Eden?" As an agnostic, Leo often neglects to capitalize deific pronouns. "Because I ate of the lamb of knowledge, he's gonna cast me forth into the land of Nod with Winkin' and Blinkin' and all the other damned and indiscrete, and put enmity between the two of us, man and woman, and damn our seed with eternal resemblance to

194

your wacky brother? Huh? What's he gonna do, Betts? Cancel my World Wildlife membership?"

"No, but he may cancel a species or two in you name."

"Well, that'd be mature."

"Ba-a-a-a-a!" she tells him.

VII

A WEEK LATER, BETSY IS STILL fretting over David, over Taylor, over, she says, the well-dressed crackpot who now frequents the religious stacks — somewhat religiously — no doubt researching his next novel. Leo tries to tune her out: considers Yoga, a brief guy's vacation on a dude ranch, a raft trip down the river of no return.

Without an in-depth vetting hashed out by her staff, Cory Ann makes the rash decision to accompany Taylor to the Fiftieth Anniversary Rail Extravaganza at the Inland Empire Trolley Museum. She has no idea what to expect. Perhaps some minor adventure. Although only twenty minutes away, *depending on traffic*, she considers it an expedition worthy of provisions and has depleted the local Super A — imperiling the next emigrant wagon train that rolls through town — grabbing up a sack of *chicharrones* taken from a kindly pig that would — did, actually — give you the skin off its back; a Hershey's milk chocolate bar requiring a low boy to transport; a case of Dr. Pepper's; a half dozen little hockey pucks coated in a dark brown compound from a secret lab by the East River, beef jerky — health food that is ninety-seven percent fat free — and a large can of assorted nuts with extra sea salt. She is as knowledgeable about diabetes, borderline or otherwise, as she is about cogwheel inclines.

When Taylor shows up on her porch, her heart drops to about pancreas level. He is in all-out full, vintage motorman's attire of black suit, vest, a prominent watch chain over his belly, lines of brass buttons flashing bling in the morning haze, and a uniform cap with a Pacific Electric pin in the center: SPEED COMFORT SAFETY.

He causes quite a stir from the continual porch party swelling out onto the walkway of the court. Someone has hit up Taco Bell for a *carreta's* worth of breakfast *burritos* and little plastic containers of hot sauce, generously napalmed with *Tapatío* all around. A wolf whistle follows Taylor up the walk.

Cory Ann yanks him inside by the arm; is tempted to put her cigarette out on his hat badge. She's admitted to an occasional smoke, and this is certainly the occasion. "The fuck, cupcakes, ya mention anything 'bout a costume party?" She is costumed herself in a uniform that might get her an interview at the Northeast Precinct Division, near where the train did the ultimate Flat Stanley on Helen.

"I'm a member," he says. "You're fine. I might run one of the cars for a while and you want it to look period authentic."

"Who does?"

"Well, everybody."

"Not *every*body. What's the Derringer for?" She points to the tiny holster on his belt.

"Ticket punch," he says.

"Should a known. Gotta have yourself a ticket punch. Ya know, I gotta live'th these cannibals here. They don't go nowheres, like work or nothing, so all they gotta do all day's sit around an' notice shit they can get all pissy about." She steps back to not exactly admire him. "This one's gonna get some traction, can see that."

"Traction it is," he says with a grin, basking in the warm glow of their compatibility.

East on the Two Ten, he bemoans the fact that they couldn't ride the PE out to Duarte, as in the old days. He rehashes his favorite conspiratorial canard: that GM, Standard Oil and Firestone, under the spell of Mordor and the One Ring, hatched an evil plan to destroy electric transit through an orc-run front company called National City Lines. A good theory, possibly with some modicum of truth that conjures spirited dialogue amongst the rail crowd, the devil's advocates of which will insist that the automobile had committed trolleycide long before William Crapo Durant was running GM. Even the Broward skeptic, Ruben Goldenberg, allows that the dybbuk is in the details.

Cory Ann is practicing an admirable level of indifference, is concentrating on getting through a stick of jerky without sacrificing her nicotine-stained teeth, and won't be distracted by ancient crimes.

They pass by malls and clones of malls, hangar-sized home improvement stores, car dealerships with computerized billboards, and chain restaurants that repeat themselves like a very bad meal every five miles. The sky gets thicker, the gray congeals, the nearby San Gabriels loose their definition, and Taylor lectures on in foamer confabulations.

"Nearly one thousand red cars, eleven hundred miles of track and line: to the Valley, to Balboa, up Mt. Lowe, the beach, Riverside. The PE had more track right here in the Southland than the Western Pacific had from Salt Lake City to Oakland." The latter: a fact worthy of David Valverde. "Hon, take note. At one time, I'm talking nationwide, every little town had a streetcar line and was linked to the next town by an interurban. Why, did you know, that there was a time when you could ride from Portland, Maine, all the way to Milwaukee and beyond just by streetcar and interurban, just by getting off of one and on to another? All across Indiana on the same car!"

Cory Ann has to admit she didn't know that. Her schooling, after all, was irregular. Fiddling with the AM dial, she says, "Got any CD's? Garth Brooks? Waylon an' Willie? Whatever?" She feels a pissyness of her own arising, is starting to wish she was back in bed, alone. He doesn't even have a CD player.

He takes the off ramp alongside a brewery with a siding of tank cars, turns left under the freeway parallel to a spur track, then left again back the way they came on a dirt road vaguely informed by the loop of the spur, near an old quarry that once supplied river rocks to landscapers, up onto a flat with the car facing Mt. Wilson's punk-spiked peak of antennas, and parks in the dust along a dry river bed pocked with smooth boulders just aching to become porch posts in Bungalow Heaven.

The lot is filled with vehicles, mostly SUVs and vans and pickups. A chain link fence with a looped crown of glistening razor wire separates the cars from the trains, 2008 from 1940, the dust funk of Taylor's tires from the festive chaos of clanging trolleys sucking juice from the maze of wires. Red cars rock by, yellow ones, geriatric machines with trussed under carriages and clerestory roofs, wooden side boards flaking like fish scales, riveted metal exfoliating, a rusty molt of lead paint, old numbers, serifed letters saying LA Railway, San Diego Electric, Key System, Muni. Wheezing complaint around a tight bend of rail comes a sleek PCC car from Vancouver, a funeral car from East LA, work cars to mend tracks and repair wire, to oil, to ballast, a trolley locomotive from Yakima to drag freight, a military diesel on stand-by to inch them all along when they fail.

The cars sit on loops and straight arrow tracks in every degree of decline, from newly restored to barely composed. The redeemed ones issue from great corrugated sheds like new butterflies from cocoons, the redeemable ones warehoused and prioritized for cosmetic intervention or full operable restoration, and the iffy, the forlorn, the already lost left outside to endure the weather. There is a vast ward of organ donors missing doors, window frames, controls, supporting trucks. They rot like the hulks of autos that never seem to leave the desert where they were last parked. A few are stacked in pyramids like a circus family, just as they were laid in state pre-rescue at the scrap yards on Terminal Island.

Taylor steps lightly from the Cadillac, as lightly as Taylor can step, practices his breathing routine, calls back to Cory Ann, "Let's do it."

She is slumped in her seat, unsure in the snack debris, thinking up headaches, cramps, escape routes across the forbidding cordillera, a death march over salt flats, a sagebrush lunch or a trade with a pack rat as last resort. She makes a long project of reapplying make-up, hoping for the intervention of lightning bolts or temblors, a locust invasion, an errant air raid siren, killer bees, the sudden Mitsubishi buzz of a distant kamikaze setting his Zero on a course with the museum's electric power plant. She senses the onslaught of a pivotal moment.

Reluctantly, slowly, she emerges from the train-free security of the car body, as Helen has proven, an illusory time out at best. Taylor, waving his uniformed trunks of arms at all the electric excitement, babbles, in paleo-infant, "Ho ho, d'ya think, huh?"

He thinks she is wowed, can't catch her tongue, as she pauses to consider whether or not *ho ho* is some sort of back door endearment. Then she says, "Don' know, not exactly what I expected."

"I know," he says. "That and more."

"I thought, y'know, museum? Big gray building with pillars? Things on stands with ropes 'round 'em an' signs t'read an' buttons to press to make'em sound like they was working? I remember fieldtrips, guess I had that on my mind.

I remember the time Mom was supposed t'go along because it was her turn t'be room mother'r something and they wouldn't let'er on the bus after her flask fell out on the four square court. Put an end t' her fifteen minutes a motherhood." She breaks from her reverie, a stall if ever there was one. "The fuck is this place? 'S like a goddamned wreckin' yard."

He doesn't hear her. The ions electric sting his nostrils; he is lured by the buzz on the wires, high on the ozone in his lungs and is already clumping along in great puffs of over-sized black-shoe-generated dust storms, heading for the entrance. Tickets are sold on the platform of an old yellow Southern Pacific station that was trucked to Duarte in pieces and lovingly reassembled by volunteers.

In fact, the whole facility is held precariously together by unscheduled weekenders and diminishing donations in a fading fabric of nostalgia. The station, most of the cars themselves, the track, are donated, as is the time to make them whole. The entrance is through the gift shop, the station's old waiting room, where are sold wooden train whistles, picture books on such household favorites as the San Joaquin & Eastern and the Oklahoma City-Ada-Atoka, and Andy Rooney metal signs sporting the logos of lost corporations.

Behind the station, itinerant vendors are set up inside the inner track loop; card tables of the usual memorabilia, antiques, models and toys; it is Stockton *al fresco*. Other tracks set out toward the foothills — a narrow gauge line skirts the jagged course of the wash — all traced by an overhead from a line of long-armed poles. Streetcars are running circles and dead end there-and-backs. A five-piece band, costumed in straw boaters and stripes, croons train songs, *Casey Jones, City of New Orleans, Chattanooga Choo Choo*, from the labored floorboards of a flat car.

Hand in tenuous hand, Conductor Taylor and waitress Cory Ann step gingerly across creosoted ties and into the measured pace of senectitude. The middle aged guys generally do the heavy work, the gray beards in their anecdotage — some in uniforms like Taylor's — do the tours behind the motorman's controls. Barely heard above the screaming friction of steel on steel is the jargon of movement. *B-o-o-a-a-a-rd*, is crooned, *Dew-ar-tay, D-ry Stone Gu-u-u-lch, San Ga-briel Moun-tains, Mo-unt Wil-son View Junc-tion*. Waist-level coin changers are clicked for effect, custom-shaped holes are punched into the tickets. Folks who remember these things in the streets, sons and daughters of those folks who've heard about them from Huell Howser, a few children who have seen something like them at Disneyland pulled by horses crapping in bags, are boarded. They pretend there is destination afoot, that they are actually going somewhere other than a dead end into the sand and brush landscape or on a loop like an American Flyer set around a Yule tree.

Taylor gives Cory Ann a hasty peck and his Lifetime Pass, tells her to ride and mingle for an hour or so, and runs off in giddy anticipation to take up his responsibilities. Today he is to pilot a huge red "blimp" with portholes from the Long Beach Line. She notices that he has removed the earring in the spirit, no doubt, of authenticity.

She lights up a cigarette, finds a bench in the shade of the station platform, and strokes her ire, alone and abashed to be here with a guy that looks to her like a Keystone Cop, brewing up her own little piss and vinegar cocktail, warding off the occasional luring stare from some ancient prune with a hearing aid, or a scornful matron rolling her World War vet down the roadway to admire a newly painted 1908 Jewitt combine with oval stained-glass windows.

And, as if to add insult to injury, there is Darouche, ambling out of a car barn, a security arm-band splitting its seams on his plentiful triceps with just enough visual oom-pah to produce that extra hint of inner-Nazi he nurtures, striding her way in his gunfighter's swagger, as if he's about to blast her off the platform, twirl his six-shooter on his pinkie, and thrust it stock forward into his holster.

"Can't even see you," she says as he approaches. "Don't even know you're here."

He steps up on the platform, looks out over the wholesome crowd, says, "Funny place t'solicit tricks."

"Rent-a-cop has wit. *Dim* wit. Look, asshole, I'm already'n'a bad mood. Whyn't you jus' go on along an' bust some terrorist threatin' to hijack one a those streetcars an' run it into the Liberry Tower Downtown or some shit?"

"Hey, CA, I didn't come over here to get ragged on. No hard feelin's, okay?"

"Last thing I expected a you, dickhead, was anythin' feelin' hard."

"You don't let up, do ya?"

"No, I don't. An' I'll tell ya this," she says, flashing long shellacked nails shaped like the rear ends of old Auburns, pointed and honed razor sharp on the grindstone. "See these here? These're for you. Ya get yourself in Taylor's face today an' I will personally whip your fat ass red front a all these nice people, an' I will use these ten little ticklers t'slice out your kidneys an' sell 'em on the black market."

"Have it you're way. Give ya all the extra space ya need. But if ya get into any trouble today, one a these old horned toads grab your buns or give ya a little tweak on the implants, don't go calling for security, because that puppya'll be burying his bone elsewhere."

Darlene Geldorf, black-leather-slick, be-wigged, a pony tail as long as Seabiscuit's swishing across the sun glare of her ass like a windshield wiper, a massive Union Pacific belt buckle hung like a hat badge above a pudendum well-delineated in cow hide tighter than it was on the cow, helmet in hand, a sandpaper-swish to the rub of her thighs, boots her way down the platform, and says, "Nightstick, m'lad, I believe there's a kitty stuck on a trolley pole somewhere. Why don't you go see about it?"

"Should a known you two'd find each other," he says in retreat. "Birds of a feather!"

Darlene says to Cory Ann, "Don't let that fool get to you."

"I look got at, hon? Don't let *me* get t'that fool."

"That's the spirit. I'm Darlene. I bet your Taylor's squeeze."

Cory Ann is squinting up into Darlene's shades, canopies her eyes with an arm. "We know each other?"

"We do now. It's a tight community. Fishbowl clarity. Where's that cutie a yours?"

"Dressed like a dork an' runnin' a train, I guess. Left me here t'fend off the lechers."

"Same here. My Jack's all spruced up and off to Toonerville. I'm about due for my shift peddling chili dogs. We could pool our respective attributes and see if we can't up the ante. What say?"

"Well, can't says as I don't know the business end of a wiener. Cory Ann," she says, offering her hand. "I'm in food services."

Taylor the motorman and Jack the conductor, their watch chains dangling in step with *The Midnight Special* in a blue grass rendition from the band, end their first shift, and head for the girls with their dogs. Jack orders a Turkey Jumbo, *hold the chili*, and an iced tea, *unsweetened*. Taylor opts for two Hebrew National's with the works, one Polish with only mustard and onions, a bag of Lay's barbecue, and a Diet Coke. Taylor knows as much about diabetes as Cory Ann.

"So how'd you land the big one?" Darlene wonders aloud, brushing the steam tears from her eyes.

"Wasn't all that much fight'n 'im," says Cory Ann. "Shoulda been a sign, but it's what I liked about 'im."

"It's ages we've been trying to hook Taylor up. Most eligible bachelor in the group under eighty-five. We've had great grandmas in walker's trying to slip roofies into his drink."

"Wouldn't know it by me. He don't drink all that much. Anyhow, he was in the net as soon as my bare toes run cross his manhood. An' we hadn't even left the joint where I waitress."

"Next to the High Ball?"

"They's both the same level, as I recall."

Darlene studies her for a smile, a twinkle, anything. There is none. After an hour of scorching dogs, she says, "Tell ya what. I see our replacements coming this way. Why don't we go somewhere and bitch and gossip like good girl friends." Two matronly woman in Kirkland jeans are tottering down the gravel path towards them.

"I'm easy."

"Wanna see my secret hideout?" Darlene opens the cooler and fishes out four canned Miller's still in their plastic porpoise trap, waves to the men at the picnic table, signing to Taylor that there is a smidge of brown deli mustard kicking back on the edge of his mouth, and leads Cory Ann into the back lot, through the derelicts, down a foot path crossing a small ravine and into a clump of prickly pear cacti and an windbreak of mature eucalyptus. An old Asbury motor coach sits on blocks in relative seclusion, an obvious segregation from the master race of flanged wheels. No one else is anywhere near them and bells and voices are muted and indistinct.

They squeeze through the semi-fold of the bus door, proceed to the wide back seat re-fitted with chaise lounge cushions and surrounded by curtains with daisies. "My damsel's tower. Whaddya think?" They sit feet up at either end of the bench. Darlene pops two of the sweating cans, hands one over to her guest. Cory Ann likes the feel of the cold aluminum, rubs it along her cheeks with her eyes closed before drinking.

"I guess you spent some time out here, Darlene."

"Sometimes, y'know, ya just gotta get away from the little boys. A while back, when Jack came back from being away, which, just coincidentally, was about the same time I was considering the promising career of hygienist, he landed a position as a watchman right here at the museum. They said he was over-qualified. That's 'cause he lied on the app. He felt he could handle it anyway. See, a lot of this stuff gets stolen, so there always has to be someone on the property. And then there's the kids with spray cans to run off now and then."

"How'd'ya rip off a streetcar?"

"The parts. The collectibles. A Pacific Electric whistle, looking pretty much like the piece of brass pipe it is, recently bid up to near four-hundred bucks on eBay. So you see, there was an opportunity here among the wreckage for a bright, over-qualified, felonious pharmaceutical dealer. You tell me when you need a refill."

"Set 'em up," Cory Ann says with a good college chug.

"So, anyways, I answer Jack's ad for a roommate, and off we go to Duarte to live upstairs in the station. He was doing community service, too, but that's a whole nuther story. The job doesn't pay much beyond minimum and room and board, mostly all you can bang out of the vending machines, but there were certain advantages."

"Like?"

"Well, love was new and insatiable. I'll tell you a secret you won't find in the museum's newsletter. During the next two years, we made love in every one a those street cars that could stand a seismic episode. In the red cars, in the yellow. Back seats, front seats, floor, up on the roof. I developed my own connotation of the term *museum piece*. That was all before we got married, decided to grow up, and joined the ranks of propertied Americans with monthly obligations. We bought a trailer."

"'Bout that chaser?"

"Aren't you the guzzler? I've got better." She reaches under her seat for a baggy with several previously rolled joints. "Never know when the moment'll be right. Shhh. We're not supposed to smoke in here."

"I'll take that t'mean *suck softly*."

They wheeze through several tokes. Cory Ann says in Don Corleone's voice, "This shit ever get old?"

"*This* shit? It was iffy, leaving it out here."

"This *train* shit?"

"It's already old. That's the point."

"No, I mean, gettin' dragged off t'all these...*e*-vents. Taylor says they go on all the time. And he's asked me t'go with 'im t' Baltimore t'see some train museum and somewhere's in West Virginia for *photo run bys*, whatever the fuck that is. First of all, I didn't need t'see more'n one episode a *The Wire* t'know I'd sooner spend an afternoon in Bagdad with a dynamite girdle under my sheet, than tour the sights a Charm City. You know what I mean? Don't these guys ever wanna lay on the beach, or screw around at some nice air conditioned mall suckin' a corn dog, or go to the Auto Show or somethin' normal? I mean, this train thing's pretty fuckin' freaky. Been t'Chicago once, with one a my exes, an' I didn't see nobody buy an el ticket 'cause they wanted t'take its picture."

Darlene shrugs, offers a puzzled little twitch to her Zig-Zag-indented lips. "All hobbies are kind a nuts, don't you think. I mean, they could be passing around little postage stamps with tweezers, or re-building classic cars so they're no longer street legal, or turning tree trunks into coffee tables."

"Jack as gone as Taylor?"

"Taylor takes the cake. No one's as obsessive as Taylor. Oh, maybe a few, but Taylor's king of the foamies. Jack, Jack's kind of what they call a renascence man. He's into everything. We drag each other, really. Cactus shows, bonsai, monster cars, living history up at Fort Tejon, cake making classes, you name it, Jack's got his boots on and kickstand up. We even breed tortoises together."

"'Course you do. What else would you breed 'em with? Christ on a bun, how the hell can a man *eat* so many fuckin' hot dogs?"

"Sounds good to me, about now, though I gotta tell you, I haven't eaten a hot dog since I read The Jungle in high school. They make you read that?"

"In high school, I only took classes where ya didn't have t'read. Never been much a the literary type. Too much a my own attitude t'deal with t'read 'bout someone else's. Was kin'a a snippy little twit. What got took out on me at home, I paid back at school. Those teachers! Gave the hardest time t'the nice ones. The ones that maybe could a done somethin' for me. Then, 'course, there were the subs, but everyone fucked with the subs. So, what was I sayin'?"

"You didn't read The Jungle in high school."

"Oh, yeah. Didn't read much a anything except the room numbers on the summonses. Gave me a lot a service classes so's the Dean could keep an eye on me. Eye or paw, it got pretty confused. Only got t'walk at graduation 'cause he fiddled with my cum record. I was a looker then. And a fiddler myself. Anyway, service was a pretty slick deal 'cause they got you as a slave for fifty-five minutes an' all ya had t'do was deliver the summonses instead a gettin' 'em. And the blow jobs. Don't think they were in the curriculum guide but each kid excels at somethin', right? I wasn't gonna win a science fair with some kind a rocket to *Your*-anus or something. Me? I got lips, Hon. Magic lips. And *suck*-tion! Anyway, best thing was, you got the same amount a credits for service as the geeks did for Advanced Placement. They didn't have t'suck off the Dean, but I didn't have t'read. And after the geezer fiddled with my cum, among other things, I was up on that stage with my tassel in play just like everyone else. Everyone takes away somethin' different from each step a life, don'cha think?"

"You poor thing! This is all true?"

"Here and there. More I tell it, the more convinced *I* am!"

"You are a woman a wisdom." Darlene has eyes that look like gunshot wounds under glass. "You stuck on Taylor?"

"He's stuck on me."

"What about you?"

"He's a sweet guy. An' contrary to appearances, he can handle his trolley. The last man I was *really* stuck on was that creepy Dean with his pecker peepin' out a his suit pants and that ping pong paddle with the holes drilled in it that got his rocks off when I was in PE doing detention 'cause I wouldn't dress with all the fuckin' lesbos glarin' at me"

"Shit! This is all very revealing, Cory Ann."

"Maybe, but *I* never done it in a streetcar, clang, clang."

Toby has closed up his table in the vending section; asks Taylor to help him retire the Jewitt to the barn. They roll down the trolley, deposit the controller in the lock box under the car and sit across the aisle on reversible wooden seats. Toby asks if Taylor is avoiding Nightstick; Taylor says he hasn't seen him. "That's good," Toby says, "Bygones have an important role in human interaction."

Toby begins to drum on a seat back, the rhythm to thoughtful silence. Then he says, "In your opinion, Taylor, how's the store doing?"

"You see the books, Toby."

"Humor me."

"I'm only there a couple of days a week."

"And what are you seeing those couple of days?"

"I don't know. Customers?"

"How many? A lot? A few? As many as there were, oh, say, five, ten years ago?"

"No. Yes. Look, Toby, I don't want to hurt your feelings or anything."

"I'm a business man, Taylor. This is not personal."

"Well, no. It's been…sort of quiet. You know, I don't think you guys ever should have put us in the back room. Never should have opened the store to the toys. We had a high end shop."

"Okay, I know how you feel about that. But you're looking at things through the lens of an enthusiast. I have practical considerations to make that don't really concern you. I have an investment to protect. A bottom line. A guy's got to put food on the table. You know what college costs these days, Taylor? I am telling you this because I consider you a friend. We go back, you and I. Fact is, if you did see the books, you'd see that the front room is where the profit is. The front room keeps the back room afloat."

"Maybe because we're in the back."

"It started before that. I saw the trend. That's why I went with the toys in the first place."

"You're not closing down the High Ball, are you, Toby?"

"Heavens, no! But I do, as a man in business, need to realize a profit, or what the hell am I doing with the whole thing in the first place? I do need to take a cue from what's going on in the economy around me. No business is an island, if you'll forgive a little corn. Tell me, Taylor, where do you go to buy a CD these days?"

"Ads in the train mags."

"I don't mean locomotive sounds. I mean music."

"I don't know much about music, Toby. I don't buy CD's. Why, just in the car coming over, Cory Ann asked me to pop in one of...of...well, I've never even heard of the singer!"

"Fantasize. Where *would* you go to buy a CD if your were to buy one?"

"I don't know. Don't they have stores?"

"That's the point. They did have stores. There are still some. But the big ones, Warehouse, Tower, they've gone under. So where do people get CDs?"

"I don't know, Toby. Last music I listened to was on a record. Somebody named Utah Phillips who sang train songs."

"The Internet. They buy on the Internet. And even that's evolving. People are downloading songs, not ordering CDs. And that's not all. Bookstores are hurting. Stereo stores are virtually anathema. So whose next?"

"Well, they can't send you a hot fried chicken dinner over the net."

"No, but they can ship you a helluva model of a B&O station or a nice brass Tenshodo 'Big Boy' ready to haul your freight if you don't mind waiting three business day."

Taylor looks at him blankly, removes his cap and palms the sweat on his shaved scalp.

"What I'm saying is, it may be time to make some adjustments."

"Am I fired?"

"Absolutely not! Just hear me out. Why should I have to deal with real estate? With the upkeep? With permits from the city every time we change a bulb? So we can be the venue of choice for a few fogies with money to burn? This is a business of attrition at this stage, Taylor. Why should I put out for stock I don't know if I can move?"

"You're closing the back room?"

"Well, not closing, exactly, for now. Trimming. Modifying. Entering the Twenty-First Century. And then? Who knows! We'll see. Here's what I'm thinking and here's where you come in. We expand the web site. Keep a few things in stock for the regulars, in abbreviated form. Use some of the space for more toys. Cars, maybe. Planes. Transportation-oriented video games. Reach out to kids because that's obviously where the money's going to be. I mean, Taylor, who coming into the store is going to lay down one, two thousand hard earned bucks in this economy for an HO locomotive? I mean, these days, that's what, ten, twenty trips to the gas station? These older guys...think of it, it's probably something of a chore for them to get out anyway, would be delighted to sit home in front of their layouts and do some virtual shopping. Longest trip they've got to make is to the doorstep to let the FedEx guy in."

"There's a personal thing, Toby. The contact. The only people in the world who talk about what I...we talk about." It is a plea, as personal as it gets for Taylor. He runs through his medley of tricks: perspires, breathes in and out, worries, surprisingly, about the demise of his contact with prototype human beings, absently checks his fly with a pass of his hand.

"More people talk through their computers these days than face to face. I'm not visible to my family anymore unless I'm pixilated. I mean, look at all these kids on MyFace or FaceSpace or whatever-face. Even railfans. Some future stage of evolution, we won't even have faces. We'll be brains with fingers and there will be more communication than ever before. Frankly, we're way too late getting into the game."

"So what do I do?"

"You're the go-to guy. Look, Taylor, no one knows more about the product than you do. Not the business, mind you. No offense, but we both know you've no head for business. But you know the stock like you made it yourself. You know who offers what, how to modify. You can trouble-shoot like no one's business. We add to the web site a new page. *Ask Taylor. Taylor the Railer. Train Talk with Taylor. Getting Started for the Rail Virgin. Layout and Throw Down.* Just casting around some ideas. You can pick your own moniker as this thing develops. Look, I will fix you up with some state of the art computer set up you will keep at home, and you run the page…the rail chat page from there, basically, of course, pushing the products, as you have always done, that you feel meets the client's needs, and then you promote us as the one stop shop for railfans. Gives you time for techno talk, history, publications, whatever, but with a worldwide train community. What do you think?"

"I can't come into the store anymore?"

"Of course you can come into the store. As much as anybody, you *are* the store. People ask for you, Taylor."

"Not Darouche."

"Count your blessings. But you won't *have to* come into the store."

"I want to come into the store. I like the store."

"Then come to the store. Who's stopping you? But work at home."

"I don't know, Toby."

"Look, Taylor. I've talked to my wife. She's with me on this. I've talked to my accountant, a few other people in the business, the distributors. This is all but done. Nothing left but to tighten the bolts. Without the overhead, I can pay you a little more."

"I don't need more money."

"Give it to charity. Taylor, I can think of no one better equipped to handle this job and for whom virtual communication will be…well, kind of a comfort."

"I'm okay in the store."

"I didn't say you weren't. But I always have the feeling that if you could just *be* in the store without ever saying a word while eye to eye with another human being…even now you're looking away from me…from *me!* Let's give it a trial run, okay? See how it plays out?"

"I can think about this?"

"We're changing gears in about two weeks. I'd like to have you on board by then."

"Jeez, Toby. I didn't see this one coming. I really didn't."

"It's less change than you think. You do the same job. Only the logistics are different. Change of venue. What the hell!"

"I want to talk to Cory Ann."

"That would be good."

"My brother-in-law, Leo."

"Talk until you're blue in the face. Let me know by the end of the week."

"I'm not real computer efficient."

"You're an engineer. You'll learn it. Even three year olds can email."

"What if I can't do it?"

"I sincerely hope you can."

"What if I can't?"

"Well, like I said, I've got to move the business forward. I'll have to find someone else if you push my back to the wall."

"Like who?"

"Why don't you think about it? Save me the trouble of going elsewhere."

"But who would you get?"

"I don't want to rattle any cages, Taylor. Shake up the old hornet's nest. Most of the guys at the store don't have the experience. I might have to look outside."

"Do you have someone in mind?"

The left corner of Toby's mouth displays a subtle twitch, a slight tug of adjoining cheek and appropriate eyelid. "We-ell, I don't really think I should be talking about that," he says carefully. Taylor's face is a story he just can't put down.

"That's *yes*, right? Right, Toby?"

"You're the guy I want, Taylor."

"Thanks. Whose second?"

"Well, push comes to shove…you're going to twist my arm and all…I need you to try to see my side of this. It's you I'm asking. But…I have bounced this around a bit with…Darouche."

"Nightstick?" A crow-squawk from Taylor's dry lips, rasping without spittle.

"One and only."

"He's nuts!"

"Computer's a good filter for a guy like him. He doesn't actually have to be with anybody to get the job done. I won't have to worry about cracked skulls."

"But, why?"

"He's a long timer. He knows trains."

"I'll do it."

"You sure? Because a minute ago, you didn't seem so sure."

"Yes. I'll do it."

"You don't want to talk it over with…?"

"When do I get the computer?"

"Why, thank you, Taylor. That's a load off. Sure you don't want to sleep on it?"

"I'll do it."

On the ride home, Taylor is more animated than Cory Ann has ever seen him. He tells her all about his conversation with Toby; doesn't ask her advice. She is pensive one minute, giggly the next. And *very* hungry.

"This is what I want to do," he says. "I know this barbeque place. I want to pick up some dinner and take you over to my place to eat it."

"Why the sudden switcheroo? Thought the place was a mess."

He tells her that they shouldn't have to pretend with each other. She's not so sure.

He stops at Bertie's on North Lake, orders The Hog Wallow Trough for Two — two what, it doesn't say, but Grendl is a good guess — four beef ribs chiseled out of the rock at Dinosaur National Monument, a half rack of spare ribs, another half of baby backs, half a chicken, a hogshead of slaw, corn bread, corn on the cob, three tubs of sauces in varying degrees of thickness and spice, a forest of napkins, and sealed envelopes of hygienic cleansing pads. It is all packed away in a leaking cardboard barrel printed to look like it is made from wood slats. If this doesn't recruit Taylor into a diabetic coma, he will likely operate as long as a New Orleans streetcar. Cory Ann smiles beatifically like Jesus just showed up: thinks she can eat it all.

The mood, if not *blackens*, grays at Taylor's door.

Cory Ann leans back against the wall; feels a movement in the floor, a dry knot in her throat, the crushing sensation that something is badly amiss here, out of place, a bristle lodged between teeth, a label's rough edge at the nape of the neck. She doesn't fully comprehend what she sees, the blur of contour growing right up from the floor boards, the painted backdrops like a ride at Universal, the pandemonium of color. She feels her way along to the control platform — *The Tower*, he calls it — eases down to flatten the rhinestone hands on the buns of her Blue Jean pockets, swallows a wave of paranoia that runs like acid down her throat and settles as a weight in her gut. "The fuck is this?" she says, her voice betraying some of that anguish Charleton Heston implied when he discovered Miss Liberty half buried in sand.

"This is it! This is the layout!"

"Ya told me 'bout this?"

"Sure I told you about this."

"Ya never told me about *this*."

"I know I haven't been keeping it up to snuff, but…"

"This is your livin' room, Taylor." She calls him by his name; it sounds ominous, a bit brash, here in the dim light, all the tiny people within earshot.

"It is…It was, yeah. What do I need a living room for?"

"Hel-*lo*-uh! Uh, livin? An' that's what?…The dinin' room?"

"It was, yes."

She wonders where he eats. Where ever, he guesses.

"It…this *thing* goes on int'the hall?"

"Uh, huh. Pretty impressive, right?"

"The bedrooms?"

"Yeah. Well, I only use one of the bedrooms for a bedroom. Part of it anyway."

"Y'have part of a bedroom?"

"Bed, desk, file cabinet, you know."

"No, I don't. Ya did this all yourself?"

He tells her he's very proud of the layout. She allows that he should be but wonders what else there is to his life. He cites the store, the museum, the trips and photo runs. And, of course, her. "Yeah, there's me." There follows a moment of graveyard silence, the lull of death, the grim reaper riding the rails. At last he asks, "Is something wrong?"

Her eyes glow like red Frisbees in sunlight. "I'm a little fucked up, 's'all." He admits it's been quite a day, says, "Sometimes I just sit up there in the Tower and marvel at it myself."

"Think I need t'go home now, Taylor. Work in the mornin'."

"We didn't eat."

Her hunger has vanished like smoke from a joint. "Throw it in the fridge. I gotta get home, okay?"

"Sure, but, Cory Ann…"

She's out the door, purse in hand, leaving an Avon shroud thick across the land.

The ride over the hill to Highland Park is a very short ride that takes a very long time. They sit in icy silence. Taylor drives on autopilot; doesn't remember how to get there but the car does. He won't remember the ride when it's done. She sees their relationship flash before her eyes: the culture class with his family, his consumption of hot dogs as if he has to better some skinny Japanese kid at Coney Island, his initial clumsiness in bed, Steven, David, Nightstick, the parade of ancients and the rumble of trolleys, and the layout. THE *layout*.

She starts to get out of the car. He wants to open the door for her, but she is out before he can. He wants to talk; she feels that they have both done sufficient talking in vehicles today. She doesn't want him to come in, says, "Just wanna get t'bed an' catch a few. You go on home an' gnaw some ribs."

"They're for the both of us."

"Yeah, you save me one a them baby backs."

"You want to come over tomorrow night? We can finish them off and then I can show you the layout up and running. You didn't see it running."

"Taylor," she says. She puts her hand on his cheek. "Maybe we ought a slow this thing down a smidge."

"What does that mean?"

She mentions a need for space. Once, by whatever name, he had enjoyed space. But now, though he lacks the experience to comprehend the cliché, it doesn't sound good. Space is a vast, lonely place, he thinks. There are unfathomable distances between those who dare venture there. At the moment, he prefers modes of transit that bring people closer together. He turns from her, looks to the windshield, fiddles with the wheel, the gearshift. "Did I do something?"

"No. You're fine. Been a big day. I'm tired. We'll see tomorrow."

"You're breaking up with me?"

She doesn't answer, pulls away her hand, clutches her bag as if she fears he will take it. Men always take something from her.

"We were going to be married."

"No, Taylor. *You*'re gonna be married. Ya just needed somebody t'slip the ring to."

He says he found her. She says she doesn't think so.

"I showed you the layout!" It blurts out like confession.

"Yes, ya did. Thank you."

"Nobody sees the layout. Nobody. Not Betsy, not Leo, not the guys from the store. Well, I did show it to this guy next door, I told you about him."

"I don't think ya did. See, Taylor, ya don't talk 'bout people. Ya don't listen t'people. You're in a world a your own makin'. A world you're good in. A world you're sure of. Got your little people. That's where we kin'a part company. I need big people. Real people. I'm not real comfortable'th this whole train thing. With your family."

"It's Betsy. She did this."

"Betsy's fine. 'S'not Betsy."

She leans over and kisses him lightly, red lips to red cheek. He doesn't feel it, does not respond, doesn't notice her walk away from the car, pass the porch party, hear someone call, "Hey, Cora Bora, w'happen t'Sergeant Pepper?"

The next recalled moment will find him in the Tower, absently clicking switches. A train starts, a train stops. His world is unformed, a void, a darkness on the deep. Click, the moon moves, the moon stops; click, now the stars, breathing in, breathing out; click, a sawmill buzzes, stops buzzing; there is day, there is night, there is more night; click, there is the High Ball, there is not.

He runs his hand over the bristles of his hair, the motorman's cap sitting badge-down on the angled panel for the second bedroom; click, was a bedroom. A whistle blows, once, a horn, three times; click, sound off, day night day night; click, click, bare bones in a trough, two beef, five spare, a rack of baby backs plundered of flesh and gristle and sucked of marrow, the Diet Coke sweats in little beads over his thumb; click, his meaty palm soiled in Bertie's St. Louis Kick-ass Fire Sauce pondering lazily the field of switches; click, a cogwheel engages a toothed center rail; click, click, click, a lone tank engine stutters forward, jerks back, jumps ahead to tangle on an un-thrown switch; click, a very slow local freight — three box cars, a gondola, a caboose — eases off a siding, poses itself on the single track mainline, and moves purposely in the direction of the oncoming Fast Mail, click; Helen, dead on the track, an eviscerated statistic, the cop at the door — *Are you Mr. Bedskirt?* — mangled steel, dissembled body parts, the

J. David Robbins

interminable seconds of silence, the vacuum between impact and death, wheels angled to rail, the ground rising, David's Sling askew through the shattered windows.

Mrs. Gettzleman across the street jotting in her notepad, *1) Who was the floozy? 2) Why such a brief visit?*

THIRD HELEN

She takes the Orange Grove ramp too quickly, looses a hubcap to the curve, races down the road in reverse parade route direction on her way to the Pasadena Freeway. She is getting angrier as she drives, stewing in juices of malice, the car a slow cooker to eventual meltdown. She's popping Valium like M&M's, palm to mouth, eased down by a thermos of cold coffee. Okay, so men have silly hobbies. How was I to know? Am I a seer, for shit's sake? Some like to spend their evenings under a hood, some collect comics or coins or fucking butterflies run through with straight pins. Some spend every waking hour watching football or golf. So he has trains! So what? Some guys never get over the comforting toys of their youth. But most guys can separate a little, participate in the fucking marriage a little. Act like you're there. Here's a guy, though, spends his whole day designing ways to make toys talk, and his whole evening controlling this miniature world of his. Or it controlling him. That was supposed to be a kid's room, wasn't it? Wasn't that the plan? Who knew the kid would be a six foot three simpleton with a choo choo fetish? I ask you, who fucking knew?

UNCAS FALLS

I

OFFICER MCCALLUM, THE BROAD SMILE OF a satisfied new father appliquéd across his well-scrubbed face, greets the Mayor with a cigar so inferior the latter plans to dispose of it at the first discreet opportunity. He opens the back door of the unmarked city car — a 1930 black, Dodge Brothers Cruiser — and with his charge seated, places himself behind the controls, revs the engine, and smoothly shifts gears. The officer is in civvies today, a collegiate look of plus fours and sweater, badge concealed on the inside of a cheap tweed coat, its polished face against his chest. The Colt Police Positive is betrayed by the bulge of the shoulder sling. He is gleaming and boyish, projecting a general good cheer that puts him in stark contrast to P-R's half-lidded severity.

"What'll it be, sir?"

P-R stifles a yawn. He suffers a rare headache, like a lump lodged in the right side of his brow. He is thankful for the continuing gloom: not sure he could endure the levity of sunshine. "Go over The Camels. Don't hesitate to give it some gas. I have somewhere to be."

"Yes, sir." McCallum shows the pedal the weight of his shoe. "Uncas Falls today?"

"You just drive. I'll let you know. And, McCallum."

"Sir?"

"Congratulations on the new addition. Mrs. P-R sends her regards."

"Thank you, sir."

"I assume mother and child continue to do well?"

"Oh, yes, yes they do, sir."

With basic instructions and pleasantries out of the way, P-R closes his eyes, leans his head into the side of the cloth headliner and pursues a nap that is not to be. He feels very much compromised by the unprecedented rudeness of T. Rail Ferrous's choleric summons, by an ominous change of mood percolating out from a disquieted Mrs. Brown, and by his own reciprocal lashing of the Chief of Police. Just this morning, he has heard from Prezhki again, the cop's insubordinate tone lambasting McCallum's chauffeuring when all officers are on alert. *We got ourselves a ruckus here,* he had complained. He catalogued fires, thefts, fisticuffs, the detritus of a seething undercurrent he was expected to quell while already under staffed. *I've got an officer shot here!* P-R, insufficiently regretting the imprecision of his own Sweet Briar remarks, defensively responded, *We are all pawns in the wiles of greater events*, and hung up.

P-R had decided that a train trip was out of the question: too public. What if someone had caught a chance glimpse of the woman, a tincture of recognition, and started putting two and two together? He checks himself. He has become a worrier this morning, plagued by unpleasant possibilities, as if he has lost the knack of his famous self-possession, as if subject to executive directives of a much higher order. Perhaps he should have driven himself, made himself small, inconspicuous. But he didn't want to show up like a cat burglar, incognito, sneaking into Uncas Falls, an uninvited interloper, or, fedora in hand, on tip toes for his fawning appearance before "the great man." Not exactly the P-R style. *Unless they are bathed in perfume and scented oils and emulate the alabaster curvaceousness of an Aphrodite, I kiss no behinds,* he reminds himself. It is an axiom for him to live by. Yet here he is, lips nearly pursed. It is no wonder his head is in a vice.

Of necessity, the railroad follows the gentle grades from Uncas Falls to Tishomingo in a wide arc that adds miles to the crow's direct hop. The Camel's Backbone Highway — a more adventurous puzzle of switchbacks — is another story: a pandemonium of steep rises and falls undulating over The Camelhump Hills; flattening only briefly in the numerous clefts between the mounds; skirting unfenced drops; assuming geologically ancient summits; roller-coasting back into trenches; and up again. It can be a nauseating transit that leaves deposits of vomit along the narrow shoulder like markers of the limits of human endurance.

On such rides, P-R likes to stop at The Cleavage, a low trough named by an early settler nostalgic for pleasures left behind in more welcoming environs. A small bronze road sign marks the site, a place of history, locked between two more or less symmetrical treeless protrusions. Each of these is topped by granite outcrops that stand like druidic monoliths: the off-color joke of some previous force of creation.

Here, in the War before the Great War, a recon team that included a great grandfather of P-R's was ambushed by the Springfields of a cowardly enemy in this very bosom of earth. They were slaughtered to a man. P-R, seldom sentimental in the worst of times, uncharacteristically feels the pang of connection here, a sense of historical presence and entitlement, and often has McCallum stop so he can read the plaque again, run his fingers over the cold raised letters, THE BATTLE OF THE CLEAVAGE, AUG. 18, 1863, polishing to a sheen the name, PHIPPS, so that it jumps out of the deep bluish brown corrosion and joins him as he wanders through the headstones put up later by the Sons and Daughters of long gone forefathers, united in their futile confederacy. Today there is no time for pilgrimage. Co-opted by urgency, he simply stares out the window, notices that stones have been overturned and ugly scrawls painted on those left erect. Broken bottles are strewn with impunity.

McCallum shakes his head under trim blond hair, under the scruffy hat with a lopsided crease that refuses to even out, says, like some old seasoned hand, "Kids today! No respect for nothin'." P-R nods. Feels no need to respond. *When were kids any better? How will McCallum's be any different?*

Ahead, on one of several plateaus that grace the range, they are stuck in a line of cars with engines running. Too, they are caught in the fragrant aftermath of a sheep flock, itself in a wooly amble up the road, its daily testimonial, as carefree and oblivious as if the animals had all recently retired as the domestics of men. Two dogs from the antipodes, trained in sheep crowd control, are frantic at the edges; yipping; nipping at hooves; a relentless harassment that the future mutton take in quiet stride, at most an occasional baaing complaint interjects their ruminant conversation. Mikel, the old Basque shepherd, lazes on his mule, slowing the pace, ignoring the honking behind him.

"This here's the game. This is what the bastard does," says Officer McCallum. "He will walk those sheep up and back all day on this road forcing drivers to offer him some sort a gratuity to move them outta the way. Old pirate. Ought a be a law."

"I'm sure there is," says P-R. "Pull around these cars here and show him you'll run the stupid things down. He'll get them out of the way. I'm going to disappear below the window for a while. Even pirates get to vote in this country."

Officer McCallum lays into the clutch, does a delicate balancing dance with the gas, gooses the city car inch by inch into the country flock. "These here sheep could give a shit," he mumbles. They bleat, shuffle, gather into a dumb knots with the dogs wedging them into disunion. A strong, feral essence enters the car. Old Mikel turns his mule, waves his arms in distress and offers a crash course in Euskaran expletives.

Later on, they are stopped again, this time at the front of the line. There is a State Highway Department truck backward on the shoulder. A man in a brown uniform is standing on the running board, observing the rockslide that has eaten half the road. Traffic is routed by a flagman, and a crew of chained black men — striped like monochrome barber's poles — are lethargically breaking up the larger pieces. In fire brigade fashion, they transfer stones to the back of the truck, pivoting on a common chain secured to their ankles. The bull sits mounted on an old horse, shotgun at the ready, a blade of some indigenous weed stuck in his mouth.

"Is there no end to this?" says P-R. He pulls a banknote from his monogrammed billfold, hands it to McCallum. "See if you can't persuade that nice corrections officer to reverse the flow of traffic. Display your shield if you need to. I'm not here."

McCallum sidles up to the horse, arches his neck upward, exchanges pleasantries with the captain, reaches up to shake his hand. The captain blows a whistle, his breath as visible as the signal is loud, and the flagman immediately motions them forward. Cautiously, McCallum negotiates around the debris. He tells P-R, "Driver can hardly progress at all for all the hands stuck out along the way. It's these hard times, what does it."

P-R thinks, *when aren't the hands extended along the road?* He can practically hear his own cranial veins pounding.

The windshield starts to show clusters of droplets. These quickly muster into a steady shower and McCallum sets the wipers into their monotonous head-banging routine, thus adding to the Mayor's discomfort. There are puddles now, full enough to slow the most expert of drivers, depressions of mud that erupt up onto the doors of the car; a brown dirty rain mutating to sleet that thwacks onto the hood, the roof, and slows the car to a painful crawl.

"I'm not getting any younger back here," P-R tells him.

"Visibility, sir."

"If y'all can't see, *feel* the goddamned road!"

McCallum cracks the door just inches, drenching his left arm, tries to get a fix on the pavement, alternates this view with that beyond the wipers. A dark hulk rises up before them, becomes an old pickup, with a tarp tied over its load and flapping madly, spanking the fenders. The whole of it is angled up against the hillside and blocking their way. It is an area once resplendent in loblolly pines, long since logged, allowing the dirty effusion of instant streams, of mudflows that slog unabashedly across the macadam.

"Christ! Someone has misaligned my stars today. See what the hell's happening now, would you?" Again, McCallum stops the car, steps out into stinging arrows of ice, approaches Choc Bonjour behind broken glass, contemplating a bloodied buck struggling to free itself from his crushed hood.

"It jus' come out a nowheres, Of'cer."

McCallum returns to the city car, motions for P-R to crack the window. He is spackled with blotches of white; an icicle forms from his brim. He is stamping his feet, slapping his palms together like an appreciative audience. "Colored fella hit a buck," he shouts over the tempest. "Neither one a'em's going anywhere. You want, maybe, we should just turn around and do this here some other time?"

"I haven't the luxury to want. Push him out of the way."

"Responsibility for the car..."

"The city orders y'all to sacrifice its damn car for the greater good." He rolls the window back up.

McCallum shrugs, reaches inside of his coat for his service weapon, moves quickly toward the buck's head, sees the blood streak over its great black lips, the big wild eyes imploring him, the puffs of steam from its nose. He stretches his arm, turns his own head away, fires once into the skull. The pop is muted by the storm. A black crater opens in the fur, ruptures with dark blood, a flotilla of rudiment gray matter and bone shrapnel, trickling onto the crushed hood.

He says to the old man, "Y'all ain't going to be doing much more traveling in this old crate. Could have gotten yourself a winter's worth a venison off a this fine fellow, could you a hauled it back. I'm going to give you a shove. Y'all okay to steer?"

"Seein' it ain't hung up on no fender. Shove t'where?"

"Just outta the way. Put her in neutral then. Stay in the cab and see you don't freeze to death. Traffic's backed up a ways behind us, but someone's bound to be along by and by."

Getting back behind the wheel, he observes to P-R, "No rear bumper. Ought a be a law about that, too. We're gonna get banged up a bit."

He crunches up into the Ford, two big steel animals rutting in the gloom, pushes the truck forward with its load of dead dear and whatever is tarped in the bed, nearly shoves the truck body up over the under frame caught on the mud slope. The noise is ugly, urgent, finds its way directly into P-R's throbbing head. McCallum says, "Too bad about the buck. I'm no hunter myself, but I don't pass up a nice steak when offered."

He disengages when enough of the road is clear to pass, sets off around the truck, continues down the slippery grade, out of the hills, out of the storm, demarcated from Uncas Falls like a line on a map — a dash, two dots, a dash — rolls the mud-strewn Dodge out of its jurisdiction and into the sunshine of the city. P-R cups his hot forehead in his hand, squints his eyes into chicken foot wrinkles. Behind them, the gunmetal sky mourns the loss of edible haunch, the sweetbreads, the oily ribs. Over the city, delicate feather clouds fan the immaculate sky.

II

CHOC CONTEMPLATES THE CURRENT NEMESIS.
"You an'me's 'bout eben', 's'Ah sees it," he says through the mottled glass. He stares along the road into an endless mist, down the slope at the stumps of piney woods lost to the band saw, a line of flat topped gnomes disappearing in the shroud. Vacant orbs of dead eyes stare back. "Wha' Ah gonna do'th dis dinin' room table, dese nice ol' chairs? What Ah gonna do 'th'out no wheels? You'n'a better place, you is, buck. Don' y'all whine t'me."

Several cars pass, slow down — edge around him, the white drivers shaking their heads in *wouldn't ya know it* expressions — getting well past him, grinding into first and escaping up the hill, into the cloud and out of compassion, as if human interaction is a quality elevation dissipates in the thin air above tree line. Finally, a weathered Ajax converted to a Nash Light-six, headlights blaring like spotlights at a movie premier, throbs up next to him. A young black man peers out through the slit of open window. He is wearing a dark coat, but the white collar of starched shirt is visible at his throat.

"Whadda we got here, ol' man?"

"What'cha see! Ford'th one a dem big Packard hood ornamen'."

"We tote that buck there off onto the road, ya still gonna have some fixin' t'do. Ya'll's hood crushed right down t'the block, seems."

"Where y'alls got so smart? Mus' be one dem Tuskegee boys. Ah sure is glad you come 'long t'share yo wi'dom."

The young man sits silent for a moment, considers the old man's rudeness. He says, with some caution, "I can carry ya on over to 'Mingo. Leave you off at a fillin' station."

"What all Ah got t'fill?" Choc is spitting angry, mists the windshield, his palsied fingers tap-dancing on the wheel.

"They could tow it down. Maybe not a total loss."

"Y'all's too young t'letchur me on total loss."

215

"Suit yourself, then. I don't figure t'sit out here arguin' with ya'll 'till supper. Ya wanna ride or ya wanna freeze your stubborn ol' bee-hind off on this here mountain?" He covers the bite of words with a headshake, affirms his own good nature.

Choc flings his door open, punishes brown ice under his shoes, grumbles over to the Nash, "Yeah, Ah's fixin' t'freeze my ol' black ass up here on de mountain. Das why Ah's up'n here d'firs' place." He gets in and slams the door, like he's doing the young man a reluctant favor, mumbles to himself, and sits as close to his side of the car as he can. The driver hands over an old thermos; Choc lets it warm his hands but doesn't drink, and insists, "Ah's fine."

"Matter a perspective."

"Well, Ah done took care a myself dis long."

"An' look'ee here where it got y'all!"

"Y'don' know shit, chile."

The young man sucks in his chapped lips, lowers his lids slightly, lays down the law. "We get one thing straight, hear? None a this's 'cause a me. I'm just a man goin' t'work, 's'all."

Choc turns to him. He is a good looking young man, a smooth milk chocolate not yet plagued with Bonjour's pallid gray elephant wrinkles. He is as clean as a waxed LaSalle on the showroom floor, fairly sparkles in the perfection of haircut, the neatly honed nails and trousers in such perfect crease as to suggest the assistance of a t-square. The Nash is just as immaculate. Choc feels bad for him, considers that the poor fellow has not yet reached that mature understanding that there are not nearly enough flatirons to smooth out a future for a young Negro. Choc had been young and scrubbed once himself. "Habin' m'self a bad day," he offers in apology. It comes as a mumble and he is not sure it is conveyed. His voice, his body, contract in the cold like produce in frost, shrinks him down to a skeletal bundle minimal in the young man's seat.

"Can see that," the young man allows.

Their way is mostly downhill now. The driver works out with brake and clutch. In a short time, he tries again to be hospitable; feels it is his right in his own car to enjoy invited company if he so chooses. With strong, pampered hands on the wheel, he says, "I'm called Charles," a happy music to his voice, as if being Charles should mean something.

"An'y'all works at where, Mr. Charles? All gussie' up da'way?"

"I work for Mr. Pullman. Sleepin' car porter, yes sir," he says with some pride.

"Don' say," says Choc. "You too young t'be so far 'long 'n life."

The young man grabs his own lapel, folds it over in Choc's direction, displays the pin with the Tishomingo T inlaid with the number Four. Point made. He continues to offer small talk, details of his job, his young family and how he dreads the weather on the road. "Don't I know y'all?" he asks suddenly.

"You does, why y'askin'?"

"I've seen you over at Brother Salvation's, right? Ain't that it?"

"How Ah't'know wha'ch'y'all seen?"

"I knew it. I seen the truck too. You that handyman." The recognition seems to allow Charles a new familiarity and he begins to tell stories of passengers he has served. At a lower elevation, he nods his chin towards the boundary sign: WELCOME TO TISHMINGO, THE HON. SOCRATES PHIPPS ROUGE, MAYOR.

Charles says, "Speakin' a the devil, that there good ol' boy gonna get his one a these days. See here, when I'm workin' the X-press, oh, not every time, but a day here an' a day there, a police come up the firs' class, goes down the aisle handin' out Tom Jeffersons t'all us colored, an' tells us, over each time like we too stupid to have memories, Mayor P-R's got a seat on this here train. Anybody ax you, you seen 'im depart off at the Capital Station. Not once has I seen that man get up on my train. Not once."

"No bidness a mine."

"Mine neither. But it smells a catfish, you ax me."

Sharing such thoughts, he hauls the old man past the road gang, through the sheep, down into Tishomingo and drops him off at the Depot and Main car stop. He reaches into a trouser pocket and offers Choc a buffalo nickel for the streetcar. "I gotta get me on down to the depot. This here trolley gonna carry you 'bout anywheres ya need t'go."

"Do tell? Dis 'lec'ric"car boun' fer glory? Ah don' needs no charity."

The porter lowers his shoulders for the first time since he picked up the old man; is at ease for the first time. "I'm sure ya don't. But y'all might need carfare. An' it's colder than a meat locker out there, so do me a favor an' take it so's I don't have t'worry 'bout'cha'll."

"Y'ain' gotta concern yo'self wid me! I ain' ast ya fer nuttin'."

"What I done to you, old man? Jus' take the coin, take the trolley, an' get y'all's self on home. An' God bless."

Choc takes the coin. "If 'E do, it somethin' 'E makin' no partic-a-lar habit ob. Don' know where dis here ride goin' get me, but Ah tanks you for de 'sideration."

"Well, now, I'm here to serve, ain't I, boss?"

Choc gets out, stands by the platform, follows the porter's purple exhaust until it fades from his vision. The sky is the blue of the deepest mountain lake, bisected by the electric lines. An ascendant hum conducts itself along the silver rails that trickle like veins in the street.

It is line's end, or start, depending. There are no loops here to turn a car, just like at the other end in Thebes where he had dropped the woman who had cancelled what little luck he had. The car, therefore, is a double-ender — no front- no rear or two of each — designed to fluster an old colored man who has never ridden one because he has been driving since long before Mr. Ford dug deep into the street railway's revenue and forced it to invite aboard people of color. Both trolley poles are down in Jim Crow conspiracy, and the two white men in official caps are offering Choc no hint as to protocol. One is sitting in the door frame with a boot removed, scraping the sole on the step to release some unwanted annexation of gum or worse, and the other is enjoying a pipe, as well as the sport of an old

217

black man trying to decide what to do. Choc is blessed with the example of a maid snug under her a bonnet, eyes set on the back of the rattan flip seat in front of her, and several rows up, a white laborer in overalls, buried in an Afternoon Edition, and indifferent to black man's plight. It is safe to assume, Choc thinks, that the colored woman knows her place, and he is free to wonder by what Caucasian magic front will become back, and back will become front, and by what order of orthodoxy seats will be purified and sanctified to make them wholesome for the tailored behinds of white folk. He remembers, *Da firs'll be las', an' da las'll be firs'*.

Mort Ringer is navigating his old hand-me-down Model A out of the alley behind the drug store at the corner of the Glassworks road when he spots Choc Bonjour, stiff legged and humped over, make his way from the car stop and cross the street in his direction. It is a slow crossing — sails in the doldrums — annoyed with the pitfalls of age on a damp day. Mort has known Choc all his life, has often helped him unload the day's catch up at the junkyard. He pulls up to the curb to wait.

"Looks like someone could use a lift up this here hill." Mort is still strapped into his Roadhouse apron decorated in molasses-based sauce, a pale skinned boy with green eyes and half a dozen freckles on each cheek.

"Ah gots dis far." Choc is leaned up against the Mail Pouch ad painted on the wall of Poole's Drugs. There are paint chips on his back.

"Hop on in, Mr. Bonjour. Just a minute outta the way."

Relieved, Choc struggles with the door, gets it open, braces on it to drag his unforgiving limbs into the car. "Hoppin' days's gone."

"Happen to the truck?"

"Got 'tacked by a moose size a my las' woman's rear en'."

"Moose? Never heard a no a moose around here! Piney Woods moose, y'say?"

"Dat'r one a dem booffaloos like dey gots ou'wes'. We gonna sit'n'chat 'till a cows come'ome or y'gonna tote dis here wet ol' colored up d'hill?"

Mort shakes his head, runs Choc up to his front porch. Yuletide makes an effort to bark: nothing comes out but rancid air. She settles for a half-hearted snarl and a near-lethal dog fart.

"You want me to come in and get the stove going?"

"No, Ah don't. Ah can't stoke up m'own stove Ah don' see dat warmin' me up's gonna do nobody no good, leas' a all me."

"I could come on back later and check on you?"

"Wha'Ah looks like t'you, son? Babe'n arms?"

Mort waits as Choc negotiates the three steps. "Y'all got what to eat?" he calls.

Choc doesn't turn around, just waves him off back handed.

He is fish-wet when he gets inside. He removes his clothing, drops it to the floor, and wraps an old wool blanket tight around his emaciated frame. He partakes of the brandy but has little appetite for it or anything else. He lets Yuletide in, throws her a pig's foot which she can barely lift, spills the rest of the brandy into her water bowl. Everything in both of them that has once bent, now stiffens. Their very marrow clogs like pond ice. Choc's five remaining teeth attempt alignment in order to chatter. The cold in his marrow matriculates into pain. He eases slowly into his bunk, nearly a swoon, sees the dog collapse on the spot, looks up at the triangular flaps of paint struggling to stay cocooned to the ceiling, coils into a fetal figuration, thinks about life after truck, a possibility of forced retirement, living off the kindness of the boy Mort and a few other decent souls in rag-tag Thebes, and says quietly, "'Nuff surely be 'nuff!"

III

"SO THE BEAH COME OVA THE mountain," says T. Rail Ferrous. "At last." His office is paneled in nearly black mahogany kidnapped from West Indian jungles, the gloss worn off with age. The single Tiffany shade splays light down upon a great tomb of a desk with carved lion's feet and inlaid leather blotter the color of long dried blood. There are thick floor to ceiling length damask drapes drawn over the windows, old and patternless, with the dust colors of their dyes shedding on the carpet below. A sturdy bronze, an engineer at the throttle perhaps, sits silent in the gloom. Cigars have had the run of the place —surely better than the one P-R has forgotten to discard — as do cuspidors. The leaf has imbedded the softer surfaces and gives the room a stale, olfactory, political ambience.

"The prodigal beah come home," says Ferrous. It is a dour proclamation to match P-R's mood. The implication is clear. P-R excuses, "I have never before seen The Camelhumps as they are today. A virtual tempest. Herds of sheep. Rock slides. Tantamount to Scripture. I half expected brimstone. My driver wanted to turn around."

"It is well he di'n't." There is no inflection to his monotone. Ferrous himself is a grim man who casts a shadow from a low sun. Risen out of the gator swamps of Terrebonne Parish, the bitter nature of his family's poverty excreting into the hummocks, the moccasins slithering through the tannin bogs; these are the things that whittled him as if he were a tupelo twig, *suckled by the bog* as he tells it, fed the angry resistance of *hu'cane thrashed wetl'nds.*

Ferrous is a little man, one step above dwarf. He compensates with muted stentorian tones from an out of body depth, with just enough volume for the listener to feel an inch beyond earshot. It is an unequivocal sense of superiority that turns stronger men than P-R into puddles of excreted fluids.

"May I sit down?" P-R says.

There is no answer. Perhaps Ferrous nodded, blinked an approving eye. It is too dark for P-R to judge inflection. His vision is doubling, tripling, patterning like one of those toys with the colored rocks children look into.

The spring of Ferrous's desk chair stutters. His form retreats into a drear soup without perspective. "A course, y'all'r'quainted'th Mr. Humbo'dt?" The voice bubbles up like bottomland ooze; the words pureed through a sieve of algae muck.

There is a stirring from a large Victorian couch next to the wall on P-R's right, the trick of shadow, the cracking of old leather, a puff of deep blue smoke.

"Yardley?" P-R can't see him. "If I'd have known y'all were joining us, I would have given you a lift."

From the darkness comes an elastic expulsion of air, a hiss ending in a breathy growl, a sound like an effluence passing over gravel. "Ah'd sooner ride with the Devil, suh."

Humboldt's voice is a tenuous warble — some say, effeminate — which serves to hearten P-R. The Mayor is not prepared to remain standing while the cuckold sits. He sinks into a leather chair opposite Ferrous and adjusts his trousers; the condition of a man's pleats, in P-R's judgment, is an insight into the condition of the man. He is nearly overcome by a sudden urge to sleep right there in the troll's cave.

"Now, now," Ferrous intervenes. "Ah'm sho Mr. Humboldt *'preciates* the consid'ation."

P-R cups his chin, rubs it slowly. It is a posture he is unaccustomed to. He sets his hat on a neighboring chair. "One, unfamiliar with the good natures of the principals involved, might suspect, in the offing, something, perhaps, in the nature of conspiratorial redress."

"Oh, deah, mah good friend," says Ferrous. "We'all intend t'portend nothin' a the kind. We intend t'*portend* not at awl. In def'rence t'the *late* 'oweh and the 'con'my a time, a which Ah ahm myself a zealot, Ah shall be succinct." Something gleams on his desk in a metallic loop.

"Of course, I had nothing else on the agenda today. I'm here to be of service?"

"Se'vice? We ah heah'n'a woodshed, P-Ah, well b'yond se'vice."

"I've offended y'all? That's a swell thing. I thought *I* was offended. You have me at a loss. I am not a devotee of loss."

"Then we shall *pro*ceed ont'the enlight'ment segment a ah little *soirée*. 'F'Ah may, Mr. Humbo'dt?"

Humboldt sniffs and shuffles from the offstage darkness. "Ah trus' y'all's judgment, Ferrous. Yore sense a timin'." There is a palpable malice in his tone, the complaint of a wounded animal. One can nearly hear him trembling, rubbing a cottony tongue over dry lips like sandpaper on raw wood.

"Mr. Humbo'dt brings me news that saddens me t'the quick. Ah ahm taken aback. A sense a...s'prise...shock even...*en*sues. Y'all have, in Tishomingo, a six membuh council, have y'not?" He doesn't wait for an answer. "Awl d'voted public servants; shrewd, an'lytical gen'lemen, who un'erstand the su'cessful, an' 'casionally nefar'ous, marriage a commerce an' fruitful 'nicipal man'gement. A course, t'spurn the neg'tives a such 'rangements is t'swim 'gainst the tide, t'disturb the nat'ral orduh a things. We'all're given these pa'ameters as an inhe'itance and are in'cent a deceit in their construction. Ower only guilt 'crues from ower se'f-righteous 'buse a prec'dent. So, it lands as quite a bombshell that such a stalwa't body a in'ivid'als, Mr. Humbo'dt 'ncluded, have d'cided, Ah b'lieve, fo' t'two, t'reject the comp'ny's 'ntreaties t'xtend ower sho't street runnin' branch outta y'all's colud distric' seven tenths of a mile t'the brew'ry, a prop'sition, y'all has 'sured me, Mr. Mayuh, was...how did y'all put it? *In the bag?*"

"It was three to three, last meeting. Mine is the tie breaking vote," says P-R with relief. "Someone has misinformed you'all. I suppose the fox is always worried that some one will outsmart it. You UF folks, y'all live in a cesspool, so it is no great feat to muddy the waters. 'Mingo's a different animal entirely."

"Ah think not. Ah do not allow m'self the tr'vail a misinfo'mation. Ah find it too time consumin', awl the rep'tition it 'ntails, the c'rections. As it happens, Councilman Dailey is 'ngaged in, oh, somethin' of an upstart drayage oper'tion, the type a skeeter so ir'tatin' t' the sens'tivity a railroad skin these days. Councilman Stein, a Hebrew gen'leman Ah have nevuh had the pleasure a meetin'...nat'rally, we travel in dif'rent circles...Mr. Stein has a lit'ny a complaints, awl a which sound like New Deal pand'rin' t'the common classes. He cites safety conce'ns, health conce'ns, sooty loc'motives *rampagin'* — his word — down city av'nues, the cacoph'nous 'ncursion on the peace a mind a neighbors, oh, a whole host a soc'listic bull pucky 'pon which he has 'nointed hi'self true believuh an' champeeon a the colud. Claims he has the symp'thetic eah a that rag that passes fo' *The Press* 'n'yore neck a the woods. They ten' t' get that way, *those* people. Act like they boa'din' a subway'n New Yo'k City'th all they constant pushin' an' shovin'. An entire race a peddluhs with they pushcarts an' they ca'pet bags jammed'n the do'. Leave it t'them t'sidle up t'ower Nigros. As fo' the routin' in question, Ah s'pose they is no need t'remin' y'all that we ah talkin' 'bout nothin' mo' than your colud dis'rict wheah, Ah dare say, a loaded freight might be a 'mprovement on the qual'ty a life, and, this 'ditional tiny 'ntrusion inta a secta that is in itse'f ma'ginal at best...Well, as they say, this'ain't no way t'run a railroad. Who knows better'n Ah? Then we have Mr. Kaiser who is truly a *tab'la rasa* on the issuh. The perplexin' bein', Councilman Kaiser pr'fesses deep an' abidin' 'fection fo' Councilman Humbo'dt."

"Then we're fine. Yardley has several times assured me...Well, Yardley, it is not my place to speak for you'all." He thinks now, despite Humboldt's stewing in hostility, that he has been called in to mediate some misunderstanding between the other two men. "Mr. Ferrous is simply looking for assurance that we, the City of Tishomingo, will do the honorable thing. We will keep our word."

Humboldt fidgets, a brush of fabric on wood, but holds his tongue.

Ferrous says, "Ah have 'proached Mr. Humbo'dt'th'at vera arg'ment. And, a course, they ah yeahs a tradition t'adhe'e to. It is the railroad that has transfo'med Tish'mingo from a backwoods lumber camp inta a thrivin' metrop'lis a retail commerce an' qual'ty res'dential tracts. Ower little street runnin' op'ration's'a drop'n'a bucket when y'all considuh the full scope a ower reach from heah down t'the Gulf, but it has been a tidy an' l'crative one, t'be made awl the mo' so by inclusion a *revenue from the evuh-pop'lar suds an' hops. Y'all follow me, a course."

"But Yardley..."

"Ya'dley this, Ya'dley that. Mr. Humbo'dt has 'nformed me that he 'ntends t'veto ower little 'fair a honuh, that he will carry Mr. Kaiser 'long with'im, an' condemn t' imp'tence...a condition hard t'quate 'th y'all, Mr. Mayuh...yore prowess as a tie breakuh...Mr. Humboldt, t'void fu'thuh discomfituh on y'all's part, as yore host, Ah'd be remiss not t'suggest that p'rhaps now is the time fo' y'all t'low the Mayuh an' Ah t'ponder fu'thuh the details a yore complaint...in s'questration."

Without comment, Humboldt arises in the shadows and leaves the room. P-R has the sense that he has given him a glance of some disapproval and is beginning to suspect that he knows why, but, not yet, how he knows. "Let's cut to the chase," he says. "The son of a bitch was on board last week."

"Last week was, alas, last week. He seems t've gotten off at the wrong station. P'rhaps ya have an inklin'as t' why."

"As I said, I'm at a loss."

"Oh, Ah think not. Ah think not 't'all. But a loss, assur'dly, is threat'nin' in a near future. It would ease mah symp'thetic pain, as it weah, 'f'Ah di'n't have t'spell out the details a yore...*adven'u'es,* P-Ah. Do me this court'sy."

"This is about a personal matter?"

"'F'on'y it was. And though we ah prob'bly both hintin' at the same swayin' caboose, Ah must remin' y'all that public fig'res, such as ya'se'f, have no pers'nal mattuhs. That is why the wise man, when in the limelight, practices *dis*cretion at awl costs, at awl times. Gives not unta temptation, as it weah."

"And who would be so...scurrilous as to advertise such...indiscretions?"

"Why the cuckold hisself!"

"*Really!* The little weasel! Has the man no shame?"

"Have y'all? Cuckolds've nothin' else."

"I am surprised you have even entertained..."

"Ah ain't the object a humil'ation heah. Get a grip on yo'se'f. He is threatenin' t'leak this heah scandal. *I*rrational, p'rhaps. But he is inju'ed t' his core, and Ah can't say as Ah blame 'im. This is not an age when such mattuhs ah han'led on foggy mo'nings on a field a honuh, ower own little Weehawkens, though I dare say much 'n'fficiency would be 'voided 'f'it was."

"What does the SOB want? Surely..."

There is no answer to the aborted thought. P-R senses that some alteration has come upon Ferrous' now secret face, some change of line work, some deviation of emotion under cover of the dark room and shielded by the nearness of the floral shade. "Y'all have me at a disadvantage. If you are going to gesture, at least turn on a damned light."

"The shyness a the dimin'tive. Da'k room, big desk. Fo'give me. O' don't. Yore mention a dis'vantage has its merits. Ah 'spect that what Ya'dley wants is gone fo'evuh. Wouldn't y'gree? But, fo'tun'ly fo' y'all an' the great tradition a street runnin' freight, he has broached...oh, somethin' of a cons'lation, some minuh alt'ation a plans, some reroutin' as it weah."

"Of the route?"

"No, too easy. Of yore commingled careers. He is damaged, chagrinned t'the *de*gree that can on'y be rect'fied by placatin' cov'tous ambition. 'F'is domestic peace is to be shattud, surely they is compensation 'n'a alte'nate venue."

"To wit?"

"He's gonna run fo' mayuh at te'm's end. And you all ain't."

P-R rubs at the point of pain in his forehead. "That sniveling little prick! He comes to you with this? He cares less for that pious cow of his than I do! The damn, inconsequential usurper! This is not going to happen." He stands, leans ape like, his knuckles on Ferrous' great desk. "This is not going to fucking happen. This is my birthright. This is no caprice of democracy, I tell you. Or did y'all plan this?"

"Sit'own. Sit...down. This unb'comin' mel'drama, not t'mention yore haughty tone, is not t'my liken'."

P-R returns to the chair. "Haughty tone? You have the gall? After that absurd phone call of yours. Do you not understand the porosity of the wires? Let me make something crystal clear. The office of mayor in my town is a hereditary obligation."

"Oh? Cert'inly they is a disgrun'led Cromwell o' two lurkin' in the galluhies. Look at y'all. I nevuh seen y'so...*beyond* yo'se'f, so outta char'cter, so d'tached from yo'own ch'rade."

"You can see that? In this murk? How can that be? Fucking coal mine in here!"

"Beware a dead canaries."

"Or equally tuneful councilmen."

"Ah imagine the mole sees quite well in'is own den. Mattuh a su'vival fo' the smalluh species. B'lieve me, Ah have some 'xper'ence. So, d'rect from the mole's mouth, heah is what's gonna happen *di*rec'ly. Fi'st, they'll be no mo'...'nuendos. The woman in question knows what's good fo' her, Ah am 'sured. Ower friend's dis'ppointment'll be eas'ly 'suaged by a promise a suppo't 'n'a nex' 'lection, in which he will be *un*challenged. Y'all can go off an' enjoy the num'rous fruits a yo' labuh...and 'nheritance, an'f'ya still feel the sac'ificial call af'er fo' yeahs a rural gentil'ty, yore cou'se'll be a y'own choosin', an' with my blessin', fo'all it's wo'th. And P-Ah, as God is mah witness, Ah will have my spur track, an' it will run deep with spirits."

"These are your machinations. All of it. The curt phone call on the open line. The gloom in here. Probably engineered the council vote. How can this be so important?"

"Y'all needn't know too much a the innuh workin's a this corp'ration. But Ah will, 'spite mah abs'lute disgust'th yore rathuh arb'trary goin's on, this se'f-destructive procl'vity ya seem t'have, an' with an estimable church woman, no less...Ah will let you in on some inside 'ntell'gence, the knowledge a which, 'f'ya don' squanduh it, might save y'some furthuh humil'ation. In a seemin'ly *un*related mattuh, ower much-touted co'po'ate pres'dent, the ven'able Mr. Talbot, has s'cumbed t'what I am tol' is quite a debil'tatin' stroke. He is t'be *re*placed by one a the young lions, a vera mode'n fella who seems t'have skipped a few rungs, college man, Ivy, knows all about the ways a the wo'ld us grunts can only 'magine, has no sense a her'tage, a the log'cal ev'lution a things. Y'see, Ah'm of a differ'n' breed. Bigguh than most men. Ah have t'be. My fathuh, rest his soul, blamed me fo' the bantam condition Ah 'nher'ted from him. Ah could be bittuh. Ah am not. He taught me resil'ence. Toughness. Ah learned t'be on'y as small as Ah 'lowed. T'this day, Mrs. Fe'ous, a good six inches by the ruluh talluh than me, speaks t'me on'y when sittin'. No one, not even my d'voted companion, speaks down t'me. We have lived this pretense so long that it has become fact. Ah am talluh than her. Ah am actu'lly *talluh than her.* She thinks a me that way, and so do Ah. And so do most men a my 'cquaintance. Ah learned at a tenduh age that a good long crowbar an' a steady swing added a good foot t'my posture. Y'see, P-Ah, Ah come up through the ranks, how it was done'n them days. At fo'teen Ah was a mess'nger boy fo' a tel'grapher. Latuh, Ah labuhed on a track gang. Little as Ah am, Ah hogged, stoked, came outta the age a link'n'pin c'upluhs'th no loss a finguhs, no small 'complishment in itse'f. Ah was smart too, see. Ah took a look at the broken men all 'roun' me an' decided they had a be some sort a ceilin' on this kin'a vocation, that one way'r 'nother many a mah co-workuhs was not gonna enjoy no rockin' chair on a po'ch in they dotage. Ah got inta payroll, rode a AhPO as a sortuh, a clerk, sol' tickets, el'vated m'se'f t'bottom man'gement'n'a steam shop, become the juniuh 'sistant t'the 'sistant a the 'sistant a somethin'r othuh havin'a do 'th purchasin', t'sistant d'vision head, t'no'thern d'vision head, t'jus' b'low ower droolin' Mr. Talbot, God protect him, an' this snot nose'n spats an' a pan'ma hat comes outta th'ether an' trumps me. Y'think y'all got somethin' t'whine 'bout, fuck y'all, P-Ah! Some a us built ah own 'nher'tance an' still they ain'no 'ntitlement, no God-given certainty. It don't mattuh that y'learned the bus'ness inside out, how many passengers y'delivered safely t'their des'inations, how much tonnage y'brung home t'market? This little cocksuckuh'th'is eastern ped'gree was shittin'is diapers when Ah had three thousan' men workin' un'er me. An' y'know what he wants t'do? Y'know what he thinks is 'propriate'n hard times? Consol'dation. Aband'ments. Reachin'out t' truckers. Cut staff. Cut yore losses. That's what they teach in them iv'ry towuhs a theys. Stroke they dicks 'til they gotta hard on fo' eve'y pensioned wida who got two shares a stock hole' 'way 'n'a Maxwell Brothuhs' can. They don' un'erstand the hist'ry, the pr'gression, the contex'. They don' see the human'ty in it all. How can this be so impo'tant, y'ask? This piddlin' seven tenths of a street run mile? It vera well may be all that's left aftuh these morons has they say. He's mergin' with Gulf & Northuhn. FCC's got it on the table as we speak. He sees them's the most vi'ble route, seeks t'shut down the Tish'mingo south a Tish'mingo itse'f, reroute all passenger runs t' th'G&N mainline, reduce th'great 'Mingo road t'a twice weekly 'ndustr'al spur. He's comin' a take a look-see t'morruh. Him an'is boys. That's why the hurry t'see y'all. Red ca'pet time. Linen toilet papuh fo' they satin asses."

"Can't be."

"Famous las' words. Quietly let go a yore stock. See what y'can d'vest 'n a way a trackside real'state. A word t'the wise, y'see. An' y'ain't hea'd it heah."

They are both quiet for a while. A clock ticks somewhere in the arc of a pendulum.

P-R says, "We'll be a ghost town."

"Y'all won'be no Chicago, but Ah don' think it'll be as bad as awl that. Tish'mingo gotta have somethin' e'se t'rec'mend itse'f. Why, jus' y'all'a proxim'ty t'Uncas, which by the way's gonna boom like all get out, 'll len'y'all a role'th light in'ustry. 'Fore y'know it, y'all be a thrivin' bedroom t' ower mo' robus' man'fact'ries."

"I need to think…A lot to digest in one sitting."

"Don't take too long. Nail 'n'a coffin, P-Ah. Keep yore pants button' an' peddle yore assets. Someday, y'all thank yore lucky stars Humbo'dt's such a quin'sential jackass."

"That son of a bitch!"

"So ah we awl, don'ya think? A curse on mothe'hood, even the best a us. The wors', though, 's'at each SOB's but a microcosm of a greater ill, of a un'versal fam'ly a like 'ndiv'duals. Was Ah t'draw the curtains, not a likely prop'sition, an' we spent the time t'djust t'th' brilli'nce a th' day, we might 'njoy the passage a great steam locomotives, a new fangled diesel'r two, p'rhaps the poles bein' delivered fo' the caten'ry des'ined t'lectrify the tunnels 'long th'gorge edge neah the falls. Like microbes 'n'a bloodstream, we glimpse ahterial America. What it was, a hint a what it's gonna be. But they be othuh phan'oms 'n'a pi'ture. Rollin' on rubbuh. The unity a great systems, linked by steel shattuhed inta component pa'ts, an ana'chy 'thout el'gance. We might see an airaplane go by. Progress, P-Ah. Led by lads bugguhed in prep schools. Ah fo' one'm a'ready n'stalgic." Ferrous opens a desk drawer. P-R can hear it slide. "Buy y'all a drink?"

"You'd better."

A cut glass decanter and two shot glasses appear under the Tiffany. They twinkle briefly in the gloom, as does Ferrous. P-R sees shadows on the desk, the glasses set down on some sort of platform, the decanter sitting lower after being poured. As P-R begins to wonder how the little man is going to conquer the big desk, a pinprick of a light informs him, as does the whirring of tiny machines. The drinks jiggle lightly and move forward, secure in a tin gondola, the Lionel engine following the arc on the desk, and come to an abrupt halt in front of P-R.

P-R obliges by taking his glass, allowing the freight to continue in a loop back around to Ferrous. "Beer?" he says.

"Not just *beah*. Lone Feathuh!"

"You hinted at *drink!*"

"Ah 'pol'gize. Ah keep nothin' heah. Wife wouldn' heah a'it. She compliments my sobri'ty."

P-R sets his warm glass down on the desk. "A card, are you?" he says.

Ferrous holds his glass toast-like. "This li'le piggy goes t'market."

"Knock off the wise guy stuff. Look, I'm not a dense man, Ferrous, not even in this perpetual night of yours. The meaning of the toy wasn't lost on me."

"How's the fam'ly? Sarah? It is Sarah?"

"Sarai, actually."

"Sounds 'xotic. Indi'n sub-cont'nent. Moham'dan."

"Old Testament."

"Ah'as certain it was Sarah."

"I should think I'd know!"

"Yes, yes. So, how is the fam'ly?"

"We persevere. I learned from my daddy the skills of survival. And Sarai, she's developed a taste for animal fur, summers in Capri, fish eggs on toast. She knows what's good for her."

"Nevuh been t'Capri. Vacations ah fo' those a us'th spoons prenat'ly 'nstalled. I been so busy gettin' heah Ah see no possibility a leavin'. Y'see, P-Ah, Ah ain't a rich man. A comfortable man, yes. An 'mpo'tant man, maybe. But not a rich man, like y'all. Why, 'f'Ah had a nickel fo' eve'y dime y'all make, Ah'd still have me half a what you do, woul'n't Ah? Even so, *Ah* summoned *you*. An' you came!" He pours two fingers each, as if he offers something potent, lifts his glass, and says, "Heah's t'knowin' what's good fo' *us*."

And P-R says, dissimilar thoughts pulsing in his head, "And to doing something about it." They do not clink glasses at such a distance across the vast playing field of Ferrous' imperial desk. P-R sets his glass down on the O gauge track, hoping, perhaps, for some future derailment.

In the elevator, P-R pays no notice to the black man who masters the cables. He is visited by his flask before the doors open to the lobby.

IV

CHIEF PREZHKI AND MR. RED SIT enfolded in their slickers, hat brims low against the chill, Prezhki's ear flaps tucked down into his collar. Red sucks a bottle that Prezhki has refused with an abrupt wave of his hand. Company housing is directly behind them — neat rows of identical clapboard cubes — as is the Chief's patrol car on Railroad Avenue.

They sit at the peak of the slope looking down on the rail yard, watching a big Bucaryus steam crane and tender pushed up on the southbound track, the line here briefly doubled, then compounded as it mutates into a yard. The crane is on loan from the G&N: the Tishomingo's inelegant homemade rig has derailed and requires a favor from its occasional sibling.

Prezhki is nearly bowled over with fatigue spiked with pique. He is reaching the point where caring about damaged maintenance equipment seems less a priority than a good goose down pillow as far away from a telephone as he can manage. He presses a thumb and a forefinger to the corners of his eyes and says, "Tell me what you think happened here and then tell me why the Municipal Police should give a good goddamn." Red wants to know if that should be the order of the telling, and the Chief answers, "Tell the end first so's I can leave without suffering through the preamble."

"This here's still Tishomingo, y'know," says Red.

"No shit! Then just what do *you* do for a living?"

Red takes a long, loud swig. "I call you all."

"Yes, you do. And do you know why it's me here, and not some knucklehead on a bike? Because, I have no one to spare. Because every young pup with a shield is out with needle and thread trying to sew the seams together. So, you got me, Red, and I cannot but emphasize how put out I am to be here."

"Someone's got a badge up his rear this afternoon."

"Unless you're prepared to remove it, I'd just let that one go, I was you."

"Y' should take yourself a swig a this here. Settle y'all's nerves."

Prezhki stands abruptly. The bottle seems to be everybody's answer to all questions. "Next time, ring the Sheriff." He turns to leave.

"I forgot. The *te-e-e*-totaler. Wanna hear what I think?"

Prezhki stops, examines his watch. "Nope. But I already made the trip."

"Union agitators. Commies. From up North."

"You know, Red, what belongs to God belongs to God. Everything else belongs to the railroad. I don't see myself in this picture."

"Your town, last I heard."

"Not really. I just work for it. I thought, this sort of thing, you get your super to squeeze the governor, National Guard bayonets a few troublemakers, and everybody's point is made, pass the ammunition and praise the status quo." Red reminds him that everybody's got problems. "So, these agitators?" Prezhki asks. "The findings of your superb sleuthing intuitions or are we falling back on the old *that's what it was then, that's what it is again?*"

"We got doin's up an' down the line. Fires. Pried spikes. Debris'n shit on the right a way. I see coordination. I see outside financing. Y'all gonna wanna get involved in this here before it boils over."

"No, I won't. You find some *rubles,* a poster of Eugene Debs, call J. Edgar Hoover. This kind of thing's beyond my expertise, and I got a city up ended at the moment. And the city doesn't pay me to keep your fucking trains on the track. Your problem, see…you and people like you, is you see every event, every little aberration in your perfect vision of a head-splitting Eden from the half-full bottom of the glass. A good cop sees a pried spike, a fire, what ever, some punk kids fucking around, some employee with a grudge, a butt burning in a wood pile, a wino's camp fire getting away from itself. There is nothing inherently preconceived about a crane knocked over on its ass. You work in an industry that competes with mining to see who can kill the most employees per annum, you don't need Trotsky to piss in your porridge. Call me when there's someone to arrest. Room and board's on us." He hasn't turned; talks to the open air.

Red gets most of it, decides it justifies an additional swig, a phlegmy spit off of the slope. "What you know 'bout this old colored junkman? Name a Choc?"

Prezhki feels a churning in his gut, starts toward the car. "Why, he some kind of Bolshevik too? Or are you just fishing in my stream?"

"This's a different matter, though the Reds have their share a colored. Colored and Heebs. You know Moses Brown?" Prezhki leans against the squad car door, waits for Red to continue. "Moses Brown's this hogger. Thought you might a known 'im." Prezhki admits he might. "That's where he stays, back a where y'alls parked." The officer concedes a glance at the house. "Him an' his wife. A looker. Like one a them Hollywood types. Only not in black an' white, heh."

"Don't know her."

"The funny thing, an' I ain't suggestin' nothin', 'cause Mrs. Brown's a real nice lady, but there's talk she sneaks out at night when Mr. Brown's on a long one. And the other night, an' here's the thing, she meets up, I hear, in a fillin' station with this old colored junkman I was tellin' you about."

"Yeah? So what?"

"Nothing. Not a damn thing. It's just, this Moses Brown's on kin'a a short fuse, see, an' I don't need none his personal shit. God's business, not the railroad's, an' none a my own, that's for damn sure. Just relaying what I hear is on the wire with a bunch a old biddies got nothin' better to do than tell tales 'bout people they don't even know."

"And what tales do they tell?"

"Well, y'all didn't hear it here, okay? But it's goin' 'round like them chicken pops that this coon, this Choc, gives 'er a lift over to Thebes."

"I'm hearing no code violations yet."

"No, guess not. But it is outta the ordinary, wouldn't ya say?"

"Probably just doing her a favor."

"Well, I don't know about that. There's favors, an' then there's favors. Not that I'm suggestin' nothin'…outside a the laws a man an' nature or whatever. Some things just look funny 'till you get them figured out."

"Yeah, well, I got some things of civic interest to figure out myself. See you around. Watch out for the Bolshies. They even get into the plumbing, I hear. Bite you on the ass, you don't watch where you shit."

"You see, folks is sayin' he drops her off over to the end a the car line near between The Roadhouse an' the motor court. Say, you still got that old clunker Willys you used t' keep?"

"Not for sale."

"How many a those you think we got around here?"

"Few. I'm not in the business of counting automobile models."

"I only asked 'cause a the coincidence. She gets out a the junk man's truck, walks on down to the motor court, doesn't check in or nothin', just heads up to a room an' goes in. Now on the way down, 'tween the old man an' this room, she passes a vehicle that someone who sees the whole thing insists is a Willys-Knight, kind a knocked about, 'f ya know what I mean, an'…well, I know whatever car I'm driving an' I happen a see one just like it, I kind a, automatic like, just look over an' wonder whose drivin', whose got one like me. Not that it means nothin'. Just a natural curiosity most folks have. So, I just thought, maybe you'd seen this particular Willys-Knight, or that you'd gone an' sold off your own."

"Like I said, it's not for sale."

"Well, anyway, after she goes into the room, a fella gets out a the car and goes after her. Right into the room."

"Who's the fella?"

"Oh, well, I ain't the copper, am I? Just a humble yard bull. Thought maybe y'all might a heard somethin'."

"Heard *you* just now. Still, no laws broken."

"'Course, if this fella with the Willys-Knight an' Mrs. Brown…"

"I gotta go, Red. Nice chewing the fat with you." He gets into the car and rolls down his window. "You know, sometimes it is the wiser course to keep stuff buttoned, including one's lip, until there's something verifiably worth sharing. I haven't studied the matter, but it seems likely to me, that longevity is largely due to an innate ability not to use yourself up running your maw."

Prezhki, parked in front of Moses Brown's house, rolls up his window. He is annoyed with the railroad and Mr. Red and more than a little irate over P-R's threats. At the same moment, the Mayor exits the company offices in Uncas Falls, replete with a sense of unease, an insistent fly buzzing quizzical nothings in his ear, and a growing mistrust in T. Rail Ferrous' veracity.

Officer McCallum is taking a break at the lobby newsstand, two steaming dogs attired in mustard and kraut behind him on the marble counter, his thermos hot with Yuban. He is studying baseball scores and P-R can see the front page headlines in the <u>Uncas Clarion-Express</u>:

FREAK STORM WRECKS HAVOC
TWISTERS KILL SEVEN IN TRUKAHOE COUNTY
MILLARDSVILLE LEVELED
HAIL SIZE OF GOLF BALLS
EMERGENCY CREWS ON WAY
CHILD TRAPPED IN SCHOOLHOUSE WRECKAGE

~

TELLER FOILS DELTA SPRINGS BANK HOLDUP
TWO SLAIN IN SHOOTOUT
ROBBERS GET AWAY

~

FREIGHTER RAMS PORT LIMON DOCK
INVESTIGATION LOOMS

McCallum says, "Dog, sir?"

P-R experiences a wave of nausea. "Dog of a day! No. You go ahead. Shit'll kill y'all."

"If it ain't this, reckon it'll be something else."

"Pretty pessimistic for a youngster with a baby. You know the Beauregard?"

"By the lake?"

"Let's get out of here then."

The car is just down the block, diagonal to the curb. P-R gets in the front this time. McCallum settles behind the wheel, sets his lunch on the back seat and the coffee between his legs. The car fills with the smell of steamed meat; vaguely, P-R is reminded of a slightly soiled diaper. Flashbulbs are pulsing in his skull.

The engine rolls over, once, twice, three times; *awooga, awooga, awooga,* doesn't catch; whines apologetically like an old dog in mid-wretch.

McCallum whacks the wheel. "For cry'n' out loud! Would you a believed this?"

"Today, I'd be more surprised if it did start. Y'all a God-fearing man, Officer?"

"Was good for Paul and Simon, I guess it's good enough for this flatfoot."

"Is this some sort of personal God? A God that knows y'all? Hears your prayers? Does right by you? Gets into a dither when y'all screw up?"

"Do I believe He hears me? Yes, I believe He does."

"Hmm! Such a God must have my number today. Either that, or He's not paying attention."

"Lemme get under that hood there. Have you underway 'n'a jiffy."

"Do what you like. I'm walking, maybe ease up on this head of mine."

"You sure, sir?"

"Surety, at the moment, is not a commodity I would recommend investing in. Tell me something. What's your opinion of Lone Feather?"

"I'm on duty, sir."

"In general. There's beer and there's beer, of course. In your opinion, how does it match up to other domestics? Out of town stuff?"

"Well, sir, I'd say it goes down well."

P-R wants to know if the officer is going back over the hill or if he is staying in town to tote him back in the morning. McCallum says he'd rather come back "'cause a the baby and all." Also, he's worried "the Chief will blow his stack."

"Okay, you come for me at noon. One more thing. I've got a hunch y'all can help me with. Before you get your hands dirty, take a walk around the block to the County. Before they close up for the night. Go in and check with real estate registration, commercial. See if there has been any change of ownership at Lone Feather, oh, this year, last, go back until you find something. Don't mention who'all put you up to this. If anybody sticks their nose in, just say *police business.* If there's nothing in the way of a sale or incorporation, whatever, ring up the Beauregard and leave a message for Mr. Tagus, T-a-g-u-s, that simply says...oh, I don't know...*No such record.* Got that?"

"Yessir."

"And what's the message?" McCallum repeats it. P-R says, "If you do find something, just tell the clerk *thanks* and don't call. You can tell me in the car in the morning."

McCallum reiterates his concern about the Chief's rath. "He's gonna bust a gut if I'm not at work tomorrow. With all the goin's on."

"Y'all're on loan to me right now. Prezhki has a problem, you just tell him to carry it across the street and leave it with me."

"Yessir."

"And Prezhki is not to know about your visit to the County." P-R slips a bill from his wallet and hands it over. McCallum protests that it isn't necessary. P-R tells him to "buy the kid something."

They both get out on their respective sides and proceed in different directions. Down the street, P-R sees a crowd. A spout of water has its attention, like a whale has beached itself in the middle of this landlocked city. As he gets closer, he sees black water spreading on the street, reflections of buildings suddenly materializing, a line of phone poles reaching a manhole-vanishing point; then he can see, through legs, the van, upended, its front end up on a broken hydrant. There is a police car and a fire truck.

A sedan skids around a corner beyond, hydroplanes over the puddle, looses traction, scattering the crowd, jumps the curb up onto the short lawn in front of First Methodist, and takes out a marquee that reads: **"FOR WISDOM IS A DEFENSE, EVEN AS MONEY IS A DEFENSE; BUT THE EXCELLENCY OF KNOWLEDGE IS, THAT WISDOM PRESERVETH HIM THAT HATH IT."** (Eccles. 7.1)

McCallum, on assignment, heads up Court Street, is passed by a wailing stake truck with Sheriff's badge emblazoned on the door, the bed packed tight with grim looking men and shotguns. He is told at Records that there is a hullabaloo brewing just across the city line at Southern Cracker and Biscuit — labor unrest of some sort — and that a mob of lock-outs is threatening to pick a scab or two. McCallum thinks, *better them than us,* and asks for the appropriate file.

V

DOREEN, THE WAITRESS FROM THE FIVE and Dime in Tishomingo, gets a day off to ride over to Uncas Falls to visit her older cousin Eula, and over a cup of tea on Eula's veranda, talks about all the troubles that seem to have visited themselves upon the state, "all the plagues except the death of the first born." "These are signs," says Eula, "no doubt about it. Get your soul in order, dear." "And get this," adds Doreen, "it is common knowledge in my neck a the woods that our illustrious Mayor and our respected Chief of police are having a, ahem, *thing*...with the *same* woman...at the *same* time."

With Doreen back on the interurban, Eula drops in on her neighbor, Mrs. Morse, asks her if she's heard the news about the two notables. Mrs. Morse hasn't, but at dinner, shares with her husband a sordid tale of UF's Mayor Constantine's and Chief Winterfield's involvement in running a brothel.

Mr. Morse, sitting in his glassed-in porch with Meryl Dent and enjoying a Lone Feather, happens to mention, as an aside to their conversation dealing with the corruption running rampant in Uncas Falls, that, "fer 'nstance," the Mayor and the Chief are partners in a huge prostitution ring that services policemen throughout the state. Meryl says, "Ah ain't all surprised!" That evening, at the General Lee's Horse, Meryl downs several shots and tells a total stranger, "Every 'lected 'ficial from here t' the Gulf's up t' their necks in white slavin'." The total stranger staggers home and accuses his wife of hooking at Columbus Hall, a known den for local politicos of the Democratic Machine, as well as hooligans from the D'Scalucci Family.

Avoiding a thrashing, his tearful wife catches the interurban to Tishomingo to visit her mother and to moan about her marriage to the total stranger, enduring the expected, "Told y'all so. Moment I laid eyes on that good-fer-nothin'," and then tells the old woman that the Constantine Machine in UF is apparently some sort of front for illegal activities involving woman transferred about the state on the railroad, with the railroad complicit.

The mother, in a state of agitation, calls her sister Edna in Thebes and explains that the Mayor and his cronies and "a Mr. Ferret from the trains" are sneaking about with scarlet women, "wouldn't ya know?" Edna is at once titillated and shocked, rings up her niece Livonia, a waitress at the Five and Dime, and lets the cat out of the bag, "They're sayin', the Mayor's havin' hissself a *uh*-fair."

Livonia hangs up, wipes off the marble counter, hands the check to June the operator who has come over the hill for a very late supper, her shift having just ended, and shares the scoop and a good laugh, and says, "If that ain't the cat's jammies!" to which June responds, "This I know: 'F'I had an Indian nickel for every story run by me that I already knew, I'd be richer than that Rocky-feller, though the added sweetener of Uncas is intriguing. A web of intrigue, you ask me. Countywide epidemic is what we got, oh, and, dearie, would you mind wrapping up this other half of sandwich for later? Mus'n't be wasteful in times like these."

After flipping the CLOSED sign and cupping her hand to receive the last holdout crumbs of white bread from the counter, Livonia hangs her apron neatly on its chosen hook and rings up Doreen just coming through her own front door. As best as she can recollect, she recreates her conversation with June, right down to the *richer than Rocky-feller*, and adds, "or God." Doreen asks, "Just what does God do for a living, anyway?" to which Livonia opines, "Railroads."

"Oh, yes, indeed," says Ethel, the operator at the Tishomingo exchange, who is listening in while picking the meat from the walnut shell she has just cracked. Ten minutes later she is happily on the line to Cynthia Dahlhurst. Under the *nom de plume* Gabby Quidnunc, Dahlhurst writes the weekly "Truth Be Known" <u>Clarion News</u> gossip column, which, although taken with some misgivings among the literati, is held to the highest standards of journalistic excellence by old women who meet after church for egg salad and limeade and to shut ins and younger housewives who swallow it as placebo to the daily grind of floor scrubbing, diaper changing and the husking of corn.

VI

THERE IS LITTLE IN UNCAS FALLS to remind of the bucolic, small city splendors of the middle and upper class neighborhoods snuggled on the hilly outskirts of Tishomingo: the curving lanes and wide parkways, the grassy trolley islands, the neat wood-skinned ante-bellum homes upon local granite foundations, the draftsman-trimmed hedges. One sees Negro lawn jockeys, expanses of unfenced greenways, crisp Grecian and Deco municipal structures, and the tree-roofed streets of gentlemanly commerce. Surely, there are other sides to the tracks; real estate to visit only to manage laborers or to collect rent or track down a ten cent hand job. But Tishomingo, with its manicured parks and gentle traffic circles, its monuments, its playgrounds and golf courses, trim little cemeteries and public gardens of seasonal foliage both indigenous and exotic, is considered an ideal burg for the raising of families and the slow drift into dotage.

"The children in the *finer* parts" — says the Chamber of Commerce brochure — "seldom leave but for college or war, and surviving either, often return to set out shingles and join lodges, to marry off their children, pamper their grandchildren, and fill a plot at Peaceful Meadows or Whispering Pines."

All of which, P-R is proud to extol. But kept close to his chest, is his secret admiration for the larger, more pedestrian grime of UF. For the Mayor is a man who appreciates the aesthetics of well-oiled machines, of carbon run stacks that spell MONEY in the air like sky writers, of row upon row of company-owned Log Cabin Syrup houses in prototypical scale, set in the greasy soil and repeating themselves ad nauseam. P-R dotes on the action, the jazz and blues throbbing out of the honkytonks and the jukes, the jet spring slide of the register drawer, the hustlers and grifters with their decks and shell games and Florida land deeds, the flop house hookers, the no-frills concrete buildings that scream function and utility.

He envies UF its terminus and junction. Witness the lines of freight cars from everywhere to everywhere else; Great Northern mountain goats on their sides, Central Vermont pine trees, the sweet whiskered face of Chessie the Cat. UF is an ant colony of vans, a seventeen-year cicada confabulation of sound. It is a pack rat city of acquisitiveness that makes his own town seem like a tractor stop in Kansas replete with feed bags, irrigation supplies and the Sears-Roebuck catalogue as a convenient but diminishing read in the privy.

Whereas in 'Mingo, the worn gets repainted and people are born and expire in the same bedrooms, UF is of the bulldozer mentality and structures there seldom last long enough to be redecorated; where things are new, up to date and refreshingly artless. Even the river is ugly, damned fifteen miles below the Falls to form a large dirty lake for fish to die in, with tar splotches in the still water of the reservoir to ensnare waterfowl in its mummifying goop: lake of sludge, river of slime. In places, it is chemical pink with white lumps like beet borsht, oily cut logs rafted and half submerged under the stink of the pulp mill. If you're not a bass, if you're not a duck, there is a cancer surgeon's urgency to getting things done, ripped down, cut out, planed, molded, sliced, ground up, patted down, pureed, packaged, pickled, preserved, sent on its way to Tacoma and Key West, to Bangor and San Diego. On a good day, when his head has no complaint, when his eyes can focus, P-R is one with it all, sucks it in with the abbreviated oxygen, the acidic, eye squelching, gut churning, tympanic thrill of a savory buffet set out by Mammon. Tishomingo is an aside in a history that will be written about Uncas Falls. "Hot damn," he would say, "What a country! What a fucking cornucopia of a country!"

✳

But not today. Today he shields his eyes, palm to forehead, elbow bent, looks like he's saluting. The sounds of commodities being exchanged grind in his skull, plunder his reason, set him to reeling as he grips the rail on the Alexander Stevens Bridge, vomits over the side a near-dry breakfast that is welcomed in the water as a kindred spirit to industrial detritus.

It is an old bridge that sits on stone pilings at the edge of the neat, ten-foot plunge, cutting in razor sharpness across the man-made lake. Were it not the property of the state, Uncas Falls would have replaced it with something more startlingly modern, something steel with a bronze plaque commemorating Mayor Constantine and his murky band of thieves; something with a short half life, a span costly enough to tariff drivers and cheap enough to need rebuilding in the living memory of its engineers. At the far end, it crosses to conclusion the old towpath and the sewer trench that was once the Great Uncas & Atlantic Canal, in those brief halcyon days before *The DeWitt Clinton* and *The Best Friend of Charleston* changed the way the world moved forever.

Beyond the littered trail, its forged historic landmark sign a State Registry gift to the target shooting set, stands the Beauregard House; anachronistic on the UF skyline, but excusably ensconced in the jurisdiction of North Uncas Falls. It boasts five gabled stories like an old French roadhouse fattened in cream sauces and set before a dry fountain in a circular drive. No longer does it rate the label *institution*. Guests complain of the fetid canal stench — or is it the kitchen? — the occasional corpse rotting on the banks where mules used to shit. Oysters on the half shell are no longer served in the dining room, and the dedicated railroad spur is now trackless and tangled in weeds. Seen from the penthouse, the roadbed seems nothing less than a effigy mound left by some snake worshipping tribe that predated DeSoto. The golf course is un-mowed and a venue for gophers, the pool filled only with rain runoff, mosquito larvae, and water beetles enjoying floating Mekong villages of pine needles. The guests are few and haggard, the poorly vented rooms keeping them awake at night in summer and frozen stiff at all other times, and the torpor sticks like skin to the peeling walls, the threadbare carpets, the tarnished copper ceilings. A perfect place to offer P-R the very anonymity required of dalliances with the Mrs. Brown's of his experience.

He checks the front desk. The clerk's lack of reaction to his appearance belies the fact that the current clientele consists of lightning rod salesmen and widows of husbands struck by lightning. No one has rung for Mr. Tagus. "You're certain? T-a-g-u-s?" "Lawd strike me f'I'm not, suh."

He is prone on his bed, his coat forgotten on the floor, his collar torn open so that a button is launched to oblivion, his tie hanging on the bedpost, a wet washrag swathed over the pain with the hotel's name bleeding onto his temples. His belt is open, the tongue hanging useless, and his shirt is dark in the pits of his arms. His laces are untied but his shoes remain on his feet. For all his monograms — *SP-R* — he smells unlike the gentleman that had set out with Officer McCallum that morning, has surrendered to a rank, feral aroma that makes of him, perhaps, more common than he intends to appear.

"I heard y'all come in. Why didn't you come fetch me?" She has come in through the door between their modest rooms, an accommodation intended for families needing some elbow room, as if a clan of Boone's were to check in.

"Keep the light off," he mumbles. "I haven't felt this bad since binge drinking was *de rigueur* at my frat house. Jesus, what a day!"

She sits on the side of the bed. "What can I do for you?"

"Move as little as possible."

"That's a new one from y'all!"

Much later, he is well enough to complain of hunger. She feeds him cold cuts from a basket she has brought, lukewarm now, and just this-side-of-soggy cheese. He watches the dizzy sway of her breasts, white as death, through the opening in her robe. By candlelight, she draws his bath, stoops with her knees in the puddle he displaces, lathers him, gently sponges him down. She gifts soft kisses on his soothed brow, follows with an explosive massage under water that sets him near to swooning.

He tells her, "You asked once if I believe in God." She corrects, "In anything at all." He says, "For a third of a second when I reach my peak, I believe in God. I do. But it's fleeting. That's why, I suppose, we have to keep doing it over and over. Least God feels ignored. Lonely. We couple as an act of faith."

"What did y'all tell your wife this time?"

He cradles her in his arms on the wet bed. "Uh uh. State secret."

"I could torture it out of you."

"Hot lights? A brick across the knuckles?"

"I was thinking more...*Lysistrata*."

"You do, and there will be nothing to tell my wife at all."

"Y'all act like there is a certain uniqueness to all of this. As if this is somehow a variance on y'all's usual chaste behavior."

"You are important to me, you know?"

"So is air. It's why we breath. Did one of your advisors suggest you tell me that? I'm an opportunity, I know that. You've taken advantage of my unhappiness."

"That's not true. I *need* you. In the office, there are times...that I could take you right there on your desk, fling your Underwood to the floor, spread your stocking legs, right there in front of a bench full of petitioners, and fuck y'all into unconsciousness."

"My, my! You should get these headaches more often. Does wonders for your prose. Nevertheless, it's desire, not need."

They lay laughing for a while, each with a mental picture shocking in its degree of abandonment.

"I need to tell you something," she says. "I think it comes after *you're important to me*."

He is already regretting his teasing. He needs no more meandering pathways on a day riddled with detours and obstructions.

"You could leave her. Set her up handsomely. She won't care."

"I'm a man of position. I can't just pack a duffle and jump a freight."

"You could. If the need was great enough."

"And by what stretch of the imagination would the need be great enough?"

"If y'all were to lose me."

"You should be on stage. Look, I don't want to discuss this today. Not... to*day*. I am raft-less and the waters are rising. Christalmighty, not today, Mrs. Barrymore!"

It is still dark when he awakens. The candle has extinguished itself, lays flaccid over the nickel holder, looks like someone has melted the dripping ceiling of nearby Smuggler's Cave, where, not so long ago, bootleggers gathered to concoct their thin stews away from the nose of the revenue man.

"You don't care for me," she says. "You say you do, but you don't. Y'all don't even speak my name when you say it. I need *you*. Everyone is *you*, P-R. Without a name, what does it mean? Your wife is *you*, other lovers are *you*. I am the *you* of the moment. Interchangeable, like a Ford crankshaft and every bit as soiled. And most of all, my love, y'all are *you*."

"What does that mean?"

"That you are so enamored of yourself there is no room for the rest of us."

"What adornment have you attached to what we do? I'm not a used car salesman, after all. Y'all knew what you were signing on for. I have broken no promises and do my best to afford you all the affection the present situation allows. And there are no other lovers. How ever did you come up with that bit of fable?"

"I've been afraid lately. You don't know."

"I'm a very careful, man. Meticulous. What is there to fear?"

"Moses."

"Please. The man's density is his greatest virtue."

"He suspects something."

He stares up at the brown, damp patches in the ceiling. "Like?"

"He thinks I'm having an affair."

"Are you?"

"Damn you, P-R!" She sits up. It is her first sign of anger since entering the room.

"Well, are you?"

"Y'all're a bastard."

"So, here we are then. You can accuse me, but when the tables are turned, you self-righteously lick your wounds. Look, y'all can be damn sure he doesn't suspect *us*. How many times have I told you about the lengths I go to...to...Why do you think our brave engineer is always in the cab when we have these little encounters. Y'all think Providence favors our deceit? Look, have you maybe slipped up with somebody else you're seeing?"

"What do you think of me? I've risked everything caring about you. Do you leave me cash on the dresser? Have I ever even asked you for carfare? What do y'all think I'm here for? I have never...never, before this, been unfaithful to my husband...nor to you."

"Sleeping with Moses isn't unfaithful to me?"

"He is my husband. Do you not fondle that prissy bitch of y'all's?"

"I haven't been so encumbered in years."

She presses the robe closed, tight over her breasts, averts her eyes from his, a hint, he sees, of cunning. "You know what you can do to get me out from under Moses."

"And you know what I can't do."

"Won't do. It's a matter of priorities."

"Yes, it is. And, a certain tradition of behavior. I am my father's son, and my son's are my sons. So it goes."

"Sneaking is a family tradition?"

"It trumps constancy, that's for sure."

"What if he hurts me? You should see the way he looks at me. The way he questions me. He suspects something."

"Of course he does. He lives in a house without love, just like I do. I've made my peace with that. And so will he, if he's got any sense at all."

"And this? This thing we do? An inconvenience? A...what did y'all say?...A little *encounter?*"

"You're twisting my words."

"I'm telling you, I'm afraid of him. I need to get out of that house before..."

"Before what? Has he ever laid a hand on you? Ever gotten violent? I can send someone around to set him straight, you know."

He stands, proceeds to the toilet to urinate, notices that the floor is not as cold as he would have imagined on a day like this. He pads back into the room and looks out over the curtain. The glass doesn't fog. He touches it lightly with his fingertips and feels only a cool indifference.

"I wish he *would* lay a hand on me," she says. "It's the waiting, you see. It's going to happen. It's building. I see it in his face and he knows by mine that I see it. Like I'm tied to the tracks and I can hear the whistle. Moses' whistle. What am I going to do?"

"Go to sleep. I'll think of something."

"Will you? Some thug with a bat? Or will y'all just send me off on the trolley tomorrow? I will not continue in harm's way, P-R. Y'all owe me something...some way out of this. You haven't ruined my life, I grant you that. You took me out of my boredom and made me feel alive, and I will not return to either that lassitude, that sleeping sickness of a marriage, nor will I set myself up for abuse. Y'all *will* think of something. Rather than the wrath of a spurned women, you will expend a great deal of effort thinking of something."

Damned women, he thinks. He is tired of threats, of premonitions, the various knives poised at his throat. His thoughts wander back to a conversation he once had with Prezhki. They were seated on the running board of a squad car, pondering a crime scene in which a woman was badly bludgeoned and left to be found in the briars. She looked like a vision from an old country song, *her hands lily white, her long golden tresses like an elfin queen, the fairest maid 'twas e'er seen. Women, see,* he had lectured, *the bane of man. Providence's reminder that we all are humble and fallible and greatly in need of certain luxuries. What with the monthlies,*

the hissy fits, the demands unending, they resemble nothing less than she-wolves braying at the moon, and jackass-ornery to boot. It is no wonder that, in His infinite wisdom, the Good Lord blessed man with hands and stuck them on arms long enough so he could reach his own pecker, to carry him through those fallow times when, for love or money, which is usually enough, that gash-comfort warmth just can't be had.

With such bitter wisdom, and forethoughts of reckoning, P-R's day comes to its eventual end. Tomorrow threatens to be somewhat less gentle.

VII

H E THINKS HE HEARS SONGBIRDS; SITS up in the bed and cocks his head. Otherwise, it is quiet. A smile crosses his chiseled face as he remembers P-R squirming over the mutiny of his council stooges, the projected harm to his investments. He is a firm believer that a solid, heartfelt gloat is a superior balm with which to begin the morning; even excels over a good breakfast. It is the sort of exultation that can easily prime his day, if only he has the opportunity to avoid the rest of it. He parts the curtains, hears the birds again, and sees fireflies in celebration low on the lawn. He steps into his slippers, shuffles out of his room and over to hers, taps lightly on the intricate faux mahogany grain of the oak door.

"That you, Captain?" She calls him Captain, a term sometimes used as honorarium for locomotive engineers.

"Yes deah, it is. May Ah entuh?"

He comes quietly into the room and proceeds to her window. "Ah 'ntreat y'all t' join me. Strangest thing Ah evuh seen!"

She reluctantly rubs the sleep from her eyes and stands well over him, even unshod.

"Mothuh, you rec'lect evuh havin' song birds an' lightnin' bugs this time a yeah?"

Automatically, she sits back down on the edge of the bed. "It is indeed queer. What do you suppose it means?"

"Ah am the Supuh on a railroad, deah. Don't suppose Ah am privy to such phenom'na." A milky streak edges up on the eastern horizon. "Oh, well," he says. "Ah might as well stay 'wake now. Kinde'gart'n fo' ower visitin' easte'n brats, y'know. And the ignor'nt shall 'nherit the ea'th, 'though, with any luck, not today."

The birds become louder, more fluent even. The glow flies stagger off home to nurse their hangovers.

As the sun lifts, more birds appear: not in flocks, but singles and pairs — Tennessee and Kentucky warblers, Northern saw-whets, indigo buntings, brown-headed cow birds — as if they had been hibernating, waiting for the unseasonable cold to surrender to a precipitous temperature rise and an equally unseasonable warmth.

Scoffers beware. A couple on skates will venture onto the seldom frozen ice of Phipps Lake, unaware that the glassine skin has thinned over night, and will go to eternity mitten in mitten. An early bear, still grumbling from broken sleep, will overturn a trash can in Thebes, and wake half the town to witness his first breakfast in months. A crew firing up a switcher at the G&N yard will note two butterflies on the oiled roadbed enjoying a sauna from the steam valve; somewhat more machine than required to humidify their fragile wings.

Brother Holynation Salvation will say in meter, *It d'worl' turn' upsi'e down*, and Arpachshad Shem will orate at length on the Lord's strange ways and the sagacity of acceptance. There will be talk of witchcraft, of some celestial fallout from Tesla's long ago experiments with unnatural lightning in distant Manitou Springs, of an imbalance caused by aggressive Huns in Europe, of sunspots and potential comets. Perhaps the earth has experienced an adjustment in tilt: perhaps some covert Soviet experiment in the Siberian tundra. Later, a government meteorologist will write an erudite but ultimately inconclusive paper about the effects of carbon emissions on climate that will thrust him into momentary notoriety, and make him the subject of ridicule in the scientific community, of those who will find it, at most, the half-baked stretch of an unstable mind.

Geographic disparity will not be an issue. Mr. Red will say unequivocally that *commie northern unions are no doubt, no possible doubt, behind some a this here*. A Michigan radio priest and a Dearborn columnist will collude to inform of the complicity of Jews, that it is absolutely no wonder that the Lord's wrath is undiminished since the deicide on Golgotha, that those who drive spikes into the gentle hands of The Son will know The Father's wrath, and that nations that give sanctuary and profit to such fiends will too suffer divine judgment. On a Gulf Coast island, an itinerant preacher, risen up from medicine show and burlesque clowning, pitches a vast tent fit for Barnum & Bailey, and exhorts the paying public to repent, that already the frog kings have descended from the mouth of The Beast, that the temple is being rebuilt as evidenced in the Zionist murmurings, and that the lost will find eternity a lake of fire. One smart aleck departs asking, *If it's prophecy, why don't the Devil have the good sense t' change his plans?* At the University, Professors A and B, recently the principals in Reverend Shem's parabolic Sunday humor, ensconce themselves in Professor A's study, parry to and fro on matters of pressure, vapor, friction and flux, the conclusion of which finds Professor B, wiping his forehead with a wrinkled hanky, admitting, *You'll excuse my French, but as to what's going on, I still have no fucking idea!*

Early that morning, a UF dispatcher, who Moses knows only as Mr. Hatch, offers him a cup of joe, checks his board, and asks the engineer to run the Express up to the capital.

"You're foolin'!" Moses says.

Hatch indicates the board. "It's chalked. See for your own se'f."

"I just come off a twelve hour!"

"I know. I had Danvers up, but he called in sick."

"I run sick many a time."

"Dif'rence 'tween you an' Danvers. Anyways, he says he broke somethin'r some such hooey. Damn well bettuh have the doctor ver'fy or I'll have his ass flushin' boiluh tubes. Anyways, I need y'all today."

"There's no one else?"

"You know there ain't no one willin'. Eve'y man jack a 'ems gonna get Union Fevuh soon's the phone rings. You hea'd what happen down at Southe'n Crackuh. This kind a stuff's catchin'. See, Brown, you the only one I don't get this crap from. That's why you my sweethea't."

"Ain't really safe. I'm all done in."

"Hell with *safe*, Brown! I gotta a schedule heah. Some big wigs commin' down t'ride too. See that li'le crummy out theah?" He points to a four-wheel caboose. "Broke axle. Ain't goin' nowhe'es, but I don't 'magine it d'tracts any from the bunk. Go catch yo'se'f a few winks an' I'll holluh y'up when I need ya." Later, Hatch bangs on the door of the caboose, tells Brown apologetically that he's given him as much of a rest as he can, and that, "Band's tuned an' awaitin' the maestra." It is a bitter pill for the engineer, this punishment of reliability. Hatch promises to relieve him down the line.

Moses approaches the big engine from behind. The fireman has his long oiler poking in all her tender spots. The engineer pulls a red rag from his overall pocket, nods to the stoker, takes the stork-beaked can and completes the lubrication himself. Behind him, the varnish is being loaded — mail, baggage, people. The conductor is martineting to and fro, a soldier in a mechanical clock. A group of men ambles around the front of the locomotive, generous with admiring glances. They are in suits, hats, except for one in overalls. One appears to be a dwarf and has a labored gait. "Y'all Moses Brown?"

"Who are you?"

"Fe'ous. Ah'm yore boss. These gen'lemen ah from Central back east."

One of them says, "We were admiring your train set. She's thing of beauty."

"She is," Moses agrees.

"Let me borrow those gloves, will you, Brown?" He is a young man, slick and clean, very sure of himself. Moses imagines that he is expensively dressed, though he has no experience of such consumption.

"Go 'head," says Ferrous.

With suspicion obvious on his sullen face, Moses takes off the gloves, hands them to the younger man, who then removes his jacket, hands it blind faced back to an associate, places the big dirty gloves up over his immaculate sleeves, and points to the oil can. "May I?" Again, Ferrous nods *yes*. The young man grabs the rungs and pulls himself up into the cab.

"Want I should show you around?" Moses asks.

"Thanks, no. I'm no neophyte. Get myself on the high iron any time I can."

Moses looks helplessly at Ferrous. The little man shrugs, mumbles, "Not mah idea of a good time."

"Bo-*ard*," from down the line. The trainmen are preparing to remove the portable steps.

"I need to be up there you want to run on time," Moses says.

"He's takin' it. B'ought his own man fo' back up." Sure enough, the young man is slipping into coveralls.

"This here's nuts! This is a gag a some kind, right?"

"'F'on'y that was true," says Ferrous. "Alas, Ah'm a man'th as much a sense of humuh as a case of gangr'ne."

"This is against company regs, ain't it?"

"Don't le'tchuh me, young man." Ferrous turns away, rubs his forehead, then swivels back. "Ya know, they's a rivuh in New Brunswick, hits the sea at a place call Saint-John, if mem'ry se'ves, that, dependin' on the tide, runs both upstream an' down. At the *same* time. Now, *that's* 'gainst the regs. Whi'lpool 'n a middle's wo'th stayin' outta."

"What about these passengers? They got reason t' expect a real hogger's takin' them in hand."

The whistle blows, loud, long, shrill, recognizing no pattern entered in the rulebook. The man at the throttle yips and haroos like he's at a sporting event.

"Respectively, this's f..."

The curse stops at Ferrous' full-sized palm. "Paid vacation, Brown. Y'all's lucky day. In 'dition, heah's a li'le somethin' fo' the cab home. Wheah to? Heah in town? 'Mingo? Live a little. Lea'n what it's like to be a pass'nger. Y'all 'bout due a new pai' a gloves anyway. Gotta ya'se'f a fam'ly? Somethin' f'them too. Unus'ally mild day. Take the 'ho'e brood fo' a taxi ride. Day at the Cave, the Falls."

Moses backs away from the outstretched hand. Ferrous moves forward, reaches up and puts the money into the front pocket over the chest of his overalls.

"Good day, Brown, and God bless."

With minimal conversation, Mrs. Brown and Mayor P-R go their separate ways; she, off to the interurban station to await big green cars, the size of mainline coaches — they will feed off the overhead in a gentle sway learned, perhaps, in the company of finely hewn wooden boats; he, for a short walk in the decay of the towpath to summon an appetite, and then back to the Beauregard to sate it.

He sheds his overcoat; the heat is untimely and nearly mystic. She stuffs her shawl into her cross-stitch bag, buys her ticket and climbs on board. He orders steak and eggs, toast, a coffee; the beef comes burnt, tough as an old chair cushion and lined with gristle tubing. People in the room share the collective embarrassment of being over dressed, prickly-hot in wool and flannel, as if they had just fallen out of a more northern adventure. They speak softly, eat slowly with disinterest, wondering how they had slept through invisible months of transition.

At the first stop out of UF — a general store with gas pumps and a PO, a place known as Dogtown Ferry — Mrs. Brown sees a telegrapher sweating in long sleeves bunched in arm garters, who comes on board and announces that a

241

freak wind has blown down the wire a mile down the road. "Crew's working it as I speak. Be up and running in no time and we'll get y'all on your way. Meantime, theirs hot coffee and yummies over there at Beale's, so y'all make yourselves welcome."

P-R has managed three bites and a fourth pass of his knife when the first siren calls. He is contemplating the yoke spilling out around the crackled fat like rust, when he hears the second. It comes from up the road on this side of the lake, but the third, the fourth, wail out of UF itself. There is a new urgency in the dining room. Mrs. Brown sees a Forest Service fire truck race down the highway back toward the city as she dips a stale powdered donut into her coffee; the sugar sinks like old expectations. P-R is at the window. Emergency vehicles of every type clog the byways on both sides of the river: ambulances, pumpers, wrecker upon wrecker. A work train is being assembled across the river. He is joined at the window by the others with their cigars and cigarettes held carelessly aloft, some with coffee cups in their hands. "What do you suppose?" "Sumpin' big, I reckon". The Lukenheimer on the work locomotive sucks more steam than can comfortably escape its open mouth. He hears its hectic blast from North Uncas Falls. She hears it's bark a moment later in Dogtown.

VIII

(The following essay is excerpted from Wincook Darvin's introduction to, When the Reaper Rode the Rails; A Compendium of Articles and Literary Passages Exploring Fatalities in the American Railroad Industry, Cassidy, Jason W., & Winton Horschtadt, Illinois Institute of Railroad Technology, Chicago.)

It is no wonder that America not only grew up with the railroad, but that the histories of the nation and the industry form a close parallel. Going back to the 1820's, we find a young nation itching to escape the tedious limitations of draft animals and water-driven transport, a muscular economy palsied by natural barriers, and a technology more in concert with tradition than the principles of commerce. It took weeks, sometimes months, for a letter mailed in New York City to wend its way to New Orleans, if it got there at all. Passengers were made to suffer the indignities of the coach, i.e., overcrowding, crude roads, wretched wayside accommodations, and motion sickness that overpowered the sensitive. Freight depended upon the fickleness of the seas and rivers, the load limits of the horse and oxen, and the vicissitudes of vast, hostile distances. The country itself, despite inroads over the first of a subsequent series of ranges, clung largely to the Atlantic, and thus to its European genesis.

The endless annexations beyond the Mississippi remained much as they were when acquired.

As every schoolchild knows, all of this was changed by the railroad. Who can forget those idealized text book images of engines racing horses, of the meeting of the Central Pacific and the Union Pacific at barren Promontory signifying the linking of the continent and the opening door to Asian-Pacific riches, or the New York Central's 999 moving man faster than he had ever gone? Railroad folklore was born: Casey Jones, John Henry, the fearless engineers of the dime novels. Every boy in the land dreamed of the throttle. The railroads became, along with the aligned industries of steel, coal and then oil, the highest pinnacle of capitalistic advancement; forming the prototype of the modern corporation; initiating health care for workers employed in the hundreds of thousands; advancing technology; moving everything manufactured from tin cups to the spans of bridges, everything raised from Texas Long Horns to wheat; opening vistas heretofore unseen by the traveling public; civilizing primitives; transferring the deeds of great tracts of fertile land to both immigrant and emigrant. The railroad was the conveyor of civilization, of democracy, of, ultimately, God's Word. No longer need manufacturers and consumers exist within sight of each other. With their steel threads, the railroads stitched the country together in a fabric of ingenuity never before seen in the annals of the world and advanced the coffers of wealth and democracy to degrees previously unimagined. Is it any mystery that the Civil War was won, was destined to be so, not only by the side of arguably superior moral fortitude, but by that which possessed the most consistent track gauges and the greatest mileage, held a monopoly on the manufacture of engines, and constructed a superior density of service for its industry and its military to enjoy?

But to every coin, there is both an obverse and a reverse. So, too, the railroad. There are countless contrary images to those referenced above: nostalgia for the lone Indian with his ear to the track listening for the rumble of annihilation or the corporate greed that prompted at least one major line to build so hastily in winter that track was set on snow, a practice proved wanting the following spring. Eastern Robber Barons bilked the government, bilked the farmer, raised many towns while destroying many others, and were the industrial bulwark of racial segregation. The Jim Crow Car, after all, was a railroad innovation.

243

But perhaps most striking of all on the tail side of the toss, was the incredible loss of life. During some decades of recent passing, more Americans died by railroad than by disease. They were killed by fires meant for wood stoves in wooden cars, by collisions, by poorly laid rail that could spring from the roadbed like a snag under a steam boat and impale a coach, by the horrendous "telescoping" of cars loaded with human commerce, by washouts, flukes of nature, avalanches such as the one that removed two snow-stranded trains on the Great Northern's Cascade run in 1910. People fell from trains, were crushed between them, and were broiled by exploding boilers. The workers suffered the most: thus the company health care systems. Trainmen lost fingers, legs, vision, and all too often, their very lives.

A case in point: Days short of two years prior to this writing, and soon to be commemorated in a highly publicized memorial service, the industry, and, indeed, the nation, was shocked to hear of the events to strike the Uncas Falls, Tishomingo & Gulf at a previously obscure facility known as David's Sling*. The Sling (the name's biblical derivation has been obscured by time), occupies a riverside flat, bounded on the east by a series of scenic cliffs, and bifurcated by the Tishomingo's main line. At the time, it offered little more than a small yard for empties, a run down shanty with a handful of cots for crewmen on break, a telegrapher's office, a signal tower, and the now infamous siding. All in all, it was a timeless, and generally peaceful, cameo of the rural railroad setting. The oft-told tale unfolds during an exceptional day of weather conditions that, to this day, has climatologists puzzled, but, alas, is not germane to the present discussion. Suffice it to say that amongst more primitive societies, such aberrations of the natural order would surely have been taken as omens and precautions would likely have been made to placate the deities.

The official company version of the incident, as read into the transcripts of the subsequent investigatory commission, indicates that the Tishomingo's first class train set was in tiptop shape. Indeed, it was comprised of new, well-maintained streamlined equipment, and was considered the pride of the line. The other train involved, as we shall see, was another matter entirely. The assigned engineer for the Express, having been hospitalized during the night, was replaced by the veteran Moses Brown. Brown had yet to be scheduled for the day. For unknown reasons, Brown showed up to work only minutes before departure. The Division

Superintendent, T. Rail Ferrous (as of this writing company president and due soon to retire), testified that while offering a tour of the shops to Acting President Acker Maelstrom, a promising young bright light from headquarters, and the latter's entourage, Maelstrom requested a cab ride on Brown's sleek train. According to Ferrous, Brown demurred, then became surly, and resorted to profanity. Ferrous felt compelled to order him from the cab and eventually had him escorted off of company property. A suspension would ensue. Testimony of employees who knew Brown tend to support Mr. Ferrous' version of events. A cab mate described Brown as moody, overly serious, always preoccupied and arrogant. "He looked down on the rest a (sic) us. Thought he was God's gift," complained one fireman. A company security officer, who claimed to be a friend and neighbor of Brown's, would offer, reluctantly and under pressure from the commissioners at the inquest, that Brown seemed troubled of late, was perhaps involved in a serious chain of incidents involving vandalism of company property and provoked by outside labor agitators and that, perhaps even more damning, seemed to suffer problems at home of a domestic nature. Brown himself would stick firmly to the story that he was concerned only with the strict procedural rules of the company and the safety of passengers, crew, and his train. His subsequent dealings with local police seem unrelated, but do underlie certain deficiencies in the man's state of mind.† In any case, no authorized engineer rode the cab when the Express left the Uncas Falls station. Instead, Acting President Maelstrom, not only a respected, sober and forward looking businessman, but an enthusiastic railroad buff who had taken the helm of locomotives on numerous occasions to enjoy successful short runs, was at the throttle. Several engineers who had run with him in the past verified the railroad's claim that Maelstrom's operational knowledge and skill equaled or exceeded their own. And, besides, Ferrous would underscore, that although he himself was uneasy with Maelstrom's decision to take the train even if only as far as Tishomingo, he was in no position to countermand his superior. As such, none of this was as yet the final ingredient in a recipe for disaster, except for one crucial failure of communication: the dispatcher, now deceased, insisted at the inquiry that essential train orders were given to Engineer Brown and, on his way to the engine, they were repeated to him by the conductor. For whatever reason, be it a lapse of memory, pique, a sense of revenge for some perceived sleight, or simple distraction, such instructions were never relayed to Engineer Maelstrom. As it was, the Acting President had no knowledge that he was expected to slow to a crawl at Three Mile, allowing the tardy northbound local to plant itself on the David's Sling siding.

The second train was a mixed, a short consist of a few freight cars and a passenger combine, that had been hastily added to accommodate residents displaced by flooding during the previous night's freakish storm. The equipment was old, standby rolling stock. The late nineteenth century 4-6-0 was assigned for scrap within the coming months. As this was not a regularly scheduled run, neither Maelstrom nor the firemen on the fast train expected to encounter any northbound traffic until Tishomingo station.

What ensued was neither the first, nor will it be the last of such horrific high-speed encounters. However, certain specifics mark this event for particular infamy: 1) The fast train was piloted by the highest ranking officer of the railroad, a man neither professionally trained for such a task nor involved in anything more than, it seems in retrospect, an arguably irresponsible joy ride, 2) some of the equipment on the slow train was unsafe at any speed having long since suffered obsolescence, and, 3) head-on collisions are in general particularly grizzly affairs and thus appeal to the darkest nature of the public imagination.

At sixty miles per hour, Maelstrom's southbound Express crested the blind ridge just north of the flats at the exact moment that the late scheduled northbound local was accelerating past the holding track at David's Sling at an estimated twenty-five miles per hour. Vision was limited by the opposing grades and a glade of pines that blocked the light, so one can only wonder the dismay of the drivers when they realized they had ominous company only yards away. The collision was great enough to explode both boilers and scorch a considerable plot of woods. Witnesses wrote of steel frames arching upward into the tongues of flame and the black plumes of coal smoke. The smaller locomotive catapulted up and forward over the larger, landing on its back atop the baggage car, its tender crushing the first coach. The wooden cars on the slow northbound telescoped from the force of the oncoming streamliner, and everything else left the track and skidded into rocks and trees, thrown helter-skelter like toy electric trains at the mercy of a petulant child. The carnage was ghastly, to say the least. The few survivors say they will remember the sounds and the sights, the smell of burning flesh, for as long as they live. Without being unduly

or morbidly perverse, suffice it to say that body parts littered
the scene and blood flowed freely on the tracks. The reaper's
booty was immense that day.

*Theories about the name's derivation are explored in
Appendix C.

†The character of Moses Brown is further illustrated in Ch.
12 of this volume, as attested to by contemporary newspaper
accounts and more recent interviews of company personal.
Brown is at once described as "cold," "indifferent," and a "day
dreamer," even on the job. "He was a stern taskmaster," said one
railroad employee, "a stickler for rules and no sense for people,"
and, said another, he was "admired but little liked."

IX

WITH FINGER AS CENTER POST, P-R constructs a little tent with his
napkin, gingerly dips its peak into his water, and dabs at a small spot
of egg that has discovered his shirt. He has been uncharacteristically
careless this morning. Yet, he is aware that a shadow has come over him.

"Your Honor," a voice says.

P-R turns to see a thin man in a overlarge suit, lapels like running boards, a
screaming tie the man can nearly hide behind. His eyes are slits in a craggy horse
face, with the long nose warped from an old break. "I'm afraid y'all've got the
wrong fellow," P-R tells him. The man consults a photo cut from a newspaper.
He has slick black hair and slick black shoes that give him vertical symmetry.
"'Fraid I ain't, pal."

"Pal? Y'all're not from around here?"

"Everybody's from somewheres they probably ain't no more, no? Bud
Constantine'd like t'see ya." The connection is clear to P-R. Constantine is not
exactly P-R's cup of hootch. Not that P-R disapproves of a politician living high
on the pork barrel, but Constantine's disdain of tradition disturbs him. The two
have never been as close as their respective town lines. Like his father before him,
P-R likes a certain order, one that more closely reflects the will of Tishomingans
even if the voters need to be prodded toward an understanding of what that will
entails. Constantine is all UF: modern and short of memory. He runs his town like
a competitive business. He lacks civility. Lacks inborn class. Plays government
like he played football at State: all offense. More New Orleans than Charleston,
Constantine looks like Herbert Hoover, talks like Huey Long, and operates like
Big Bill Thompson. It is no wonder that the man disturbing P-R's breakfast seems
like he just took five from a Cagney set.

"How does he know I'm here?"

"We got bunches a these here snaps. He's waitin' in the car."

"I'm having breakfast."

"Maybe you're done." The man puts his hand on the back of P-R's chair and motions him out. Then he takes the unpaid bill in its leather wallet and hands it back to the waiter, who thanks him.

"I need to get my things in the room."

"Already got 'em. You travel light."

P-R squints into the horse face. "This behavior may come back on y'all... Pal."

"Does, it does. Whadda'ya gonna do?"

Constantine shakes P-R's hand in the back of a big Lincoln. The sedan is the color of the thin man's hair, but not as expertly waxed. Constantine himself is a pasty looking man who sweats through expensive suits as if they are toilet tissue. His bodily functions are as un-nuanced as his administrative style. Not an imposing figure, rarely leaving Columbus Hall, he is well respected, and even feared, because of his propensity to employ an entourage of rough characters as bargaining chips.

"I don't appreciate the strong arm tactics, Bud. Like I told the goon, this kind of shit can come back on y'all."

"Take a breath, will ya. This here ain't 'bout us. Y'heard yet?"

"Is this about the railroad?"

"Sharp as a tack."

"Did Ferrous sick you on me?"

"Ferrous? We talkin' 'bout the same thing? Y'heard the sy-*reens, ain't ya?*"

"What's going on?"

"I don' know what all yet, but we got us one hell of a deal up at the Sling. Head on. Couple a choo choos'th their noses in each other's business. Hear it's an ugly one."

"Jesus! Are there fatalities?"

"How should I know? I'm sittin' hear talkin' t'you! What I'm thinkin' is, reason we butt in on your mornin' *re*-past, since ya already here by some amazing coin-*ci*-dence I don't wanna stick my schnoze into, we take *ad*-vantage a the sichiation. Have Marvin here take us on up the service road t'see what's what. Kind a show a united front. How neighbors comes t'gether when the public need arises, an' all that malarkey. Waste a few flashbulbs. Whaddya say, P-R? You wanna go back in and sink you teeth int' a little more pussy or ya wanna give our reps a good crank? Guaran-fuckin'-*tee* ya, there's more beavers in the pond."

"Give it a rest, Bud. I don't exactly smell reform on your breath either. Sure. Of course. Tragedy like this. How did you know I was here?"

"Marvin, the horny bastard, was doin' a ewe jus' yesterday up'n'a Camelhumps, an' afterwards, over smokes, the sheep tells 'im P-R an' his driver jus' nearly turn'er int' chops. This here's my town, P-R. Y'all crap here, I'll know ya flushed, an' I'll tax the water y'soiled. Behoove ya t'put some miles 'tween you an' your chums y'wanna go borrowin' other people's sugar. Or d'y'all tote your own sweets?"

The service road begins where the street fades to gravel, skirts a ragged path roughly midway between the river up stream from the dam, and the tracks. An officer has been stationed at the RR PROPERTY KEEP OUT sign, swings open the gate for the Lincoln.

It is not long before they can hear more sirens and see the smoke bend in ugly tufts, before they are caught in a jam of ambulances and fire trucks, wreckers and cop cars, and behind them, the honking press. "Hyenas," P-R comments to no one in particular.

"Bottle flies t'shit," says Constantine.

"Even that bitch Quidnunc," says Marvin, "see'er there? A little a the 'ooman interes' t'swalla wid your mornin' tea."

Indeed, the gossip columnist — in near drag, sports coat and tie, men's hat with press tag — is scribbling away with the swarm.

"Shut up, Marvin. The shit y'know 'bout no tea?"

They slow to a halt, sit in a warm cloud of exhaust alive with frantic wings, then creep along the rough lane with rocks crunching beneath them. The sky is black now with lightning flickers of reds and yellows, the ground cluttered with hot little meteorites seared and steaming.

"Marvin, you pinhead, it's the gas makes the car move."

"'M'I suppose t'do? Ain't exactly Broadway."

"That's why the turnouts, wiseacre. G'wan 'n pass these here shit-heads"

He does, but the going is still slow, the road narrow with only an occasional widening of the shoulder. Soon there are telling odors of burnt things: metal, wood, tissue, a hissing of anxious vapor escaping, and dark carrion birds circling over the river and casting shadow wraiths on David's Sling. Whole things begin to diminish to parts of things: trees to limbs, limbs to bark, unrecognizable shards of metal, dark fluids bubbling like pitch, perhaps a man or woman or child turned to liquid. Ashes float on the warm, noxious air like little black kites. Through his window, P-R sees half a bronze builder's plate hacked into a tree like an ax head,

-aldwin Locom- Works

-adelphia

"God in heaven," he says.

The field of debris expands. Ant men in uniforms, bandanas tied to their faces, hustle in all directions, prying up heavy things, carrying limp bodies. There is a sense of mortification on all of the faces. A fireman has black tears running down his cheeks. An officer is puking into a thistle bush. Incinerated blocks of wood flame suddenly, then die out, become dust demarcated by the sizzle of minium design.

A woman's voice says, "Sweet Jesus, sweet Jesus, sweet Jesus," over and over, a question? A prayer? An invitation? "Sweet Jesus, Son of God, sweet Jesus," she implores into the chorus of, "Help me, help me," like a round,

"Sweet Jesus

Help me

Son of God

> Help me
>> Down by the riverside"

Constantine says, "Looks like Flanders Fields. Y'there, P-R?" P-R was not; when America acquiesced into the war the president promised to keep it out of, P-R's father told him to ignore it, *you're too old,* and that crawling in trenches was all right for farmers' boys and such, but that he was intended for greater things, some of which he had already attained. Indeed, P-R himself had by then grown to disdain most sweat and blood activities. "The stink," Constantine continues, "Y'can almost smell the mustard gas." There are parts of people that voted for him in the trees, the Pompeii fossil of an engineer dangling out of the engine that has jack knifed through the baggage car to litter trunks, suitcases, gifts for loved ones; crude flag decorations string the pines: dresses, shirts, feathered hats, corsets, long johns marinated in red sauce, strung midway up the trunks at half mast. "Fuck me! I know some a these people," says Constantine. He sees substances, shapes, pieces of flesh or fat or incised organs hanging like sleeping bats from the roof of the parlor car.

A man is hunched on the roadbed, rocking, rocking; the few rags on his body still fuming lead-gray ribbons; moaning like something cave-like, unnatural, something wronged beyond comprehension.

Marvin says, "Want I should show a face? Get out an' lend a hand er somethin'?"

"Not that face! Anyways, y'wouldn't know what all t'do! No, y'go on over there an' pet the buzzards. Tell 'em UF an' 'Mingo are in this here together, even if it ain't technically jurisdictional for neither a us. Tell 'em, time like this, we're all brothers 'n arms'r some shit like that. Spare not any expense, 'cet'ra 'cet'ra. These folks here'll have their justice if we have t' turn the whole county upside down. Make sure they know we're here. Make sure they know we're moved t' e-motion an' moved t' action. Anybody from one a them socialist union rags, y'point them out t' the others, say somethin' vague but clear, like, *we gotchur number, we do.*"

There are quick blasts of photographic light — life spans shorter than bees — bespeaking expiration. Thoughts go, memories, passions trickling into the thorn berries, genealogies cracked asunder, histories erased like mastodons, futures pinched like candle flames, called home, called home, left only in photons on silver.

> "Down by the riverside
>> Sweet help me Jesus Row Row Row your boat
> A continuo of escaping vapor
>> Ssssssssssssssssssssss
> Metal heats, metal cools
>> Thawk tic thawk tic thawk tic
>> Gonna lay my body down"

"I ain't never seen the likes a this," someone admits. There is a girl impaled by a brass whistle and neither can find breath. "Easy now. Easy. Don't drop'er now."

The trucks keep coming. Work trains from both directions. The small crew from the shanty. A hermit awakened in the woods. Reporters with pads. Oil smoke folds into bales; the water, the air, an ebony night, raining little pins of steel down upon the tourists amassed on the opposite side of the river and stinging their skin.

"Hal-lo-o-o. What happened? Y'all wan' dis a heah skiff?"

"Row, row, row,
   Sweet Jesus
    Sssssssssssssssss
     Son of God
      Thwack tic thwack tic
      Down by the riverside
       Gently down the stream…"

X

DURING THE FIRST HOURS FOLLOWING THE disaster at the Sling, the body count rose at a breathless pace. In the days following, it began to slow, then even off, then to stagger both up and down. Divine Providence, consistent with Its history of "mysterious ways," decided not to lessen the burdens of rescuers any time soon, and a total list of passengers proved elusive. In some cases, survivors were so badly injured that it took weeks to reconstruct a seating roster. In others, passengers and crew either never regained such memories or they locked them away in the deep recesses of their subconscious minds. A few who seemed near death attained an amazing level of recovery: some who walked out of the wreckage died later of undetected internal injuries. Not a few of the dead were burned so badly as to defy identification, others required re-assembly by the coroner. One man wandered off in a daze, walked home, and managed to remain un-tallied for over a year. Officially, the total of those who perished instantly, and of those who expired at a later date from injuries incurred on that fateful morning, numbered one hundred seventy-three. However, this is a number of compromise; high enough to engender a series of crushing law suits that would make fortunes for a number of attorneys and finally force the teetering Tishomingo over the edge and into receivership. Undeniably, when the great engines met head on at David's Sling on that unusually sultry morning, the man who should have been at the throttle, after extracting a twenty from his overall pocket and dropping it into the hand of an overwhelmed legless war vet outside of a soup kitchen, was buying a ticket for the ride home on

the Camelshump Crescent Electric Interurban Railway.
(Wincook Darvin)

(Presented below is an excerpt from an article entitled, "Trolleys Round the 'Hump'", by L. Leonard Cruiskshank, Vintage Traction Journal, Vol. VI, Issue 24.)

As with most inter-city traction operations, the Crescent had by now been bleeding traffic at an unsustainable rate. Once a powerful conglomerate of older companies that fed three counties, management had been degrading service just to stay afloat, shedding the more unprofitable lines, reducing others to one man Birney Safety cars, ripping up rails and employing trolley busses, and finally, during the last decade, aggressively abandoning its signature rail operations to a fleet of motor coaches. And still, revenue receded as more people took to the roads, and agents from a very hungry National City Lines were snooping about the car barns with open note pads and barely concealed salivation. The electric line forming the inside curve of the crescent, noticeable on contemporary maps for skirting the eastern arc of the hills, as opposed to the Tishomingo on the west, serving Uncas Falls at one end and, by way of Tishomingo, the resort community of Devil's Glade, bisected the bus lines, fed them, gave them succor as it were, and was fodder for the handwriting on every embankment wall. Having hemorrhaged capital and property, little was left of a once admired system.

XI

THE TICKET AGENT PEERS OUT THROUGH his bars, through his thick lenses, tells Moses about the delay at Dogtown Ferry and about the progress of the line crew, and that he's invited to wait on the platform or in the car.

Moses decides on the car, settles in three benches behind the motorman, who wishes him *good morning*. He slides up his window to let in the suspect warmth, and closes his eyes. When he opens them at the Ferry, the first leg of the ride is over, the previous car has been reversed on the passing track, and the repair work is said to be completed. The conductor begins leading a small group of passengers out of the trackside store and as Moses looks to the steps to watch them board, his eyes lock on those of his wife. She is frozen still, silhouetted, framed, too late to retreat. The conductor says, "Make some room there, ma'am. We fixin' t' load up an' get goin'."

She forces herself to inch forward, the knitting bag clutched to her chest. Moses is patting the seat next to him and there is nothing for it but to sit down.

For a moment, neither speaks, she staring forward in a mental fog, he fixated on the blush at the side of her face. Then Moses says quietly, "Why, ain't this the damndest thing!" His left hand is drumming rapidly on the windowsill — *tatatatatatatata* — and he seems to have developed a slight tic of the jaw. "Been some spell since we been able t' spend time t'gether, husband an' wife, take in the countryside."

"I thought you were on a run," she whispers. It gets lost in the buzz of generators. There is no moisture in her throat.

"'S'that? I can't hear you."

"I thought you were working."

"Betcha did!"

They are both looking forward now at the motorman's short neck hairs, Moses, tapping, she rocking slightly forward and back. The car starts up, its meager population scattered widely throughout the coach. At the first milepost, he says, "Thought *you* was home."

There are tears in her eyes. She is anguished, afraid, humiliated. *I can explain*, she thinks to say, but goes no further. She can't really.

"Funny thing is, I never took much t' conversation on a train. Now, that Sardo, he can talk up such a lot a nothin' that it's all a man can do t' keep from pitchin' 'im off the viaduct. Me, I like t' take in the scenery, listen t' the rumble a wheels on rail."

"What do you want me to say, Moses?"

"Nothin'. That's the point, ain't it?"

She notices that he does not say her name, that he, *too*, does not speak her name. Are they talking to themselves, these men who have held her, been inside her? Is she not here? Is she a fiction? And, if so, whose? She turns to his profile, to make sure he is there, as if, somehow, seeing him validates herself. She wants to touch him as evidence, dares not for fear of how it will be received.

"We can have us a little chat at home," he says. "Mean time, think on this here. Y'all thought I'd be on a run. Tell the truth, I thought I'd be home in bed."

The car rocks noisily on its way; woods to one side, an occasional cabin, livestock, furrowed yellow-green fields; granite hills to the other, the line car and crew relaxed on a siding, animated, discussing something of great import. At Schlager, a man gets off, leading a child. Two women get on, pass the Browns in great excitement: "*I heard they're all dead, that it's the worst*" — fading down the aisle — "*in the history of...*"

Side by side and silent, they stroll downhill from the Railroad Avenue Terminal to the car stop, then from the final stop to company housing. She clutches her bag still, but when they are in front of the house, he suddenly grabs it away, looks inside, and hands it back. Two doors down, Moses sees Mr. Red running out to the street, still hooking up his suspenders like a fireman on call, his coat and hat under his arm, and getting into his Ford.

"You go up in the house now and make some supper," he tells her.

"Y'all want supper!"

"Man's needs 'is strength," he says rushing to catch up with Red before he can drive away.

Red sees his approach, his arms waving, lowers his window, and says, "Horrible thing, ain't it? Kind a God let's this happen? Christ, Brown. My God! What kind a management! Should a never happened, this thing. Should a never!" His eyes are scarlet and he is trembling.

"Gotta ask y'somethin'," Moses says.

"Not now. I gotta get down there, for chrissakes!"

"That junkman. Where's he stay at?"

"Whattya'll think? We're social? We visit one another? Step away from the vehicle, would ya."

Moses clutches the door. "He live in town here? Down'th the colored?"

"Some people ain't gotta ounce a sense. Didn't figure y'all for one a'em. The old coon comes from up over in Thebes. I guess, 'f'y'all go on over there an' ask where's the junkyard…Now move on outta my way. *I'm* needed, see, 'f'you ain't."

Moses finds her in the warm summer kitchen, still bundled for winter and clutching the bag. Her lips are covered with a gloved hand that betrays a visible tremor.

"I don't smell no cookin'," he says.

"I don't know what words you want me to say. I don't know what I'm supposed to do."

"I ain't a educated man. I can't give ya words. You're the book reader." He speaks calmly, in a monotone, his eyes blankly darting about the room. He begins to remove soiled garments, to drop them onto the floor and head for the spigot in the mudroom where he stands naked in the open doorway. He is muscular, a great compact package of strength, with thick arm muscles linked like a string of sausages, the sinew forming the banks of rivulets. "Things I wonder, though. How'f y'all could think I was s'posed t'work, see, what with a knittin' bag full a what t'wear, how it is my wife come t' be on a car out a UF so early in the a.m.? That there's my concern. I may come 'pon more, directly. You got all the words I'll need."

"How should I tell you things you know?"

"Not much contrary t'tellin' me what I don't. Y'all can put it together."

"I never meant…."

"No, no, not now. Not today. Like cider, some things are best mulled." He shuts the door; she hears only the shower.

XII

L IKE BROTHERS IN ARMS, MAYORS CONSTANTINE and Phipps-Rough are bundled together in the crush of dignitaries and arrayed before a bank of winking Speed Graphics. They are solemn, reverent, confederates of relief. Each enjoys the company of underlings: Constantine, his police Chief, his fire Chief, members of his council, two of which, including Marvin, hail from the

D'Scalucci family, various heads of departments this and departments that. P-R submits to an unfamiliar tremor. Prezhki holds him in place and studies his own feet shuffling and tapping so that when the images later appear in the chemical trays, we will see the top of his hat, the obstructing brim, and only the shield to identify him. Ferrous is there, the height of a child, looking ashen, bent like an ancient forest creature and exposed in afternoon shadows; as are assistant superintendents aligned in descending importance on a large flat rock. Most of them, secretly, desire to be here, need to be. It is a moment in history, an event about which, one wants to be able to say, *I was there, one of the first on the scene, witness to the carnage, why, I helped to pull a poor child from the grasp of a dying mother, bless her eternal soul,* to be able to tell it at family gatherings, picnics, reunions, to future chroniclers of history, *imprinted indelibly on my mind, can't get the smell out of my nostrils,* to ask constituents, *who was there when the chips were down, my friends? Whose hands pressed the wound to assuage the dark flow? Who bears this scar on his arm from the hot press of steel? I keep still the bloodied shirt, to remember.*

Constantine tells the scribblers that, "All a us is inspired by these unfortunate innocents, by these willin' heroes, one after another dousin' flame', luggin' stretchers, comfortin' the torn an' the pained. I wanna thank the generous sacrifice a our own, an' them that's rushed down from 'Mingo like there was no distance 'tween us at'll. The Sheriff, God Bless, Arvin, I never seen a fella jump t' action so swiftly, and Warden Prim, who can't be here hisself, but who hustled over these here trustees y'see 'round ya'll who are heart an' soul with us all today." Except, he fails to mention, for the three who duck into the river and are caught, a week later in another county, borrowing a chicken from a rural coop, or the one who skirts the banks and is found the next day with black leg swollen purple from the fangs of a water moccasin.

P-R talks of grief, of the difficulties "in comforting the families of those who are gone, the logistics of identification and notification" and "locating the Jewish passenger who must be buried with observant haste." He ponders "matching infants with mothers, the mobilization of hospitals, *and let's not forget the timely intervention of Col. Farragut at the base who has sent over these wonderful young patriots to help with the heavy lifting.*" He says it in a daze, not thinking; it comes through him from whatever administrative center of operational thought.

Ferrous speaks up, his voice like broken glass, wipes a great glistening tear from his eye, assures that "'spons'bility will be 'stablished and all 'prop'iate action taken, *whethuh it be t'wa'd 'narchists, soc'alists, commonists or un'on agitators,*" and that, "trains will be runnin' 'gain'n no time," and passes the baton to the assistant superintendents to stammer out how.

The churchmen come; the priests for last rites; the ministers, including Shem; a rabbi for unity and the one Jewish victim. They offer prayers and a word of reflection to shield God from blame; men of the cloth that "is the celestial gridiron, God's defensive linemen." They preach of *"a coming together"* and *"a commonality of need and solace and a delving into the mystery of it, the horror of it, the acceptance of it,"* creating a grim camp meeting of shared anguish that *"stirs the very roots of what it means to be a society."* They ask the forgiveness of sins, the bestowing of redemption, the kindling of hope. They kneel, they pray, they entreat, they sway on bent knees, they genuflect, they make ancient tracings on their chests. The Negro pastors, including Salvation, gather to a side to comfort the surviving porters, the dining car crew, the passengers from the COLORED ONLY car. And they sing, oh how they sing: *"We shall meet again by an' by,"* and invite *"that great gettin' up mornin',"* and, *"Yea, dough dey walks 'n d'valley a d'shadow a death,"* souls are restored like heirlooms from an attic.

The flashbulbs ignite, blister, get spit out onto the field of slaughter. The reporters race across their yellow sheets of paper and more than a few pencils go pointless and discarded.

And steam hisses on, and the dying groan on, *fare thee well, fare thee well.*

XIII

FERROUS MOTIONS P-R AND PREZHKI TO his modest conveyance: a long, blue '25 Buick Six, powder-dusted like confection from the crude road and airborne debris. He gets into the back, followed by the Mayor. The Chief sits in front. Ferrous seems smaller than ever on the spacious bench, like he's waiting to grow into the vehicle, or maybe it's just the events of the day that have diminished them all. Shades are drawn from the soft top.

P-R pulls off his hat; wipes his forehead with the back of his hand, the hat still in it. "God All Mighty. Hell of a thing!" he says. It is the closest he ever gets to a whine.

"Keep them shades down," Ferrous barks. Prezhki protests that it is "kind of close in here," and Ferrous says, attempting closure, "Y'all wanna read 'bout this heah conve'sation ove' mo'nin' coffee, leave 'em up."

"Why should I care who hears?" Prezhki says, then, reluctantly, with a nudge from P-R, obeys, and is instantly sorry in the fetid air of the old man's car. Ferrous is of that age where he briefly leaves a memory of his presence wherever he has been. It is an essence in no way abbreviated by money or power or the arrogant thrust of his chin, a reminder that Samuel Butler knew what he was talking about.

The Superintendent removes his own hat, points it at P-R's chest. "Ah wanna know who'all's been fiddlin'th mah trains." He sounds like an irritable child on Christmas morning, one who gets a new necktie instead of the lead soldiers he had asked for.

P-R says, "We are all on edge here, Ferrous. Now's not the time..." His voice is raspy, a cataract of soot hindering its passage.

"The time? The time y'say! Up y'all's'th the god'amn' time, P-Ah! Ah'm the railroad. Ah *am* the time. 'F'there wasn't no railroads it could be five a.m. in Brooklyn and seven-thi'ty'n Queens. Who'd ca'e? The trains has turned g'og'aphy to time, distance to time. *Ah* will tell *you* when it is *time*. And then Ah'll tell ya *what time* it is, and what this time is *fo'*, and wheah y'all 'll get off and at *what time*. And, at this *pa'tic'lar* time, Ah wanna know who'alls screwin'th mah trains."

"I've never before encountered so many people in one day who thought they'all were the voice of Providence. We are all overwrought," says P-R, "and I've had just about enough of y'all's condescension."

"Ah'm jus' now firin' up. And you, Chief? What say you? Ah got a me dick in the 'Mingo Yards who 'nsists y'all're an 'cquaintance a his."

"I don't need to sit here for this," Prezhki chokes, his hand on the door handle.

"The hell ya don't! Ah could go on out an' spew awl ove' the vultu'es outside, o'you can fix yore ass wheah it is and heah me out. Ah am tol' that y'all've spent some time'th a certain dispatchuh down theah, that whenevuh ya do so theah is a gene'ous 'xchange a cash, foll'in' which, a ce'tain 'ng'neah gets sched'led t' haul va'nish as fa' 'way from Tish'mingo as possible. Two days 'go, ya made such a visit. A note was written. It got relayed down to a dispatchuh 'n UF. A pe'fectly hea'hy 'nginneah, chalked fo' t'day's 'Xpress, is listed sick. The othuh 'ng'neah, a Moses Brown, gets off a twelve-hou' shif' and is set up t'run the 'Xpress. These ower not the da'k ages a railroadin', my frien'. We treat ower 'mployees'th a ce'tain level a human'ty. Ower stan'a'ds, with a li'le boost from that pinko uni'n a theys. The 'foremention' gen'rous 'xchange a greenbacks gets pa'tition' 'tween the two dispatchuhs, who've al'eady spent some time'n the company confess'nal, and the sick 'nginneah who's right now singin' 'The 'Nternation'l' and hidin' 'hine the fat reah end a some Yid rep from Chicaga."

P-R asks, "What does this have do to with anything?"

"Y'all tell me, Mayuh. No one fiddles with mah trains, Ah tell ya."

"Damned nonsense!" Prezhki says.

"Walter," P-R says, "I think Mr. Ferrous..."

"*I'm* getting a little put out with you too, P-R! Had it up to here with this business," Prezhki says.

"The co'lition begins to crack, eh, gen'lemen?" says Ferrous toning down. "We all get so pulled this away an' that. Sometimes ha'd t'member which side we' on. So beah'th me, and let's see wheah this heah goes. My people heah out the ya'd dick, see, and he goes on'th a sto'y 'bout y'all, Chief, that Ah find somewhat 'ncred'lous in light a yore rep'tation as a highly reg'rded and eth'cal public se'vant an'a fam'ly man a the fi'st o'duh. The pa'ts ah not connectin' fo' me. Then Ah get a bit a news from that scoun'el Constantine through one a his penna ante hool'gans that, ho ho, P-Ah's still in town..."

"Now wait just a minute."

"Mah minute, 'membuh? P-Ah's in town, funna thing, an' has rese'ved not one but *two* rooms, 'djoinin', in some ol' fleabag 'cross the rivuh. Now, knowin' yore rathuh cel'brated rep'tation the way Ah do, P-Ah, even an ol'relic like me can put two an' two t'gethuh, so Ah ask Mayuh Cons'antine if he wou'n' min' havin' one a'is hounds sniff out the occ'pant a the othuh room, an' a desk clerk is on'y too eaguh t'blige. Not that it's none a mah bid'ness, a cou'se, but ya nevuh know what'all'll pop up that might prove handy 'n the future. She a ciphuh, a Della Cant'ell, 'cordin' to the res'vation made at the same time as a Mr. Tagus, which tu'ns out to be a so't a *nom d'baiser* fo' you, P-Ah, and, also, as it tu'ns out, has

257

stayed theah sev'al times 'fo' un'uh diff'ent mon'kuhs. Both a'am have, she's *a coluh*, he thinks, *Blue or p'rhaps...Brown?* Now, mah ya'd bull fig'res the Chief heah has a taste fo' a ce'tain 'ngineah's private stock, but me, the skeptic, I get t' thinkin'. And y'all know what? Eureka! *Brown:* coinc'den'ly the name a the 'ngineah that... well, long story sho't...Is this heah cleah t'y'all yet?"

"Brown is as common as white in a snow storm. Has nothing to do with me," says P-R, "or either one of y'all, as far as I know."

"As far as you know?" says Prezhki. "I warned you about skating on thin ice."

"Gen'lemen, gentlemen. Win'uh dive'sions ah not really the co' issuh heah. No' is the despoilin' a Mrs. Brown. The real issuh is, that if the two a ya have, on the contr'y, been screwin'th mah trains to the tune a what we see heah out the winda, so that you, Mr. Mayuh, could indulge yore lack a grace in the agein' process, I can tell you that this railroad cert'nly ain't gonna pay fo' it. Whet yore whistle on y'own dime. They will be a' 'countin', gen'lemen. We all learn t'pay's we go."

"He was at fault, this Brown?"

"He weren't even on the train! The man was ravin'. Ah sent him on home."

"Then what's this about?"

"Had the 'signed 'ngineah been theah, eight hou's a log-sawin' reada fo' the hea'th, he'd a been on that train as back-up and a whole helluva lotta people right now'd be enjoyin' suppuh on white linen as the pines zip on by."

"Why back-up?"

"Anothuh sto'y enti'ly."

"You and Constantine, you've got this wrong. I was here to see a man about a horse and that's all I'm going to admit to."

"A i'on one at that."

"So what happens now?" P-R asks.

"What happens now is the two a y'all get outta my autamobile." He taps on the door for his driver who has been waiting nearby nursing a cigarette. "And ya do so'th th the knowledge that, no mattuh how well shod y'all may be, P-Ah, the 'to'ney y'all hi'e'll be the company 'to'ney's mentee. I won't say *good day*, as all hope a that has 'vap'rated. And not just fo' us, God knows."

Prezhki gets out, turns and leans back in the door. "Just so you both understand. I won't be the fall guy here. Just so you know."

P-R catches up to him, suggests that it might be a good idea to compare notes. The Chief dismisses him, says, "A smart man puts nothing on paper." P-R says not put too much stock in Ferrous' ranting, refers to the super as a "piss ant, a maggot under toe." Prezhki spits into the already despoiled earth, palms up to P-R like caution signs at the roadside, trudges into the greater turmoil.

The Mayor is left with Shem approaching, looking stricken. They make remarks of condolence before passing by. Shem suddenly grabs the Mayor's arm, holds him steady, a clutch really. "I may have lost a parishioner," he says. "We'll see, maybe more than one. We'll see. We all bear responsibility in this." He is flour white, trembling, looks like he's seen the Devil with his hand in the tithe basket. "We'all do this to ourselves."

"Stow it," P-R says. "Can't you see...? Can't you?"

"Conceived in sin, by sin. Our guilt runs like blood into the soil. Consumed by sin."

"Save it for Sunday, would you?"

P-R sees McCallum through debris-sodden air, wrenches himself away from Shem. McCallum has found a coach bench to sit on. It has flown into low underbrush and is perched like a box seat to disaster. The officer has blood on his hands, his starched shirt, and his chest heaves in asthmatic rhythms. P-R sits with him, asks, "Y'all able to drive?"

"A minute...a minute."

Prezhki in motion spits out the taste of the old man into the stew of human fluids that have commingled into the Sling's geology. He moves toward the action to give a hand, pushes his way through the reporters, particularly avoiding Quidnunc who is jabbing at him with a finger and shouting angry questions he does not take time to understand, and comes face to face with Mr. Red. The bull blocks the Chief's passage, whispers into the his pallid face, "Next time y'all'd be smart t'listen t' a fella officer."

"There is no indication of sabotage, and if I hear you've been running your damn fool mouth, there'll be hell to pay."

"Seems like there is already. Y'all need any he'p out a this here mess?"

"You see this as a time to gloat?" He waves his arms about him, an acknowledgement of the carnage. "Do you see this at all?" The Chief's fists are bulging, the knuckles white. His eyes narrow to hyphens as he checks his emotion. He is feeling a powerful urge to act out, to break rules, smash protocol, to hurt someone. And here is Mr. Red, ideal candidate if there ever was one. Prezhki wants to lure him behind a singed box car perpendicular to the tracks that brought it there — a place beyond the notice of rescuers — lure him with a promise of something he needs to see, a mock alliance of the minute, a curiosity the bull can't resist; lead him in professional collusion over rails tortured off of crossties, to the far side of the car, to say, *see here, this is telling,* invisible bait to the world's most credulous fish. He wants to have Red place his big head up into the car to see what he can see while the back of the same thick vessel keeps a recently scheduled appointment with the stock of the officer's pistol; crack, serrated knife edges of lightning run the circuit of Red's transmitters, flag stripe-white to mineshaft black, with Prezhki gently settling the big hulk down on the road bed and cuffing the yard bull's hand to the tension bars of the car's under frame. Instead, he says, "You're interfering with an officer. Get yourself out of my way."

"Seems y'all in mine, by jurisdiction."

Prezhki gives Red a restrained shove and moves on to the wreckage.

The drive back over the hills passes with little conversation. P-R closes his eyes, tries to sleep, but is troubled by escaping steam and mortality, betrayal, and the sudden juxtaposition of the conditions of life. He has never even imagined a day approaching this one, let alone experienced one, and he feels seared to the bare bone by the horror and confusion of it all. How could this happen to him, how to bear up to Ferrous, to Constantine, to Prezhki, to the woman who is somehow central to it all.

The trip seems silent, its event quotient depleted, though that cannot be. No rocks slide in their path. The sheep seem to recognize the car and cling in neighborly fashion to the shoulders of the highway. Even the very weather is chastened, retreating to shadows at the periphery of all the day's travail.

P-R has them stopped at the battle marker, strolls blood-fertile soil, touches fingers to the plaque and feels the grit of the raised letters, *in memory of, to the brave souls, victims of treachery and cowardice, hallowed be,* etc., etc. It could be anywhere in the cleavage of the great disunion — Gettysburg, Wilson's Creek, Atlanta — so conventional are the tributes. But, of course, it's not; it is here between The Camelhumps, midway between Uncas Falls and Tishomingo, on two lane macadam of the type that will one day be four, will grow a center divider, turn lanes, a parking lot and a small visitor center for a ranger to dispense a pamphlet for the self-guided walking tour, a ten minute video on the battle, a diorama of the action under glass, minié balls unearthed at the site.

He invites himself up to the front seat. "How's the wife getting on? The baby?"

"Well, you know, everybody's kind a in shock. Not the baby, a course, though I do think the little ones sense the stress in the rest a us."

"I think they do. How'd you find me?"

"I came up to the hotel like you said. When you didn't show, I went inside and asked for Mr. Tagus. They told you went with one of Constantine's apes. The rest was easy, with all the commotion and such."

"It occur to you what I was doing up there? At the Beauregard?"

"Don't figure it's none a my business."

"No, it's not. And Mr. Tagus? Have you anything for Mr. Tagus?"

"Well, kind of. A little over my head so I'll tell you what I wrote down." He pulls a brown stained notepad from his pocket.

"I'm told the smart man never puts anything on paper."

"Yeah, well, I'll leave that to the smart man t' worry about. Me, sir, I don't write it down, you don't get to hear it. Anyhow, they was very cooperative over there at the county. Clerk kind a guided me through the files." He relays data on several exchanges that P-R hastily rejects. Then he says, "Five months past, the brewery was bought out by a firm called...Mar-you-rit-ee-us, And-a-man and Seashells, or something like it, Holdin' Company...Damned queer name!"

"Not if y'all're an island in the Indian Ocean."

"Sir?"

"Nothing. Go on. You may have something."

"You know these fellas?"

"I've got a pretty solid hunch on one of them. Perhaps, two."

"I hope I didn't overstep none on this here thing, but I took the liberty to enquire into just what...this company, I'm not going to try and say it again... does. Seems that the brewery is their sole asset. This company was only recorded three months prior t' the purchase. The papers' was filed by post, but everything was in order, the clerk said. Down at the bottom a the last sheet, M.A.S. Holdin' Co. is signed off by a Cookie Praejean, Gen'l. Manager, but a who they got no other record on. But the clerk said he checked with Lone Feather and they said it was on the level."

P-R's mouth drops. He pumps upward in the seat; feels an emergence of sorts, as if someone had chipped away the concretion bottling up his thoughts, as if Shem had floated by and elevated him to the rafters. "I think I've been played for the fool! Three partners, my ass! More like three walnut shells. Two are empty. So, who's the bean under the third?"

XIV

S HE HAS LONG SINCE RETIRED WHEN he enters the room. She feigns sleep, hears him remove his clothing, ball them up for the chute. He has brought an alien aroma, of dirt and grease and coal, a sour pinch of whiskey, as if he is a machinist or a miner returned from his labors, delayed at the tavern for some convivial relief. She hears him run a shower, hears him dripping on the tile floor. He hits the bed still damp, moisture on the monogrammed pajamas, lies still on his back. "You've been drinking," she observes. "Who hasn't?" he answers. She asks if he was there and was it as bad as they are saying.

"I don't know. How bad are they saying?"

She remains with her back to him, the crosstie pattern of spine clinging to her narrow form, her elegant ballerina's neck straight and smooth like fine stemware, smelling of newly bloomed petals. She has always seemed luxuriously fragile to him, as if she could be broken in one abandoned embrace, a cold ceramic surface in danger of scratches and nicks. He thinks of her as socially graceful but sexually alien, a keepsake best left displayed on a mantle or a coffee table.

"Are there many dead?" It is whispered; a tenuous question. "Do you have names?"

"No, not yet. Some, yes. I don't want to say. They are being withheld until all of the family members are notified."

"Are you okay?"

"Compared to what? I wasn't on the train."

"Where you were is your business. It's been years since that was of any consequence to me."

"Then why ask if I'm okay?"

"I don't know. Occasionally one simply yearns for a little conversation."

"A *little* conversation is what one gets. I'll tell y'all this though, in a pile of garbage a good digger can unearth a gem."

"What good can come of such carnage?"

"Not of the carnage itself. But there was a certain element of the day I may find useful." He props himself up on an elbow and turns to her. "Let me ask you something," he says. "A name came up. Not from the train. But it's a name that rings a bell. And somehow, I think it's the name of a colored woman. Could you ask the girl if she knows a Cookie Praejean?"

She holds his gaze in hers. There is a nearly imperceptible twitch at the corner of her mouth: a warning he is familiar with. The fine ridge that defines her upper lip hardens. He has always admired this knife-carved feature of hers — once in intimacy, of late from afar — a feature designed with the dual purpose of seduction and challenge; now it says, touch me here, and I will slice you bloody. "I can tell you right now, she does. But it's not a bell rung in this house. Cookie is a cousin of our Clara's. She is employed by the Humboldt's. I've met her. They used to ride the cars together and Cookie sometimes picked her up in our kitchen after work. I think Praetoria has her living in these days. No doubt you've met her too, but not here."

"That was insensitive of me, wasn't it?" he says. He thinks, *that's two, but it is the third shell that holds revelation.*

"I would expect nothing less." She sounds more weary than peeved, relaxes her china face. "Neither one of us will lose any sleep over it."

"Actually, all things considered, it might ease my sleep somewhat."

"I don't want to know. You have this uncanny ability to turn a profit from a dunghill, so good for you. I *really* don't want to know. Anyway, that insipid gossip writer for the paper rung you up three or four times this evening. She's like a rabid dog. I'm afraid a quick bullet to her temple is the only solution."

"I'll keep that in mind. What did she want?"

"I didn't ask, not being as inquiring as her. You'd think, with all that's happened, that it would involve the wreck. But she had other fish to fry, and insisted on using my pan. It seems, once again, you've managed to become something of a curiosity. The same old boyish pranks, I hear. People seem to have lost the ability to whisper in all the cacophony of modern times. I really have no interest in knowing, but you might take some caution in the fact that there is a persistent buzz about town."

"This bothers you all of a sudden?"

"No, not at all. I'm a realist, P-R. I like the life. I'm not willing to give it up because of some banal carnality from the likes of you. I like the club. The servants. So enjoy all the dalliances you want. But if you endanger my peace or my luxury, I will cause a stink that will have angels swooning and falling from the sky."

There is a silver letter opener on her nightstand. She's been opening envelopes. Her birthday: he has forgotten. "Don't worry," he says. "No one's washing away y'all's little sandcastle."

"I'm happy to hear it. And one more thing."

"Always is, Sarai?"

"Tell your trollops not to call here either."

"I'm not sure I know what you're referring to."

"Perhaps you mean, you don't know *which* trollop?" Her hands go up, a sort of wave. "Don't say anything. It doesn't matter to me so long as I don't have hear their voices on my phone. Anyway, there's something else. Not because of the calls. I've been thinking about this for a while. I've decided to convert the boys' old room for my own use. There is really not much sense in us sharing a bed, do you think?"

He rolls over on his back, thinks for a moment. "I really don't dislike you, Sarai."

"You have a great capacity for being magnanimous. Actually, I really don't dislike you either. I'm not a dullard, you see, I knew what I was getting into even as a girl. You're not the master of surprise you think you are. Anyway, I've gotten what I wanted."

"Yes, you did."

"Yes, *we* did. You could not have found a more tolerant, to say nothing of presentable, wife. We do understand each other, something, I think, that is more valuable than a bond of affection. Still, we might enjoy a more substantial geographic demarcation."

"No, no. I'll take the other room."

"Please! A little late in the day for gallantry. Actually, I prefer the boys' room, the way the light comes in through the bay window. There's a softness to it. A certain femininity. It would distract you. Femininity always does. I will have some one come in to do the work."

"I can..."

"No, don't trouble yourself."

"But I have access to maintenance crews that..."

She quiets him, a gentle touch of her finger almost to his lips.

The Chief feels gravity, as if his skin has been entered through hundreds of tiny incisions and weighted down with small stones. His hands are red, chafed, the fingertips scraped and inflamed. A burn has penetrated his shirtsleeve, sits raw on his wrist. He has lost track of time, of comprehension.

The phone hasn't stopped ringing in the outer office. Everyone wants news. Everyone has a name to be looked into. He has shut the door but can see the desk sergeant silhouetted in the pebbled glass between them.

He puts in the call home. Her *greeting* is husky on the line.

"Tennie? Did I wake you?"

"Not really. How could anyone sleep?"

"Sleep? I could sleep. Nothing sounds better at the moment. Have you been crying? Your voice."

"I'm fine. Really, I am. Walter, John called from school. He was worried that maybe there was someone we know...Well, frankly, I am too. He wants to come home."

"There's no reason for that right now. Look, Tennie, there's not a lot to tell yet." They are both hedging, well aware of the porosity of the wires. "Call him back, will you? I'm up to my ears here. Tell him I'll call tomorrow and fill him in. Tell him that names are just filtering in. I've got officers out talking to families. Until that's done, well…"

"There's some talk of anarchists. The unions."

"Talk's cheap. A lot of it foolish as well. Looks to me like an accident, plain and simple. People in shock seem to find comfort in the most ignorant recesses of their heads. I don't blame them. I'm just not in a position to partake."

She asks if he's eaten, but he can't remember. She scolds that he will be of no use to anyone if…He knows this, he acknowledges. Says he not really hungry. That he has seen things this day that exceed his experience. She asks him to wake her when he gets home, that she has dinner in the box to reheat.

"Probably won't get home tonight. Who knows?"

"You'll need some rest, Walter. It was already a difficult week, even before today. Have someone bring in a cot for you. Maybe you can catch an hour or two."

"You know, Tennie, my dear…" He wants to talk details — of the maimed and the dead, of his disgust with the Mayor and the railroad people — but he doesn't dare. Instead, he says, "A day like today, coming on top of a week like this one, underscores my deep-seated skepticism as to the existence of a supreme being. Yet, all I can think of to do is to fall down on my knees in prayer, *To whom it may concern,* and so on. I am in a mood of utter futility."

She listens, waits, then says, "There has been some trouble in the neighborhood today. Have they told you?" He admits he's not registering everything right now. She tells him that the fish man was on their street, that boys — ruffians — were teasing him, that they pulled fish from the back of the wagon and pummeled him with his own stock. When he struck back with the whip, they pulled him down to the road and tipped the wagon. The horse may have been injured. Fish and flies settled on the pavement and there were no officers to respond. "Until *I* called.

"I'll ask around. See who's responsible."

"No, don't. No one's to blame. I don't imagine they knew where to go first."

He is quiet for a while, his head hot and spinning. "You know, Tennie, sometimes I think that at the end of the day, when it's all said and done and I am in repose no wiser than when I was in diapers, I will look back on it all, run it through all the knowledge I think I have amassed, and wonder, *Just what the hell was that all about?*"

Officer McCallum enters the three a.m. stillness of his kitchen. There is a chill in the room that he hopes has been heated away where they sleep. He leans against the ice box, opens it, scans the offerings: a saved meal under wax paper, a slice of apple pie adrift in crust debris, a bottle of milk. He retrieves a Lone Feather, rolls the frosty bottle over his forehead, snaps it open in a single motion on a wall mount that says Nehi. He leaves the empty on the counter, repeats the ritual with a second bottle. The house is quiet, the usual ticking of still things moving, a subtle grind of weight, the whisper of a mouse along the baseboards.

He will have to set a trap in the morning. He should do it now but has no wish to see anything else dead today. Even if it is no longer today. Even if just a mouse. Midnight seems artificial, a thing of schedules, devised of man for some sort of continuity; of labeling, a place mark that can never be found again. Without sleep, it is still the same day it was yesterday. Sleepless men have their own chronology, follow their own star-studded charts.

There is a hat rack in the entry hall. He removes his gun belt and hangs it there. It is a thing separate from his family: this gun, this belt. They hang ominous over the umbrella stand, ferocity diminished by neighboring bonnets and tiny mittens. He looks in on Victoria, sheets askew in troubled sleep, beads of perspiration on her milky cheeks, hair loose in fine yellow strands that glisten like silk when the moon shines. There is no moon tonight. This too, this lunar absence, underscores the seamless passing from one to the other of this day and this night.

The baby is muted in grayish innocence. McCallum is careful not to breathe too loudly, shuffles in stockinged feet over domestic geography where he knows the planks are most secure, where the squeaks that awaken are fewest. The child is smaller than he has remembered, almost not a person at all, somehow diminished in a day of such import. It is as if the sand of innocence has emptied from a glass that begs upending. He leans forward, sees the thick cover sway with the minimal heave of abdomen.

He sets the second bottle down on his nightstand, strips down to his long johns, marvels at how weary and yet sleepless he feels, a magnet drawn to both poles. The bed is softer as the baby is smaller. Victoria's warmth fills the room like perfume. Were it up to him, he'd freeze time in the moment.

XV

THEY COME UP ON THE FIVE Car from Thebes to pray in Tishomingo and to mull the imponderables of Uncas Falls and David's Sling; old crones awaiting final judgments; finding some comfort absorbing themselves in the uncertainties of other people's lives; women in black, somber, with parasols tucked under their arms, lacey ebony collars tight around hoary, wrinkled necks squeezed out like paste from a tube; powdered, colorless faces with lips pleated over sullied teeth, magnified myopic eyes; come to hear the Father recite his cloistered Latin, to eat egg salad on white bread, limeade, *a piece of that rhubarb pie —fore that there fly eats it all, if you please, dearie;* picking at crumbs, morsels, remnants, phrases, suggestions, hints, could be's, trying to make some sense, some contiguous sense, perhaps with chronology, of train wrecks, the wiles of needful men, loose women, the whole great undercarriage of society. The waitresses are rapt with elbows on counter as the old birds peck away at this meager, disjointed feed, and offer the following discordant cacophony:

This comes directly from Mrs. Red, who gets it over the pillow directly from the horse's mouth.

J. David Robbins

A woman who shares a pillow with a horse has some way to go on the road to credibility.

Well, after all, to hear her tell it, her husband is the Chief of the Railroad Police and therefore the Chief investigating officer. I should think he'd know.

To hear her *tell it!*

I don't doubt her. I just meant that her command of the English language is no better than most foreigners. Why, you'd think English wasn't the lingua franca *of the world to hear the way some of these people mangle it.*

So the horse woman says?

The horse's *woman says.*

My husband, when he was alive, of course...

Of course. We will save the ghost stories for our next campfire.

...almost went into the horse trade once. But, dear man, he had no head for business what so ever. Got entangled with a slick fellow from down on the Gulf who had him invest in dog meat for horses. Had him investing our savings and collecting strays until his brother was able to convince him that horses don't eat meat.

Silliest thing I ever heard! So, Mrs. Red says what?

Mrs. Red's horse.

Well, the railroad is trying to hush up the fact that there were three *trains involved.*

Three trains in a collision?

That's what she said.

How could...Are you never prone to skepticism?

Well, she should know.

You tell me how three trains collided. One fall out of the sky?

The Lord's trains move in mysterious ways.

I don't know the logistics, but she insists it was three *trains.*

Claptrap, you ask me.

Maybe one was following too closely.

I'd be more interested in the number of bodies than the number of trains.

Give me the names of the bodies and you'll have my attention. I been lookin' all over since it happened to see who's missing. Milkman's five minutes late, I'm thinking, uh huh, poor Mr. Stanley.

Well, it's not official yet, but I hear some high-ranking nabobs were on the Express. Someone, even, in city government.

Which city?

Why, she didn't say.

Seems germane, don't it?

I don't think the Germans have anything at all...

My dear, I have heard the oinks of pigs that were more enlightning than your Mrs. Red.

Or the horse she rode in on.

And sleeps with!

Well, I've heard that the Mayor was already in Uncas Falls when the trains hit.

Which Mayor?

You know very well which Mayor.
What do you suppose he was doing there so early in the morning?
I'd like to know what he was doing there all night that took him 'til morning.
I don't know about him, but Mrs. Red insists that our mysterious paramour is indeed Chief Prezhki.
My money's still on the Mayor. Now, there's a horse with more'n a few laps to go.
Always was a skirt chaser, that one.
Could be you're both on the wrong track.
Someone was on the wrong track, all right!
We talkin' rails or races here?
Who will deliver the milk if Mr. Stanley's...?
Mr. Stanley's fine, dear. I was just supposin'.
I have heard it alleged, that it was a member of the City Council who strayed from the connubial bed for a little taste of UF's iniquitous dens.
And the dens, it seems, are county-wide. A confederacy of municipalities and eastern gangsters. White slavers, the whole kit and kaboodle.
Seems the closer we get, the farther away it is.
Isn't it always the case?
If there were three trains, where did the other one go? Wouldn't someone notice it was missing?
Railroad swept it under the carpet before the camera's got there.
Is it warm in here, or is it me?
It's you. I'm perfectly comfortable.
Why, I hardly noticed if it was warm or not. How would you describe this weather any way?
What weather?
Myself, I hadn't given it any thought.
Milquetoast weather, I'd call it. Neither here nor there.
Sky's about as colorless as...well, it's colorless, isn't it, girls?
*It can't be colorless. It's just not...color*ful.
Neither hot nor cold, ya ask me.
A vague day. Does that make sense?
Nothing you've said for the last sixty years makes sense!
No, I think she's right. There's a kind of torpor. A vague day indeed. Neither sun nor gloom. I barely have any sense of feeling the air around me.
No breeze, that's for sure. I noticed on the way up. Leaves are as still as a picture.
So is it warm in here?
It's not warm.
Is it cold?
Definitely not cold.
Then what?
Hard to say.
Like Someone forgot to turn things on.
Could it be? Could it really be?
Please! Are we all going daffy?

Could there be no weather at all?
Could there have been four *trains?* Five?
Oh, my! I'm afraid I feel left out. I feel as if God doesn't like me.
Well, that's two a u(U)s.
If there is no longer to be weather, how will we know what to put on when we go out?
Watch what Mr. Stanley's wearing. If he shows up.
Aw, gowan and eat your pie, dear. That's what the hole's for.

PASADENA

A GREAT, JAUNDICED ORB RISES SLOWLY on the horizon, it's fullness gnawed by silhouettes of steeples, ashen smokestacks, water towers, the hangar-like hulk of the Hefaestus Locomotive Works with its corrugated siding and lanky grids of windows, the clerestory of vents emerging from the roof peak, its naked boilers dangling from gargantuan cranes on overhead rails. There are heaps of un-burnt fuel, the stilled trucks and cars, the cloned power poles spewing wires; the workers' housing unlit; the heaps of discarded boiler sheathing and miles of sere piping; the yard of steamers lined for the paint sheds; the flats bedecked with wheel pairs and axles, primed running gear, tender shells, pistons.

The Man in the Moon, for those who accept such fables, is looking across it all, his vast hedges of eyebrows rising above the static people: the doctor, the lawyer, the Indian Chief bent forward with offered cigars in hand, a woman with a shopping basket and perishables tucked under gingham, the traffic cop with directional arms outstretched, the teamsters loading a truck, the hobos lolling in a boxcar door, the boy with his dog, the girl with her doll, the arabers and the fishmongers with their swayback horses and wagons, all of them with soles fixed on the balancing stands like small islands of stability.

The nose waxes — the size of a Model T — the nostril hairs the length of snakes, the caverns themselves nearly able to accommodate a grown man and his mistress in adjoining chambers. He breathes in, he breathes out. There is a wind to loosen leaves, swing a trolley wire, propel a tumbleweed to tumble along into a sunset that has been extinguished. The hand, nearly the size of a city intersection, begins to right a derailed reefer, loses interest, instead, sends a thumb to polish a dulled section of rail, forgets its mission, picks up a gas pump, discards it, sets it to rolling into a school bus out under the moon for purposes no one can imagine, for no one here imagines anything at all.

Then it is dark, then bright daylight, as Taylor flicks lazily at switches and sends trains to tragedy at grossly out of scale speeds. He is lost, without purpose, without orders, without motive power, without traction, without juice, without the concise timetables to tell him where to go and when, without need, without longing, without Cory Ann Kowntertaup. She is as gone as if the Metrolink took her, repackaged her, redesigned her, shipped her down the line to the dining room, the bedroom, through the kitchen to the workshop; snuffed her in a heartbeat, put her down, turned down her lights, flattened her like a roach under the server's boot, sent her down the track, never coming back, got the lost love, runaway, broken hearted, whose-got-my-honey-baby-now, railroad blues. O-o-o-oh, yeah!

The phone rings. It barely cautions him away from puerile distraction. He will leave it to the answering machine Cory Ann had foisted upon him, just about elevating her to Betsy's canonization nomination list.

–Hey, Taylor. Toby. The kid tell's me you called in sick. Just wanted to see what's what. See if you need anything. Lemme know, okay? Oh, yeah, and about the thing? Thought we had an understanding. I've got to know when you can start, like yesterday, so if you're sleeping, I hope to heck that's what you're sleeping on.

He stands up and pads listlessly to the kitchen, studies the refrigerator, decides he's not hungry. He ventures off through the former dining room, down the hall to fall with the weight of his pain into the single bed, wondering as to the heaviness of being empty, something so contrary to physics, to boxcar loads, endurable grade weights, foreign to himself from all approaches. The phone rings. Betsy — not for the first time that day.

–Here's the thing, brother of mine. The machine lets you know who called so that you can call them back. *Some concept, huh?*

He stands, grabs his wallet, his keys, leaves lights on, sun off, in his shorts and Milwaukee Road t-shirt trudges out to his car, soon forgets whether or not he's locked the house, forgets to care. He drives all the way out to the Union Pacific classification yards to study the nomadic graffiti on the big yellow locomotives, the freight cars spray-vandalized like old New York subway trains, instantly loses interest. He ponders a stop at the market for a few essentials: Cheese Puffs, ready-formed beef patties, Diet Coke. Rethinking, he drives home.

The red light on the phone is red, *red*, RED.

–Hey, boy-o. It's Leo, probably with Betsy on the extension. Wanted you to know that I confiscated the train. Felt like the damn FCC. It's good to be the king! I'm writing Steven off. Maybe disown him. Want him? Let me know before I post him on Craigslist. Anyway, he doesn't know what he's missing. I've been puttering in the garden, and I need some technical direction. Roadbed consistency, grade limits, curve radii. Tried the store but they said you didn't come in. What say you get over one day soon and enlighten me? We can burn a couple a t-bones and see if we can't beat the Central Pacific to Patrimony Point? Really, I need your expertise. Give a jingle. I'm one desperate New Mexican.

–Hey, Taylor, dude. This's me, Billy. Look, I know we got in some a those Amtrak Superliner Coaches? Only, I'm like tearing the place apart and I can't find 'em? And, I thought, maybe you stuck 'em somewheres? So, maybe, you could like call me? Like soon, 'cause I gotta guy comin' in wants to see 'em? Anyways, I think the boss is gonna be trimmin' the fat around here. I'm not even gristle so I don't know how long I'm gonna be on board. Them's the breaks! It's all real, bro. Later.

–Taylor. Betsy. Remember me? We shared a womb.

–Me again. Look, I'm worried sick. I don't deserve this from you. Just let me know you aren't dead or some shit. You aren't dead, are you? I'm fucking imagining all kinds

of awful shit. You know, if there's something wrong…Well, that's what family's for. I mean, not to cause awful shit, to help you out of it. Supply the TP. Wipe you off. We're here for you. Leo and me. Unqualified love, like I always tell the kids. Blow up the house, I'll still love you. Of course, I'd kick their little asses if they blew up the house, but I'll love them all the way to the ER. Did Leo call? Did David? Look, Taylor, I know we don't always see eye to eye, but I do love you and….

-We got cut off. Can't you set that thing for a longer message? Anyway, it's me, Betsy. I'll sit by the phone. Hunger strike 'till I hear from you."

-Uncle Taylor? This is me. David. Your nephew. The little one. The Baltic tank locomotives built by Montreal weighed two hundred seventy-five thousand pounds and had a pissy of two ten. Cool, huh? What's a pissy? Steven says it's something I'm not supposed to say. They spell it p-s-i.

He browses a few brittle antique timetables: Cincinnati, Hamilton & Dayton, Atlantic & Pacific, West Shore, then loses interest and leaves them unattended, not even slipped back into their glassine map sleeves. He tries eBay; collectibles — over nineteen thousand entries — transportation, railroads/trains, hardware; there are two thousand six hundred forty-eight entries scrolling before him. They include bills of lading, matchbooks, bar car swizzle sticks, fuseé cases with red signal flags poking a nose out, cable car tickets, REA dollies and wagons, logo mugs, a live steam locomotive — local pick up only — an oak ticket box, and enough kerosene lanterns to light Canada. Nothing of interest. He decides to open a stack of packages from bids he has already won, but, once again, the phone intercedes.

-Asshole. It's Betsy, in case you've forgotten the voice. I'm out in front. Pick the fuck up or my next call's to nine one one. I'll tell them I think you've got you head in the oven. Don't humiliate me. You do have an oven, don't you?

He takes the phone, plods slowly to the window, inches back the shade, shields his eyes from the light. A black Lexus SUV is at the curb, a prominent Jesus fish pasted on the rear-molded-plastic of what passes for a bumper these days. Betsy is leaning against the front fender; a scarf tied around her head with her hair swirled up like whipped cream on a sundae, tight jeans, loose blouse, a stream of smoke zigging and zagging from her lips like a voice balloon screaming *I'm calling, @$#%!* The phone is displayed as evidence in her hand. He didn't know she smoked.

His cordless rings again. "What?"

"Thank God! Can I come in?"

"No."

"Why not?"

"Same as always. I just don't want to have to try to explain it all to you."

"Then you come out."

He hangs up, slips into sneakers but lets the laces hang loose. When he gets outside, she has the passenger door open, motions him in. She goes around the front, crushes the cigarette into the asphalt, and gets back into her side.

There is a thermos in the cup holder. "Want some coffee?"

He shrugs.

"Want to just sit here? Talk here?"

"Okay. But I don't want to talk."

"You look like shit warmed over." Betsy's news isn't always DSL fast. He hasn't shaved — around the goatee or on his scalp — makes his head look like the crown of a barrel cactus. He is thinner, drawn, pasty, dark sacks drooping from his eyes. He smells like an old sock. She cracks his window, then her own.

"You forget how to tie your shoes?"

"No need. I'm not going anywhere."

"You could have tripped off your own fucking porch, you know. Like ninety percent of all accidents occur within a block of home."

"I think that's cars."

"Cars, schmars. If anybody can get themselves killed over a shoe lace, it's you. So what's up?" she says.

"Nothing."

"You haven't been to the store."

"No. Under the weather."

"Too sick to pick up the phone?"

"Me and phones. You know."

"She dump you?"

"Who?"

"Dolly Parton! Cory Ann, the Kraft CEO. Who do you think?"

"Look, Betsy. You got me out here. Now you can go home. Hi to Leo and the kids."

"You're better off without her."

"I was better off without her before I had her."

"Too cryptic for me."

"You can't miss what you haven't had."

"Sure you can. It's called envy. You can miss what other people have."

"I never did."

"There's plenty a fish in the sea."

"I'm done fishing."

"You say that now. When you're already in the shitter, anything that's likely to come at you isn't going to look all that good." Jesus nods from the dash. He agrees with Betsy; probably why she likes him.

"I'm going to go in now."

"No, you just stay put. Look at you. You look like one of those fucking shopping cart guys with Da Nang tattoos and no veins left. Have you been eating? You're bulimic skinny. Or is it the other one? You know, anorexic?"

"I'm not dead, am I?"

"So you say. What have you been eating?"

"Heck, Betsy! Take out. Delivery. You can get anything you need on line, over the phone. The only person we really need anymore is the guy who delivers."

"Then you still haven't learned what need is. Heavens, Taylor, look, let me take you home, my home, get you cleaned up, swim in the pool, help Leo with his fucking train before he destroys my whole garden. I'm going to make my famous *enchilada* casserole. Your favorite."

"I've never had it. Anyway, I've got a pizza."

"Taylor, Taylor, Taylor. We all go through this shit. Pizza outta the box. Part of the plan. It matures us. What, you think Leo was the first to get me in the sack? Gives us a better take on the next one."

"I don't want to hear it. And there's no next one. I was fine before."

"A person can't be alone like this. It's not natural."

"I like being alone."

"How can you like being alone? No one wants to be lonely."

"I was alone. I wasn't lonely."

"Six a one, half…"

"No. I was alone and happy."

"What about when Helen died? You were beside yourself."

"No, actually, I was happy when Helen died." Her jaw drops. Quickly he ads, "Not that she died, of course. I was just happy I was alone. Like before you introduced us."

"Don't even go there. Don't fucking lay this on me. You married Helen and then you drove her nuts with your dip-shit obsession. Forgive me for saying so, but you drove her to an early train as much as if you were behind the wheel."

"And you drove me to Helen."

"*Me? I* made you get married?"

"You never let up. You had me convinced there was something wrong with me."

"There is!"

"See? That's what you did. That's what you still do. And when I brought… someone around, just to get you off my back…"

"Just to get me off…Look, asshole. You had your hands all over the skank. I thought you were going to do her right there on my fucking rack of lamb. You brought your shitty little X-rated affair to my dining room table. To my children. This is *my* fault? How is this my fault?"

"It *is* your fault. I was just trying to shut you up. At first, it was about you. I couldn't handle all the badgering. The phone calls. I thought I'd bring someone over and that would shut you up."

"Well, I certainly didn't make you comb the wharf to find someone, did I? The depth of your search was your own doing. You want to know something? I'm glad she's gone. She was trash, that one. You're a fucking college grad, after all, and you're doing the dirty with Ms. STD of oh nine! God knows what incurable gift she's given you."

"I'm glad I've made you happy."

"This isn't about me."

"Good. Then you don't have to be part of this conversation anymore." He gets out of the car. "Don't call me again. I'll let you know when I'm ready for…well, when I'm ready. Tell Leo…when I can, I'll give him a hand. Don't go looking for me at the store. Don't come here. Don't bribe David to call me. Which one *is* David, anyway? I'm going to stay alone until I no longer feel lonely."

She watches his wide backside lumber up the walk. Her hands are tight on the wheel and she's going to have to redesign the mascara that's flowing like syrup down her face. She shuffles in her purse: Kleenex, make-up, Tic-tacs, pocket Bible, swings the rear view her way. Glancing out her side window, she notices that she is being observed by an old woman on a porch swing, a notebook of some sort across her lap. The woman smiles, throws her a wave and a wink. It is the same nosey old crone that caught her attention in a previous stake out. Betsy revs the smooth six, leaves a millimeter of tire DNA on Taylor's street.

Taylor has slammed the door. It is a new experience and it feels good, gives new definition to the phrase *giving off steam*. He paces, mumbles things to himself, places blame, feels the elevating psi, takes aim on an innocent locomotive headlight, swings a foot back, the force of which jettisons a tennis shoe he hasn't removed to catapult over towns and prairies, and lodges it toe-long into purple mountains majesty. This causes not exactly a tectonic fissure so much as an impact crack in old flour-soaked newsprint. The swung foot, in ignorance of the launched Nike, describes a punter's arch that leads directly into the antique headlight housing, klonk, twang, "*F-u-u-u-ck!*" Now's he's said it, after Betsy, Cory Ann, Blake: It makes him feel ordinary, connected.

This may not be the hallmark of a good thing. The headlight decides it has given all it is going to: there are limits to the quantities of human emotion that inanimate objects can be expected to absorb. Taylor goes hopping in a stew of self pity; reaches out for someone, something, anything for balance; and — with his large, flat palm capable of assembling so many wonderful, tiny things — hits modeled terra firma with the force of a meteor, taking out two trains, a length of track, and several old growth pines. And don't wait for FEMA to make this one right.

Clutching the abused foot in one hand, an abused locomotive in another, Taylor Bedskirt — now having lost two women to trains, one gratefully, the other grudgingly — sinks to the floor, and sheds tears to end a three-point-five-millimeter-to-the-foot scale drought.

Mrs. Gettzleman hears the *f-u-u-u-ck!* all the way across the street and through durable nineteen twenties lath and plaster, as does Mrs. Devore limping along on her aluminum walker with pruning shears snug under her arm. It comes louder and longer than it seems to Taylor, somehow magnifying without the editing interference of foot pain, as it trumpets through windows and doors, rattles around the jailhouse porch like an excruciating fanfare, sets itself to rhythm over the quiet street, up Mrs. Gettzleman's walk, past her plaster ducks and deer, the green hose reeled up on a portable plastic dolly from Home Depot.

"At first," says Mrs. Gettzleman, "I thought it was the contractor home to strangle the wife."

"Gettin' interestin'," Mrs. Devore remarks. "Yes-sir-ee-bob!"

"All this time," adds Mrs. Gettzleman, "the man never has a visitor. And now...these women? And they all seem to go away looking like their implants just collapsed."

"Ha! That's a good one. In my day, you know, we worked with what we had. You want to stuff a little tissue in there, so what? But now, if you haven't had something rebuilt they think you're old fashioned."

"I know just what you mean, dear. Sure would like to be the fly on the wall over there."

"I think they're...whaddya call 'em? You know, prostitutes that do house calls?"

"Call girls. There was something on Oprah. Everything's so out front these days."

"'Cept Mr. Weird over there. And what *do* you suppose is going on with his friend next door? Not a bad looking young man actually. But such going's on! A screw loose, that one. I told Sidney not to drive on it least he pop a tire."

"Oh, I know exactly what you mean. Beware of the fallout after the blast. As you know, I have my theories. I certainly do," says Mrs. Gettzleman with a thump to her notebook.

FOURTH HELEN

The Pasadena Freeway sinews its way Downtown on the bed of a gully designed for a rousing thirty-five miles per hour, valium-free outing. She is slowed only by the traffic, weaves in and out of lanes, flips off half dozen impatient commuters. The pavement itself seems to have lost some definition, the painted lines fade, the shoulder collapses, and distances and speeds begin to elude her. It's all a simple segue from her marriage. The monotony of the trips to the State Railroad Museum, narrow gauge rides in Colorado, streetcars on the coast of Maine while anybody with any sense is there for the lobster and the outlet malls. When she was finally allowed to choose a destination, she chose Amish Country — visions of hex signs on barns and cutesy craft shops with horse and buggy hitched outside between the rental cars — only to wind up riding behind a steam engine on the Strasburg, "the Road to Paradise." Some paradise! This marriage, this life. The jerk could wax poetic about a fucking short line to a fucking nowhere Paradise but couldn't remember their anniversary. The last gift he brought her was a bouquet of obscene calla lilies on the fix-up double with Leo and Betsy. No doubt, the flowers were in answer to Betsy's nagging. The yellow spadix powder stained her blouse as he clumsily thrust it toward her. It made her sneeze. She should have known right there and then on her front porch. A guy who makes you sneeze! A guy who brings out your allergy to impress. Give me a break! Why hadn't she known? Was she that hungry? Was she that far removed from the romantic loop? Horns are doing what horns do best. All the other drivers are as pissed as she is, a serpentine confederacy of Japanese sedans. Here's the thing, she decides: Be careful what you wish for, or at the very least, describe it in some detail before wishing it.

TISHOMINGO, THEBES

I

THESE PAST FEW DAYS, THERE HAS been less talk than weather at the Brown house. Conversation is reduced to convenience, aborted phrases, grunts, subtle body language, comes out as: *more, are you done, pass that please, may I get by or can you turn down your light?* Contact is the result of mishap: passage in the narrow upstairs hall, an accidental brush of hands at the coat closet, an errant arm thrown across a distant partner in sleep; all such subject to instant withdrawal, embarrassed coughing, turned heads, eyes cast wall-ward.

She does her usual. Continues to scrub all sorts of surfaces, to polish tarnished vessels, and to scrape the visible filth of their accumulated week. She dallies on the way home from her part time employment at City Hall, walks the many blocks rather than ride the cars. She makes a slow study of store windows, the unyielding feminine shapes of manikins, the design of a cast iron window frame, the scroll of letters on the glass at the beauty parlor, a display of leeches in brownish apothecary jars, derbies on stands, rings on cigars; reads the labels on the grocer's shelves and the binding at the booksellers. She tries things on, thanks the girl, moves on to the baker to spend thirty minutes savoring the smell of bread.

She makes it a point to leave early and return late. She practices opening doors so as not to awaken him. Noises startle: the catarrh of old plumbing, the complaint of floorboards, anything, any tick, any scratch, any whistle of escaping pressure that claims life in the dead house. But she fails to recall the sound of her name in a man's voice.

He sits. Often, on the front porch, or slumped on a yard chair under a stream of water in the mudroom. The bad pipe vibrates with the ill vapors that envelop the house. He is seen at the edge of the backyard, overlooking now forbidden trains, on the living room couch, the edge of the bed, at the wheel of his car mute in the driveway. And he walks, first in overalls down to the dispatcher who tells him he is suspended until further notice, from tie to tie along the main line all the way over the viaduct at Thebes. He wonders, what would happen if a train came: would it hurt, would the lights just go out, would there be a painful interlude, a transcendence, a descending, a futile change of mind, a consciousness of the alteration of matter, a sort of re-composition, a passage to a place better or worse, sounds of horns, choruses, more trains, harps, more harpies, or just more disillusionment from wives and bosses. Would he be able to look down and see her with him, able to look up and see up her skirt, see what the other man had seen, and where he'd been.

Up and down Railroad Avenue he tramps, up and back, changing sides of the street. He passes through the engine house under the watchful eye of Mr. Red, up through Darktown to peruse the hookers, all around Downtown in his summer around-the-house casuals: fix-it clothes, old jeans and soiled shirts and paint-splattered boots. He talks to no one. No one notices. He has never been a talker. *The fireman's got a mouth on him but the engineer's carved from stone.* There are no friends to miss him. His parents are deceased, his brother works construction somewhere in California, and his sister is making babies with a John Deere salesmen in Northeastern Iowa, one Mississippi short of Minnesota. He is a sullen man being sullen. A serious man devoid of purpose. A sober man who nervously enters a liquor store, points in ignorance to a bottle, drinks it out of the bag in an alley, so that she finds him asleep on the front lawn in the morning as she steps over him on her way to work. He has little tolerance for spirits. She has little tolerance for him.

P-R has the window open. The air is like death: without substance. They exist in a vacuum. She is smartly, but economically, dressed, a small tilted ladies hat of the kind one finds on the heads of chaste wives, a suit of muted colors, and efficient lines cautious in their revelations. P-R offers her a cigarette from a silver, monogrammed case. She refuses.

"I think," he says, "the wisest course of action would be something of a sabbatical from each other."

"Y'all reduce it to such an academic triviality."

"I'm thinking of you as well."

"You know, P-R, sometimes I think y'all seem more naked here in the office than you are when making love."

"What do you expect from me? What right do y'all have to expect anything?"

She pauses to staunch her eyes, offers a modest heave of chest. "I'll need some money."

"Talk about reducing things to trivialities!" He fumbles with a cigar box on his desk: flips the lid open, then closed. "You know, I could've just left it on the dresser. Or is this just y'all's garden variety blackmail?" His voice has taken on a near sinister tone, a color of alarm, just short of an odor.

She nearly swoons in his disdain. "I'm scared. I've got to get away from here. I have an aunt in Boise. Moses doles out the cash like he's my executor. I need train fare. Some setting-up money. Something to tide me over."

"This is why you committed the cardinal sin? How did you get my number, anyway?"

"My God, P-R, I work here! Did y'all think I was too insipid to breach a little file protocol? What you must think of me!"

"*That* I must think of you is, at the moment, of considerably greater import than what."

Her fists are gripping the sides of her skirt. She is determined to remain outwardly calm: has already failed, a realization that nourishes his venom. She says quietly — what she thinks of as quietly — "Y'all's fangs are showing. Just give me some money and I'll be out of your hair."

"Christ, I don't have it on me! What did you think?"

"What about that bundle you're always flashing around?"

"It takes a hell of a lot less to impress a bunch of jesters than it does to ship a woman off to Idaho. I'll have it tomorrow."

She steps back to leave, dabs a cloth to her eyes. He is moved to call to her as she reaches the door. "I don't mean some of the things I say." He has summoned a sympathetic tone. He is good at summonsing. "It's been quite a week, see. I enjoyed our...I enjoyed being with you."

"Yes, me too. Doesn't say much for my judgment, does it? Please, just have the money, P-R. I won't bother y'all again." She is speaking with her back to him, her hand tentative on the brass knob.

"Too bad. I had hoped I was worth just a little bother."

"Two sides of the same coin, we are. This was never going to be anything more, was it?"

"No. We both knew that."

"Still, one pretends."

"Half the fun, the pretense."

Cookie Praejean is an efficient woman who has served the Yardley Humboldt's for twelve years. She escorts Arpashahad Shem through the French doors, somehow leading by following, depositing him on the flagstone where Praetoria Humboldt, in unexpected summer attire, sits at a glass top table, alone, staring off on her winter garden in its confusion. The sky is almost white and she labors to find shadows.

She nods to him, says, "So good of you..." but doesn't finish.

"May I sit down?"

"Of course. How rude I've become."

"Not at all," he comforts, pulling out the chair next to hers and turning it in her direction.

"We shall have tea. I'm presuming. Do you prefer coffee?" she says, and Cookie scampers off to the kitchen without another word, is already scampering before it is said. Cookie runs the house, knows it better than the lady who couldn't find a tea bag if it was hung like a cameo about her neck. There are two houses really, the Humboldt's above decks, packed with extraneous conceits to awe and comfort, and Cookie's boiler room which keeps it all going on it's merry way. She is the lubricant that stifles friction, the fuel that burns in the soul of the structure, the commissar, the breather of life unseen and un-praised, the guardian angel of domestic logistics. Cookie drifts unseen through the pleasure dome with just this

side-of-tan toast and prisms of butter, three minute eggs, rare steaks, the latest
<u>Life Magazine</u>, an inscribed set of hair brush and mirror, a pipe and tobacco,
a ham bone for the dog. She is near as things of the most intimate nature are
discussed, dusts around private papers, hears the expressions of their lovemaking,
the flushing of their toilets, the whimpering of breakdowns, the harsh profanity
of displeasure. Neither of the Humboldt's has been to the kitchen or the pantry
in over four years when an unfortunate swelling of the front door frame caused
them to rely on the back door for an excruciating period of hours.

"Tea would be just fine. Look, Praetoria..."

"Shhh!" She holds a finger to her lips. "I was watching an owl a moment ago.
Quite remarkable, don't you think? In the middle of the day. Quite the handsome
fellow too."

"This is difficult, Praetoria..."

"Ah, here's the tea." She says it as if it has come by itself, floated from the
house on its magic silver tray with its matching pot and tiny China cups, women's
cups really: delicate with painted peonies and set upon near-translucent saucers.
These are heirlooms, no doubt. Having done what was bidden, Cookie vaporizes
back into her vessel to reappear only upon the next cast wish.

Praetoria says, "We'll let it steep. It's a brew from our trip to India, what
the Brit's call the Raj or something. Yardley's a great fan of tea. Did you know
that?"

"No, I don't think I did."

"He seems so gruff, so rough and tumble. It would make you laugh to see
his big finger stuck in such a delicate cup, sipping away like some grand dame at
a *soirée*."

"I'm sure it would be quite the scene. May I say...?"

"I'll pour. Sugar? Cream?"

"Just as it is would be fine. I must insist..."

"Don't bother." She is speaking rapidly, as if there is a deadline to meet. "I
know why you're here in the middle of the afternoon. Don't let my verb tense
deceive you. You've already gotten our contribution to the building fund, so I've
deduced it's the other thing."

"The other thing?" His brow raises, wrinkles like wind-blown sand.

"You've come to minister to the widow." She doesn't look at him when she
says this.

"Someone's been here? I shouldn't wonder. The time that's past and all."

"Someone hasn't. That's the point. I knew what train he was on. And he is
very long overdue." She seems to tremble just slightly, a quiver of lips, of nostrils,
a less than expected command of the teapot as it overshoots his cup and fills the
saucer.

"I'm so very sorry," he says with seminary-taught compassion. He gently pats
her free hand.

"Thank you. Yes, sorry...I wonder why you were told before me?"

"Oh, I think, because it was a matter of some delicacy. I suppose they wanted
you all to hear it from a friend. Having a policeman come to..."

"Still, still." She doesn't continue.

"Shall we pray together, Praetoria?"

She seems distracted. "What?"

He pulls a small, worn Bible from his coat. "Would you like me to pray with you?"

She is puzzled. "I wouldn't know what to pray for."

He is taken aback. "Pray for the knowledge to know?" he offers.

"I wasn't a very good wife, as you can attest. I got...distracted."

"He would have forgiven you all. Perhaps he already had."

"Oh, I doubt that. No, no, no, I very much doubt that."

"God will forgive you."

"Easy for Him. I wasn't cheating on *Him*."

"Then who else but Him, when we sin?" It comes a bit sharp; reminds him to soften his tone.

"You are well meaning. I know that," she says, almost as if she is here to soothe him. "And you have always been a comfort to me in times of my... waywardness. But spare me this...redemption. That is what's afoot, isn't it? I don't deserve it. I don't want it. It would only add to the guilt. You see, Pastor, while you are deceiving someone, in the very act of deceit..."

A lump, not sugar, gathers in his throat. He remembers taking Yardley by the arm, whispering in his ear, *We all need to talk.*

"...I mean," she continues, pacing her words, cautious now, "while you are being unfaithful, you do not think of the person you are hurting, you do not expect that there will be no time to make amends, no time to move on, no time to prove yourself. You just do it because it's a thing of the moment. Because it feels good, if you'll...I was going to say *forgive*. How silly! You think it's a fleeting thing. You have absolutely no indication that something will happen to make it permanent. When I feel myself redeemable, if...if, I will get down on my knees with you and beg, beg, beg for whatever it will be that I will find myself in need of. Or deserving. Now, I need to bury my husband and endure my remorse."

There is a thumping and a groan from out of the earth. The house strains behind them.

"What's that? Do you feel that?"

The teacups, with tea unleveled, patter across the saucers. The saucers soft shoe on the glass table. Inside the house, all manner of things seek escape; ball jars bail from shelves, losing beans, flour, grains; cereal boxes topple; a lamp meets the floor; doorbells loudly announce no one.

Cookie, engaged in both dusting and research, maintains the presence of mind to return to a drawer a stack of documents in Yardley's study, then materializes out through the French doors, having grabbed props of soup pot and washcloth, and allowing the terror to appear on her face, and says, "Y'all gotta haint here, y'ax me."

Praetoria is wide-eyed, likely from the movement, though it appears she is going to ask, *Who's that black woman?*

Shem directs the maid to sit on a bench equidistant from them and the house. He takes Praetoria's icy hands. The shaking stops and leaves a stillness that is suddenly as palpable as the movement before it. "Why, that's a new one for me," he says, catching his breath, his shoes firmly on the patio stone.

"What's happening?" She is frightened, momentarily feels she is the subject of some divine imprecation, and is gratified that Brother Shem seems as unsettled as she herself.

"Well, I'd guess we all just experienced an earthquake."

"Here? In Tishomingo?" She wants to laugh; deems it inappropriate.

"It appears so."

"What do you suppose all of this means? Earthquakes? This...what? This weather? The train? Even before the train, the sirens were going every fifteen minutes. Is this some kind of precursor? Has God abandoned us?"

"If anything, it is us who have abandoned Him," Shem informs, just a bit too smugly. "Maybe He's reminding us to pay attention."

"You're becoming predictable," she almost snaps.

"Some truths are worth repeating," he jabs back. Are they arguing? The widow, the comforter?

"So what does this all this mean?"

He clears his throat, recovers his truant demeanor. "Well, as you know, Praetoria, I am not of the school that is prone to eschatology. There are things best left up to God for explanation."

"Sometimes God keeps things a bit too close for me."

"It is not for you all to judge." He tries not to sound the scold.

"No, I suppose it's not."

"When these things happen..."

"These *things?* Which things, exactly? Yardley in, what? An upturned parlor car perhaps? Or, my...moral detour with P-R? Or, these phenomena? Which *things?* They're beginning to run together, the things, don't you think? Like those watercolors I'm so bad at. I tried to sing this morning. A hymn. Couldn't find my voice. It was raspy, lifeless. I'd lost the melody." She stands suddenly. The ground offers one more queasy complaint. "If you'll excuse me, I'm going to lay down for a while. All of this is...well... Thank you for coming. I will want you to officiate, of course."

"Of course," he affirms as he watches her totter off to the house.

"Please feel free to stay and finish your tea," she calls.

"Do you think it's safe?" he calls, but she doesn't answer. "In the house, I mean?"

Cookie is still hugging herself on the bench. "Welcome to California," he teases, more to relax himself.

"Was fine where I was at, thank y'all the same."

"I'll show myself out then," he says.

He walks back through the house, rights an upturned vase on his way, adjusts an oil of the Humboldts with their grown children. No doubt at this very moment, they are seeking transportation for the trip home.

Out in front, he feels the first burst of air returning, along with a thickening of the sky as if it was a brew being churned over a flame by a spoon. Pine needles have showered down on his car, have presumed to land inside the open window so that he has to brush them out onto the street. Looking through the windshield, he perceives a darkening, the thinnest veil of cloud overhead, and to the north, like Sherman's army, a black, unappealing thunderhead introduces itself. He feels a sudden chill, buttons his meager coat, rolls up the windows, and shivers. At the moment, he wouldn't mind a bit more divine transparency himself.

Holynation Salvation is out on the lawn to the side of the chapel, a cold wet rag pressed to his wife's forehead to calm her, a quiet psalm or two whispered in her ear, "*Save me from the lion's mouth; Yea from the horns of the wild-oxen do Thou answer me,*" yeah, from the sudden quaking of the earth. He notices the change overhead, a distant rumble, like horsemen coming, a grim chilled rain, needles of sleet, and finally pea-sized hail stones dropping like a shower of sparks from a forge, and then proceeding on its way south to build on its own calamity. This on top of a call no more than an hour earlier, a frantic report from his sister downriver, of dead eels washing up by the hundreds around her catfish pier and spreading a stench so fierce as to bend the boughs of trees hanging above the water.

Sarai watches the storm pass from the gazebo where she is reading, trying to forget the tumble of earth. It flickers and scowls and is gone as fast as it has arrived. She runs for the house, runs from room to room with the girl shutting windows, and grabbing an afghan along the way to cover her shoulders, tripping over a telephone that has slipped to the floor during the tremor and scraping a well-scrubbed knee. Her eyes are as round as two moons and as white as truck headlights in the dark gorge below Thebes. She and the girl are both sobbing. The mistress raises her arms to the servant, says, "Come," and they hold each other to dampen tremors. Eyes closed, they are not privy to the scene out the window where a flock of starlings is falling from the sky like the dark bombs so recently rained down upon Spain.

Officer McCallum surges into the office drenched like a boat's bottom, and tells Officer Voorhiis at his desk, "Damndest weather I ever seen. I'm about to collar this old boy, see, tries to punch a clerk and takes on out a the A&P with a box a corn flakes don't belong to him, an' he starts gettin' clobbered by hail, falls down on his face screaming, *don't shoot no more, don't shoot.* So whatta I got? Grand theft cereal! Who's got the time for this shit?"

"Yeah, who?"

"I give the bastard some change, march him back up to the clerk and make him pay and say he's sorry. You're probably full up in here anyways."

"To the nose hairs."

"Damndest thing!"

"Can say that again. One to remember. I just heard over WTUF they had a twister…go on, say it. *This time a year? A twister!* Heard it right there on the Philco. A twister comes outta nowheres, goes ahead an' sets it's gnarled ass right down in Tom Pinckney County, high tails off with two milk cows, a barn, an' a small crossroads town. Drops the whole mess over to Red Stick County like it was all made outta twigs. Has its way with a pin factory up over in Dexter and then it rains pins ten miles as the crow flies in Gale's Bluff. And that ain't the half a it. Hail the size a grapefruit killed a farmer in Stonewall."

"Yeah, well, was they there? The radio guys?"

"Well, I suppose they can't say it if it didn't happen."

"I suppose. But you never know."

"You never know nothin', but, like takin' a dump, you still gotta answer the call when it comes in."

"Ain't that the truth. Damndest thing I ever saw, these last few days."

"So what's it like outside? I feel like a U-boat captain, locked up in here."

"Mostly a lot a shattered nerves. Starts shaking, everyone runs outside like roaches when the lights come on. Storm comes up, everyone runs back in. A real tennis match out there. Could wrench your neck trying to take it all in. Masonry in the streets. Horses runnin' every which a way. The usual malarkey when stuff that can't happen does anyhow."

"Phones're ringin' off the hook. Pard, you don' even wanna know! They're asking *me* what's goin' on! Like I got an in with the Big Fella. A lot of it pretty imaginative. The earth opened an' a house got swallowed on Stevens Drive. A tree's *bend*ing so much, it's doin' a full one-eighty. Bang, hits the ground on it's right, bang again, comes slappin' down 'n it's left! A pond's gone empty. There's a spirit in some ol' boy's rockin' chair. *B-o-o-o-o!* Invasion a gnats. Loonies come'n out a the woodwork along with 'em, ya want my opinion. A little worse over in UF, I hear, though some a the lines are down. They lost some structures, seems. Maybe some casualties. Don't know no more'n that."

"So what you all doing about the phones?"

"Pretendin' I can't hear 'em. Look, the girls run off when it started shaking. Everyone's been sent out on a call 'cept the janitor, an' I gotta eye on him. Not a badge'n the joint, suits, uniforms, the whole kit and kaboodle. Even the Chief's out patrolling for looters. And if you all don't haul your sorry ass off a that there chair and end your shift, I reckon I'll have t' notice, an' send y'on out t' nail up the cross back top a First Lutheran, or refill the reservoir, or some shit 'er other."

"I'm not even here. Never was. See you in the mornin'."

"Yeah, if there is one."

"Well, there generally is."

"Gener'ly."

⁜

How's it over there?

Oh, just the biggest mess I ever did see. Don't know what I kept all this junk for anyways, an' now I gotta sweep up the pieces. And with you?

I don't really know yet. I just got in when the storm started. You'd think you'd get a minute to breathe between events, now wouldn't you?

Expectation is the mother a disappointment, I always say.

I'm afraid I may have lost my mother's china.

When's the last time you used it?

I've always been afraid to use it. It's quite fragile, you know.

There ya have it then. Ya lost somethin' ya couldn't use. Better'n losin' something ya could.

True, but still, it was my mother's.

You okay over there? Sound like the teenager who just found out she's with child.

I don't know. I do feel strange.

So'd the teenager. How, strange?

Like I've been abandoned, left to my own devices. Set adrift. I don't know what that means, but it's what I'm feeling.

I'm feeling broken glass beneath my feet. What next, do you suppose? Frogs, water to blood?

Young Mrs. McCallum is married seven months when the baby comes to term. She and David pretend the child, all eight pounds of him, is premature, and most everyone else pretends to believe them. After rushing the swaddled infant onto the street with the flood of neighbors, and then shielding him from the ice, she has put him back in his cradle and is attempting to call her mother in Uncas Falls on a candlestick phone with a recently chipped mouth cup. She tries many times before service is restored. Because she is so occupied, she is unaware that seven minutes into the calling, the baby stops breathing.

II

SATURDAY BRINGS FROST; LIKE SOMEONE HAS laid thick comforters on the lawns. She walks carefully up the glazed sidewalk with breakfast groceries, but none for lunch or dinner. As soon as he disappears on one of his mysterious walks, she will slip the already packed bag from the attic, remove P-R's substantial contribution from an oatmeal box in the pantry, and make her way quickly down the wooden stairs to the yards and the station. Her face is heavily powdered over the bruise. It wasn't exactly a beating, she tells herself: one punch only, one swift out-of-the-blue engineer's powerful throttle fist below her right eye to send her reeling to the floor and to upturn the laundry bucket. Neither of them spoke a word, before or after. He turned quickly and went out the front door with his suspenders hanging, like he'd just be back momentarily with the paper. She lay there, damming back angry tears and thanking him for the affirmation.

The kitchen is in shadow on this gray day, the dim sunlight still prone on the house's eastern front side. At first, she doesn't see him sitting at the table with his forearms extended and resting on the wood. He is gray too, nearly formless, a ghost man, lost in his own self-pity and plagued with recrimination.

She reaches for the light string over the cutting block. "Leave it," he says. He is quiet but definite, and she stands in the middle of the floor hugging the bag like it is offspring.

"I'm done mullin'," he says. She tries to answer but has nothing to say. "Who is he?"

She forces, "What difference does it make?"

"Makes none at all. But you will tell me."

It is then that she sees his gun on the table, sees his fingers edge closer to the butt. She says, "You don't have to do anything like this."

"Same as I'd a tol' you, had I sufficient warnin'." He pushes the chair back and stands, lifting the gun with him. She is frozen as if tarred to the linoleum. He comes forward and shoves the barrel into the bag and pokes the things inside, breaking an egg or two.

"I'll leave," she offers. "You wont have to put up with me anymore."

"I don't have t' put up'th ya now."

She can smell the alcohol. It flares her nostrils. He senses her revulsion and blows vintage breath slowly into her face. She starts to tremble, feels she is turning to powder, lets loose a warm trickle of urine down her legs.

"Look'ee here! The whore pisses herself on'er own kitchen floor. Give ya something t'mop up 'till I get back."

He moves around her, around the puddle. He turns at the front door, shoves the gun into the back of his pants, says, "I'm gonna go see me a junkman."

"He doesn't know anything."

"Well, we'll see. 'Course, I see the coppers beat me up there, I'll quietly excuse myself. An' I will know why they're waitin'."

"He doesn't know anything. He's just an old colored man."

"We'll talk on this later, you an' me. You be here. I gotta boy down at the depot waitin' on ya, 'case y' got ideas. So you stay put, hear?"

She steps back to the wall, sinks to the floor, still hugging the market bag. She sees the door shut, hears him start the car, flood the engine, struggle to start it again. It is quiet for a while before he resumes, turns it over, and backs out into the street with part of a hedge spinning in his spokes. She can smell the congealing yokes, her urine on the floor, the aftertaste of his whiskey breath.

As he rides through town, shopkeepers are still sweeping up the last of the glass, removing goods damaged from broken pipes. Some stores are boarded, and pedestrians seem careful to walk on the curb edge of sidewalks. He focuses on the hood ornament — an undistinguished knob of chrome with his own twisted expression looking back at him — drives cautiously past the many patrol cars that are cruising watchfully around roped off-debris. It is the same in Thebes, but less so; fewer walkers; only one black and white passing him the other way; smaller piles of brick from less ambitious structures infringing upon the street.

He shifts with effort, takes the hill as if he is driving for the first time, and nearly loses traction on a mud shoulder. He parks well below the old man's rail car.

It is graveyard quiet in the pines. He takes a bottle from the glove box, endures a swig of fortification, and weaves unsteadily on rubber feet up to the porch steps. There he is hit with an overpowering rancid-sweet stench that sends him twirling backward, has him dry heaving great yellow compounds of drink and digested burgers. Hunched over, hands strutted to knees like eaves, he dry-heaves long stalactites of rejected material when all else has escaped him. He has had rats in the house before, has left poison for them to consume, to drag their dehydrating rodent asses back into the walls for one last, odiferous insult. He knows the smell of dead things.

Quickly sobered, he gets the car down to The Roadhouse. He calls the police on the pay phone Prezhki had used on the night of the motor court run. "I think there's a dead man," he says, causing the cooks to peer around the corner at him. He turns away from them, cups the bakelite mouthpiece. "Why you need t' know? I ain't the dead man? Huh, huh? Okay. Moses Brown. Okay. I'll wait up here at the Greek's. You just send someone up t' that ol' shine's junkyard an' take a look. Yeah, I will. I'll be right here. No, I hadn't nothin' t'do'th it. I just went up there for some…pipe fittin's. No, I didn't. But I know that stink…okay." He looks over at Anatoli who is leaning on the counter, watching him intently. "Wants t' speak t' you."

The Greek comes around for the phone, says, "Uh huh, uh huh. Breakfast on you fellas then. Uh huh." And then to Moses, "Getcha hotcakes? Y'want? Eggs? Bacon?"

"I ain't goin' nowheres," Moses says.

"I know that. Waffle? Sausage?"

"How about coffee?"

"Coffee we got. Come with breakfast."

"How about just the coffee?"

"I think we got just coffee. Drink down slow."

Prezhki himself, Mike Voorhiis on the bench to his right, responds to the tip. They are heavily wrapped for the day, brims low upon foreheads, the Chief in his trademark cap, Voorhiis in uniform. Frost shrouds the junk in the yard. Prezhki gets out, leans up against the cold hood. Thinking better of having his ass frozen to the squad car, he steps away and tells Voorhiis to go up and take a look.

"Sure thing, Chief." He steps around the bedsteads and pieces of old farm machinery, privy tanks, a barrel of mismatched oars, a box of used rifle stocks. "Someone's been sick over here," he calls.

"Put it in your report," Prezhki calls back, lighting a cigarette.

"Oh, we gotta ripe one, all right," Voorhiis says, still twenty feet from the door. He pulls a hankie from his pocket, covers his mouth and nose. "I gotta knock?"

"Just kick it the hell in."

He does so, peers inside, jumps back out gagging, a stream of spittle hanging from his lips. "Oh, man, oh boy! Y' gotta see this."

"Whatta we got?"

"Part of a dead nigger an' one mighty fat old cur."

Prezhki pulls out his service revolver, drops the cigarette and crushes it in the damp earth. He grabs his own rag, dips it into his gas tank to take on the smell of petroleum, covers his nose, and marches purposely up to the door and inside. Voorhiis hears a growl, then two quick pops and a yelp, and sees the Chief come back out looking satisfied with a job well done.

"Never did like dogs," Prezhki says.

"Whattaya think, Chief?"

"What do I think? I think, now they're both dead."

"I mean, how'd it play out?"

"Dog did it for the insurance. What's the difference? Old people tend to die. I'm going to go down and call this in on the box out by the drugstore. Using a phone around here's like going on radio. You hang around and wait for the undertaker. I'll pick you up directly."

"Chief? Ya think dead white folks smell that bad?"

"Next time we got one, let's just leave him to set up a bit. See what happens."

❉

Prezhki goes down to the call box and tells the deskman to ring up one of the colored preachers. "See if they can't send up one of their own to pickle this guy." Then he proceeds down the gulch towards the viaduct, makes a wide circle past the trolley stop into The Roadhouse lot.

The place is nearly empty. Brown is at a corner booth, with the Greek nearby making sure he has plenty of coffee and doesn't bolt. Anatoli motions Prezhki over to the bar, steps behind it himself, whispers, "Peckerwood not so hungry."

Prezhki finds himself facing snake eyes, black with evil gray rings, the end of prominent barrels.

"He totin'," the Greek explains.

"Why, that's thoughtful of you, Toli. I don't think it's going to come to that, so you just go on check the kitchen and let me earn my keep."

"I be back there you need, Chief," he says, hoisting the shotgun up over his shoulder for Brown's enlightenment, and carrying it around to the kitchen.

Prezhki steps over to Brown's table and says, "You'd be Moses Brown, I figure."

"That's right."

"Well, I'm sorry for you, Moses Brown."

"It against the law t' be me?"

"Well, we'll see, won't we? You the one that called?"

"I am."

"You the Moses Brown of David's Sling?" The engineer doesn't answer, sits rigid, expectant. Prezhki sits across from him. "You've managed to piss off some powerful folks, you have. You know who I am?"

"Nope."

287

"Chief Walter Prezhki. Ring a bell?"

Moses leans uncomfortably back in his seat and stares into the officer's face. "Not really."

"Want some breakfast?"

"Y'all been up there yet?"

"I have."

"And y'gonna eat?"

"I am."

"You got some cast iron stomach, y' ask me."

"Comes with the territory. Give it back on retirement. Tell me what you know."

"Nothin'. Like I tol'em on the phone. I went on up there for some pipe fittin's an' I smelled…whatever I smelled. Then I come on down here an' called y'all. Ask the Greek."

"What kind of pipe?"

"Huh? What?"

"The pipe fittings. What kind?"

"Just your standard plumbin' kind."

"Incoming or out?"

"In."

"What for?"

"Gotta saw into an ol' shower pipe. Let them air pockets out."

"What pieces?"

"Couple a elbows. Length a straight."

"Male or female?"

"Why?"

"You're an engineer, right?"

"I am."

"Then I guess you know pipes. Not that it's any of my business, but don't you guys usually lift that sort of thing out of the shops? Kind of stuff disappears all the time, I hear."

"I don't steal."

"That's very righteous of you. Do you lie? You sure you don't know who I am?"

"Heard some stuff."

"You heard bullshit."

"Could be."

"You carrying a weapon, Mr. Brown? Seem to be sitting a ways away from the seat back, kind of aslant. Why don't you hand me that pistol you've got there, stock first would be nice, before you put a second crack in your ass." He takes out his own weapon as he says this, handles it casually, generally in Brown's direction.

Moses says, "Ain't done nothin'."

"Let's us just make that the status quo."

Moses reaches back under Prezhki's careful scrutiny, hands over the gun, butt first. The Chief takes it, inheriting rust flakes to brown his hand, sets it in his own belt and returns his own gun to its holster.

"Should never keep a good weapon buried in the yard. You ever fire that thing?"

"Not too recent."

"No shit, you say! You always go armed to pick up a few pipe elbows, a length of straight?"

"Man's gotta right."

"A man does. Usually a man has a reason too."

"Things've been funny 'round here lately."

"I noticed. You stop in to visit us tomorrow morning and help us with some paperwork. You can have your antique back then. That work for you?"

"It does."

"Bullshit in, bullshit out, you know what I mean?"

"I guess so."

Prezhki rocks his head once forward and back, gives Moses a bent streak of smile. "I thank you for doing your civic duty, Moses Brown. You and I have nothing more to say to each other."

Moses hesitates. Can this be all? The officer affords him no further clue. Then he stands and exits slowly, as if considering a diminishing number of options. Prezhki retrieves the old pistol, places it on the seat next to him and watches the engineer through the window; does not stop doing so until he sees the man's car proceed out of the lot and up the main street of Thebes.

"How it go?" says Anatoli emerging from the kitchen, the shotgun slanted across his broad shoulders like he's carrying the cross to Golgotha.

"You were right. He wasn't hungry."

He has a short conversation with the Greek about the loss of power and perishables during the quake, then treats himself to what he considers an extravagant breakfast: three sanctimonious eggs staring up in judgment, a steak as thin and tough as holster leather, potatoes chopped up and fried in lard with onions and green peppers, several thin strips of crisp bacon, grits. He coats it all with enough salt and pepper so that the condiments are all he can taste, and washes it down with two cups of black coffee. It exiles the petroleum stink from his nostrils.

When the Chief arrives back at the junkyard, Voorhiis is sitting on an old streetcar seat as far from the corpse as he can. The officer is shivering, but remarks that for once he is thankful for the cold.

Prezhki sits next to him and offers a cigarette. "No takers yet?"

"Nary a one."

"They'll be by directly. Been a busy week."

They smoke quietly for a while. Then Voorhiis asks, "'Bout the witness?"

"Nothing to witness. You know this Moses Brown? He ever give us cause to pay him attention."

"Not that I know of."

"He just stumbled on this here. Let's leave it at that. You run across his name, though, you let me know. At the very least, Moses Brown is an angry and very poorly informed man who I suspect's made a deal with Johnny Walker in the resent past."

"Not the best a combinations, y' ask me."

"No, it is not."

They are quite again. A slight breeze is awakened. It stirs the saw grass all these discarded memories sit in. The summer birds seem to have taken their leave as quickly as they had appeared.

"We...some a us 'n'the office...we got us up a collection for McCallum's kid. You want in?"

"Sure."

"Hell of a thing!"

"The innocents. One minute they're all demand...teat, diaper, a warm hug... the next, they're gone."

"A tragedy, y' ask me."

"Yes. It is."

"I said a prayer for the little one. Guess he's 'n'a better place."

"Better seat to view the action, anyway."

"Sir?"

"You read your Bible, Lieutenant?"

"Not to no scholarly level. I don't read much a anything's the actual truth a the matter. Paper, magazine, maybe. I've no attention span for anythin' longer."

"That's okay. Some times the more you find out, the less you know. Here's a for instance. It says in the Book that God called on Moses and Aaron and commands them to parlay with Pharaoh, right?"

"I suppose. I'm kind a ignorant a these areas."

"Trust me. That's what it says. Then He says, He will *harden Pharaoh's heart* so's He can awe him with some chicanery he's not likely to forget anytime soon. This is because He wants Pharaoh not only to know his place, but to know His place. A kind of sublime one-upsmanship, if you follow. So Moses and Aaron, God's boys, arrange for an audience with Pharaoh and by some slight of hand, turn a stick into a snake. Not to be outdone, Pharaoh, who, remember, has already had his heart hardened like Herbert Hoover, brings in some of his boys to turn their own sticks into snakes, and probably, I don't doubt, pull a few rabbits out of their turbans. So God, as if this is news, tells Moses and Aaron that Pharaoh is stubborn. The boys are probably thinking, *well, shit, it just wasn't such a awe inspiring trick if they could match it*, but God is kind of an unpredictable guy, so they keep their mouths shut. He sends them back to turn the rivers to blood, another stunt that Pharaoh's boys seem to equate with your garden-variety card trick. No wonder Pharaoh is a scoffer. Long story short, God's boys and Pharaoh's boys match wits with frogs, with gnats, all of which by now is making the land of Egypt a pretty tough piece of real estate to unload on even the most naïve of crackers. Then we get flies. Pharaoh's boys can't do flies. They are up against a wall here, see? And they can't seem to do murrain, boils or hail either. It seems about now that God's corner has come out on top in the pissing contest. He's made his point and even stubborn old Pharaoh should read the handwriting on the side of the pyramid. But God, not yet sated, reaches into His bag of tricks and pulls out locusts. And, you guessed it. Pharaoh's heart is hardened. Now me, if I was God, I'd say, *okay, why kick a guy who's already down?* But what do I know about being God? So God, in His righteousness, slays the first born sons of the Egyptians. See, in God's view, this is a good thing. We recoil in horror and take up collections for the family, but God is righteous, so this sacrifice of lambs is righteous. I don't get that? Do you get that, Voorhiis?"

"Sir? I don't know. Not mine t' question."

"No, I guess it isn't. And here comes our wagon. But don't you wonder that if God could harden Pharaoh's heart, He could just as easily've softened it? Could have just gotten His flock out of town without all the fuss? Pharaoh, see, was set up. Framed. By God. Which makes it seem like the time you spent praying for little McCallum might have been better served were you occupied with something else all together."

The van sputters into the yard followed by a trail of dust and perhaps some resident gnats, though it is not the time of year. Pharaoh's boys probably can't do gnats either. The tappets sing like cicadas. So much for seasons in Thebes. A sign on the side panel reads: RETURN TO SENDER FUNERAL HOME, P. Q. SUTTLEY & SONS, UNDERTAKERS. Young Abel Suttley comes out the right side, his brother Ahitub on the left. When they open the back doors, Holynation Salvation, grim faced, jaw set, steps out with his Bible, a perfumed cloth, nods to the officers and proceeds with the suited young men carrying the box to retrieve the parts of Choc Bonjour, both inside and outside of the dog. The Good Reverend gets just to the door, recoils as if hit by grapeshot, comes back to the truck and leans over the hood to retrieve his bearings.

"Y'say," he says, clearing his throat, "there's some sort a moo-tilation a my good Brother Bonjour?"

"I'd say that," Prezhki owns.

"What ya r'portin's the cause a death?"

"End of life, as with most of us."

"'Spectfully, boss, you be a the same notion that be a white man up'n there?"

Prezhki is suddenly hot: feels he's been struck. *"Respectfully,* you say? Look it here, preacher man, you see evidence of something untoward, you write the fucking report. Maybe you should be Chief of Police. See how that appeals to the voters."

"But the vi'lation a the body?"

"A snitch fingered the dog. Dog resisted arrest and we were compelled to use force. Dog has learned crime doesn't pay."

The two cops move off to their car. Voorhiis says, "The balls on that darky!"

Prezhki sighs. "Honestly, Officer, if I was him, I wouldn't trust us either."

Up on the ridge between Thebes and Tishomingo, Prezhki turns off onto the gravel firebreak that leads to the flat spot where lovers park on starry nights. He gets out of the car, leaving Voorhiis inside to warm himself with the engine running, and looks out over his jurisdiction.

Tishomingo curves and bends and slants down toward the river valley like the diorama of itself at the Chamber of Commerce, the punched up knolls of the Camels across the valley, home lots receding, as does the elevation, through Downtown, through Darktown, past the brewery, skirted by the ridge overlooking the classification yard with its identical company houses, along the spur of the saw mill which seems to be on fire again.

In fact, Prezhki can see there are three fires raging. They send up columns to meet in a communal vapor of cloud and ash. He sees chimneys down, a steeple very much askew, hears a din of hammers and sirens and, he thinks, a shot or two. A crowd has gathered at the depot, perhaps the threatened wildcat strike the agitators have exported from the mill towns of New England, the longshoreman on the Hudson, the stockyards of Chicago, the steel mills of Pennsylvania, the coal seams of Colorado. *Damn them and their hardened hearts,* thinks the Chief, taking in toy town with its manicured geography, its contrived decay.

There is a smell of friction, of electricity, a hum of transformers. *This is how God sees it,* he thinks. *And now, that baby too.*

PASADENA

I

—Taylor. Toby. Look, guy, the bulldog's chomping at the bit. I've got to tell him something. You in or what?

-Okay, okay. You're right. I shouldn't've come to the house. That was our agreement and I blew it. But, you're doing it again. And the silence scares the shit outta me. I understand if you don't want to talk to me...I mean, for a while. Just show that ugly mug of yours so we know you're breathing. Run the flag up the pole. Anything. Call Leo. Just say, Hey, Leo, and hang up. But, Taylor, fuckin' surface already!

-Me again. Forgot the most important thing. You wanna come to dinner? Friday? I'm making *ropa vieja, albóndigas.* Leo's mother's recipe. *Auténtico.* Your fave. You don't have to call. Just show up.

-Hey, bro-in-law. I'm stuck driving spikes in poisonous oleander. Help!

-Last chance, my friend. Can't hold up the march of progress. I need your answer to-day or I turn it over to Bull Conner. It's Toby. I'm at the store 'til six.

-Look, Taylor, it's...what?...Six thirty? I'm going home. Call me at home tonight and give me the thumbs up, because, first thing in the a.m., I'm giving our wacked-out friend the keys to the city.

-You missed some kickass *comida.* A coupla a fuckin' *mariachis* and you would a thought you were in Mazatlán. Please stick your nose above water. Something. Did I say, please?

-Hello. I'm calling for...Taylor Bedskirt...Do you know that you can probably lower your mortgage and borrow up to $200,000 on your equity with just one phone call. And with our licensed, professional...

The calls keep coming. Taylor disconnects the answering machine. He takes it and deposits it in the trash under the kitchen sink, where a sneaker-sized water bug displays its displeasure by emitting an astringent chemical odor. The phone rings again. Eleven, twelve, fifteen rings. He pulls the plug from the box on the baseboard. The voices die in the wire: truncated waves, expired pulses.

He putters around the parcels filled with things won on eBay. There are cap badges, rule books, and locomotive builder's plates. He moves them here, stacks them there, but can't muster the excitement to open them. The sellers will be awaiting feedback. Some will withhold theirs until he rates them — *a pleasure to do business with; nice seller; quick shipment and well packaged; highly recommended eBayer.*

He lies under the layout table and contemplates loose wires hanging like eviscerated intestines from the plywood, but shuts his eyes for sleep rather than repair. It is no great task to numb his mind these days. But driving out the discomfort expels all else with it, until there is no layout, no childhood home, no weather to express variance, no color. It is a time unanimated, as monochromatic as Buster Keaton making off with "The General". He tries to sleep himself into, not death, but limbo: a purgatory for the absent.

The house is littered with half-empty Diet Cokes waving finger tabs like flags, others not even opened, pizza boxes still with pizzas — some slices with just the crust gnawed off or a few discs of pepperoni selectively appropriated — untouched cartons of cashew chicken, solidifying *war won ton, moo shoo* pork, and a gelatinous *fettuccini alfredo* that is growing mold greener than *pesto*. It is all starting to make its presence known. Unshaven, unwashed, Taylor has long since started to emit as well. In recognition, in appreciation, a squadron of Blue Angel flies is putting on an air show and circling targets, intrepid Special Force roaches have emerged from the nearest gutter, sent off on exploring expeditions with curious feelers a-wag. You can almost hear them celebrating the booty.

It is dark when he is called to attention by the sirens and the flashing lights — first one set, then another — bringing diesel fumes, shrill skids of steel radials, slammed doors on fleet Crown Victorias. His back aches from the unforgiving floor and he suffers a dull pressure headache. He has forgotten to take his blood pressure meds, is equipped with what his ancient doctor calls, *exquisite sensitivity* — he can feel the silent killer.

He carefully crab walks his way out from under the platform, sits up slowly, and rubs his eyes with his knuckles. He grips the side of the layout, carelessly crushing a chain link fence and the mother and child freeze-walking along side, manages a dizzy uprightness, slogs off to the john, the medicine cabinet, downs a colorful collection of statins and diuretics from the last loaded day of the pill box, and studies the red flashing lights splashing across his mirror and the old, cracked tiles.

He hears static voices, breathy and abrupt, instructions: "Easy now, easy". They intrigue him out of his stupor, compel him to trudge off to the front door and observe from his porch just like Mrs. Gettzleman and the walker lady, and the guy down the street with the hound who is baying at the fire truck and the paramedics. It is as if the neighbors too have been summoned by the roach general, up out of their respective gutters for an evening of adventure, happy conjecture, a social gathering of people who share fences, and an instant block party drawn by the extravaganza over at the Blake's.

A police car with a big rose decal on its doors has come right up onto the perfectly edged dichondra, laying waste to asparagus ferns and birds of paradise. The front door at the Burke's is wide open and people in uniforms are going in and out, while others are firmly requesting that the gathered fans retreat across the street where everybody can enjoy an unobstructed view of the action. First of the principals out is Blake himself, arms drawn behind his back, head down, a large uniformed hand in a vice lock on his elbow, brought over to the low retaining wall that separates lawn from driveway, and set down briskly and with a practiced lack of gentility, so that he is facing Taylor, now peering through the TJ bars on his porch. His faces flashes crimson in the spinning lights.

A female cop comes through the door with a package, a bundle — the baby cooing obliviously in her ear — swaddled tight despite the heat, her hand massaging what must be its back under the pastel pink blanket. Then the gurney speeds in over the three tiled steps, through freshly stuccoed arches, over the threshold, presumably to carry out the wife where she was once carried in. She is wheeled with fluid-bags held aloft, a tube glistening in the porch light and the rotating red flashers, slid into the red and white **ECNALUBMA,** and carried away with a siren's urgency. The hound has about lost his mind by now.

A cop in an unbuttoned sports coat is consulting with a uniform who wields a clip board and occasionally points towards the house or to Blake or to the wagon making haste up the street.

Suddenly Blake's head pops up and scans the crowd. "Semper-fucking-fee-fi-fo-fum, assholes," he yells. "Better fucking turnout than we got at fucking Bethesda, thank you very much."

An officer is cautioning him, upbraiding him. "See over there, Ocifer, sir." Blake is pointing with his chin. "Behind that fucking cheap-ass greaser wrought iron shit I offered to...anyways...where was I? That's my man, Taylorific. See 'im. Taylor's a guy's guy. *The* fucking guy's guy. Tails the man. *El Hombre.* Man with the plan. Head honcho. The big mullah-rulla. The big dawg. I tell you, sir, you can only look and hope. You wanna see what your independent motherfucker can do when he ain't pussy whipped, you go on over with your fucking clip boards and take notes 'till your balls grow back." He is lifted by the cuffs, escorted to the squad car that sits on his lawn lowering property values, cries out, "I love you, you fat schmuck, Taylor Bedshit. Fuckin' King-a-Men. Fuckin' God, sir! Fuckin' God!"

There is pressure on his head and he is squashed down into a back seat and the door slammed shut. Cops are interviewing a few neighbors, taking notes, measuring things, pacing off distances, bullshitting with each other. The woman cop is rocking the baby, gets in shotgun — no car seat, definitely a misdemeanor — while her partner takes the wheel, chokes out a few siren bleats, edges out to clear the crowd. Kids in PJ's, teens making out, a troop of seniors sharing what they know with Mrs. Gettzleman, skate boarders shaking loose zits on a makeshift ramp, a woman snapping pictures with a phone, a man in shorts and nothing else trying to pry news from a mute cop, just about everybody with a cell stuck to the ear or narrating away into little dispatchers mics strapped to their heads like they're Air Traffic Control. Together, they populate the sidewalks. A copter circles, News at Eleven, *thackadathackadathackada.* Another cuts in, shines a monster beam down on Blake's lawn just as Blake himself, crated in the back seat like a chicken on a truck farm, is driven off to get his picture taken: front, side, *say cheese, cocksucker, and then we'll let you make that call.*

Taylor feels ill. Should he have said something? Warned someone? He slumps to a porch swing.

A uniform comes up to the grating, says, "I ask you a few questions?" The face is chiseled, displays a neat mustache that dares not reach below his lips.

"Why?" Taylor says.

"We like to be thorough. Just a minute of your time, okay?"

"I guess."

"How well you know your neighbors?" He nods towards the action as if there might be some question as to which neighbors.

"Not well at all. I'm not a real social guy."

"I see. So you know them a little?"

"No. Not the wife. I mean, I've seen her, of course."

"What about the mister?"

"Just to say *hi* to."

"You never hung out?"

"He came by here a couple of times."

"Inside?"

"Huh? Here? No. I'm really not very social."

"Never? Neighbors, after all. Borrow some sugar, cup of milk, screwdriver?"

"He's a contractor. He has his own tools."

"What about the sugar?"

"I guess the Blakes have their own."

"So you've talked to him?"

"Just in passing. He has his company name on his truck."

"Yes, he does. Can I get your name, sir?"

"Taylor Bedskirt."

"Bedskirt, huh? Don't think I've heard that one. Spelled like it sounds?"

"How does it sound?"

"B-e-d-s-k-i-r-t?"

"That's right."

"So when he came over, what did you two talk about?"

"He really didn't come over."

"I think you said he did."

"No."

"But you knew what he did for a living."

"The truck."

"And he seemed to have a certain...what, admiration for you. You could hear that just now, couldn't you, Mr. Bedshirt?"

"Skirt."

"Yes, *skirt*. Sounds like he thought you were *the man*. So what else did you guys schmooze about? He talk about his marriage at all? He seem angry? Some of these vets are. Not their fault. You ever in the military, sir?"

"No."

"So he's an angry guy, you think?"

"I have trains."

"Uh huh."

"You know, model trains?"

"Yes."

"He came to see them just this once and we talked about the trains."

"Your house is what? Fifteen feet from his? Ten? Just the easement, right? Then the driveway?"

"I don't know."

"Gentlemen on the other side says there were…*sounds* now and then. You must've heard them too."

"No. These houses. Lath and plaster. I generally keep the windows closed and the air on. Quiet as a tomb."

"Oh, I bet. So, like, maybe one day you're taking out the trash or you're kicking it on your lounger in the yard, you hear something. What was that like?"

"I don't really use the yard."

"You do take out the trash?"

"No. I mean, yes."

"I hope it's *yes*. I got my kid that Silverstein book about the girl who never takes out the trash. You know the one?"

"No."

"Well, you wanna take out the trash, believe you me. Look, I'm gonna set my card down here. You think of anything that might indicate domestic troubles between Mr. and Mrs. Blake…well, don't be bashful. You don't need to ask for me. Just tell who ever picks up what you're calling about. I'll write the case number. Will you do that, sir?"

"Sure. If I think of something, though I can't imagine what it might be."

"You don't want to know what happened? I mean, you're out here on the porch along with the rest of Pasadena. Everybody else is asking. Or sharing a theory. But you don't want to know?"

"Isn't that okay?"

"Lack of curiosity? It's not against the law or anything. It's just strange, don't you think, like you've kind of figured out what happened from what's been happening all along? Could that be it? That this kind of thing has happened before?"

"I have no idea."

"Okay then. I see. Here's the card, the number. Don't be a stranger. We're freeway close. Thanks for your time."

The officer folds his notepad and walks off, is met by another cop in Blake's front yard, and tells him, "This end of the block must be at a lower elevation than the other, 'cause, buddy, they're all rollin' this a way!"

Taylor is left wishing that he hadn't listened to Betsy when she told him to mind his own business. As if Betsy, of all people, knew anything about that. There was nothing illegal about his inaction, he supposed. And how could he have known how far Blake would take it all. He barely knew the man; the wife not at all. Still, he was too embarrassed to admit to the officer what he had suspected.

He gets up slowly with a grateful squeak from the swing, and sees Mrs. Gettzleman across the street. He imagines she is acknowledging him in some way: a slight nod, maybe a whispered greeting, secret hand signals, a sequence of blinks, the affirmation that she knows what he is about, how he shunned involvement, how he let this happen. *This is what involvement is,* he thinks, this involuntary sucking in, this gravitational whirlpool of other people's issues, this never ending second guessing and should-have-dones and having to own responsibility for things out of his control. Taylor enjoys a smaller world: one that doesn't judge and ask back, where you can pull yourself up from the underworld and crush an innocent woman and child with impunity.

Inside, he searches for the phone, snaps the cord back into the jack, and dials Cory Ann's number. The line is disconnected. He puts together basics — keys, wallet — slips out the back door to his car and speeds over to Highland Park. The court party is small tonight. There is a young woman with bare midriff who would be more appealing in a muu muu, and two scruffy teens he has seen before, pants low on their asses as if they are an ad for striped boxers.

"Hey, Sgt. Pepper. 'S'up, homie? Bitch's gone, y'know."

Taylor gets up on her porch anyway, knocks, rings the bell which offers hallow echoes around the room, leans over to look in through the window. There is an upright Hoover, a mop and bucket, a can of paint, and nothing more.

"When did she leave?" he says.

"What I look like, *cabrón*, attendance monitor? Bitch's gone. Who gives a shit how long?" The girl is tugging at his sleeve. The other boy is laughing into his *cerveza.*

"Did you see her go?"

"Yeah. We got it on the sky cam. Couple a friends in a van helped with'er shit. *¿Qué pasa*, dude, no *adiós?* You're lucky. Who needs the fuckin' drama, know what I'm sayin'?"

"She say where she was going?"

"*Chinga, pendejo!* Too many *preguntas.* I look like fuckin' Google t'you?"

Lost in the slowly gentrifying barrio, Taylor drives for a while with no purpose. He follows York Blvd., up into the Avenues, back to York and over to Figueroa, until he finds a Bun King. It is costumed in faux Craftsman's river rocks, protruding faux wood beams, posters of faux burgers as big as the steers they supposedly came from. He decides he is thirsty. The drive-thru line looks like the northbound border crossing at Tijuana, a long parade of lowered Datsuns and Chevy Suburbans circling the building and hugging the curb up the block.

Inside, it is nearly empty except for fifteen overweight teens LASER-ing the pre-formed patties. Taylor sees the colorful pictures on the back-lit menu, now decides he is hungry, a sensation he had thought lost forever. He orders a combination of triple burger with triple cheese and a pig's ass worth of rippled bacon smothered in spicy barbeque sauce the color of old motor oil. It comes with fries and a diet Coke. He studies the process of assembling the components; the layering of meat Frisbees; cheese squares, denuded of wax paper partitions that keep them from reproducing; frozen fries; a measured cup of shredded lettuce.

He is number one oh seven eight four two one. They call *twenty-one*. Maybe they don't recognize the rest of the numbers. Maybe they don't have the energy for seven digits, or the ambition. He sits at the plastic table with his plastic tray lined in paper, hefts the triumvirate cheeser, and bites its heart out with grateful relish. The grease goes down like honey, a sweet sense of broiled release with the healing powers of chicken soup, an artery-plugging one man celebration at the end of a long desert crawl, the Lassie-lift from the well, the beam of light and the influx of oxygen in the collapsed shaft, the comforting high ball seen from the locomotive cab.

Here is the fucking king-of-men in the house of the fucking king-of-buns. He is one with his oneness, guiltlessly feeding on everything that's bad for him: in your face, diabetic coma. He is free to wipe his mouth with the back of his large, hirsute hand. Heartily, he breathes in, breathes out, and unabashedly scratches his crotch, performs a sauce-lubed finger adjustment of sour wax in his ear, releases a hearty belch that feels like rebirth, and loudly farts like he's all alone.

And, as it happens, he is.

II

No matter what Betsy's God recommends, Leo refuses to offer up David to the sacrificial altar of shrink or, worse yet, church counselor. "We're not playing Abraham and Isaac here. You're not dropping a C-note so some Austrofile with lacquered diplomas can ask *how does that make you feel* for a full fifty-minute hour. Tell you what, Bets, I'll ask the kid how it makes him feel and I won't charge you a dime." Betsy pleads, cajoles, nags, threatens, almost gets his attention with a rare sex act that may still be illegal in certain southern states, and finally compromises on a visit to the school counselor.

Sierra Academy is an upscale Pasadena private school that occupies a classic old Greene and Greene in a neighborhood of proud trees and old money. Leo has bought David in with a generous donation to the Land Acquisition Fund — Sierra has it's covetous eyes on three adjacent properties — and David has contributed some exceptional scores in a battery of entrance exams that should get him into Stanford as well. "New money can be laundered into old through the ringer of a large playing field", Leo boasts. "If you pay for it, they will enroll."

Harry Pleck's quaint, dark space was once a carriage house, then a pantry for a mother-in-law suite, now charades as a head master's office from an English boarding school where children are unmentionably cruel and everyone is experimenting in homoeroticism. It has exposed wood beams and a dumbwaiter, the only thing of that description in the entire school.

Harry has a teaching credential and a license to do social work. He is an easygoing guy who likes the kids and who is liked back. Thirty, thirty-five, middle American white, he's nurtured thinning blond hair, a sleek athletic frame that has chucked a bale or two in its day, well-proportioned hands firmed at the udder, and a level slit of mouth parallel to the flat horizon he has come from. An altogether nice looking Methodist with a kind demeanor, he enjoys the equalizing quality of sitting on the same side of the desk as his visitors. He offers coffee or milk, depending: a soda if he's feeling particularly risqué.

Counselor Pleck believes strongly in the eclectic nature of the human mind, believes in whole child guidance, a variety of learning experiences in as many disciplines as possible. He decries the stifling test-oriented curriculum with its political appeal and the specialized focus geared away from the production of learned citizens. *We learn in order to know, not for the buck,* he tells recent inductees, staff and pupils alike. *We are here because of the inherent value of knowledge. All else follows naturally.* On one wall, between hand-tinted glass sconces, are hundreds of sketched portraits from "The New York Review of Books" — serious Eastern European authors arm to arm with Naipul, Henry Roth, José Saramago, Amos Oz — united by literature and a bristling network of map tacks.

"So you're little David's folks," he says, as if to remind them. They are seated in a triangulated circle with Harry's desk behind the Valverdes.

"What makes you think that?" Leo deadpans.

"I'm going to have to ask you to forgive my husband. Because *I* won't. He thinks he's auditioning to host the Oscars. Always." There is an almost imperceptible adjustment of her jaw, noticeable only by the molecules it displaces. Harry and Leo feel the chill. "Of course, you're correct," Betsy adds with haste. "I'm Betsy Valverde, and this man is David's father, Leo." They have already touched hands. Her phrasing cracks like expanding ice.

"Call me Harry. Betsy and Leo okay with you guys?" He is cast in baggy tweeds, loafers, an old sweater vest he shares with moths. There is actually a pipe propped up on the ashtray behind him.

"Tell the truth," says Leo, "I'm partial to Buck or Rock, Skeeter's good too, but my parents were old fashioned." It earns him a mild reproach from Betsy's pointed toe.

"That's very good. *Buck or Rock* Valverde. I like that. Think of getting stuck with a moniker like Harry. A guy like me losing his hair. I'll be Harry the Hairless before long. The kids don't let you off the hook. So what can I help you with?"

Betsy assumes earnestness. "We're concerned about David."

"Correction. She is."

"You're not concerned about your son?"

"Are we talking *concerned* caring, or *concerned* worried?"

"Of course, you're a caring family. No one who didn't care would put up with our enrollment gauntlet if they weren't. Not exactly like a membership to Costco, is it now? Mug shot and you're in. Nope. We don't start at first base here."

Betsy cringes at the baseball analogy. She's starting to feel hemmed in. "I'm worried, yes. He's such an…unusual boy."

"That's a good thing. Not to blow our own horn, but if he were ordinary, you'd be playing the lottery to get him into the public school of your choice. We don't do *ordinary* here at Sierra."

"I'm sure you have a population of very special students." She wants to be agreeable, to win him over, to have him join enthusiastically in David's castigation. Or, as Leo wonders, is this about David at all?

"All students are *special*. Sleeping beauties. Each and every one. Ours are just *more* special. All of them."

"I know. Yes, of course. We did considerable research before applying. But even within that context, David, God love 'im, is…I'd say…as his mother who adores him…well, you know, *strange*." She has inched forward, lowered her tone, become conspiratorial.

Harry squeaks back in the desk chair he has wheeled around from behind the desk, locks his hands behind his neck with his elbows splayed like the compass points: two of them, the points. "How so?"

Leo shakes his head. "My wife tends toward the hysteric. David's a normal, special kid."

"Quite frankly, Betsy, I would tend to agree with Leo here. I plowed through his cum and I find him quite the young scholar. Surely you've seen the progress reports, the teacher's comments. He's never been referred for disciplining. Homework's always in on time. Teachers all like him. Some actually rave. All in all, a credit to the school. And at this school, that's saying something."

Betsy squirms in her seat, feels like she's testifying against her own child, will have his sentence on her conscience at the end of days. "But he behaves so oddly sometimes. And he has no friends. Not that we know of."

"Nor enemies, apparently. He's not the kind of kid that gets nudged in the hallways. Not the butt of abuse that children can sometimes sink to. I'd say, a content, well-adjusted young man with remarkable potential. And at Sierra, we're all about potential. You know, if you can shine here…Harvard, Yale, watch the heck out, ha, ha!"

"He's in the fourth grade," Betsy points out.

"Not forever."

"One hopes," Leo says.

Betsy clears her throat. Her lips are constricting like quicksand around her concerns. There are little wrinkle lines, almost corduroy with lip-gloss. "I'm sure all that's true. But shouldn't a boy have friends?"

Harry shrugs as if he's never thought of that. "If he wants them, I guess. Does he appear to you…lonely, depressed, moody? At home, I mean? I've spoken to staff, and none of that seems to come up here."

"Well, no. He doesn't. But I should think he would."

"I'd think you'd be delighted he wouldn't."

"Told'er," Leo tells them. His finger marks one on an invisible scoreboard.

"He has an older brother. Steven. Steven has a million friends."

"Steven's not particularly…what's the word? Cerebral," Leo adds.

"What, smart people can't have friends?" Betsy protests. "Steven's bright enough, really. Maybe Sierra's not a match for him, but he's certainly got a good head on his shoulders."

"I'm sure he does." Harry comforts, though he has no idea.

"Actually," Leo admits, "he's kind of a slacker at the moment, the victim of his pubescent demons."

"Well, weren't we all?" Harry clears his throat, conscious that he may have just confessed to something sinister in his past. "Betsy, tell me, is it because Steven has friends that you think David should have them?"

"What are you asking? Shouldn't *everybody* have friends?"

"How about you and Leo? You seem to be reasonably congenial folks. Do you have a wide circle of friends?"

"Well, we're not a family of hermits!" It is a statement borne on spittle. "Of course, we have friends. And all of our friends have friends."

"Of course. They have you." His pencil-line lips quiver with his own cleverness.

"And their children have friends. That's normal. Isn't it?"

"That's *usual*. Different thing entirely."

"How can you be happy without friends?"

"I couldn't tell you. I have friends. I'm thinking, you need to ask David. He seems happy without them."

"You're saying it's okay for him to be alone?"

"Yep. If it's okay with him. And if he's not lonely. We don't all have the same needs. If David's content in himself, with himself, well…even people with friends can't always claim contentment."

"Human interaction. Connection. What about that?"

"He has you. Steven. He's very conversant with the staff. Seems to fill his bucket."

"Bucket?" Betsy is leaning forward now, Harry farther back. "We're talking about a young boy who barely ever sees sunlight. Like an earthworm. Who'd rather surf Wikipedia than throw a ball."

"Throwing balls is overrated. A fine thing for people who enjoy it, I guess. Should David throw balls because that's what the other kids do?"

"He should throw balls so that the other kids can catch them. Maybe throw them back."

Leo informs, "Dogs can catch balls. Right, Harry?"

"Have you really talked to David? Do you know him?" she asks.

"Oh, yes. Many times. We're all about knowing the kids. Really knowing them. We have a very small student population. As you've seen, we're extremely selective."

"Do you have conversations? Or does he just share obscure facts no one really needs to know?"

"Well, now that you mention it, the other day," Harry chuckles. "he stopped me in the hall to tell me, and get this, that Peruvian Indians high in the Andes once subsisted mostly on potatoes seasoned with ground limestone."

"That's normal?"

"For the Indians?"

"For David? For a young boy?"

"It's not *ab*normal. Unusual, yes, but nothing to worry about. I'm not a clinical psychologist or anything like that. But I've worked with a heck of a lot of kids. Look, we had one kid here that collected license plates. Carried around several at all times. Nice kid. Very articulate. Another child was an expert on walking sticks, you know, the insect. Knew every variety. Had a collection under glass. Learned to dissect them. Hand her a grasshopper, a housefly, a carpenter bee, she wouldn't give it the time of day. Some kids can memorize all the presidents in order. Some can give you baseball scores back to the game the White Sox threw with Shoeless Joe. *Say it ain't so, Joe?* You remember, 'Darn Yankees'? I've seen kids memorize the capitals of all the countries in the world just because it gives them some sort of satisfaction. And the things these kids can do with computers! Don't even go there."

"Okay. Capitals, scores, presidents. These are things kids understand. Even license plates. They're everywhere, right. But David, I'll bet, doesn't even know what limestone is or how it could possibly have some nutritional value. Frankly, I don't either. Not in one of the food groups as I understand them. He's just parroting the facts without understanding anything."

"Actually," instructs Harry, "we're learning that parrots really do understand the words they use. There was an article in <u>Geographic</u> recently. Did you see it?"

"You're distracting me."

"Am I? Sorry. It's just that here at Sierra, we like to go with the cues. If this was a class, say, right now, here, we'd ask, oh, maybe, *why parroting?* As a verb. What's the derivation? We're all dissectors here."

"Well, Harry, dissect this," says Betsy. She has adopted a *tone.* "Why are facts more important to my child than relationships?"

"I can only offer you conjecture. Hopefully, educated conjecture." He nods towards his diplomas, unreadable in the glare of the ceiling fixture. "My best guess is that the facts keep him company. Maybe the facts are his friends. And those of us who listen to him repeat them are his friends by extension. It's the facts themselves, see, the feat of memorizing them, that gets his adrenalin flowing. In time, I'm sure, this aspect of your son will evolve into something that will seem to you a more productive application of his talents. But now, he's a child, and though, I think, a very special child, like all of our pupils, he does things, albeit not the expected things, the way a child usually does. And in that, he is very, as you say, *normal.* Gosh, Mom, Dad, am I making sense?"

There are no takers.

He goes on. "Do you worry about…Steven, is it?…Do you worry about Steven as well?"

Leo rolls his eyes as Betsy smiles knowingly, and says, "There's not much to worry about on that score."

"As a mother. You know. My mother worried over me about things that never happened, weren't even in the cards. Just because."

"Let's get real, folks," says Leo. He has given his forehead a light tap with his open palm. "With Stevie, see, you worry about everybody else. The kid's a crazed sperm factory, a zit field of triggered craters ready to blow with pent up human fluids. We don't worry about Steven, huh, Betsy? We're like, let *their* mothers worry!"

Pleck offers a paternal smile. It is dismissive, a much-to-do-about-nothing gesture, suggesting he has switched to his we-are-reaching-the-end-of-our-little-discussion mode. Leo has learned that the mention of sperm at parent-school conferences can be a game breaker.

"Gee, Betsy," Pleck says, "I don't know what you want me to tell you, but I find David to be a very well adjusted young man and my recommendation, for what ever it's worth, is to just let him evolve into who ever he is."

"Isn't he already who he is?"

"Well, by definition, I suppose. I stand corrected. Into who he will become."

"We, his parents, have no role in that?"

"Of course you do. It's called DNA."

As they maneuver into their seat belts, Betsy asks, "The hell was that in there?" She has her face to the side window, and though he can't see the gestating pout, he knows it's there: can hear it pucker and swell, a malaise upon the land.

"You didn't like the guy? I thought he was okay," Leo says.

"Of course, *you* liked him! Me? I didn't go there to like him. I'm feeling ambushed. Should I?"

"I don't know what you mean."

"Did you call him first? You two work out a game plan?"

"You're kidding, right?"

"You were like what's-her-name's father and Charlie McCarthy. *Maybe the facts are his friends!* Vintage fucking Leo, you ask me. You're so damned smug."

"How would you know? You're not looking at me."

She turns forward, still doesn't look at him. "You stink of smugness, Skeeter."

"Next time I hit the car wash, I'll have them change the air freshener. Maybe they've got Contrition, Humility." He works the silent car out into traffic. "Look, there, right now...I'm getting what, sixty, sixty-five." Betsy hates to converse with him when they are in the Prius. The car is selfish, insecure, demands all of his attention. He is constantly referring to the mpg indicator, adjusting his driving, his braking, so he can later email other hybrid junkies and tell them how well he has done. Never mind that it takes him twice as long to get anywhere, that he generally has a fleet of horn punchers on his sloping tail, that some of them are armed just in case the opportunity presents itself to bag a guy with a car pool lane sticker, dress the Toyota right their on the shoulder, and strap the meat to the hood for dinner and taxidermy.

She says, "If you get *seventy*-five for two fucking seconds, so fucking what?"

"We drive with the law of averages, Bets. Some day, I will achieve that penultimate millisecond when I will, in the blink of an eye, get the best mileage anyone has ever gotten. Anyway, I need to make up for the fact that my spouse is draining Kuwait dry clumping about town in an amphibious attack vehicle that ekes a rousing two miles per."

He refers to the SUV. It has a bumper sticker that says, JESUS WOULD HAVE A BIGGER FAMILY CAR BECAUSE THE WHOLE WORLD IS HIS FAMILY. Little white cutouts of Leo, herself and the boys are lined up on the rear window over their names. Such postings, Leo rails, "are endorsed by pedophile support groups." She defends, "These days, a family needs a big car."

"When we were kids, folks had bigger families and smaller cars. The kids aren't any bigger! So what's the deal?"

"Every contemporary family has a big car. Kids have a lot more shit to carry around these days."

"Yeah, if they're the Jonas Brothers, they have amps and roadies and such, but our two, moderately-sized kids?"

"They have car pools. Friends to lug around."

"Not David!"

"I don't want to talk about cars any more."

"I didn't start. I was talking about mileage, not cars."

"Again, I say, so fucking what? You're just all about diversion."

On the way home, chagrinned Betsy accuses smug Leo of secretly increasing his contribution towards the purchase of the Spanish revival villa adjacent to the school or of promising access to his box at Staples. Leo tells her to worry about climate change, the Middle East, the poor folks who inhabit the mangrove swamps of Myanmar, "Something real, Hon."

"Did Taylor call you back?"

"Inflation in Zimbabwe, the Roberts court, the abduction of women in Juarez."

"After all these years, I still don't understand why everything has to be a joke to you, Benito."

"Nothing particularly funny about any of those things. But, humor does have its advantages. And it's a helluva lot better than despondency. Look, maybe, in some ways, it's better not to need friends." A Grand Marquis is honking impatiently into his tailpipe. "Asshole!" he says.

"People who need people are…"

"Thank you, Barbra. Look, don't get me wrong. I have lots of friends, as you know. I love my friends. Well, some of them. I love having friends. That's because having them's part of my make-up. I'm a guy who needs friends. But having friends isn't always a piece of cake. First of all, they cost a lot of money because you're expected to go out with them. And what do you do when you go out? You eat. You can't fucking talk to friends unless your mouth's full of *tapas* or *dim sum*. No one's friends just want to go out for a walk up the block just to talk. Or, you go to the show, where you can't talk anyway, or a play in some crappy little theater with a one stall unisex john so you spend the whole intermission in line waiting for the old guy with the prostate to have a little consideration. If you didn't have friends, you wouldn't be in that line. You'd be home with the flat screen and a snack, and when you had to take a leak you'd TiVo whatever's on and choose from any number of fine toilets with European fixtures and disinfected by a Mexican on a far lower rung than you yourself. Or myself, anyway. Friends have problems, and then you have their problems if you're any kind of a caring guy. Like you don't have problems of your own! Friends come down with things, have things removed, and you gotta show your face in the hospital, a place you never, ever want to go to begin with. With no friends, you only go there when you need to. And then they die. They fucking die and you have to put on a suit and go listen to some asshole who's spent all of fifteen minutes with the family making sense out of a life he's had absolutely no contact with. Cemeteries are the places you don't want to go more than hospitals. When you go there, you want to go when you don't know you're going. Hospitals, cemeteries and the DMV. With no friends, you'd only have to be conscious at the DMV. Bad enough, right? When my old man was in the hospital with the bypass, there was this constant stream of people 'cause he was a gregarious old guy. It blew him away, knowing they came. Knowing they cared. Knowing they were missing 'Bonanza' so they could bring a little light into his life. He was very grateful. And he couldn't wait for them to go away. He told me so. He looked like shit and felt like something even less attractive. Tubes up the yazoo, steel wire keeping his chest together, pain like a motherfucker, and so stoned on morphine he's having conversations with Poncho Villa whose in the next bed with hemorrhoids. Poncho says, *I shoulda had the federales shoot them out,* then proceeds to seduce and marry all the nurses right in front of Papa who can't even get up to pee. And this is going on in the next bed, and he's got the Serillos bringing him *flan,* the Trujillos showing him the latest pictures of *mija's* daughter out of wedlock, and the Tapias making plans to take him river rafting on the Kern. Who needs it? A guy with a tube up his dick does not want to float a tube down the Kern! You know, I envy our little guy. He won't have to do all that shit. Listen to the stories, comfort the criers, loan them money, get them laid. Shit, Betsy, when you have friends, you're like some community service agency you would never think to patronize yourself. 'M'I making any headway?"

"That's the biggest crock I've ever heard."

"Not enough wool to pull over those big peepers of yours, hon."

"You're so full of shit, Reynoldo!"

"They gotta store it somewhere. Nevada doesn't want it. So what's the plan for the rest of the day?"

"I think I'm depressed. Before I slit my wrists, I'm gonna need to have something with three scoops and about sixteen ounces of whipped cream."

"A little glob of Red Two on the top to keep the planes from crashing into it?"

"You have long ago approached your last cherry, Humberto. Find the soda fountain before I fling my body from the car."

Leo could call Suicide Prevention on his cell, instead heads for the retro soda fountain in South Pasadena. As he pulls up to the curb, he says, "Not a bad theory, though. And I think it works for David." He gets out of the car, turns to see if Betsy is out yet so that he can hit the remote, notices she's reclined her seat, has a forearm over her eyes. He opens his door again. "Bets? Coming?"

"This works for you?" she says. "This Harry guy? A kid doesn't need friends unless he needs them? The fuck is that, Leo?"

"Tell you what. Like Harry says, why don't we just let David grow up as he is and see who he turns out to be? If, upon reaching his majority, he becomes Taylor, or anything remotely resembling Taylor, well, then..."

"Well then what?"

Sheepishly, a tilt of head, a squint, a deep shrug hoisting shoulders all the way up to his ears, Leo says, "You win?"

"What exactly is the prize?"

"Your wish is my command, princess."

"For one, keep David away from that fucking train you've got spilling toxic fluids in my garden."

"But, he's helping me. We're having fun."

Betsy thinks of her father, the endless trestle photo ops with Taylor. "Don't get me started, Ponchito."

"You *don't* want him to go outside?"

"Skin cancer. Look at the Australians. And he's allergic to bees."

"All of which pales in comparison to the threat of...*r-a-i-l-s.*"

"You got it, wise ass. Let's get that sundae before I go into withdrawal."

And they do — Taylor-sized, two spoons, a dish the size of a canoe — a trough really, three gi-mungus scoops, the Grand Tetons in winter, chocolate syrup gushing like Spindletop, sprinkles in a Benjamin Moore of color, little jagged nuggets of nuts, and, of course, three of the last cherries extant on this most promiscuous of planets.

III

TAYLOR LABORS SEVERAL DAYS TO CLEAN the house and make it habitable for generations of pressure-molded Americans. It is a chore delayed too long, even for a man of such minimal hygienic discrimination.

He carts out fat black trash bags that would have brought joy to the questioning officer in, what Taylor has come to call, "the Blake thing." They are jammed full of cartons and flat tray boxes with corners jutting through the plastic. He becomes drum major to a parade of mourning flies, stuffs the garbage bins to overflowing with little regard for segregating refuse and recyclables — he will keep this lapse secret from Leo — removes all items in the refrigerator that appear datable only by carbon fourteen techniques or show evidence that they have evolved into other life forms entirely.

He sweeps, he vacuums, he crawls on his belly like a reptile, scrubbing floors, even under the vast platform that wends from room to room. He punishes the waterline out of the toilet bowl, applies grout cleaner to tile joints, lays waste to haphazard cob webs, exiles tub stains, even does a bacteria purge of the phone.

He buys aerosols of Raid dedicated to particular pests — one for ants, one for roaches — that seems not to discriminate against the water bugs, hangs fly paper in the doorways and windows, connects an electric zapper to the front porch to entertain the moths, spends an entire afternoon big game hunting with a brand new swatter that is quickly bent and battered to uselessness and soaking in indiscriminate carnage. He runs out to Ralph's to pick up a half dozen more: to beat the invaders senseless, smear their little bodies onto surfaces that will then be Lysol-ed until he can eat off of them — the surfaces — sucks the corpses into his mother's old drag-along Electrolux with its deco chrome panels, inserts the flex hose in the ass end and blows dust off the layout, above and below, and for good measure sets several rat and mouse traps generously laden with Skippy's Chunky Style, even though he has seen neither rodents nor droppings.

He bundles clothing from his unimaginative wardrobe up off the floor, sets them to spin in the aging Kenmore, *hot-cold, extra high,* rearranges them when the washer loudly complains of overloading. When he is done, a man like Blake might say there is almost a woman's touch to the sparkle of the place, his betrayed estimation of Taylor sinking like the *Andrea Doria.*

Then Taylor showers. It is a good long skin-puckering baptism. He details cracks and crevices like they do cars at the hand wash; scrubs and scrapes the undisciplined flesh that overhangs natural borders with a zest of eradication. Dirt off, stink off, guilt off, moping regret off off off, he watches the last week of pain suppression swirl down the drain like Janet Leigh's blood. You can almost hear the screeching strings of Bernard Hermann. Afterwards, he scrubs down the shower, even gets a toothpick, undulating walrus-naked to the kitchen and back, to clean out the shower head holes. He dries, he combs, he shaves off the ridiculous affectation of beard and leaves the sparse stubble on his scalp, anoints his underarms with aluminum chlorohydrates, clips nose hairs, gargles and spits, and shines like a newborn.

It is time to tackle the layout.

Though not given to philosophical insight, and despite odd manners that cause him to diminish in the minds of others, Taylor is not a stupid man. Ignorance he hoards aplenty, but what he does know he has more than mastered. So it is no surprise to him to note that while the natural world, left to its own devices, tends to thrive, the built world is another thing entirely. It is prone to disconnections, expansion and contraction, all manner of decay and wear; it fades, it splinters, it clogs up with gunk; parts fall off or inexplicably cease to perform designated functions; it corrodes, it anodizes, it peels and congeals; it cracks, it weakens; it sucks; things uninvited knock it down; it dents, it scratches, it suffers from viruses as if it contained living organisms; it blows away, it blows up, it burns down; it suffers the debilitation of dust and grime; it spills; it looses the age old battle against gravity; it sometimes just breaks.

Taylor has a great deal of penance to perform in order to assuage his sins of omission. One can only assume that the Master of the Universe is on call twenty-four seven. One can see it here at work. So much for your day of rest.

He organizes his tools: tweezers, needle nose pliers, strap-on magnifier, miniature screw drivers, camel hair artist's brushes, probes, soldering gun, drills and bits, knives and saws. He puts them all into an easily identifiable progression for use. He cleans first, light feather brush where possible, air can elsewhere. He removes the battered section of mountain concussed by the flying shoe, re-glues the tilted steeple, performs emergency CPR — not to be confused with Canadian Pacific Railway — on the mother and child and tools a new fence for them to pass by. There are several trains to be united with rails, WD-40 to lubricate the orbit of sun and moon.

And when he is done, several happy days later, after re-forming the firmament over the waters, and waters under the firmament, and separating the waters from the dry land, and setting the days and nights alight on their trams, and placing all the non-living things in the earth and on the earth, and seeing everything that he has made, he decides, it is good. And, if you were watching, which he won't let you do, and because you are made in his image, you'd probably think it was good too.

⁂

Retreating to his workbench, he mends the open platform of a Pullman parlor car. This was the car he brought home that — like the butterfly in Africa that eventually destroyed the Ninth Ward — initiated the storm that caused Helen to loose her tenuous hold on lucidity, and several hours later decide to take the car and the pills and make a whole lot of folks late for work. *Just what we need,* she screamed, *another fucking toy train! Where are you going to put it? Why did you need it? How much did that piece of shit set us back?* That was the beginning, the overture with its preview of thematic material to come. It escalated, crescendo-ed, set the hair he still had on end, sent chills with bumps up his arms, made him breath in, breath out. She said, *I can't fucking do this any more. I can't spend my life with people no bigger than toes. I need some human interaction. Some warmth. I have nothing. Absolutely nothing.* And he said, *You have me.* And she replied, *You are less than nothing.* In the morning, for all we really know of such things, she would be considerably closer to nothing than Taylor.

A knock on the front gate rescues him from the specter of Helen.

"Who could this be?" he says aloud, putting down the resurrected coach. He takes a quick sip of his Diet Coke, and walks cautiously to the door, peers through the peephole, can barely make out the small form behind the exterior bars. "Who is it?" he calls.

Something is mumbled.

"I can't hear you."

Something is mumbled louder.

Reluctantly, he opens the door, just inches, figuring that actual confrontation will be the best way to rid himself of the nuisance. "Yes? Can I help you?"

"It's me."

Who's me?

"Blake's wife. From next door." No name: just *Blake's wife.*

He swings the door wider. She was right: it is Blake's wife. He says, "I thought it was political. Or, you know, someone asking for money."

"I have your mail," she says, slipping some bills and a supermarket flier through the bars. "I put the baby down finally, so I thought I'd just slip on over for a minute and give you these."

She waits quietly, perhaps for him to let her in. Instead, he squeezes through the doorway, shuts the door behind him, comes out on the porch, and faces her through the wrought iron. She is bruised, displays the fossils of stitches that trail up her face like track symbols on a map, her face ashen and unhappy. She wears no make up, has cropped her hair like Joan of Arc, looks drawn and emaciated, a weak little thing in a rumpled Hello Kitty t-shirt and blue jeans, barefoot, her soles black like tar.

He thanks her, and she says, "No problem." There is a pause; they share an intimate moment of indecision. "Well, how are you doing?" Even before he finishes, he is sorry he asked, doesn't really want to know.

She shrugs. "Okay, I guess." She works through a mumble, credit of an unbending scab on her lip. "It's pretty weird. I just had this thought...us talking like this...that the last two men I've spoken to were behind bars. Funny, huh?"

"Oh, yes. I guess. I'm not the one to ask about funny. Do you need anything?"

"That's nice. No. What I need, I don't think you keep over here."

"Well, if you do..." he says, wondering what mischief has gotten into him now.

"Yeah, sure. I'll keep it in mind. Anyway, my Mom's helping me out while... She's helping me out."

"Great to have a mom," he replies stupidly.

"Oh, it is. I don't know what I'd do without her right now. You're Taylor, right?"

"Yes. Taylor Bedskirt."

"I don't know why I asked. Of course, I read the name on the mail."

"Okay then, thanks. I've got to get back. Big project. I'm right in the middle."

"Oh, sure. Hope I didn't disturb anything."

"No, no, not at all. It's just that...You're sure you're okay?"

"Oh, me. I'm good. Yeah. Do you want to know what he said?"

"Who? What who said?"

"Tony. You probably know him as Blake. He tells people, just Blake."

"I don't know. Was it meant for me to hear?"

"No. But it's about you. He said that you're the luckiest man in the world."

"He said that?"

"Yes, he did. More than once."

"About me? You're sure?"

"Oh, yes. About you."

"Well, thank you for telling me...I guess."

"No biggie. Can I ask you something?"

"A question?"

"Questions are what people usually ask, aren't they?"

"Not usually of me."

"Are you the luckiest man in the world, Taylor Bedskirt?"

"Well, I never gave it much thought...In the whole world? I don't know. Yes. Yes. Well, maybe I am. Who knows?"

"I never see anyone else here. Not that I'm prying or anything. You see people come and go up and down the street. But not here. Are you married?"

"Oh, no, no. I was. Quite some time ago."

"Didn't work out, huh?"

"Kind of. She died, actually. But also, it didn't work out. And then she died."

"Enjoy your luck, Taylor Bedskirt. Don't let the envy of others go to your head."

Across the street, Mrs. Gettzleman, strategically ensconced behind pearl inlaid opera glasses, says to herself, *Third broken fly in the web. What a dirty old spider! And with the hubby just off to the farm to hammer rocks!*

IV

THE NEXT MORNING BRINGS THE CHEER of sunshine, a vista of the San Gabriels nearly smog-less. The newly-crowned Luckiest-Man-in-the-World makes the short hop over to the High Ball. He's feeling a bit tenuous here today, a reduction to guest status, not entitled to the designated spaces in the lot. He parks his scruffy behemoth down the street at an hour meter, and four quarters lighter — an Illinois, a Wyoming, a Rhode Island and one vigilant raptor — proceeds up the street past the Dining Car. Enrique sees him through smudged glass, and calls out, "Tailpipes, *cómo está?*" Taylor, annoyed, finds himself beckoned to the doorway.

"You jus' gonna walk by — 'thought sayin' hey? Where ya been, fool? Toby's been askin' if you been in here."

Taylor stands in Enrique's doorway, shuffles his feet, anxious to move on. "Got busy with some stuff. I was just off to see Toby." His eyes measure the room; a couple with soup bowls, a man reading The Times over a plate of rye crust and a cup of coffee.

"So, bro. How's it hangin'?"

"Okay...I guess. How are you?"

"Same ol', same ol'. So, you eatin'? Y'want companionship, I gotta kick-ass *basura burrito* stays with ya for the next month."

"No, just need to take care of some business next door. Place is kind of empty."

"Whadda I care? I ain't on no commission."

Taylor hesitates, tries to capture an essence of nonchalance, leans in the door frame, absently scans the signed photos of local TV Hundai salesmen, a realtor in a red jacket, a guy who had a one liner on a sitcom that lasted three episodes in the days of "Maverick." He says, "So, uh, where's...the...you know?"

"Easy come, easy go. Beats me. You know how they are. What's that old song, 'Blowin' in the Wind?' Like fuckin' candy wrapper litter on the shoulder a life! Know what I'm sayin'? Particularly that one! No offense, bro. They got a new chick comin' in this afternoon. I think this afternoon. Maybe, maybe tomorrow. Someone said she was handicapped. Hope she was born 'thout no mouth. Me an' my retard nephew been holdin' down the fort 'till last week. *Mi hermana,* you know, she texas me, like right in the middle a the fuckin' lunch rush like I'm on *siesta* or somethin', an' I can like read the tears, see, says he got mixed up in some bad shit. Like what's new? Huh? Seems his PO violated his dumb ass right there in that discontinuation school they got for punks like him. I ain't mad at her, see, 'cause I seen what she put up with tryin' to raise the little shit, but, with the bitch gone, and him in juvie, I'm bustin' my ass here. I guess you two ain't a thing no mores."

Taylor can only shrug. "I'm going to go see Toby."

"*Mira,* homie." Enrique is hesitant, braces his feet behind the counter. "You an' me, man, we're cool, right?"

Taylor works a brief smile. "Okay."

"*Mira,* was like this, see. I saw you comin' at me, I'm thinkin', shit, fuckin' deer in the old headlights, car broke down on the tracks. Taylor the wailer, in motion, comin' my way like *el toro diablo.* Y'know what I'm sayin', *no?*"

"Oh, yes, I know." He hears Helen hissing in his ear. "I'm sorry about all that. Don't know what came over me," he says.

"Betcha don't! Look, man, sometimes I gotta mouth on me. I shouldn'a said what I did. All the race shit? Kind a gets to ya. Y'know, the bitch wasn't really that bad. Sometimes she got stuck up, like she was all that an' all. But, she was okay. We got under each other's skin, but, it didn't mean nothin'."

"The bitch?"

"I don't mean, like, the *bitch* kinda bitch. Just a bitch...a chick, you know, man."

"I'm going to go see..."

"Yeah, yeah, *amigo.* My man Tobias. *No problema.* You know, the whole thing was 'cause a that dickhead Darouche."

"Yes. Okay."

"You believe he came in here couple a times after. The *cajones* on that fool! After what went down. He ast if I seen you. I act like he ain't even there. Fuck him, right?"

"Okay."

"'T's'all good, bro."

Taylor thinks, *yes, it is. And getting better.*

The store is nearly as quiet as the cafe. Toby himself is behind the counter, checking a spread in <u>O Gauge Magazine</u> and looking distracted. "Well, would you look what Chessie dragged in," he says as the door activates five seconds of recorded train sounds. He doesn't look overjoyed to see Taylor. "Thought I saw you drive by. You've still got the clunker, I see. Would've thought you'd've euthanized the poor thing by now."

"Hello, Toby."

"Hello yourself. I've burned through a cell phone battery calling you. You out of town, or what?"

"Yeah. Kind of."

"You were kind of out of town?"

"Kind of."

"Okay, so it's none of my business. What happened to Cory Ann? I thought maybe you two had run off together or something."

"Oh, no. We just sort of...you know."

"No, I don't think I do, but if you want to tell me sometime, I'm not a bad listener."

Taylor pretends to look over some new S gauge stock, asks casually, "So, what did you decide? About the computer thing? I guess you gave it to..."

"You're kidding, right? Can you imagine that lunatic working with the public?"

"But you said..."

"I say a lot of things. I'm feeling the pressure of fiscal desperation. I thought it would motivate you. Christ, Nightstick! Give me a break! I know twenty other guys I'd give it to before that nutcase."

Taylor glances around the room, advances to the counter while Toby has returned to his magazine. "So how's the store?"

"What you see is what you see. More action at Forest Lawn. I'm not going to make the rent and the utilities this month. Not unless I dredge some pretty deep pockets. I had to lay off the kid, but still..."

"Barry?"

"No. I had to lay off my own kids. Things are that bad in the world. They're out pounding the streets right now, lugging resumes, looking for new parents. Of course, Barry?"

"How come?"

"*How come?* This is the part where I'd say, if I was talking to anyone else, *you're kidding, right? How come* is that there are a total of about thirty-five octogenarians who still regard the steam engine with a certain degree of nostalgia, and they're selling off their stuff on eBay so their widows won't be burdened with it. *Thinning the collection,* they call it. What it's thinning is my next downhill in Mammoth, the family's traditional Carnival cruise to Ensenada. Looking like Community College for the kids. And then, there's this recession thing. I don't know when we're going to see the end of that little bump in the road. I tell you, Taylor, and I've told you before, the only way to keep my head above water in this biz, in these kinds of times, is to go on line. There's no overhead to speak of and you have an international audience. Wife's breathing down my neck too. Wants to turn the back room into a Thai massage or something. You in for the big change-a-roo?"

"You still want me?"

"Not really. You've been sort of unreliable. Truth is, though, my back's against the wall. The twenty other guys don't want it. So, who else am I going to get? You don't take it, I'm closing down and going into plumbing fixtures. Everyone flushes, right?"

"What do you know about plumbing fixtures?"

"Jesus Lord, Taylor! I see you weren't off to Oz to beg a sense of humor. Look, I want you to meet a guy I know does web site design. Kind of a nerd. You'll like him. Come in tomorrow, we'll have some lunch and map this thing out. My treat."

"I'd rather avoid next door."

"Of course. Too rich for these times anyway. If I dip into the till as a business expense, expect nothing classier than the roach coach after its pickup at the animal shelter."

"I like the truck," Taylor says.

Toby closes the magazine, taps on its cover, offers Taylor a weary smile. "Look, I didn't mean to bite your head off. But you should have called."

Taylor runs his hand across his broad pate, as if he is searching for something gnawing at his flesh. "I had a problem."

"Yeah, well, welcome to Earth."

"I'm okay now."

"Glad to hear it. See, when you popped in just now, well...you got me at a bad time. Luck of the draw...yours. Business is in the crapper and I didn't foresee this happening about now. I guess I've been lax in padding the nest. Anyway, it gives me kind of a vulnerable feeling."

"Okay."

"Is it? Okay? Yeah, well, who hasn't got problems?" Their hands reach across the magazine, across the counter, Toby initiating, Taylor's hesitant brush locked in Toby's velvet grip. They are both tentative but resigned, and the thing is consumated.

V

MRS. GETTZLEMAN SLIDES THE TWO OPEN-FACE melted cheese sandwiches from the yard sale toaster oven, sets them on the tray with the thrift shop Seattle World's Fair teacup, brimming with tea and an opaque clump of honey. She is not supposed to have the honey — there is some medical rational — but since she has outlived her last two physicians, she considers their advice theoretical at best. Despite some minor palsied annoyance of fingers that have enjoyed better grasps, she balances the tray well enough to reach her roll top in the center of the living room, and set it carefully down so as not to trouble her stacks of papers in manila files.

Her living room is tailored to be exactly that, a place where she does most of her living, crammed as it is with, besides the big desk, her bed, her dresser, a couch, a twenty-one inch TV on a wheeled cart, an armoire, and assorted oddments discarded at estate sales, garage cleanouts, or set out with the trash under hand-made signs proclaiming, FREE. Most of the large pieces have cats reposing on them, some porcelain, others made from the usual genetic material that all felines share in some combination or another. If she still retained the power of smell, Mrs. Gettzleman would know that the litter box has needed changing for the last four days.

Through the French windows, she can see Taylor Bedskirt's fortifications, framed by her own row of arches reminiscent of Mission *San Fernando Rey de España*. She can log Taylor's movements, the drawn faces of the lovers who he cavalierly dismisses one after another, the visits from the wife-beating alcoholic from next door, the frequent UPS and FedEx trucks, the mailman weighted down with large envelopes and priority boxes.

This is her garret, her study. She rarely leaves it unless to leave the house, visit the kitchen, or to do what must be done at the commode: like the forced march to Nod, an eternal penance for the sin of harvesting. She eats here at the desk, having covered the dining room table with things she has collected and never discarded: carnival ashtrays, cast iron banks, colorful aluminum plates and cups of the kind used on redwood picnic tables in the fifties, vases of all tastes between none and wouldn't-be-caught-dead with, old post cards of natural bridges and ostrich farms, Niagara Falls from the Canadian side, and caves that Jesse James holed up in. Likewise, she has stereopticons with boxes of duplex cards from around the world, Keystone views of the Grand Canyon with overdressed tourists on over-burdened mules, Old Faithful being faithful, Indians dressing up like Indians. There are layers of amateur oil paintings crushing each other against the walls, a collection of Burma Shave signs, a model of the "U.S.S. Constellation" on a voyage in search of a mizzenmast.

The hall, the three bedrooms, are worse, with barely a fire path between the piles of ancient LP's: Belafonte, "Carmen" excerpts, the Four Tops. There are even seventy-eights of big bands from World War II. And books. And books. And more books to thrill the earwigs and fertilize the mildew. There is a stench here of more than cat shit: the odors of memory, a lifetime of nasal sensation.

Mrs. Gettzelmen prides herself on being an early and continuing practitioner of the green concept, having converted long before people were sorted by the color wheel of their ideas: green, red, blue, pink, gray. She feeds herself primarily from the ninety-nine cent store, clothes herself from Goodwill, hordes from the things most people are only too glad to be rid of. It is her contribution to the earth, to the future generations she'll never know.

But most of all, and most economically stored, Mrs. Gettzlemen is a collector of people. She logs their faces, their forms, their back stories which she generously annotates with copious notes. She imagines them over honeyed tea at the roll top desk. A perpetual toter of notebooks and pencils, sometimes her little subversive camera for which she occasionally lands a deal on outdated film, and the antique opera glasses that help her spelunk into the cavernous lives of others, she goes on field trips like a private eye. She sits at the zoo to watch the people. In the market she peers over pyramids of rock-hard avocados to study the shoppers;

on the bus bench she studies the sad faces behind the dirty windows etched in graffiti. And on her scribbled yellow note pages, she gives lives to them all, justifies their unhappiness, builds foundations for their levity, gives them imaginative connections to other lost souls like a pre-JDate *yenta*.

Lately, she has developed a special favorite, who she observes, and records, and builds upon, gives him a plan, connects the dots that she herself has mapped. And Taylor, as with many other secrets of life, and lost to his own insular designs, hasn't a clue.

FIFTH HELEN

She is creeping down San Fernando Blvd. at non-speeds to shame a low rider. At times, she is nearly going backwards. Cars are honking, passing. Drivers are gesticulating, hurling insults. She rolls past the Northeast Division police station unnoticed. She's either driving on instinct or the car knows where to go. It's been there before. Everything is run down: small industrial businesses, welders, wood strippers, retreaders, a speaker cone replacer. Some kids are rolling a drunk asleep on an MTA bench. She is straddling the lanes, fixated on the white line. Boy oh boy, wouldn't that asshole like to know where I'm going? Where am I fucking going? Everything's different. Used to be nicer. Last week it was nicer. This is all Taylor's fault. He probably decided to rearrange everything. Turn a decent upscale neighborhood into a run down slum. Wouldn't that be just like him? He likes things used, weathered, a sway to rooflines, tattered curtains, exposed tarpaper. Taylor's been moving the buildings around. This calls for a Valium. Girl's best friend. Whoops, out of fucking Valiums! I'll be there soon. If I can remember how to get there. If my batshit husband doesn't pick it up and put it somewhere else. A lot of power to risk on the lame, if you ask me. How can I compete? How can I? Why should I? Married to a loser who likes his women diminutive, no more than eighteen millimeters tall. I'm too much woman for the asshole, that's what this is all about.

TISHOMINGO

I

OFFICER VOORHIIS CAUTIOUSLY NEGOTIATES THE SQUAD car down the ridge between Thebes and Tishomingo proper. A sharp aftershock has left a cleft in the crest, setting in motion a slide of earth and stone and flora. Parts of the oil-slicked macadam have crackled like dried lakebed, and phone poles have been set askew. A power company crew is busy righting them.

The collective mayhem has put the officer in a contemplative mood. "Sometimes the Good Lord is hard t'figure," he says.

Prezhki, taking partial exception, says, *"Sometimes?"*

"I mean, he calls home an old colored junk man 'thout no family, who's t'wonder? Right? Probably just some sort a correction anyways."

"How's that?"

"Wasn't much sense in him bein' here in the first place, way I see it."

"That so? That's for you to decide? You know, son, even the housefly has a part in The Plan. Wasn't for it, we'd all be knee deep in shit."

"Don't prevent ya from swattin' 'em once in a while."

"It surely doesn't. Someday, we may come to regret that."

"But a little white infant from a proper family? Hardly makes no sense, now does it?"

"Not for me to know. But I'll tell you this: some of today's newborns will grow up to take a life, some will embezzle, some will rape, and some will go into politics. Gotta give the Lord a little credit. Maybe it's a prevention. The child, not the old colored man."

Voorhiis has an urge to turn to the Chief, to offer at least an expression of protest. He is troubled too by a sudden chill commuting up his spine, sending his shoulders into a single involuntary twitch. He concentrates on the road and keeps his thoughts to himself. Perhaps this was Prezhki's intention.

Back at the bottling plant, the brothers in their mourning suits trundle the undigested remains of Choc Bonjuour, secure in pine box with nail heads protruding for a future extraction, into the back of the wagon with the words painted on the sides. Late as it is in Choc's final repose, it is like cleaning crumbs from a plate. They are big men, with broad shoulders from hefting dead weight. Rev. Salvation is also of commodious proportions, but he rams himself into the front seat with them so that their elbows are wedged stiff, and the act of steering and shifting becomes a social agony. He is not about to sit with the box, reeking as it does.

"This some powerful *per*-fume!" says Salvation.

"Ya gets accustomed," says the nearest brother solemnly.

"Da real ol' ones likely t'die 'lone. Dey outlive' all der peoples.'"

"One ol' gen'leman got took las' week lib alone on an' old hardscrabbly farm back up on a wagon track up pass' da falls. No one in, no one out 'cept hisse'f. Some fambly out on Highway Sickteen calls in t'da sheriff dat dere's dis suspicious large num'er a buzzards wid a more'n usual interes' in some acreage sout' a UF. Da hu'band, he a hun'er. He know what dem happy buzzards celebratin'. Talk 'bout puttin' up a stink! Dis breeze come up an' we gettin' altogether too familiar wid dat ol' boy 'fore us eben leaves da road an' hikes on up dat weedy track."

"An' dat ain'all, no suh. Da ol' boy keep a flock a dem guinea hens an' dey be puttin' up a squawkin' like it guinea hen jub'lations day. Some folks sez dey better'n mos' dogs fo' watchin'. Hadda shake twigs at 'em t'get 'im t'scatter. Same on d'ways out. I prefers t'have me a dog m'se'f."

"Lawd mobs'n 'sterious way, yes 'E do."

"Another piece a th' great puzzle. Warn folks t'stay 'way, trumpets out t'critters t'come an' get it, an' to cleans up this human mess despoilin' this tarnish' Eden."

"Prosaic way a puttin' it. M'self, ah don' think 'bout it all dat much. He," nodding back, "don' neither. Papa say, ya'll wants t'put ya se'f 'n concert wid da clien'."

"An' Papa say, be sure y'all snap out a it quick so's y'can be a some use 'fore it's yo'own turn a'raise a stink."

"Amen!"

"An' t'y'all, Pastor!"

And, ahead, Prezhki wants to see what's going on in town, navigates the officer on a circuitous auto tour of hot spots seen from the ridge. There is action everywhere, the cleanup from the fires, a steeple cabled and coaxed into place, glaziers cautiously transporting invisible sheets, sign artists with stencils, masons and hod carriers, an army of painters and street cleaners, all the king's horses and all the king's men in their happy, clamorous festival of correction. "We live on egg shells," Prezhki muses. A brief preview of sunlight calls attention to itself as a brass band oompahs Sousa in the gazebo at Memorial Square.

The Square, as it is almost always referred to, is the geographic and political hub of Tishomingo, surrounded by the spokes of the various neighborhoods: business and residential, prosperous and depressed, and the limestone ostentation of administrative offices: the City Hall, the Police Station/Jail/Municipal Courthouse, Fire Company Number One, the Chamber of Commerce. These are stately expressions of promise, cut stone wishes and dreams of boosters. The Square itself, with geometric disobedience, is actually rectangular, modified in recent years by rounded corners to facilitate faster and more plentiful traffic. What in particular it is a memorial to is confused by its plethora of monuments, added at different times and not necessarily in regards to historical chronology. One admires the essential Civil War soldier on his pedestal, from which he can see the enemy swarms cresting The Camels, or the frontier family breeching the Appalachians with oxen in heroic strides. There is an alabaster-white Indian fighter in buckskin with musket and powder horn astride a wary mare, a Rough Rider in mid-leap — presumably toward a Cuban trench — the determined doughboy on his crutch, all mourned by a weeping angel with exposed breast, her face covered by a bent arm, a brass plaque with the names of dead men corroding green at her feet. There are smaller memorials in the shapes of fountains, busts, simple placards, an etched stone, a handsome frieze on a retaining wall, and benches named after mayors and other local sons. No human woman is represented except for the frontier mother who obediently trails her strident husband, her breasts concealed with a sense of decency angels apparently lack. There are no people of color. There are emigrants, but not immigrants. The remaining rock and bronze speaks of men who have done well for themselves: planners, builders, pioneers in all their many disciplines, inventors; the kind of men that rouse lesser folks, promote awe, instill order, and keep the gears of commerce rolling, and the nativist juices boiling like a witches brew.

From the passenger seat, Prezhki directs Voorhiis east on Grand Street toward the station, all the time taking inventory of aftermath. He sticks his hands through the crack of window to experience a warming in the air. Enjoying depleting unease, he starts thinking of lunch. It has been some time since his pointed rebuke of the engineer at The Roadhouse, and he looks forward to the deferred release of a good long piss before anything else.

The Civil War Monument looms ahead on the right, the station in stern red brick and the weight of law on the left, and before them the open office window behind which P-R entertains the gossip columnist.

The Mayor thanks her for visiting, attempts to pull a chair out for her. "Always an honor to celebrate the First Amendment."

She pulls the chair away and seats herself. "You may find that premature. Flattery," she says, "in this case will, in fact, get you absolutely nowhere. Tell the truth, I'm little put out with it. Medieval as chivalry, don't you think?" She is wearing a flat black hat with a brim, wire-rimmed spectacles, resembles a Dutch pastor with a fish net purposely concealing her countenance. She leans forward as she talks; threatens to take his eye out with her busy pencil.

"It generally works for me," he says. "I don't tinker with that which works." He remains standing, a comment on how much time he is willing to spend with her.

"Good thing you're not in my business, then. Wouldn't make it out a personals."

"I suppose I wouldn't. That's very true. But alas, I was never very good at scribbling. So, what service can I offer the press today?"

"I don't pull punches, either. Be forewarned."

He smiles. Hopes she is. "We all on the record at this time?"

"Always. All's true is fair game."

"And all that isn't?"

"One prays for the wisdom to discriminate."

"Does one, now? And innuendo?"

"Innuendo can be true. Sometimes you hear the body of the truth, sometimes just a limb. Sometimes just a tiny toenail of innuendo leads you to a foot, a foot to a leg, a torso. Stick a head on it, a couple of arms, embellish with ears, nose, hair, and if I may be so bold, a few telltale private parts, and, oh well, you have enough truth to go to press. Are you a Catholic, sir? Lapsed?"

"Heavens, no! No, no."

"You say that with some relief."

"Do I?"

"I only ask to clarify as to what we are about. It's like eating the host. The flesh. With each morsel comes a little wisdom."

"Is that what the diminutive wafer does for y'all? I wonder: do you ever get your fill? Do y'all ever comprehend the whole picture from this...nibbling?"

"Wouldn't know. I'm not Catholic either. So I stick to the diet that keeps me fueled." She juts a square, masculine jaw and in the right light reveals a trace of goatee. P-R considers offering her a cigar, perhaps the poor one that McCallum had bestowed.

"Am I expected to understand what it is y'all're talking about? I mean, not in the abstract, of course, but just what it is we are really discussing beyond not being papists?"

"We can make it easier. Would you like me to be more direct?"

"Until you are, I'm hardly in a position to know if I would or not, am I?"

She squints, nods. Appears to be enjoying herself. "Suppose we just get to the yolk of this egg, Mr. Mayor. A little bird tells me that a couple, or more, gentlemen of some note around town have taken to transporting a young lady, or ladies, as it may be, to a certain place of rendezvous for purposes not in the best interest of the community. Another member of the flock has revealingly chirped that these two or more functionaries employ an old Negro to provide the actual transportation of the young woman-slash-women. Maybe there is more to this. Maybe not. Maybe just a chance tryst. Maybe an operation. More geography covered. Now, see, if you will, if you can help add a little color to this otherwise gray tale?" She's rolling the words about in her mouth, looks as if she is about to spit, and he wonders if the cuspidor is within her trajectory.

"What color exactly? Scarlet?"

"Scarlet sells a paper. And there are the coincident fatalities. The Negro sans parts that might at least have revealed a cause of death. And his dog. And, a young upstart at the railroad who apparently was not a favorite of certain local company officials; this last death owing, at least in part, to the untimely dismissal of Engineer Brown, whose wife, it is rumored, took a ride with the old Negro. And, if it was Mrs. Brown, wouldn't it be a treat to know where she was going, and why, and who was waiting for her when she got there? I'm practically salivating to find out! And, of course, Yardley Humboldt, dead on the train after some tiff with the very local company official who was himself less than enamored with the young upstart. Now, under the cloak of a certain legal invisibility, it is revealed that the local railroad man and Mr. Humboldt were involved in a questionable business proposition that also included a preacher of the Baptist persuasion. By the way? Doesn't Engineer Brown's wife work somewhere in this office?"

His lips part, his eyes narrow; just slightly, but enough to cue her.

She says, "Which part of this didn't you know?"

Quickly recouping, he says, "Any of it. And which part of it do *y'all* think you've closed the book on?"

"Oh, I'm still reading."

"Then, I've caught you in time. Your editor? Tom Maze, right? Good friend, Tom. The wife's cousin, actually. Quite the hunter. We've spent many a pleasant afternoon together running the dogs and wantonly killing off things with obsolete defenses. You can imagine how much an adhesive hunting can be for the sporting man. Brothers in arms, as they say. His boys played with my boys. Bridge for the wives every Thursday. At homes. Tea on nice china. That sort of thing. I can't think of anyone I'd rather consult when threatened by an angry she-boar. Y'all hunt, madam?"

"All the time, Your Honor. You threatening me?" It comes lightning-quick, as if she had it ready, part of an oft-played arsenal.

"No more than you are me. How colorful is that? Tom and I are just an operator apart."

"You *are* threatening me." She is defiant, but less at ease. She shifts her narrow buttocks on the hard wooden chair.

"No, no, no. You must learn to look on the bright side of things." He is. He has gained an advantage she has shed, the prerogative of enjoyment. And, a piece that may well complete the puzzle. "See, chivalry still works here at City Hall. We are an administration conscious of tradition. No, no. We don't work that other way. It's just that, well, one who communes with fowl, will wind up with information that is for the birds."

"Wasn't born yesterday, Your Honor. I know what's going on."

"Then I can't be of any help to y'all, can I? Sorry to have wasted your time."

"I will write this story."

"Waste of a perfectly good ribbon. It'll never get to press."

"I can color it in with you, or the Chief. Or I can implicate you both."

"My dear woman. I can access an impressive body of libel law, you know. If you had the skeleton to support your parts, it would long since have been shouted from every rooftop in Tishomingo. *Read all about it. Ancient truths revealed in dirt.* But this, this has a touch of hokum: the Cardiff Giant, the sea serpent in Long Island Sound. Real discovery involves some serious digging in the soil of record. I strongly advise y'all to get your nose back on the trail, locate some more substantial…if I may, excrement…before you go about town slinging the meager allotment you have been given."

"I'm not done with this." She is one step toward the edge of complacency.

"I think you are." He is lecturing now, gesticulating, a scholar of his discipline. "Tell me something. How long can a daily subsist without advertising? See, it's not all about news. About innuendo. About the little parts of the bigger truth. It's about the buck. Cash on the line. The great big bad world of finance, of which I am a denizen, and y'all but a nibbler of discarded seed. Or, wafers. Good day to you."

Outside, officer and Chief cross Electric Avenue, a rudimentary partial pavement of an alley that runs along the west side of the station toward the trolley car barn, and Prezhki's attention is drawn to a familiar green Chevy up the lane outside of CONTRELL'S HARDWARE BUILDING MATERIALS AND FIRE ARMS. With it, he catches a brief flash of a man walking toward Grand, toting a long package in brown packing paper, and cries out, "The hell's he doing here?" Voorhiis takes a sharp shoulder jab and is ordered to, "Make a U up here. Get me as close to the corner as you can without showing yourself to the alley."

Grand sports a median of grass and hedges. Voorhiis asks, "Whadda we got?" He gets no answer, lets the tires whine through the traffic break and spins around over the greenway to the displeasure of beleaguered horns. He pulls up, half on the sidewalk just short of Electric, on the inside of the cars parked in neat diagonals.

"Give me some cover," the Chief orders, haste ejecting him from the car, over to the somber wall, edges toward the cornerstone — EREC. MCMXXVII, CHAS. ROUGE, MAYOR — Voorhiis coming up behind him with loaded gun, feeling a bit foolish not knowing where to point it.

Prezhki can hear the engineer's boots clop on the irregular cobble, dance cautiously around puddles, all the time getting louder until he can hear the breathing as well — quick nervous bursts — can nearly smell the anxiety, as he steps suddenly out before the man and says, "I appreciate you dropping by so soon."

Moses is startled, rears back a step, and tightens his grip on the linear package.

Prezhki sidesteps out to the mouth of the alley but remains in Voorhiis' view. He has one hand held up like the cutout policeman on the stop sign, the other snug on the butt of his service revolver displaying itself from under his coat. "Contrell stock those elbows?"

"He does," says Moses unblinking, his eyes, steel blue and unrevealing, locked on Prezhki's. Slowly he loosens an end of paper to reveal the casting, shows its masculine threads circumscribing a length of pipe.

Prezhki, relieved, allows a meager smile, and says, "A man might've thought you'd been to Contrell's for a different manner of cylinder."

"A man might," says Moses, returning the gesture with an easing of his own jaw, breaking tension, watching as Prezhki tends to relax muscles in his neck, his cheeks, the taught fingers, and with no warning what so ever jabs the angle-ended pipe forward in a ferocious thrust to the Chief's abdomen, deflating him, causing him to crease in the middle like an empty suit, earning time to swing the pipe rearward and form a wide arc toward the side of Prezhki's head.

Voorhiis moves into view and fires off an ill-considered shot that chips a corner brick, shatters it to red powder, triangulates over the stricken man's head no where near the aggressor, and deafens Prezhki's right ear. Prezhki recovers enough composure, sucks enough air, to fall on his back side, hopefully avoiding the smooth loop of the pipe, only to have the weapon's ankle end send his nose into his far cheek, spin him into Voorhiis' face in a spectacular display of very red blood pumped by an overcharged heart.

All the while, blind with pain, Prezhki locks onto the engineer's knees and drops him backward. The pipe flies over his head and hits the wall with a resounding clank, and Voorhiis, after an eternity of indecision, coming around with the gun, orders Moses over on his belly, and slaps on the bracelets.

An officer peers out of a third story window, then ducks back in. In the park, the band plays on, and across the street and up a flight, the report pierces the chill silence of the Mayor's office, sending him, and the reporter, in a race to the window. *"Now* there's news!" P-R tells her. "Fetch!"

Prezhki engages a blizzard of acerbic speech, screams, "Jesus puck! Puck be!" extracting the gasoline-perfumed hanky and sponging his face, leaning forward shedding blood-mucous confetti streams onto municipal property, and yet finds the sanity to wave on slowing vehicles with his free hand. Rivulets of pain are flowing from his newly asymmetric face, hot magma tendrils grasp his chin, his cheeks, right up through milky, insensible eyes, and cut throbbing fault lines upward into his skull. He has never known such physical agony, nor such total surprise. "Geb dis piece ob shit ibto duh car."

Voorhiis yanks Moses to his feet. "Sir. We can just take him on inside."

"Car," snaps Prezhki. He staggers over himself, yanks open the back door. Voorhiis follows, dragging Moses Brown, shoving him inside.

"Lemme get ya over t' 'Mergency."

"Look, ooh puckib retarb." He is talking through blocked passages, seeing through tearing eyes. "Geb us ober to duh garabzh. Bow."

As officers come out of the front door, Voorhiis, hoping he understands the order, takes the car off the sidewalk, turns right, and races up Electric, around Contrell's Hardware, spins around the next block and down the ramp under the station. Prezhki pulls himself out, the rag to his face, walks at a right angle to his nose into the motor pool office, where two grimy mechanics are enjoying sardine sandwiches and Crush de Oro soda pops. He orders them out of the garage, and takes over the office. Motioning for the officer to bring the prisoner, he locks himself in with Moses. Voorhiis is on the outside. "Doe bub cubs ib."

"Sir?"

"Doe... bub... cubs...ib."

Moses is huddled in a corner, hands bound behind his back. He is rigid, determined not to show fear. Prezhki exchanges hands for the staunching of blood, secures a large wrench from a tool rack, hefts it, gets its feel, motions through three or four practice swings — slow, even, assessing distance and velocity. For a brief moment, he freezes the pose. Then he drops himself backward onto a desk chair and wheels up close enough to anoint Engineer Brown with prolific, crimson fluids.

"Ooh dub sub ob a ditch," he growls, expelling tissue, cartilage, a random tooth, shaking the wrench for emphasis, "I bill say it bub tibe. I ab bot habib relashubs wib oor whore ob a wibe. Look whub ooh dib to by puckib nobe, shib braibs! I'b goib to bake sure ooh gob bleby a tibe to 'onder ooh ib. Ooh bet ooh 'istle, Casey puckib Jobes!"

He stands, towers over Brown, kicks the chair backward, advances with the wrench, and before returning a recent favor, says, "I habe bo 'ords to tell ooh 'ow buch bis 'urts." He flings the wrench into the wall next to the prisoner, and spits. "I shoub kill ooh, 'ut bat 'ould 'e obercobinsatib", and swings a swift, bunched fist, turning Brown's head in a vermilion flash, lands it dead center in the porridge of the engineer's former nose. The prone man buckles, yowls like a wolf to the moon, falls to writhing in his own stain. Prezhki finds the doorknob in his liquid fog, tells Voorhiis, "Book 'ib. Abb resistib arrebst. Hab Doc'er 'Alsey tabe a 'ook ab hib."

"Dr. Halsey?" Halsey is palsied, nearly blind. There has been a mix up in his retirement papers. Voorhiis wants to protest further, but dares not.

Prezhki leaves a trail through the service door as he goes seeking poultices and patching materials, packings for his nostrils, and a clean suit. Nose wounds can look and feel worse than they are; the office girls shudder when they see him, rush over with hankies of their own, ignore his protests, escort him maternally into his office, over to the leather couch where they lay him out lengthwise, apply tender pressure to his wound, raise the blinds, and let in a sunshine they have all but forgotten. It comes on the wail of sirens.

One says, "Should I phone up your wife?"

"On'y 'f 'oo bana be 'ookin' 'or a job duri'g a depression."

At an equal elevation, an avenue's width away, P-R escorts the woman out through the front office, then rings her editor to chat. There are assurances offered before Maze is called away by some excitement in the newsroom. "So what do we know?" P-R calls through his open door.

"My God," says a aide on his way in. "They're saying Chief Prezhki's been shot in the face in the alley. Right next to the station. We can't see a thing through the crowd. They've called in an ambulance but it might be too late."

P-R grabs his hat, trots through the outer office, into the marble corridor, trying to sort out the meaning of this latest event, putting it in the perspective of the repairs he is engaged in, emergency measures to staunch rumors and secure his control on the flow of information, fancied and fabricated. There is room for loss here: he is not immune to the ramifications of human suffering. But P-R is a pragmatic man, and for every friend fallen, there are gaps to patch, allies to be mined, and opportunity to snatch. He comes out onto the fresh air of the portico, sees the hubbub of citizenry and press gathering at the station doors, seeks to avoid notice by pulling his hat brim low over his forehead and cutting out on an angular approach to the building's garage door. Almost there, he is intercepted by two young men in summer suits and straw hats, one with pad, one with Graflex blinding him into submission.

"A statement," Mr. Mayor. "A statement."

P-R summons his concerned public mask. He keeps an interchangeable set, mirror-tested, on his person at all times, files it in gray matter with babies' names, old ladies petitions, plots of land registered to this one, medical procedures performed on that one.

"Let me say this," they let him say. "The City of Tishomingo will provide its police department with all resources necessary to get to the bottom of today's events. My administration and law enforcement are cooperating in full. Our strategy is to move forward on this. Thank you, and God bless Tishomingo."

With that, he is allowed to escape into the garage, to see the telltale trail of blood, the detritus of foul play, and to follow its lead through the service entrance. He finds Officer Voorhiis, pale and distraught, coming out of the men's room.

"Where's the body?"

"Sir?"

"The body? Certainly it wasn't left where it was found."

"Did you know him?"

P-R leans close in to Voorhiis' face. "Are y'all out of of your mind, Officer?"

"Sir?"

"The body?"

"Suttley & Sons picked him up, sir. Just the sons, actually…I think."

"Who the hell is Suttley & Sons? They from out of town?"

"Local, I think. They take care of a lot a the colored. Chief hisself gave 'em the call."

"The Chief gave the call? He must have been delirious. Poor man. But a colored undertaker? That's unacceptable. How long did he last after the event?"

"No idea, sir. He was dead when we got there."

P-R steps back and stares carefully at Voorhiis. "Officer, just how many bodies are we discussing?"

"Just the one, sir."

"And that might be?"

"Colored junkman, sir."

In the front of the station, the weather has warmed and men are slipping out of their coats, slinging them casually over their vest shoulders, their watch chains glinting in the crystal afternoon. The sky is an intense blue, nearly artificial. Officers are culling the reporters from the avocationally curious, bringing them inside for a briefing in the small conference room at the rear of the building. A coffee pot is brought in — cups, napkins, cubes of sugar, a pitcher of milk. The room is warm and one of the officers yanks the ceiling fan chain and the napkins begin to blow off of laps, scatter about the room like moths under incandescent bulbs. Everyone looks worn, on edge, an insomniac's convention waxing. These are not folks who make anyone's best dressed list on a good day; today they are unusually shabby and uncombed, and only Miss Quidnunc, straight from her interview with the Mayor, has managed a passable Windsor knot in her tie. There is a general, yet wearisome, consensus that, as newspeople, they are enjoying too much of a good thing. "This here's been a plague of opportunity," one says.

An officer in a suit, sporting a shoulder holster with a snub revolver poking out and a prominent shield polished new on his belt, comes up to the podium, nods to a few familiar faces, and says, "Ah think we can get underway, heah, boys. Hell w'this," he says gruffly, pushing around the podium to set himself closer to the group of fifteen or so anxious men, and one woman, setting himself authoritatively but firmly down on one of the front tables, in the process overturning a cup or two and ruining a cub's gabardines. The officer is over indulgent with weight and whiskers; his breakfast could be ascertained from the stains on his shirt.

"Ah wanna thank y'all for yore patience while we piece t'gether just what is an' what ain't. Happy us'all'er able to oblige y'all with a little sunshine t' stand out in while we're *in*vestigatin'. Anyways, Ah'm Capt. A-i-m-u-s Gunze... z-e at the end. My mama had somthin' uva *un*fortunate sense a humor...Chief a detectives." There are smiles. He has broken ice, as if they are bergs floating in a cocktail glass. The loosened crowd knows him already, which he acknowledges with some redundancy, "Some a y'all, Ah ain't had the pleasure. Chief usually does this sort ova thing, so bear with me if I seem a tad rusty. What Ah can tell y'all's this here: Chief Walter Prezhki and Officer Voorhiis was comin' back t' the station after a *rou*tine *in*vestigation havin' nothin' t' do'th this here current fuss. That's how we're seein' it. We'll look into all a that further, a course, but as a right now, we got us two separate e-vents *in*volvin' *en*tirely dis*in*terested parties. Now, Ah know you're gonna ask, why's the Chief out on patrol, an' I'll tell ya n'all honesty that, fellas, that's just simply the kin' a public servant we got here. A hands-on kin' a leader. Ain't a day passes he don't go out an' see what's what his own self, make up his own mind. You might say, his is one desk chair in this town'at don't stay warm."

This gets him a few chuckles: they all know their Chief, these City Desk boys and girl. "Now, I know y'all're *con*cerned, an' we thank ya, an' the Chief thanks ya. I have heard a rumor 'bout some shootin'. Lemme put that ol' houn' t' rest. No one's been shot. We don' know the *ac*tual cause a the pop some a us think we heard, but we will an' we'll let you all know what it was jus'as soon's we know. Backfire, piece a brick fall off a *fa*çade, somethin' that there band did, kettle drum maybe, who knows? How these things get started, huh? How they take on a life. Chief did *in*volve *his*self 'n'a little scuffle, being the hands-on kind a fella I already said. Little nose bleed for his valiancy. Nothin' t' write home about, or'n your papers. Don't' go waistin' no precious newsprint ya don't have't'. But heck, people, as the wise man said, y'all should see the other guy! Huh? Huh?" There is some applause, a little complicit nudging.

"Who was the scuffle with?"

"Well, Henry...It is Henry, right? I just come up from lockup an' they seem t' be *of*ferin' a little *hos*pitality t'one Moses Brown. Y'all *re*call Mr. Brown as bein' somehow *co*lluded'n that awful thing with the head-on down toward the Sling.

How that *re*lates, we don' know. Maybe it don't. Mr. Brown's a bit down'n'a dumps at the moment an' has *his*self *de*clined our offer a *con*geniality. What I can tell ya is, that for no ap*par*ent reason, Mr. Brown sought t'cause harm t'the person a Walter Prezhki usin' some plumbin' he just *ac*quired for such a purpose down at *Con*trell's. Mr. Brown has no previous record'th us here, an' prior t' the wreck, as we all've read, was a 'xemplary *employee* a the railroad. So who knows? Maybe he thought the Chief uz someone else. Maybe he jus' up'n' snapped an' uz mad at the world. Could a *as*saulted who ever'd the *mis*fortune t' come 'round that corner the same time as him. Tell ya this, though, he made *his*self one very bad *de*cision'th the choosin' a this particular victim."

"How's the Chief gettin' on?"

"Did Brown resist capture?"

"Why do you think this isn't related to the crime spree?"

"This Brown. He a Union man?"

"Well, y'know, *my* first thought 'xactly. Dug in my own self, but so far it don't pan out. But I tell ya this. Don'ya rule out no *a*gitators. I don't."

"What's Brown charged with?" Dalhurst shouts.

"At the least, *as*saultin' an officer a the law. 'Course, after we gather all the facts, we may jus' wanna build on that. Look'it, fellas," — he is indignant that the woman is slogging through the mud with the men — "I'd take y'all's questions," he says, edging to escape, "but I got no more answers at this time. So ya'll call in what ya got, *en*joy the brew, an' have yourselves a pleasant *after*noon. Keep in touch now, heah," and he is out the door.

Cynthia Dalhurst, primping her tie, beats him to the hall with long, athletic strides. "Succinct," she compliments.

"Is what it is, missy."

"Wasn't it Mr. Brown's wife that is alleged to be involved in some behavior that…"

"I don't know nothin' about no dame, honeysuckle. I hear somethin', y'all be the first t' know."

"You don't know a lot, do you? None of you do."

"Well, now that there's a value judgment, ain't it? We know what we know. We find out what we need to, then we know that too. Beyond that, we have the good people a the Third *Eh*state t'fill in the blanks. Don't y'all usually do *en*gagements, comin'zouts, births, that sort a thing? This here's a little *be*yon' such terrain, ain't it?"

"You tell me."

He shrugs. "That ain't part a what we know, now is it?"

II

*S*O, GIRLS, WHAT DO WE REALLY *know?*
I know I don't like egg salad.
Yes, you do. You're just being ornery.
I am not! I don't like it. Never have.

But you order it every week! Just like the rest of us.

I do not!

Throw me a life jacket, June.

Let's just move along. I made a list. Would you like me to read it to you?

No. I hate being read to. Obliges me t' fall asleep.

And then she snores. Great big wallops a hippo grunts bouncing off the stone walls of the chapel, each and every Sunday. I can barely hear myself pray!

At your age, dear, being awake obliges you to fall asleep.

And, you can barely hear, period!

Here we go. Just read it, okay? If she wants to put her head down in her egg salad, let'er.

I really don't think I ever before ordered egg salad.

Oh, dear! Let me just continue, okay? Thank you. Okay, One: Choc Bonjour, our dear junkman...

Poor soul!

They say the dog ate him.

Swallowed him whole.

Jonah in the whale.

Choc in the dog.

May he rest in peace.

Or get belched out in one piece.

He wasn't like the others.

No, he wasn't.

You don't know that.

Well, he always was respectful around me.

That's how they do, girls. They learn that kind a guile as pups. What they think *is a whole nuther ball a wax, I'll wager.*

Ahem. Remember me? I was reading, One: Choc Bonjour obliged a white woman with a ride from Tishomingo, starting at the Signal station on Seventh over to just past the last car stop in Thebes on the Thursday night in question.

Nothin' questional about Thursday night. We generally get one once a week about the same time. What she was doin' there's a whole nuther can a night crawlers.

Speaking of which, if you don't mind, hon, I'm setting the scene.

Well, excuse me for livin'! Do go on, Mrs. DeMille.

Two: We have established that this woman was probably the wife of Moses Brown, the Tishomingo engineer complicit in the recent tragedy and the alleged attacker of Chief Walter Prezhki.

Alleged? Good heavens, why the man took a pipe to the copper's mug!

Uh, huh. Seals it for me.

That's not conclusive. We don't know how come. What this Brown knows.

Or thinks *he knows.*

We don't even know what we *know!*

All the same as to motive for damage done to the Chief's face.

What's more, we don't know what we *know.*

I just said that!

Did you? I thought you said something about egg salad.
That was a while back.
Which is the reason we are reviewing.
Egg salad?
No, no. Eat dear. That's a good girl. Fill your mouth. Open the hangar for Mr. Lindbergh. So, if I may, Three: Chief Prezky's car was parked just past the car stop when Choc Bonjour dropped off the alleged Mrs. Brown.
You didn't say alleged *before. You said* established *if my memory serves.*
Therein is a whole different discussion.
Who has allergies?
The wax is building as we speak!
No one, sweetie. I said alleged. *Hush up and push your lunch around the plate. That's a dear. Let's move on,* again. *There were two men in the car. Four: One of the men got out of the car and followed the alleged…followed the woman who may have been Mrs. Brown into the Motor Court for a pre-arranged…well, I just don't know what all to call it! Not that I could put to paper anyway.*
I'd call it illicit sexual commerce between two people with wanton disregard for public morality.
Goodness, I can't write all that! How about reciprocity? Illicit reciprocity?
What does that mean?
Figure it out.
Whatever makes you feel good, dear.
That is what it means?
I don't like your tone.
Been some time since anything made me feel good, illicit or not.
Ladies. We were approaching Five.
My, my. How the time flies! Five already!
Number Five, y'silly old fossil!
Five: Days later, Chief Prezhki makes a few visits down to the rail yards. Six: P-R receives an angry summons from the Section Supervisor in Uncas Falls. Seven: P-R answers his summons on the same day Mrs. Brown travels to Uncas Falls. However, Eight: Mrs. Brown returns to Tishomingo with Mr. Brown, who has missed his assignment at work, which would have put him on the train that collided with that other train…
Or trains.
…had he not. Nine: The late Choc Bonjour gets picked up by another colored railroad employee up in The Camels…was seen bein' dropped off by the trolley.
They sure do for each other, don't they, the Nigras?
And is given a ride to Thebes, where he is encountered by my nephew who carries him up to the junkyard. You all remember me telling you about Mort.
This the same nephew with the telescopic peepers?
I only have the one. Six beautiful nieces though. One prettier than the next. There's Maybelle, Daphne…
What happened to Ten? We were comin' up on Ten.
Ten already! Why, I should be in bed!

329

If you'd all just listen!

Thank you, dear. Ten, then: Choc Bonjour up and dies, poor man. Eleven: Prezhki shows up days later at the junkyard. Let me remind you, this is the Chief of police out investigating the death of an old colored man in the midst of a crime wave and I don't know what all else, like he hasn't a care in the world. And you know what? The call in was made by Moses Brown himself! Seems Mr. Brown discovered the body.

Did he now? Like I said, enough for me.

Twelve: Moses Brown attacks Chief Prezhki and nearly kills him. I rest my case.

And your laurels. You've proved nothing other than your impressive mastery of all the single digit numbers.

Plus two of the others.

Playing Devil's advocate?

Not on the Lord's day. I'm just not convinced, is all. *What're you saying? That Prezhki or P-R are involved, reciprocally, with this same hussy? That they or the railroad did in old Choc to keep him quiet? Or this Moses Brown did him harm, though I hear he was already considerably ripe by the time Mr. Brown went pipe hunting. Maybe your nephew was involved. Maybe the Iberians at The Motor Court. In revenge, Brown tries to kill the Chief? You know what I think? I think we have wasted a lot of precious hours none a us at our age can well afford, and we've come up with nothing other than some pretty thin broth in search of a chicken.*

Now chicken salad, that's a different thing! I can't abide egg salad, though. Brings on the gas.

Well, don't that add a whole new element to our discomfort.

Thar she blows! Fire in the hole!

I think you're making light.

I think you're making gas.

What does your reporter friend say?

She says she can't say. She says she's been instructed to drop the whole matter.

By whom?

She didn't say.

Perhaps there is just nothing to say.

I'm still troubled by sexual reciprocity. *What exactly does that have to do with the price of egg salad in China?*

Nothing that's likely to trouble you too much longer.

What does any of it have to do with anything else? P-R moonlights? No banner edition there. An old man dies after spending half the day on a frozen mountain. Where's the wonder? A policeman is seen at the rail yard, where all sorts of riffraff come in on the freights and congregate like Coxey's Army. A man with marital concerns is late for work. Like he's got nothing else on his mind. Eat up, girls. Because no matter how much we pretend to know, egg salad is about as exciting as our old lives are going to get.

I find that disenchanting. As you know, I despise egg salad.

I think that's cruel. I think you're being dismissive.

Next time, I'm getting the steak sandwich. You just watch me.

Better get some teeth to eat it with.

I think we're a bunch of old birds trying to squeeze out one last egg.

The hen's just fine. It's the egg that's the problem.

I really don't like your tone!

Well, then. What shall we talk about?

Keep this under wraps 'cause I don't want to speak ill of the dead, but I heard that poor Mr. Humboldt was on that train because he had spent the night in UF too.

That same night?

That's what I heard.

With the same strumpet?

What trumpet? I didn't hear any trumpet.

Just the eggs salad giving voice to your innards, dear.

Is every man in town pokin' his whatsits where it don't belong?

Girls, girls, girls. While we have been so obsessed with all this hanky panky, did it ever occur to any of you that the world around us seemed to be coming to an end?

I'm so confused already. Can we deal with that another time?

Well, that's a bit of an exaggeration, don't you think?

Is it? Or is it just because things seem to be settling down?

The public has a short memory. Our little corner of the public has none at all.

Speak for yourself!

We have witnessed some strange things lately, with the crime and the weather and I don't know what all. And now that we are getting something of a reprieve, well, don't we wonder what was going on?

Myself, I don't want to know. These are the kinds of things best left undisturbed. Hopefully, it'll be some sort of a wake up call for those folks who've wavered from their faith, I mean, the mystery and all that. Me? I'd just as soon make my peace with the Lord and let bygones be bygones.

Do you think maybe the engineer attacking the Chief is part of some bigger design?

Lack a design, y'ask me.

And Who might you be blaming for that? Might be, you could use that wake up call yourself. Such talk, and on the Lord's Day, no less!

No one is asking you. And we're back to square one.

Prattle, prattle, prattle! D'ya really think He's got the time t' listen in on the Sunday dribble a four old goats He's gonna call home any minute now? Reach' is fingers down an' tweeze us on up like old burnt match sticks?

I like to think He does, yes.

You like to think?

I think I heard somewhere Moses Brown's got a nose the size of a yarn ball.

When did that happen?

He didn't have it at the hardware, so they say.

Must be something going around.

Something carried by plumbing fixtures? Like cholera.

I heard, resisting arrest.

I heard there was a crazy man running around in the altogether.

Must a just finished visitin' Moses Brown's wife. Better watch his nose too.

Gracious me! Better watch more'n his nose!

Lord, give me strength!
Whatever would you do with it?
Well, I'll tell you this. I wouldn't waste it masticating egg salad.

III

YARDLEY HUMBOLDT, ON ICE, AWAITS HIS departure with the pliant complacency only the dead can afford.

Living relatives, after all, need time to prepare, to put things in order, to locate someone to feed dogs and milk cows. They need to engage a trustworthy hand with the where-with-all to watch the store and make sure the help doesn't rob them blind in their absence. They need to steer Mother out on the wheelchair, gather up her medications, to secure train tickets, endure the long haul — up to three days for the British Columbia contingent — cross mountains, deserts, time zones, meeting Pullman connections in smoke-seared train sheds marinated in burnt fossil scents. Clickety-clack haste over states and countries; the motion memory which refuses to abate even on junction platforms; the water glasses and the coffee cups with the fluids see-sawing for level; the tight bunks for sleeping; walking the charging aisles to iron out the kinks; dozing upright in coach chairs, necks as stiff as rail; feet cramped; cinders and sludge raining down on golden fields and great mudflows of river; endless queues of creosoted poles; the light-flashing steel girders of bridges; the hind sides of towns with their mills, and scrap yards, ripple-sided tractor sheds, classification yards, pyramids of coal, signal towers with wary scanners and rows of long throw levers, buildings smudged and rusted, road beds littered with Coke bottles, bean cans, scraps of paper, cardboard boxes, sleeping hobos with their bindles, a hillock of rubber tires burning in a sickly stink that stays with the train for hours. All the while, dark hands are bringing wool blankets, an extra pillow, matching company china refreshed in a transient kitchen. For these things, they need the time.

Yardley Humboldt, frozen fresh like a side of venison, placid in his waxy reconstruction, mutely calls them all; soon gone, lost to the trains; eviscerated by the torn steel skin of a parlor car; his suit ruined so that he has had to be re-attired for the viewing, his city council pin gleaming on his lapel, hair combed in even furrows. He has called in the obligations of loved ones to make haste for one final salutation, one last parting of ways; called them by telegraph, by phone: *pack light, it appears to be coming on Spring here, but then, who knows?*

They come from out of a closer past: brothers, sisters, mothers, fathers, cousins, aunts, uncles, tykes and geezers, a boy in uniform, a girl close to giving birth, the uncle that hasn't been seen since he went off to the Klondike, a friend who happens by once a year anyway, a salesman who incorporates it into his route.

Mr. Pullman is good enough to carry them home so that they can send Mr. Humboldt on his way. They patronize the carriers of choice, the trunk lines, the living tethers of mortal transport. They bring what they have in black, Sunday clothes, mourning suits, veils to hide the tears, starched and scratchy things that cry penance. They gather on the Tishomingo platform in dribbles of humanity, grab cabs, are met by friends, cluster in spare bedrooms, hotel rooms. They are *so very sorry*, they note, *he went just as he reached his prime*, that *there was so much life left in him*.

Mr. Humboldt can only lay there on his ice pack, unresponsive in preserving juices, and remark to himself, *apparently not*. He is not in the same hurry as they. He is all resignation: *all this carrying-on, my, my, it all seems so beyond the point from this perspective*. Not to be the spoiler, not to bring them all down, not to be the monkey wrench in the punch, the worm in the fruit salad, he politely keeps his thoughts to himself. He will be meeting the worms soon enough and with them he will talk it over at length.

A mile away from where he lies, shadowed in Gothic steeples that extend in jagged grays along the verdigris field, up and over the headstones, St. Augustine of Hippo's church yard — referred to in the local blue collar lexicon as *the Hippos' Burying Grounds* — is a lonely place of profoundly silent loss. Officer McCallum has flowers in one hand, his wife's arm as snug in the other as the briar and the rose in old mountain songs. His mother-in-law is the diminutive figure treading a few steps behind. They are visiting today, a sad trinity bereft and beaten. Slowly plodding their way, they can be, indeed, are being, watched from any number of dormers on small boxy houses that repeat each other beyond the iron fence.

They come to a place of fresh turned earth, a small grassless patch shorter than a mother's arm, and chase away a garrulous squirrel. There is as yet no headstone: such a recent death, hardly a death at all of one that has hardly lived. *Do you leave a mark if you die unknown? Is there a record somewhere? An accounting of infantile accomplishments: a first bowel movement, a screaming demand for the breast, the lesson of gripping a giant's thumb? The recognition of a comforting face that assures a full stomach and a familiar beating heart?* Officer McCallum ponders such things, gripped by the hope that to all things, as to seasons, there must be some meaning, even to brevity, to a truncation, to the cruel tease of the thing.

And across town, at a lower elevation appropriated from primeval gators and water moccasins, and still awash in mosquito larvae incubating in un-reclaimed pools, prime cuts of Choc Bonjour decompose in a pine box in the abandoned carriage house behind Suttley & Sons, as far away from sensitive human traffic as the acreage will allow. In the converted Victorian, Beales Suttley, father of the Sons, is complaining over-loudly on his candlestick phone to Brother Salvation that the body is emitting vapors that are no longer healthful and that, beyond the five dollars promised by the city, no one has come forth to either claim it or provide for its disposal. Salvation, knowing nothing of mortuary science, asks, "Can't ya jus' put somethin' on the body t'arres' the pro-cess?" which causes Suttley to erupt in a whine of professional slight, "We by da book here, Pastor." Salvation insists that he meant no disrespect, did not intend to suggest inappropriate measures that might be construed as less than reverential to the departed, or less than legal to those with jurisdiction. Salvation's options are reduced to prayer, which even he realizes is a hit or miss proposition. "We a very po' congregation, as ya knows, Brother Suttley," and Suttley, breathing a frustrated fog into the mouth cup, says,

"Ain't no money growin' on my tree neither," and, "Ya wan' da dear man's remains put t'rights, someone's gotta up an' pay fo' da time an' da labor."

Salvation has searched to no avail for a relative, a close friend; he is told one day that Brother Choc was always a solitary soul; that he was married three or four times another; that one or two of the wives up and died many years ago, that *could be* none of them was really married; that some were and some weren't as that old Choc was quite a dashing fellow as a young man; that the women were all childless; that there were several children who have all gone away; that some children remain in town but don't know who their father is; that there was only one child, a daughter, *da name a which 'scapes me,* who married a Tuskegee graduate and went off with him to Nantucket where they were known for many years to operate a Negro boarding house for vacationing *high yellas.* No one has an address, a direction, a tangible lead, or, Salvation tells Suttley, "Da slightes' clue." "Den I sugges's," says Suttley, "We put da gen'leman 'n groun' soons we can gather up d'diggers. I knows a coupla a good boys dig ya a nice hole for two bits each an' don' tender no oldfactory complaints."

The day brings sunshiny warm picnic weather at Contemplation Hill, weather so totally unfit for mourning that the bereaved promenading up the cobbled grade seem to inherit a sense of levity not generally associated with the living as they stroll among the dead. An unusually carefree buzz of conversation erupts, a family reunion amongst the monuments of weeping angels and mordant carved poetry, and vacant marble benches suited more for quiet tears and lonely vigils. It is a great throng: the relatives, the many friends, constituents, lodge brothers, people in the public limelight there to be seen paying respects. Some of them will be in the papers tomorrow. A photographer is busy recording the event as if he were at some socialite's wedding; Quidnunc is jotting names. Here comes the widow, reinforced with grown children, shaped like an African termite mound shrouded in black, an angel of death floating up the trim lawn, an imperceptible and smooth gait as if on wheels, a macabre float in a melancholy parade, an entry from the cult of the bereaved.

Here come travelers refreshed, Humboldts and in-laws, friends from the neighborhood. Here from the club, the church, political venues, the remaining council members. Here comes the Pastor and Mrs. Arpachshad Shem, here city and county department heads, the chamber of commerce weaving its way to graveside. Two hundred folding chairs are unfolded, yet there is standing room only by the time the Mayor and Mrs. Phipps-Rouge arrive with a parcel of judges in tow, all heads downward, as if not wanting to trip over residents in slumber. They snake around the stones, the wrought iron fences, the bunches of wilting flowers returning to the earth. Their shoes thump and tromp, vibrations tickle the grains of soil: the dinner gong of subterranean gourmands — *oh, happy day, come and get it, dust to dust to the mouth of* Lumbrididae, *one man's footsteps another worm's dinner, your loss our gain* — a happy crawling and wending in anticipation that brings such overwrought joy to the tunneled nether places of cemeteries.

Mrs. McCallum, overcome by her feminine nature, collapses quietly, eased down by the professional hands of her husband. With Mother, they form a teepee of entwined bodies, their substance draining from them until they seem as non-skeletal and formless as cephalopods. Someone in a window notes the toppling to a companion. They become a gallery, joined by others in other windows; what to make of three adults evaporating into a church yard, when all around them is summery torpor, lazy bluebottles circling, dragonflies in the lilied fountain, birds flirting with thoughts of families.

The Old Negro Burying Ground is well stocked with weeds and tiny worn crosses. Virtually a potter's field for the segregated, demarcated by a low chain link fence, a trash barrel set at the gate for the good souls who come to clean the detritus left by the camping hobos from the nearby train yards. The Suttley brothers lug their pauper's box, set it down next to the hole where the two shirtless men have been sweating for hours. Four good women from the auxiliary — one the preacher's wife Elisheba, another a porter's spouse — have answered Salvation's call to proxy as mourners. Because of them, the placement of ten unmatched and aged chairs seems not so futile.

A brown Model A — not of this congregation — pulls up to the gate, ejects a young white man from the driver's side. He walks around the back to approach the passenger door, offers his arm to a woman in black, skin color concealed, but possibly of some relationship to the man who waits on her.

Salvation indicates the chairs set as four, four and two. The man and woman approach the latter two but Salvation intervenes, says, "Ain' no Mr. Jimmy Crow up'n here. We all's one an' welcome. Praise Jesus." "Praise Jesus," they say, the man, the woman, the ladies auxiliary four; member five has begged off with a painful case of shingles. Seats are exchanged as bidden. Then another car of some official bearing pulls up in front of the chain link. Chief Prezhki emerges, his nose swaddled and taped, dark blue crescents below each eye, and enters the forlorn yard, hat in hand. He hangs back near the gate and the two diggers study the ground at their feet.

Pastor Shem ahems like a grade school teacher striking a single piano key or giving the light button two quick punches. Watches are already being consulted and the sun is promising a bit of uncomfortable whimsy on the suited flock at attention before the Humboldt Family Plot. He sails through the too-familiar Twenty-third Psalm, *shepherd, not want, pastures* and *waters, the shadow of death* and *the house of the Lord forever,* and for good measure as well as a preamble, taps the Twenty-fifth for *Let integrity and uprightness preserve me.*

"It seems I've been doing this forever." Shem's voice is a weary quiver. "Burying the lost. It is something I will always do until that inevitable time when someone else will do it over me. And each time, secluded in my study the night before, reviewing the life that has slipped from us, I search Scripture for some phrase, some minute gift of divinity that defines with some clarity, some personal recognition, the one who has been taken. Let me say it again: *Let integrity and uprightness preserve me.* Makes one wonder, does it not, if the psalmist prophesied Yardley Humboldt?" There is a compliant shaking of heads, a few smiles, glistening trails of tears silver in the sunlight. P-R tries to shake loose a dry distraction of phlegm in his throat: releases it into his monogrammed hankie.

"We are here to bid farewell to a husband, a father, a son, a friend, a mentor, an example of how life should be conducted, and we rest assured that it will be integrity and uprightness that this fine man will bring to his work at the right hand of the Lord, just as he has done these last forty-three years as he awaited the call. Nourish your loss with profound tears. Enrich your life with the gifts he has given us all. In the Ninetieth Psalm, Moses prays, *Lord, Thou hast been our dwelling place in all generations.* When we live, we are with God. And when we die, the same. And we are the progeny of others who have shared this experience. Our friend has gone nowhere, the lost, essentially not lost. He dwells in the same house, and ere long, in joy, we will, each and every one of us, once again visit with him in the house of the Lord."

"Stand, love," McCallum says, the grass is damp. "There can be no sense to this," she says.

Reverend Salvation thanks those in attendance for their kind gesture. He is sure, he tells them, that Brother Bonjour is appreciative. "Was a fine ol' man, p'raps not as pius as one might a had hoped, but a generous an' a blessed soul. We reads in 'C lesiastes, *dere be no man 'at hath power over da win' t' retain da win'; neither hath he power over da day a death.* Had'e a had such a power, he might a jus' up an' chose dis day hisself. Dis brother'uz rea-*de-e-e.* Dis brother'uz *tired.* Ti-i-i-erd a it all. Da toten an' da fixin' an' da 'aches'n' pains. Da *yessirs* an' da *no ma'ams,* da resi'nation, da very tran'parency a his life. Dere ain' no throng here t'day. No great parcel a witnesses t'da brother's passin'. Dere weren' no throng in'is life, neither. If dey was, dey lo-o-ong since pass dey own selves. Re-*joice* fo' dis man. He in a better place. No mo' arthur-itis, no mo' a dat rumbly gut, no mo' a dem sad ol' fingers bent like branches, stiff an' useless. No mo' fog 'cross da eye. He defin'ly'n'a better place. He be sittin' at da fron' a the train. Firs' class. He 'biden' on the hill. When his train be comin' int' dat final station at Glory Junction, he be loungin' in the parlor car, suckin' one a dem big ol' Cuban *cee*-gars long's your arm."

The good sisters *amen,* affirm his every comment, "Das right, oh, yes, Lawd, oh yes, my sweet Jee-sus, no mo' crossin' da stree', no mo' watchin'da groun', no mo eatin' di-rect outta tin cans."

"No mo'," says Salvation, loudly, clear as a bell even to Prezhky in the back. "vigilance a da wiles a unkin' folks, no mo' boss man, no mo' boss lady, no mo' a the man wid'is big six shooter." His voice scampers like lambs in the hills of the Basque, up down, wave slide roar, tear and spit.

"Uh huh," say the ladies. "Das righ'."

"Brother Choc Bonjour, dear sweet, tire' soul, *choose* dis day t'end it all so's all da res' can begin a' las', lugs hisself up outta dat cushy parlor car seat, steps of a dat train, an' be met by a throng a radient angels. *When da wirlwin' passeth, da wicked be no mo'; But the righteous be an everlastin' foundation.* Go in peace Brother Choc, go in comfort. For it be best t'be 'membered in Heaven even as you been forgot on earth." He ends hoarsely, authentic tears curling over his heavy lips, and the two diggers move forward with their shovels to ensepulcher the abomination that is left of an ancient junkman.

From the elegant parlor in the Humboldt house, Brother Shem looks across the entry hall into the dining room, wonders if it is yet appropriate to take a plate, assault the cold cuts and fried chicken, the potato salad and sliced fruits, all set right by a dark apparition that flits unseen between the bereaved. Sister Shem is nudging his arm, *"I am on the verge of starvation,"* and he is relieved to see that the surviving council members have resolved to partake, have hewn the way like good pioneers, have secured the punch ladle, and a knife to carve the roast goose that has just migrated in seasonal harmony. Momentarily, voices are hushed, but the repast seems to liven folks up. The conversations become louder, denser, overlaid with dozens of subjects. "I will sorely miss that bastard vetoing my every measure." "So sorry for the wife, such a good woman." "They certainly done a job on this joint, remember how it sat on the market for over a year?" "You never saw a more devoted couple." "I've heard there were problems." "Can you believe the Phipps-Rouges have the nerve?" "How would it look if they didn't show up?" "Hell of a spread, you ask me." "Once again, Pastor Shem, you've outdone yourself."

The widow has appropriately turned down a plate. "Just a little something," she is urged, "a bite or two to keep up your strength." She reluctantly agrees to have it set down upon the table in front of her, as she sits on an heirloom sofa holding court. A line forms her way, a son keeps it moving, just short visitations, showing the face, "We don't want to tire Mama." They kiss her cheeks, pat her black-gloved hand, display a lachrymal convergence with her, and they apologize as if they themselves were responsible for train wrecks.

Sarai leans in, her eyes a-glisten, brushes cheeks softly as if the widow were breakable, and Mrs. Humboldt whispers to her, "So very gracious of you to come, I neither deserve nor expected it," and Sarai, diplomatically, righteously, replies, "'Anger resteth in the bosom of fools.'" Then P-R leans in and says, "If there is anything at all I can do…" and she says, "Can *you* turn back the clock? Can you get on the train instead?" He smiles modestly as if he has been thanked for his concern.

Mother has taken to her bed. The McCallums have retired to their porch swing with a pitcher of lemonade. "It is a punishment, you know," she says. "No, no, I can't accept that." They rock slowly. "But it is. For what we did." she insists, and he counters, "For loving?" She tells him, "No, not for loving, for breaking the rules, for the sin." He sets down the frosty glass, wraps an arm about her thin shoulders, offers a resting place for her head. "I can't accept that. If I did it would destroy my faith. I could not cleave to a god that would take an infant to punish the parents. I'd rather it be indifference. Chance. Just something that happens. I see things all the time, and people ask, why us? Well, why not us? Why anybody? Do I know? Do I know? Christ, whatta life! And what would the knowing do for us? What could we possibly do with what we'd know? No, it's random, see? It's gotta be. We're all ducks in a line. And the good Lord is just as broken up about it as we are."

The white woman lifts her veil, introduces herself and her nephew to Salvation. "We are from Thebes," she explains. "I work for the telephone exchange. We have known Choc for many years. He was well liked." Salvation smiles, says, "Was he now?" very much as if he doubts her word. "Oh, yes, yes he was. By everybody." He looks about quizzically, explains, "I don't see them." "Well," she offers, "you know how things are." He rubs his hands together, holds them as if to pray. "Indeed, I do know how things are. And you all, and you young man, aren't you just a bit uncomfortable in this here weed patch for dead Negroes?" She holds his gaze, says, "Actually, I am. This is a…departure for me. We hope we are not intruding." He assures them, "I would surely tell you if you were. Your visit gives me hope that someday we may even be able to lie dead together."

The woman and the young man move on, and Prezhki blocks Salvation's way up to the gate, saying, "You seem to have mastered more than one language." The preacher laughs. "When in Rome," he says. "Know your audience," from the Chief, only slightly nasal now. "That too," Salvation concedes, "and how is it you have sought this audience? We have all the required paperwork. Very nearly civilized, us church niggers." Prezhki takes the taunt in stride. "I gave the old boy a hard time. I guess that wasn't necessary." Salvation shakes his head slowly, nods in agreement. "A rare meeting of the minds, Captain. But I'm afraid you're in the wrong place to do your penance." The Chief ignores the titular slight. "I should have told him when I could, I guess. Sometimes you don't think too far down the line. You get so caught up in…oh, well, I've got to get back." He turns to leave and Salvation says to his back, "Old Brother Chocolate, he knew what was what. I'm sure he thought no less of you for it." Was this a kindness, a barb? Either way, Prezhki is stung, clenches his fist and keeps on walking up to his car, thinking, This is what you get when you try to do a good turn. These people. Well, fuck them. Salvation smiles at the members of the ladies auxiliary and observes, "Brother Prezhki's nose be wider'n mine! Ain't dat a rebelation?" Sister Salvation observes, "An', no doubt, longer."

VI

Socrates Phipps-Rouge, third term Mayor of the City of Tishomingo, the fourth Phipps or Rouge to hold the office, is not unaware of his circumstances. He knows not what to credit, but he is expansively grateful, even if somewhat confused as to whom. He is in his shirtsleeves, on the back lawn overlooking the pond, sacked like produce in his hammock, a glass of locally brewed whiskey propped on his affluent belly, counting blessings in lieu of sheep. And while he is not one to propel misfortune upon others, not wishing to profit from the ill nature of events, he certainly knows how to take account of whatever happens to land in his lap, and mold it to his advantage. Sarai once accused him of *feeding at the trough of despair*. Responding glibly to such pedantry, he had said, *It's true. The muse of opportunity lacks a certain circumstantial sensitivity.*

Of course, there is the horror of the train wreck, which had plunged him into visible despair. You see it in the newspaper photographs, heard it in his failing voice. And there was the portentous weather, the pull of the moon on the gravity of the criminal mind, the arsonists, the threatened labor actions, all of it synthesized by an editorial in the <u>Capital Daily Voice</u> as the "fifth season of 1937."

This was a time when Providence seemed to avert eyes, to let the chips fall where they may, to defy physics and reason and meteorological certitude, to loosen the glue of sanity and order and function: God on Spring break, God preoccupied with other celestial matters, God in absentia with no one to watch the shop, God nursing a wound to the exclusion of all other cares, God in deep, impenetrable mourning. It happens to gods who exist in such solitary omnipotence, gods who are top-down deities, micro-managers, unable to trust the operational lubrication left in their absence. Things happen, go awry, boomerang and swerve; tracks rust, signals mix, the skins of solids flake like piecrusts, and the systematic staples of human experience are shuffled and diced and dealt into excusable mysteries.

And, P-R is cut to the quick by the loss of his mistress, pain nurtured piteously by authentic affection, concerned sick over the rocking of continental plates, the killings, the senseless demise of an infant, the continuing suspicion of his own fidelity, the badgering of the pastor, the verbal slugfest with the Chief, the humiliation in the Superintendent's office, the omission of his steady dysgenic hand on the wheel. He releases himself from the hammock stretched between two sweet gums that were old when his grandfather claimed the estate, wanders down to the water's edge to skip a stone or two, assures himself, *P-R, my man, y'all're better off without her, source of disquiet as she became; and the tremors are gone and civic response was both rapid and efficient; trains are running on schedule, a new signal system, and rewritten rule books on the press; that gossipy woman has been effectively gagged; the central witness has wound up in the bowels of a dog; Sarai knows her place and will get over it if she hasn't already; there is no viable candidate to oppose me; and two unscrupulous associates are about to pay some dues.*

There is a stillness on the land, a warm sun and a cool, whispery breeze, a lubricant in the running of machines, an unwound spring in the machinations of men.

※

As bidden, Prezhki meets P-R in Memorial Square. They sit on a bench gazing up at the marble angel. P-R is emancipating peanuts from their shells, offers to Prezhki who characteristically begs off.

"On duty?" P-R says. "Not even peanuts! How's the face? Appears to be healing adequately."

Prezhki is alternately splaying his fingers and balling them into a fist. "I'm *literally* up to my nose in your shit, P-R. This wouldn't have been any more your fault if you had swung the pipe yourself."

"That's a terrible thing to say. *I* didn't lead Moses Brown astray."

"What do you want, P-R?"

"This is my question," P-R ponders aloud, turning his head to appreciate the stone-cold angel. "Why do they always sculpt them with one tit bare?"

"Do they?"

"Pretty nearly always. Y'all've seen them. You have this toga thing draped over one, and the other, pert and sassy, pointing the way for all to follow. Why do you suppose?"

"I don't spend much time concerned with marble tits, P-R."

"Hers were like that, the woman. Pert and sassy like a young girl's. Well, nearly. Gravity always wins, of course. A bit more give, I'd say, a smidgen more heft. Such things are the great imponderables."

"I have spent too much time concerned with this woman. In my job, see, we focus on facts. I leave the imponderables, as you say, to the politicians. Hers are a couple of tits I don't want on my hands."

P-R turns to him in surprise. "Well dealt. So y'all have a sense of humor after all."

"I think so. But that wasn't it."

"Anyway, it wouldn't be like y'all to so waiver from commitment."

"No, it would not. I obey a certain set of standards when I can. Look, get on with it. What is this about?"

"I wanted to apologize."

"You don't anymore?"

"I *want* to apologize."

"If I'm going to owe you something, I'd rather stay angry."

"My ill temper was the product of certain distractions. I'm sorry I was so detached as to take out my chagrin upon y'all."

"Are you now? Well, I'm sorry you were too. I'm sorry you ever lured me into your dirty little adventures. I'm sorry we're having this conversation. I'm sorry that within five minutes you're going to ask me to do something I don't want to do. I'm sorry that I'll probably do it, things being what they are. Then I'll be sorry I did. So, Your Honor, shove your *sorry* up your sorry ass and serve up the current humiliation while it's still warm."

P-R brushes something from his sleeve, a piece of feather, an insect, a speck of soot. "*I'm* sorry you feel that way, Walter. I think it's in both of our interests to present a united front."

"Christ! That again!" Prezhki has his wrist twisted, his chin resting in the palm. "Maybe, maybe, but it doesn't have to make me happy."

"Think of the alternatives."

"Why do you think I'm still sitting here?"

"Then this will be simple."

"It had better not involve that woman!"

"Oh, that? No, sadly no. There have been tears shed, I'm afraid. It's hard for the women, you see, to leave well enough alone. Give them a hand, they want an arm. Comfort them, they want a ring. They place considerable, and I might add, usurious value upon their favors. It's a natural thing, of course. Even single celled life forms felt compelled to evolve. No, this particular project shouldn't get you *lured* into anything…well, lurid. I have a sealed envelope in my pocket. There is nothing inside to implicate anybody in anything, in case the *federales* stop y'all at the border. It's just an invitation. A few simple lines in my best cursive. Only the recipient will understand the gist. I am going to hand you this envelope and I am going to ask you to simply deliver it to someone you solidly trust down at the Tishomingo Depot. With the envelope will be a nice portrait of Mr. Hamilton, folded across the nose, which y'all will offer to that same person without further explanation other than he is to deliver it immediately to Division Headquarters, Superintendent Ferrous, before the office closes this afternoon. That's it."

"That's it? Pick up some groceries for you? Stir your coffee? Sit on your lap and take dictation? Why don't you deliver your own goddamned invitation and leave me out of it?"

"With an extra hand, there's a tendency for the waters to muddy more rapidly. A benefit, in this case. Besides, I'm the Mayor. A bit beneath the office, don't you think?" He removes the envelope with the ten neatly clipped to it. "So, how is the beak?"

"Can still smell shit."

"I certainly hope the odor in no way impaired y'all's reason when dealing with Moses Brown?"

"What are you asking? Did I tell him? Let's say I attempted dissuasion. But he's a stubborn cuss, that one."

"Dissuasion, but not redirection?"

"Whatever he thinks he knows at the moment, he didn't get it from me." Prezhki stands and snatches up the offering. "Last time, P-R, so I hope this is important. No more of this crap, understand? I'd rather get flat feet on a Darktown sidewalk than share a bench with you again."

"Now, now."

"Yeah," spits the Chief, shoving the envelope into his jacket pocket, stomping away in a pique. "Last fucking time! You remember."

Prezhki makes no secret of his displeasure as he surges into traffic, waving down cars, jackknifing in between them in utter disdain for their very presence. He skips steps up to the great mahogany doors with etched-glass traceries and gold leaf print, into the marble hall where complainants doze on benches, waiting to be seen, up the arc of steps that lead to the gallery, and into the anteroom insulating his office.

Old Mansard, on the force longer than the Chief, is at the desk, phones quiet, his large pink head stuck in crime pulp, and McCallum is seen entering the locker room to store his civvies. Prezhki leans into Mansard's magazine — "Detective Stories" — says, "What's he doing here?" He points with a head nod, the anti-directional nose out of sync.

"Suh?" Mansard's breath is all garlic and tobacco.

"Christ, man! What do you do here anyway?"

"Oh, McCallum. His shift, Ah reckon."

"You reckon? Good. What do you *know?* Does he have a shift?"

"Don' us all?"

"Wasn't he given some time?"

"I ain't in charge a no roster?"

"Keep up the good work, Mansard. Crimes to fight!" Prezhki trots over to the locker room, calls in, "McCallum. Keep me company," and bangs his way into his office with the young officer, now half uniformed, behind him. The Chief sits on the edge of his desk, says, "Sit down."

McCallum does so, posture-correct in a blond-wood chair. His shirttails hang askew.

"Why're you here?"

"My shift."

"Didn't they write you out for a few days?"

"I asked to come back in."

Prezhki circles around the desk, settles into his own chair, scans a few papers on his desk, says, "Nobody told me."

McCallum thinks the remark requires no answer: either that, or he can't think of one.

"I think you should stay home for a few more days. Finish out the week, and then we'll see."

"I can't."

"Wasn't asking you."

"Need to be doin' somethin'."

"Go fishing. Paint the house. Jesus, Officer, stop beating yourself up!"

"I'm not. Just need to be busy."

"What about the wife?"

"She feels guilt. I told her she shouldn't, but, well…this all's a helluva thing."

"Go home and hold her hand."

"She went with her mother. To the coast for a few days. I didn't wanna go. I need to be doin' somethin'…familiar. I need to start…you know, goin' on. Ain't one to sit on the beach, anyhow."

Prezhki nibbles a thumbnail, lets out a long breath. "How you holding up?"

"Okay. This kind a thing…Knocks the wind outta a fella."

"Knocks the wind out, huh? That's a way of putting it. I guess it does. Look, McCallum, my heartfelt sympathies, but all the shit goes on. I've got a department to run and I can't have an officer on the streets whose mind is elsewhere."

"I can't sit in no empty house all day. I'll be fine here."

"You in a position to say?"

The officer's face is one of agonized petition. He is at the edge of both his chair and his wits. "I need to do this. I need to kind a locate myself. I'm without bearings. I'm ramblin'."

"Don't play on my sympathies. I am a heartless son of a bitch. Look, you screw up and I'll ship you off to the doc. We take it a day at a time. You don't go out on calls until I okay it myself. You can clean up some of the paper around here. Put a dent in the backlog while things are quiet. Can you do that?"

"Rather t'be out on calls."

"I'd rather you stay home. Final offer. Can you do that?"

"Yes, sir."

"Good. We don't stick our necks out here. We play by the rules. No one's a hermit here. Our lives depend on each other. So find a pencil and get to work."

"Yes, sir."

"One more thing. Your buddy, the Mayor, needs you to deliver a message to someone trustworthy down at the railroad station. Someone who can follow directions. Keep his yap shut. Who do you know?"

"Several guys. He asked for me? Why he don't just gowan'send someone from his own office?"

"You've been his cabbie long enough to know there is no straight line between two points. Just keep your mouth shut, take this letter and five bucks down to the depot, the other five's yours, and get it delivered to the division super in UF before they close up. Don't report back. I don't want to hear about this again. I can count on you, right?"

"I don't need the five."

"Give it to someone who does. Fucking depression, remember?"

"This is not police business?"

"If the Chief of police tells an officer to do it, it's police business. Sometimes the boundaries get a little fuzzy, don't they? Police, politics, acts of man, acts of God. This'll be the last time we extend this particular courtesy, okay?"

"Yes."

"You all right?"

"Yes. And you?"

"Me?" He can think of no misfortune of his own that wouldn't pale in lieu of McCallum's.

"The nose?"

Prezhki touches palm to wound, is suddenly self-conscious, likes to think of himself as a vigilant fellow, someone who can see things coming from a long way off. "Oh, that. Fella made a mistake about a dame. You have yourself a good day, officer," he says, immediately regretting the casual courtesy, its relative banality, the pain pronounced in the abbreviated grimace on McCallum's ashen face.

As a practical matter, of course, it's all okay. McCallum is a trusted hand at running interference, clandestine night rides, the delivery of sealed envelopes with suspiciously rectangular cargoes, and the dispersal of Canadian whiskey at Christmas time. It is the stuff of police tradition: the straight face, the averted eye, the favor returned in the form of a positive review or a crisp new bill rolled into his holster. McCallum considers himself a good cop and an ethical man. He is not troubled by journalistic conceits such as graft, patronage, nepotism, or any one of a thousand different names for inferential tasks. It is all part and parcel of the job, and he does it with the same due diligence as he does the issuance of a traffic citation or the arrest of a scoundrel.

He finds an unclaimed squad car in the garage, just at the end of a trail of bloodstains leading from the shop office. It feels good to be behind the wheel, the static of the radio that seems only to work a mile or two from the station, the heft of the Police Special on his waist. A couple of suits in an unmarked car nod as they pass him in the entrance way — them coming in, he going out into the light of day — feeling his sense of authority and responsibility as he casts a wary eye at other vehicles, at a man selling hot roasted nuts by the square. McCallum sends a cautionary chill up and down the avenue by his very presence. It all feels good, these mundane signs of life.

He sees a street cleaner tugging a wheeled can, harpooning spent tissues, half a hot dog; the carpenters putting the last touches on a new plate glass window frame; a welder correcting an errant cast iron column at the Tishomingo Trust Co. The usual line of scruffy men meanders from the soup kitchens. There is a sense of normalness. There are trees in bloom, a wholesome aroma of hot donuts, the busy harmony of traffic. All is becoming right at last for Tishomingans. There are fewer of them than there had been a week ago, jarringly obvious to the young cop, but even loss is subject to its own attrition.

He hones in on Mr. Red. All the local cops know the bull. Like beer on tap, he's a fixture at the Copper's Baton, a saloon rising up from sawdust, brass foot rails, cigar smoke so thick it mutes voices. Uniforms and suits clink mugs here, share spittoons, unload on each other and McCarnagin working the bar with spritz and cloth, carouse the kind of women that are attracted to brief dalliances with less than gentle men. Red comes here for kindred belonging, envious of the blue and brass brilliance of their attire, the neat repetitive caps with shoe-polish beaks reflecting the stained glass lamps. It is a dark place of dark wood, advertising mirrors, dim booths; there is over all the perfume of painted women, warming peanuts, Lone Feather, and vomit. Were he a younger man, Red tells himself, he would be one of them. As it is, he is able to share tales told in the manner of fishermen. He speaks of busting heads and kicking asses down embankments from moving freights, and likes to contribute a punch or two when the inevitable brawl commences to redecorate the room; throwing big, ham-fisted wallops of jaw-cracking intensity, gamely receiving the random chop to his kidneys, the sorry organs already knee deep in hops and suds. He's a head cracker, Mr. Red is, a plug of hard flesh designed to dismantle framework, to re-sculpt cheekbones, re-socket eyes: a teller of masculine tales celebrating belligerent glee that the cops, once appropriately inebriated, can relish as if the product of one more nearly their own. McCallum has spent many an hour teasing him on.

The officer runs the car along the service road that skirts the mainline and offers grade crossing access to the yards and shops. The tappets click like cards in bicycle spokes. He sees Red in pursuit of two kids with stolen fire buckets, gives a short yipping crank to the siren so that the concave-bottomed red cans drop to the coal blackened soil and the boys disappear into the underbrush along the embankment leading up to Railroad Avenue. McCallum pulls up to Red who is breathing heavily, tucking in his shirt and leaning on his knees as if he will find his breath on the ground where he has dropped it.

"There's your cans," he says through the window.

"Oh, I would a caught 'em, alright. You di'n't...have t'do that. They're... not supposed...t'steal the...fuckers," says Red sucking sooty air. "That's why the bottoms...are curved. Not supposed t'be...a use t'no one. Damn kids these days'll steal your drawers an' run 'em up flag poles before you...feel the breeze."

"Betcha was a time you'd a had those two scamps layin' track 'til their mamas come to claim 'em."

"I still could a had 'em. Anyways, was…a time, aw-right. I guess I ain't so young no more." He straightens, adjusts buttons, hat, tie. "How're y'all gettin' on, McCallum?"

"Oh, as well as need be, I suppose."

"Tough break there. Me an' the wife're awful sorry. Never had none a our own, y'know, on account a the wife not sparkin' all 'er pistons, as the Doc said, and I cannot imagine the loss of a little one. Listen a'me blowin' smoke. We're just awful sorry."

"I appreciate that, Red. I will pass that on."

"I give to the pool, y'know. The c'lection. I hope it helped with expenses 'n'all."

"We're gonna be just fine. Everybody's really come through. People at the station, neighbors, folks 'long the beat. Everyone's been real considerate."

"Brothers in arms," Red says as he retrieves his flask. "Little pepper-upper?"

"I'm working."

"Me too, friend." He takes a hearty slug. "I need you to do me a little police favor."

"Can count on me. This official?"

"What I'm told."

"I get t' know what I'm about?"

"Wouldn't know t' tell ya."

"What the hell, huh! Secrets a the trade."

"Way I see it."

"So?"

"Little delivery."

"Who to?"

"Division Supe."

He wipes his mouth on his sleeve. "I'm impressed."

"Don't be. I get the feeling this is just some routine matter."

"They don't have no phones at the PD? Access t' Western Union?"

"Whatta I know? Couple a grunts like us, huh? Take the envelope, get it to the big man before he leaves his office, and get yourself a steak for your trouble."

"Might jus' be enough t'fill the flask too."

"Might be."

Just after noon, Mr. Red flashes his employees pass as he gathers himself up on the boarding stool, lodges himself facing backwards on the first bench, the unmarked envelope snug in his pocket, a crinkled ten in his billfold. He is already snoring when the northbound local huffs out of Tishomingo on its last lap to Uncas Falls. He dreams happily of being hustled along by a trio of angry German shepherds, frothing and straining at their leashes, a gaggle of bums dropping their bindles and abandoning the warmth of a burning trash barrel. He is unaware that the train passes uneventfully through David's Sling, sways like a rumba down the grade towards the terminal and the junctions of the river and the competition. Out through the vaulted waiting room with its four-sided hanging clock, down a cascade of broad steps, onto a trolley with open sides to let in the latest incarnation of spring.

He is deposited in front of the Tishomingo Lines Building, proceeds up the caged lift to the top floor and is directed to a seat with magazines — <u>Railway Age</u>, <u>Life</u>, <u>National Geographic</u>, <u>The 1936 Tishomingo Lines Annual Report</u> — and remains there with his secret parcel for nearly two hours.

Finally, Ferrous lopes through his door in swift child-strides borrowed from a younger man. His umbrella and overcoat are tucked under his arm, and he is end-of-the-day hatted. He darts for the door with not so much as a goodnight to the ladies behind their Underwoods. Mr. Red, barely awake, calls out, "Superintendent Ferrous. A minute, please, sir," and drops his periodical with black and whites of pygmies with waist-length mammaries.

"Who the hell ah you?" Ferrous doesn't slow, ducks into the men's room with Red on his heals. The little man is easy to pace. Red turns his coat, taps his badge for Ferrous to read backwards in the mirror as he rinses his hands. "Y'all one a mine?" He wipes his hand, tosses the damp towel to the policeman, says, "Shine that theah thing. It's a *dis*-grace."

Red tells him he has something for him. Ferrous says to make an appointment and races out the door and down to the lift. The bull is panting. He towers over Ferrous but feels diminished nonetheless. "I been waitin' goin' on two hours."

"Then Ah thank y'all fo' yore patience," says Ferrous getting in. "Ma'vin," he says, nodding to the operator, then telling Red, "You got 'til we get t' the lobby. This is the 'xpress, is it not, Ma'vin?"

"Cer'inly dat, Mr. Ferrous, suh. Cer'inly dat."

Red holds out the envelope. Ferrous says, "How y'all know it's fo' me? Ain' nothin' on it Ah can see?"

"Tishomingo PD business, sir."

"Why ain't y'all on a job, anyway?"

"Lobby," Marvin says.

"I am, sir. We often work in conjunction with TPD."

"Do y'now? That come from me? We'all'll be lookin' inta ower 'lationship'th our southe'ly boys in blue." He snatches the envelope, stuffs it negligently into his coat pocket, leaves Red letter-less and insignificant and accompanied by the echo of footsteps ricocheting off of marble.

It is long after a dinner servant-served that Ferrous recalls the envelope, decides to leave it until the next day, is tickled with the slightest feather of curiosity, and proceeds to the entry hall closet to retrieve it. He holds it up to a great floral Tiffany — vivid grapes, forest green leaves — but it remains a mystery. He carries it back to his desk, produces a brass letter knife cast with the company seal, gives the envelope one authoritative swipe, unfolds twice, reads quickly, and says, "Shit!"

"My deah, Cap'ain?" remarks Mrs. Ferrous from the hallway.

"So vera sorry, Mothuh. Ah seem t' have fo'go'en mahse'f."

"Indeed ya have. In'all these yea's, Ah don't b'lieve Ah have evuh hea'd such language in this house. What could pos'bly be the cause?"

"Oh, nothin'. Nothin't'all. Ah…In ret'ospect, Ah ovuh'eacted. A trifle. That mayuh they'all got up theah'n 'Mingo's been gettin' un'uh mah skin. The 'mpe't'nence a some people!" He tears up the letter. "Ah won'uh 'f'it ain' jus' bes' t'nore 'im 'nti'ely," he says without certainty.

But, before retiring, he makes a phone call, orders a Special made up for the morning. It must include his private car *Eunice,* named in honor of his wife. He wants it stocked with breakfast for three: eggs, rashers, fresh trout if it can be gotten — beefsteak if not. He wants the car on the far side of the Junction yard, the engine uncoupled and waiting far enough away to reduce soot to a non-issue. There is to be security on the platform front and rear, the windows latched, the curtains drawn. He makes second call, so that the next morning finds P-R wielding the big Buick past the empty lots on White Meadow Road, the hood ornament lining up with the steeple of Pastor Shem's chapel.

The Mayor pulls onto the dirt lot, steps out into fresh air and the first peek of sun over the Camels, wipes a spot of churchyard dirt from the rear fender with a personalized hanky. He is in time to see Shem, in overalls and straw hat, tripping out of a tool shed behind the rectory, wielding a hoe and rake and a large watering bucket with a spout as long as a swan's neck, and looking overly rural, as if he is going to suck on a long blade of grass or take to whittling. P-R catches up to him soon after he reaches a small vegetable garden, finds him kneeling with shears in carrot and lettuce furrows, tomato vines on skeletal wire supports, several families of squash. Not far away, Shem's grandchildren are enjoying the swings, the teeter-totter.

"Am I interrupting prayer?" P-R inquires.

Shem says he thought he heard a car, that he didn't know P-R to be such an early bird. P-R responds, "Y'all being the worm, the telltale soil clinging to your skin, I thought I'd catch you casual and defenseless."

"The worm? I see. It's really early, Socrates, for such threatened Socratics. I don't know that I'm up to it." P-R tells him, "If you can dig in dirt, you're just where you need to be." Shem pivots on his knee, sits back on his rump pockets in the irrigated soil, says. "I don't like the sound of this."

P-R looks around to see if they are alone, secure, far enough removed from the child's play. Assured, he removes his hat and shields his eyes from the closest ascending star in the east. Then he squats, runs a hand through the dirt, inspects a clod and discards it. "I always thought the green thumb was the wife's."

"No, no. Mine all the way. It is sort of prayer, you see. A communing, as they say."

"Do they say that?"

"They all might as well. I find it liberating. Back to paradise. But it's not horticulture you all're here for, is it?"

P-R glances up at the chapel eaves. The same flaked shingles sit askew and overlapped by neighbors. Several have shattered on the ground, asks if he's that easy to read.

"Like a primer."

"Well, read this then." He pulls out a garden stake, and, to Shem's dismay, a bean vine with it. He uses it to trace BREWERY in the soil. Irrigation seeps into the script so that it seems written in liquid. Shem calls it cryptic. "Y'all's stock and trade. Not mine. Maybe you can weave a little parable. The satanic evils of drink. Something to emphasize that good men, men of conscience, men of God, neither imbibe nor traffic in. Am I getting your attention?"

"What is it you think you know?"

"I know that within every silver lining there's a cloud. I know that politicians are disingenuous, that lawyers are self serving, that cops are crooks, and business men greedy, and that leaves hypocrisy for the wholesome likes of a man who preaches morality while stealthily copping a feel from a nubile bosom. The kind of fakir who lends his sanctified name to both sermons and suds while one pen doesn't know what the other pen is signing. What else do y'all need to know that I know? See, we're all subject to the great sport of taking. When we behave, we credit morality. Religion. But really, we'd most of us eat our own progeny if it suited us and we wouldn't get caught. Should be insurance for getting caught. The capitalist solution, you ask me. Ethics, you see, are only the output of guilt. That's why God can be such a capricious bastard and still we fall on our knees before Him. God can rant and rage, take your first born, unleash the floods, rattle the earth and get away with it because who's going to complain? Who's going to implicate God? God, alone amongst us, has no ethics, fears no condemnation, because God can't get caught. God is above suspicion."

"You all've become tiresome, my friend. I suspect you're trying to back me into some kind of a corner. I'm a little lost here, outside...cornerless."

P-R stands, says, "*Lost but not forgotten, darling Clementine.* It's going to be a lovely day, my friend. Go on inside and slip into something less *rube*-ish. We'all're going to quibble with a business partner of y'all's. Not God, the other one."

Shem is struck dumb. He doesn't know whether to adhere to denial, to act offended, to spew denunciations, or just throw in his hand. Receiving no divine inspiration, he does the latter, slumps sadly back to the house and appears shortly in mourning black. He tries to convince himself that it is for the sake of curiosity only.

In the car, P-R, fat with contentment, nearly giddy, does all the talking. It comes fast and with the punctuation of excited spray that dusts the wheel. "See, when I started to suspect something smelling of long dead bass, I had no idea you and I would ever be enjoying the passing countryside together on our way to Oz. A guy like y'all, so good at what he does, should never dabble in what he doesn't. This county of ours is not exactly an IRS office. Y'all want to be bored to tears with the records, you just pay a small fee and a friendly clerk is only too happy to open its transactional heart and soul. So here's the question: what do y'all get when you have street running plus hops plus one hundred bottles of beer on the wall? If my calculations are correct, and the county affirms they are, you get one covert wheeler-dealer with bituminous eye shadow, one pureed councilman with a wife as loose as syrup, and a preacher who bears false witness and covets his neighbor's ass, in a way of speaking. Y'all an end-of-days sort of preacher, my friend? A believer in red cows, great rewards, the final battle, the culmination of time? Because, my long suffering childhood companion, today is a day of reckoning, hellfire and brimstone, the clash of lance and sword, the thrash of a chair cane, just desserts, the twisting of the knife, the culling of the saved from the sinner, the temple rebuilt on the temple mound, the gallop of the horsemen's quartet, hallelujah, Brother Shem, in this *great gettin' up mornin', fare thee well, fare thee well*. Sing it with me, brother. *Fare thee well, fare thee well*. If only that bell-timbered nightingale Mrs. Humboldt were here to lead our happy congregation. *Fare thee well, fare thee well*. I can almost see the life-pump of alabaster bosoms heave with melodious balm up from that hallowed diaphragm. Can almost feel them breathing their all into my cupped palms." He is tapping the wheel in time, dancing his foot across the peddle.

"Next car I get is going to be a convertible! Let the sun shine in. Let the Lord look down. And God help the bird that dares shit on me a second time!"

VII

T. RAIL FERROUS HAS LITTLE USE for the present, much less the future. He enjoys upright clouds of black coal smoke, disdains the stink of diesel; believes brass and velvet and dark woods from tropical rainforests proclaim luxury and stability and hint at bedrock foundations — chrome is cold and artless — prefers vertical to horizontal, the Victorian to the Prairie School; would rather listen to Elgar on his Victrola than "The Rite of Spring" on anything whatsoever; enjoys William Dean Howells over the pornography of Theodore Dreiser; champion's Hoover's laissez faire to Rooseveltian socialism; a chaw to a smoke; parlor cars with vestibules to the industrial minimalism of streamliners; top down decisions to collegiality; experience to education; trusts to regulation; the Bishop of Usher to Charles Darwin. The late Aker Maelstrom once said of him: "It is time for the dinosaurs to retire to their tar pits."

Therefore, Ferrous' taste in private rail transit leans toward Wagner Palace Cars — defunct, absorbed by Pullman thirty-eight years ago — all that golden tracery and colored glass lamps, varnish thick like cake frosting and transparent as the skins of ghosts, gleaming hand rails, the evidence of artisans, and the muraled clerestory panels. The detail: the exquisite, unrestrained conceit of curvaceous detail.

The company had offered him the use of a stout modern business car of sleek, steel simplicity, a sensible car that bespoke economy and efficiency. He complained that he couldn't ride in it, that mobile bunker, that he felt like it required of him an iron helmet, consultations of roll out charts and volumes of

Clausewitz or Mahan. "It's bleak, mundane. Don't impress, don't draw y'on in. Says *caution*, a Spa'tan lack a aht. Yore p'ivate car, now, ought a boldly proclaim *p'ospe'ty*, 'ngu'f y'all'n its lux'ry, cha'enge y'all t' keep up'th partic'luh Joneses what rides'n they own. It should *awe!*"

To underscore the point, he had his property people locate an older car at his own expense; had it stripped and remade until it looked showroom new for 1893; had it painted a deep regal maroon and numbered it with a Roman numeral "I" and had the name *Eunice* scrolled within an intricate lacy frame on its side. They sat it on a new undercarriage, installed two decades worth of retooled safety features to keep the Feds smiling — Westinghouse air brakes, knuckle couplers and new trucks — and found room for a generator and a full kitchen and imported chef. They stocked it with stogies, champagne, a glassed-in bookshelf with buckram bound editions of Gibbons, Plato, Hawthorne, Trollope, Irving and a great dark, foreboding tome of Dante for good measure and self-effacement. Silverware from Tiffany was inscribed with the Tishomingo crest and the table was set with a special gold-teased edition of the company's trademark, dining car china. Small original oil paintings from the Hudson River School occupied the minimal wall space.

The *Eunice* stands proudly alone on the farthest western siding of the yard, a figurative diamond in the literal rough, the cook fires of a nearby hobo camp visible from the platform, the ground oil slicked with waste. The locomotive, conjoined with tender, is catching its breath a hundred yards up the track, ticking like a massive clock, aspirating in big heaves and sighs, clunks and pings, a huge recovering animal after a run, shuddering. The crew is tweaking with wrenches and lubricating cans. All can be seen from the service road where P-R enters the yard.

Red hails the Buick, a passé derby insolently cocked across his forehead, his heavy boot extinguishing a cigarette in the polluted soil.

"Gentlemen, gentlemen," says Red with cheer. "Superintendent Ferrous's expectin' y'all. Ya don't mind, I'll ride along."

P-R inches forward in a quick roll, says, "Can find our own way," and leaves Red chagrinned in a cloud of exhaust. In the distance, on the station platform, he sees two woman with baggage awaiting northbound traffic; wonders if one is the now-lost Mrs. Brown. He pulls up next to the opulent coach and is greeted by another bull who opens P-R's door, and motions toward the back platform. The sky is ablaze with blue, almost black at the fringes, several nascent puffs of moisture adrift and wispy white. It is a picture postcard day, *wish you were here.*

Shem, not feeling the spirit, says, "I pity you P-R." It comes quiet, solemn, more uneasy than superior.

P-R tells him to save it, gets out, turns and says, "We'll see who requires pity, we will."

Behind them, Red is attempting a frantic run in their direction, is seen stopping, bending at the waist with hands on his knees. Another bull joins the visitors up the steps. He knocks cautiously, questioningly, on the door, and opens it for them.

It is dark inside, typically Ferrous. The shadows crunch size and numbers as factors of contention. "Good mo'nin', gen'l'men," he says from his seat at a gray, depthless dining table. It is elegantly set for four. Again, the broad tones of his voice fail to betray his size, as if, on his railroad, he can manipulate acoustics. It seems as if his very office has been set on wheels.

P-R peruses the shadow table, says, "Good morning yourself, Ferrous. Who else we'all expecting?" Ferrous credits the fourth chair to eventualities, a nice touch, symmetrical, balanced, dimensioned to the "fo' ca'd'nal *directions*," a memorial to the fallen partner, a metaphor akin to the rider-less black horse. P-R antes, "Or your ascendant partner, *the Widow* Humboldt?" This gets Shem's attention.

"Patience, P-Ah." Ferrous cautions. "We got a who'e mo'nin' t' draw conclusions as well as swo'ds. Ah hope y'all saved room fo' some b'eakf'st."

Shem's eyes are adjusting, targets Ferrous' on a level with his own. Perhaps the little man is perched on a padded seat, congealed in gloom; perhaps it is not his torso that is responsible for his diminution. "Thank you, no, I've eaten."

"Too bad. Mr. Denvuh sets a tant'lizin' table. An' y'all, P-Ah? Y'all ain'gone let a ol' man eat ahl 'lone?"

"You wouldn't be making a subtle play to have me removed from the next Mayoral contest, would y'all?" Ferrous admits that such has crossed his mind but finds poisoning too melodramatic. P-R says he's probably not the one to ask.

"So...what? Greek! Pois'nin'. S'pose y'all don't get up t' The Roadhouse down theah in Thebes, do y'all? Speakin' a Greeks an' poison."

"I don't know it," P-R says. "Not my favorite part of town."

Ferrous rings a small crystal bell. The chef, Mr. Denver it is assumed, appears in white toque, a clean towel over his arm, sends a young black boy, also in white, to pour the champagne, place napkins in the gentlemen's laps as if they are helpless quadriplegics. Shem waves him off.

"Jus' two a us," says Ferrous. He holds up his glass to P-R who does not return the courtesy, sips on his own while cocktails of succulent cubed fruit appear, perched on tall stems like flamingo legs. Ferrous skewers a geometric pinch of cantaloupe, downs it quickly, says, "Ah's thinkin' t' have us all place ower hands palm up on a table."

"To summon Humboldt?"

"No, suh, t'see who got who by the tes'icles."

P-R rolls a piece of fresh watermelon in his mouth, spits the seed into his napkin. "My hands are feeling awfully heavy this morning. If you've plotted to get me to let go in the act of lifting utensils, you will force me to boast of my famous ambidexterity."

Shem says, "I really don't know why I need to be a party to this. I have no idea what I'm doing here."

"Perhaps," says P-R, "if we segue from the topic of testicles, you will feel a greater sense of belonging."

Shem is about to protest P-R's behavior when they are interrupted again by the boy bringing out the serving tray. It is set on an argentite stand and supports

351

platters of poached eggs, fried trout on a bed of rice and julienned vegetables, toast, jams, thick sizzling bacon, all decorated with sprigs of parsley, and then a large bowl of spiced potatoes, chopped, garnished with minced green and red peppers, circled by a ring of pearl onions, and finally, oysters shivering on a bed of ice. A pot of coffee is poured, to which temptation even Shem yields.

"Ah 'pol'gise, Pastuh Shem," says Ferrous. "Did w'all fo'get grace?"

"I'm not here to be mocked."

"'Fraid the Mayuh heah has othuh *i*-deas. We both heah t' be mocked."

"Mocked, humiliated," P-R stammers, "such a fine line. Let's say, at the risk of cliché, that the only thing served this morning better than Mr. Denver's elegant breakfast, will be revenge." He holds the cocktail dish up for the boy. "Pass me the eggs there, will y'all? And two or three strips of that bacon." He looks to Shem. "If y'all're not going to touch that trout…" It gets passed. He thanks them both.

Shem says, "Look, Socrates, who are you all to go threatening anybody? Not exactly a babe in the woods, as we all know. And, besides, nothing illegal has been done by any of us."

"We'll leave that to the barristers when, and if, we come to it. I wasn't yet up to that. I was thinking…Mr. Denver," he calls, "my compliments. I was thinking more on the level of the unethical, the kind of thing that gets up the dander of those to whom we are answerable."

"We are all likewise answerable. You no less than us," says Shem. "What about Mrs. Humboldt? What about a young mother in my church? What about the rumored woman in black who takes a nighttime jaunt with a Nigra down to the red light end of Thebes? Not your favorite part of town, indeed! And who else will come crawling out of the woodwork once the finger is pointed? How many in all, Your Honor: wives, daughters, whores?"

"You give me altogether too much credit." He passes platters to Ferrous who is enjoying the repast as well as Shem's discomfort.

Ferrous says, "Mr. Denvuh trained in Pa'is, Rome, Vienna. Cost a p'etty penny t'ntice him out t' the piney woods. Nea'ly had t'shanghai the po' fella."

"I'll bet you did. But oh, the spread! Some things are worth the sacrifice. Women, I think, are worth the sacrifice. You see, many men carry a grudge about women. Blame them for their own failures, the taxing of their self worth. The whole Eve issue. Easily swayed by any clever Tom, Dick or serpent that slithers by and seduces in a voice of melodious temptation. Most men make the life-long mistake of choosing to dwell forever with the one with which they made passion-driven promises in the first place. Not that passion's the problem in itself. Passion is good, with parameters. And passion does come with parameters. Parameters that you can measure in years, days, sometimes minutes if you're over anxious. That's why, when it's gone with one, the wise man finds it elsewhere. The parameter is the diversion. Don't think they'all don't understand, the women. They hiss and stomp and spit for effect, but they'd rather be done with all that tussling as long as the man continues to pay the rent and doesn't take to lashing out with blunt objects, doesn't beat silverware into projectiles. Me, I'm an old hunting hound, I am. There is no sort of fence that will keep me in the yard when there is a bitch in heat within a reasonable sniffing radius. So what, exactly, *do* y'all know about me, my friends, that isn't at least imagined by everyone else in the county? What could y'all possibly hold over my head? That I'm a scoundrel? That I whore about town with abandon? And who will bear witness? The women? I think not. Sarai? She is long past private rage and does not relish the idea of public humiliation. The cuckolds? The ringleader of that sorry lot was lost, as we know, at David's Sling, poor man. As for the others, it's not the sort of thing a man wants scrawled on walls. The colored fellow, I'm told, has passed on to his reward. Several of the assignations in question are said to be the work of another public official entirely. Tantalizingly, he shall remain unnamed for our purposes. Ask that deranged engineer Brown. He'll cough up a tale or two. The papers won't touch any of it because several businesses in which I am part owner are prolific advertisers. Others occupy property I own. This should be particularly meaningful to y'all, Shem. Suppose you lost your lease, say. Suppose I decide that a buck a year is too generous even if for a worthy cause, and during a depression yet. My town, my rules. What is this in the rice? Is this jasmine? My God, Ferrous, it's a wonder y'all're not as big as a roundhouse!"

"Ah pa'take spa'ingly. Too rich fo' mah system, Ah'm 'fraid. Was a time though, Ah could polish off a b'eakf'st like this heah one an' do *e-qual* jus'ice t'lunch not an houh latuh."

Shem says, "Mr. Ferrous and I are blameless in all of that."

"Well, let's see. Let's see. Suppose, we hear, through the usual lines of gossip, that a prominent man of God has purchased one third of a large brewery. There's the ethical question. This man is a public teetotaler, though some of us know better. His parishioners are a…how should I put it? A very small 'c' catholic group, for Protestants. The preacher? A virtual Carry Nation at the pulpit. And then, there is the question of the money. It is a healthy congregation, but by no means wealthy, except for some of the new money that hasn't deserted for more cavernous haunts. How much can the sheep be paying the shepherd? Not all that much. So where, oh, where, has the little dog gone and dug up so much legal tender? Imagine questions. Investigations. Imagine an outside auditor tracking down the recipe for the cooking of books. The collection plate is full to bursting week after plentiful week, and still the shepherd is forced to seek out the good nature of others to fix the perpetually leaking roof. Where has all the money gone? To hops? To suds? To precious amber grains? To purple mountains majesty of cartons of chilled Lone Feather bottles? I have *nothing* on y'all, my very old and dear friend? Is *that* what you think? Cross me again, and y'all won't find a hospitable soap box on skid row."

Shem huffs. "What would that get you? We'd all be brought low. Do you all think I'd disappear quietly?"

"Might as well. You'd lose your reason for being. The Reverend Brother Irrelevant. If I can't find my way out of it, which I'm not so sure I can't do, I only loose the office. I can live with that. I still own what I own. Of course, Sarai will find all of the publicity a bit unnerving, but then, she's chosen her bed to lie in and it's rich with goose down and vermin free, excluding yours truly, if I may be momentarily self-deprecating. Anyway, that's no longer the issue."

"Ah'm feelin' so vera p'riph'ral," complains Ferrous. "A bit a yolk at the cornuh a yo' mouth, P-Ah."

"A bit of crow on yours, Ferrous. But say, you too have a cross to bear."

"Ah'm bu'stin'th 'ntic'pation."

"Bet you are, bet you are. And at y'all's age, even anticipation must be consumed sparingly. First of all, you're a damned old codger who'd like to retire out with a huge pension and stock options and all those perks the truly selfish strive for all their lives. You have the wife, the boys and their daughters to leave something to. Not too likely that the Ivy Leaguers back east'll feel philanthropic, after being let in on a little fiscal adventure of yours, in which you try to manipulate a municipal election in order to get the city's permission to extend a siding, at company expense, to benefit an external business in which you have become one third proprietor. Those corporate attorneys are sharks, Ferrous. They'd devour a little man like you: a minnow, an appetizer, something spread thin on a cracker. A cracker on a cracker, if you'd like. There is not an organization more vituperative than a Class One railroad scorned. Puts a shrew to shame. It is a steel thing, see, driven by pulverized mastodons. There is no beating heart, no warmth of blood, indeed not an ounce of humanity in the whole thing. It rolls on over tamed land and wild, unconcerned, driving prices up or down as the whim takes it, dropping the hopeful off in pitiful bottomlands of rock and scrub until they succumb to foreclosure so the process can start up all over again. If y'all think such a machine could find a sympathetic hinge or bolt for an old dwarf, I bid you pleasure in your naivety."

"Y'all 'n'erest'mate me," Ferrous protests quietly.

"Tit for tat. What, you're not a dwarf?"

"Ah 'nuhstan' when a need for negotiation is at hand. Ah'm not a stubbo'n man."

"A little late in the day for the League of Nations, as Mr. Lodge once said to Mr. Wilson. I'm puzzled though. Why was Humboldt being such a jackass?"

"'Bout the council vote?"

"A snip at his own nose, wasn't it? Not to mention bad business."

"He was at that point, b'yond ration'l *pur*-suits."

"Blinded by betrayal. How silly. Betrayal, after all is one of the few eternal truths. Am I right, pastor?" Before he can answer, Ferrous bids P-R to look under his plate. "What? Party favors? Have I won the centerpiece? Had I known, I'd have brought Mrs. P-R along for the festivities."

"Or any one of the fillies in the stable," says Shem bitterly.

"Ah, the scorn of the envious. How y'all wish the tables were turned. How you've always wished it."

"I've made peace with who I am."

"That will be harder for the community."

"Go on, now, look unduh yo' plate theah," urges Ferrous. P-R lifts the plate carefully, sees a plain white business envelope facing up. He waves an arm about the coach, as if to introduce companions to new vistas. "This is all very grand, Ferrous," he says.

"Yessuh, ain't it? F'om a bettuh day. Back then, us'all'd be eatin' pheasant'r bison steaks, shot f'om these vera windas'th the on'y shaduh 'cross the land bein' the en'less flock a pass'nger pigeons."

"My understanding," says P-R, "you project back far enough, you'd be the one sent out to drag and dress the meat, and a bowl of cold beans for your trouble."

Ferrous leans forward, they think, nearly grumbles, "Go on, open it a'ready."

P-R does so, pulls out a blank check on Ferrous' account. "What's this here? A bribe?"

"Nothin' so crude as that. Jus' a note a'preciation."

"It's good to be appreciated, certainly. But y'all leave me at a loss."

"'F'anythin', Ah leave ya at a gain. Fo' pushin' the sidin' 'xtension, street runnin' an' ahl, th'ough the council."

"You know, Ferrous, I'm not exactly here as a supplicant. I am quite well heeled. You see, here in Tishomingo, when times are tough for God, He hits me up for a little change to carry him through." An angry grunt from Shem follows; goes all but unnoticed.

"G'won, write in a amount. Ah spect y'to be not *un*-reason'bly 'xtrav'gant."

"You're not grasping the situation." He slides the check over to Ferrous, pushing it with a fork, as if it is unclean. "I'm not a cast off in the municipal flea market. I'm not for sale."

"Oh, come now! This can't jus' be *re*-venge."

"Why not?"

"That'd be chil'ish. Po' bid'ness. Would make y'all seem as stupid as Ya'dley."

Shem protests. "Gentlemen! The man is barely interred!"

P-R ignores the pastor, says to Ferrous, "I'll leave business to pirates like y'all. In politics, revenge is the quid quo pro of success."

"So, what 'xactly d'y'all want?"

"First, more of those heavenly potatoes of Mr. Denver's. Thank you. Second, there will be no viable challenge to my reelection."

"So it *is* a value to you?" notes Shem.

"Of value, certainly. Critical? I think not. I'm the Mayor here whether I'm behind the desk or not."

"An' whatta y'all do fo' me?" says Ferrous.

"For us?" says Shem.

"Nothing. For you or *to* you. We go merrily back to the status quo, you at the pulpit, you at the office, me in the dealer's chair at City Hall, and may we all forever hold our peace."

"Silence for silence," says Shem.

"Or an eye for an eye. At this juncture, nothing gained, nothing lost."

"An' whatta 'bout mah sidin', damn it?" Ferrous pounds the table with his standard-sized hand. China and silver are set to motion.

"Off the table, for now," P-R says quietly. He waves his arms above the table action. "No room for it now, in any case. We'll see how y'all behave. Perhaps there will develop some motivation to revisit the issue at a later date."

"Pretty damn' one sided, y'son 'va bitch!" Ferrous says.

"Yes, it is that," says P-R. "As it was when you two snakes and the dead fellow conspired behind my back."

"Y'all fi'ed the firs' volley, P-Ah, damn y'all! Ah 'spect yo' the one'at sought a 'nfluence the council 'gainst us. You broke the faith. You're duplic'tous."

"Bygones, Ferrous. Spilt milk. Water under the great stone viaduct. Had you more foresight, had you split your original pie in quarters rather than thirds, well, who can say what influence the shared dessert might have had on subsequent events? But a pie once cut is like a virgin once probed...Oh, well. The blood is on the sheets, gentlemen. Our reputations hang by a thread. Avoid sharp objects and stay out of the wind."

Shem says, "A proud look, the sowing of discord...these are abominations in the eyes of God, Socrates."

"As is a false tongue. Y'all're not going Papist on us, are you? Will we be hearing talk of contrition next?" He wipes his mouth, a bit too extravagantly, drops the napkin over his plate and looks to Ferrous who is seething quietly in the dimness. "I've got to tell you, Superintendent, best breakfast ever in my experience. Food's passable as well." He stands and says to Shem, "Ride home?"

"You all'er not serious!"

"I wouldn't leave you stranded. What sort of friend do you think I am?"

"I haven't the words to tell you. I'll walk up to the depot and flag a taxi."

"Won't that appear extravagant? No more levitation, you know. You're feet will trod the oily ground."

"I'll weather the storm."

"Yes, you will. As always, y'all won't even get wet." With that, he stands, nods, and says, "Gentlemen."

Ferrous grips the fine tablecloth in both hands, practically snarls, "Y'all a vera stupid man t'so capriciously bu'n y'all's b'idges."

P-R stops on his way out, turns, feigns anguish with lowered lids and a chilled recoil of limbs. "That y'all think ill of me cuts to the quick. But then, you are neither a constituent nor a tax payer in my town, so who really gives a shit!"

"Ah *am* a taxpayuh, damn you!"

"Shhh. That's a secret best kept in the dark of private compartments with drawn curtains. With some restraint, gentlemen, this will all blow over, all will be returned to a comfortable norm, and, perhaps, down the line a bit, when tempers wane and memories meander as memories tend to do, we can all gather somewhere in the happy comradeship of conspirators, and drink a good, local beer together."

"When hell f'eezes ovuh!"

"Whenever. I'll even claim the tab."

P-R steps out onto the back platform where Mr. Red is sharing his flask with the other bull. His elation is palpable, and with a broad, toothy grin he pads Red on the shoulder, and says, "Good man! You made it."

"Yes, sir," says Red. "I was supposed t'show ya'll the way."

"Perhaps I was abrupt. You a voting man, officer?"

Red likes the sound of *officer.* "A man does his civic duty, sir."

"You know what? I can always find a niche for a man that votes who also displays law enforcement experience. Y'all come on Downtown and see me when you get a chance. I'm sure we can give these penny-pinching railroad sharks a run for their money. Don't disappoint me now."

The varnish of *The Eunice* reflects in the ice-sheen wax of the Buick; *TRF* scrolled in Hebraic reversal across the door, just below a fluid left to right *SP-R.* The sun is very bright, allies with the luster of the hood in blinding indifference, and P-R positions the visor for optimum highway myopia. He enjoys piloting the big eight on a nice day like this: relishes the snug caress of leather, the smooth roll of rubber from the wide whitewalls, the command it gives him of road, of town, of all the smaller folks with feet stuck in the static social strata of their plastic stands, from here, to there, all the way to the horizon and the abrupt edge of the known plywood world.

HIGHWAY 99

I

TAYLOR IS IN A DEEP SLUMBER as Magic Mountain trails backward. He misses all the excitement of such world class hot spots as Castaic Junction, Gorman, and Ft. Tejon: historic headquarters of the U.S. Army Camel Corps and other pivotal shrines in American military history. He misses the eighteen wheelers burdened with toxic Chinese commodities struggling in the right lane, up to the Summit; misses them again creeping down the same lane, nursing hot brakes, hoping once more to avoid a possibly lethal vault up the emergency truck escape ramp. He misses the CHP drum-majoring a line of travelers through the snow flurries.

When he wakes, his stomach is telling him it is four or five in the afternoon. He notices long shadows edge their way up the rounded plein-air hills, the darkness of the smooth ravines like space between the prone limbs of mountains at rest on the valley floor; the lonely vigil of sparse oaks, ancient and bent, claws heavenward in supplication. They descend from cloud to a tule fog as thick as a colony of krill.

Taylor and Leo are immersed in Leg One of the First Ever Bedskirt-Valverde Guy's Weekend Adventure, a five hour — anyone else driving, six hour with Leo at the wheel — drive through corporate agrarian boredom; the endless bleak fields under the endless bleak clouds punctuated by Shell, Best Western, Wendy's; the stink of damp fertilizer, the tinny buzz of crop dusters. So it goes, all down the bleak gray road, a ruler drawn incision whose monotony is broken only by the frequent breakneck stunts of cars passing the commercial traffic, the pickups warning WIDE LOAD behind someone's half-a-house trundling along at forty-five, or the flat beds with tilted camper shells and unashamed McCain-Palin bumper stickers: Leo has to turn his head and look up into the grizzled ear of the driver under the John Deere cap, just to see who'd be unabashed enough at this late juncture to keep on advertising.

Leo has incrementally manipulated himself into Taylor's world, but Taylor understands the pressure he's under. "Okay," Leo admitted, "so I'm Bush to her Cheney! Doesn't mean I don't enjoy throwing out the first ball of the season."

He hugs the right lane, creeps with the semis, eyes positioned on mushy red taillights. He is humming along to the fourth movement of the *New World Symphony*. In Leo's rendition, what he calls, *Variations on a Theme of Ethnocentricity*, only Leo recognizes the melody. Taylor wouldn't know it if it came direct from

Deutsche Grammaphone; *Pacific 231, Little Train of the Caipira* maybe, but not Dvorák. "Supposed to sound American," Leo says as the defroster shushes him, "but it's all Czech to me. Y'know the movie composer Tiomkin?" Taylor, half awake, doesn't, grumbles and sniffs in answer.

"Now this is better," Leo remarks as the fog becomes haze and mild clarity with a suddenness he has never before witnessed. Neon perks up like cold nipples along the shoulders and hand painted signs for prime agricultural acres punctuated by rotting barns and JESUS SEES YOU NOW. "Tiomkin wrote some of the best scores for Hollywood westerns: *High Noon, The Big Sky.* He wrote *Rawhide,* for chrissakes! *Rawh-i-i-de.*" Leo produces a single-note drone when he sings; it would be easier for him to carry plutonium than a tune. "When asked how he managed to write melodies so evocative of the cowboy, he said he hadn't, that the music, just like him, was Russian."

"I don't see movies." Nor the point. Leo slaps a palm across the padded wheel of the Prius. "Therein lies the answer, my friend." Taylor doesn't know what the question is.

An annoyance to all the drivers behind him, Leo has become responsibly aggressive, is clogging the lane one to the left of the trucks at a greenish fifty-three, his eyes constantly scanning gauges, seeing if he can't goose a little less than a gallon out of the next hour. Cars are passing with festive horn and finger demonstrations, a virtual ASL communal rant. "They say this baby'll do one oh four. I wouldn't know. I wasn't thinking salt flats when I was lucky enough to nab one at a mere five thou above sticker. The tack-on's a bitch, I admit. But, shit, Taylor, I'm doing my part, right? Right? If you were a sled dog in Greenland, you'd be thanking me now."

His voice is lost in the rumble of a passing Safeway truck about the length of Visconti's *Death in Venice.* "Them's a whole lotta Twinkies," Leo says. Taylor has little interest in the vehicles big people drive: Twinkies are another story. Cars, after all, prematurely killed the streetcar, and trucks, with their government-built right-of-ways and generous subsidies, did near fatal damage to the common carriers. This was all a while back, but in Taylor's monomaniacal world, forgiveness moves like the "Sturbridge Lion." Instead of following Leo's lead, he says, "I'd like to eat soon."

"How about we cover a few more kilos? There's cookies in the bag. Tide ya over. Betsy made 'em. Your favorite. Chemical sugar subs. She says you always had this thing for chocolate chip. Carob, in this case." He refers to a large paper Gelson's bag in the back seat, stuffed with thermoses, napkins, a first aid kit, and, of course, the cookies.

"She said that? How would she remember?"

"What? You don't like chocolate chip?"

"I like them fine. How would she remember that?"

"Mind like a pachyderm."

Taylor plows through three saucer-sized cookies. "I was actually thinking of dinner," he adds, fiddling with crumbs settling in the creases of his shirt.

"Too early! It's uncivilized to eat so early. So, what?...Broward County! Anyhow, Ninety-Nine's paved with batter. Not to worry. You know, Taylor, you should see a flick now and then. I mean, everybody sees movies. This is California, after all. Without movies we're left with earthquakes and Disneyland. Probably not even Disneyland. Without celluloid, what are we? Fuckin' Kansas! Everything else is flammable chaparral. Movies are our own personal lost and found. Where we lose ourselves, where we find ourselves again. Window to the actual. Transit to the fantastic."

"I'm okay without the actual. Could use something to eat." He watches evening things splat and career on the deeply sloped windshield, creatures that thrive in the hot muck of the crop bottoms, leaving short liquefied *auto*biographies splayed across the glass. "I don't generally see the point of movies."

"Yeah? How about *Union Pacific? Broadway Limited? Ring of Fire?*

"I saw *those*."

"Yeah! And?"

"I liked the trains. *Ring of Fire*, though, I think they shouldn't have destroyed a train...and a great trestle...just for a movie. Kind of a shame."

Leo gives him a brief, exasperated stare: not the extended in-car movie stare that lasts far too long for safe passage even at a sluggish fifty-three. "You're like a fucking space man, Taylor. Like you just got here. And you came on the train. Who the fuck comes on the train anymore?"

Taylor sits quiet for a while, reaches back for another cookie. "I'm okay without movies. I have an imagination. Scripts in my head...It's not important."

"Is to Betsy. Like a tithe, you're ten percent of her waking day. It comes on slowly, the anguish, sort of like Mt. St. Helens. A series of rumbles, huffs and puffs. A stubborn codger like that Harry Truman guy, not the one who dropped the bomb, the one who wouldn't leave his cabin, he says, *What the hell! You don't scare me!* But me? I've seen the signs before. Know what's coming. I don't see it in her eyes. This is no literary omen. I see it in her brow. This furrow come-on. An undulator, creeping across her forehead like an Etch-a-Sketch. It is the brow of doom. Gives me chills. I know what's coming. *Taylor's coming.* And I know how. By train. I call this furrow *the eerie canal.* And then, kaplowee! There you are. In my den, my office, on any one of a number of finely-appointed toilets. And before I know it, there's hot angst flowing down the slopes in total disregard for the humanity it's about to consume. Tell the truth, every time I hear your name mentioned I feel like flushing myself down one of those many toilets. If you were around, I'd feel like flushing *you* down the toilet. Who am I kidding? We've opted for low flow. Can barely flush water! You don't crap at our house after one of Betsy's lead-inspired meatloaves without Ready-Rooter on the red phone. Anyway, you should only know what I gotta go through being your brother-in-law."

"I'm a little sick of it all myself, of *pretending* I'm okay. Because, actually, I think I *am* okay. Which makes it harder to pretend."

"Nigh on *impossible! I* know that. *Live and let live.* Betsy thinks you're depressed. Depression is her answer to all behavior she can't understand. Jesus cures depression, by the way. Jesus and big pharma. Besides, nobody's anymore okay than you are. We've all got our little peccadilloes. They're road kill all over Texas, the peccadilloes." Leo gives Taylor a little wink that says that at least he is pleased with himself, and perhaps, on his most generous edge, with both of them.

"I'm not depressed. I wake up each morning anxious to start the day."

"Ah, anxiety. That's part of the depression. Look, seriously, Taylor, me, I never thought otherwise." He is enjoying the jogging LCD bars on his dash, like a light box from the Sixties. He wants so to be greenishly correct, sometimes threatens to get out and push the car along. He economizes past Bakersfield — SUN FUN STAY PLAY — and the Hank Owens portal, the Central Valley's answer to the *arch d'triumph*: Graceland of the San Joaquin.

"There's a Micky D's up there." Caltrans has planted a convenient road sign with the logos of the several upcoming artery-close eateries.

"Again, I never thought otherwise. How about someplace with waitresses?"

"Whatever you want. I just want to get something to tide me over. I'm not used to being the passenger."

"Middle ear thing, huh! Don't you hurl in the Prius, Taylor. That would be so fucking un-green. Like pissing in Walden Pond. We'll pull over and you can drive. Would that be better?"

"Okay. Just go up into the drive-thru and I'll grab something and we can change places."

By now, the windshield looks like a Jackson Polack canvas, the vivid yellow and green lumps and streaks on a safety-glass battlefield.

"I don't do drive-thrus, just so you know. Waste of gas."

"It's a hybrid, Leo. You won't be using gas."

"It's the principal."

Above the parking lot, the lights go on. They are hissing in the unseasonably warm lowland evening, attacked by moths the size of combat choppers. The air is a toxic mix of grilled beef, aliphatic hydrocarbons, and the various crops sweating off their last engineered nutrients. The lot is busy and the car line wraps around the building with idling sixes and eights. Queues inside back into the table areas, and the receptacles are overflowing with briefly used paper and stained from sticky streams of fructose.

Cars and lines, Leo thinks. Civilization visits the hinterland: French fries to the breadbasket, the rural richness of irrigated soil cratered and super-sized with food on the run. Even the salads are in plastic boxes. Yum! Diners lift their feet as a young Latina mops the floor and sets out a yellow easel; *piso mojado.*

Taylor gets two Big Mac meals to tide him over, and a tankard of Diet Coke that wouldn't fit in the cup holder of a Seven Forty Seven. They sit amongst the crumbs and smeared ketchup of a departing family.

Leo remarks that it feels like the cafeteria at Ellis Island. People are speaking Spanish, Armenian, Thai, Mandarin, Hmong: maybe about where they've come from, where they'll be, if they made good time or bad, if the car is running right, "'Cause y'don' wanna have t'get somethin' fixed by one a these pirates on the road. Fuckin' fan belt'll cost ya an arm," or if this was the last time they'd see Tia

Concepción in Los Banos, "She di'n't look so good" even for a woman living in a place named after a convenience. They wonder if they should have stayed away from the blackjack table at South Lake Tahoe, or if they'll be back in Hawaiian Gardens in time to see "I Survived a Japanese Game Show," which they forgot to TiVo. More than a few mention the weather, have shed jackets, sweaters.

Leo says, "I guess you didn't really want me to come along, did you?" He is studying his Filet-o-Fish, looking for telltale signs of fins, gills, a mouth, a tail, anything to indicate that it once swam in schools and picked on squares of fish smaller than itself. "It's not that," Taylor says, to which Leo responds, "You gave me quite a hard time." Taylor explains that he feels like he's dragging Leo off to something he really doesn't want to be at.

"Dragging me off! I *begged* you. You should have seen me on my fucking knees with the telephone. How do we know this is really from a fish?"

"It says *fish* on the sign." Taylor points. Leo says, "So what?" Taylor protests that they couldn't say it if it wasn't true. "Ever get Chinese that's supposed to have crab in it," Leo argues, "or the pre-mixed seafood salads *with crab* they sell in the markets, and what you get is kind of a rubbery white cylinder the diameter of a pre-school crayon, and it's got a crab-like red streak across it? Kind of a fantasy crab?" Taylor guesses he has, but isn't certain. "Of course you have. And you know what? It's something called pollock fish and it's about as closely related to a crab as I am. So, how do I know this is fish?"

"Trust?"

"Trust a fish? One that uses an alias? I don't know! Bet ya haven't seen *Jaws*. Not a train in it. Now, *that* mother was a fish! The Kingfish. The spokes-fish. I'm afraid I'll choke on this...*coaster*. It looks like a coaster. Should I pull it out of the bun, wipe it off, set my ice tea down on it?"

"You don't need a coaster. See," he taps the table, "Formica. And the fish... It's a fillet."

"Bones would be too much to hope for. Actually, I was worried about the corners." Leo bares his teeth, takes a macro-nibble of crust, ponders why the breading doesn't sog as the animal wends its way through coral reefs; decides not to share the thought.

Over wide-mouthed, enthusiastic chomps, Taylor says, "I don't think I did see that one."

Leo says, "Shouldn't eat cow, bro-in-law."

"I take a pill for cholesterol," Taylor mumbles through mastication, certain Betsy has written Leo's three by fives. Leo is playing *good cop*.

"Not only your health I'm worried about. You know what eating that shit does to the environment?"

"I don't keep up," he says, triple rows of needle sharp teeth honing in on the kill.

"You will when the Arctic flows through Pasadena like a parade float. Cow farts, Taylor. The foul gasses from your burger's ass are a large part of the climate change problem. And not only that. Think of all the trees cleared for pasture. Each time you bite into that thing, hundreds of acres of trees cease to produce carbon dioxide. Shit! You're a scientist. You should know this stuff."

"Engineer. I was an engineer. I designed stuff."

"Still. Why be part of the problem?"

"These burgers come from dead cows, right? Steers? Dead steers don't fart."

"Sounds like a Mailer title. I'd call you a wise ass if I thought you had the capacity. Your excuse doesn't exactly make you David Browder. And — speaking of trust — how about trusting me that I really wanted to come along? You got me hooked on that shitty garden railroad and I want to see what's on the market."

"I didn't buy it for *you*."

"Possession is nine tenths of the law, or something. The little cretin bolted and what was I to do? Anyway, it's mine now."

"You could have gone into the store and…"

"Not the point. I wanted to be in the thick of things. Smell the coal fires, hot oil, schmooze the train guys."

"The trains are electric. They smell like…like Norelcos."

"Let me enjoy this. It's a chance for us to bond. To be away from Betsy and her Taylor nonsense for a while. Let me have some fun, okay?"

"You want to be away from Betsy?" Taylor has put down his crepitating burger.

Leo surrenders the apparent fish to its wrapper. "Don't make more of that than it is. Everyone wants to get away from someone once in a while."

"I don't."

"You have no one to get away from."

Taylor smiles wisely.

"What happened to that hot little number with the bazooms?"

"Cory Ann? Didn't work out."

"What didn't work out? The sex? Did she snore? Did *you* snore?"

"Not during sex. The sex was fine."

"Then?"

Taylor runs through a few minimal breathing exercises, quickly, the Evelyn Wood speed version. "I had to break it off. Too time consuming."

"A retired old fart like you is too busy for pussy! You have some sense of priorities!"

"We had very different interests. I have the trains, and all."

"And all?"

"The trains, you know, the store, the layout, the trains."

"And, don't forget, the trains. I see. And what about her? What was she interested in?"

"Cory Ann?"

"The very one. Who else we talking about?"

"Oh, I don't know."

"You don't know? You shared her bed, right? You dined together. Talked. You must have talked about something."

"Well, yes. Those things. Yes."

"So what was she, Cory Ann, interested in?"

"Well, she liked to have her feet rubbed."

"Did you rub them?"

"C'mon, Leo. I don't want to talk about this stuff."

"So you rubbed her feet and presumably certain more entertaining anatomical features. That's not exactly an interest. Rubbing feet."

"She liked that."

"What else?"

"I really don't know what else. I guess I just wasn't that taken with her."

"Can I fix'er up with Steven? He was very taken."

"You're kidding?"

"Of course, I'm kidding. So you broke up with her because…?"

"We were very different."

"You don't like having your feet rubbed?"

"No. Yes. I don't care about my feet. And, I'm ticklish."

"Borderline diabetic, Taylor. You'd better care about your goddamned feet!"

"We had different interests."

"How do you know? You don't know what she was interested in."

"I know what she *wasn't* interested in."

"Lemme guess: t-*rainz!*"

"Yes," he says, feeling, and trying not to sound, defensive. "This is a subject that is very important to me."

"No shit! Aren't trains what came between you and Helen?"

"Yes." There she was again, chewing over his shoulder. "Not exactly *between.*"

"Trains. Helen."

"One ran over her."

"I know. The railfan's penultimate, serendipitous moment. Like a hero's death in battle. Off to choo choo Valhalla, poor Helen. So why didn't you want me to come along?"

"With Helen?"

"No! With *you!*"

"Well, in part, because I don't like talking about this kind of stuff. I don't like talking very much at all."

Leo turns his head, arches his neck, shields his eyes with a flat hand. "See? You *didn't* want me to come. The ubiquitous trainman, chugging off into the sunset, friendless, self-contained, insular. Kind of like John Wayne framed in the doorway at the end of *The Searchers*, which, of course, you didn't see because there wasn't a goddamned train."

"Okay."

"Think of me as the sidekick. The fireman to your engineer. Leopold to your Loeb. Once we're up there, you won't even see me. We have separate rooms and I'm only interested in perusing the G string."

"Gauge. It's G *gauge.*"

"I finish up there and it's off to the pool to wow the common folk with my Mark Spitz feats of aquatic derring-do and see if any of the unattended ladies with loosened bra straps needs someone to rub sunscreen on their backs. Or feet. Or fronts. Whatever."

"Winter, Leo."

"Was an hour ago. Now, I don't know."

"It's not you, see. This is…just something I'm comfortable doing alone."

"Like masturbation."

"What?"

"I almost left Betsy once. Bet you didn't know that. Well, maybe more than once."

"Does she know this?"

"Yeah, sure. We're very up front with each other. She tripped over the suitcase, read the note, listened to the message on the answering machine, and saw it on Facebook, and," snapping his fingers, "got it just like that! Had to cancel the blimp."

"I don't want to hear this."

"Grow up, Taylor. Shit happens. Shit wears out, wears off. Sometimes the neighbor's grass looks greener. It's a big lawn out there. Hard to avoid. You can obey the signs, KEEP OFF. But you can't help but wonder what it would be like to set the timer on someone's else's sprinklers."

"This is about grass?"

"Why am I telling you this?"

"I have no idea."

"No, you don't, do you?"

"I don't even want to know."

"But soon, you will. See, Taylor, what I'm saying is that what's expected, what's normal, isn't…always…enough. I don't mean *enough*, enough. Satisfying. That's not it either. We, men, are just biologically tuned for variety. Try as we do, well, as some of us do, we can't help our selves any more than a puppy can ignore your socks on the floor."

"You cheat on my sister?"

"No, no, I don't. But I sure as hell *dream* of cheating on your sister and I wish it was okay to do so, that we called it something other than *cheating*. I don't chew on her socks though."

"Why *are* you telling me this?"

"I guess…I just have always wanted to tell you that it's okay to be you. Not to Betsy, of course, she thinks you were put together with stolen body parts from Transylvania. But it's okay by me that you're you. Does that make sense?"

"I don't know. It seems you're telling me more about you."

"By way of telling *you* about you! That sometimes what other people expect and want of us is not always the stuff that best suits us. I don't want you arriving at any harebrained conclusions here. I love Betsy and when all's said and done, I'll die a happy man with her holding my hand and telling me how worried she is about you. But, if I could, in the interim, just kind of experience something… well, exotic. A different touch. A different smell. A different approach."

"Betsy smells?"

"Everybody smells. She doesn't stink, if that's what you're asking. It's just that I know Betsy as well as I know myself. I miss the mystery."

"Mystery?"

"Newness. Novelty. I don't know. An escapade without guilt. But I just can't. Not without guilt. Not without fear that the things I want to change will irrevocably alter the things I don't. You don't feel guilt, do you?"

"Well, sometimes, a little. About Helen. But then it goes away."

"Blessed are the devoid. I know you're not a hermit. I know there are little things each day that you have to do because we live in society. But, Taylor, do you ever avoid doing anything you really want to do?"

"No. I don't think I do. What's the point?"

"Exactly! You wanna work, you work. You wanna stay home, you shut the door and don't answer the phone. You wanna go off and ride some train somewhere, that's the thing you do. Alone, guiltless, and fearing nothing other than the light won't be right when the thing gets up a good head of steam and you're photos are a wash. Am I right?"

"I think so. The light is very important."

"Okay then. We've got some miles ahead of ourselves. You want this fish thing? I haven't touched it. Almost." He stands up and tosses Taylor the keys. Athletically, Taylor has the eye-hand coordination of the blind, drops them to the floor. Briefly, he ponders what they were talking about, what caused Leo to let go like that, what it all meant. But only briefly. Tonight, his heart belongs to Stockton. He grabs Leo's pre-owned filet and follows him out the door, warm with the bovine methane that is somehow bad for narwhals.

Taylor drives past the next two exits before Leo relieves him at the wheel. "I can't watch you flit away my mileage like this," he explains.

They entertain each other with a car game. More like, a Pullman car game. Taylor says, *Orient Express,* not quite the whole title, but Leo is feeling magnanimous, and nails an easy S: *Shanghai Express.* Taylor: *Strangers on a Train.* Leo: *North by Northwest. The General."* Coming up blank encourages them to rotate articles: *Lady Vanishes, The. Station Agent, The.* Alas, this is not a game with much staying power.

A quiet hour of the identical junctions follows, the same non-service stations, the same gritty glitz, counties upon counties of in-convenience stores with self-serve microwaves and jerky and Slim Jims as long as arms. It is a flash of Modesto before Leo collects his thoughts, says to Taylor, "Taylor! You know, I do get you? You know?"

"Okay."

"Really."

"Really, okay."

"I do take you seriously."

"Okay."

"I don't minimalize you…*or* your train thing. Your passion. It's what you do. It's you. I respect that."

"Okay."

"Okay? Really?"

"Yes. No."

"No? That I take you seriously?"

"Yes. That."

"I'm at a loss. Help me out here."

"I just don't want to be taken any way. Anywhere. I don't think I want to be taken."

"Kind a what I meant."

"Okay."

"A matter of articulation."

"Okay."

"*Polar Express!*"

"Easy. *Shanghai Express.*"

"Used. Try again."

"You're not going to leave my sister are you?"

"Never! Promise. As they say, one needs occasional *space*. Of all people, I'd think you'd understand."

"My *sister*, Leo!"

"Yeah, I know. Blood thicker than sludge, the Bedskirts, despite all the shenanigans. Don't you understand the meaning of fantasy?"

"*Me?* Of course!"

"When I was a wee *niño* herding my flock in the Sangre de Cristos, I'd fantasized that I was some kind of Zapata, super hero to the *peones*, bane of the rich, and all the pretty *señoritas* were frothing over me like un-skimmed *sopa con pollo*. It was fun to pretend. I never thought it would happen."

"Well, okay, I guess."

"So, we're good?"

"Okay."

"I need a pit stop. You hungry?"

"Okay. Sure. Just be good to my sister."

Leo gives him a quick, exasperated glance. "Christ! Be good to my wife! And see if you can't find one of those signs with the glow in the dark utensils."

"Okay."

Leo mutters, "Jerk!"

"Okay."

II

THE CHIVALRY TIMBERS SUITES, AND THE gangs all here — all of them that have survived another six months.

After a pit stop in Merced, a bite at a well-known all nighter — Taylor refueling with a chili size and a Diet Pepsi, Leo with an open-faced tuna salad sand on wheat with a wicked side of sliced tomato — they do the last lap in a weary silence. Well after midnight, they sink into queens in adjoining rooms. Taylor watches a few heart throbbing minutes of "Railfanning in the Fabulous '50's," while Leo avails himself of an in-house rental featuring girl-on-girl action in Memphis. *Why Memphis?* he asks himself. *These babes could be from Milwaukee, Buffalo. Anywhere. What'd I expect, coonskin caps? Couplin' with a grizzly bar? Christ on a scone, why am I torturing myself?*

⁂

Harlan Brewster looks like death un-warmed. He sits behind a ensemble of loose scrambled eggs, sickly yellow to compliment his pasty skin, and coffee so black that it could suck in planets. He has gained weight, puffed out, is covered in a thick blanket of meaty corpulence which puts some strain on his shirt, let alone his heart. He is pumped like something off the line at Voit. He cups his shoulders firmly, separates his shirt between buttons, the spaces in the shape of the Jesus fish people like to paste to their bumpers, now vertical as they swim in a line down Harlan's belly. Taylor sighs with a memory born of such labor.

"Taylor Railer," Brewster calls, a poor attempt at enthusiasm. "Heap plenty room. Come rest those box cars a yours."

Reluctantly, Taylor complies. He sets down his tray and prepares to put his statins to the ultimate test. Until now, Harlan has managed to be alone: for him, no great feat. He has cleared bigger rooms than Ye Olde Buffet.

"How they chuggin', big boy?"

"You going to set up?" Taylor asks hopefully. As in, *now, right now! Please!*

"Nope. Not sellin' this time. Got turned over by a new leaf." He does a little flip with an adipose hand, representing the leaf, or the hand, or perhaps just muscle relief for fingers too long gripping utensils.

"You looking to buy then?"

"Nope. I drove six grueling hours for the fuckin' buffet! Whaddya think? If I ain't here to sell, of course I'm here to…Aw, forget it!" His voice is cracked like an eroded desert floor.

Taylor wonders why Harlan invited him to the table. Maybe he didn't. Maybe he had heard him wrong, misinterpreted what he meant by *box cars*. Once in a blue moon, when Brewster isn't smashed like Pompeian pottery, he can be counted on to be obtuse *au natural*. Taylor hopes Leo will come down and rescue him, or that a fire alarm will short circuit and send them all out into the parking lot. "So, how'er you doing?" It is not a question that goes out of its way begging for an answer.

"Like I said, new leaf. Tenuous. More like a new pine needle, if you know what I mean." Taylor doesn't. "I'm off the sauce. Wagons ho! Clean as virgin snow. Ho, snow! Now there's a thought." Taylor glances over at the ketchup menstruating all over Harlan's eggs, hasn't an inkling what sauce he refers to. "Been pure for two months, one week, seven days, and, well…" he says consulting his pocket watch, "almost five hours."

"That's pretty good," Taylor compliments, finally getting the gist.

"How the fuck'd you know? You ever been on a binge?"

"Me? No."

"Then you don't know shit, do you?" The rasp peppers nearby tables.

"Well," Taylor says softly. "I had a neighbor…"

"Second-hand craparoo, Bedwet. Like I said, you don't know shit. That's why I'm not selling. Can't sit at the fuckin' table all day waitin' for some cocksucker like Nightshtick to jew me down. Every minute of every day's a struggle, see. You can't go nowhere's without seeing a fucking ad with some shithead topping off a brewski, or a neon cocktail glass, or a case a two-buck Chuck at the Trader's. The old lady clicks on the Food Channel, and whaddya see? Some fruit making a rum cake. No chance he's gonna make *chocolate*. Marble. Dotty says she liked me better before, liked it when she could hear my footsteps squish like I was walking in puddles. Now, she says, I sneak up on her. And I have this attitude. Fuckin' bullshit! You think I have an attitude?"

"No. Attitude! No, no. You're going to let those eggs get cold."

"No biggie. My third dip in the trough. 'Cause, you wanna see attitude, I'll give ya attitude."

"So what floor you on?" Taylor asks, hoping to change the subject. He is thinking he prefers the pickled Brewster over the bitter one.

"Right now? Ground floor, just like you."

"I mean, your room."

"I'm down the street."

"Down the street?"

"At the Mo'Six. I landed the Bridal Suite."

"Everybody always stays *here*."

"What? I can't have a little variety now and then? It's cheaper at the Six. What am I gonna do in there anyway, but sleep? For the price, I ain't gettin' any luckier over here." There it was, that word, *variety*. Leo had talked of *variety*, as well. "Thing is," Brewster continues, "and you should remember, they gotta funny way a doin' business here. Last time, that broad at the desk was downright rude. No sense a humor. God's gift, know what I mean? Like every guy'at checks in wants the key to her pants. You know what, trolley boy, she ain't even hot shit in *Stockton*, you ask me. She stood still in LA, dogs would piss on'er. To say nothin' a that basmati-breathed swami in the red blazer. Who needs to get dicked around by a bunch a Third World retards when the shower's just as hot down the block?"

Taylor is stuffing his mouth as fast as he can. He is considering buying Harlan a drink. Something double, with a little paper umbrella, a tall frosty glass, immobilizing, anesthetizing. If Harlan won't bite, he could drink it himself. Where the hell is Leo? For the first time in memory, he wants *more* company.

"So, tell me, Tailgate. You got yourself a new gig, I hear. What's that like?"

"A gig?"

"Job. Vocation."

"Oh, you mean the computer thing? You know, huh?"

"The toy monger mentioned it. Not to me. He don't talk to me. I heard him tell that blowhard Nightstick. Nightstick didn't look all that thrilled."

"Kind of still in it's embryonic stages."

"Yeah, well let me know when you go into labor. It won't work, y'know? Dead hobby, dead business. Christ, Look at these people! Looks like the boardroom at the *Prostate Pacific. The Erectile Dysfunction Express. The Cardiac Caboose. The Flatulent Flyer. The Brain Function Limited. The Senile Special.* 'Cept for those two fucking out a season hippies, Jack Sprat and that hot shit lesbo a his. You don't see any train buffs shoppin' at Banana Republic, wearin' their caps backward like fuckin' retards, or showin' off tattoos that don't have anchors in them. Young people today, Taylor, they're too busy coverin' their dicks with their laptop loin cloths and stuffin' nose candy. They don't get hard over clouds a steam and rotary plows in crisp mountain air. Fuckin' business a nutrition, ya ask me."

"*Attrition*," Taylor says.

"That's right. You know what I'm talkin' about. Asshole Toby's got cinders in his bonnet. Well, shit, he wants to pour his savings down the swirly bowl, *please, do not flush in station*, well…it's his to clog."

"I'm looking forward to doing the work," Taylor says.

"Don't wait up for *you got mail*. Smart thing'd be to offer multiple, comprehensive services. *Coot's R Us*. Trains, Senior Living, and six foot plots a real estate on hillsides with views a Horseshoe Curve. Your all-in-one shop. Literally, shop 'till ya fuckin' drop. Coffins shaped like hoppers, stock cars, some plain pinewood cabooses for the Yids. Complete with HO layouts to wile away eternity. Y'might as well market leeches, eight track tapes, whale bone for corsets."

"Well," says Taylor, pushing away the plate. "That hit the spot!"

"So what about this neighbor? He kick it or what?"

"Well, yes, he did."

"So he's fine?"

"Well, actually, he kind of regressed, I guess. Beat up his wife and the cops took him away."

"Thanks for sharing, Taylor. No wonder your old lady parked on the tracks."

There she was again, rising from the yoke slime on Ye Olde Plate. If he's going to be visited, he'd much prefer nearly *anyone* to Helen.

Silently, Darouche has landed at their table. He sets his tray down, but stands behind his chair, dimming light, railfanning's dark lord. It's the double whammy for Taylor, who briefly pines for Helen. Harlan looks none the happier. The bull says, "You guys'er a bit loud, doncha think?"

"All I need now is a tumor and my day is complete," says Harlan.

"You are a tumor," Darouche tells him. "People are starting to notice." He is wearing a sports coat over a black t-shirt, the neck stretched threadbare, his Adam's apple scurrying under it like a gopher.

"What people?"

"People. You're too loud."

"Ya know what the kids say, *If it's too loud, you're too old.*"

"Kids who said that, if my memory serves, are now older than us."

"So what're you? The fuckin' hobby police?"

"I think it behooves us all to maintain a certain decorum."

"B-hoofs? The fuck, Nightshade! B-hoofs us to behave?"

"We all represent the organization. We don't want to be an embarrassment."

"How do you know what I want? Maybe I do wanna be an embarrassment. I think you take yourself a little too seriously. Ya haven't kicked a hobo from a moving train in years. The rust is beginning to wear through."

"Was a time, a good yard bull had the same authority on company property as a public cop."

"Was a time, you weighed fifty pounds less and didn't limp from gout. I need to get to a phone. You've driven me to a meeting, the both a ya. That, or I'm rollin' off the wagon here and now." He stands as a tremor agitates his hands, then sits back down like he's forgotten where to go.

Darouche stands firm, says to Taylor, "Figures, you two found each other."

Taylor keeps his eyes on his plate as if he fears Darouche will steal it. "Okay."

Darouche places his hands on the table, framing his tray, leaning his face down nearer to Taylor's. "You get yourself a moment, Bedbugs, you and me still got some things to go over."

"Okay."

Darouche is tapping the table now, reacts poorly to such pacific reactions, retreats with his food to another table.

"You're not afraid a that piece a shit, are you?" Harlan asks. Taylor shrugs. "Key-rist, Taylor, a brick shithouse like yourself, the prick gets in your face, I don't know, like, fuckin' roll on him."

Taylor sees his cue, excuses himself as the double doors open to the conference room. There are the familiar faces, the familiar folding tables, and all the toys of attrition arrayed yet again in an iron horse kitchen *midden*. But, even as he walks away, he has the sense that Brewster hasn't stopped talking, now standing unsteadily between the table and chair, hunched over, grumbling about this and that, fidgeting with the silverware and pushing his food around the plate. Taylor nurses a quick image of Blake: hopes Brewster doesn't go home and reconfigure his wife. But such hopes are short lived, and, without another care, he dashes off to catalogue the memorabilia.

Leo sleeps in, languishes in a rare solitude: no garbage disposals to repair, no touch up painting in the great room, no strip of insulation to replace under the kitchen door. He can afford to pay someone to do it — a handyman, a Salvadoran illegal outside of the lumber yard — but Betsy doesn't see the point of big bucks for little jobs when her husband is perfectly capable, if uninspired, to do it all himself. She has him hanging rain gutters, peeling old wallpaper, dragging steamboats over mountains in South American jungles. *You don't do your own nails,* he would complain. *That's different. That's therapeutic, and you don't carry your own golf clubs.*

He'd protest, *No, that's different. They're heavy, unlike nails. I do tote my own balls, however. When you're not using them.*

He has turned off his cell phone; can always say he was recharging the battery. He retrieves a small bottle of Chardonnay from the courtesy bar, engrosses himself in the first ten minutes of *Mayhem in Montgomery: Alabama Girls Cure the Blues — densely plotted, subtly nuanced, an all star cast of barely legal nymphets, I laughed, I cried, I came* — then proceeds enthusiastically to abuse himself until his hands are covered with warts, he is totally blind, and an eternity in hell is a given.

He stretches out across the bed, first on his accustomed left side, then the right, then smack dab in the middle with his bare legs splayed and staking a claim. Just for the hell of it, he gets up and unmakes the second bed, lounges in its tract of cushiony lots. He takes his well-worn, oft-read copy of Edward Abbey's *Desert Solitaire* from the nightstand, reads it for inspiration as other travelers might turn to Gideon. He daydreams of selling the house, ordering a prefab log kit and assembling it somewhere near Jackson Hole, installing a windmill, solar panels, bamboo floors, or building a sail boat in the meadow out back; or moving to Ketchikan to save the salmon, to sit with his coffee out on the back deck, bundled for the cold mist, and watch the orcas play in the Inland Passage.

Betsy would never go for any of it, is not a big fan of snow, sun, fog, rain, insects, things that swim or crawl for a living, bears that eat women having their periods, the smell of canneries and pulp mills, pine smoke, and driving thousands of miles to get to Whole Foods. The last time they went camping as a family was before they were one; just two young folks dating and, he imagined, enjoying a sunset over the Pacific on a state beach near Oxnard. Betsy said, *Never again,* complained of sand fleas, concrete block bathrooms with no hot water, wood ash in her eyes, stones under her sleeping bag, and sand in her panties. Leo complained that sand was the only thing that got in her panties that weekend, but, all things considered, loved her, and loved being there with her.

Reluctantly, he pries himself up, straightens the second bed to shield against embarrassment when the *mujeres* come in to make up the room, and heads off to the bathroom. It goes against his grain to take a long shower in perpetually evaporating California, but he certainly won't tip the ecological balance if he compensates by flipping off the light and mandatory vent fan that is about as loud as a Boeing engine. He offers a silent apology to the Delta Smelt; later enjoys a slow toweling. Dressing slowly in a Chivalry Timbers polo shirt and khaki shorts he had sent up from Ye Olde Gift Shoppe, and his beloved Birkenstocks, he uses the stairs down to the lobby and proceeds to enjoy the last morsels of breakfast. The kitchen crew is cleaning up to prepare for the onset of lunch. Leo eats alone. He knows no one. It is a satisfying breakfast.

Taylor, on his way to the Squire's, comes bounding in, says, "There you are."

Leo is still nursing his coffee. "Here I am."

"Where were you?"

"Do I detect concern? Will the real Taylor Bedskirt please stand up?"

"It's not that. Do what you want. I had wanted to introduce you to some of the guys."

"It is satisfying to know that you are acquainted with someone other than your sister and I."

"Actually, Leo, I'm kind of well known in this crowd."

"You want something to eat?"

"I ate. Everybody ate. You're missing the show." Taylor is a bit breathless, an excited heave to his chest.

"I'll get in there, don't worry. Kind a easing my way in. Acclimating. Know what I mean?" Taylor doesn't. "How'd you sleep?"

"Me? Oh, not well. I get kind of excited when I come to these things. So much to look at. So much neat stuff. You?"

"Like a man without a conscience. Best night's rest I've had since my honeymoon. Not once did anyone wake me to ask if I had talked to Taylor lately, was he taking his blood pressure pills, how were his triglycerides, what damage was he doing to the old Bedskirt homestead?" Taylor denies being at fault. "Am I blaming? It was just sort of a happy departure to have you sleeping in the next room instead of in the bed with us."

"I've got to get to the bathroom and then back in. I've got some people holding things for me."

"In the bathroom? Say, Taylor, how *are* your triglycerides, anyway?"

"Jeez, Leo!"

"It's not for me. You know it's not for me. I don't give a shit about your congealing blood stream. Can turn to fuckin' concrete, for all I care. Not that I don't love you dearly, but when the choice is your plaque or my rest, I'll take the shuteye any day. Fuck, you want ribs for dinner? My treat. Duck fat fried in bacon? Knock yourself out."

"I'm not telling you details of my medical history."

"Why not? I'll tell you mine." Taylor doesn't want to know. "I'm not going to put it on the internet or anything. The crawl in Times Square. Do they still have a crawl in Times Square? Probably not. Look, Taylor, give me a little love, okay. I had to finesse this trip. It took some delicate maneuvering. The mistress of the universe had other plans. She wanted to look for a new sofa for the den. Do you believe it? The house has seven, eight fucking sofas! Who can sit so much? Between the sofas and the toilets, you'd think we never got off our asses. She says, maybe if we had one of those convertible sofas, Taylor would come and stay over once in a while. Like you're from outta town. I say, we have three convertible sofas, which she says are all old crap as comfortable as washboards. So there's this sale at Ethan Allen this weekend and all the Green Mountain Boys are mustering there, so I tell her, look, take plastic, buy whatever you want, and I promise I won't say anything about it even if it's the ugliest piece of furniture since they sat on stones. Like, even if it's so hideous you couldn't sell it in Tehran. So, Taylor, you gotta give me something to take back so it won't be a total loss."

Taylor looks around the room, afraid someone is listening, that someone other than Betsy might care about the condition of his arteries. "Is this why you came?"

"This is why I was *allowed* to come."

"Truth is, Leo, I haven't been for some time."

"Been what? Been to the doctor?"

"Yeah. I feel fine."

"You never get a check up? They don't look up your ass, tickle your prostate... my fave, suck your blood? You're of an age, you know. Gotta watch yourself. Who knows what evil lurks beneath the skins of men?"

"You too?"

"No, no, of course not. I told you, I could care less. Well, not really *less*. I do want you to be okay. Look, Taylor, have some pity. I can't go home and tell her you don't go to the doctor."

"Tell her I don't like the needles."

"Is that why? That can't be why. Big guy like you."

"Well, I *don't* like the needles."

"Nobody likes the needles. So what? But when you think of the options, it's probably the best way to get some blood out of you. So what am I going to tell her?"

"Well, if you have to tell her something..."

"What'er you, nuts? We're talking about your sister! Sure, it's your ass, and you know she'll be on your case like *tarna* on Glendale, but I don't think I should have to run interference for you. Make something up, for chrissakes!"

"How about you go onto the Internet and find out what's a good reading for triglycerides, then just give her a number?"

"That's lying. I'm shocked!"

"You're asking me to give you something I don't have."

"So? Why should *I* be the liar? *You* look on the Internet, give me the number, tell me you got it from Dr. Moreau, and I'll believe you."

"You'll believe me?"

"In a manner of speaking, yes." Taylor doesn't get this either. "If I tell her that you said this particular number is your actual, verified reading, then I'm not lying, am I?" Taylor thinks he is. "That doesn't matter. If *I* believe I'm not lying, it works for me."

"But you are."

"Not technically."

"Does that matter?"

"If found out, it's always easier to explain away a technicality than an outright whopper. I can say, *This is what he told me. Why should I doubt him?*"

"I was on my way to pee."

"Call 'o' the wild. Take a specimen cup so Betsy can have a souvenir of our time together. So? We're agreed?"

"I'll think about it."

"No, you won't. You'll Google it later and give me a number before dinner or I'll leave you in the godforsaken Central Valley with nothing but your thumbs to get you home."

"You wouldn't do that."

"I wouldn't *lie*. I *will* leave you."

Leo catches the last flicker of the show. Some displayers are already packing up. He pads down the aisle with very little comprehension of what anything is and no idea what so ever why anyone would want to take any of it home. Of course, a lantern is obviously a lantern, but the guy in the corner has about two hundred of them, and why is it that the one that looks primo new is going for forty bucks when the rusty, dented one next to it, a smoky glass chimney in a corroded cage, sans handle, is priced at two fifty? He thumbs through some old timetables, brochures, all hermetically sealed as if they carried toxins, wonders why anyone would want to bargain down a hundred and fifty dollar Soo Line folder with chipped paper, torn seams, foxed corners, and a coffee stain, to, say, a compromising one-twenty-five. The Soo Line, whatever that is, is probably defunct, and the trains listed haven't run for years. So who needs to know what time they're not coming?

Most of these people look fairly normal, people you could be sharing a doctor's waiting room with, or pass on the street. There is the occasional character decked out for Engineer Bill's Halloween, but eccentricity is certainly no stranger anywhere else in the Golden State. *What gives?* Leo asks himself, probably the only person in the room unable to answer. *What is it I'm missing?*

Without even getting to the model and toy room, Leo bolts back upstairs, ties himself into some loose fitting trunks — also procured from the Shoppe — grabs a towel, and heads for the blistering inferno of the pool deck. It is supposed to be cold. Cold enough to worry about frost on the crops. He chooses a chaise, does a few smooth laps dodging toddlers sticking out of inflatable dolphins like aquatic parasites, and retreats to his spot in the sun. More and more cars of road-weary families are pulling into the adjacent lot or easing up into the drop off lane, and soon folks come oozing out to the pool with their lotions and domestic racket. A big man with a shag carpet chest is abusing a young boy by throwing him screaming into the pool and not retrieving him until the kid's swallowed an amount of water equal to what Shamu displaces. The air smells of diesel fuel from the freeway, sweat, chlorine. The cacophony is only slightly insulated by the water: children scream, mothers admonish, there is a constant chain-cranking torture going on at the mini-coaster in the fun park next door, and the deep throated gut rumble of diesels out on the road.

Leo studies the women. This is not exactly Cancun. In all probability, Cancun is not exactly Cancun. There are a handful of recently attractive young moms sporting stretch marks like map boundaries; but none of them are the folks one sees on prime time TV: stealing husbands, tracking down perps, reading the news, discussing frequent urination. There is more fat here than one is taught to admire, more legs like Doric columns, large, panoramic, overwhelming gelatinous breasts, and tiny mounds you'd feel *after* the pea if they shared a place under your mattress. Here is a montage of varicose veins, formulaic nose jobs, bowed legs, fat asses, tummies shivering like Jello, brown wrinkled leather skin — hides really — tanned and dried for Richard Henry Dana to write home about. People who really should wear *more* clothing: *burkas,* perhaps. *But, oh, what self esteem!*

Real people, us, Everyman — and -woman: ordinary women, with the usual families, one two three, splashing and perspiring, snug behind sun glasses with rhinestones and the latest paperback by the currently in vogue Asian-American author. And they have ordinary husbands, guys with neat trimmed hair, wedding rings, the signs of one too many six-packs, and pasty hairless legs. They are probably sales managers for auto parts makers or civil servants, on the adventure of a lifetime at the Chivalry Timbers Suites on Ninety-Nine; teaching the kids to float in a heated half urine solution; bussing soda cans; reading the sports page in <u>The Sacramento Bee</u>; and remarking to each other, *Christ, you believe this weather? You couldn't a made this up!*

And Leo knows he is not in Jackson Hole or Ketchikan or Lake Geneva or climbing K2, and that to look at him is to imagine just another guy taking a brief reprieve from exceeding the speed limit. He is starting to miss Betsy — compact, taut, stylish, looks younger than she is really. Everyone is surprised when they discover her birth year. He misses her touch, her scent, maybe even, just a little bit, the nagging, the nail biting over crazy Taylor. He thinks of retreating to the room, remembering the cell phone, hearing her messages, excusing. Well, kind of lying: *Sorry, babe, I didn't know I'd left it off.* What the hell was he doing in Stockton in November turned August, hemmed in by a bunch of old farts enamored of obsolescence?

When he calls her, she complains that she is worried sick, that she has called five times and left messages. Which he knows. She has searched the paper for one of those multi-vehicle, fog-induced collisions that are so frequent in the San Joaquin, was ready to start calling hospitals where people go when they're run over by harvesting machines or get pitch forked in bar fights while the band covers Garth Brooks. This is all to be expected, and he lamely excuses that his phone was off, which *she* already knows.

"Besides," he says, "the service is kind a iffy up here."

"Bullshit. You're hearing me now!"

"Comes and goes. Only one bar."

"You're not in the fuckin' Gobi, Miguel!"

"Have you been here? Anyway, while it is true that Agent Mulder can reach Pennsylvania Avenue from a cave deep under Antarctica, you and I are children of a lesser satellite."

"You know, I agreed with this little fantasy weekend of yours so you could keep an eye on the *putz,* maybe scratch the surface a bit on what's going on with him. So what happens? You're as unreliable as he is."

"Hey! Not fair. I've done everything you asked me to. Do you think this is a good time? Not exactly Club Med here!"

"Did you broach the subject of some sort of dating service?"

"Consider it broached."

"And?"

"And what?"

"How did that go?"

"It went. What did you think? I bounced it off him."

"And? I want to know exactly what you said."

"Why? It didn't float. What more do you need to know?"

"Maybe it's the way you brought it up."

"Jeez, Bets, I pulled the nine volt out of the car, clipped the cables to his testicles, and gave him the juice. He can be pretty stubborn, your brother."

"Cut the crap, Leo. Did you mention a service? JDate maybe?"

"Taylor's Jewish?"

"It's not only for Jews."

"No? Then why's it called JDate?"

"Other things begin with J. Like *jerk*, or *jerkoff*."

"Elegantly put. *Jerkoff*, huh? I don't think he's into Russian authors. Look, I'll meet you half way. I'll write him a personal for the <u>New York Review of Books</u>."

"Write yourself one while you're at it. I'm that pissed off."

"No, really. This'll work. Listen: *Looking for serious relationship. Overweight elderly male, thinning hair, terminal dandruff. Abhors skiing, walks on the beach and other physical activities. Has no intention of ever going to the Hamptons or Cape Cod. No spirituality or politics. Reads <u>Railroad Model Craftsman</u> cover to cover. Passionate about trains, trains, trains. No sense of humor. Junk food gourmet. Looking for steamy, coal-fueled gal. Would love to meet woman of any age who is still reading this ad. Pasadena area. Willing to commute as far as Alhambra.* Whaddya think?"

He can tell she is trying to keep a straight face. She says, "What is it about trains, anyway?"

"Believe me, it's not the trains. Everybody else here seems to be pretty solid. It's mostly your brother who's made it a religion. Some a these guys'er even here with their wives."

"So Taylor's the only freak?"

"Not anymore *only* than he'd be anywhere else."

"The fuck's that mean?"

"They kind of broke the mold after Taylor. But folks here seem to know him. He kind of fits in. Some a these guys defer to his knowledge. He's having dinner with his posse tonight at some steak house in town. People seem to like him, even the women. What the hell, Bets, he ain't hurtin' nobody."

"Himself. Don't let him eat the steak."

"Not even himself. What about the lamb you proffered?"

"It was roasted, not proffered. That's different. I shop for lean. Whole Foods. Only the best. Anyway, with Mom in her grave and all."

"She has an eternity to get over it."

"And me?"

"I'm not sure that's *his* problem."

"He say that? I'm not his fucking problem?"

"No, no. He just doesn't seem to think either one of you is a problem, and, I gotta tell ya, I'm more and more of the same mind."

"That's the scariest thing I've heard since Norman Bates spoke to his mother!"

"He's okay, Betsy. Pig in shit. He's not a slasher. He's not going to wind up on some tower somewhere with a high-powered scope, either."

"His health?"

"Stats better'n mine. Pressure's under control, could loose a few pounds, but who couldn't? We're Americans. We're supposed to be fat. Brash, greedy and shaped like *tamales*. Africans are supposed to be thin. Humble."

"I'm not an ignoramus, Ernesto. I read the health section in The Times."

"The Times still has sections?...Betsy?"

"What?"

"I miss you."

"Is this the lead in to something I don't wanna hear?"

"I miss you. That's all."

"Well...kind a dead around here too."

"When I get back, maybe we take an evening, leave the kids to their own scatter-brained devices, and maybe go somewhere and do in a pair a lobsters. Whaddya say?"

"I say, watch the tab on the courtesy bar."

"No, really, Bets."

"I don't ever know if you're pulling my leg or not."

"Tell me over a crustacean that's gotten itself in hot water."

"Drawn butter?"

"What else?"

"We'll see."

"What's to see? If I still love you in the morning?"

"When you get home, we'll talk lobster."

"Have Erlinda iron the bibs."

III

DALE AND PATTY MONCTON, NOW EX-PRESIDENT and ex-first lady of the S&TSHA, oblige Taylor with a ride to the culminating group event: a combination reunion and working dinner. The Moncton's are deep in discussion about the future of the meets. Occasionally, as a courtesy, they ask Taylor what he thinks, to which he contributes a discretionary, *"uh huh,"* an authoritative, *"okay with me,"* or a discriminating, *"I'm sure I'll be fine with whatever the group decides."* Taylor talks infrequently in cars, even less than when his feet are on the ground, or if Leo is there to work words out of him like he's squeezing the last plug in the tube, rolling up Taylor's feet, his legs, squishing out his essence.

Instead, he studies his surroundings, looking for ideas to model for the layout. He registers an old brick corner drugstore with front door aligned forty-five degrees to either street, the detritus along an abandoned grade crossing, pre-plastic signage, the freeze-frame placement of cars and trucks in mid-progression on the pavement, an ancient ice house converted to antique shops with battered chairs and farm tools and patriotically painted milk cans displayed on the freight platform. He sees them in balsa or strip pine, molded styrene, painted subdued period colors from Poly Scale half ounce bottles, decaled with circus posters, and in all the various stages of progressive decrepitude. His brain records details few others see: a mangy red dog asleep in the shade of stacked pallets, an amputated RAILROAD CROSS... Sign — *stop look listen* — a forlorn Plymouth gas locomotive sitting on blocks in a junk yard, a collection of restored wood stoves set as yard art in front of a neat bungalow, a pair of tennis shoes tied together and looped over a power line, a root beer drive-thru peeling lead-based paint onto the surrounding picnic tables. There are no definitive explanations for these things and the conditions they are found in. They are a potpourri of chance, the middles of stories that no longer begin nor end. They have no context in time, are shorn from the little tale they were once integral to, are isolated fragments of the broken continuum.

But in our modeler's imagination the red dog becomes a runaway, as most Irish Setters are, exhausted and hungry from its extended adventure away from home. The crossbuck breaks when a trucker suffers a seizure and loses control of his rig, veers up onto the sidewalk just outside of the intended grade, flips onto the tracks with the trailer arching outward just enough to skim the ING off of the sign. A rail fan with backyard space for a narrow gauge loop purchases the engine *as is* from a local fertilizer processor, intends to restore it only to be hit by a major medical bill from his wife's cancer, and is forced to sell it to the junker for scrap. Stove guy evolves into a retired mechanic, who locates his first Peerless abandoned in a field, enjoys cleaning it up so much he goes out and finds another at the local drive-in movie Sunday swap meet, then another, and another, until they overflow the house into the yard, and he gains some indigenous notoriety as an eccentric. The tennis shoes involve a pair of skin heads in a hydraulic Impala and a place of interest on their turf GPS. The owner of the fast food dump suffers from Parkinson's and none of his five children want a decaying hovel of a business far from their comfortable lives in the Bay Area and Seattle.

He could make it all come alive again, Taylor could, set to period, miniaturized, customized, plagiarized from the actual, lifted intact as if by Kansas tornado, set it down upon an extended veneered planet and fed by wires without end. He could move the sun and moon over it, set it aflame, cover it in snow, animate it, take its lives, hear the prayers of the static bereaved. He can give it back the linear attachments it has lost. The themes. The stories. He can make it whole.

J. David Robbins

THE GADSDEN PURCHASE, STEAKS RIBS CHICKEN, BUFFALO
BURGERS, SINCE 1987, is a favorite of Stan's, who has once again found
himself roped into administration. Dale and Patty have pleaded grandparently
responsibilities before it's too late to enjoy the kids. *They grow up so fast, you know,*
Patty explained, *and neither one of us is getting any younger.* Stan Franco said,
What'm I? Peter Pan?

The Gadsden was originally a car barn for the Central California Traction
Company. Next to the front door is a small plaque proclaiming it a National
Historic Landmark. It is a big hangar like affair, part brick, part wood, with a
long clerestory across the rooftop for ventilation. It had gone through several
reincarnations before a Mr. Gadsden from Corpus Christi bought it, had it
gutted, and over the years converted it to a popular family dining room in
search of a theme. He has scattered sports memorabilia around the room to
complement the recently added wide-screens. Also, there are branding irons
and hand plows in profusion; saddles set on posts ringing tall bar tables; poster-
sized prints of Commodore Stockton, John C. Fremont, Brett Harte, Joaquin
Murieta, Snowshoe Thompson, and Three-fingered Jack. Along with Black Bart,
the versifying stagecoach bandit, all are in no particular order as to their relative
merits. And in the center on a pedestal, a full sized streetcar — a short, open-
sided Brill four-wheeler that never ran anywhere near Stockton — lettered, THE
GADSDEN TROLLEY, with a big number 1 on the front end. Along the
walls, in a dissonant meld with the footballs and the bats, the hand pumps and
the irrigation valves, are Gadsden's cloudy eight by tens of streetcars in LA and
Sacramento, Denver, Boston, Holyoke, Salt Lake City: an eclectic mix of soft
focus sepia that seem shot through cataracts.

Gadsden's has no menus, just a large hand painted sign behind the bar
announcing various WORLD FAMOUS steer and pig extracts, deep fried
chicken, baked beans, potato salad, slaw, *all the fixin's that are fit to eat,* on individual
plates or in buckets to cart home.

Stan knows ahead of time that the barn will be full on Saturday night, the
testosterone pickups overlapping the compact-only lines in the lot, the overflow
spread across a gravel field. The TV's will be on, the kids queued deep at the
video games, and Patsy Cline will be belting it out over the several scattered
Bose satellites. The acoustic muffling comes from the concrete floor, which,
despite intentions, offers an absorbent carpet of sawdust and peanut shells, and
the clientele itself. Everyone here is sound-mushing: overlarge and corpulently
insulated, shaded by cowboy hats, denim behinds defined by tractor seats, trough-
fed buckaroos that look like they were born and raised at Home Town Buffet. The
buckarinis all but moo. Even the kids are big and gelatinous with slow bovine eyes
nearly crushed shut by fleshy lids. They look like someone has blown glass-wool
insulation up their asses. Stan has wisely reserved the old machine shop which
masquerades as the back room, has had the tables aligned boardroom style. The
thumping woofers pump through the walls like the big barn's heart beat.

Stan gets up, clears his throat. He is a heavy set but compact man, a former
medic in the army, with serious narrow eyes and a wide slit of a mouth, and very

substantial Abe Lincoln ears. He wears his gray hair in short stand-up bristles and sports a brief villain's mustache. Before him are stacks of bones, stripped naked, gnawed, the results of a cave man meal or a brontosaurus dig. "Up at this end of the table," he says, "I feel I should deliver a benediction."

"You're just the one!" Dale calls.

"Bring it on, *padre!*"

"He who has not sinned, cast the first stone..."

"I did," Dale replies, and Patty gives him an *aw you pinch* on the thigh.

"Anyway, we better get this road on the show. Some a you have lengthy drives in the morning, so let's be the heck gone at a civilized hour."

"Here, here," says Ruben Goldenberg. Ruben has had the trout, guaranteed to sizzle on a segregated grill, and his hull of needle-thin bones pale in comparison to Stan's.

"I want to say at the get go, I never thought I'd get railroaded into this deal again, excuse the pun." Mr. Cramer belts out, "Don't get sidetracked," to boos and hisses. Jack Geldorf chimes in with, "Stay on track now, Dr. Stan." Groans, catcalls. Someone does a middling air horn with hands cupped to mouth.

"Bunch a damn juveniles! Don't blame me if you're here all night. I'm gonna count on all a you, and the general membership, to volunteer, volunteer, volunteer, or I just might up and draft ya. I don't type any more, 'count a my hands, and I haven't got the wind for long proclamations, so we make this a group effort or I'll opt for early retirement."

"We're with ya, Stanley," someone says, accompanied by seconds and more *here here*'s.

A waitress comes in to remove the plates. She is wearing a cowboy hat and kerchief, a short skirt and spurs on her boots that jingle jangle jingle. Her belt holds bullets and two big six-shooters that dangle nearly to her knees. No one knows why.

"What else can I getcha y'all?" she calls, a tiny high school voice, pepped up, perhaps on Cherry Coke, cheery, like she's trying to interest a bunch of pre-schoolers in a hamster. Bill Stiles points to the pistols, says, "Anything you want us to have, hon!" Stan says, "How about a ream a those napkins, doll?" Dixie says, "Where y'all from? Ain't y'all got no pants?" "Used 'em up on the ribs," Stan says. "And we'll see about some a that lemon cream pie after our meeting."

Darlene says, blinking road map eyes, "Toss the pie in the air and see if Annie Oakley here can shoot out the slices before they land."

"First time I seen a bunch a folks schnockered on barbeque sauce," says Dr. Stan. "Now, c'mon, people, let's move the agenda along. Jack?"

The bus boys are wheeling in a cart with which to haul the bones back to the Natural History Museum. Jack waits for them to clear the table, then asks, "You want the minutes read?"

A few scattered boos. "Naw, let's just get done."

"Oked-e-dokety, all right," Jack says. "First up, sales report."

"That's me," Gus says. He talks his robot warble through a hole in his throat. "My quick survey shows we are down about twenty-five percent in attendance and about another ten in sales. I'll tighten that up when I see the numbers, but that's the ballpark. And I haven't been off since I voted for Dewey in forty-eight."

"That bad, huh? Welcome to four-seventy a gallon, kids," Jack intones.

Mr. Cramer mumbles something about bloodthirsty "A-*rabs*," which Ruben hurriedly concurs with. Someone else suggests, "A-*holes, y'ask me!*" Ruben concurs again.

Jack says, "You can't discount the age of the membership, either."

"Whattya you know about age?" from Cramer.

Dr. Stan pounds the air gavel. "I think we can all agree that things are slowing down. We're all kind a running out of gas. And if you check the obits in the newsletter, I think you'll see Jack has a point."

"And the gas," says Ruben.

"Oh, Jack has plenty of gas, too," says Darlene.

"And the gas. Okay. So, do we need to make some adjustments? I thought it might be a nice touch to have a list available of all the rail attractions within a convenient radius. The museums, the photo sites, you know. This is a pretty rich area."

"Nearly the same folks each meet," Ruben points out. "Doesn't everybody know where the Jamestown roundhouse is, the Rio Vista trolleys?"

"Hey. Everybody's ridden in a Chevy. They still advertise. I just thought it might give a little more impetus to hauling your behind down here."

"Fine. But for my part," says Ruben, "I'm going to cut back to once a year. With the X-raying, the luggage limits, the lines, flying's not what it used to be. I want to take off my shoes, I'll go to Japan."

Jack says, "We need to lure in the kiddies."

"How ya gonna do that, Jack?" Dale wants to know. "Let 'em blow up trains on a monitor?" Stan scratches his head, cups his chin, sniffles. "Jack's right. We need to think about it. Put all of our ideas in the virtual suggestion box." Ruben ads, "Virtual waste of time!"

"I think", says Darouche, "we just go back to *one* annual event per year. Cuts the security issues way back. No brainer, ya ask me."

"What security issues? Not exactly a rave!"

"I see things," says Darouche. "Almost had to break up a punch out at the buffet this morning." He sends a chilled glare Taylor-ward.

"G'wan!"

"I was there. I didn't see anything."

"Let's vote," Jack says. "Do I hear a motion?"

"Motion," shouts Darlene as she gives her torso a suggestive wiggle.

"You go girl!"

Jack seconds and Gus accuses them of nepotism.

The vote is taken and the bi-annual annual event is halved like World Famous drumsticks in Gadsden's Special Hades Sauce.

Nightstick sidles up to Taylor in the lot. His face is red and the neon glistens on his lips. As Taylor faces him, Nightstick steps back several feet, out of the floods, a tilted shadow favoring his right hip. He flicks a match off his left thumb; lights the cigarette already hanging from the corner of his mouth, snuffs the light with his fingers. He starts talking mid-context, as if continuing an old conversation. It takes Taylor a second or two to locate the segue. "You owe me an apology, Batshit." He says. "You threatened me and you were rude. You displayed physical intentions and I want some satisfaction on this thing. Right now."

"Okay," Taylor says.

"Okay, what?"

"I apologize."

"You what?"

"I apologize."

"Just like that?"

"I think so, yes."

Night stick flips the cigarette to the ground where it performs a brief pyrotechnique display. "Why's that?"

"I'm going to miss my ride."

"That's not a reason."

"Okay."

Taylor's hears a whip crack. *Thwack.* A shit-kicker's band has assembled in Gadsden's bar, their electric cover of Frankie Lane, adopted by a breeze, wafts through the swinging doors. An errant dirt-devil dervishes through the light beam.

"I don't think you mean it," Darouche says.

"I'm sorry for that too."

A form spins low over the lot. A plastic bag? A tumble weed?

"You know, I'm not too old to take you down."

"I know."

Two headlights bathe them in high beams. A car engine chortles to life. Taylor and Darouche are both bright and blind.

"This is pretty chicken shit, Bedibye!"

"Okay."

"Okay? Okay? Don't you go all New Testament on this old boy, fucker!" His eyes are flashing red, like someone's flipped his emergency signal.

"Okay."

"Y'know, truth is, Toby wanted *me*. Not *you*. *Me*. But I turned 'im down flat. I got principles, y'see. Not like some folks. I had no intention a whoring out to this new-fangled, store-less kind a operation. You won't see me selling out the railfan community like some fuckin' Benedict Arnold. Not me."

Stan and Patty skid up next to them. Stan leans out of his window and says, "Meeting adjourned." Taylor gets in, and Nightstick stands alone in the lot working his fists and watching tail lights disappear into the warm night. There was a time he would have flattened the big man right there on the pavement, lifted him by his shoulders and slammed him up against a nearby eucalyptus. There was a time. A grand old time. Before Starbuck's. Before faggots. Before women drove locomotives and went to war and became cops. When a field of honor — whether a barroom floor, an asphalt lot, a boxcar roof, or a shady meadow paced out by seconds — was the venue to decide who indeed the real men were. In that time, the Taylor's of the world knew to bow out politely or endure injuries they would eventually carry to their graves. A tear forms in Nightstick's scarlet eye: the transport of something lost. And he says out loud, "We're not done, shithead," but he doesn't believe it.

And from the bar, the lead croons, *M-o-o-o-l tra-a-a-a-a-a-in.*

IV

L EO COMES DOWN EARLY THE NEXT morning, his bag already packed and locked in the hatch. He has filled a bowl with Cheerios, some cantaloupe, an apple. Taylor joins him with another cordillera of fats and starches. Much of the group has already left. Brewster is nowhere to be seen, and Darouche is across the room, aimlessly poking at his eggs, snake eyes glued on Taylor.

"There's this guy over there," says Leo. "I think he's sweet on you."

"Don't mind him," says Taylor. "Kind of a crank."

"Your prescience amazes me. A whole new Taylor I'm seeing."

"Tell Betsy. They don't keep me in a straight jacket."

"How was your thing last night?"

"Great food. Thought I'd never get up off the chair."

"And here you are, like yesterday never happened. I landed a couple a chicken tacos from a local mom and pop. Spent the night in the can."

The Geldorfs join them, zipper pulls dangling in leathery pageantry. Taylor introduces them to Leo.

"So, Taylor," says Darlene. "How'er the ladies?"

Taylor blushes. "No ladies."

"No shit! A cutie like you?" She sounds honestly surprised.

"No room in my life right now."

Darlene is pensive as she schmeers a half of bagel with cream cheese from little plastic cups. She looks over at Taylor with one eye. Leo notices she is stuffed into her slick, protective pants like sausage in *derma.* "Cory Ann says, *hey.*"

Taylor puts down his fork. "Who?" Cory Ann has come to breakfast with all the ill-considered finesse of Helen.

"Cory Ann, *pendejo,*" Leo says.

"Where did you see Cory Ann?"

Jack says, "Excuse my wife while I extract her petite boot from her Moffit Tunnel-sized mouth."

"It's no big deal, is it, Taylor?" says Darlene. "I mean, after all this time."

"But where did you see her? I don't care really. We weren't a match, so I let her down easy. I was just curious."

There is a heavy, discomfiting silence. "You've gone this far," Jack tells Darlene.

"Well, see, Taylor, this is awkward. I shouldn't've brought it up."

Leo asks, "You want me to leave?"

"No, Leo, no big deal," Taylor postures, hoping Leo *will* leave.

"Okay, then. Cory Ann and I…at the museum…we kind of bonded. And she, Cory Ann, seeing no career future at the greasy spoon, asks if I know of anything out our way. So, I said, I think a truck stop in Beaumont is looking for someone full time. I didn't think anything would come of it. But the next thing I know, she goes out there, charms the shit outta them, lands a full twenty percent more than the last cheapskate was paying her, and, with an ass like hers, those truckers are giving up change like broken slots at Stateline." Darlene leaves a Cheshire grin hanging in the air and tries to disappear behind it, no mean challenge.

Taylor cops Nightstick's expression from the lot the night before. "So she lives out there?"

"You didn't think she drives in from the *barrio?*" Jack grumbles. He is giving Darlene the *we-will-talk* glare.

"She's got an apartment, or what?"

There is more silence from Darlene. Jack hums a catchy *Dias Irae.*

"Taylor," says Darlene. "Cory Ann and I, you see, we got on *real* well. And Jack too. It's hard to explain, but, she kind of completed us."

Leo says, "I left something in the room," and vaporizes as fast as steam. No one notices, even here where steam is a big deal.

"And, you know," she continues, "we got this double-wide because Jack was going to set up his trains in there but…"

"Who has time?" Jack says.

"I do," Taylor says.

"You're retired."

"Do *you* work, Jack?" Taylor is sounding testy.

"I consult."

"About what?"

"This and that."

Darlene interrupts, spits out, "SoCoryAnnmovedinwithus."

Jack says, "Just tell him already! We're a *thing.*"

"A thing?"

"A couple."

"There are three of you."

"Yeah, well, kind of an extended couple."

"With Cory Ann? I don't get it."

Jack smiles. "I'm getting enough for both of us. No hard feelings, bro?"

"The math is bothering me."

"Think outta the box, big guy."

Taylor says, "I think I left something in the room too."

"It's the age," Jack says. "You're all so brain dead. My excuse, I'm just half stoned all the time."

Darlene says, "I'm sorry. I shouldn't have told you."

"Why not?"

"Well, because, you look...stricken!"

"No, I'm fine. It's just...well, the t*hree* of you?"

Darlene asks. "You want me to tell her, *hey?*"

Taylor looks her in the face, a deer to her headlights. "I don't know. Whatever you think."

❊

In the car, Leo says, "It's a new day in America."

"I think I'm relieved," Taylor says.

"Interesting reaction."

"I wouldn't want her to be alone."

"I would, but I'm an asshole. You? You're a fuckin' prince! You wanna talk?"

"About what?"

"That. Her. You know."

"We just did."

"That was it?"

"I don't know what else to say."

"Okay, then, Taylor."

"Okay, Leo."

They pull out onto the service road and approach the intersection. A rent-a-cop in brown striped jodhpurs, drops his kickstand and stops traffic with his palm. A line of cars with FUNERAL window stickers solemnly slide by like a presidential motorcade.

Leo feels a need to bust Taylor out of any possible reverie. He brakes, says, "This is something I will never understand. Everybody's gotta stop for the stiff. People going to work, maybe a guy driving his laboring wife to emergency. Thieves fleeing the cops. Where the fuck does this guy, behind the curtains, need to be in such a hurry as to hold everybody up? There's gotta be a better way a gettin' rid of us than wasting time and real estate, or polluting the air with ashes. What if morticians had big shredders? They'd feed us through and we'd come out in little flat strips they can unload on farmers for fertilizer. Whaddya think?"

"And we'd eat the things they fertilize? Isn't that kind of like cannibalism?"

"Oh, sure, make light of my innovations. You're just like your sister. Emasculating. See, when they send you up in smoke, someone's breathing that very same air, aren't they? Through the nose, you are consuming particles of dear old Auntie Carmelita. Nasal cannibalism, Taylor. You can't escape the dead. Chances are, and this is fact, right now you're breathing in molecules that Ghengis Kahn once breathed. The dead'er gonna stay with you no matter what."

Taylor knows only too well.

Leo rolls the Prius forward, all EV now, noticing that he has failed to keep Taylor from private musings. He says, "So did you know she was bi?"

"Buy?"

"-Sexual. Bisexual."

"No, I guess not. I get them mixed up."

"You get what mixed up?"

386

"The sexuals. Bisexual, homosexual, heterosexual, trans-sexual."

"Did you never share your junior high locker room with other pubescent males? Bisexual. Kind a like the Unitarian Church of gender. A little a this, a little a that. Whatever works. Everybody's welcome."

While Taylor ponders, Leo turns on to the underpass below the freeway, takes the U-shaped ramp, joins the parade of global warmers who flip him off disgusted with his trendy greenery, gradually depresses the pedal, gets the horn from a big toothy Dodge RAM with STP stickers, and proceeds into the second lane from the right. He yearns to be home, caves to a barely socially conscience sixty, and gets passed by Expeditions — *ka ching!* he thinks — Hummers — "Ka ching, he says — Suburbans tugging power boats — "Ka ching, Ka ching" — a Mountainer, a Tundra — "Ka chingerooni!" The only vehicle that doesn't pass him is the forlorn Winnebago, flat footed on the shoulder, a Corolla hitched to it's rear end right under the Good Sam smiley face and halo, and providing a millisecond of shade for the rest of the traffic. Leo says, "Winnebago, lose a bago."

The big neon knight moves backward, followed by other corporate stanchions, across the Stockton City Line-*ya'll come back now, hear?* Soon the fields reappear, corrugated by plows, run down farm houses, *braceros* hunched to stuff burlap bags, and then the long pipe lines intersecting the axis of a series of irrigation wheels and raining sunlit mist on the crops. The air is jubilant with compounds, organic fertilizers, and the sizzle of bugs frying on the pavement. Long freights stacked high with potatoes slog by.

And Taylor thinks, *A funeral procession. I could do that. A line of boxy old sedans and cabriolets with a cop in front and a cop in back. Have them coming from the Chapel, up through town to Contemplation Hill Cemetery.*

V

THE TRIP SOUTH IS BUSY WITH talk, none of which matriculates into conversation. Leo describes frames from his favorite films — *Viva Zapata, Amores Peros, Captain From Castille.* He talks a little real estate to liven things up. Taylor has heard of none of the films and doesn't hear of them now. He is concerned only with properties measured in inches. Taylor vocalizes in intervals, those between lost railroads that once plied their trade along and down to where Ninety-Nine bisects nearly the length of California. He reminisces about the San Joaquin & Eastern, the Visalia Electric, the diminutive Sunset line, tells it like he'd ridden them. Leo hears, *clackety-clackety-clack, and* remembers nothing. One hybrid, five sets of seat belts; a pair of brothers-in-law, out of kilter, as if the spheres have rotated in opposite directions, as if time moves at a different pace for driver and passenger; complimentary universes crammed into cabs comfortable for individual Asians, halves of hands-free phone calls, abridged chips of fact and opinion that go unanswered in the current discordant planes; different layers of being in the vast, agricultural facade nourished by mountain glaciers. As if Taylor and Leo themselves are happening in different eras, in different consciousnesses, looking out of different Safety Glass windows onto alternate realities.

Leo observes, "Two halves of different conversations do not add up to one." Taylor says, "I guess," only because he knows that Leo has said *something*.

✳

Leo has popped the hatch door, but they sit, exhausted from the drive, in the silent electric air processed into the Toyota. A need to speak hangs between them over the console. Absent a muse, it is a phantom waiting, waiting. Leo drums on the wheel. Taylor tries to adjust his large form for comfort.

"Well," says Leo, barely heard over the roar of austerity. Several more minutes pass before he says, "So!"

"Uh huh!" Taylor affirms.

"Here we are."

"Yes, we sure are."

Next door, the wife beater's house is still, the lawn the color of hash browns, a rain gutter tilting loose from the roof line: perhaps loaded with leaves and pods from neglected trees and a ravenous oleander that has reached up over the peak. A gyrating sphere of gnats cavorts in the shadow of an unclipped shrub.

"So what's on for you tonight?"

"Me?"

"We're alone in here, right?"

"Oh, I don't know. Relax a little, I guess. You?"

"Well, I think I'll be enjoying the tribunal."

Taylor shrugs. His house is alive with a selection of brown packages. They are segregated from the inner porch by its wrought iron gate. A pair of rolled throwaways, belted by rubber bands, lounge in the grass. No one will read them. Their parent trees have died in vain, lured into service by a lie about the wrong cause.

"Questions will be asked."

"Yeah."

"Hot lights. Bamboo under my fingernails. Fingers removed at selected intervals."

"Yeah. Sorry."

"Yeah, easy for you. So what do I tell her?"

Taylor shrugs. He is getting very good at shrugging this weekend. Finds that a good, shoulder-jogging shrug covers more ground than he would have expected. "Tell her I'm fine."

"Right. But the cross exam's a bear, Taylor. How to convince the adjutants-general? How to get them to take my testimony seriously?"

Taylor shrugs yet again.

"You do that shoulder thing once more, I'll be tempted to dislocate one of them."

"Okay."

"Yeah. Well."

"Uh, huh."

"Look. I had a good time."

"Yeah, okay."

"No, really. I really did."

"You don't have to say that. I know it's not your thing."

"Not true. I love a good time. Look, we each get what we get. Take home what we got. Each on our own level. Measured from where we came in at."

"Sure. Okay."

"You?"

"Me?"

"You have a good time?"

"Always do."

Leo thinks, *Was I there at all?* He wants to say he feels like chopped liver; tries to remember what chopped liver is supposed to feel like. Tries to remember what it tastes like, if, in fact, he has ever had chopped liver. *Why chopped liver?* he wonders. Why not *albóndigas, moo shoo* pork, *ravioli?* What subtle quality of chopped liver is it that represents insignificance, being passed over — in no Biblical sense — that makes diced organ meat in a generous puree of chicken fat the grand cipher of all metaphoric foods. What does it all lose in translation? Leo wonders. Being descended from folks who entered New Mexico in armor, he feels that he should have some insight. *Probably a crypto-Jew somewhere in the lineage. Wouldn't that drive Betsy and the snake charmer over the edge?* These are the kinds of things being with Taylor puts in his head. "And," he announces, thinking of filters, "gotta take a leak."

"Is that a question?"

"Why would I care if you had to take a leak? Betsy might, but not me."

"Okay."

"Well, okay what? My leg's vibrating like something sold on late night cable. I'm drowning here."

"Nice try."

"What?"

"You can't come in. You know that."

"I don't want to come in."

"You don't have to pee?"

"Nope, not anymore. I had to pee for Betsy. But you said I can't. So that's that. You know, funny thing?"

"Yeah?"

"When we were up there, in Stockton, I missed her. I really missed her, being up there with you. Now, I don't know. Now, I've gotta go home and talk about you, and…I don't miss her so much. I think…I think, Taylor, you're not the part of Betsy I miss. I think you're a great guy in your world. And I like you there. I liked you in Stockton with all your train buddies. I don't get the whole thing. I don't understand really. But it was nice seeing you in it all. But, now, minutes away from the hot seat, my darling wife, your fretful sister, in *her* world, and your business, is just, somehow, not going see the nice. Not your fault. Not her fault. Not my fault for that matter. None of us controls the world, huh?"

"I don't know."

What's to be done, huh? Anyway."

"Yeah. Say, Leo, you two okay?" Once again, Taylor is instantly regretting asking a question he may not want to hear the answer to. This is the problem with family: you ask them how they are and they tell you.

"Which two?" *A little payback for the terminally dense.*

"You. And my sister."

"Oh, *those* two! What are you asking?"

"Oh, I don't know. Forget it."

"No, no. Outta the bag. Go ahead."

"You said some things."

"Yeah, well, Taylor, that's what happens in conversations. Yeah, we're okay. I'd say we're a great deal more than okay. We're working on a better landing. We're a hell of a lot better than I'd rate much of the competition. You know what she's like. You should see the shit she gives me over David." Taylor manages not to ask what is wrong with David. "But she's okay, see. And when it's all over, she'll be with God and will only have to see me on weekends and holidays."

"This God thing. I don't remember her always being like that."

"Always a little spark. Since I know her, anyway. But that's a majority of her years, isn't it? But losing Helen…"

There she is, stuck to the headliner of Leo's car like an errant mosquito, hanging over them, listening, seething. "Is this going to be my fault?"

"Shit! I don't know. Is it? I mean, we…you and I never really talked about it, did we?'

"Because I don't really see how this is my fault. If Betsy does, if it drove her to God…"

"*Closer.* Closer to God. Wherever he is. She always had the germ."

"You'd think, something like what happened to Helen, that it would not bring you *closer* to God."

"You'd think. But the worshiper moves in mysterious ways. So. Tell me, why did the marriage end?"

"My wife got hit by a train."

"No, I mean, what led up to her bolting out the door at that hour? Winding up over in some dumpy industrial blight?" Taylor tells him of her constant anger, the broken railroad car, in deference to which he feels more entitled to anger than she was.

"No other signs, huh? Depression? Sleeping all day? Talk about counseling?" Taylor thinks hard for a moment, then shrugs. "We weren't real happy, I guess." Leo shrugs. He is conscious of doing so. This is the kind of moment he would expect himself to say, *If you ever need to talk…*but doesn't, says instead, "Okay, so get your shit and I'll see ya when."

Taylor thanks him for driving. "No *problema.* You want to come by and help me with my track plan one a these days?" Taylor hoists himself out of the car, stretches, leans down to the window and says, "Sure." Neither of them expects it to happen. Then he takes two slow steps hatch-ward, pivots and comes back to the window. "You know, Leo…" He stops, as if he's lost his words, breathes a big breath in, lets it out again. "If, you know, you've really got to use the bathroom…"

It comes out muffled, compressed, forced through a cringe, as if he is both offering and holding it back.

Leo angles down over the console, looks through the passenger window to see if it's still Taylor standing there. "That would mean I'd have to go inside." Taylor, in retreat, says, "Yeah, well…" stops in mid-shrug as if to denote that he thinks better of it.

Leo opens his door and carefully sets one sandal down on the pavement. He sits that way, staring at nothing in particular over the dash, then hoists himself out as Taylor turns again to retrieve his gear. Leo sets his arms down on the roof, his chin down in his arms, says, "Taylor, I don't know. Maybe that's not such a good idea."

"I just thought, if you have to use the bathroom…Maybe, it's time we just got this whole thing over with." Once more he plunges himself into a well of instant regret.

"Funny thing about it is, if we do, and I do come in, the cat's outta the bag and keeping the neighbors up. I don't know exactly what the cat has to tell me, or why it was in the bag in the first place, but I do have an imagination. And I'm guessing, what I don't know won't hurt your sister, and what I might find out…It's like science, see, each new discovery carrying its own baggage of wonder. She'll say, *He's done* what *to the place?* No, actually, she'll say, *My asshole brother's done fucking what to the place?* I'll try to convince her that it wasn't so bad, wasn't bad at all, this remarkable thing you've done. And she'll say it's remarkable only in its abnormality. Up and back, back and forth, to and fro, to grandmother's house we go. Get the picture?"

"Not exactly." He is both relieved and vaguely disappointed. He breathes in, he breathes out, fidgeting with feet and hands at the side of the car. Revealing the unfathomable secrets of the layout to Blake and Cory Ann seems not to have played to his advantage.

Leo says, "Neither will she. Let's just turn the clock back a bit to the point where you said, *nice try*, and I'm outta here."

"Okay. It was our parent's house." Leo knows this. "Not our grandparents." Leo knows this too.

"Okay."

"Yeah?"

"Sure."

"I'm right, huh?"

"Dumb idea."

"In a perfect world, maybe." And Taylor thinks, *that's what I've got. Made it myself.* "Leo," he says. "I like you in your world too."

"And never the trains shall meet."

"Twain. It's twain."

"You're sounding a bit like Elmer Fudd there, *amigo.*"

"Because you said…"

"I know. I know. So, okay then." Leo eases quietly away from the curb, getting over a hundred per right now, all fifteen feet of it.

Taylor calls after him, "I don't have a cat." Leo stops, buttons into park, waits for Taylor to amble over to his window, says, "Nope, you don't have a cat. You have trains. But, the thing is, after all I've seen this weekend, I'm still clueless. Why trains?"

"Why *trains?*" Taylor sounds incredulous. Who doesn't know this?

"Why not stamps? Coins? Antique bottles purple from the desert sun? Little silver spoons engraved with places you've been and hanging on a specially-made maple rack? Why trains?"

"Trains don't ask you stuff."

"Stamps don't ask you stuff. So, give me a real answer."

Taylor is looking uncomfortable. He puts his weight on one leg, then the other. He breathes in, he breathes out. "I don't understand the question."

"Sure you do."

"I don't know what you want me to say."

"Just tell me, why trains? Tell it like you want to tell it. Tell it like you want *me* to understand."

"I don't…"

"I know you don't. Just try. For me, bro."

"I'm not good at this kind of thing."

"I know."

"This talking about feelings."

"Talk about trains."

"And my feelings about trains?"

"I wouldn't put it that way, but if that works for you, go on, test the water."

"Water?"

"Just do it."

"Okay…I guess. Let's see. Trains. Trains. They've always been with me. It goes back to Dad."

"Yep. So I've heard. Go on."

"Dad had this thing, see. He'd take me up to Cajon and shoot pictures. Weekends, we'd ride the red cars. Cahuenga Pass, where the Hollywood freeway is now. There were sheep on the hillside that became Universal Studios. I hardly recognize anything anymore. We'd go down to Long Beach. One Christmas, Dad got me a locomotive kit. Mantua. Little cast iron job. Oh-four-oh switcher. He helped me with the detail work. The painting. It was hard to tell if it was his or mine, but that was okay. The locomotive became a train. We built a table and a four by four layout in the garage. Simple oval. A switch and a siding. A mountain in the middle. Mom was unhappy she couldn't park in the garage anymore. Little trains became big trains. We'd, Dad and me, sit on the porch swing and listen to the Super Chief or the El Capitan blow by. We had the timetables. Knew when they'd be at the Pasadena station. Twenty minutes before, we'd be on that porch. We'd pop some pop corn and take it out there like we were going to the show."

Taylor is looking dreamy. He is no longer talking to Leo. "It was the sound of…of connection. To everyone, everywhere. Some kid in Pawtucket or Spokane was sitting with his dad on his own porch swing." His eyes cloud; moisture develops. "It was the normal thing to do. The way things were. And the whistle... It was like...the sound of...dreams. Ends of the earth stuff. Adventure. And the power. There was still some steam then. There was muscle to it, clouds billowing out of these massive machines. It's what made hearts beat. It made you want to ride. And keep on riding. Riding all your life. Riding your life. The sway of the cars. That repetitive sound of wheel to rail, ticking off miles. It pumped your blood. The rush of speed. The rush!"

His eyes glass over like duck on a tray. The lids swell. His face turns flush, a hand nervously checks his capricious zipper. "It was all so alive. So...what, what do I want to say...integral? I think integral." His arms begin to flail, his big hands forming the letters like a mute. "It held the country together in a big knot. It touched everybody in some way."

Taylor's lips pump up like puffer fish. His moist words settle on Leo's injection-molded plastic trim. "It brought you things. It took you places. It carried your circus, your relatives back east, your mail, your news. It carried...*you!*" His voice has become shrill, cartoon-like. "And I've watched it going away. The busses. The trucks. The piggybacks and these big box cargo things they just yank off the ships. I've seen the logos disappear, America's greatest companies. Snap. Just like that. Logos to graffiti. Design to vandalism."

Stains form under his arms. "Long haul to slow death. I've been to the scrap yards. Terminal Island. You betcha, *Terminal* Island! Seen the streetcars stacked like soda can empties. Stripped. Eviscerated. Waiting for the crusher. Train guts. Piles of trash for the dozers. The big Missabe engines waiting on the torch in Duluth. The whistles, the number plates, everything removable, gone to poachers. Squandered! A whole network...the fiber, see, the sinew...squandered."

He points to the house. "But there. It's alive. I keep it alive. I keep it stoked and generated. I revive it. Breathe into it. Light the fires. Make it all stay on track. I give it...I give it...I don't know, continuity. A continuum. I *resurrect!*" He puts his head down, his chin to his chest. He is embarrassed by this sudden possession. He wipes the dandruff from his shoulders. Breathes in. "Christ, Leo, I don't know what you want me to say." Breathes out.

"Wow! Me neither." There is a moment of silence. For trains? For Taylor? For time to gather thoughts, have them crated and shipped down the tracks and warehoused for consumption. Leo has his fingers splayed along his lower lip, pulling it down, stretching his mouth into an incredulous oval. "I'm blown away. I never heard you so passionate about anything."

"Have you been listening?" Taylor asks softly.

"I guess not."

"Leo?"

"Yeah."

"Don't tell Betsy I said *Christ,* you know, in vain."

Leo tweaks the end of his nose with thumb and forefinger, says, "I'll tell her I brought you home in one piece. I'll tell her you're fine. I'll tell her we didn't have this talk because you had to get inside, that you were needed in there. I listened, *just now.* Top of my class. An avalanche, shock 'o' the day surprise earful...I would a taken notes had you given me a thumbs up. I don't know what to say either. But still, I guess, I gotta admit, I still don't get it. But mum's the word. That's all she'll know. What do the kids say: *It's all good!"*

Across the street, Mrs. Gettzleman, who does have a cat, has an ark-load of cats, refreshingly not kept in bags, holds a long-spouted can, is watering several pots of jades and other succulents that have long since proven that even drought resistant entities can no longer survive in Mediterranean climes. She waves to Taylor, studies Leo, shakes her head as if she knows something she thinks they know.

SIXTH HELEN

As she passes the Home Depot, she realizes she has gone too far, does a loop in and out of the lot, considers hiring a day worker to get her where she's going, then makes a left out of the right-turn only exit. A Civic veers out of her way. Two blocks into her backtrack, she remembers that she's seen all of this before, and negotiates an indelicate U-turn where none is permitted. The world has taken on a fuzziness, a softness, all the lines defined by the arm hairs of an infant. It comforts her. She thinks about Harry Stork who she met in an Old Town bar after a previous rupture with Taylor. Harry isn't much to look at, but he knows how to talk to a woman. He should: he has been married to enough of them. He is attentive, complementary, patient with her timidity. Harry has money and a nice Spanish Colonial on a hill above Los Feliz. He likes good wine and good food and he wants her to like them too. He gives her gifts she can flaunt at home because Taylor never looks at her. Out of habit or tradition, she keeps it all secret, doesn't want Betsy to find out. It has been going on for months while Taylor diddles with his toys. It is so easy, it feels guiltless. Where is that damned left turn anyway? He must be worried sick by now. Harry admires punctuality. He says he likes that in her. He tells her she is pretty, that he's convinced that she's younger than she admits, that he hasn't seen better bodies on twenty year olds. He hungers for her. Strokes her. Harry is an intoxication. Taylor is the hangover. Harry is just the right dram for the dog that bit her.

THE RIGHT OF WAY

I

During much of the long history of technological development, the most complicated mechanical advancement was not an object of war or work, but rather a medium with which to commune with God. We speak, of course, of the mighty pipe organ, a complex mechanism of pumps and tubes and an array of keys and stops so sophisticated as to shame to simplicity the vast panoply of contemporary invention. This was all to change with the advent of the steam engine and its locomotive offspring. Simple enough at first, hardly more than a large teakettle with a linkage to wheels that sometimes failed to outrun a horse, the locomotive became the focus of educated men with an interest in transportive power, efficient commerce and the wiles of pressure cookers. From a clumsy platform with vertical boiler, the steam train engine evolved into a behemoth with multiple drive wheels and an unsurpassed ability to haul tonnage.

Our focus, in this second volume of the U.F.T.&G. saga, is with motive power and the infrastructure it demanded. The Tishomingo, with its tortuous right of way through hills and flats, a red line on a map rarely straighter than a strand of cooked spaghetti, its steep grades, and its weighty revenue loads of coal, all combined with a need to move freight cheaply, people comfortably and mail swiftly, to say nothing of competitively, tried nearly every type of iron horse in existence from the line's inception on. Initially, it prided itself with a smart fleet of American Standards, evolving toward the waning days of steam when big articulates struggled along with one hundred loaded hoppers in tow. It tried awkward little tankers, low slung Moguls, high stepping Pacifics, the mighty Mallets; specialists all in their assigned tasks, right up into the age of the diesel. And though, with some peripheral exceptions, the line was slow to modernize, it did eventually adopt a fleet of second-hand diesels which hauled the company into eventual abandonment. However, it is with steam, the road's mainstay through most of its history, that this volume is primarily concerned.

Big, complex machines require big, complex maintenance facilities, and the Tishomingo had no shortage of these; both major for general repairs, construction and rebuilding, to more regionally designed plants equipped to deal with the local quirks of the line. Rods were thrown, boilers rusted through, pressure lost. Steam engines derailed, exploded, corroded and wore down iron tires. Parts had to be forged, bolted, and kept operationally clean. Miles of tubing required flushing, gauges had to be attended, pistons lubed, and corrosive waste matter removed. And finally, the pride of the line resided in the cosmetic application of paints and color schemes: primers, burnished woods, and gleaming brass fit for frigates. All this on an undeniably dirty leviathan belching soot, leaking oil and hot water, and all manner of pollutants from the Gulf to the Central Shops at Uncas Falls.

(Excerpted from the introduction to, The Undulating, Fragmented, Troubled & Grunge: A History of the Uncas Falls, Tishomingo and Gulf Railroad, Vol. II, The Motive Power, by Turner M. Hattfield, Prof. of History, Capital Institute of Technology, CIT Press, 1957.)

All along the railroad, from Uncas Falls to the Tishomingo Station, and the coal seam down to the Gulf, the world returns to normal. This is not to say it gets back anything that it had lost, but it moves on: hurdles jumped, rapids forged, the record expunged, and history laundered like bad money. Which is good for some, but not for others.

One that it is good for is T. Rail Ferrous.

Ferrous prides himself on reading every word of the morning Uncas Falls Republican-Advertiser. In particular, he likes to monitor how the railroads are portrayed, and assure himself that the Tishomingo's advertising budget is wisely spent. A retrospective op-ed piece, penned by Peyton Marsh — more than coincidentally a nephew of Ferrous' — commends the line for its rapid structural repair and modernization of the northern leg in the post David's Sling environment. It lauds the company for its compassionate response to the needs of the victims, both payroll and revenue, and their bereaved families. For particular notice, Marsh cites the division super for his rapid deployment of medical and insurance personnel, the nearly immediate clearing and cleansing of the tragic site, the onslaught of work crews, and the timely restoration of service.

Moses Brown is not mentioned. He is one that all of this is bad for.

Ferrous makes a mental note to renew Peyton's rail pass, attach it to a nice bottle of something well aged by Frenchmen. He runs his approving eyes over the banner at the bottom of page one, an elongated rendering of the Thebes Viaduct crowned by streamliner with smoke slithering like a kite tail. The type is bold: **THE TISHOMINGO, WE GET YOU THERE!** Not always true, as recent events can attest, but Ferrous is looking more for message and visual impact than veracity.

A mild breeze decomposes, finds its way through the screen around the veranda. It is careful not to reveal its secret to the insect commandos looking for an approach. Ferrous hears the tired whistle of the eight-thirty freight as it slogs out of the yard with a heavy load and in no particular hurry. He sees the dark plume blooming out above the warehouse roofs. He anchors his teacup on the corner of the telegram, then re-reads it slowly:

TAKE NO ACTION INSTRUCTIONS PREVIOUS PRES STOP OPERATION AS USUAL STOP WOULD YOU CONSIDER TOP TIER PROMOTION STOP REPLY 48 HRS

Ferrous thumbs through his file of business cards, places a call to the Tishomingo City Hall. P-R says he's surprised to hear from him. Ferrous ignores the observation, bets he *is* surprised, says in his steady, unconcerned tone, *"How'd y'all like t'heah some good news?"*

"From y'all? I am hesitant. The subjective value of *good* suggests that I pace myself."

"Re-lax, now, P-Ah. Wadn't the fi's' time we got un'uh each othuh skin."

"Oh, I am relaxed. I'm very relaxed."

So is Ferrous. He sits at the top of the heap that is Uncas Falls, at the end of a willow-ribboned drive that ambles in under his *porte cochere*. He looks down on lesser estates: simple homes with one-tree yards, apartments, shotgun shacks and dog run shanties, and a disheveled business district be-smudged by tall stacks from the factories along the river. He looks down on the steeples of God and Mammon and government. He taps his toes tunefully on the decking, a little song from his childhood that has re-entered his head and refuses dismissal. It is with effort that he manages to get his feet to reach the floor.

"Call't y'all t' bura the hatchet."

"Exactly where?"

"Now, now, P-Ah! The both a us got a li'le off a the beaten path."

"I didn't. I had you in the cross hairs and I took the shot."

"Yessuh, y'done'at ahl right. Well played. Ah c'mend y'all on yore ma'ksmanship. That bein' ai'ed, Ah ain' partic'la'ly fond a y'all eithuh. But us'all still gotta wo'k t'gethuh. Ower 'spective in'eres', y'une'stan'. Look, Ah'as thinkin' a takin' a ride. Good t' get outta the smudge an' inta the count'y ai' oncet'n a b'ue moon. A'ways *en*-joy the view from The Came's this time a yeah. Hopin'a catch the wild flowuhs in bloom on the bat'field. Late aftuhnoon's bes', when the sun gives jus' the right slant, the long shadas, the vivid col'ation. Plannin' on bein' up theah 'bout fo', fo'-fi'teen."

"Y'all enjoy your jaunt, then. Don't let that Basque slow you down."

Ferrous sets the phone down, notices that the song is back, a lullaby, *hush little baby*, nothing his own mother ever sang to him: perhaps just the whiff of a tune he had heard on the street while passing a pram. He stares at the silent phone, as if Western Electric has advice to give him, considers a second call to Tishomingo.

A uniformed driver, slick, knee high patent leather stiff, nods to P-R as he pulls into the gravel lot. Ferrous is the deep yellow dwarf snug on an overlarge stone bench, a mote in the gleam of a long angled light, still as the rusty caisson behind him. The golden speck at his abdomen comes from the hinged top of his pocket watch. "Fo' twen'y-se'en," he scolds. "Coul'n't make it on mah' crew."

"As what? A train?" P-R calls out, halfway between his car and the bench. "The world is considerably more haphazard than the latest time card."

"Oh, we'all'll see 'bout that, we will."

"I wouldn't want to wager. Y'all're not running suds down my streets while I'm around. And, odds are, you will be the first of us to check out." P-R is in full stride, begins to cast an elastic shadow over Ferrous, dilutes the yellow to cream with a mere touch of yolk.

Ferrous owns that unpredictability is the funny thing about life. He cites Humboldt for effect. P-R says there is no mystery to the future of street running in 'Mingo. This seems petty to Ferrous, but he concedes the point, notes that P-R has added curiosity to his expansive catalogue of vices, that he wasn't sure he would come. P-R puts his foot up on the bench, rests an elbow on a knee, a chin on an elbow. He pulls a monogrammed hankie from his pocket and rubs the dust from first the one shoe, then the other. The wild flowers — sedge, ginseng, Virginia wild rye — are ablaze around them. "I like it when I'm asked nicely. Anyway, what the hell! Slow day. I expected y'all'd be in the car with the curtains drawn."

"Ah'as hopin' fo' a bit a transpa'ency. Whaddya say? Ah'm thinkin' a unloadin' mah in'eres' anyhow."

"So what's the *good* news?"

"Y'all still hangin' ont' y'all's rail'oad 'nves'men's?"

"I'm sure you already know."

"Fo' the sake a conve'sation. What Ahm sayin' is, Ahm offe'in' y'all an olive branch'n the fo'm a some 'nside 'nfo'mation."

"I'm all ears."

Ferrous tells of route changes, a management shift. P-R doesn't hesitate to deny credulity.

"Ye a li'le faith."

"Almost none at all."

"We'suh, Ah done mah good deed fo' the day. Do what y'all will with it."

"This is the word of the eastern boys?"

"Well, as y' know, numbuh one easte'n boy has become the pat'on saint a hub'is. The scut'butt bein' he gonna be su'ceeded by someone'th mo' ma*tour* views. Someone who see a good faith off'in' as a foundation t'a so't a...*rebindin'* b'tween company an' mun'c'pal'ty."

"You're not getting your street running."

"'Nothuh a yore vices — stubbo'ness. Look'et heah now. S'pose y'er t' 'qui'e mah sha'e a the tho'n in both ower sides? Ah think this could be 'ranged unduh vera civ'lized te'ms."

"What are we talking about?"

"Well, who'all knows? We jus' talkin' now."

"Why would I want your share if y'all don't?"

"Oh, Ah jus' thought that'f y'all held a' 'nte'es' a y'own...p'haps the street runnin' might seem, from a new, mo' p'op'etary pospective, in the bes' 'nte' es' a y"all's constit'ency."

"And the railroad writes the tariff? No, not in the cards, I'm afraid."

"Ah'm ce'tain that the rail'oad can be mo' than 'comm'dating."

"Accommodating?"

"So t'speak."

"I like things as they are."

"Spite's a might po' subs'tute fo' p'ofit."

"Oh, I don't know. Spite has its virtues. I can't say I'm not enjoying myself."

Ferrous scowls. Says P-R could have a pretty good time as well a product marketable and transportable, that though he himself is no imbiber, he hears that the Feather is a fairly respectable brew. Possibly a pleasant compliment to an an *étouffée* on the Coast. And, if so, P-R wouldn't want to haggle with the drayman to get it to the railroad and allow the local foot and rubber traffic to impede his profits. "Bu' then, y'alls a bid'nessman, fi's' an' fo'emos'. Ya know awl this heah. Me, Ah'm jus' a ol' crack the whip boy, gettin' things f'om heah t' theah." Ferrous stands up, breathes in the sultry elevated air. "Back t' the big city fo' me. A bit too sombuh 'round heah. Sleep on it, P-Ah."

"There's an outside chance."

"Don' sleep too long. Is, 'member, a 'tractive p'ope'ty."

P-R doesn't watch the little man go down the path, continues to stare off over the consecrated ground. *With at least one attractive partner,* he thinks, then calls out, "How about the prophet of God?"

Ferrous stops, turns halfway back toward the Mayor, says, Shem will pray at this juncture, and the Good Lord will give him the wisdom to divest the "fuck outta hops" before an all-too-public head forms on the mug. "Cheahs, P-Ah, an' may the same God bless."

P-R turns, follows Ferrous up to his car before the chauffeur can let him in. "The thing that gets my goat," he says, "is how y'all...all of y'all...underestimated me."

Ferrous cranes his neck. He is in P-R's shadow and P-R is bright in the descending sun. "P'haps yo' too thin-skinned. P'haps, we'as me'ely ove'est'mated ower own cleve'ness."

"I think both. You know, you might have gotten away with it if you hadn't bawled me out in your office that day." He has his fist up over his chest. "And in front of the emasculatee, no less."

Ferrous blames a chain of events, not of his making. Not to defend that fool Humboldt, but it was P-R who voided the sanctity of the marriage bed. Once done, a careless word, an indelicate gesture, perhaps, oh...he doesn't know, the creak of the connubial floor as the maid passed in the hall, and the wronged husband smelled blood? Humboldt, he complains, leaned on him to lean on P-R. Or, perhaps, he heard it from someone in whom the abashed wife confided? Someone who provided her counsel? Someone tired of begging alms in order to keep...say, a roof over his head to protect from the elements? And how did Ferrous become involved? "Ah'as the fi'st victim," he pleads. That spur was as good as spiked. He'd promised Yardley something for his vote, and Yardley opened the door to the vulture of God. And then P-R dropped his trousers in the midst of all Ferrous' plans, and the jig was up. Yardley came sniveling. He reneged. "Ah'as b'side m'se'f. 'Fraid mah 'motions got the bes' a me."

"We're on hallowed ground. If tears well up in my eyes, don't flatter yourself that they're for you. Did y'all think that I'd be so taken aback with your challenge that I wouldn't have the wherewithal to ponder the motivation? That the brewery would not stand out like a sore thumb? That the profit motive would lie immersed in the brew?" Ferrous admits he hadn't thought of everything. "No, you didn't. You didn't think that Humboldt would be such a simpleton as to use his housekeeper as a shill. Or that, in one of my many social calls, either dalliance or legit, that I would have heard the name of the maid"

Ferrous smiles with serenity, says that such is life. That when all is said and done, he hasn't done so poorly. And P-R? "Buy me out," and he can either enjoy a partnership with a man who has the ear of God, or he can leave him to drown in his own chapel." Ah'm a Meth'dist, mahownse'f."

Later, from the summer porch, Ferrous calls, "Mother. How'd y'all like t' live in a place enjoys a sea breeze? Place wheah y'all could walk for taffy?" Fireflies adorn the lawn like the lights of a distant landscape.

There is noise of movement from inside, a shuffling, a soft tapping. It is a long while of cautious baby steps before Mrs. Ferrous attains the threshold, grips the doorframe and relies on the support of her cane. There is a slight downward droop to the left side of her mouth, likewise, her left shoulder. Both seem to be improving daily. She says, "Someone's chippuh this evenin'."

"Someone c'ainly is. Ah feel the compassion'te wisdom a Prov'dence t'day, my deah. It d'scends on this heah house like the wa'mth a summuh."

There is a slamming of car doors. He sees first Rev. Shem, then Chief Prezhki, ascend the stone path leading from the drive to the garden behind the house. Ferrous primps, follows them out, is pleased to see them, offers refreshment. Prezhki demurs, but Ferrous knows he has peaked his curiosity. Shem paces nervously.

II

DAVID'S SLING BATHES IN MORNING SHADOWS, muggy from the slow river and the palpable air. It is an atmosphere that, though recently cleansed, takes on the ambiance of a museum diorama, with primeval ferns and low-wasted mangroves, and the calls of lesser, unseen things. The ravenous mosquitoes are laden with moisture.

Suited men debark from long, black town cars, slapping at their necks, their cheeks, move up toward the tracks away from the dampness and into a waxing patch of sunlight. It is a bit more civilized here, a tool shed and the old bunkhouse, newly scraped and painted, the silver poles of the new signaling system just beginning to suffer the condensation.

Mayor Bud Constantine indicates a flat area on the bluff over the river. "This here's where I'm thinkin'," he says.

Stanley says, "I like it."

"The pinhead likes it. Like I give a shit! Any a ya'll wanna chime in?"

A long freight — cut timber, coal hoppers, bright yellow reefers of cool produce — rumbles by at a lazy pace, ascends to the top of the low ridge, and paces itself noisily down the opposite slope, leaving a harmony of water and pine warblers, and slouches in the yard on the other side. Late orders handed up by message hoop call for delay, a wait for a switcher to come up from Tishomingo, assemble some empties and work cars, and tuck them in between the caboose and the last loaded flat.

Renato D'Scalucci, tonsorial perfection, richly draped and pin neat, says, with — what he imagines is — *Hahvahd* intonation, "Ahs the donah, my fahthah's name would be on the plahque?" The accent's derivation is one of general concensus; why Renato speaks with such affectation is anybody's guess. Of course, no one asks. But some do wonder if his attempts at non-rhoticity would survive serious scrutiny in The Bay State. Privately, Constantine believes he sounds like a cartoon character from an afternoon matinee.

"Whatta I care?" Constantine says. "He wants 'is name, he gets 'is name. He wants a carved relief, sculpted mountain, we call in Gutzon Borglum."

"He will be pleased to hea' it, Mr. Mahyah."

"Here t'serve, ain't I?"

"He will be even mah pleased to heah about the rewahding of cont'acts. Notahiety alone, ahftah all, hahs its limits."

"We do the usual no bidders. Sure, we throw in a couple a shills for the press, but a course, ya'll's people get all the contracts."

"Ahnd the railroad?"

"Mr. Ferrous tells me what's good for the gander's good for the goose."

"Mr. Fehous is ahn expaht on fowl?"

"Mr. Ferrous'll soon be 'n'a position to do all the carvin'. Don't you worry none."

"Ahnd exactly what scahle ah we tahlking about?"

"Big. Not Stone Mountain, for God's sake, but not that pitiful Civil War pile a blocks they got down there in 'Mingo, neither. See, I envision somethin' bronze'r marble'r some shit like that. Maybe both. Hell, maybe all three it comes out the most economical. Marble pedestal, bronze statue. The shit's'n'a the details. Somethin' heroic. Emphasize the contributions a the railroads while 'mortalizin' the unfortunate victims a the *e*-vent. And labor. Don't forget our good brothers a the hammer an' sickle. No finger pointin'. Everyone comes out smellin' like roses. They wanna maypole to dance around, so be it. An' we don't wanna go overboard on the carnage side. A few tear invokin' images, yes-sir-ee, but we ain't here t' piss no one off. Right Stanley?"

"Yes, sir."

"Ya'all're a rock, Stanley. We pave the road from town. Nothin' that's gotta last like the pyramids, jus' somethin' t' get by a few inspectors that'll do their reports *in absentia*, enjoyin' the comfort a they offices so's they can think clearly. Further, ya'll get t' pour a little extra *cee*-ment with the parkin' lot, maybe a coupla a crappers…not too close t' the memorial. I want a certain reverential kinda settin'. Comfort considered, but reverential. The river behind. Emphasizin' flow. Goods, people, current. Hard work. I want the fuckin' veins on the workers arms t' pop, cast shadows. I want benches. People can sit an' med'tate. A little shop t'hawk *soo*-venirs…miniatures a the thing itself, them pitchur post cards, the color ones'n them little foldout books. Burgers, dogs, sodas. We wanna get folks on out here. We make it all a mun'cipal park. Put up a little gatehouse. Two bits a car. This somethin' ya'll think ya can do?"

"Oh, I think we cahn gahthuh the resahces. We'll hahve something for you on paapuh. Pahliminahy pahposahl. A rundown of pahbahble costs."

"Like I give a shit what it costs, huh!" Constantine reaches forward and shakes D'Scalucci's manicured hand. It is firm and cold. D'Scalucci seems not to sweat, as if he is encased in a protective coating immune to the forces of man and nature, a substance with a dull sheen, like Bakelite. "I think this'll please the Big Guy," Constantine jokes, pointing skyward with his eyes. "A fella can always bank a few extra points."

"Points, Mistah Mahyah? When the time comes, Ah thought Ah'd just cahy ah little extrar cahsh to lub'icahte my way through those restrictively nahrrar gates."

With that, D'Scalucci walks back to his car followed by an entourage of blank faced goons, all of them slapping themselves like over-dressed flagellants.

Constantine pats Stanley on the back. "Points weren't for that son of a bitch! When the time comes, pinhead, I hope t' have a large enough constit'ency up there t' challenge the powers that be."

"I'm sure you will, sir."

"Yeah, well, the fuck you know 'bout it?"

Stanley adjusts a trouser crease, smiles through the thin blue lips of the near dead.

III

AT IN HAND, THE YARD BULL walks the line of recent arrivals. It is a
hand-carved bat, honed with affection, sanded and shellacked with the
bull's initials carved at its thickest surface. He checks for empties, a
suspiciously opened hatch on a refrigerator car; checks undercarriages for un-
ticketed passengers: those embalmed in a particular level of desperation. He
exchanges a few comradely insults with the crew complaining about the coffee
in the caboose. A young trainman in overalls comes out onto the platform, calls
out, "That there your pecker in your hand, redskin?" and Mr. Red waves the bat
at him and responds, "Was this tiny, your mama wou'n'a had me a second time."
The trainman spits down onto the ballast, says, "Shit, y'fuckin' Polack, y'was a real
man y'woul'n'a had a had one made a wood. Anyways, knock one out a the park
for me, bull dog." Red throws him a middle finger, says, "The old lady complain
a splinters? Not t'my knowledge."

A switcher, nudged by a sloped-back tender approaches to weed out the
locals, the empties, reassemble the train with the addition of a Lone Feather load
and miscellaneous freight. There is a cacophony of couplers releasing, the shrill
traction of wheel on rail, the shifting of weights, the strain of metallic tension,
then the brute union of the new cars jamming into the weighty hoppers. The
prodigal caboose returns, just a little more crimson as the sun nears its zenith.

Red moves on around the other side of the lengthening freight, poking the
truncheon under the cars and into doors. In the distance, he can see another
bull up on the pedestrian trestle above the train. The man is gesticulating in his
direction, and, when he catches Red's attention, points downward, then holds up
one finger. Red takes cautious steps to the indicated M-K-T boxcar. With effort,
he hoists himself up the ladder on one end, peers over the top at a prone man's
Swiss cheese soles. There is a great deal of noise from the asthmatic switcher
grumbling by, so Red is able to hoist his ample carriage up to the roof and reach
the man before he is found out.

Red sneers, "Okee-dokey, freeloader. Here's your pass back t'earth," and with
a swift swing downward plants the club onto the roof from which the hobo's spine
is so recently evacuated. The man reaches for his boot and Red catches the glint
off a blade, rears back with both hands and brings his slugger down decisively
on the man's ankle. The crack is like a firecracker, is heard over the wrenching
anguish of valve gear and whistles. "You on the wrong train, shithead," Red says,
giving the hobo a hefty crunch in the ribs, flipping him over and off the roof and
watching him thud onto the grease-slick earth. The flyer lays face down, silent,
stifled by either pain or impact.

A small but appreciative audience has gathered. The freight's brakeman kneels
over the bum, shakes his shoulders roughly, as Red releases his bindle. Tattered
rags pennant out over the wounded man. The brakeman says, "This here boy still
enjoys the gift a life."

"Risen up like Lazarus," says Red peering down. "Y'all take care now. He had hisself a sticker up'n'is boot." Red has stepped back on the roof, out of sight, has his hands on his knees and is laboring for breath.

"So what we s'posed t'do 'th'im?"

"Well, I suppose y'all could show him where the ticket winda is, help 'im check his luggage. Or, ya might could heave him up on the caboose platform an' give him a lift over t' them woods past the Thebes bridge. Your'all's call, I figure."

"Well, I do thank ya'll for the inter-departmental courtesy, Red, but why couldn't ya just a kicked him off an' let him run down to that rat's ass hobo camp over at the river?"

"I wanted him t' have a souvenir a his travels. Something t' remember Mr. Red by."

"I think you done that, aw'right," says the brakeman, hefting up the tramp with the help of a few other workers. The man winces, glares up angrily at Red through coal-black eyes.

Red says, "What we got there? Some kin'a Mesican? How's that ankle, *amigo*? Don't you boys get all greasy an' drop 'im now. Hey, Poncho, remember the Alamo."

The brakeman says, "Aw g'wan an leave off, Red, or come on down an' give a hand."

"Uh uh. I already demonstrated my professional expertise. I'll leave the grunt work t'you fellas in the freight department, seein' y'all's used to totin' shit around."

Red is a man satisfied as he marches off to the security office to fetch his lunch pail. It was a job well done, with the added gratification of laming a leg browner than dirt. He isn't adverse to laying violence upon a white man, but he usually tries to limit it to something less incapacitating. The bones of darker folk, he is certain from experience, brake easier, crack louder, as if manufactured from some inferior material — perhaps a lesser grade of calcium — and poor workmanship. He enjoys the brittle splintering of such junk bones, the quick loss of fight from the victim, the resignation that life is shit and this is just another calamity to be borne with stoic acceptance. *Oh, to be me'th my stick'n'a box car load a darkies!* Red muses.

Zolt Korda, the dispatcher, swivels in place at his roll top as Red marches in with triumphant strides. Zolt wears a visor and a black vest over his white shirt. The room is decorated in paint chips, browning pin ups and company bulletins. The Zenith is filling the room with Jews and banks. "A little ruckus. I seen through the winda," Korda says.

"I needed the extrasize," says Red, dousing his face at the washtub. "Turn that down, would ya? Can't hear myself think."

"That there's Father Coughlin, Red. Someone yells *fire*, a fella oughtta pay'im some mind." Red is unrepentant, and Korda turns the priest down to a halcyon whisper. "You gonna wanna write a incident report."

"Hell, no. What for? Just a greaser."

"Still. Upstairs, they're fond a paper."

"Whaddya think, Juanito's gonna sue? Jesus, give a fella some slack, Zolt!"

"Don't say I ain't told ya."

Red retrieves his lunch pail from a shelf of similar containers, sets it down on a long table and settles into the bench.

Korda says, "Dunno why ya don't eat home. Just up the ridge."

"Thank you, Korda, but I know where I live, don't I." He doesn't say he avoids the stairs as much as possible. "I can't have me a little male company at lunch? Discuss somethin' other than curtains?" He reaches in the box. It is shaped like a blimp hanger, now with its roof flipped over and has Red's truncated name painted on the front. Inside is a sandwich of homemade sausage on dark bread, a pickle that fills the room with its sour bouquet, and a spiked soda in a thermos. Mrs. Red assembles the lunch: Mr. Red fills the thermos. The club lays between it and Korda like a papal line of demarcation.

"Y'took some swing at the bastard."

"He was fixin' t' pull a blade on me. Gonna have t'do better than that t' stick this ol' dog. Had it *con*-sealed up'n'is boot."

"You might wanna put that in your report."

"I eat in peace here?"

"He alive?"

"If ya call that life." He takes a generous bite of the sandwich. "God Bless America. Where else can a man beat the *tacos* outta a wetback, sit back down an' enjoy a hand-stuffed Polish sausage, an' shoot the shit with a fine Hunky such as yourself?"

"God's country, all right."

"Ya bet your sweet Magyar ass."

"They're sayin' you been up t' see the brass."

"Who's sayin'?"

"Odell Lutz."

"Who's Odell Lutz?"

"The conductor you rode on up there with. Says ya talked up a blue streak. Before you dozed off."

"Company business. He don't know nothin'."

"You're supposed t'sign out if ya leave the yard, I guess y'know."

"What're rules for, Korda?"

"I don't care none myself. But ya get ya'self caught an' they gonna wonder why I ain't nailed y'on it."

Red sets down the sandwich. "Lookee here, pal-o-mino. Some shit, y'all don't wanna know."

"Like for instance?"

Red makes a show of getting up, looking out the window, swinging the door shut and setting the lock.

"I was on some secret bus'ness," he says as he sits back down.

"Jeez, Red. You about t' spin me one?"

"Ya wanna know'r ya wanna poke fun an' stay i'norant?"

"If it's so damned secret, why ya gonna tell me?"

"T'get you off a my ass. Ya gotta promise t' keep your mouth shut. Can ya do that with your head full a *ghoulash?*"

"Who'm I gonna tell?"

"Y'ain't gonna tell nobody."

"Suits me."

"'Cause you're my favorite bohunk, you are." Red moves down the bench closer to Korda, drags his tray with him, "I'm gonna let you in on just the surface details. See, I was deliverin' a important message t' the big guy."

"T. Rail? No shit!"

"None what so ever. Y'can bet I had his attention."

"What kind a message?"

"A *secret* fuckin' one! You listenin'?"

"Why you?"

"Why me? Who ya think I am, some no 'count gandy dancin' knockabout lookin' t'make a few bucks t'spend at the saloon? I got my contacts, ya know."

"Aw right. You're the big man in town. G'wan'th'r story."

Red lowers his voice, tries to sound mysterious, covert. "Ya know, I gotta shit-load a city cop friends."

"Those guys laugh behind our backs. Think we do this 'cause we can't get on the force."

"Yeah, an' I set them straight. We do the same shit as them 'thout the politics an' the rule books."

"Take a ride up t' the colored an' you won't see no city cop consultin' his handbook on how t'serve the citizens."

"Well, that don' really count, does it? Just like I ain't writ up no paper on this thing'th' a greaser. Anyways, I got contacts. This ain't the first time I been sent on some critical bus'ness. This time, it comes direct from," in even lowered voice, "the Mayor." He is fabricating: has no idea he has hit upon something solid.

"I was hopin' FD-fuckin'-R. Ya disappoint me."

"Up y'all's! This bit o' correspondence seen the hand a only three people. The Mayor, Chief Prezhki an' yours truly. You seen me an' Prezhki talkin' here in the yard, I bet. And I'm the only one trusted t' get it up t' Ferrous 'count a he knows me an' has some trust in me."

"Tell me this. You so tight with the Chief, was it him bangin' Brown's ol' lady?"

"I don't rat on my 'sociates. Whaddya take me for?"

"Just thought y'might know."

"'Cause I *know*, don't mean I gotta tell. An' I'm tight with P-R too."

"Safe as a bank, you are. 'Course, banks ain't what they used to be, with your Dillingers and your Nelsons and such. And your Jews." He acknowledges the radio with a nod. "And you're tellin' me you're tight with The Mayor an' ya got an audience with Ferrous?"

"Hey. I ain't beggin' you t' believe nothin'. You the one wanted t' know."

"So go on."

"I go on up t'Uncas, up to the big guy's office. Natur'ly, they know me by now. The gals'n'a office. We exchange a few pleasantries an' Ferrous hisself comes out t' *es*-cort me in. After some brandy an' small talk, I give him the message, we shake hands, an' I'm off."

"With Ferrous? You *handed* him the message?"

"Don't none a'em write shit like this down, Korda! Christ on a jackhammer! No wonder Hungaria was on the wrong side a the Great War. I *spoke* it direct to'im!"

"Well, the gods surely blessed you all! Hungaria, huh? Y'all's one dumb Polack, Red."

"Yeah? Well, just you wait'n' see how long this dumb Polack gotta walk this shit hole here. None a these UF big shots live forever. New blood's on its way. And, Korda, keep this here under your hat."

"Visor do?"

Not twenty minutes later, Mr. Red is unscrewing his well-worn flask for a quick slug. He repeats the story about Ferrous to the engine house mechanics and the hostlers. The air smells of alloys, fossils and oil-leached aggregate.

"I'll be damned," one of them says.

"Good chance a that," says Red. "I'll see if I can't put'n'a good word for y'all'th St. Pete." And then, "I'll trust y'fellas t'keep a lid on this here thing."

Just then, Sardo Cardineli comes out of the toilet, tucking his johnson into his overalls. "Had my shovel, I'd follow you around, Red, tidy up a tad."

There is some general laughter. Red says, "Hey sourdough, weren't you pluggin' Brown's old lady, was it?"

"Ain't had that particular pleasure."

"Who ya stokin' for these days?"

"A fella name a Hauser. Real nice fella too. Sure don't miss that old sour Brown. At least Hauser don't look down his nose. Not so long out a the stoker's seat his own self. A man enjoys a good conversation t'pass away the miles. That Brown…fuckin' deaf mute! No wonder the missus made the rounds a mun'cipal gover'ment."

Red says, "I'm the one that seen her run off that night. Pretty as a winter pitchur outta Currier an' Ives. Real nice red glow on'er cheeks too. I seen her hitch up with the 'boo."

"Yeah, well," says Sardo, "save it for someone who's *im*-pressed. I got me a furnace t' feed. Mr. Hauser's a fine gentleman an' all, but he does like promptitude. Glad t' be rid a Cal Cooledge as a cab mate, though. I reckon as y'all heard what 'e done t' the copper."

Red gives a knowing grunt. "An' what the copper done back. Both a theirs nose's wide 'nough for a minstrel show."

This gets another good chuckle from the shop boys and Red feels magnanimous enough to pass his flask around. It comes back appreciatively diminished and wet with backwash. "And, 'nother thing I know," he says, the generosity just oozing from his pores, "the engineer's ol' lady ain't givin' it away'n 'Mingo no more. Took it down the track. Her an' another sportin' type."

This gets Sardo's attention. "How you know so much?"

"I seen what I seen, ain't I?"

"Brown in on it?"

"Well, why'n't ya just get on up t' the jail house an' ask 'im? You bein' his cab mate an' all."

Sardo reaches for the flask again, but Red restores it to his jacket pocket. Sardo says, "Was! That Brown. He got some fuse on 'im. He don't say much, but I sure don't wanna be the one there when he does find a need t'speak. Fine where I am, thank ya. Anyways, I'd jus' love t' hang around an' shoot the shit'th you all, but I got me a hog t'slop."

Great rays of dust and filth light the men from the transoms. The building is tall in order to accommodate the smoke; cathedral like in the beams. Outside, hot water and steel are coming alive and there is the unmistakable report of couplers ramming together. Loaded boxcars are rutting in the sunlight like feral dogs.

It can all be heard in Darktown, at the neat white box of a house with precision-cut lawn, the little Nash Six all agleam, two little boys with willow-stick Winchesters staving off the Indians screaming around the picket fence, staunching flaming arrows, these two decorated Buffalo Soldiers. The porter is coatless but neat as a pin on the screen porch. He expertly folds his newspaper to the desired article, sips lemonade from the family's unmatched set of glasses.

His wife comes out from the house, brushes his forehead with pouting lips. "You never tol' me 'bout the sending-off from the other day," he says. "No, guess there weren't all that much t'tell," she admits. He asks, "Who was it got sent home?"

She wipes her forehead with a rag she keeps in an apron pocket, stares through the screen at their small garden, asks without looking at him, "Y'ain't watered out there today? Them squash a mine, they dry as old bones. A ol' junkman, what Salvation said. Just the ladies. No one that know'd 'im. We had a copper come by but he hung back and talked to the pastor after. An' a white lady an' a boy from up Thebes where the departed departed hisself from. Don't see that every day!"

He puts down his paper. "I think I know the po' man. Ain't all that many a us peoples down in Thebes. He gone an' run into a deer up there in The Camels, so I carried him down to the car stop in 'Mingo. How he pass?"

She turns to go back inside the house, and says, "Alone."

IV

WALTER PREZHKI DRIVES OVER TO THE Five and Dime for a quiet lunch. It is close enough to the station to walk, and he could use the exercise. Tennessee tells him he's acquiring a paunch, probably from all the sitting he does in the squad car and behind a desk. He has, she says, lost that youthful athleticism that had first caught her eye. *The youthful part is beyond my control,* he complains. He wants to please her, should have walked, has such little spare time to do so, but, even more, he hates the turned faces as they take in his battered and scabbed nose, the stitch marks, the purple half moons under his eyes. He sits up on the round stool at the counter with a menu from behind the napkin rack. It is one sheet of heavy card stock in a thin cloth frame with brass triangles in the corners, and is sticky from repeated use.

Doreen comes along with fire engine-red smile and makes a cursory sweep with a wet rag, leaves a stink from other swiped places in his small counter territory. "Ouch! How's that face?" she says. It is a cheerful bit of small talk, no real interest intended. "How's it look?" he says. He keeps his head tilted down at the menu, as if he is reading, though he's certain he could recite the offerings blindfolded.

"Even so, you're still the best lookin' flat foot in town."

"And you, the best looking counter girl."

"I heard what happened."

"About what?"

"About your face, that's what."

"You and everybody else."

"So, what's the scoop, handsome? The engineer have a gripe, or's he ready for the loony bin?" A coquettish tease, her elbows on the counter, her back arched forward, big green eyes a flutter.

"I'll have this open face roast beef with mashed and gravy, hold the conversation. Some a that two-cents-a-cup coffee like it says on the sign. Like pitch. You want to put that down on your pad or you think you can remember it all the way to the kitchen, sweetheart?"

"Sweetheart, huh! Y'all gettin' fresh?"

"Let's not abet the gossip. I'm getting hungry, is what I'm getting."

When she brings the order, she brings an extra coffee for herself, comes around to his side of the counter and sits on the stool next to him. She is a recent teen brewing sexuality, flirting with a middle-aged man behind a smashed nose. The man is not yet hormonally immune, but is a rule follower as well as enforcer. He has never betrayed Tennessee and doesn't intend to do so now.

Doreen doesn't talk for a while, just wends her spoon in circumnavigation of the cup. Then she says, "Ple-e-e-se," and bats a millipede of lashes his way.

He doesn't look at her. "If he has a point, it's not about me. That's all you get."

"Way I hear it, your car..."

"Look it, Dory, there must be some law against interfering with the nutrition of an officer." He is snappish now, official.

"Well, if that's the way it's gonna be," she pouts, taking her cup and retreating down the counter. "Nuts to you."

"That's the way it's going to be," he mumbles, pushing the plate away barely touched, throwing down some change, and leaving for the solitude of the car.

⁂

He sits in the car out in front of the lunch counter with his hands on the wheel, as if watching for a stakeout target. Generally a patient man, he realizes he has exceeded his tolerance level in this affair of P-R and the engineer's wife. He is dogged by suspicion where ever he goes, leaves a trail of sanctimonious leering in his wake, carries on his face the visible insignia of the whole sordid episode like some modern day Hester Prynne.

And what of all the others enduring the wounds of P-R's not-so-original sins? It is as if P-R himself slithered out of the garden he had once walked, to toil away at the nibble of others; the Humboldts, because the patriarch sought amends and a short ride home on the train; the innocents sitting along side him in harm's way because of an anguished husband who should have been steadfast at his throttle; and the abbreviated families of them all.

And P-R, in spic and span, magic, levitating shoes, seems to float over the muck with Shem's trapeze ease, gliding like a combustible balloon over the field of his damage. A better politician, Prezhki knows he's not. A better man? Does Roosevelt spend his day in a chair? And yet, has he not allowed himself to follow the path of least resistance at this particular juncture? And how then does one change direction?

Deep in such thoughts, he returns to the station, heads straight for the holding cells, has the guard escort him over to the engineer. There are several bunks, but Brown is alone since the decline of the freak crime wave. He sits on the corner of his bed, leans against the wall, stares at the lurid inscriptions left by previous occupants.

"Well, Mr. Brown," the Chief says, "ain't we got fun!" Moses glances over, shows no emotion. "If I come in there, you going to take a swing at me?"

"Not likely," Brown says softly, moving his feet down off the bed. He is wearing old prison garb straight from the laundry, makes him look like a monochrome candy cane.

"That's good news," says Prezhki as the guard unlocks the door, drags in a wooden chair, and closes the door behind him. Prezhki sits down, says, "You look like last year's shit." They study one another, the twin purple-blue under the eyes, yellow blotches on the cheeks.

"You ain't winnin' no beauty contest your own self."

"No, I don't suppose I am. At least I'm not wearing Paul Muni's old costume. Jesus, look at the two of us, Brown! We look like we've been hawking elixirs off the back of a wagon. You getting everything you need in here?"

"Oh, yeah. Place t' recommend."

"Good. Glad to hear we're keeping you happy. You know, Brown," says Prezhki, feet clichéd flat on the floor, leaning forward, "as I go through my day I am offered constant reminders of how much you piss me off. I don't like that. I don't like you. You are a hot-headed, narrow minded, violent man, with less sense than a horse fly, and considerably wanting in the noble art of self control."

"You hadn't ought a took up with other men's wives." There is a dryness to the words, a flutter of voice.

"And that's just the thing, bonehead. You've made me for someone else. Got your tin ear to the wrong wire. You're not hearing the right notes. Are you following me?"

"I ain't a idiot!"

"We shall have to part intellectual company on that score. It is no genius that introduces the Chief of Police to a length of plumber's pipe because a person unknown has allegedly taken liberties with his old lady."

"I heard from people who seen things."

"Everybody in town's seen or heard things! On this side of the law, we call innuendo, *hearsay*. Not legally admissible. And we tend not to beat shit out of people for hearsay."

"What was your car doin' there?"

"I don't have to tell you that. You don't get to ask the questions. My car could be any-fucking-where. I am the police here, see. You might find me on your street one night, or in your bedroom closet. But you will not find me in your marriage bed and that is all you need to know."

"Why should I believe you?"

"That's a question, isn't it? I'll answer that one. Two reasons. One, you might wish to live the rest of your life a little less ignorant than you've lived the last part. That would be reason enough for most folks. Of course, most folks've got more than a lump of anthracite in their heads. So, two, I would like to wash my hands of this whole annoyance and get you out of my hair."

"To save your own damned ass, I s'pose."

"Suit yourself, Mr. Brown!" Prezhki stands up. "Hope you can swing a sledge as easy as a sink pipe. You know, I try to be a reasonable man. You should know that by now."

"How would I?"

"You're still kicking, aren't you?"

"Wait, wait," Moses says. "I'm listening, okay?"

"I'm surprised you know how that's done," says Prezhki returning to the chair. "I've been checking with the railroad and I find nothing but commendations in your records. Co-workers speak highly of you, even though some think you've got a considerable length of rail up your ass. And you have no previous history with law enforcement that I can find. All of this, of course, before your major screw up in that whole David's Sling matter. But that's no concern of mine. Out of my jurisdiction, and glad of it. The railroad wants to go legal on you, that's their call. So this is the deal. I am willing to drop the charges and get your very sorry ass out of my jail. Tell the truth, I can't stand being in the same building with you, besieged as I am with the aroma of your uninlightenment. Your job is to go home and collect your things. I understand the missus has disappeared like a passenger pigeon, and the railroad is going to set all of your crap out on the sidewalk if you don't come to tote it away. You pack your bags and move elsewhere. Uncas Falls or Timbuktu, I don't give a shit. But if I see you in Tishomingo again, ever, I will not treat you kindly, no sir. And one more thing. If, before you leave, which will take place no later than this evening, you provoke any violence on your fellow man, myself included, if you so much as threaten, curse, accuse or berate, or if you attempt to strike anyone within my hearing, I will see you up at the county farm as sure as I'm sitting here. Am I impressing you, Mr. Brown?"

"I jus' get t'walk outta here? Jus' like that?"

"You'd better be walking a little farther than just out of *here*. So, tell me something I want to hear or get yourself a very competent attorney."

"Was it you'r not?"

"You are trying my patience, Mr. Brown."

"I need t' know."

"No, you don't. Because anything you know is just likely t'leave you in more shit than you're in now."

"Where did my wife go to?"

"The moon. She ran off with Jules Verne."

"Who?"

"A dead Frenchman."

"I didn't never intend to lay into you'th that pipe, y'know."

"I get it. You just had some plumbing needed doing."

"That's right."

"And you meant to do me no harm?"

"I didn't say that."

"You did mean to do me harm?"

"Not'th no pipe. An' not there on the street."

"Well, now that's a comfort. So, how about now? We have ourselves a deal? Because I'm not talking anymore."

Brown considers and says, "Yeah. I think we do."

"I think we'd better. And make no mistake: when I hit you? *I* sure as hell meant it!"

Prezhki goes up to his office, passes McCallum on the way, says to him to write up the paperwork on Moses Brown's release, that he'll sign it, and then to take Mr. Brown home to retrieve a few personal belongings, and then set him free somewhere up in The Camels well past the city line. Someone else will get Brown's car up there, leave him with enough gas to get at least to Uncas Falls. Better yet, "Impound the piece a junk for our troubles."

McCallum momentarily steps up from his grief, registers puzzlement: he says he doesn't think the prisoner deserves such a generous amnesty, if any at all. "After all, sir, he did try to kill a cop." Prezhki, sensitive to the man's ongoing distress, reminds him kindly that he is speaking out of turn. McCallum persists, asks, "How come?" Prezhki considers leaving him to wonder, then says, "Sometimes things get so out of kilter that, to follow the normal progression of crime and punishment, seems like one just perpetuates the other. I hope that makes some sense to you. If it doesn't, you'll have plenty of time to share your insights with our Mr. Brown himself. Don't make too much of this, Officer, but don't you ever think that there are some things that just aren't ours to decide? I don't need an answer to that."

The Chief heads for his office. McCallum in a slouch, heads off in Voorhiis's direction at the front desk, and says, "He really wants me just to let'im go, right?" Voorhiis confirms, "That's how I read it. If he wanted ya t'otherwise dispose a the son of a bitch, he wouldn't a been so damned mysterious about it. Maybe the Chief's gettin' soft, maybe he's found religion. Seems to do a lot a spiritual puzzlin' lately. Anyhoo, whadda I know? I was you, though, friend, I'd cuff that bastard 'till'is wrist skin peels off.

The phone is ringing in Prezhki's office. He picks it up, and says, "Prezhki," and then, "Well, well. Pastor Shem. What's leaking now?"

V

BROTHER SALVATION'S ONE ROOM CHAPEL IS close enough to the rail yards that, as he sets down the receiver, he can hear the exhausted moan of an old freight whistle as a train prepares to continue on south toward the capital. He adjusts collar and tie one last time in the fun-house mirror curve of an old teapot. He is a bit nervous. Feels the hatching of caterpillars in his gut, the dryness of his throat. Dealing on any level with white people always inaugurates one or another degree of agitation; though he lives in a cross-hatched world, with fine-line shading and historical traditions of stratification, intimidating a prominent Caucasian minister calls forth a whole new category of anticipatory unease. He leaves the building, returns for forgotten keys, finally gets out to the Model T he has washed for the occasion, and produces a soft rag from the trunk for a once-over of watermarks and missed soot deposited by a breeze felt earlier at the engine house. The condition of a man's automobile, he believes, reflects the condition of the man.

The ride to First Baptist is a blur. More than once he is tempted to turn around and forget the whole thing. It is so little he hopes for really, the worst of the stack of old pews awaiting, sadly, a junkman at the side of Pastor Shem's rectory.

Shem hears the catarrh of the old careworn Ford, comes to the door, thinks, *Who's this?*

Salvation stands up straight before the steps — not a tall man, but big boned, mostly West African in heritage, an ancestral history perhaps of capture by a river king, the despair of a Portuguese coastal fort, the lowest tier of steerage in an unknown sea — a slight tilt to his head to align his eyes, black pupils in a yoke-colored field. Shem's eyes are two thirds of the flag: blue on white.

"Yes?" Shem asks, opening the door with caution. He has just completed his short call to Prezhki, thinks perhaps he may soon have some cause for thanks.

"You are Pastor Shem?"

Shem hesitates, takes a step back from the door. "Yes. Who sent you?"

"I'm Pastor Salvation. I called earlier."

Shem runs his eyes over the man. "Oh, yes. But I didn't expect..."

"A colored man?"

"No, I didn't. On the line...well...I expected..."

413

"Diction can be misleading. The telephone only gives you a fraction of the picture."

"Indeed it does. So what is it? You mentioned an important matter you all needed to discuss. Quite frankly, this church has had very little interaction with our colored brethren. Certainly, we practice a mutual tolerance, but such moderation is a product of our separateness, as well as our separation. It is a tradition we intend to maintain in everybody's best interest."

"I understand. I ask only a few minutes of your time. May I come in?"

Shem is a bit taken aback by Salvation's brazen request. He pauses before answering, considering his options. "I suppose. But I'm very busy," he says curtly, and steps out of the way, allowing Salvation to come inside.

"I am sorry to be a bother. You didn't mention on the phone that you were otherwise occupied."

"And you all didn't mention being a Negro, Mr. Salvation. So who is the most disingenuous?"

"*Touché!* May I sit?"

"If you must. I'm not planning this to be a protracted encounter in any case." Shem is stiff, defensive, a slight arch to his back, a lowering of lids as if he is about to take Salvation in through crosshairs.

"I assure you that I am no more comfortable than you are. Perhaps less so."

"I'm quite comfortable, thank you. But I am busy." Shem motions him towards two wooden cane-backs placed in front of his desk, sits down in one, taps impromptu rhythms on the blotter. "So?"

Salvation takes this as invitation, gives a slight bow of his head, and sits humbly with his hat alert on his lap: to put it on the desk would be presumptuous. Far be it from him to be presumptuous. He glances quickly around the room, envies the spaciousness and comforts, yet is surprised about the apparent shabbiness of it all: the water stains, the pungent growth of mold, paper absently scattered across the desk top and crumbled in rejection on the floor. He is aware that Shem offers no apology for the state of the room.

He clears his throat, works the saliva around in his mouth, searching for suddenly elusive voice. "Mine is an impoverished congregation. A storefront affair, no more than an empty room at present. It makes the worshippers no less devout. They have been toting their own chairs for the older folks, the pregnant women. Some stand. Children sit on the floor."

"God hears the prayers of the needy along with those of the well-heeled." Shem sounds absent, bored even. He avoids looking at Salvation whose leg is now vibrating with urgency.

"Ah, but the prayers of the needy seem so much more exigent. Perhaps He will heed our prayers for proper pews."

"Are you here for a handout?" He is taken aback by the man's language, shows his disapproval in the deepening crinkles of his face.

"I prefer to think of it as Christian charity," Salvation says.

Shem begins mechanically to fiddle with the detritus on his desk, ruffling papers, tightening the lid on an inkbottle, brushing away invisible specks of something he may have nibbled while scribbling a sermon. "We are not exactly a for-profit institution ourselves. Look around you. Our roof leaks and we can barely afford to patch. And we give generously to a plethora of selected causes, both as a congregation, and as individuals. So don't think to move me with talk of tithes. We, here, are well versed in such teachings. Anyway, we have always enjoyed a pleasant reciprocal relationship, as I've said, with our Nigra neighbors." He is nearly beside himself with wonder at his own need to explain. "That said, I think our business is at an end."

"But your members are able to *sit* through Sunday worship." Salvation has leaned forward, overtaken by an apparent earnestness. His eyes are direct, demanding.

The gall! Shem thinks. "I am not unacquainted with the needs of the poor. Nor am I unable to prioritize them in categories of urgency. In Africa, in your own motherland, there are those who have yet to be introduced to the True God. And though I am impressed with your apparent attempts to haul your people up by their bootstraps, I find the need for pews comparatively paltry. Now, I am out of time. And *you* are out of place. And I'm beginning to take umbrage with your tone."

Salvation is aware of no particular tone, has tried hard to moderate his voice so as not to overtly offend. Shem's remarks unleash him, defy his better judgment, his natural caution. His eyes thin, his lips compress. "A case of the shepherd's not wanting to mix the black sheep with the white. You've made your point. Now, let's get to mine."

"I had thought you all'd made it. Not that I'm interested. Look here, now. I don't even know you and yet you come banging on my door with your hand out."

"I called to request an appointment. You seemed only too pleased..."

"Because you disguised your voice as a white man. As it turns out, that's a bit of falsehood, isn't it?"

"I have a degree in theology, sir. This is how I normally speak. Most days, I disguise my voice as a Negro."

"You are taking advantage of my hospitality, Mr. Salvation. I am about at the end of my tolerance." He too is now leaning forward in earnest. "If you persist, you may find yourself in serious trouble."

"Nevertheless, you have a stack of pews outside that you are discarding."

"They are spoken for. I have contracted with a used furniture dealer who will contribute to our building fund for the pleasure of carting them away. Not that I need explain that to you all."

"I would ask again that you reconsider my plight."

"And I would ask that you consider mine. If you are prepared to outbid the man, I see no reason why we couldn't make some sort of accommodation. Short of that, well..."

Salvation leans back in his chair. "You know I can't do that."

"There it is then," says Shem standing.

Salvation smiles broadly. "Money! I have nothing to give you but good faith. Were it otherwise, I would not come begging hat in hand."

Shem stands, points toward the door. "Then I wish you well in your quest. Have you ever seen the circus, Mr. Salvation?"

Salvation stands as well, slowly now. He won't reward Shem with the appearance of being pushed, but he is puzzled by the question, alert for some slight of hand. "I've neither the time nor the inclination, I'm afraid."

"Might do you some good. It's educational, really. Illuminates much about life itself. How we dress in our gaudy clothes barely concealing our perceived needs, our lusts, the bombast of our horns and drums, while we challenge the norm, defy, we think, death, push ourselves just that little bit past the position we have been assigned, our natural habitat, so to speak, to fly higher, to be a tad more foolish than is conventional, to tempt the teeth of ferocious beasts. As an audience, we laugh, we thrill, we cover our eyes in horror, and we envy these...what?...these... *gladiators,* their unnatural feats. These ventures they take beyond divine intention. They are like gods, small g. Defying gravity, fear, security, risk. We're told they are death defying. And we *all* want to live forever. Yet, to live forever, how wise is it to fly? How wise to feel the breath of a big cat on our face? It is only through deliverance that we live forever. And the saved are humble. The saved recognize that which is greater than themselves. The saved are conscious of their station in life...as well as in death. The saved don't say, *Were it otherwise.*"

"An eloquent sermon, I'm sure, for your genteel flock. It is over the head of this po' ol' country preacher. I'm at a loss for relevance."

"Oh, but you have a degree in theology! No doubt from some backwoods Negro college where they teach you a trade, how to turn peanuts into automobiles, what fork goes where when in the company of carpetbaggers who've come down here to tutor you all on how miserable you are in our medieval rebel stronghold. This is how I imagine a trapeze artist learns his trade. First, he is taught how to fall; that learned, he is taught how to avoid falling."

"Again, I'm sorry to have wasted your time. You see, though, near the bottom, where I have spent my humility, the drop is not nearly so intimidating as it may be at a higher rung. I'm sorry, too, you've taken this position. Perhaps the Lord has hardened your heart. Perhaps I do have something to...well, I was going to say...*exchange*...More to the point would be to...*demonstrate.*"

Moving towards the door, a sweep of his arm encouraging Salvation to do the same, Shem says, "I really *have* consummated a deal with the furniture man."

"Probably so. From what I hear, you are no stranger to deals."

"What impertinence is this?"

"A certain brewery comes to mind."

Shem moves back into the room, sits slowly back down, gathers his thoughts, looks up at Salvation and responds in quieter, more measured tones. "This has gone far enough. Who sent you all here?"

"I like to attribute to the Lord even the insignificant events of my existence."

"I will know if someone's put you up to this."

"You would deny us even the equality of imagination?"

"As a son of Ham, it is you who wandered off into the darkness. And, so, this is your *good faith!*"

"God helps those who help themselves."

Shem offers an incredulous laugh. "So, what is it you think you know?"

"I know what you don't want me to know. More than that, I know what you don't want *anyone* to know. Tales of street running, a certain lady of your acquaintance and her late husband, T. Rail Ferrous of the Tishomingo. You see, while I don't recommend it, being a Negro in this state has some often overlooked advantages. One is the camouflage of insignificance. Not something one would choose if one could decide such things, but it does have it's uses. It makes one's very presence an act of stealth. One hears things, while serving a course of pheasant, that the average white person is not privy to. One encounters letters, scribbled notes, documents, while employed in the menial task of dusting. Witnesses emotions better left constrained, records incriminations, takes notice of an innuendo here and a secret discourse there. Whole circuses collide through a sponged window. It is not the walls that have ears, *Mr.* Shem, it is rather the dark shadows you have invited into your lives to fan away your flies and wipe the excrement from your privies. The access of the unseen is subject to neither privacy nor modesty"

"How dare you talk to me like this!"

"The pews, sir. The pews and I'm gone like so much filtered light in your lovely stained glass windows. We only have room for ten or so. I will leave it to you to pick the least of them. And you can still make your salvage man happy, if that can really be. Myself, I have only known unhappy junkmen."

"Is this a tenant of this theology you learned? Blackmail? Is this the embodiment of the word's origins? Why does such a man as yourself choose to minister to others?"

"There are two roads open to a young, respectable Negro man; he can work for Jesus Christ and serve his own people, or he can work for George Pullman and serve yours."

"Nonsense! Look, how do I know the pews will be the end of it?"

"Have faith. Pray. I do."

"I will not deliver."

"We're only too happy to pick them up."

Shem offers a sly sneer. "Am I your only target?"

Symbolically, actually, Salvation replaces his hat upon his head. "For now. However, it's always good to have a little socked away, don't you think, a little something for that rainy day? And we have had such taxing weather."

After Salvation leaves, Shem pulls a flask of brandy from his desk, takes a quick swallow. *Well, well,* he thinks, *not the end of the world. Nobody really wanted the damn pews anyway. But to be so used by a big mouthed Nigra! Sweet, Jesus! Is there no end to these travails? Comforts me to know though, that Ferrous may get hit next. Or P-R, somehow. Wouldn't that be the icing on the cake? To be the fly on the mayoral wall! Or, better,* he laughs, *the dark shadow polishing his baseboards.*

Salvation's chest heaves. But it is a premature relief that comforts him.

He licks his thumb and rubs a small smudge from his car's fender, sees his own diffident smile in the polish: black on black, the edge of invisible, negative space. Down the road comes a squad car, a young officer at the wheel and, refreshingly, a white man in the back, perhaps shackled. The prisoner looks familiar. Salvation sees him in the pixels of newsprint, something about the David's Sling disaster flits through his mind. He gets into the T, sits behind the wheel in prayerful thanks, begs forgiveness for his deception, and asks a blessing for the common good. He does not stop trembling until he is safely — one more premature comfort — back in his own churchyard. Later, he will tell Sister Salvation that the difference between himself and Pastor Shem is that one turns to rock-solid Scripture for his sermonic muse, the other to the itinerant carnival.

McCallum had registered the colored man examining the car in front of the chapel. If he hadn't so urgently wanted to be rid of Moses Brown, he would have stopped to see what was going on. He will check it out later at the station, just to make sure there is no funny business. He isn't particularly obsessed with Negroes, but he is a good cop, and you just never know with some classes of people. Different mind set, different rulebook, *a whole nuther* ledger of commandments from a less punctilious god. Perhaps, even, one without commandments, just suggestions.

He gets Brown up into The Camels, passes P-R going the other direction down the road, pulls up to the Civil War plaque at the turnout, and orders the prisoner from the car. The engineer struggles, but asks for no help. The cuffs are chaffing his wrists. The officer gets out and opens the trunk, orders Brown to, "Come get this here shit a yours." Silently, the prisoner steps around to the back of the car, still shackled, removes the two bags one at a time.

"Put them over by the marker stone," the officer tells him. After which, he says, "I take back my jewelry, y'ain't going to take a swing at me or anything, are you?"

Brown shows his first signs of fear, a twitch at the corner of his mouth, an unconscious two-step on the gravel back away from McCallum. "You gonna say I did? That the idea?"

McCallum tells him to suck in his tongue and hold out his hands. It seems an eternity to both of them before he does so. The engineer's hands vibrate as if they clutch the live throttle. "Hold still. Can't very well get the key in a movin' target." There is a loud click, a cool salve of air on the bruised wrists, and McCallum returns the cuffs to his belt, himself taking a few cautious steps backward.

"Y'really just gonna lemme go?"

"I am. A gift from God, y'ask me. An all too generous one too."

Something migratory passes over, casts a moving shadow momentarily between them. The sky it travels in is a deep-lake blue, almost black. McCallum walks around to his side of the car, gets in, doesn't take his eyes off of Brown any longer than the split second that the doorframe obstructs his view.

Brown hunches down to look through the window at him. "Ya just gonna lemme go? Just like that?"

"You know, fella, I was you, I'd stop asking questions, be thankful for my good fortune, and start totin' whatever I got left in the world north, before this particular copper takes heed a his better judgment."

"D'ya know what happened t' my wife?"

"I know nothin' about nothin'."

"They say she up an' left. I lost my wife, see."

McCallum's sad eyes look into Brown's. "The world's a dark place. Your's ain't the only loss come outta these strange times. Believe you me. Maybe you hit her too much. Maybe not near enough. Not my concern. Besides, it could be worse."

"How's that?"

"Bitch could come back."

The squad car makes a U-turn, heads back to Tishomingo. Moses Brown is left to nurse his wounded wrists and deflated ego together in the quiet battlefield. He could sneak back down to town and try to find her, only that, like Prezhki said, would probably land him in more trouble than he already has. He has descended a long way and needs no more tribulation. Nor does he want to be seen in UF either, stick his neck out at the railroad's pleasure. Perhaps he can make it out of state, find a logging company with a few geared engines in need of an experienced hogger. It could be worse. It *could* be.

Anxious to be active again, McCallum plays his hunch as soon as he is back in the office. "The plate on your T," says the clerk at the capital, "is registered to a Holynation Salvation."

"That's what?" says McCallum. "A charity? A church?"

"A person. That's the guy's name."

"You're kidding me?"

"This is Motor Vehicles. I could direct y'all to Vaudeville?"

McCallum hangs up, takes the given address, drives out to the black man's home to see if there has been a problem with the car: was it stolen, loaned out to a relative from out of town, sold and not reregistered? But when he gets there, the T sits shining in brilliant late afternoon light, and he recognizes Salvation from the earlier sighting. The minister is raking leaves around the chapel, still dressed for formal visits.

"I talk to you a moment?" McCallum says from the car. "Not really a question, is it?" Salvation says, standing fixed at his distance from the officer.

"Y'might not wanna sass me, boy."

"How can I he'p y'all, of'cer?"

"A little bird tells me you were nosing around over at First Baptist this morning."

"Was dere. Weren't doin' no nosin', boss."

"You got a attitude, boy. How about we take a ride?"

"Can I go on up's t' da house dere an' tell da wife? She be a worrier, her."

"We'll ring her from the station."

Salvation knows not to argue. Hopefully, he hasn't overplayed his hand and this will all be over soon, just another of the casual pleasures of the world's great melting pot. Nor is he surprised when the officer cuffs him and slumps him down into the back seat of the squad car.

Prezhki comes out into the office for coffee, spots McCallum on the phone, that prideful colored preacher sitting in front of him with his hands clenched in his lap. He sits on the edge of the desk, says, "What have we here, Officer?"

McCallum cups his hand over the mouthpiece. "I seen this boy out at First Baptist. He say's he was visiting with the preacher over there. Don't take an alley cat to smell the fish in this one."

"Whose on the phone?"

"I'm waitin' on Pastor Shem."

"Hang up. Pastor Salvation and I go way back. Does your wife know where you are, Pastor? Officer, call the Pastor's wife and tell her you are going to have her husband home inside of the hour. Do your damnedest to treat her like a lady."

He invites Salvation to his office, uncuffs him, closes the door hard enough to rattle the frosted window, sends the lettering to tango across the glass. The Chief sits down, invites Salvation to do so also, and says, "We're seeing quite a bit of each other lately."

"Another one of those unfortunate misjudgments that seem to occur so frequently between the races."

"Without generalizing way beyond the moment, see if you can't give me a plausible explanation as to what business you had out there at Pastor Shem's."

"A charitable man, Brother Shem. Took pity on my struggling flock. He has offered me the use of several abandoned pews."

"And?"

"And?"

"Do better. I know Shem."

"You know about the brewery?"

"It's getting around. But I suppose you know that. You blackmail the minister, Salvation?"

"We bartered."

"I bet you did. You dare tell me this?"

"Have I misjudged you, sir? I seem to have recognized a glimmer of decency."

"Whoa, careful you don't overstep. We talk of blackmail and decency in the same breath? You gotta just love the faithful, Pastor!"

"Oh, yes, I do. And so does Jesus. The faithful and the sinner alike."

"Look here, now, don't push your luck with me. And talk less. Officer McCallum can drive you home now. Sit in the front seat this time."

"Please. I'll sit in the back, if I may. Cuffed. I have my own sense of propriety. A reputation to maintain."

"Suit yourself."

Prezhki reaches into the coat that hangs over his chair, pulls out his billfold, hands Salvation a crisp portrait of Hamilton.

"What's this? I'll have no special pull on the final day."

"It's for the hat this Sunday. Put it toward a stained glass window so's you don't have to leverage one out of Shem. A risky hand in a dangerous game, I think."

"I thank you for your consul and donation." He does not thank Prezhki for his civility; this, even if rationed, he considers deserved. "But, if I may share a confidence, gentleman to gentleman, do not think that I have suffered the sin of pride in my encounter with the Reverend Shem. That I have, as they say, stepped out of my place. What I *wanted* to say to him, right after he uttered the word *Nigra* was this: 'Such a curious term you use.'" He clears his throat, does a nervous tug at his necktie. He imagines himself at the pulpit, perhaps for comfort, perhaps, for the moment, to forget the current surroundings and all of their implied hazards. "'As many times as I hear it, I remain puzzled, enough so that I have consulted my dictionary and can find nary a mention. Initially, one thinks that perhaps it is from the Spanish, the feminine of Negro. But, no, a similar search of the *diccionario* offers no further enlightenment. A shame. For I can only conclude that Nigra, therefore, is a distortion of Negro, an aberration, a bending for some nefarious purpose. To use the proper form, to say Negro, is to advertise either one's good breeding and education or to at least show some awareness of the feelings of those to and about whom it is said. But in your mouth, Reverend Shem,' I wanted to say, 'a mouth that seems to betray only a gentle regional lilt and that I venture has no trouble correctly pronouncing, oh, say, furrow, or Cairo, or any one of the many words ending in the long o,'" pursing his lips as if a man blowing smoke rings, "'must be responding to some hidden emotion when confronted with *Negro*. Perhaps it catches in the throat like a fish bone, brings that sudden panic of cutting off breath, makes one think, oh no, I am in a room, choke, on nearly equal terms, with a, cough, gag, Nigra! Good breeding betrayed. Nigra is a transitional term, approaches something intended to be less of an accommodation.' That is what I would have said if I had wanted to overplay a dangerous game. And sadly, I shall always wish I had. But then, my purpose was the pews."

Prezhki is at a loss for words. When he finally recovers his voice, he says, "Yet, you thought it better to say it to me!"

"Yes. I did. Not because I think you will understand, but because I think you would like to understand."

Prezhki is embarrassed, feels the heat radiating off of his face. Salvation digs deep under the skin. "Yeah, well, see if you can't keep yourself out of trouble. We don't need to make a habit of this."

"In my experience, trouble's the seeker, not otherwise."

"Did the junkman tell you anything about…well, anything at all?"

421

"Let's say, I know enough to admonish a certain engineer as to his lack of judgment."

They both stand. Prezhki says, "I think we have done each other a service today, Pastor. If there is anything I can assist you with in the future, don't be bashful. I'm here to serve. But...use the mail. You don't want to be on the phone and you don't want to spend any more time up in here."

Salvation holds his arms out before him with mirror-image fists. "We really don't need to do that," Prezhki says quietly.

Salvation says, "In this part of town, I'd feel naked without them."

Prezhki shows reluctant palms. "Suit yourself then," he says as he hands over a pair of bracelets. "Tell me something. What part of the moniker is your given name?"

"None of it. You see, since the first Africans came to Jamestown as chattel, we have learned that nothing is ours to give, not even a name. Holynation Salvation is no plantation hand-me-down. It is my *taken* name."

McCallum stands waiting at the door, bewildered by all the great and small events of the recent past. No less worrisome is the kind smile that Salvation bestows upon him when delivered back to his home, and the comment, "I am sorry for your misfortune, Officer."

Tennessee carries a tray of breaded pork chops in creamy gravy, adorned with corn bread and cooked carrots, and sets it atop the wicker table on the front porch. They eat quietly, other than the commotion of Walter's enthusiastic mastication. Their view of the avenue is obstructed by the work of a Golden Orb Spider, the size and hue of a Double Eagle coin, the gauze of web filtering strands of sunlight and hosting egg-shaped translucent beads of humidity like strung Christmas lights. There is a clicking of lawn mowers and playing cards clothes-pinned to bike frames, queens and jacks slapping themselves silly. Little girls are jumping rope and playing hopscotch in the chalky squares of driveways. The cicadas are loud enough to drown the tempered volume of ordinary conversation. There is a slight odor of fish from the street.

"So, Walter, there's cobbler next or talk?" She is a handsome woman of conservative, some say passé, attire, contrary to the rumors of her atheism and penchant for free thinking.

"Hold the pie, Tenny. I've had an interesting proposition today. I'd like to discuss it with you."

"More coffee?"

"Not just yet. I got a call from Rev. Shem today?"

"What did the old fakir want now? A new porch step? Replace the old cross? A relic from the True Christ?"

"No. He didn't ask for anything. Seems he wants to do something for me. Wanted to meet in his car."

"Did you?"

"Why, yes, I did. You know the phones."

"Wooden horses are best left outside the gates, Walter."

He neglects to tell her of the visit to Ferrous, is a bit unsure of the distance he has already traveled down this alien road. "I'm not naïve. You know that. But the offer was interesting. He is in league with someone high up at the railroad. I'm not to discuss it just now. Nor are you. But, see, they've asked me to challenge P-R in the next Mayoral contest."

She puts her hand over her mouth. "Oh my!" she says. "I hope you said *no thank you*."

"Well, actually, I didn't. Not *yes* either, but...I don't know. Why not?"

"Because, Walter, then you'll owe them."

"And now I owe P-R."

"Frying pan to the fire. Why are they doing this? And where exactly is the financing to come from?"

"I don't know why for sure, but I suppose I could put some pieces together. There's enough credible folklore out there. I realize that it's probably not for my benefit, but if something positive could be made of it, well, then, who knows? The money? I don't imagine it comes from the church coffers. My guess would be the railroad."

"That can't be good. This marriage of God and Mammon."

"Throw in City Hall and you've got more a trinity than a couple. No, it can't be good. Not in and of itself. But I can be my own man, don't you think?"

"What do you think? You seem to have no such independence at present." It is a stern jab she deals.

He leans back in his chair, folds his arms and studies her as she evaluates him. "That's a hard judgment, Tennessee."

"I don't mean it to be. I'm trying to be realistic. This is not about your competence. This is about powers we have no control over, no matter what trust is put in us. Do you trust these people? My heavens, Walter, hands-out-Shem! The railroad!"

"You know the answer to that. But I'm so under the thumb of P-R right now I imagine seeing his imprint on my face when I look in the glass. I find myself doing all kinds of things that are against my better nature, all related to P-R and his foolishness. Anyway, this is just a possibility I will have to mull. I sure wasn't expecting it and I'm caught a bit off guard."

"And they, these forces, they will back you openly?"

"Well, no, not Shem, not the railroad. There will be proxy support, of course. Shem is particularly leery of P-R getting hold of this. They're in cahoots on something unsavory, I'm pretty sure. Let them cut each other's throats, I say. Somebody needs to be left standing when it's all said and done. Might as well be me."

"I don't know, Walter. Politics. What do we know of it? Why, some of my very well known views could be a liability in a campaign."

"I got this far." It goes unsaid as to how: for him a sin of denial, for her an act of charity. "The voters accept us as we are or we lose. Nothing gained, nothing lost. P-R's dirty laundry waves over the streets of this town like Stars and Bars on Confederate Memorial Day. Anyway, no decision has been made. We'll see how this all plays out. Now, you sit still, and I'll bus these plates and see if I can't locate that pie." He stands, forks refuse into one plate and stacks the two plus the serving pieces. "Mayor Prezhki! Doesn't sound all that bad. Boy oh boy, wouldn't P-R hate the ring of it?"

She frowns, just slightly, but it seems to drown out all else, even the roar of approval from the collected cicadas in the ravine next to the house. But cicadas are an under-voting constituency. He knows her long enough to read her face. In the kitchen, he sets down the dishes, finds the pie tucked neatly into its tin on the stove, is intoxicated with the aroma from the filling in both the crust and his mind. She is right to disapprove, he knows. He doesn't see himself as a vindictive man and wonders if he can serve the public unselfishly while at the same time enjoying the downfall of his tormenter. Not that he thinks P-R conspires to harm him: it is simply his misfortune to be set in the Mayor's path. He rinses the frying pan of seared pork crisps and congealed tallow, and finds it to be a harder task than he expected.

VI

P-R PARKS HIS CAR IN THE alley shade behind the Humboldt house, where the white petals of magnolias flail down upon it like confetti after nuptials. He is entertained by the ancient routines of black and yellow songbirds out for late summer evening flirtations. And, he is enjoying, in Mr. Harding's words, "the return to normalcy," which gives him leave to promote a bit of mischief of his own making. He observes entrances for a time, neighboring vantage points, runs through several cautionary scenarios, then implores the choke and turns the key, and rides around town until he is satisfied that the time is right. Hours pass, and he returns to the alley, now all in dark shadow, and parks once more up against a moss-encrusted fence. He feels like a scrappy kid on the make, sneaking about to the obvious displeasure of parental guidance and social norms. He is swept away by the adrenalin pump of risk as the dark congeals about him. He unlatches the back gate at the side of the carriage house, works his way around to the backdoor service porch, and taps lightly on the screen hidden in the pitch dark.

"Back away from the door where I can see you," she says. A light goes on in an upstairs bedroom and the curtains part. He sees dark, double-barrels extend through the open window. They scan the yard as if they have sight.

He raises his arms half in the air. "Are you going to pepper the Mayor, Praetoria?"

She inches her head out over the sill and over the shotgun. "A little seasoning might do you good. Darned if y'all aren't one nervy son of the devil, P-R."

He lowers his hands. "One tries to latch on to what works," he says. "Why don't y'all come on down here and unlock the door?"

"Why ever would I do that?" She doesn't lower the gun.

"Getting a crick in my neck trying to get a look at you. Let me in, or I'll huff and I'll puff."

"Are you drunk?" Her voice is full, cushiony, hangs like a laden cloud above him. It is both siren's call and warning.

"If I were, I wouldn't exactly know it to answer, would I?"

"Everything you've ever done is calculated, even inebriation. What do you want? I'm in mourning."

"Just a neighborly inquiry from an old friend. Y'all were on my mind and I wanted to see how you were getting on. I'm here to comfort you in this dark time."

"*Dark?* Dark of night! Like a thief. And at the back door yet!"

"Please, Praetoria, understand, you've troubled my mind all day. It speaks well of my uncanny sense of discretion that I've held off this long."

"My Lord, P-R! Sometimes I wonder if anything you say even makes sense to *you*. Well, y'all've seen how I am. Now go home to your wife. She's probably wondering where you are."

"I very much doubt that. A shrewd woman, my wife. You alone?"

"Just the girl. But that's neither here nor there. And the shotgun, to which I consign considerably more significance."

"Y'all wouldn't shoot me!" His voice is pitched high with injury. There is an extra blood-pumping thrill, a frosting to his prankish cake, foreplay at a story's distance.

"Oh, I don't know if I would or not, but I sure could take to the idea. If anybody in this town deserves to collect a few pellets, it's y'all. And such a balance it would bring, to perforate y'all with my husband's weapon."

"As I recall, y'all used to coo sweeter."

"Before you killed my husband."

"Me? Something of an exaggeration, don't you think? Wrecking trains is somewhere beyond my purview."

"You know why he was down there in UF. You know it was about you."

"I'm a simple man driven by basic needs. Passion's a complex thing. Machinations all it's own. In any case, I didn't think there was all that much of it left between you and Yardley."

"Humiliation is a whole different animal. Please, go home, P-R. Y'all've done me enough damage."

"Never intentionally. I wish you only the best. There is a special place in my heart for you. Y'all know that."

"A bit too crowded for me. Your heart. Like a boardwalk on the beach on a fine summer Sunday afternoon. A Balkanized heart, y'all's, of overlapping claims and ancient wrongs. Go home, go home, go home. My Lord, have you no shame?"

Palms up, he throws his arms in the air. "Apparently not. Nor was that something that previously troubled you. Look, how can I tell you? I'm lonely. Y'all know how it is with Sarai. I thought, perhaps, you'd be lonely too." He hears her sigh. The night is that quiet. There is the rustle of a small animal in a hedge nearby, something sensitive enough not to intrude upon the privacy of others.

"You sound hopeful. Do you think by mocking me you're going to pity yourself into my bed? Is that what this is about?" She tries to sound quizzical, fails to do so. She is not at all surprised to see him beseeching her in the moonlight, nor is she surprised at how fetching he can be, the boy he can seem, bent to distraction by his yearnings. He can make her, if not discount, at least ignore his deviousness. She pictures his secret war room, entombed somewhere beneath city hall, a stark bunker with maps and charts pinned with the locations of vulnerable females. And, there is an uncomfortable truth to his visit: she is not all that put out that he is here.

"I'll try anything once. At least once," he says, "and there is some history to pity's aphrodisiac side." He is feeling a sense of accomplishment already. She is surrendering quicker than he had imagined, albeit, a weary sort of capitulation. Not surrendering had not entered his reckoning.

She sets the gun down by the sill. It is hard to tell, but he thinks she smiles. "And just what manner of comfort would y'all offer a lonely widow in the throws of grief?"

"Hopefully a sort more robust than the palsied advice of Pastor Shem."

"That's unfair. The poor man's not even here to defend himself."

"I feel it coming on, the huffing and the puffing."

"I will let you in for a drink in the parlor. Then you will go home. I am lonely too. It's a big house to be alone in. Don't pretend that there will be any continuity to your visit. If you fill a momentary void, good for me. Y'all can spend the rest of your days in hell, for all I care."

What a dark vocabulary of seduction, he thinks, and wonders if it assuages her piety. He likes religious women. They have license to blame their own personal Satan, a quality which lends them a certain becoming abandonment.

He sees the light go off in the bedroom. Other lights go on elsewhere in the house, descending from the upper floor. She brailles her way along the kitchen walls looking for a tactile memory of a light button.

He stands haloed in the twinkle of lightning bugs as she opens the door. She doesn't have the gun any more and he can see hints of familiar landmarks beneath the sheer translucence of her nightdress. He begins to walk past her, turns, grabs the full fabric of her auburn hair, lightly tugs back her head, and kisses with all his civic authority the soft crest of the constituent's lips.

"It must be sweltering inside," he says. "There's the slight cooling tremor of air in the yard. A bit sultry, but pleasant. A moisture on the skin."

He steps out onto the stoop again, begins to undo his tie. She sheds the nightdress defined in a thin tracery of backlight, and walks slowly out to the lap pool and slips in quietly. He takes his time neatly folding his garments, placing them gently down on a lawn chair, tests the water with his toe, shivers, slinks in nearly as quietly as she, and watches her do a slow lap out — apparently impervious to the water temperature — then back, her buttocks' golden crescents in the moonlight, her shoulder blades tensing with each stroke of lassitude. There are leaves in the pool and delicate creatures that dash across the surface on spindly legs.

One would think a body of water would insulate against sound; one would do well to think again before putting such a theory to practice. The sounds of their union careen about the yard, send tendrils up the rain spouts over the carriage house like itsy bitsy spiders. Blinds are parted there. The dark night melds with the dark window glass, the dark glass with the dark face taking it all in. Their coupling is recorded and stored for Brother Salvation or whomever can find a use for such intelligence. In the telling, she will have them hand in hand dripping their way across the patio, the man not too incapacitated to remember to take his neat square of clothing with him so as to protect it from the humidity. It seems an effortless intercourse, well rehearsed, and without the oblivion often associated with such behavior. The blinds fall parallel again, and the shadow woman thinks, *Dat's white folks for ya! Woul'n'a wanna hurt demselbs.* And then, *I knows dat good ol' boy. Bare bottom an' all. Thank you, Jesus!*

It will be more than an hour before he gets the promised drink. The parlor has been sidetracked. He is working his fingers on the small of her back, the smooth spinal trough that bisects her waist. The bed is large, a lamentable collection of pillows to cry on, and to clutter to distraction their lovemaking. He finds it taxing to work around such obstacles.

"Y'all are good for one thing beyond nothing," she admits.

"Just *one?*"

"One is generous. Anyway, it's been better."

"Well, familiarity breeds contempt, they say. Anyway, I'm not an untalented man in more mundane matters. I have education, you know. Ongoing administrative experience. I've made a pretty penny in business matters."

"Easy to make money when you start out with so much of someone else's. It's late to drag out the old resumé, P-R."

"I just want to say, in all sincerity, that if there is anything else I can help you with, I'm at your service. Anything at all. Moral support. Financial advice. Anything."

"Anything *else?* How do the amoral offer moral support? Let's not pretend we'all're something we're not. I'm tired, P-R. Go home now. Y'all got what you came for."

"Like the practical snail, I carry my home along with me. Praetoria, because I have great affection for you, I was wondering if you have someone to advise you on…well, the details of a husband's passing. A widow is suddenly burdened with the business affairs of the deceased. Things your husband might not have confided in you. This is in your interest, you understand. I was wondering, have y'all had the opportunity to review the estate?"

"What are you getting at?" She sits up, a sudden angry modesty overcoming her, pulls a cover up over her breasts.

"Widows need to guard against shysters. It's as simple as that. Y'all're an easy mark in your condition."

"And what condition is that?"

"A condition of vulnerability."

"I'm not a dolt."

"I'm not suggesting you are. But there are some shady operators out there with bridges to sell and swamp land to build upon. I'd hate to see y'all taken in that way. I'd hate to see you so finessed by some unscrupulous grifter as to succumb to unwarranted charms, and lose a great deal in the process."

"I've already done that! A few thoughts: One, *unscrupulous* is a redundant adjective when defining *grifter;* Two, this seems to be more the kind of conversation people have with their clothes on. Perhaps a discussion in a paneled room with some sort of desk and very serious papers strewn about. Pens for signing. And, Three, if I'm looking to be the victim of the shrewd, the unscrupulous, the charmed, I have only myself to blame for the surrender of my bed. He knew about us. Yardley did. From the time he knew to the time he died, he didn't speak a word to me. But you could see it eat at him. You could see the shame. He withered like a leper."

"He didn't hear it from *me*. Did *you* speak to anybody? One of your lady friends? Someone to lean on?"

"Of course not! I'd be too humiliated. That's much more the male's gambol, don't you think?"

"Then how would he know? Perhaps you sought spiritual advice?"

"Brother Shem would never share such a confession. How dare you!"

"Please, Praetoria, receive this in the manner in which it is intended. We'all're friends, and no matter what reputation I have accumulated as to how I deal with opponents, I do know the meaning of friendship."

She huffs. "Yardley considered you a friend."

"And I, him. We had a very comfortable working relationship. My affection for you has nothing to do with my fondness for him."

"And my behavior with you...has nothing to do with affection. I loved my husband."

"I'm sure you did. You've an attorney, of course?"

"My husband's."

"Y'all's now. An accountant? Your husband's too? He wasn't the wisest of wheeler dealers, you know, your husband?"

"He got by."

"Not a guarantee that you will. And what is *getting by* anyway? Sounds like resignation to me."

"What do you want, P-R? I don't like where this seems to be leading."

"Y'all know about the brewery, of course."

"Yes. I didn't know you did."

"You know who was involved?"

"Just Yardley, I suppose."

"And Shem."

"I don't believe that. That's ridiculous!"

"A mediocre investment, considering the cost of the draymen. All those suds carted down hill to the rail yards, reloaded from truck to car. Labor intensive and expensive. But, suppose, there was a rail siding snug as a bug along side of the plant. Am I going too fast for y'all?"

She stands and finds a robe draped over a chair. It makes her look sleek and shimmery, aerodynamic even. She would be perfect sculpted, an opaque glass shade in floral over her head. Still, less perfect than Sarai, as are most women of his acquaintance. "Get dressed and get out." She is hissing like a snake, her fists clenched, the shotgun remembered where it leans.

"The company may dry up without the siding," he continues without emotion. "It was thought incumbent when the venture was launched, but the slow wheels of municipal government call for occasional lubrication. I would like to buy y'all out. There, it's out in the open. I will give you a fair market price. Consult whom ever you wish of your husband's associates. Though I'd leave Shem out myself. And a certain railroad executive. We can even haggle a bit if you'd like. That might be fun."

"It might be *fun?* Did you have to sleep with me to broach the subject?" She gathers up his clothes, throws them to the bed: silk, monograms, Italian leather shoes and all.

He protects his face from the projectiles. "Apples and oranges. I would have had to sleep with y'all whether you owned a third or not. You know, sweet thing, there is much we can give each other."

"How d'y'all live with yourself?"

"I've no choice, do I? It's Sarai who has the hard row to hoe."

"Don't think I don't pity her, you smug bastard. Get dressed and go. I won't say it again."

She leaves the room first, makes an audible point of stomping down the stairs.

P-R dresses slowly, comforted that the gun remains in the room with him. He concerns himself with creases, symmetry, the unified perfection of each slick hair. He is pleased with himself. He knows this conversation has only begun, that before it is a happy evolution that can only end in the presence of a notary.

He comes downstairs and sits across from her in a parlor insulated with books. There is one light on: a small table lamp with a glass shade that allows for a kaleidoscope of soft colors on rich mahogany. The table has a transparent sheen, much like the domestic who rubbed in the beeswax.

She is curled up on a large stuffed chair, great wooden lion's feet protruding from its skirts. "You make me feel unclean," she says. It is stated matter-of-factly, an announcement of inevitability, acceptance. He detects no bitterness, no emotion what so ever. "I hate you for that. I should have shot you."

"Go ahead. Gracious me, I hadn't intended to leave you unfulfilled."

"No, not now. It had to be a thing of the moment. I've lost the mood."

"So when shall we talk again?"

"I'm so very tired. I can't think. Go home."

"Drop by the office. We can have a respectable lunch somewhere. I can make y'all a very comfortable woman."

"By leaving! And, you'd better. I sense the mood returning." She is wiggling a delicate trigger finger.

He stands, demonstrates a little cosmetic brush to his hair, and a tug at the one lapel that rides slightly higher than the other. It jogs the lodge pin and cloisonné American flag. "You need me, Praetoria. I can be of great assistance. I can navigate y'all through the snake den if you'll let me. I'll look forward to our next chat."

"I know about the engineer. About the tramp," she tells him.

"Then you should speak to Walter Prezhki."

"I think not. Such things bear their hallmarks. Again, as the snail, y'all do tend to exude a rather public slime."

"How can I convince you? You've got this all wrong. Prezhki's car was seen. The woman must have confessed to the engineer. How else can we explain his violent outburst? I even hear that the old colored man identified the Chief. Perhaps, even, the engineer killed him in a rage. Or Prezhki...or one of his minions in blue. So there you have it."

"Well, we can't ask the colored man, can we?"

"In that sweet by and by, my dear, if that's where they'all wind up. Away from us, of course."

"Will I need to be avoiding you and Sarai at church?"

"I make the rounds. Haven't been to mass lately. And I suppose I should show my face to the Hebrews. The colored. The colored always seem to have the best food and the best time. Speaks well of poverty, doesn't it? And anyway, it might be a good idea to warm our dark brethren to the idea of an occasional short freight bringing good cheer to that dusky bottomland of indolence. Will y'all be singing any time soon? After all, your lovely soprano is the high point of my religious experience."

"Let yourself out," she says. "I will put the shotgun back in its case when I hear the back door latch. It has a singularly loud crack that echoes through the house, the door latch. I think I'll forgo the singing for a while. Seek ecstasy elsewhere, P-R. Good night."

On his way out, he cautions, "Mind your shoulder. That weapon of yours is capable of considerable kick."

He's feeling restless, not ready to go home, wishes the bars were still open this time of night. He'll have to see about such blue laws that require a man to be home at a decent hour. After all — and after David's Sling — who on the council would deny him an extra hour or two in the congenial society of like-minded men, or women?

VII

HALF WAY THROUGH THE NEXT MORNING, Chief Walter Prezhki gets up from his desk to stretch his legs. Through his open window, through a mesh of phone and trolley wires, he can see P-R's window across the street at the municipal building. He approaches the sill, crimps the blinds out of his way for a better view. Once or twice in the past, P-R has appeared at the very same moment as the Chief, causing them to exchange nods. But not today. P-R's window is closed, the shades drawn. *That's okay,* the Chief thinks, as he is in a forgiving mood.

There are joyous sounds to cheer him: hammers tapping out restorative tunes, the comic grumble of a dump truck hauling debris through the streets — blocks of shattered concrete, brick, segments of cracked wrought-iron facades — taking it all away to be plowed over and forgotten, out of sight and mind. Prezhki's attention falls on the hot dog man working his cart across the street to roll parallel to the front of the station, so as to set up by the news stand a block and a half past Railroad St. He can almost smell the uncooked dogs, figures to give the dog man a half-hour head start to get there, set up, boil his pot of water. He is hungry, and in better spirits than he has been in weeks. Maybe he'll have two dogs; one with kraut, one with chunks of raw onion awash in mustard. A cup of joe, *a step up from the sludge here at the station,* or maybe even something cold. A triangle of geese plays follow the leader in front of the sun, a pool rack in full flight and too bright to look at. He can hear them honking like airborne DeSotos.

He tells the deskman he's going fishing *and* strides purposely out the door. When he reaches the corner of the building, he slows, peers vigilantly around the corner toward the hardware store, smiles at his foolishness, and proceeds to Taggart's City News. He sports a mug wealthy with discolored skin.

Taggart is immersed in a racing form. He is the very worst of the samplers he rails at: reads all he has his considerable time for, sets them back on the shelves creased and foxed. The racks are bright with <u>Collier's,</u> <u>The Saturday Evening Post</u> with a new Rockwell cover — an Indian at a mailbox, the cheap paper stock of <u>Railroad Man's Life</u>, comic books, <u>National Geographic</u> in its formal printed frame. The stand tunnels down an alcove between two buildings, the passage now in full view, the air dense with the aroma of boiling sausage from the cart opposite Taggart's.

"You a sporting man?" Prezhki asks.

Taggart says, "A wager now an' again. Nothin' extravagant. Basement winda at the track." Taggart is a slovenly man with a bristled double chin, gray sacks under his eyes like RPO bags, and unkempt black hair thinning from the sides of his forehead. There is a smell about him: of cabbage, old socks, just a hint of skunk, and newsprint.

"Nice day."

"Wouldn't know. Been slavin' here in the tomb."

"Christ! A man can see out, can't he?"

"If he looks. All the same t'me stuck behind the counter. How's the shiner, Chief?"

"What Shriner?"

"Shiner. Okay, I get it. We all over that thing with the engineer's woman, I'm guessin'."

"What woman? You want to know something, buy yourself a paper. And I'll take that <u>Mercury Ledger</u> you got there."

"Don't worry none. You ain't in it."

"Sweet anonymity. The faceless public figure. You ought to get out here and enjoy the day, Taggart. A man gets all pasty and irritable holed up like you are."

"What? I forgot what it's like on the outside?"

"You never know until you immerse yourself in the ether."

"Well, look who's waxin' poetic today. Get y'self some nooky last night, or what?"

"You ever pass a kidney stone, Tags? I hear it's like getting kicked in the side by a steel-tipped cowboy boot. Only, point of impact stays with you for the duration. You don't know how good you can feel until the pain stops."

"A metaphor in regards to nothin' I can figure," Taggart says to Prezhki's back. "Y'ain't gonna subject your system t'one a Shorty's dogs, are ya?"

"Two," Prezhki says holding up that number of fingers. Shorty has the pot at a boil. A bottle fly is helping itself to the steam, sending smoke signals to its kin.

"I gotta copy a The Jungle here abouts somewheres, y'might wanna peruse durin' lunch," says Taggart.

"One with kraut," orders the Chief. "One with mustard and onions. If you've got a cream soda on ice, I'll wash them down with that."

Shorty struggles with the tongs, stirs up juices in the form of cloud. He is palsied — a cruel quirk of birth — and just a little bent in the middle so that he stares past your ear when he faces you. Shorty stutters, "D-d-d-don't listen to Professor L-l-l-it, over there. I g-g-got nothin' but p-p-prime wieners here. H-h-hit the sp-spot. Him there, h-h-he reads h-h-his self a st-st-story about Chic-c-cago, he thinks it's gotta be like that in T-t-t-t...."

"I got it. I know. The long jump to righteous assurance, huh, Shorty?"

"If you s-s-say so, Ch-Chief!"

Taggart calls, "One on the left there, I drove over that one on my way in this mornin'."

Prezhki waves him off, jaywalks his dogs and soda on a diagonal over to Memorial Square, and chooses the bench with the least bird shit. The dogs are comfortably hot; nothing harmful could live in such an environment. Pasteur would eat them.

"Why if it ain't the cop 'o' the hour!" It is Cynthia Dalhurst, looking mannish with her pageboy, slacks, white shirt and vest bisected by a cheap, plated watch chain. She is wearing a man's striped tie as wide as a tablecloth. "Mind if I sit down?"

"Public park...Dog?"

Her lips curl, settle when she considers he probably wasn't meaning her. "You ever read The Jungle?"

"It's a muckraker's morning. What can I do for you, young lady?"

She settles down on the bench, retrieves a pencil stub from behind her ear, a spiral pad from her vest pocket. "Answer a few?"

"What's on for today? Fact or fancy?"

"Once the ink dries, it's all fact. So, from my perspective, the more you give me now, the more fragrant the wind blowing in your direction."

"This an ill wind we talking about?"

"Depends."

Prezhki asks, "We on the record here? *Read All About It. Chief of Police Eats Lunch in Park. Extri extri. Seen With Wounded Soldiers, Half Dressed Woman. What Does It All Mean?*"

"I heard you sprung the engineer."

"We needed the bunk."

"Kind a odd, don't you think? Man whacks you with a length of pipe and you kiss and make up."

"I don't get kissed all that often." He takes a hardy chunk from the bun, wipes the mustard from his mouth with a napkin.

"Not what I hear. I know what's going on."

"Do you? Want to give a peek to an officer of the law?"

She narrows her eyes, forms an appraising sort of smile. "I couldn't trump the competition if I was giving it away, now could I? People eat the dogs in your world, the dogs eat each other in mine. But in the interest of civic responsibility, I suppose I can throw together a few tidbits and see how they come out in the wash? You ever see that painting of the Indian with his ear to the rail?"

"No, ma'am. Not that I recall."

"He's listening for news of the train. Of what's coming at him. Of what it's bringing. He doesn't yet know what it portends, but he knows enough not to be happy about it. The rails are abuzz here in 'Mingo these days."

"And they're saying?"

"Suggesting, more than saying."

"You've conversed with this Indian? So tell me, from one Chief to another."

"A higher-up at the railroad demands that the Mayor comes down to UF to see him. Which the Mayor does, tail between his legs. The secretary at the higher-up's office is instructed to send him in upon arrival, even though the higher-up is in confidential take-no-calls mode with a 'Mingo entrepreneur and councilman. The councilman exits first, in something of a tiff. In the meantime, a policeman, under your purview, is tapping into files over at the County. A snoopy clerk straightens up after him, and discovers the apparent object of his curiosity. A change of ownership at a certain brewery. Involving, see, a certain higher-up at the railroad, a certain entrepreneur and councilman and a certain respected man of the cloth. All under aliases. Am I ringing any bells?"

"Not in this parishioner's steeple."

"The next day, a certain engineer and his wife…the two of them the subject of certain other buzzings of late…are riding the cars *together*, her from an assignation with the Mayor of recent mention, him from being *removed* from the cab of a train he was assigned to drive. Removed by the higher-up. The train, with an unscheduled exec at the throttle…a bit of a joyride, that ends, as such things tend to do, badly. The exec is dead, which seems to open a career path to our higher-up who, in the current comparison, is the *lower down*. But not for long. The Mayor, who has to get back to his responsibilities at City Hall, is not, thank God, on that train. It would have been his most likely path back to town, but he has fortuitously chosen to have the policeman come all the way back to UF to carry him home. Also dead, is our councilman. Curious, huh?"

"Not really."

"No? How about this then? The councilman's widow, a parishioner of the well-respected man of the cloth and the new third partner in the brewery, gets a late night visit from the Mayor. She greets him with a shotgun. Her distress is soon replaced by a warm night romp that sends the two of them to the pool *au natural.* There's more of course. I don't want to bore you. There's a profitable visit by a colored preacher to the aforesaid clergyman. The preacher is the very same one that buried the old fix-it man who supposedly carried the engineer's wife up to Thebes for a liaison with a certain gentleman or gentlemen unknown. Unknown, but hardly unsuspected. And then we hear, those of us with our ears closest to the rail, along side the Indian, that the other clergyman is casting his net for a few new allies. Hearing those chimes yet?"

"Not a one! Look, you think you know what's going on? Print it. See if you're not counting cow flaps for The Kansas Daily Sod come morning."

"One and one makes three. Two and two makes five."

"Not in a depression, lady. What exactly does that mean, anyway?"

"Well, I guess it means that what it winds up to be is not necessarily the sum of its parts"

"Well then, here's something for you, okay. Set down your pencil. You're going to need your fingers to count what this doesn't add up too." He puts the dogs down on their waxy wrappings, places them neatly on the bench. Swats away flies. "What exactly do you know that makes you such a math wiz? Overhear something on a party line? Pick up a little gossip over at the five and ten? Christ in pajamas, even you ought to know that a good story really is often *less* than the sum of its parts."

"*Even* me! I'm listening to man who's poisoning himself while reading the Ledger. Here's a headline for you, *Chief of Police Ends Own Life, Dies Ignorant.*"

"To each his own favorite rag. Look, here's what we know, or don't. On a certain evening, so-and-so's automobile, being the only one of its kind in the known world, is seen by a hawkeyed teenage busboy on a dark night at the wrong end of a certain down-in-the-dumps burg. Earlier in the evening, a woman in black, perhaps the only woman in black about that night, gets a lift from an old black man. In a black truck. Or, perhaps, the old black man has loaned his truck to an eighteen year old buck known for a prominent endowment. The woman in black, who is of course white, unless of course she is colored, appreciates the taxi ride from the old black man. Or, she's giving the old buzzard one last reminder of what it once was like. She gets a particular thrill from misogynistic, geriatric gymnastics. Some people are like that. I've seen things you can't pretend people'll do. Or, she's a working girl. Plans to earn her two bits and then roll him for the rest of his change. Maybe. Maybe not. Maybe he doesn't have any change. Maybe, she's enamored of a certain cantilevered architecture promised by the young buck. In any case, this very same woman, if not an all together completely different one, gets dropped off near so-and-so's one of a kind automobile, finds her way over to a certain motor lodge of some considerable and nefarious reputation among the locals. Mr. so-and-so slides across the seat, follows her to her room. Could be her estranged daddy bringing her guilt money because he left her a babe in Mamma's arms, could be a john, could be someone who was sitting on the passenger side in the first place and leaves so-and-so to twiddle and nod behind the wheel. If it *was* so-and-so who followed these gyrations, he must have completed his business in an embarrassingly record time as, moments later, he is reported being seen ordering a burger at the Greek's, back a block and across the road. Perhaps he got the burger for the woman in black. Perhaps getting the burger was his cover and he tossed it on the way back. I'd search the brambles, I was you, for that burger, missy. But then again, boy wonder with the night vision says the fellow getting out of the car has the singular physique of a well-known what's-his-whosits. Matter of fact, if you take the time to notice, you might find that so-and-so and what's-his-name have very similar, singular physiques. Much like ten or fifteen other fellows that might come to mind. Might be that it would be pretty hard to remember a man's physique with the accuracy one would of his face, especially when spied from a block away and down the street in the pitch dark of a moonless night clothed as he must have been in heavy winter outer garments. But young people do tend to see like Galileo, don't they? Maybe so-and-so and what's-'-is are in this thing together. Good pals that share and share alike. Maybe they don't. A working girl wouldn't give a hoot either way. We have no complete dossier on the preferences of a certain engineer's wife, who may be the woman in black, or she may have just been visiting her sister who lives in Thebes, not all that far from the site of the alleged indiscretion performed by a party, unlikely, or parties unknown, if in fact it wasn't an innocent meeting of some unknown nature that, by the choice of venue, may look to be more sinister than it appears. Maybe the two men, or two other men, or the old Negro, or all three in cahoots, were pimping a stable of young women in black, young white women in black, young black women in black. Maybe these women are striped like zebras, are black or white depending on your perspective. What's-'is-face has a reputation, after all, however secretly admired by those without such bragging rights. But does a reputation prove behind a shadow of a doubt a man's culpability? Or a woman's? Even a woman in black driven by a Negro or Negroes in the dead of night? Or, was it early evening? Or, hot damn, was it at all? Does the busboy have an imagination? How well does he see? Do we have a cabal of evil men leading young virgins into a life of sin? Do we have a bunch of old biddies with their jaw motors running like racecars? Did a higher-up at the railroad purposely cause his own train to crash so he could kill his superior to clear the career ladder? Did he do it to better his stake in a brewery? Who is this nefarious colored preacher? Did he send the woman in black to ride the junk truck on her way to carnal sin? Is the copper in the county files going to get his ass chewed by the owner of the car so amazingly luminous that everyone on the planet can see it in total darkness? Did the owner finish his burger? Does two and two really make five? Or three? Is the bear Catholic? You're not getting any of this down." He takes a deep breath.

"I'm counting on my fingers. Proud of yourself!"

"Reasonably."

"You're wasting my time."

"*I* was having lunch! You swooped down like carrion on road kill. How am I wasting *your* time? So, you don't like that story? Let me tell you another one." He lifts a dog, chomps into it, sets it back down as he chews. Several of the flies connive to file a complaint.

"Do I want to hear it?"

He holds up his hand; a pause to swallow. "I think you should. It's a better story. More germane to the topic at hand. Based on truth, not the snake oil nonsense you use for confirmation at the script factory."

"Germane? My, my!"

"You expected a country bumpkin, did you? Should I spell that out for you?"

"I don't know what to expect. In my experience, you don't generally say all that much."

"I may not be saying all that much now." He performs another large amputation on the dog, makes a deliberate show of chewing slowly and pleasurably. "My God, the lowly wiener!" he says around a stuffed cheek. "You can have your Delmonico's and your caviar. It doesn't get any better than this! You can quote me when they promote you to reviewing pushcarts. Anyway, my good old daddy, bless his soul, had this oft-repeated story of how he came to understand America. Back in the old country, things were worse than Oklahoma in a dust storm. Kind of a permanent depression. Folks worked hard to make ends meet, and when they couldn't do that, they ate the ends themselves. Ends of breads, ends of tubers, the leafy ends of a carrot stick, *odds* and ends. And plastered all over everywhere were these colorful posters, put up by the steamship companies, white angels of Clara Bow-sweetness pointing toward America where they were serving roast beef on silver platters. Oysters Rockefeller, you name it. And land was cheaper than locusts in a cornfield. Lots of folks went to find Clara Bow, though I may not exactly have my chronology right. Maybe I mean Lilly Langtry. The point is: none came back. So folks are thinking, *over there must be better than over here.* Right? Huh? Right? So my granddaddy packs up the family and they steam their way in vomit-crusted steerage to Castle Garden. In Castle Garden, eveybody's trying to get out to Manhattan or Brooklyn. Jersey too. Nobody comes back. So it must be something over there in Manhattan or Brooklyn. The genuine article. This is before Ellis Island, see. Before Lady Liberty and her tired and her poor. Milk and honey turns out to be a two room, walk-up firetrap full up with seven people and five treadle Singers. But they had a pot to piss in. Yes, they did. Because, you didn't want to go down five flights in winter to relieve yourself in the cholera garden. And everywhere, the railroads are plastering these big color posters of Clara Bow floating across the plains with one perfect white bosom exposed and pointing west at a stream of Pullmans. And once again, anybody who went, never came back. So things must be great out there with Clara, and the bosoms, and the redskins all reservationized. As a kid, my daddy remembers his life in the rattrap with fondness. See, they were all poor. No one he knew had it better. But then, there were those posters. And word leaked down of Carnegies and such, names that weren't exactly the stuff of Plymouth Rock. They got out and didn't come back. On Daddy's twelfth birthday, Granddad managed to scrape together a couple or so Indian Heads, sends Daddy off on the cars to the American Museum on Broadway. Phineas Barnum, the sucker-a-minute fella. This is like coming to America in the first place. The novelty. This is like getting out of Five Points. This is Uptown. *Up*-town. Up out of those streets of European effluence, floodwaters of Bohunks, Polacks, Ruskies, Wops, Yids, you name it, they were there with their pushcarts and their foreign stink, their garlic and their sausage, their *borsht*. But not Uptown. Daddy enters the land of milk and honey, the big rock candy mountain, the shores of the Jordan. P.T.-Sucker-chump magnate-Barnum. The Cardiff Giant, the world's tallest and shortest men, the wild family from Borneo, the two-headed boy, all the great wonders of the modern world. Take that, you Colossus of Rhodes, you Hanging Gardens of Babylon. And then Daddy sees the signs. Big, bright, eye catching banners bedecked in prominent arrows, **THIS WAY TO THE EGRESS, DON'T MISS THE AMAZING EGRESS, THE GREATEST EGRESS ON EARTH.** Well, Daddy still struggles with his English. He's too shy to ask, *What in God's creation is this egress? Is it really worth seeing?* He *knows* it's worth seeing. Why would so many people be *see*-ing it if it wasn't? Why such elaborate signs if it is nothing? So Daddy, passes through the wondrous door clearly marked, **EGRESS,** and winds up outside in the alley without the change to get back in." He stops talking, smiles. He is proud of himself. He wonders if he tried, could he levitate?

When he doesn't continue, she asks, "So what am I supposed to do with that?"

"The readers love a fable, ma'am. See this hot dog here? Without the bun, it's still a hot dog. Less than the sum of its parts. Take away the bread, though, the mustard, the kraut, the relish, the onions, it is complete for what it is, but it sure doesn't eat as well. I'll look forward to your by-line in <u>The Nebraska Weekly Manure</u>. P-r-e-z-h-k-y. Get it right. I can't tell you how many times someone slips in an s where the z is supposed to be."

"Thanks for all the help," she says, and walks off with pad and pencil toward the street. With her back to him, she asks, "You gonna cite me if I cross here in the middle of the block?"

"Me? Naw. I'm going to sit here and finish my lunch. And I'll go you one better: you go and get yourself hit by something out there, I won't even cite the driver."

She crooks her hand behind her back, forms a structural right angle with her wrist. Prezhki is certain that she has also extended a middle finger, just briefly, a punctuation, an entire editorial from a hand overlarge for a lady, its elongated digits pregnant with substantial knuckles. He doesn't recall ever seeing a woman make that particular gesture. He imagines they may think of it with a certain frequency, but keep it under wraps like their actual age. He will have to ask Tennessee.

She crosses the street to endure an angry horn from P-R as he speeds toward City Hall, nods at the dog man as his steam wafts across her eyes, tells Taggart, "Wanna check up on the competition. Give me one a each except my own." He puts down a periodical he has covered in brown bag paper, folds over a page, then closes it. As requested, he assembles a stack of news rags from the capital and Uncas Falls, then late editions from the locals. She ads a Baby Ruth from the rack in front of the counter, hands Taggart a paper dollar, from which he subtracts the change.

She begins to peel the wrapping off the bar. "So, Taggart, tell me, if a tree falls in the forest...does it or doesn't it?"

"We on the record here? 'Cause I don't wanna lose the upcomin' pool a wisdom like so much flotsam on the wind."

"Sure. I'm doing a piece on what people think about stuff they can never prove."

"Why'd anybody wanna read that?"

She shakes her head and frowns, nibbles the end off of the candy bar, leaves a trace of chocolate on her otherwise unadorned lips. "What about you? You ever read my Quidnunc column?"

"The occasion 'rises."

"Why do you?"

"Look, sister, in this particular profession, a man's got plenty a time on his hands. I'd read the candy wrapper you left it on the counter."

"You must be a very literate man then."

"Yeah. I must, huh? That's why the *flotsam*. Wiener boy o'er there can't read HOT-COLD on a faucet, but me, they ought a hand me one a them PHD's or somethin'."

"So, smart guy, what about the tree in the forest?"

He scratches the stubble on his chin. "Well, I'd say, the wise thing would be t'question what's your definition a sound."

"Okay. That's good. How about this: If a tree falls in the forest and there's a guy napping under it who wakes just before it falls, and it falls on him and he dies, does it make a sound?"

"Same answer."

"Too easy. There's really no way to know, is there?"

"No, I guess not for positive."

"But see, Taggart. The public is curious. What was the last sound this unfortunate napper heard? Did the hearing of it cause him to try to shield himself, to dodge out of the way? Or was there no sound at all? Then splat! No more napper."

"Well, like ya just said, there ain't really no way to answer that, now is there?"

"Nope, there isn't. But what of the tree? What can the tree do for us? All that newsprint? All that ink? We've gotta print something."

VIII

THE LENGTHENING FREIGHT IS A DAY late when it crosses the stone bridge over Thebes. Back in the yard at Tishomingo, the engineer had fretted about a pronounced wobble in the pilot truck, passed on his concerns to the shop foreman, who requested a substitute locomotive. The train is a tardy sight as it makes clouds over the Motor Court, hangs a transient vapor film above The Roadhouse, and rattles every bone in every mortal up and down the trolley line to the ridge. Walls crack, chips of lead-based paint clutter floors like corn flakes at the bottom of the bowl, pictures shift, the barber withholds his blade from the pulsing throat of a customer, and liquids in glasses struggle to level; all in a familiar, time worn routine that neither surprises nor rattles any one at all. The Tishomingo is a rail line and a fault line all at once: the bringer of tectonics, the mover and shaker, the rattler and rocker of this tipsy landscape.

Thar she blows!

A long one, too. Near fifty cars.

A day late and a dollar short.

You count 'em?

Why no, I didn't.

Then how could you know how many?

I don't know. It just seems.

Well, if all you got is just seems, *don't go and get so precise and all and call it fifty like you got some sort a i-dea what you're talking about.*

Look-ee here, through the Greek's winda. Which is why we are gathered at this different table, after all.

He ought to get a girl in to wash it down, you ask me. Like lookin' through hog fat. Foreigner's!

No one's asking you. What I wanna know from your nephew, dear, is how he can be so certain.

Let it rest already. My Lord, y'all are tiresome.

Not even the long nose a that reporter woman's gonna sniff this one out. What else you got, dear?

I hear the Mayor's up to his old tricks. He was seen coming out the back way of a certain widow's. I hear his automobile was parked in the alley most of the night.

A certain widow's what?

You gotta source, do you?

Well, yes. Yes I do. But it would not be professional for me to tell you, now would it? I can't imagine even Jesus loves a tattler.

He loved that there Judas.

But I will say this: Like pitchers, little servants have big ears.

They use their employer's phones! Is this what you're suggesting?

Well, you're as sharp as a tack today. I don't need to suggest it. They've figured it out themselves.

Why, I never! You bring someone into your house, treat them well, send them home with all kinds of hand-me-downs and leftovers the likes of which do not grace their tables otherwise...why, you even pay them! And this is the thanks!

I think you should report them.

And dry up the flow of information! Not on your life.

I've been wondering...

Where too?

Wondering, *dear. You know you can't hear when you chew.*

She can't chew when she hears, either. A matter of truant molars.

What I'm wondering is...is...if poor Mr. Choc was partially consumed by the dog...

Still chewing! Yuch!

...how could the police determine how he died?

Did they determine, or wasn't it worth the bother?

I don't know. But supposing he just didn't up and die.

I like the counter at the dime store better.

Supposing someone...well, did him harm. Real bad harm.

Oh pooh! I hate that old egg salad.

All the same to me. Last time I tasted anything, President McKinley was shakin' hands in Buffalo.

Oh, that poor man! He never should have done that, should he?

No, he sure shouldn't'a, and gone and let that lunatic cowpuncher into the White House.

Oh, I was rather fond of Teddy. I like what he did with that Grand Canyon. Cecil and I once caught the Santa Fe out west and..."

Is anybody listening? I can think of several people who might not've wanted the old man to speak his mind.

Out west! Out west! There isn't anything out in that there desert that we didn't have first, and better, right here where we are!

Ladies, ladies! We are losing our train.

The train, hardly lost, snakes its way through a relentless series of S-curves, eases down snail speed into the reclaimed swamp of the capital. It's six chime whistle can barely be heard in the rundown boarding house behind The Capitol dome. Miss Gossinger and Mrs. Brown née Gossinger, both registered as the sisters Smith, Irma and Mary Ann, have chosen quarters as far from the railroad as practicality allows. They are concerned more with anonymity than the layout of rooms, and are eating into their mattress money for a single shared bed and a bath three doors down the hall. They had planned to look for jobs today, had circled various want ads for domestic and counter work, but sitting under the whip of the ceiling fan in slips, they are lethargic, can think of little else than the incomparable heat that has mosquitoes sweating the blood of others and swarms of deer flies on annoyance drills, *Go for their faces,* the DI orders, *their mouths and*

noses and eyes, that really gets their goat. And be quick about it; they'd sooner slap their own mugs than let a bug make an honest living.

"When you do land a job," asks the spinster, "what are you going to do with your first pay check?"

"Oh, I got that worked out, alright. I'm going over to the hardware, see if I can't find one of those cute little lady derringers that fit so comfy in a gal's bag. It will become my constant companion, go where I go, sleep under my pillow at night. It will be my jewelry, my talisman, my good luck charm. And if, somehow, that bastard Moses finds me, God help him to walk away with all the parts he came in with."

Engineer Hauser has had much to say. He is an able tour guide who points out sites along the road: on your right: off to the left, the old bootlegger's shack on Sophie's Hill, The Bank of DeLong County where the Scarrett gang was finally ambushed by the law, Seal's Creek Battlefield, the most fecund carnage memorial to poke for brass buttons and broken bayonets, Gulich Bend where, as teens, he and his crowd would go to pet and earn the right to embellish tales of boast-worthy thrills. "So much fer ancient history," Hauser shouts over the pounding of the loco. "Comin' up on yore right, ladles an' gents, the fines' sight these here piney woods has t'offer. A partikler interes' t'the gents."

Sardo licks his boiler-steamed lips in anticipation. "Brown never even looked outta the winda. Made the run blind-fold. Like quarry stone, that one." He has a cherry-red lobster's grin. Hauser says, "His loss, boy. Take a breather an' come o'er hyer, peek on out'those hungry peepers a yours, if ya can, o'er mah shoulder thayer. That a boy. Don' let that thayer hot mist cloud ya o'er, 'cause bein' the red-blooded Southern hound dawg you is, ya surely don' wanna miss this'un. Oh, yes sir, we timed this here a one jus' 'bout right. Sunny bright an all. Lawd, she sho' could yank back on my johnson bar, any ol' time 'a'tall, she could. Bless that sweet thang, vision a pearly gates that she be."

Sardo whistles covetously through his teeth as the naked image slips backward toward the way they came. "Girl can ride my train, Captain. I'd sure as shit toke her fire box!"

Covered by the tumult of the train, Deputy Dolph Llwelyn is able to pull his squad car to within a stone's throw of a gaggle of unwary boys occupied in the provocation of blindness and damnation, the forfeit of their own fatal puberty. He recognizes one or two, overalled striplings from a local farm, fourteen or fifteen and old enough to know better, or at least to have some passing acquaintance with fear. They've squinted their eyes between the slats of the fence trying to get a look-see at the woman on the lounger, so much better framed from the locomotive window, but they make do with what is available, the hardly censoring fence. All the while they are working compliant peckers in hand in one communal, masturbatory stag party. Deputy Llwelyn calls out, "Y'all tuck them bait worms away 'fore I cuff 'em," causing the boys to limp off in a heightened wobble, stuffing their inflated selves back into denim.

J. David Robbins

Llwelyn, as he has done many times before, takes his old woolen army blanket from the trunk, unrolls it, pushes through the complaining gate into her weedy yard, holds the blanket before him in deference to the modesty he feels they both should practice, and boot taps his way up to the lounger like a blind man without his cane.

"That you behin' thayer, Dolph?" she asks sweetly.

"Yes, ma'am, it surely is." He covers her nakedness with the blanket, tucks it carefully under her backside, cautious in avoidance of any strategic contact, and sets her on the lounger. "Jilly, Jilly, Jilly. Whate'er'm'ah gonna do'th ya'll?"

She says, "What ever y'all like t'."

He tugs her up by the arm, his hand firmly clutching the wool, nudges her for direction. In her simple kindness, she goes with him through the thistles to her porch, wrapped like a squaw woman, smelling, not unpleasantly, of sweat and rose water.

They sit together on rockers, and she lets the blanket drop from picture-perfect breasts, the kind he's seen in French post cards or in Belloque photographs from the bordellos of New Orleans. He tugs it back up, slowly, drapes it firmly over her sun-browned shoulders. He feels a stirring, a discomfort, the innocent attraction of her nubile form, the soft, irresistible contour of sexuality that is beyond the grasp of her alien's mind.

Jilly Zorn, despite what some may think — and some do talk of what they think — is not a hussy, not a brash exhibitionist: Jilly is but a minimalized child of God, tea cup-delicate and snowmelt slow. "Ah declare, yore such an' ol' party pooper, you, Dolph. Ah was havin' such a nice rest an' the sun felt so good."

Dolph leans forward with his head in his hands. "Jilly, dear thaing, how many's the times I gotta tell ya folks won' stan' for y'all paradin' 'bout'n'a all t'gether like ya do?"

She pouts. "Ah weren't paradin', Dolph. What ever give ya such a dumb *eye-dea?*" It is a sincere question. It is the word *parading* that distresses her, as if he thought she were some sort of circus animal, performing for the stands.

Dolph rubs a finger through the back of his hair, soothes a kink in his neck. He talks loud over the noise of the endless train. "Jilly, girl, ah know y'all don' mean no harm, but ah jus' gonna have t' insist y'all keep yore clothes on. It ain't proper t'be par-...out'n the daylight buck naked. Ya know that! Or ya don't. No difference t'me. An' no difference t' the law which prohibits such wanton *bee-havior.*"

She says she doesn't know "any such a thing," and that she "don't care none, no how," and that she doesn't "'preciate the way he's goin' on 'bout 'er."

He wants to give her a good spanking, find a switch and giver her what for, but he is confused as to his reasons, is tugged one way to blame her for his impure thoughts, another way to blame the sinner in himself. She's growed, but still a chile he reminds himself. When she tells him she doesn't like him any more, that he's mean, he admits that sometimes he doesn't like himself very much either. "This a here's all fer your own good. Ah know some a them no 'count boys takes advantage a y'all. We cain't have none a that now, can we?"

442

She puckers her lips, causes a wrinkle of her round little nose like she smells something bad. "Some a them boy's real sweet, Dolph. Not like mean ol' you! They say I'm thayer gal. Could be y'all's gal too, if ya want. Long's ya treat me sweet."

Dolph lowers his voice, tries to scold, as he would one of his own offspring. "Nah, y'jus' get that thought outta that foolish head a yours. Ain't gonna happen, no way, no how. Y'know, Jilly, ah gotta lug this hayer blanket outta the trunk one more time, I'm gonna have t' take y'all in t' the station like we done last time. Y'all 'don'want that now, do ya?" She says she doesn't, that the boys at the jail are not nice boys. He heartily agrees, tells her he reckons that's why they're there. "Ya 'recall ol' Judge Overmeyer, do ya? Who ya got brung up afore last time?"

She shivers in disgust. "Such a silly ol' man. Ah don' wanna talk 'bout 'im."

He tells her that's not for her to decide, that the next time they slap her with an indecent exposure charge, "He gonna up an' send y'all t'the funny farm over there by the peach orchard." She tells him she likes peaches. "They's some mighty sour peaches over by the funny farm," he warns.

"Oh, you, Dolph!" she says, and gives his knee a little squeeze. "Then ah won' eat none a 'em."

Firmly, he pushes her hand away. "Look'ee hyer, now, girl, ya cain't go on an' touch me, now. Ah'm a sworn off'cer a the law, ah am, an' y'alls 'nuff temptation jus' t'sit next t', an' ya don' even know it. This hyer Judge Overmeyer ain't the kind t'take no pity 'pon no po', simple gal like ya'll. It jus' ain't in 'im t'dredge on out. What they calls a stickler, he is. Ya followin' me, Jilly? 'Cause girl, yore kin up an' chucked ya...they wan' no part a this foolishness a yours, an' town folks's had it up t'hyer. An' so've Ah, y'wanna know the Gospel truth." Her tear — born of the same innocent glycerin generousness that offers her up to anyone fortunate enough to pass — gets his attention. "Now, doncha y'all go a'ballin' on me now. Keep yore knickers on an' we don' need a worry ourselves no more 'bout this hyer thang."

She sits up in a righteous, superior posture. "Y'all gonna get punish, Dolph. Ah feel sorry fer you. Ya tryin' a get me t'go contrary t'the Lawd. Ain' a gonna happen, no sir."

Dolph smiles in pity. "Well, if ah know a'thang'a'tall, the Good Lawd'd want ya t'keep yore privates covered as well as the rest a us does." It is something of a half-disingenuous announcement.

"Ain't so. Ah am as He made me. Chile a God, image a God. God wan's me t'show what a good job 'E done. What a pretty thaing He made."

"Ya come a long way from the butt-naked koochie-koo babe 'E made ya, y'all don' min' the observation. Girl, sometimes ah wonder what ya see through them baby blues a y'all's, 'cause I gotta feelin' it ain't much like what all the rest a us's seein'."

She leans close and whispers conspiratorial words in his ear,
"Ah saw God."

"Huh? What's that y'say? Y'all saw God now? Sweet thaing, y'ain't seen no God!" She laughs at him, silly boy. She speaks loudly: everyone who happens by, who wants to hear, can hear now. It can be trumpeted, this Good News. "Ah know what ah seen. Back durin' the Trouble. Durin' the hail storm time an' all. The earth got shook like the End a Days, flipped up the lounger, me too, turns me o'er on m'face on the ground. An' Ah'm a layin' thayer'n'a'dirt an' alls a sudden now ah feel like Ah'm a'bein' touch by somethin' all smooth an' warm an' peaceable, the han' a God, Ah don' won'er, an' Ah gets picked up, ris' up from the groun' like Laz'rus from ahin' the rock, an' turn' o'er like a li'le chile, an' place' back on mah lounger by two great fingers a the Lord. Ah knows this, 'cause when Ah look on up, Ah'm stairin' right up int'Is face. Ah feel the tingles up'n down mah arm hayirs, tickles up'n down m'legs, an'them hayirs down thayer 'tween 'em too." She is sitting up straight, loosing the modesty blanket, exposing the prototype bosom, tanned to the areolas, elbows pinned to her sides, arms forming ells with the flats of her hands palm up as if Dolph were about to drape the loose blanket over them like strung yarn, her eyes turned upward and as empty as ancient desert pools. A shiver, a shake, a rhythm works inside her, nervous twitches behind her delicate ears, sudden pulses in arms and neck, eyes rolled up to whites and lost in lids like they're glaring up into her own head where God and the nice boys boomerang around in empty space. "An' 'cause 'E done that, Ah know my body is bless-ed an' bee-you-tiful an' it's somethin' He wan's me t'dee-clare t'th worl'. An' Ah do. Ah'm a good thaing. A thaing t'see. A thaing t'touch. God touched me. He did. Ah'm'Is gal. Ah am."

Dolph sits back in the chair. He feels a tinge of sorrow now, can't imagine how this free spirit will fare strapped to an iron bed in a stark monk's cell. "Tell me, darlin'. Jus' what all'do God look like?"

"Well, lemme think on it. He's very big. Ya'd spect that. Seemed Ah was but part'v a pinkie. Yes. An' pow'rful han'some. Looked kin' a like that President Harding. Mama had a colored-in pitchur a President Harding. Mama said she know'd why the ladies took a fancy t'em an' why that got'im'n trouble. Ah don' know what kin' a trouble, but that's what Mama said. She said 'e was so good lookin' she woul'n'a minded gettin' im in some trouble her own self. Then Mama'd smile an' get all dreamy an'wou'n talk 'bout it no more. God looks like that pitchur a President Harding. Only 'E keeps 'Is hayer cropped real close t'Is scalp like they do t' the kids'at got thayerselves a dose a the licey-bug. An' the light ahin'Im's very, very bright. Near blinded me, but Ah don' min'. Ah'd fall off a that ol' lounger again'th Ah thought 'Ed pick me right back up."

The Deputy re-drapes her with the blanket, a reluctance tugging at him. "God looks like Warren Harding? Y'in a whole nuther place, you are! Li'l girl, supposin' this be our e-special secret. Neither a one a us needs t'tell no one 'bout it."

She drops her hands to her lap. "Sure, Dolph. An' then y'all be nice t'me? An' not say no mean things? An' not make me see that thayer cranky ol' judge? An' Ah'll be ya'all's gal fer e'er an' e'er? Ah sure nuff will. Yours'n God's, a course."

The caboose finally saunters past, its cupola packed with happy trainmen, like tourists from out of town, taking in the sights.

Once again, a few cars are uncoupled for local consumption and the quad of pistons resumes their work on the last leg south. The air is thick with condensation; it seems the locomotive needs to try just that much harder to inch through it. *"Like runnin' through my granny's puddin',"* the engineer quips. "For my money, y'all *can have your damn lowlands."*

Karnak, Mustegee, Willow Glen, Bad Luck, Luthersville, Dickson's Ferry. Forlorn clumps of towns, places asleep, signs on a post, sometimes a shack and a T of rails for a hand car, a water tank with incontinent spout, occasionally an actual station comforting a lone farmer with overalls and an overnight bag, a dog pissing on the high ball pole, a yellow control tower overlooking the steel diamond of a junction with an east-west line.

Finally, the shipyard cranes can be seen shimmering in the swelter. The main line disappears into a maze of sidings and sidings of sidings, and an ugly, worn architecture of iron and commerce — slag heaps, rambling coal chutes, and fetid air — invades the landscape. And there, the prows of ships, freighters, tankers; the busy oh-six-oh saddle tanks shunting like ants with stolen crumbs; a centipede of wheels and axels awaiting pallets of swivel trucks; cotton baled high, tobacco enjoying the damp, crates of brand new appliances, newsprint, raw lumber with cut ends flagged red; a congress of goods called to order by the authoritative bellow of the horns and the impatience of the bells, the cacophony of friction, the rumble of movement from objects innumerable and inanimate, the crunch of gears, the stress of chains, the deranged *halloo* of dynamic distemper, the harrowing pressure of compressed air, the pulsing instability of transience. *All 'booooard,* rattle and clang, all the way down from UF and other points north, 'Mingo, the capital, the dismal gator lands and delta sewage of the Gulf, and a ship to the wide world beyond the edge of sight.

THE LAYOUT

FOUR-HUNDRED THOUSAND SCALE POUNDS OF FORGED and molded motive power finds its way to the turntable, does a precision mount that brings it to within four millimeters of the drop at either end, spins slower than a Stouffer's frozen dinner in the microwave, backs into the stall surrounded by sisters to share the gossip of the road just ridden: the idle monotony of grease jobs and rod adjustments, the intimate tickle of the oil can, the presentation of new marker lamps, the rust removal on an old worn tender.

The train is pilot-less, gets attacked by the switchers — the shufflers, the dividers and conquerors — beams glaring front and back, the amplified talk of crews, the electric bee spin of the drivers, puffing non-toxic faux smoke. The cars go this way and that, imaginatively east to Atlanta or Jacksonville, west to El Paso and Barstow, south to Matamoras and Vera Cruz. The hoppers get dragged up onto the coal chutes, fill the hulls of ships with dreams of Havana, Caracas, Rio de Janeiro. The din is small, tinny, seems to emanate as much from the tenders as anywhere. Switches are thrown, a new freight assembled behind a squat mogul, weathered with grease stains and layers of grime, a few flats ridden by tractors, identical tank car quintuplets, some aging stock cars, the caboose.

Taylor peers up out of sea level like Neptune himself, enjoys the scale-eye view, sees the tracks from a grounded perspective so that they actually do diminish toward the simulacrum of horizon. Everything looks bigger at this angle, takes on a sense of ageless mobility, the uneven details of diminished reality.

He is wearing his dispatcher's vest, a green celluloid visor, and arm garters. His thick fingers scratch out train orders, send them clipped on a wire to the nearest control module, where Taylor, again, sans beak, now in a smart new engineer's cap with a Tishomingo logo expertly stitched in front, pecks skillfully across one of his several keyboards, lights up the digitized map seen on all the accompanying monitors, smoothly manages the safe operation of six separate trains and several more interurbans and streetcars, clipping along on scale Half O track, each strip wood tie individually set with four tiny spikes by a needle nose grip.

The mogul lurches forward. Couplers strain in their order of linkage — one by one, domino-like — until the reluctant caboose is convinced to join in. Several workers, replacing a spur rail, watch it proceed, frozen in an eternal styrene mold. *Ooooooo-wa-a-a-a-a-h ooooo*, through the junkyard betrayal of the bottomland; *futa-futa-futa-futa* clacks on the conduit of rail; the amperes cast as boiling water, *S-s-s-s-s-s-s*; mock sounds sampled from life, loops of conversations, sampled excerpts of industrial bedlam. A steady roll now, up past the yard limit, a handsome show of smoke.

Smoke is the key. Smoke, the puff of authenticity, however redacted. It's all smoke, really. And mirrors. And Taylor's snatch of life just comfortable enough for him to live in; where nobody calls and demands to know where you are, what you're doing, if you've cut down on salt or have a date for your next colonoscopy; where nobody — absolutely nobody — from division super to Mayor to Chief of police asks anything at all, expects anything at all other than that the trains will run with fascist-precision, a beam will glide across the sky during the day, a smaller bulb at night, and that the Master of All Things will dutifully see that the seasons get changed with a certain regularity in a confident neo-cosmic loop of its own. Simple folks, simple needs. No explanations, no excuses, no outright lies, no breaking of rules or avoidance of norms.

Taylor is the Swiftian maker and changer of all the Lilliputian rules. The mogul and train, mother duck and ducklings waddling out of the family room that Taylor's father had designed and had built, into the kitchen, *clang-clang-clang-clang-clang, s-s-s-s, ooooowah, futa-futa*, stuttering along from one isolated berg to another, some no more than a gas station and a general store and a live bait sign, past occasional cars and trucks that never move along the roads they continuously travel, never getting closer to where ever it is they are not going, caught for eternity at the cross bucks of time, and the freight hoots on by. A long low trestle through the swamp of primeval trees and water snake pools, black still waters sullen under murky green skins.

Krk! The thwack of expanding plywood, the tectonics of the veneered earthen crust, the percussion of the electric *whir-r-r-r*-bogey of pretense. The real world should love it: imitation, after all, being the compliment — no matter how shrunken — all in the image of something greater. The dining room doorframe comes at the train like the Hoosac Tunnel portal, with Taylor's hinged bridge in place over the shapeless void of the Bedskirtissippee River wallowing its way back toward the delta. The bridge is crossed, the hall entered, the train comes to a water stop at Dickson's Ferry, where the farmer is still waiting with his bag, and the dog is still pissing like a Saturday night drunk. The tracks proceed along the banks of a feeder creek named Betsy Run, get continually more curvaceous as the stream narrows, steps back in a series of milky risers, the swirl of fast water, where one can imagine, if one were allowed entrance, the whisper and giggle of flow under the plastic silence. Mute gurgles, splash: the erosional suggestion on river rocks. A small cataract appears through the engineer's window — he doesn't notice now, notices nothing at all, ever. The drop hangs perpetual in impotent silence. The earth swells on all sides, plateaus — bubbles to hillocks — steepens in haste to talus slopes and granite escarpments, to tree-crowned ridges, looses dimension in the painted back drop of purple mountains majesty and static swabs of cumulus moisture.

Taylor said, *Let there be majestic peaks and the threat of heavy rain,* and so there was, and it was good. Taylor said, *Let there be Luthersville and Bad Luck and Willows Glenn and let us borrow Karnak from the old world like we did Syracuse and Rome.* Taylor sends the current down the rails to the pickup drivers, puts the words in the fireman's mouth, rings the bell, blows the horn, supplies the expected *clickety clack* — the whistle song of introduction, *here we come, small-footed mogul with things to buy and news of the world.* Taylor changes hats, slips into overalls, furiously pecks out the orders that only he will read, digitizes it all in precision, collision-free compliance with Federal safety regulations that he pretends govern such commerce. It is pretending so real in scale diminution, so accurate down to the brass buttons on a conductors coat, so painstakingly modeled hour after hour, day after day, year after year since the fiery consummation of Helen, that, like the oft-repeated lie, it settles as living sediment into Taylor's belief system.

Taylor decides on the Capital Cutoff Branch for the freight; he has a fast mail lurching down from the north on the main line. The cutoff provides an arboreal experience. It is thick with piney woods, shadow-sucking groundcover, dark blind curves and blasted stone tunnels.

Taylor made them all. Taylor is the Big Bang, the first fish to venture onto land, the meteor off of the Yucatan coast. Taylor is the found link and the missing, the genetic material, the formulator of change. Taylor makes the flora, paints the fauna, sets the humans on their way to a perpetuity of stillness. Taylor is the split atom, the egg, the sperm, the Idea. Taylor moves the trains, is dispatcher and surveyor, the cartographer, the gandy and the boomer, fireman and hogger. He wears all the hats. Pens all the orders. The super's Super. He makes the news, makes the time, makes Time itself. Taylor, without equal. Taylor is great. Taylor is omnipotent. He was here before it all, handed down the scripture to prophets in the desert. Taylor is Truth; Taylor is undeniable. Taylor is the master of his very own universe. Taylor is the one true Taylor.

Disheveled junctions with cheaply built industrial railroads; narrow-gauge Shays dragging ancient Taylor-made trunks of trees; dinkies like toys lugging ore cars from quarries; homely side tankers with toxic tank car tails. Back on the mainline, screeching like a banshee over the great Thebes Viaduct, an engineering marvel in simulated gray stone, over the patched roof of the motor court, a pebble's throw from the Greek's, the trolley car Taylor sends up and back with minute-long stops for the convenience of passengers who never, ever get on or off. A short, dry water stop awaits in the Tishomingo Yards, the endless search of the bulls in the box cars, the flip of the high ball signal, *b-o-o-o-o-rd*, *ch-ch-ch-ch*, a skirt of the Camels, a cautious pass up and down the grades that culminate in the infamy of David's Sling, down along the river to the chaotic hub of Uncas Falls, in the middle of Taylor's living room, in the house his parents bought, a not uncommon Spanish colonial with stucco mission arches, hardwood oak floors, pink and green bathroom tiles that have gone from stylish to passé and ugly, to retro chic in less time than it takes for the lath to separate itself from the plaster and for cracks to web out throughout the house with the visual proof of California tectonics, a few short miles from the seismographs at Caltech. Taylor's world; secure in the collective protection of bars and rotating cameras, a bolted foundation; safe, unencumbered with the cares of others, insular, impermeable, the private bastion of a solitary man cluttered with the happy sounds of all that he has wrought. Taylor created He them, man and woman, Mayor and mistress, mistress and cuckold, the accused, the abused, the mistaken, the gossipees and the gossipers, the righteous and the righted, the high talkers and the low, the venal, the detached, the clothed and the naked he delicately lifts back up to the lounge, the ones that hide and the ones that don't, the lawmakers and lawbreakers and the keepers of the straight and narrow, the solitary and the crowded, the thinkers and the dullards, the schemers and the scammed, up from rib bones and mud, apes to plastic, molded He them.

And Taylor saw what He had made, and that it was good.

FINAL HELEN

And, so it came to pass, that the Lord revealed Himself unto Helen. He came upon a mighty shuddering, a terrible quaking of the earth. She turned her face to behold His countenance, and He presented a fearsome blast of light, brighter than the one sun, so that she could not look upon it, and legions of angels about Him, cheeks bellowed like the faces of the winds on ancient maps, blew upon their horns, louder than any sound she had ever heard, earsplitting, drum-breaking, and then a whisper, a hush, and He commanded time to stop, and in His infinite approach, a calmness about her, while outside, He summoned the bile of the Nephilim, and He caused to rain down brimstone and fire, and all the morning commuters that had come with Him, put down their Times, *their* Newsweeks, *their* People Magazines, *their I-pods, and their laptops plentiful with spreadsheets, and they spoke amongst themselves, and said: 'Escape for thy life; look not behind thee, neither stay now in all the Train, lest thou be swept away.' And, lo, the smoke of the land went up as the smoke of a furnace.*

Track Three
DRUMHEAD

*T*AYLOR'S SATISFACTION MIRRORS HER OWN, INSEMINATED *through sear, bone-yellow fingers, knobbed at the joints like dying bamboo stalks, pain yielded up in electrifying neural jolts, parchment skin prints struggling with the resistant keys, even "…good" an autumnal struggle for completion against all odds.*

She runs these reluctant digits over the monitor, as if the generated words could rejuvenate their aridity. "It is good", *she says quietly, alone as she is, a shrunken gnome beneath the ramparts of cubby holes and roll top, her claw-scratched notations illuminated by a fluorescent resembling a vanilla-swirl cone, the cross-hatched shadows of the room darkening in progressive transit away from the green glass shade of the desk lamp. She wants to add her name,* Pasadena, *today's date, which she can't remember off the top of her head, has only the strength to SAVE, to QUIT WORD, to SHUT DOWN. Her teacup is half full, cold, the bag leached and the brew bitter. Evidence of her tremors are puddled in the saucer and reflect the lamp's output of eight cool watts.*

With palms down on the arms of her chair, fingers splayed defensively away from contact, she hefts herself up — what little there is of her to heft, a cocoon from which the moth has fled — and shuffles her way to the front window, like crazy Mrs. Winchester of rifle fame on her easy-riser stair treads. She parts the coffee-colored blinds, works the pearl-skinned opera glasses from chained pendant up to her prescriptions, and scans the fortified arches across the street, pocked as they are with tiny red lights of robotic intelligence.

"Not home," *she decides,* "Taylor What's-his-hoozits, whatever." *The car is always out front when he is home, gathering evidence of the parkway tree where escaped parrots congregate and scream the day's events like they're gabbing on cell phones.* "Maybe a new hussy. Or one of his mysterious weekenders. He always wanders off this time of year." *UPS, the postman, both have left a collection of brown packages to co-mingle on the portal of his secret, gated world. She would love to skulk across the street, discover the moniker of the addressee. But that would make it real, the label, make it all entirely something other than what she has molded it to be. She needs the anonymity of night, the gaping chasms of information in what she sees as demarcation from what she doesn't. Several times she has nearly edged that border, an all too obvious smile from the porch, a limp wave at the hybrid that occasionally stops down the street, a man at the wheel, a woman opposite — some sort of stakeout maybe, plain clothes detectives, some government covert ops, enforcers from a loan shark, repo agents — there to haul him out of whatever secret monastic criminality he indulges. Risky, her crossover behavior, a skewing of the purity of her task. She needs him to be Taylor Bedskirt, not Max Obermeyer, nor Bill Stein, nor Joe the Whatever, just as she needs to remain, within the context of anonymity, Mrs. Gettzleman, who she isn't, but who cannot exist without her. She has responsibility for Mrs. Gettzleman, for Taylor, for Walter Prezhki, for all of them. Their lives are in her hands: that they live at all is solely to her credit.*

She lights the electric sconces from the wall buttons — the house has enjoyed relatively little tampering since the tract opened eighty-two years ago; still has the original black and red wall buttons, the open service porch with milkman access, floor furnaces, lath-line cracks commemorating all of the big quakes since the twenties, like a redwood-slice of history.

A mantis alights on the window, preaches to the choir of ecstatic moths lost in the warm spiritual glow. It is hot outside, ashen, Los Angeles more or less on schedule, burning down with the help of desert winds.

The remodel across the street and one over sports a FOR SALE sign from a major realty chain. The truck has been back sporadically since the big night, when Pasadena's finest rousted the licensed contractor, and the paramedics whizzed away the wife. Weeks after, the estranged couple talked on the porch. It seemed she wept, he balled a fist, thought better of it, left a gift — probably for the child — and stomped off kicking over a Malibu light or two. She morphed him into a soldier, gave him a broken body, set to boil the ill will she had planted in his head like a chip from an alien saucer. She gave him a combatant's mouth too, seasoned it with profanity and bigotry she learned from films and contemporary literature and a secret email collaboration with a great nephew, gave him things to say that flowed easily from her pen if not from her mouth: liberating things, things not said in the real youth of her real life, things that reflect a seamy underbelly of a prayer-resistant existence, writing the dirt-mean words as if filling the vacuum of her own experience. She gave voice to the limping soldier she herself had conscripted. Purpose to the mock-Taylor's solitude. Pathetic anguish to the loneliness of Harlan Brewster. The talent of worry to Betsy Valverde. She rented the rooms at the Chivalry Timbers Suites. Moved the incandescence of day and night. The trains. She ran the trains.

When it began, as a curiosity, something to pass the time, an avocation you might say, she just watched, the quiet house of many eyes by the women with extra lenses, the climate of rage at the neighbor's, the big man's comings and goings in the old consumptive Cadillac. She started to keep scraps of paper near the front window, to jot things down, run them by her contemporary down the street so they could volley scenarios: where he went, what they fought over, what he did in there.

What did he do in there? He was a large handsome man, unaware of himself, unkempt, dreamy, lost in space and out to lunch and gone fishin'. His shirttails betrayed his disorientation, waved behind him like flags surrendering to the inevitable, as if tucking them in were beside the point, against nature. In his unconsciousness of self, she saw acceptance, and, with that, a certain wisdom to resist Sisyphean exertions. She had no idea what it was, but there was a comfort about him that said he had all that he needed, that he was self-contained, batteries included and no assembly required. He must not watch television, she thought, there being no antenna or dish, no evidence to falling in the thrall of commercial acquisitiveness. Yet, he was guarding something in there, some secret, some treasure, some unpatented idea that would give him control of The World, or give him a world to control.

There were all kinds of theories: none wholesome, all delicious. She took to following him in her old New Yorker — an easy mark, slow rolling, only vague reference to his surroundings beyond what he needed for his own safety — to hot dog sales at gas station markets, two for ninety-nine, 7-11's, the True Value hardware store, the taco trucks that hung around small industrial firms, a bridge to East LA where he loitered to watch the Union Pacific contribute its grand share of greenhouse gasses to the seamy local air-like product the sky hid behind. Always, a yellow steno pad and ballpoint accompanied her on the wide bench seat.

One day, she followed him to a model train store, watched him go inside, don a red vest splotched with pins of some sort, run the register, read magazines off the rack, rearrange the brass engines slumbering in glass display cases. "This it what he does," she thought, "this is what he will do." *This is where he lives/will live, a remarkable miniature world for such a big man. Scratch, scratch, ballpoint to pad. The boxes on the porch? More trains, Pullmans with silhouette passengers painted on the windows, stock cars filled with plastic cattle? So much less heinous than all that was imagined, but yet, in its ordinariness, its banality, so much more piquant; a man with hanging shirt tails not discomfited by himself, his uncombed hair, the extra heft above his belt; a boy grown inevitably large, careless of the real world, sexless; a complex savant in his own universe, hidden within a cipher that happened to resemble Warren Harding. She constructed him about this ocular frame, exposed the living core within the mundane ruse. She gave him life, and parallel life. And she named him. Shopping for linens, she saw a package — tailored bedskirt — wrapped in plastic.* "That's him, shrink wrapped, Taylor Bedskirt," *for no particular reason other than it somehow sounded like him, and that's who he became. Taylor Bedskirt. Works in a train store. Casual diner. Occasional dalliance with a trollop. Goes home alone to a full house. Absolutely oblivious to her snooping.*

Sitting in Memorial Park, brown bagging with her crinkled cronies from the Senior Citizens Center, she shares her findings. They uh huh, guffaw, you betcha, y'don't say. *They add their own readings from the forensics she presents. They are women she has known for a long time. They have shared the deaths of husbands. Women like those she had known as a child in a moderately-sized southern mountain city, women who invented worlds over egg salad and limeade at the Woolworth's after church. She co-opted them, these park women, sent them home to Kentucky or Alabama, ordered for them, gave them a phone operator with an ear to the wall, a conjurer, a stirrer of pots best left undisturbed. She gave them something to do, something to pass the time, to return them to an integral state, braise them with meaning and season them with vicarious keyholes to stare through. She read to them excerpts from the note pads, jotted things down as they talked, as much about them as about what they said. She took them home to Taylor Bedskirt, put them in his house, surrounded them with the familiar things that make an environment, flipped back calendar pages with an ardor to make H. G. Wells drool, rented them space in mansions and shanties and by-the-week hotels, and hemmed them in with track from Taylor's trains.*

She researched Taylor, the train store, interviewed his co-workers when he wasn't there, learned what she could about model railroading, railroading in general. Particularly, she developed a fondness for train wrecks. One might have thought she was writing a book. And then she was. About the man across the street who she didn't know. And about herself from before she could recall and about where she came from and the people who were already there when she arrived. She contacted the historical society back home, downloaded local news, put it all in Taylor's house and ran trains around it. She put herself, a babe, in her mother's arms in the church they attended whose pulpit passed down through a primogenitor of increasingly less restrained preachers. She fed old scandals to the old ladies with their toasted white bread sandwiches. They gobbled them up, digested them, burned their energy, and shed the waste to fertilize the seeds they'd

*planted. She abducted mayors, and mobsters, and railroaders from home, and gave them
to Taylor. She took preachers and conjurers, soda jerks and junk men, and gave them to
Taylor. She kidnapped battered wives, insensate yard bulls, doctors, lawyers, all kinds
of chiefs, and gave them, wholesale, as a lot, to Taylor. She took the ways of their narrow
and insular worlds and refined them down to a critical scale mass on a series of laminated
platforms and trimmed them like a Yule tree back home, and gave it all to Taylor. She
took omnipotence, and gave it to Taylor. Master Taylor. Luckiest Taylor in the world.
Taylor, the One Taylor.*

*She organized, ordered, laid a trail of broken continuity that calcified on Taylor's
layout. She handed out voice, language, jargon, and pastiche, that maybe Taylor, only
Taylor, could hear. Man and woman, she created them. Pissing dog and pedestrian sheep,
she created them. Hobos, dead folks, the doomed and dying, reporters, winos, hoggers,
trainmen, motormen, conductors; wives, lovers, lonely old maids; cheaters, liars; tellers of
tales and chasers of tail; the sacred and the secular, the proper and the profane; inheritors
and losers, the winners and the won; all the colors of humankind arisen out of the muck
of Africa before The Flood; the tasters and the forbidden fruit, the punctual and the
tardy, the rich, the not so rich, the never hope to be's; the feeders, the fed; the upright,
the crooked. She gave them emotion, she gave them history. She wove them a fabric of
connection within the abrupt boundaries at the ends of the world, four precipitous feet to
the scuffed blond-oak floors, the urethaned fundament of the underworld; a view from
Taylor's empyreal perch.*

*She is interrupted by a chill, thoughts of a week before and the clink of old door
chimes.* Yes? *She had called, not expecting anybody.* It's me, *he'd said,* from across
the street. *She was instantly troubled, flipped the brass lid over the peephole, glanced
myopically at the pained buttons on his shirt. It was indeed him. What could he want?
Visibility, revelation? Would he turn to ashes all her hatched plots? Would he be real, no
longer her own, born of woman, named, christened perhaps? No, no, she didn't want
that. She didn't want any part of that. She wasn't prepared to surrender him, her Taylor,
to this…this facsimile, this imposter, this counterfeit self-imprisoned in the shabby stucco
across the avenue. What could he want? Her mouth was dry. Her hands trembled more
than is ordinary. It was a long while before she could repeat,* Yes? *Would he introduce
himself, accuse her of spying? Would she make excuses, beg off,* A whistling teapot, *an*
I'm not feeling at all well. *Would he ask to come in? Would he infect her invention
with his living flesh? He stepped back from the door, told her he had some of her mail. He
made some derogatory remark about the mailman's literacy. She thanked him, more for
the relief than the missives, asked him to simply slide them through the door slot because
she wasn't decent. If only he'd known just how indecent. Without another word, he left
the mail and was gone.*

*She turned off the room light, shuffled in slippers like a neophyte skater on ice, saw
a resident Norwegian tree rat skitter along a baseboard on his way to destiny with a
sprung trap, a living example of the uselessness of cats. The sighting gave her a sense of
comfort, a dark thrill, to know the surety of a snap would leave her alone in the house,
an anxiousness to get it done, to bag the marauder before tomorrow's trash pickup. Good
to rid the world of evil things: to squash earwigs, hang-up on solicitors, turn in drivers
who illegally parked in handicapped spaces, expose the woman in the eighteen or less line*

with easily twenty items, to crack the brittle neck bone of a rodent. It was good to be in charge. She leaned over the old desk, the computer, touched the screen lightly with fusing knuckles, considered all that she had made.

"Okay, then," *she said.* "Okay."

THE END